MAXIM JAKUBOWSKI is a London-based novelist and editor. He was born in the UK and educated in France. Following a career in book publishing, he opened the world-famous Murder One bookshop in 1988 and has since combined running it with his writing and editing career. He has edited a series of 12 bestselling erotic anthologies and two books of erotic photography as well as many acclaimed crime collections. His novels include *It's You That I Want To Kiss, Because She Thought She Loved Me* and *On Tenderness Express*, all three recently collected and reprinted in the USA as *Skin In Darkness*. Other books include *Life In The World of Women, The State of Montana, Kiss Me Sadly* and *Confessions Of A Romantic Pornographer*. In 2006 he published a major erotic novel which he directed and on which 15 of the top erotic writers in the world have collaborated, *America Casanova* and his collected erotic short stories as *Fools For Lust*. He is a winner of the Anthony and the Karel Awards, a frequent TV and radio broadcaster, crime columnist for the *Guardian* newspaper and Literary Director of London's Crime Scene Festival.

D0846213

THE MAMMOTH BOOK OF

Best
New Erotica

Volume 7

Edited and with an Introduction
by Maxim Jakubowski

RUNNING PRESS
PHILADELPHIA · LONDON

First published in the UK by Robinson,
an imprint of Constable & Robinson Ltd, 2007

Collection and editorial material copyright © Maxim Jakubowski, 2007

First published in the United States in 2007
by Running Press Book Publishers

Printed and bound in the EU

9 8 7 6 5 4
Digit on the right indicates the number of this printing

Library of Congress Control Number: 2007938614

ISBN 978-0-7867-2075-0

Running Press Book Publishers
2300 Chestnut Street
Philadelphia, PA 19103-4371

Visit us on the web!
www.runningpress.com

Contents

Acknowledgments and Copyright

Introduction

Maxim Jakubowski

Is there any evidence of a seven-year itch? Or should we even be mentioning itches when it comes to a collection of sexual stories? I just ask as this is already the seventh volume of the *Mammoth Book of Best New Erotica*. How time flies.

Technically speaking, it's actually the twelfth volume, as the initial five collections I assembled came with individual titles (in succession, *The Mammoth Book of Erotica*, *International Erotica*, *New Erotica*, *Historical Erotica* and *Short Historical Novels*) before we moved to a common title and settled on a successful formula whereby I hunted down the best stories published in print and online during the preceding twelve calendar months. And I'm not even including the two individual volumes of erotic photography, which also fit into the series.

A lot of flesh, much lust, an abundance of emotions and epiphanies and thrills galore! You'd think that by now I would be bored at the prospect of swimming in those erotic seas all over again. On the contrary, the experience proves each new year to be as invigorating and provocative as ever. Good writers with an assured feel for this much-maligned genre somehow always manage to renew their inspiration and come up with stories which shed new lights and perspectives on the dangerous currents of sexuality in all its forms, and as a bystander and an editor I get caught up all over again.

Many of my (and your) favourite authors make welcome appearances in this new volume, together with new names. These wonderful tales of sex, sweat, lust and desire unbound originate from all over the world, and from publications cast wide and far. The past year has proven a particularly fertile one for original anthologies, and I counted over 20 whilst prospecting for this book, but magazines on the Internet and also of a more literary nature (and not specifically erotic) also yielded some fascinating tales.

Savour slowly.

Maxim Jakubowski

The Dire Consequences of My Libido

Tara Alton

Claude

I first learned about the dire consequences of my libido when I was twelve years old and I fell in love with my sister's stuffed rabbit. His name was Claude, but let me get one thing out in the open about our situation. He was the one who began our romance when he kept staring at my bare legs from the shelf on the wall during the night.

At first, our relationship was only a friendship. I told him all my secrets, even the deep dark ones that I never told anyone else, and he told me how lonely he was sitting up there on the shelf all the time. It was tragic really. We were two lost souls looking for something missing in our lives.

A few months later, my parents kept wondering why Claude was going bald. My father thought it was moths. My mother thought my sister was giving him haircuts with cuticle scissors because she wanted to become a hair stylist one day.

The mystery was solved one night when I was caught dry humping him in my bed when I thought everyone was asleep. Of course, there was a lot of crying and screaming, and of course, no one would listen to me about how much I loved him and how much he loved me in return.

The following day, my parents took Claude into the backyard where they burned him in a pile of autumn leaves. As my sister shed tears for the loss of her toy, they comforted her and ignored my tragic wailing. They didn't understand they were killing my best friend.

That was when I learned I would never forget the sound of a stuffed rabbit screaming.

The Big Race

When I turned fourteen, my parents enrolled me in the swim team after school so I couldn't sit at home every evening, watching old horror movies and writing morbid poems about dead rabbits.

Why they chose swimming, I had no idea. I hated swimming because my breasts were already developing beyond a C cup, and they were constantly getting in my way as I tried to perform the strokes.

As the weeks of practice went by though, I slowly began to learn how to move my body gracefully in the water, and it seemed to embrace me in return. The pool became the one place where I could let my thoughts go. No one cared what I said to the water when my head was beneath it. I came to love the water much like Claude, and I thought it loved me back.

For the first time in my life, I started to excel at something. I began winning races. My parents offered up their praise and talked about my success at the dining room table instead of my sister's accomplishments.

At the end of the summer, there was the championship race. I was the favorite to win the breaststroke, but they didn't tell me I was going to be racing against a long-limbed girl named Betty Snow.

Betty was beautiful in a way I had never seen before, and the sight of her bare legs gave me goose bumps. There was a curious dreamy feeling blooming inside me that I had only felt for boys before.

Unfortunately, she was in the lane next to me for our race. As we dove into the water, I found I couldn't tear my gaze away from her, so I was keeping pace with her. The water seemed to sense my distraction, and it made it that much harder to swim. I decided I was only going to have one more look at her when suddenly the wall of the pool was in front of me. The race was over. I had lost to Betty Snow.

I'll never forget that moment when I looked over to my team, realizing I had just lost the championship for them. You should have seen the look they gave me in return because they knew I hadn't swum my best.

After that day, my parents no longer mentioned my achievements at the dining room table. To my sister's relief, she was once more the shining star.

The Middle Finger

When I was sixteen, I tried to find a job to make some extra pocket money, but the only thing I could find was babysitting some kids who no one else wanted to babysit because they were little monsters. What made it worse was that their father brought them things like ancient jungle gyms from the junk yard where he worked. Their yard looked like a set from a Tim Burton movie.

The worst monstrosity in the back yard was the rotating teeter-totter. I thought it reminded me of a giant rotating spider that spun around, and I despised it the moment I saw it. The kids thought it was the best thing their father had ever brought them.

In an effort to get them to go to bed, I promised to push them around on it one more time when my finger slipped into the middle gear. It felt funny for a moment and then I pulled it out. The top of my finger was dangling off, hanging on by a tiny bit of skin, the bone exposed.

Thankfully, amongst the horrifying screams of the kids, I had the presence of mind to flip the top of my finger back over the bone before I passed out.

A neighbor heard the commotion and called my parents. I woke up to my parents taking me to the emergency room. In the examination room, I sat with my father, waiting for a doctor, my finger soaking in a pan of lukewarm water. It painfully throbbed every so often to remind me it wasn't a bad dream.

The nurse had asked me to take off my top. I wasn't sure why I needed to sit there in my bra, but I obeyed, trying to avoid my father's embarrassed gaze. Once I had grown beyond a C cup, my mother had gone into complete denial about the size of my breasts. I was pouring over the top of my bra like a movie star on the red carpet.

To my delight, my doctor wasn't some old man. He was young and tall, dark and handsome. I don't know what came over me, but suddenly my posture changed. As he examined my wounded finger, I felt gooseflesh rise up along my arms from his touch. I hadn't felt this since Betty Snow.

To my surprise, I realized he was stealing glances at my breasts. This was wonderful. A gorgeous doctor was actually checking me out. I felt like a real woman for the first time.

I leaned forward so he could see more of my cleavage.

Suddenly, my father cleared his throat and left the examination room.

I couldn't believe I was alone with my doctor. All sorts of sexy scenarios started playing in my head. I wanted to give him a kiss he would remember for the rest of his life when the examination room curtain suddenly opened.

There stood my father with an ancient doctor beside him. Before I could open my mouth to protest, the younger doctor was asked to leave and the older doctor took over. I stared daggers at my father as the older doctor examined my finger. Couldn't he see this old coot was wearing huge coke bottle glasses?

A week later when the bandages came off, we learned he had sewn the tip of my finger back on crooked. I wanted to tell my father this was his fault, but he gave me a look that said if I hadn't flirted with the young doctor, this wouldn't have happened.

The Sweater

For the next two years, I tried not to feel self-conscious about my crooked finger, but it was hard. I blamed it for my not having any goose bumps since Claude, Betty or the young doctor. Who would want a deformed girl like me?

Meanwhile my sister was the dating princess. She had no problems keeping a steady stream of boyfriends who adored her.

Finally, in my senior year, I came across some possible goose bump material. I was developing a crush on a boy named Ben and I was almost sure he liked me back. He was sweet and sincere, and he had the nicest smile. Every day, we met in between classes to talk about horror movies, which he loved as much as I did.

One weekend, he asked me to go to the movies with him, but I wasn't sure if he was asking me as a date or a friend. I was too afraid to ask him, but I decided if I wore something sexy, it might just give him the motivation to let me know if he was interested in me beyond being pals.

The problem was that I didn't own anything sexy. I mostly wore shapeless black clothes, like a badly dressed Goth girl. On the other hand, my sister owned an entire girly wardrobe encompassing the entire spectrum of the rainbow.

Therefore, I decided to borrow my sister's favorite lucky pink sweater without asking her. I knew she would have said no, because she secretly hated me ever since Claude.

That evening as I wore her sweater, I felt as if I was wrapped in a fluffy pink dream. It hugged my every curve, and it revealed more than ample skin. Ben couldn't take his eyes off me. He didn't even look at the screen when the movie started, and he had been waiting for this movie to open for months.

It didn't take him long to turn my head toward him to kiss me. His warm, sweet mouth lingered on mine. Immediately, I started kissing him back, my body flushing with a sudden heat. Taking his hands in mine, I pushed them toward my breasts. I hadn't felt this aggressive since I leaned toward the young doctor.

Before I knew it, he had slipped his hands under the back of my sister's sweater, fumbling with my bra hooks, trying to get access to my bare breasts, but there wasn't a lot of room because everything was so tight.

Suddenly, he gave up on getting it undone and slid his hands around the front, going right under the underwire to my bare skin. The room swooned. I closed my eyes as he squeezed my breasts.

"Oh, Claude," I said.

Abruptly, he stopped. My eyes flew open. He was looking at me in horror. I had called him "Claude". How could I ever explain to him who Claude was?

We sat in silence for the rest of the movie, and he didn't even say goodbye to me when he dropped me off at home. I wore my coat until I got upstairs, and then I hid the sweater in the rear of our closet, my sister already asleep in her bed.

The next morning, I woke to her rummaging in the closet. She said she needed her favorite lucky sweater because she had an important job interview, and if she got this job, she could move out, find her own apartment and start her new life.

I cringed. Why did she need this sweater today? It was badly stretched out because of Ben's fumbling, and I was going to take it to the dry cleaners to see if they could fix it. The moment I heard her suck in her breath, I knew she had found it. I couldn't see the wrath on her face because I was under the covers as she pummelled me with her fists.

That afternoon, I heard her in the kitchen with our mom. She was crying. Without her lucky sweater, she didn't have the confidence she needed to win the interview. She didn't get the job. She wasn't moving out. She blamed me for ruining her new life.

The String of Unfortunate Jobs

After I graduated high school, I knew I didn't want to end up working at Denny's restaurant like my sister and living at home. Thank goodness, I lucked out finding a job as a receptionist at a tattoo parlor and I made enough money to rent a little studio apartment.

It wasn't a bad job, mostly making appointments, keeping the lobby organized, and giving after care instructions to the recently tattooed. Big Mike was the owner. He was strictly appointment only, while his two apprentices did the walk-ins.

Big Mike was not only called "big" because he was one of the owners, but because he was a tall, barrel-chested man with an intense, unapologetic personality. He came across as gruff and intimidating, but it was only because he was a perfectionist.

His girlfriend treated me with indifference usually reserved for office temps. She was tall, blond, and stacked, but there was something rough around the edges and there was a rumor her breasts were fake. I'd even heard she worked as a stripper. She was a silent partner in the tattoo studio, and she and Big Mike had a volatile on and off again relationship.

After a couple months of working there and withstanding his outbursts, Big Mike started to act as if I was maybe going to become a permanent part of the studio. He asked me if I was ever going to get any tattoo work done myself. All my money was going into rent, so he suggested we stay after work one night; he would tattoo me for free, a perk of the job.

Right away, I knew what I wanted from the moment I saw it. It was a piece of artwork of a grey-shaded rabbit, and I wanted Claude's name beneath it.

We stayed after work on a Friday night. I had decided I wanted it on my upper arm, but my shirtsleeve was too tight to roll up. Big Mike told me to take off my shirt. He'd seen a million breasts before. It was no big deal to sit there in my bra while I got my tattoo. I waited for him to stare at my cleavage like the young doctor had, but he was intently focused on tattooing the outline of the rabbit on my arm.

Quickly, I realized getting tattooed hurt a lot more than I had imagined. Here I was telling customers it would be no more painful than a bee sting or an intense scratch, but it really stung.

Big Mike finished the lettering of Claude's name and he was halfway through the shading when he said he needed a smoke break. I got up to look at in the mirror when suddenly he was behind me. I thought he was going to look at my arm in the mirror when he spun me around and kissed me.

This was no kiss like from a boy like Ben. This was a kiss from a real man, and it made my toes curl. Alarms sounded off in my brain, but the intensity of his mouth on mine drowned it out.

I kissed him back, with all those years of pent up passion. Grappling each other's bodies, we stumbled. He pushed me back against the mirror, and started to kiss the side of my neck, his hand coming up to squeeze my breast from beneath.

"God, they are real," he moaned.

I started to reach around to undo my bra when I heard a distant screaming. For a second, I flashed on the other screams I had heard in my life, Claude, my sister as she pummelled me with her fists and then I realized it was coming from the front door of the studio.

Big Mike's girlfriend was standing there, screaming at us, fumbling with her keys. The moment she got the door open, I thought Big Mike might actually defend me, but she pulled out a knife from her designer purse and came after him. I ran out of there, my belongings trailing in my hand, my tattoo half finished, never to return.

The Vibrator

After the tattoo studio incident, I found it hard to find another good paying job without a reference. I had to take two crap jobs, and even then, I still wasn't making enough money to pay the rent on my studio. My parents wouldn't let me move back home because my sister was still there, but they said my great-aunt was looking for a live-in caretaker.

Therefore, I quit my two crap jobs and I moved in with her to take care of her.

Within a week, I realized living with her made me feel as if I was under house arrest. She constantly wanted to know what I was doing, and she had hundreds of poodle statues, which I had to dust every day. On top of that, she kept the house freezing cold, and it was a huge undertaking just to keep track of all her prescriptions at all the pharmacies around town.

Time had not been kind to her. She seemed like a man in drag with her sunken chest, bad wigs, knobby knees and smoker's voice. She was completely addicted to steak, cigarettes, lime green Jell-O, her daily pill cocktail and her TV reality shows.

Constantly, she harped at me to cut my hair short and to get a manicure. According to her, a young woman my age should not have long hair and hangnails, but with my deformed finger, who would want to manicure me?

One afternoon, I was so frustrated with the living arrangements that I picked up a personal massager at one of the drug stores. I needed to find some relief somewhere.

Upon arriving home, I discovered a note from her saying that she had gone to a friend's house to watch the finale of one of her reality shows. Jackpot! I finally got some time alone. I ripped open the personal massager, only to find it didn't come with batteries, nor did I find any in the junk drawer. I did the only thing I could. I raided her TV remote, thinking I could replace them when I was finished.

In the privacy of my bedroom, I gave myself a rocking orgasm, fantasizing about Big Mike coming to rescue me, fucking the shit out of me and finishing my tattoo.

After the glow of my orgasm finally faded, I padded into the kitchen wearing my dressing gown to make some popcorn. This had to be the best evening I had had in weeks.

Just as I was settling down with a novel, a diet cola and bowl of the popcorn, the front door opened. In walked my great-aunt, looking more harried than I had ever seen her before. She told me she had a fight with her friend who had asked her to leave and now she was missing the crucial moment on her TV show.

Grabbing the remote, she tried to change the television to the right channel. It wasn't working. She slapped it on her hand. I froze. I hadn't replaced the batteries yet. Immediately, she started freaking out.

Attacking the front of the television, her gnarled fingers grazing the tiny buttons that no one had ever used before, she vainly tried to change the channel. I leapt up, ready to run to my bedroom to get the batteries when suddenly, she fell to the ground.

I ran to her side. She was clutching her chest. Her eyes were rolling back in her head.

"The batteries are in my vibrator," I cried. "I can get them."

"Call 911," she gasped.

At the hospital, the doctors said she was going to be fine. She didn't have a heart attack. It was a panic attack, but by the look in her eyes, I knew I had lost my home.

Toby

After sending my great-aunt to the hospital, I decided I was never going to let my libido ruin my life again. I lived in my car for a few weeks before I landed a job at a little auto parts factory. The place was a shit hole, but it gave me enough money to rent a room at a weekly rate motel in the dingy side of town.

My life would have been completely horrible if I hadn't finally met someone a few months later. His name was Toby and in some ways, he reminded me of Ben. He was sweet and sincere, and he had the nicest smile. I had met him when I was trying to land a part time weekend job at a bookstore, and he mistook my second hand designer suit as my usual attire. I didn't get the job, but he did take my phone number.

Toby had fifteen years on me. He was a little overweight, a little bald, and he liked pastel-colored polo shirts and khaki pants. Clearly, he wasn't my usual type, but I thought I could really go places with him. He called me several times a week, sent me flowers, and he took me out to dinner every Saturday night. He wasn't all about getting into my pants either. The most he had done so far was hold my hand, call me sweetheart and give me a dry kiss on the cheek.

I told myself I was relieved that he never noticed my crooked middle finger. I didn't have to explain what happened. It was a good sign that I never felt the need to share the stories about the dire consequences of my libido. Why would a decent man like him what to hear those gory details?

Quite simply, he said he liked me. He promised me things. He used the word "we".

Most of all, he didn't creep me out like my neighbor who I liked to call The Mechanic. This man was in his early thirties and he sat outside his apartment door, wearing no shirt, while he smoked endless cigarettes every evening. The owner of the building said he worked at a nearby garage.

The Mechanic had one of those intense vibes, as if he had

seen and done everything, and nothing would catch him off guard. There was nothing sweet or sincere about him. He was probably disturbed, judging by the intense look in his dark eyes and his willingness to engage in heated discussions with our other neighbors.

Once when he was taking his garbage to the dumpsters, he had spotted me dancing in my underwear in my apartment through my front window when I forgot to close the curtains. After that, I hadn't been able to look in his direction for days.

One evening, Toby was supposed to take me to an expensive dinner at a new restaurant. I was all dressed up in a twin set and skirt that I had bought at a thrift store. Except for a loose button and a tiny stain, they were practically new. I colored in the scratches on my black pumps with a magic marker and I sat on the sofa to wait for him.

Half an hour later, he hadn't shown. My phone rang. He said he was running late and asked if I would please wait for him. Of course, I said I would wait, even though I was exhausted after working overtime at the factory.

The moment I hung up my phone though, I kicked off my shoes and peeled off the top layer of my twin set. My apartment was stifling hot and I felt as if I was going to expire any moment in these clothes. I closed my eyes for a moment, wondering if I should dig out my ancient electric fan, when I dozed off.

I had one of those dreams, the kind that had been haunting me ever since I had been dating Toby and I decided to take the high road away from my libido. It featured The Mechanic, of course, and I was doing terrible, horny, vivid things with him that would make a porn star blush.

Suddenly, I woke and looked disorientated around my apartment. What time was it? Where was Toby? My entire body seemed to be burning up. Slipping my pumps back on, I stepped outside my apartment to cool off.

The Mechanic was sitting in his lawn chair.

"So where is your boyfriend?" he asked me. "I thought you always went out with him on Saturday nights."

Trying to push the recent images of my dream to the back of my mind, I glared at him.

"I'm really surprised that is the type you go for," he said.

"What's that supposed to mean?" I asked.

He shrugged.

"Why are you even speaking to me?" I asked.

He didn't answer me. I couldn't believe he was judging my choice in men when he didn't even know me.

Teetering in my pumps on the driveway gravel, I walked over to him to give him a piece of my mind. Upon seeing him closer, I knew this was a mistake, because he was even sexier. There was a cleft in his chin I hadn't noticed before.

"You know this is none of your business," I said.

"I just thought you might go for a different type," he said.

He was baiting me to argue with him, I thought. Why did I ever walk over here? I should just walk away.

I turned to go, but my pump slipped on the gravel. My foot twisted. I tried to right myself, but I lost my balance. I fell right into his lap.

For a moment, we were both so stunned that we just sat there staring at the other, but then he kissed me. It was a surprising kiss. It was nothing like kissing him in my dream or kissing Ben or kissing Big Mike. Of course, his mouth tasted like an ashtray, but he was an amazing kisser. There was hunger, but not a crushing need to make me submit. Quite simply, it was a kiss that could last an hour, and I found myself lost in it, drawn inside it, not knowing which way was up.

Suddenly, I heard car tires on the gravel. I opened my eyes to see Toby in his car slowly passing us, his stunned face in the window. I leapt off the mechanic's lap, but Toby slammed his foot on the gas pedal and spun the car around. It fishtailed wildly as he tried to steer it out of the parking lot. He clipped the mailboxes and the car came to an immediate halt.

I ran over to his car and frantically opened the driver's side door.

"Are you all right?" I cried.

He looked over at me, blinking in disbelief. Then his gaze stopped on my arm.

"What is that on your arm?" he asked.

I froze. I had never shown him my tattoo either.

"It's Claude," I said.

He shook his head.

"I can't believe I've been dating a tattooed whore," he said.

Closing his car door, he backed up his car and sped out of the driveway.

I stood there stunned. Once again, my libido had ruined everything. I would never have a normal life, a decent job, or a good home. I would never have a straight middle finger. I would never meet the man of my dreams.

With a start, I realized The Mechanic was standing behind me. I spun and faced him. Had he been there the entire time? Had he heard everything? I bit my lower lip, realizing my mouth was still tingling from his kiss.

"So that puts him out of the picture," he said. "I never thought he was right for you anyway."

I glared at him. He leaned in closer to me. I could smell his skin.

"Are you going to tell me why you have my name tattooed under a rabbit on your arm?" he asked.

I stared at him in shock and then glanced at bunny Claude. They had the same name! I was so angry at that moment that I really didn't care what anyone thought. I was just going to tell the truth.

"I used to have this stuffed rabbit. I loved him to death, but my parents caught me humping him and they burned him in a pile of leaves," I said. "His name was Claude."

There was silence. I stared into his eyes, trying to read his reaction, but how could I read it when I hardly even knew him, and with a painful twist, I realized I desperately did want to know how to read it because of that freaking kiss.

"I don't know what this says about me," he said slowly. "But your little story just made incredibly horny."

The Protocol of La Fère

Florence Dugas

"We met at the lycée," she said. "In preparatory class, just before the *bac*."

I looked at her. She hadn't changed much, or so it seemed. If I was to believe her, she was now twenty-three years old, she'd just gained her teaching certificate, and would probably teach next year. But she had kept that very young look – it was undoubtedly not mere chance, she perpetuated her adolescence, faces talk as much as masks. Gray eyes and black hair, cut very short, with thick locks, and milky skin. Judith Salomon was rather beautiful. She beamed – though I detected signs of anxiety in that slight swelling of the veins at her temples, but that could also be a symptom of fatigue.

"We were living in Laon at the time."

Laon, its cathedral, its ramparts, its tedium, all that history gathered in a few middle-class houses and the sky of the Aisne: even when the weather was fine, something gray hung in the air, like sheets damp and crumpled in the morning.

"Doctor," she said, "can you help me?"

She half stood up from the sofa. The effect of her grey eyes suddenly full of tears was not lost.

"We had an essay to write, I had to meet him. We were attending the course, sitting next to each other, the chances of the beginning of the year, when one finds oneself in an unfamiliar milieu. The weather was still nice, in September, I was wearing a T-shirt. He took hold of my left arm and wrote his phone number on my skin, just before the bend of the elbow.

'So you won't forget it.' He had a strange way of speaking, as if he always had a second meaning in the most innocuous words. I looked at my arm and blushed."

She hesitated. Her voice had a different tone now.

"My grandmother survived Treblinka," she said. "She was thirteen in 1944, but she looked older, and the SS commandant spared her – he was obviously up to something. Three months after she entered the camp, the Russians arrived and liberated them. She was one of the very few who didn't go hungry.

"She got married, ten years later, to a French soldier stationed in Germany, who brought her here. They had a daughter – my mother – who married a young engineer from Saint Gobain in 1976, a Jew, but I always thought that was pure chance."

I refrained from telling her that there is no such thing as pure chance, and that the daughter of a deported Pole marrying a Mr Salomon is a way to recover a filiation, to go back to the tree.

"She died the following year, giving birth. One thinks that doesn't happen any longer.

"My father literally gave me away – abandoned me to my grandmother. I saw him more and more rarely. I don't look anything like my mother, but I think I am a kind of remorse for him, a suffering anyway. To make a long story short, my grandmother was still very pretty, she could even pass for my mother. Did I say I look a lot like her?

"I called him one evening. We arranged to meet at his place. Then I rubbed my arm clean. I had a lot of trouble erasing those ten absurd numbers. A trace remained. It's my grandmother who noticed: 'You've been marked with a number, too?' she smiled. Everything that reminded her of the camps made her smile. She has made a remarkable system of self-defence out of it. Sometimes there is just that smile – and I know she thinks of Treblinka, and that her thoughts are not joyful.

"She never told me anything. I examined all the photo books, the survivors' stories; I knew all the barracks, the watchtowers, the striped pajamas, the hollowed faces, the dormitories and showers. I saw all those photos. When my grandmother smiled, automatically, the pictures come back to my mind – but they are images, aren't they? Not life . . . On her arm she also has five numbers – now that she's getting old, the skin is withering a bit, and only a trace remains, exactly like that phone number badly erased on my arm that evening.

"I went to his place, no longer thinking about it. He opened the door. 'You are late,' he said. I blushed like the day before – I remembered all the more for I don't make a habit of it, and I didn't understand why his every word made me feel uneasy. He helped me take off my raincoat – it was raining, for a change, my hair was wet, he ruffled it as if to dry it. He grabbed it with his hands and pulled me toward him. I felt all weak, helpless.

"He didn't kiss me – and during those five years he never did, actually. That would be . . . how to say . . . inappropriate.

"We were in a kind of living room, cluttered with military memorabilia – his father is a colonel, today, and he collects objects, weapons, and uniforms. In his house there is even a room entirely devoted to models and armies of tin soldiers to play kriegspiel. A maniac.

"He was holding me by my hair, my legs were shaking. He made me kneel down. Then he removed my sweater and bra.

"He stepped back a little, to judge the effect. I was on my knees, in jeans, bare breasted, a bit cold. When I think about our meetings, there has always been that sensation of cold. He is very good at bringing me into damp and badly heated places. I will tell you about my weekend later on. That's why I'm here. Because it continues and it can no longer go on.

"I stared at him – his blond hair, against the light slightly, gave him a kind of halo. And those limpid eyes appeared lit from within.

"He ordered me not to look at him, to keep my head down. 'Open the zipper of your jeans,' he said. 'Yes, that's good: just open, not pull down.'

"He came back to me. He undid his belt, caressed my cheek with its leather. It was only at that moment that I realized I was literally drenched – it was pouring out of me, my belly was at melting point and I was terrorized.

"He finished undoing his trousers and slapped me across the face several times with his cock before forcing it in my mouth.

"He went in so far that I felt nauseous. He had a robust cock, rectilinear, wide at its base – thicker than my wrist. I started to go back and forth the best I could. I told myself I deserved to suck that big uncircumcised penis. It was like desired rape. I was suffocating slightly.

"It was the first time. For everything, by the way, it was the first time. Like when he went behind me and pulled my jeans down to mid-thigh. When he ordered me to lean forward, head in hands, buttocks offered. When he penetrated me with the tip of his fingers, testing the solidity of my hymen before plunging his fingers into my ass – three fingers, right away. It was just before he sodomized me – not for one moment, at that time, did I think he could take me any other way.

"And then words. When he told me to wrap my tongue tight around it, to go back up to the glans before plunging again, my nose in his pubic hair. When he came out of my mouth, he said that I was useless, incapable of making him come. He said it again when he came out of my ass: 'Incapable of making me come – what are you good at?' I crawled at his feet, told him I was sorry, I was going to make him come, I would be able to do it. He came back into my mouth – his penis had a bitter taste I learned to recognize, but again, he didn't come. He was doing it on purpose, of course.

"He finished undressing me, he made me walk up and down. We went into the kitchen, he made me lie down on the very cold white varnished wooden table. There were neon tubes on the ceiling and he ordered me to touch myself there, in front of him, spreading my legs wide. The idea that he was watching me made me come almost immediately.

"He told me off; obviously, that was the purpose of the game. I was panting, I had come so intensely that my thighs were soaked. He inserted himself between my legs, lifted them to place my heels on his shoulders. I wanted to look at him but I closed my eyes, because of the neon, and he deflowered me.

"Since I've known him, he has always liked to fuck me in harsh and at the same time gloomy lights, neon, bare lightbulbs, hanging on a wire. Stage spotlights. And on cold surfaces – lacquered woods, paving stones. Only once did we do it in his bedroom, but he had thrown some white sheets on the floor, which he'd carefully sprinkled with water, before stretching me on the damp material. He rolled me in it, only letting the part of my body he wanted to use show.

"I felt a brief, sharp pain, then my blood flowed, at least I thought it was blood. He pinched my breasts hard, and I came again. When he pulled out of me, he still hadn't ejaculated, and he said I was useless, I was good for nothing. He removed the belt from his trousers and hit me several times on the breasts and belly.

"I fell on my knees and took him in my mouth again. He didn't stop hitting me, on the back and buttocks, harder and harder, and I stopped sucking because I had come again."

I look at her carefully, straight into her face. She is not embarrassed, neither by recalling her memories nor by her use of the most precise words – it is plain that she takes delight in it. As if such a graphic confession was part of a protocol imposed by the master, and that, far from saying something on neurosis, it was part of its manifestation – its complacency, I should say. Surely not. Judith uses those words because she thinks they are adequate – and I have a very brief flash, imagining her in class, in front of her bewildered students, with those same words, spoken in that calm, balanced voice.

"That's how our relationship started.

"He told me to get dressed, immediately, without having a wash, my panties sticky, the jeans stained with the blood, which still dripped. And the rest.

"I asked him where the toilets were. He took me there, left the door open, watching me with interest – delighted, without showing it, because of my confusion when the gush of piss hit the water in the bowl, like a heavy fountain.

"He gave me, in detail, the protocol of our meetings. The exact time. The way I had to always kneel down as soon as I entered. The underwear I had to wear from now on – or rather, not wear. He ordered me to go to a saddler to buy a crop for breaking in horses – specifying that the handle had to be metallic. 'What are you?' he asked me. 'I'm nothing.' 'No,' he specified, 'you're less than nothing, you're my slave.' 'I'm your slave, yes . . .'

"The next day, seeing him in class – I had sat alone instinctively, far away from him – gave me a shock. I had spent the night thinking it all over, trying to understand why, and my nerves were on edge, as if after insomnia. I looked for a long time at my skin, covered in red patches, the exact demarcation of the belt with which he had chastised me – that's the word I used spontaneously. Chastised for some fault – and each time I reached that point, I caressed myself and came, and the question disappeared – or rather, the eventual answer – but the question remained, burning, and I caressed myself again.

"Five days later, another meeting – just after class. I had brought the crop, spotted several days before and bought just prior to going to see him. The door was ajar, I entered and looked for him. He didn't seem to be home. I took my clothes off and knelt down in the middle of the living room, in front of a heavy, low table where I had laid the crop. He made me wait an extremely long time. He was there, of course, scrutinizing my submission.

"That day he just hit me on the loins, buttocks, and thighs, in neat parallel stripes. 'Count the blows,' was all he said.

"At ten I thought it had to stop, he was doing it just to draw lines, I was not going to be able to refrain from screaming much longer. At thirty, I said to myself he will be fed up soon, the stripes are probably overlapping, forming a mesh, and it was no longer of interest, from an aesthetic point of view. I almost tried to get up, but he had stretched me over the lacquered wood, and bound my wrists to the legs of the table.

"He stopped at sixty, and I was nothing but pain – no, I was beyond pain. I had screamed of course, pleaded, cried, and still the leather rained down. I don't know when I thought, strongly thought, that I deserved what was happening to me.

"He stopped, caressed me with the metallic knob of the crop, which he pushed inside, in one orifice, then the other. 'You want it, don't you?' No point specifying what I wanted. 'Please, please . . .' 'Please what?' 'Take me, please . . .' 'Take me how, little slut?' I realized he wanted to hear the words, and I begged him to sodomize me, as deep as he could, to tear me apart. That pleased him, but he put his cock first in my mouth. My nose was stuffy with tears, and I was half suffocating while sucking him.

"That's it. It's been going on for five years."

She looked at me. Obviously, it could all be fake – all the more so for it sounded true. Psychopaths are good actors, when acting is part of their delirium. But at worst (was it then something worse than the suspicion that it could be true?), the narrative was there, and was telling something. And I felt something inside me, quivering.

"Other rituals were organized, over time. The uniforms he wore. That so-special sensation of rough material which grated against my buttocks when he fucked me in the ass. The weapons he made me lick, after having pushed them in certain orifices. The fiction of his 'army comrades' to whom he sometimes loaned me. But above all, that way to make me an enemy, the prisoner tortured to confess some unspeakable secret . . ."

I was listening to her, and I was no longer listening: there was something impossible in her story, but nevertheless I believed more and more in the reality of what she was narrating. Usually, and contrary to the old jokes on the subject, the masochist doesn't live on the same planet as the sadist. I would even say that they loathe each other. The idea that someone could sexually enjoy suffering, outside his own protocol, offends one extremely; the idea that the other could benefit from his own cruelty, canceling thus her own will, shocks the other. So Judith was suffering not in her flesh, but in someone else's – and that dirty perv who was making a martyr of her, was – grudgingly – the instrument of it.

"I'm coming to the point of that weekend," she said after a long pause. Her silence, after a few seconds, had respected mine, a rare thing with psychopaths, who love telling their story.

"I now live in Paris. I only go back to Laon for the cere-
monies he imposes on me. He phoned me on Thursday – he was
expecting me on Friday night, at the station.

"In the train, the man opposite me was nice, well-read, and
frivolous looking. We chatted, and for the hour and a half our
journey lasted, I had all that time, in my head, that second
thought – I was once again going toward that horror, and my
belly was all puckered with pleasure, and I didn't listen to
anything that nice, handsome man was telling me. Something,
insidiously, was cutting me off from the world. It's as if I'm in a
camp – a private camp, for my sole use, where the world is no
longer relevant.

"He was waiting for me. Our greetings have been reduced in
time to the essential – an exchange of looks, I lower my eyes,
mentally kneel down.

"Of course, I'm not fooled. In reality, he's a little lout who
did his studies too. And who has guessed what I am since the
beginning. Who has read me like no one else has read me. To be
honest, I've already told this story two or three times – each
time they looked at me, horrified, explained to me that I'm mad
– so? I can diagnose that too.

"For a while I visited some specialized circles, or which
pretend to be, anyway. Some *masters*, as they say, and *submissive
girls*. Poor little men, poor little wankers, always so worried at
the thought that one could enjoy suffering and humiliation . . .
yes, able to elaborate a script of submission, minute by minute,
where all the violations are codified and punished. But with no
question, ever, as to the reason, or unreasonableness, which
pushes the *submissive* to accept those games.

"We left for La Fère. Do you know it? It's a garrison town
since time immemorial. One of the last places before the east. In
crisis now that the armies are reduced.

"Whole army barracks are deserted, and that is where he took
me. Empty huts, weeds everywhere, broken windows, abandoned dormitories, watchtowers without sentries. He stopped
at the entrance. 'Step out, go to the middle of the courtyard and
undress.' November in such a place is November twice over. It
was cold and grey, I was already shivering in my coat, even

more when I took it off. The rest followed, until I was naked in the middle of a paved courtyard, near a pole which, in the past, held a flag. Night was falling, he turned on the headlights of the car to cast light on me. The headlights were very white, dazzling. I heard the car door slam, I saw his shadow moving toward me . . . The taste for uniforms, you see: he was dressed like an SS officer, from cap to patent leather knee-high boots, he was holding in his hand a cosh – I didn't recognize him at that moment, he had become so much himself, the blond hair shaved on his temples, the ruthless, limpid eyes. '*Schnell*,' he shouted. I didn't even know he could speak German. '*Schnell, schnell!*' He lashed at my buttocks, while I stumbled along, moving toward a barrack hut in front of me, sliding on the wet paving stones, bent over because of the cold, the humiliation, too. I remember feeling embarrassed because of my hard breasts, the nipples stiff with cold, and arrogant. I was experiencing again the feeling I had earlier in the train, that foreknowledge of the horror – as if everything I had lived till then was only the draft for an ultimate show . . . I fell twice, sliding over the greasy paving stones. I had long streaks of mud all over my body.

"He made me enter an old dormitory, then a room next to the showers. He hit me behind the knee and I collapsed on the frozen tiles. He grabbed me by the hair, dragged me to a corner, and tied me with handcuffs to a leaking pipe. He hit me four or five more times, I was screaming, protecting my face. Then he threw his crop on the floor, took out a pair of scissors from his pocket, and started to cut my hair – I used to wear it medium-length till four days ago. The locks fell on my shoulders and belly – he was cutting it short, hacking at the mass.

"When I came back on Sunday, my head completely covered, when I undressed in my bathroom, and my mirror showed me that poor bungled head, with the white trace of his snips, I didn't recognize myself – no, it's not that, I recognized someone who was not me – who was me only externally, but in a few snips, he had made another woman come to the surface.

"He tied me up and left me there, all night. I didn't hear the car go. Night fell, I was alone, I ended up shouting, crying, there was just the sound of the wind, the cold, the damp. All night long. For a moment I was crying so much that I felt nauseous and vomited bile. No, that is not the right word. I was vomiting myself, that's it, myself.

"He came back in the morning, he was still speaking German. He told me I had to choose between absolute submission and immediate death. It was like lightning, you know. The feeling of recognizing a scene one has already lived. The other, in me – not me, for I would have preferred death – the other said she wanted to live, and that she would do what he wanted and that she would submit.

"He made her kneel down, while leaving her tied up – the hand-cuffs slid on the pipe, he opened the trousers of his uniform and forced his cock in her mouth. She sucked him as she could, awkwardly – as if all my science had vanished. After a minute, he kicked her in the belly, telling her she didn't know how to do it, that I couldn't do anything. That she was just good enough to lick his boots – he pushed her neck down, and I licked the patent leather. I still have the smell of polish in my head. Again he kicked me, she collapsed at the bottom of the wall, bent over. Something warm ran along my back, and I realized he was pissing on her.

"He untied her, dragged her around the whole camp. It was drizzling. She was frozen stiff and she was burning inside. A little later in the old kitchen quarters, he plunged two fingers into her sex – the leather of his gloves was frozen, but he plunged them effortlessly, so ready, open, and available she was."

She is silent. Is it my turn to say something? From the start I had created for myself an attentive mask, and slightly doubtful, too. The abomination of her story must not taint my listening. The purity of her story must not provoke my own desire.

"To cut it short," she resumes, "we stayed there for two days. He barely fed her, some filthy things thrown on the floor, that she had to lap up, her hands handcuffed behind her back. He penetrated her in every orifice, without ever coming. He hit her a lot, yes. He tortured her, in fact. It's incredible what a boy with imagination can do with needles, time, and alcohol. All the time he called her a filthy Jew – and it was a red rod plunging deep into her, each time, to touch the other, the one suffering inside her – not her, for she was in the ecstasy of a fantasy realized.

"She reminds me – this is going to make you smile, isn't it? – that she thought several times about her mother, that mother she never knew, thinking she is the one who should have expiated, but that she had passed to her the torch of guilt – and it's her she blamed for being a survivor, in that long female filiation, since her grandmother, who had done what was needed to survive, in the past, and didn't talk about it, and the whole story was coming out now, and it was her shouting the shame of survival, under a low sky . . . At three in the afternoon, on Sunday, it was almost dark, and there was that sudden storm. He left her in the middle of the courtyard, chained, with rusty old chains, to the pole in the middle, like a fallen flag. Washed by the rain of her stains. He left in his car, he looked at her from far away, she could see the smoke of his cigarette coming out of his open window. He turned the headlights on, like on Friday night, to illuminate her ruin."

She is silent again.

Looks at me.

"You have some doubt," she says.

I don't know if I doubt her. I no longer know, in reality. She has that characteristic of the perverted, she knows the cause of her delirium, she has explored in detail the transferred guilt, the unbearable survival. Fifty years after the end of the war, it's still there, the memory passed on like an inheritance.

She stands up suddenly:

"You have some doubt," she repeats.

In a few quick movements, she undresses. Her body is a wound, covered in bruises, gashes, cuts, and scabs. And I look neither at the dried blood nor at the traces of blows. Only at that milky skin, or what's left of it, the very dark triangle between her thighs, then her face again . . . Time stops.

"Kneel down," I say. "Head down, come on, will you never learn?"

Of course, and as every time, I plunge deep into her mouth, up to the hilt, as far as her glottis, until she has tears in her eyes.

"You told our story really well!" I say.

And as always, for five years, it's only when I remember her story that I manage, finally, to come.

Hand-Jobs

Mike Kimera

Is this thing on? Ok. Strange, I don't normally get to see myself on video. It doesn't really look like me. So, anyway, let me read this so that I get it right.

I am subject 103. I'm male, 57 years old, 5' 11", 211 lbs, heterosexual and widowed. I confirm that I am taking part in this sociology study of my own free will and that the material in this tape can be used anonymously for academic research.

Your advert said that you wanted to hear from people with strong sexual preferences; well, I have one of those. These days it's my only sexual preference.

This is hard to say, even to a camera.

I like hand-jobs from whores.

I know how that sounds: selfish and pathetic but that doesn't stop it from being true. It's not all that's true. I used to enjoy making love with my wife. But that was as much about the love as the sex. And even then, if I'm really honest, fucking never matched the gob-smacking impact of a good hand-job.

My dad bought me my first one the week that I started as a conductor on the buses, back in 1967. "One good job deserves another," he'd said. Then he'd added, "And say nowt to your mother." Like I was going to go home and say, "Mam, you'll never guess what me and Dad did today." Daft pillock.

My first time wasn't a very sophisticated affair. Back then it was called getting a hand-shandy. I got mine from a blousy woman who smelled of beer and fags and who wore enough make-up to paint the *Queen Mary*. I sat beside her in the pub on the Dock Road with me Dad sitting opposite me, while she tossed me off with one hand under the table and supped her half of stout with the other. I sat there trying to look like nothing was happening while all the while I wanted to shout and groan and swear. It didn't take long but it was long enough for me to know that I wanted more.

I know everyone thinks that the Sixties were swinging but round our way there was no such thing as free love – you paid up front. It put a dint in my pay packet but it kept a smile on my face.

I may have been ignorant but I wasn't stupid. I'd seen mates pay and get the clap. I didn't want to wear a rubber – it was like wearing Wellington Boots back then – so I got into the habit of hand-jobs.

'Course, nowadays it's all blow jobs and that, but this was years before Linda Lovelace showed how deep her throat was. And besides, most of these girls, you wouldn't want to go near their mouths; you know where they've been.

I got tired of the buses after a year or two and did a spell in the Fleet Air Arm on the *Ark Royal* based mostly out of Malta. I was on joint Brit/Yank shore patrol, in the Gut in Valletta, cleaning up the mess when things got ugly. I saw a thing or two that taught me to keep it in my pants unless I knew I was in safe hands so to speak. Before Malta, I thought brothels were like saloons in the Westerns, something grand but tacky, not some crumbling dive filled with drunk sailors and young women with old eyes.

I came home in '73 and courted Patricia Mahon, a nice girl who'd lived down our alley since she was a kid. The third time we went out together I took her to the Gaumont to see "Don't Look Now" because she'd said she liked ghost stories. We sat in the big seats in the back, where it was dark and we could cuddle. I'd expected a bit of kissing and that but nothing more. Except it turned out that the movie was quite sexy and Patricia Mahon, while still being a nice girl, had learnt another use for the handkerchief the nuns had made her carry at school. While Julie Christie and Donald Sutherland where at it on the screen, I was getting the most exciting hand-job of my life in the back row of the cinema.

Patricia and I never spoke about sex. Not even after we were married. We just did it a lot. Then we had the kids and we did it less. Then she got ill. The thing is, even when she was ill I'd get hard. My cock has no conscience but I do. I was celibate a long time.

After my wife died of the cancer, I knew there'd never be anyone else. At least no one I wanted. And I knew I'd get sad and twisted without a woman's touch. So, when things got tough, I went back to the whores.

Of course it's all changed now. The girls don't hang 'round saying "fancy a nice time, Deary" any more. These days the whores have websites with photos and lists of services and how much everything will cost.

I prefer older whores. I'd not want some slip of a girl, young enough to be me daughter, touching me like that. And I like them to be English. Not that I'm prejudiced or anything, but you read about how some of these girls from Russia and Thailand and the like are here against their will and I don't want that on my conscience.

I shopped around a bit in the beginning but nowadays I go to the same few girls when I'm in the mood. They know what I want and they don't make a fuss. One of them even makes a decent cup of tea.

Still, it's not the tea you want to know about, is it? You want to know about the sex.

Well, there's not much to tell, really. Sex is not about the words is it? It's about the doing. And I know just how I want it done. I like to stand. And I don't like to take me clothes off. I prefer the girl to sit. Kneeling would make me feel like I had to hurry up and if she stands she gets too close and I'd have to pay her too much attention. When she sits, she can work in comfort and I can concentrate on what I'm there for.

I've always found it easier to come standing up. And better too. I stand there and unzip (I always do that myself. I hate having people fussing down there) and then I let the dog see the rabbit.

Most of the time, I'm at least at half mast when the girl starts and if it's been a while I'm fully at attention. They know I don't want them to use their mouths, not even for talking, so they pour on some baby oil and get started.

I like to hold on to something for balance, a chair or the mantelpiece or something, and I keep my eyes closed. The girls are good at what they do and soon my arse is clenching and the muscles in my thighs are as hard as my cock. Towards the end I'm up on the balls of my feet with my head tipped back and my mouth partly open. When the come starts to flow it's like flying. I feel light and happy and released from everything, even gravity. Then I thank the girl; wash up in the sink and go. I like just being able to go like that. It helps me keep the mood for longer.

Of course you don't stay free of gravity for long. After a while what you've just done feels dirty and weak and you want to tell yourself that you'll never do it again. Except you know that that's bollocks, a passing mood that wears off soon enough. I'm not proud of what I do but I'm not ashamed neither. I've lived long enough to know there's some things you just have to do, so you do them with as much dignity and as little fuss as you can.

That's all I've got to say, really.

I'm not sure it's any help to you but it felt good to talk about it. Not that I'd want to talk to anybody about it face to face but talking to the camera is like being in confession only without the Hail Marys after.

Now let's see if I can switch this thing off without breaking anything.

Attempt to Rise

Alana Noel Voth

Drowning is not so pitiful
As the attempt to rise.

Emily Dickinson

The summer before my sixteenth birthday, it was all over the newspaper, BIG BOLD headlines that announced, "Joe Wilde wanted for murder." I saw his picture once: older guy with a leathery face, black eyes, and a black moustache. The girl he took was my age. According to the newspaper, Wilde told this girl he was a photographer and lured her to his car. There, he hit her in the head with something then drove across the southwest with her in the front seat beside him. People saw them together and weren't worried about the girl's spaced-out eyes and bleeding temple. Wilde killed her outside Durango, Colorado and then dumped her body off an overpass where she tumbled through underbrush to a creek. Her head remained submerged underwater until the highway patrol found her days later.

My father used to smack me for insubordination. Definition: dirty looks, stomping, slamming doors, and wanting to know why. *Because I said so.* That was all I got from my father followed by a smack to my head.

My kindergarten teacher was a man. He stood behind me waiting for me to pick up a pencil with my left hand so he could tell me to use my right.

"No," he'd say, "use your right hand, Lena."

My whole life went like that. I was small and men seemed

overpowering, even scary. My ex-boyfriend, Nick, was six feet tall like my father and knew what I was thinking all the time.

"Know what you're thinking? You'd like to suck my cock."

I'd actually been thinking how I wanted to go to the zoo, but I sucked his cock because he was the boss, and I loathed him for it but had no idea how to tell him, "Go suck your own cock," because I was afraid of him – to make him mad, to ask him too many questions, like why. *Why shouldn't we go to the zoo today? Why can't I just leave you? Why can't I tell you to leave?*

"Hey," he'd say while I was on my knees, "open your throat. Tongue. Little harder. Watch your teeth! More tongue. Faster. Swallow it, swallow."

Four months ago, after Nick left, I went to a party. A young guy, nearly a boy, opened the door. I wore a yellow dress, and my hair was in a ponytail. No makeup. Open-toed shoes. The boy wore jeans and a tee shirt. He had hair in his eyes, terrible posture. As I passed him, I felt his finger press against my side, just a second, as if by accident, and it was unexpected, his touch, his trembling bravery, and so I turned to look at him.

Without a word, the boy ducked down a hallway. Like he was scared. I felt a pull or a chill, like when a ghost passes through your body, and I actually shut my eyes. Then I went further into the room and to the bar and ordered an apple martini. I stood to the side of the room. Never good at parties. Nick had said so. Anti-social, social phobic. A child. Late bloomer.

What's wrong with you?

I used to cry when he fucked me.

Jesus Christ, what's the matter?

I never had any idea. Sadness. Anger. Unable to articulate my problem or act upon it, I loathed Nick for his arrogance and meanness.

I set down my empty glass at the party, apple martini all gone, and went looking for a bathroom.

The boy was in there – as if he'd been waiting for me all along. I was startled and then embarrassed. His pants were a puddle around his ankles, and he stood in front of the toilet, cock in hand.

I said something like, "Oh!" and then dropped my eyes, stumbled backwards and hit the door with my shoulder. "Ouch!"

"I was just taking a piss!" the boy said. I heard him flush the toilet.

"Sorry." I rubbed my shoulder – then peeked. I couldn't help it.

The boy had bright blue eyes. He'd shoved his cock back in his pants, but he had an erection. Obvious as daylight. I wanted to smile.

The boy gazed at me, blinking, and I stared at him, not blinking at all. What a wonder. I felt something . . . like a fire inside my stomach, a rushing torrent through my limbs, like I could spring on him any minute, and so I took another step into the bathroom, him not moving at all and still blinking, and then I heard a noise – someone in the hallway behind me, clearing her throat.

I backed out of the room and pulled the door shut. "Occupied," I said pushing past the other woman, whoever she was, not meeting her eyes, and then I was out of the house and in the cool night.

There was a community college three blocks from my apartment. Every morning, I went for walks. Some of the freshman, the boys, moved in packs and blocked my way on the sidewalk, nudging each other while ogling my ass as I passed them. I kept going. Hurrying along, sweating and nervous, uncomfortable.

The other boys, the ones who walked alone, looked at me under their eyelashes. They walked with slouched shoulders, shuffling their feet.

I looked at those boys head-on, smiling in a way I could feel my front tooth hooking the edge of my lip.

I was putting a bed together. The bed frame was heavy, and I panted as I manoeuvred pieces around then drilled in the screws. I was determined to do this by myself, fuck you Nick who'd owned the bed and taken it with him, fuck you. I moved the box spring onto the bed frame, but then I couldn't get the mattress on top of the box spring. Goddammit.

The mattress was heavy but pliable and kept threatening to fold in on me any minute and then smother me underneath it. Damn it, sonofabitch. My body felt slick with sweat. I was shaking. Finally, I succumbed to sobs. After a while, I picked up the phone to call the management office. I tried to keep the embarrassment out of my voice. I tried to stop sniffling.

"Natalie? Hi! I'm trying to move this mattress and need help. Yeah, heavy. Listen, any maintenance guys around today?" My armpits had begun crying sweat to a space between my breasts.

"Elijah's here."

"OK. Great. Could you send Elijah, then?"

"No problem. Ten minutes?"

I hung up the phone and took a bottle of water from the fridge. I drank it, all of it, and then held the bottle to my forehead, between my breasts, and then to my nipples. They stung and stood straight. I made a tuna sandwich and ate it in five bites before roaring with a loud belch. I really didn't want a man here at all bossing me around, showing off. I heard a knock on the door and left the kitchen to stand on tiptoe to look through the peephole.

"Are you Elijah?" I sounded pissed off.

"Yeah." Pleasant voice, not too deep.

I opened the door. Elijah wasn't tall. He had a smear of something on his cheek. He swallowed, looking at me. "Need help moving a mattress?" Elijah reached up to scratch his face, smearing the smear on his cheek.

"Yeah, that's me." I looked at him, pleased. "Aren't you a little young to do maintenance work?" I liked the idea I was teasing him. It felt good.

"I'm old enough," he said, on the defensive. "I'm eighteen."

I leaned in the doorway, gripping the edge with one hand. "OK, sorry."

Elijah straightened his tool belt, which hung halfway down his hips. "I'm working to get a place. Maybe like this one." He gazed at the room behind me.

I stepped from the doorway. "This way, then."

Elijah followed. I liked that he followed. I could hear the clank of his tool belt as we entered the bedroom. I stepped over the tools and the directions. Elijah stood in the doorway surveying the scene and then cleared his throat and went to the mattress and crouched beside it.

"You got this frame together yourself?" he asked.

"Isn't that something?" I tensed, waiting for him to insult my efforts.

"Yeah," he said, like he was really impressed.

Nothing happened for a minute. He surveyed my progress; I surveyed him; and then Elijah took hold of one side of the mattress and I took hold of the other. Together, we managed it perfectly.

I smiled at him across the bed. "Thanks for the help, Elijah."

"No problem. It's a nice bed. I've got a lumpy old thing at my foster family's. It's a piece of shit."

"You live with a foster family?"

Elijah looked at his fingernails. He had paint under them. "Yeah, just for now. They were getting money for me, you know until my eighteenth birthday, but now I'm eighteen so not any more. I decided to work here, so maybe I'd get a place like this." He looked around the room. "It's nice. Really is."

"Where does your foster family live?" I tried to sound polite, polite conversation.

"Up the street, in a subdivision. Hey, do you think I could get some water?" Elijah met my eyes.

"Water?" Not wine or beer? We could get roasted and belch, spout of offensive words, wrestle on the floor, and then look at each other's privates.

"Yeah, if it's not a pain in your ass."

"No, of course not."

In the kitchen, I took bottled water from the fridge. "Want ice with it?"

"Yeah, thanks."

I put ice in a glass and then poured water into the glass. The bottle emptied with a chugging sound. The ice cubes somersaulted. Elijah sat at my kitchen table.

"So what happened to your real parents?" I brought him the water. My hand brushed his as he took it.

"They're dead."

"Oh. Sorry." I looked away a minute then watched him. Elijah's throat moved as he drank. I watched the rowing motion of bones inside his neck, feeling mesmerized. Aching.

Poor baby. Those big brown eyes. The stained jeans. Those rotten foster parents.

Elijah covered his mouth to burp.

"You don't have to do that," I said.

"What?" He watched me a second, his hand between his mouth and the table, a smile edging close to his lips. "What do you mean?"

"I can burp my ABC's. Listen to this."

Elijah listened, his smile now becoming a grin.

"Girls don't usually do that," he said. "Especially, you know, older girls." He looked around the kitchen. "How long you lived here?"

"Three years."

"It's nice."

"I used to live here with my boyfriend. Now it's mine."

"Oh. Wow. Where's he?"

I decided to lie. "He's dead." It would bond us forever. We'd both lost loved ones now.

Elijah was quiet. The empty glass sweated in his hand.

"All done with high school?" I broke the silence to stir him.

"Yeah." He frowned.

"What's wrong? Didn't like it?"

"It was all right."

"Were you one of those guys the girls loved?"

"No."

"I don't believe it. You're so cute."

Elijah stared at the glass in his hand, smearing water with his thumb. He smiled on one side of his mouth. "Thanks. So I guess you were popular."

I sat at the table beside him. "This guy in school, he was like a senior when I was a freshman, told me he wished I'd just shut the hell up because I was driving him crazy with all my questions in math class. Said my boobs were floppy too, and my hair was stringy, and I should just stick a bag over my head so he wouldn't have to look at my ugly face."

Elijah shook his head. "What a retard. You're like Helen of Troy, Helen of Troy times twenty."

I couldn't bear to look at him any more. My eyes watered. I was dizzy with wanting to press him against the table and suck him off, stop, suck him off again. Torture. "You know, I had a sandwich a little while ago, but I'm suddenly hungry. Want to get a pizza?"

"Ahh, I'm supposed to leave here and snake somebody's toilet."

"I'll call Natalie. I'll tell her I need your help with something else – garbage disposal, the closet doors, and the damn faucet's leaking again."

Elijah's face broke into a smile.

Boy in jeans and a tool-belt too big for his hips. Evening sun, freshly cut grass, and ripe apples. My little Dreamsicle Angel. Elijah.

Two days later, I heard a knock on the door. "Who is it?" I was hoping – hoping I knew who it was – and looked through the peephole.

The room brightened behind me. "Hi, Elijah."

"I have something for you," he said to the door.

I opened up. Elijah held out flowers, white daisies that smelled like the field outside the community college. "Like them?"

"Love them." I took the bouquet. "Thanks, Elijah."

"You busy?" he asked.

"No." I waited, making him squirm. "Want to come in?"

"Yeah, sure."

"Close the door behind you, thanks."

I went to the kitchen to find a vase and then peered around the corner. Elijah was studying my books. He leaned down then stood on tiptoe to read each title before moving his finger over the spines, letting his finger ride the spines like a track, hitting bumps, swiping dust away, touching every book. I watched him for the longest time then finally found a vase.

"You like books?" I called out.

"I don't know. I don't read all the time."

I ran water into the vase before placing the flowers in it and then brought them out to the living room. "I could read to you."

Elijah took a book from the shelf. "This one?" *Lord of the Flies.*

"Good one. Nature vs. nurture debate."

Elijah's smile was crooked. "Yeah, but . . . any sex?"

I stared at him. "You want a book about sex?"

"Yeah." He blushed.

"OK, *Fanny Hill.*"

"That sounds, you know, stupid."

"Lots of sex in it."

"You'll read it to me?" His crooked smile went straight.

"Yeah."

"Now?"

"No. Later. How's the job going?"

"OK."

"Getting money saved up?"

"Yeah."

He was lying. I put the vase on the coffee table. "They're pretty."

"When you going to read me that book?"

I went to a window and shoved it open. "Gees, I'm hot."

"Sure are," Elijah said behind me.

It was so cheesy I had to smile. He came up behind me and brushed his hand down my hip. "Boo," he said in my ear.

"You don't scare me." I put my hands in his hair. "But maybe I scare you?" Soft hair and a warm scalp.

Elijah swallowed, staring at my lips.

"Well, do it, then."

His kiss was warm and sloppy and sweet. I felt dizzy. And stopped.

"What's wrong?"

"Nothing." Out of breath.

"Lena?"

"What?"

He reached for a button on my blouse and played with it. "Could we, you know, go to the bedroom? Your bed?"

Elijah had a smooth chest and dime-sized nipples. His arms were slender and pale. He had little bunches of hair in the pits. He didn't have hair on his chest, except little rings around his nipples. His cock pointed to Jesus. His balls sprouted sparse hair. I put his hand where I wanted it.

"Wow, you're slippery," he said. "Is it always like this?"

"Heck, no. You're making me horny."

"Really?" He shoved his fingers further inside me.

I opened my legs then laid back keeping my hand on his wrist, guiding him, hearing the sucking sounds, feeling the friction, the moisture on both of us, his arm trembling, and his cock against my leg. I put his fingers on my clit, told him to concentrate there, don't stop, that's nice, I like that, oh so sweet.

"God, are you coming? I feel something. Shit. Want me to wipe it off your leg?"

"No, baby. Eat it. Tell me what you taste like."

Elijah licked his come off my leg then crawled upward and wedged himself against me before he said in my ear, "I don't know. Maybe like cornstarch."

Elijah burped, scratched his butt, and played with his balls. It was sweet, you know? He spit loogies in my sink. Outside once I said, "Oh, yeah? Watch this!" then launched a fat one at the sidewalk. Elijah rolled over it on his skateboard, wondering if it had stuck to his wheels. He glided beside me, suntanned on his shoulders, glowing around the eyes. Elijah. Five-foot-ten in tennis shoes. Square jaw and no whiskers. He loved scary movies and video games. He brought his PlayStation 2 over one night, and it never left. The grosser the games, the better he liked them. You could code "gratuitous dismemberment" in *Blood Rayne* and then she'd shoot men's limbs off, their heads. I gripped the controller, going wild with my fingers, bam, bam, bam!

Rayne's tits would jiggle with each blast.

"Look at them," Elijah said.

"Look at what?"

I lifted my shirt. Elijah spat on his thumbs and rubbed my nipples. He sucked them like a thirsty baby. "What if something came out?" he said. "That would be great."

Something did come out. He sucked; I squeezed my thighs together, tightened the muscles, released them, and then came, bam-bam-bam.

Elijah left potato chips crumbs in my bed, socks lying around, and dishes in the sink. "Clean up after yourself," I said one afternoon when he was over, half joking. "I live here."

He covered my mouth with a kiss. I came up for air. "I want to be on top of you," he said. "I want to come in your mouth. Let's get drunk. I want get drunk and fuck in your car."

For a second I thought about pushing him off, but then didn't. I felt drunk on something that wasn't alcohol and took beer out, then wine, and then my breasts. Elijah poured beer and wine on my nipples, cold and room temperature, making me shiver and sigh. He sucked it all off while I sat on the kitchen table swinging my legs. He stuck his finger inside me as frantic as if he were picking a booger. I was drunk-on-top-of-drunk and dragged him outside in broad daylight, unlocked the car, and then shoved him in. Cramped and hot. Elijah clamored on top me, shut his eyes, and then we went at it. I kept my eyes opened and looked straight into the eyes of my next-door neighbor as she approached her car next to mine.

She looked away, looked again. Her eyes bulged.

Elijah hollered, "I'm going to blow!"

The woman wasn't much older than me. She opened her purse and took out a cell phone. Elijah pumped inside me, spurting off, oblivious.

I screamed out the window. "Mind your own business, bitch! Fuck you!"

Elijah sat up, cock dripping, chest slathered in sweat.

The woman flew into her car and gunned the engine. I panted and sneered and drooled on myself.

And then Elijah wanted to move in with me.

"But you can't," I said.

I got off the floor where'd we'd been sitting, playing another one of his video games and picked up a plate he'd left on the coffee table, a half eaten sandwich left to go hard in the middle.

"Why not? I'm here all the time."

"But that's just, you know, staying over."

"So I'll stay over permanently."

"But you want to get your own place, right?"

"I love you," he said. "I never said that to anyone. I swear it."

I started toward the kitchen to put his plate in the sink, but Elijah blocked my path.

"I don't want to lose anything any more," he said.

"You're not losing me." I stepped around him and made it to the kitchen sink. I turned on the faucet, rinsing his dish with hot water. "Why don't you get a place in the same building? We'll live close."

He came in the kitchen. "I want to live here with you. Why are you being a bitch?"

I shut off the water. "Fuck you for saying that."

Elijah rushed over, standing in front of me. "Lena. I'm sorry."

I dropped the dish in the sink and then started to move around him again, but he grabbed me, like a weight pulling me down. "Please, Lena, don't. Don't be mad. It'll drive me crazy if you're mad."

"Let go of me, Elijah."

He threw his arms around my waist. "OK, wait. Just listen."

"To what?" I fidgeted, trying to ease his hands off my waist.

Elijah locked his arms around me. His chin was on my shoulder and his face was in my hair. "Have I ever told you about when my parents died?"

"No, Elijah." Not a sob story now.

"The police thought I had something to do with it."

His arms were so tight around me I could barely exhale. "What?"

Elijah lifted his face to look at me. "Just don't make me leave, OK Lena?"

And I went motionless. Like a body on top of the water.

By the Spy Who Loved Me

Maxim Jakubowski

Some women you have sex with.

Some women you sleep with.

And then there are the women you have sex with and then sleep with. A whole night. And during that night, you cannot escape the warmth of their skin close against you on every blurry single occasion you half awaken, you sense their body in the darkness of the room, soft and pale so close to you it could be an extension of your own skin, and you have to repress the urge to pull her against your bulk and squeeze her to death as the tenderness races through your soul like a sweet poison invading your bloodstream, a runaway train with its ineffable cargo of lust and affection

Those are the women who also break your heart.

Those are the women who move your heart in quiet, ardent, hypnotic, mysterious ways.

And she was one of those.

No ifs and buts; no doubts about it.

At the wrong time.

In the wrong places.

We'd met in the mountains. Snow fell on a picture postcard ski resort like a curtain of cotton buds floating, swirling down from a grey sky, minute patterns against the background of peaks and valleys. Here, France. There, Italy. It was a neutral zone, an ideal place for people to meet who shouldn't meet, away from the gaze of security cameras or familiar faces. I was staying at a luxury hotel with parquet flooring and uniformed staff. She had been assigned a room a mile away into the steep hills, some rustic inn with wooden beams criss-crossing the ceilings. Arrangements had been made to organize the exchange in the opulent ground floor salon of my hotel. It was late evening; a lounge singer was crooning a song by Coldplay, badly, his fingers flying like errant quicksilver over the electric piano keys. I was wearing black, as planned, so that she might recognize me. It was unlikely anyone in the noisy apres-ski crowd scattered across the deep sofas would be wearing the same colours, and for security, I had a copy of an obscure Italian crime magazine on the table in front of me, next to my glass of tomato juice. The red and the black. That's what had been agreed. I didn't know who to expect.

Her jet-black curls fell to her shoulders as she made a beeline towards me, her long, lanky legs devouring the floor. She sat across from me, nodded politely and ordered a coffee from the white-jacketed waiter. We sat in silence, quietly observing each other while the music played and the crowd's chatter rose and fell around us. She allowed the spoonful of sugar to float briefly on the coffee's surface before it sank. I noted a few isolated strands of white hairs amongst her darkness. Soft brown eyes. Pale uncovered shoulders. The gentle curve of her neck and slight breasts under the thin material of her white blouse.

She sank her coffee in one gulp and rose to her feet. She walked away slowly, leaving the manila envelope she had been holding in her right hand on the table. I took hold of it and walked swiftly after her.

For a moment, there was a look of confusion on her face; maybe she thought she had left the envelope for the wrong person?

"Come to my room," I asked.

The shadow of a smile crossed her red lips, and she followed me to the lift.

Room 411.

That first night she let me undress her, but would not allow me to kiss her on the mouth. Her hair fell across her naked shoulders like a lion's mane, thick, curling to infinity, heavy, dark as night. Her breasts were small enough that I could cup one in each hand and marvel at their softness, pink pale nipples blending quietly into the whiter landscape of her skin. There was a small brown mole growing inside the crevice of her belly button, another texture for my tongue to wander across before exploring further south through the unclipped, luxuriant jungle of her pubes. Unlike so many other women, she had no distinct smell down there, but the initial sensation was of an all-consuming fire that took me by surprise. Time and again, she rode me like a stallion, delaying penetration and rubbing her cunt against my cock, pressing down on my pelvic bones until I hurt, and could bear it no longer and cramped with a muted cry.

Then we slept, skin touching skin, words redundant, in the peace of the Alpine night, leaving everything unsaid, after our communion of lust.

In the morning, she left around five – she had earlier set the alarm on her mobile phone just before we had dozed off, arms tangled between crumpled sheets in the room's penumbra. I didn't want her to go, but she insisted she had to return to her own hotel, and be seen at breakfast by others. I watched, with pain in my heart, as she slipped on her black tights and then her dress. I blew her a kiss as she moved towards the door.

"Don't get up," she said, as I slipped out from under the quilt, my cock still damp with her juices, and opened the door. I imagined her path, attempting to listen to her steps down the corridor through the wooden partition, shadowing her movements as if practising my spy craft. I did not hear the lift. I stood naked with my back against the hotel room door, with a heavy heart. There was a gentle rapping at the door and I opened it halfway; it was her. She smiled at me and quickly kissed me on the lips.

"My name is Giulia," she said.

I had to stay on at the resort longer, awaiting further instructions from London. She joined me every night. On the second night, we hurriedly undressed right by the door and she suggested we share a bath, while Pink Floyd and other tunes she'd collected MP3 files of played on her laptop which she'd precariously positioned across the sink. Inside the water, she leaned against me and took my cock in her mouth; my throat tightened at her unbidden generosity and purity of desire. The landscape of her body grew familiar, her longs legs, the scattered birthmarks across her flesh, even the small pimples on her rear, the colour of her smile, the look of tenderness in her eyes when she came, the sounds she would make in the throes of pleasure, the way she would turn onto her stomach and invite me to take her from behind and the incandescent vision of my cock digging deep inside her, separating her scarlet sex lips while the puckered hole of her arse almost winked at me in complicity, the way she would say my name, or at any rate the name she thought was mine.

"It can't last."

"No."

"You're beautiful."

"Let's not talk."

We were together for now. And we fucked as if we'd never fucked before with anyone else.

But she was too young, she had another life I knew nothing of and we both were all too aware of how impossible our situation was.

When the time came to make our separate ways, we exchanged telephone numbers.

"It's wrong."

"I know."

"I have to go to New York. Join me there."

"I don't know."

"I'll book your ticket."

"I'm not sure."

"Please."

Our first row, as she and I already counted the number of hours before she had to leave and return home and the pain became too much. Her sitting in a corner of the room, all bunched up.

Making up.

Making love.

"You hurt me," as I thrust inside her with too much anger and despair.

"I'm sorry."

"Don't do that again."

A kiss at Ground Zero, the reflection of her naked body in the room's closet mirror as she walked naked out of the bathroom and we embraced, her pale nudity shadowed against my all-black outfit, the shape of her arse, the curve of her back, the fragile geometry of her neck. Memories that would have to last forever, I already knew.

Her voice on the phone.

"Pronto?"

The next time we met was months later. She'd made arrangements and rented a room in a stone house in a walled city half an hour's drive from Rome. It was, again, out of season, and the heating was on the blink and we had to stay in bed most of the time just to keep warm, running clumsily down the steps to the lower level of the small house to fetch water, or snacks to eat. I would watch her in awe as she moved between bed and winding stairs. She suffered from stomach cramps and every time I entered her, she flinched. We had only two nights and time flew like lightning. She would drink water and then straddle me and allow the tepid liquid to dribble back into my open mouth. My heart was melting and my soul was in turmoil. She drove me back to Fiumicino in her own car, and we almost ran out of petrol. I barely made my plane and there was no time for goodbyes. Which was better after all, I supposed. She'd also mentioned how much she disliked long, clumsy farewell scenes.

In Barcelona in the Spring, she told me that while she waited for me to arrive, she couldn't help herself and had masturbated herself on the hotel room bed we were about to share. Halfway through the first night, her period began. We fucked in blood with all the energy of despair, and damn the sheets. Her powerful body waltzing above me, impaled on me, and the flood of red bathing my loins as I grew softer and withdrew from her. My fingers checked my midriff in the room's darkness and then spread the blood and come and sweat across her delicate breasts, like a painter celebrating the colours of the seasons on his unsteady easel.

Flowers and books on the Ramblas on San Jordi's day, tapas, her smoking a joint, and her suitcase emptied across the floor, clothes spread akimbo. She walked with a manly gait, which made me laugh a little and just served to annoy her as she accused me of similar ungainliness. Falling in love as we argued about small, petty things, unable to talk about the future.

Taking separate cabs to separate destinations in early morning and time, again, to part and go our own ways.

London.

She had been threatening to cut her hair, shorten her unwieldy mass of medusa-like curls and I had protested.

"It's done."

A text message as I waited for her flight to arrive.

She walked down the arrivals hall with a head full of hair, with a mischievous smile across her lips, enjoying the joke she'd played on me.

Wearing a long, white billowing skirt all the way down to her ankles. Raising the skirt as I drove down the motorway from the airport and slipping her panties down so I could finger her. My hand soaking wet from her secretions.

Wanting to fuck her to death as the only way to keep her, to split her open with my love – or was it my unchecked lust – to invade her with such force we would be forever embedded within each other. Feeling harder than ever when inside her, so much at home.

Again, counting the hours to the inevitable separation. Beginning to think the unthinkable and envisage another world in which we could be together. Despite the obstacles. Age. Country. Past and present lives. The world and what it might say and think.

A beach, where we basked in the sun and she was the only woman who would not go topless.

My hand collecting her pee as she squatted over the toilet seat and the heat from her innards marked me forever. Wishing the day would come when she tied me down and scarred me with her showers in an indelible fashion, aching to receive her unholy offering in such shocking fashion. Memories are made of this.

The last time: by a well-known lake, as she told me of her childhood. Coming up against the local marathon on our way to the airport and diverting onto unknown roads and not even having the proper time to say goodbye, to kiss her, to smell her, touch her.

A final night during which our bodies were ever in contact, seeking each other's warmth and contact. A mosquito in the room keeping us awake.

Flowers for her birthday.

More flowers for Valentine's day.

Telephone calls after telephone calls, as if there was always something more to say. The endless, anguished e-mails. The not knowing. Realizing that words are never enough. Feeling her slowly, inexorably move away, changing wavelength, tempted by new adventures, undermined by the days we could not spend together, the nights we could not share, the lives we would not have.

The train will soon reach the Mongolian border. It's been a long journey for which I never had a map, and I feel nauseous. In a shower of smoke, we draw into the station. There are soldiers on both sides of the track, in grey uniforms, patrolling the bleak no man's land, weapons against their flanks.

There is a dim light.

I make my way down the empty wagon, leaving my useless baggage in the compartment; they wouldn't let me keep it anyway: just warm clothes, her letters, a CD she'd burned with photos of her, punctuating our story.

I walk down the platform.

They are ready for the exchange.

A man in uniform nods as he sees me approach. I stop. Wait.

*   *   *

There is movement behind him in the fog, and shapes emerge. She is escorted by two tall, stiff soldiers. She looks gaunt and tired, dark lines under her eyes, her long curls tangled. But as beautiful as ever. My heart skips a beat. My gut tightens. Everything comes back and I find it difficult to stop the tears.

The trio stand to attention.

I begin my steps towards them. One of them taps on her shoulder and Giulia raises her face and begins her journey towards freedom. She sees me but doesn't allow herself to react. She passes me, ever so closely; I am tempted to say something but I know it would be pointless, and even attempting to touch her, brush her cheek gently with a final act of infinite tenderness might provoke some trigger happy soldier. The distance between us widens with every step I make towards Mongolia proper and the end of the no man's land.

The exchange is over.

Now my winter begins.

Don't Look Back

Alison Tyler

I Google him. Sometimes occasionally, if I've got a minute to kill while the printer is churning out my latest project. Sometimes obsessively, staring at the computer screen until my eyes water, drinking straight vodka as the minutes blur. Sometimes recklessly – not bothering to delete my history afterward. "Deleting history" seems like too much of a cheat. It would be dangerously easy to strike out all the pages I've visited on my endless, circular search. You can't do that in real life.

I know he isn't the doctor in Minneapolis who specializes in exotic-sounding diseases, or the professor on sabbatical in the Orient who beams his latest pictures up to his website every two or three days – lovely lush landscapes that I've grown fond of viewing. Sure, people change, but not *that* much. I'm absolutely certain he's not one of a pair of Bluegrass-loving brothers who live in Utah. They hit local bars every few weeks, playing warm up for bands I've never heard of.

I've done the online White Pages searches, as well, turning up addresses from fifteen years ago, six or seven places in a row, apartments I remember visiting when I cut class to fuck him. I actually think about calling the numbers – one might be current – but I can't make myself. There was no caller ID back then. Now, I might get caught. And what would happen to my well-ordered life if he Star-69-ned me and my sweet boyfriend answered?

So I resort to Googling.

Googling takes the place of those late-night drive-bys, looking to see if his Harley was in the spot out front of his building.

My muscles tighten up the same way now as they did back then. Maybe I'll see him. Maybe I won't. So why do I even bother? Because I fantasize that one day when I type in his name, up will come all the information that I crave. What he's been doing for the past decade and a half. What he's doing now. Who he's with. How he's aged.

Truthfully, I don't know all that much about him. If I were to tally up all the facts, they wouldn't fill an index card. Or a matchbook cover. He was older than me, but by exactly how much, I don't know. Twenty-seven to my eighteen. That's what I remember, but he lied all the time. He could have been lying about that. In my online search, I found a man with his name who graduated high school in 1978 somewhere in Southern California. Is that him? His middle initial was D, but he never told me what it stood for. Donald? David? Daniel? Dean? None of those seem right, yet I've found men with those middle names on the internet. Might he be one of them?

There's a fellow in the midwest who runs marathons. I can't imagine Mark breaking a sweat unless he were running from a cop. But he had a sleek runner's physique way back when. Could he have transformed himself to an athlete? Has he given up pot in favor of healthier substances? Has he hit the pavement to kill his demons?

Googling takes my mind off my modern-day problems. Googling makes me forget about deadlines and pressures and what we're going to have for dinner. Delivery pizza, again? Sounds good. Far easier to answer that mundane query than the other nagging questions pulling on me until my stomach aches: Should I pay the $29.95 and do a search of prison records? Because that's where I'll find him. I'm sure of it.

I don't enter my credit card. I don't think I actually want to know.

After spending hours on the computer, I dream about him. My eyes hurt and my head spins. I hit the pillow and recreate his image from the puzzle pieces that I remember: the black-ink Zig-Zag man tattoo on his upper arm. The way his blue eyes could turn grey or green depending on what he was wearing.

Depending, even, on his mood. His paint-splattered jeans. His grey shirt. His body.

Oh, God, his body.

I remember our first date, if you can call it a date. A walk from the beauty supply store where I worked after school back to my home – with a lengthy sojourn in a deserted alley behind the beauty supply. And I remember our first kiss – moments into our first date. What was I doing out in the rapidly darkening twilight with him? Who was looking out for me? He was.

He pushed me up against a wall and kissed me so ferociously that there are days I swear I can still feel his lips on mine. When I run my tongue over my bottom lip I feel where he bit me. Can you feel a kiss fifteen years later? You bet you can.

His large, warm hands gripped my wrists over my head while his powerful body held mine in place. He pressed against me, and I could tell how hard he was, and I could understand – finally – what all those whispers about sex were about. I hadn't got it before. Look, I wasn't an idiot. Just naive. I knew where babies came from. I'd watched enough old movies to understand the steaminess of the looks between hero and heroine. But there'd been no appeal to me in the high school fumblings at dances. In the background make-out sessions at parties. I'd been an outsider, an alien, gazing in wistfully from a distance and knowing for certain that nothing present was right for me.

With Mark, everything was different.

In that back alley behind the cosmetic store where I was a shop girl, he slid a hand up under my shirt and ran his fingers over my pale pink satin bra. In a flash, I wished that the bra was made of black lace instead. He touched my breasts firmly, as if he owned them, as if he owned me. He took my clothes off, unbuttoning my jeans himself, pulling my shirt up over my head, exposing me for what I really was.

"A slut," he said, "You're my little slut—"

I shivered, but stayed silent. I knew who the sluts were at school. I knew that I wasn't one.

"Aren't you? Tell the truth." His hands were everywhere.

His mouth on my neck, his fingers pulling down my panties and parting my lips to see how wet I was.

"Come on, Carla. Tell the truth —"

I Google him. Endlessly. Dangerously. Desperately.

Because he knew me. I was just out, taking that first shy step out into the world . . . and he knew me.

I understand why I do it. So why the hell do I find it so odd that he Googles me, too? That I get an email, short but not sweet, asking if I'm the one he remembers.

Yeah, I am. Sure, I am. Of course, I am.

I think I am.

Mark waits for me in our spot, leaning against a grey concrete wall, looking almost exactly the same despite a fifteen-year absence. Do I look the same, too? I'm not. Not a teenager any more, not trembling with desire, not — dare I say it? — young.

But I was young. Back then, I was new.

We were inseparable for months, me, a high school kid, and this twenty-seven-year-old hoodlum. This handsome, so handsome, man with the cold blue eyes out of a Who song and the iron jawline. A man who seemed to know everything about me. What was I doing? What was I thinking? Christ, what am I thinking now, fifteen years later? He's in his forties, but still effortlessly lean and tough with only the slightest lines around his eyes and the same tall, hard body I remember. I have on jeans and a black sleeveless T-shirt that says, "I break things" on the front, something I dug out of a box filled with memories in the attic. I can pass for twenty-three rather than thirty-three if I have to. My dark hair is long to my shoulders, my glossy bangs in my eyes, as always.

He doesn't say a word. He just looks at me. I close my eyes tight and remember — the loss of him when he disappeared, the way no boy could replace him after he was gone. I spent years trying to recreate the exact connection that we'd had. I slutted myself out with a variety of losers, all of whom possessed at least one rebellious quality of Mark's, but none who owned the whole package. Some spanked me. Some fucked me in public places. None made me feel anything other than disillusioned. Ultimately, I gave up hope. Now, even though I am with someone else, I've come running at Mark's call.

What the *fuck* am I doing here?

"Carla," he says, hands in my thick hair, lips on mine, and it is suddenly summertime again, and I'm missing him.

"Carla," he says, and I open my eyes and I look at him, and see him, the man, the danger, the reason I'm who I am today. If I hadn't met him in high school, who would I have become? Some other girl. Some smart chick. Not a person who would leave a loving relationship in order to track down that fleeting emotion of lust from a decade and a half ago. Not a moron who could still go weak-kneed at the first sight of her long-time crush.

"What do you need, baby?" he asks, and I find myself cradled in his strong arms, as always, my legs shaky, my heart pounding at triple-speed so that I can feel the timpani-throb in my chest and hear the clatter in my ears. "Can you say it, now? Can you tell Daddy what you need?"

My throat grows tight. There's a man at home, waiting for me. A simple man with a true soul who does not know where I am, but who trusts me to always return nonetheless. Yet suddenly the very concept of trust seems immensely overrated. What's trust to lust? Which emotion would win every time?

"Carla," Mark says. Just that word. Just my name, and I am lost all over again, head spinning, heart dying.

"Let's go."

He has no power over me. I'm not a kid any more. You can't impress me with a stolen Harley. You can't turn me into a puddle with a single kiss. I'm only here on a crazy dare. I'm only here because of Google. I can leave him. I can run. I have a safe home furnished with faux antiques from Pottery Barn and appliances purchased only after careful consideration of the advice of *Consumers' Choice*. I have a place to be. Mark doesn't own me, not any part of me.

"Come on, baby."

I suppose I've hidden it well, the desires that burn in me. I chose normal over interesting. I chose safety over adventure.

"You know you want to."

Back then, I'd never have been so fucking lame. Back then, I'd always take the risks when offered. Jesus, I invented the risks when there were none available. Slipping out my bedroom window to meet him. Cutting class to ride to his apartment on the back of his pilfered Harley. Letting him handcuff me to his bedframe so that he could do anything he wanted to me. Anything at all.

Can I change? Is it too late?

My hand is trapped in his, held so tightly. The heat between us is palpable. Some people never find that heat. That summertime heat that melts over your body and leaves you breathless. Some people search their whole miserable fucking lives for some semblance of a sizzling kiss, and they die believing that "true love always" is just a bitter myth. But I found that heat as a teenage kid and I knew for real that it existed. Even if I'd never found it again, I'd had it once.

How many places have I looked? How many other dark alleys have I gone down with nameless, faceless men, trying to find that old summertime magic from years ago?

Mark bends to kiss my neck and I remember in a flash, in one of those blinding jolts, that he'd covered me in suntan oil one sultry afternoon. I'd spent the whole day at the beach, the first truly hot spring day, and he'd come to my house afterwards and dumped out my red-striped canvas tote bag onto my floor and found that bottle of oil. My group of friends had no fear of wrinkles yet, no worry about sun damage, not like the ladies in my circle now, the ones who Google StriVectin with the passion that I've Googled this man. We used the oil back then, for "the San Tropez tan". Mark coated his strong hands while he told me to strip, and I'd watched his hands for a moment, dripping with the oil, knowing what he was going to do.

I remember being shy, so nervous, still unaccustomed to being naked in front of a man. I could strip at the gym, in front of my peers, but taking off my clothes while he watched was something entirely different. Mark liked me like that. Not just naked, but nervous. He liked to put me off center, to make me feel as if I were always on a teeter-totter, the ground rushing up to meet me when I fell. He watched through half-shut eyes that told me of his appreciation as I slowly took off my pink halter top, my cut-off jeans, my candy-colored bikini top and bottoms.

And then he covered me with the scented liquid, until I gleamed, shiny and gold, the smell of papayas and coconut swirling around us. He rubbed the oil into my breasts, and over my flat belly, and down my hips. He coated me with the shimmering liquid, and then he fucked me like that, slippery and glistening, staining my sheets, ruining his pants.

Nobody had fucked me like that before.

Nobody's fucked me like that since.

"Come on, Carla," he says now, leading me from the nondescript alley to the parking lot in back. There is a pick-up truck waiting. I know it's his. He always drove motorcycles or pickups. They suited him. I look behind us, take one last look like Lot's doomed wife. I could go back, wander through the alley, hit the shelves in the nearby Borders, buy the latest issue of *Allure* magazine, get an iced coffee in the cafe. I could go back to beige and safety and predictability. To reviews in *Consumers'*. To my Mr Coffee machine – a six-time winner.

"What do you need, Carla? Tell Daddy what you need."

Back in high school, I'd needed to be spanked, and he'd taken care of that need with the most exquisite care. He hadn't laughed at me. He hadn't refused my desires or been disgusted by them. He'd simply assumed the role, once I confessed. Once I'd finally gotten the nerve and spelled it out:

I'd needed him to bend me over his lap and lower my jeans. I'd needed his firm hand on my naked ass, punishing me. Or his belt, whispering seductively in the air before it connected with my pale skin. Then I'd needed him to cuff me to his bed and fuck me, to flip me over and fuck my ass until I cried. Until I screamed. Is that what he'd seen on the day we met? A yearning in my eyes that told him I was in need? How had he found me? How had he known?

Most importantly, I'd needed him to show me that I wasn't a freak for having the cravings that I did, the white-hot yearnings that kept me up late at night, kept me away from the high school boys and the safety of what I was supposed to do and who I was supposed to be, and he'd given me everything I needed.

Don Henley says: You can never look back.

"What do you need, now?" Mark murmurs, lips to my ear. I know suddenly what I don't need. I don't need to erase my history with a keystroke, when history is all that I've got.

My fingertips grip the handle of his vintage blue Ford. I slide the door open and climb inside.

You know, I never liked Don Henley much anyway.

After Hours

Marilyn Jaye Lewis

Whenever I'm out with Jack I feel like I'm nothing but white trash. I revel in that feeling, though, and only he brings it out of me. He's known me too long and too well.

"Here, have a cigarette," he offers.

I take it even though I no longer smoke. It's an unfiltered Camel, no less. "Jesus, are you trying to kill me, or what?" I lean my head closer to him and let him light the cigarette with his Zippo. I inhale. It's harsh and I feel like choking, but something about it is reminiscent of sex with him and I like it. I keep puffing on it and I get the feeling I'll probably smoke all night.

"Should we bring along a bottle of something?" he asks. "It would probably be polite."

"If you want to," I say. "But if we buy something too expensive then I always end up wanting to hoard it just for us."

"Then let's pick up a bottle of something cheap for show, and a fifth of something special to keep between ourselves."

"That sounds like a perfect idea. Make people think we're more generous than we really are."

When we arrive at the party, it's already in full swing. We know just about everybody there and I'm getting a little bored with it – everything always being so predictably chic. What happened to those years when everything about going to parties seemed new and maybe even a little enticingly strange? Even when you did know everybody there?

"Remember when a Friday in New York was wildly exciting?" I ask him under my breath.

He looks at me and smiles wryly. "No. I can't remember back that far."

Jack and I are fuck buddies. We circle into each other's orbits when we're between significant others. Neither one of us is bold enough to take that step into marriage like almost everyone we know has already done – some of them, more than once. Beneath our respectable careers, our healthy incomes, and our trendy fashions, we're both still hopelessly immature when it comes to making serious commitments that involve the destinies of other people.

"Alison, hello there!"

It's my boss, Susan Krieger, the well-known architect, coming toward us. She's the female half of the very wealthy couple who's throwing this shindig. She looks astonishingly attractive. I always forget how good she's capable of looking when she's not seriously harried from too much work.

"Hi, Susan. You remember Jack? He used to work with us at the firm? In drafting?"

"Of course, Jack. How are you? So nice of you to come."

Susan is only slightly older than we are, but her fully loaded husband, Derek Krieger, has a good twenty-five years on most of us, and has more money than any of us can possibly imagine. He founded the Krieger Designs architectural firm in the late 60s and has been at the top of his game since the bulk of us were still in college. He's not exactly handsome, but for a straight guy, he's always put an extraordinary amount of effort into maintaining his outward appearance. I guess he's what you'd call striking.

"God, she's a bitch," Jack says in my ear as Susan is walking away from us.

"She's okay. She's just one of those power gals."

"Who probably likes to be down on her knees when nobody's looking. Or getting stuffed in both ends at once by a couple of grease monkeys in some parking garage."

"Jesus, Jack." I give him an incredulous glance. "Where did that come from?"

"I don't know. Come on, let's go fill up some glasses and stash our booze somewhere safe."

We steer clear of the bar in the living room that's been set up for party guests and duck into the well-appointed kitchen instead. We help ourselves to a couple of their good quality drinking glasses. We press them under the ice dispenser in their over-sized stainless steel refrigerator. The ice tumbles down into our waiting glasses with a crashing noise. At that moment, Derek Krieger comes into his own kitchen.

"Alison, Jack." He takes in the full scope of what we're doing with a stern expression. It's clear he hasn't forgotten Jack, his incorrigible ex-employee, in the slightest. "Feel free to help yourselves there."

He grabs a bottle of wine from the counter and leaves.

"I feel like we just got caught by the school principal or something. And we got a last-minute reprieve."

Jack chuckles. "Fuck him."

We fill our glasses with our own Ciroc and then stash the vodka deep in the Kriegers' freezer. Then we return to the party and act as if we're part of it. But really we retain our own little world where we watch everyone else over the rims of our vodka glasses. We gossip between ourselves, we denigrate our friends, we mock the few party guests we don't know, and eventually we start to kiss discreetly and get horny. We go out onto the Kriegers' balcony overlooking Central Park and light up a couple of Camels.

"You want to leave?" Jack asks. "We could go over to my place and fuck like bunnies."

That sounds like an excellent idea. "Okay," I say. "Let's finish these and then go."

Jack moves up close to me. "How long has it been since your pussy got good and fucked, Alison?"

"Too long," I answer quickly, practically chewing on the end of my cigarette. I follow each puff closely with a healthy gulp of vodka. Clearly I'm craving something in my mouth. Why does he always get me so horny when we're in public?

"How would you feel about getting stuffed at both ends by a couple of grease monkeys?"

I smile at him over the rim of my glass. "You're such a sicko, Jack."

He smiles back at me, his coal-black eyes searing into me without flinching. "I still think about you an awful lot, Alison. The thought of you always comes to me when I'm jerking off, when I need a pretty girl in my head to get very agreeable."

"How agreeable do I get?"

"You do just about anything, honey."

I'm hot now. My panties are starting to get wet. The nicotine and vodka are buzzing cozily through my veins. I'm curious about my exploits. "So tell me some of the things you make me do?"

The balcony door opens and more smokers come out to join us.

"Hi, Alison."

"Hi, Tina. You remember Jack?"

"Of course I do. How've you been, Jack?"

I quickly put out my cigarette, hoping Jack will do the same so that we can leave. He does.

I want an answer to my question. I'm feeling seriously horny. "Tell me, Jack, I want to know."

"Let's go get another drink," he says.

I'm all for it but I thought we were leaving. I follow him to the kitchen anyway. Before we even refill our glasses, we're kissing. Slobbering all over each other. He pulls me up close to him. I hold onto his neck. His hands are under my skirt, up inside my panties, grabbing fistfuls of my ass while we kiss. He has a rock-hard erection pressing up against me.

When we break for air, I try again. "Tell me some of those things you make me do, Jack. I want to know how agreeable you think I am."

"Oh, just the usual," he says between kisses. "Mostly."

"What does that mean?"

"You know, you let me put my cock anywhere. Anywhere, any place, any time I want it. You just come in very handy, that's all. Come on. Come with me."

"No," I protest on instinct, following him anyway. He leads me down the hall to the bedrooms and ducks inside one of them. "No, Jack, I'm serious. I'm not doing this in my boss's apartment."

"No one's going to know, Alison, come on."

He pulls open a closet door. "Come on, come in here. Just a quickie until we get home."

I both hate and love this about him. He's irresistible when I'm horny. I follow him into the dark closet and we close the door.

In an instant he's tugging at my panties. "No, don't," I'm saying. "Keep them up. I don't want to be without my panties." But he tugs them all the way down, clear down to my ankles.

"Step out of them, Alison," he insists in an urgent whisper. "Come on, take them all the way off."

For some reason, I do it. I guess he's right about my being so agreeable. It's dark but he manages to extricate them from my high heels.

"Give them to me," I say.

"I'll just stick them in my pocket."

"No."

But before I can protest further, he's pulled me up close to him again; his hands are up under my skirt, getting free rein of my naked ass.

I'm moaning deliriously into his kisses. As my eyes adjust to the darkness of the closet, I realize there are slats in the closet door, louvers, allowing air and some light to trickle in. I realize we'd better be extra quiet, though, because of those louvers.

"What are you doing?" I whisper suddenly.

"What do you think I'm doing, Alison? I'm going to fuck you."

"Jesus, are you serious?"

His cock is out and I can feel him trying to find my hole. He does. "God, you're wet," he whispers. "You little tramp."

I try to angle myself in a way that lets his cock get up me easily. I know I'm wet. I'm incredibly aroused. But this position isn't really working.

"Why don't you turn around?" he suggests quietly. "I'll try you from behind."

I turn around, leaning a little against the louvered door. His cock finds its way up my hole again and this position is definitely better. It feels incredible. I can't resist emitting a little moan.

Until the light in the room flashes on.

Jesus.

We are both instantly motionless, not making a sound. Someone is in the bedroom with us. No, it's two someones, and they're closing the door.

I can hear Jack quietly panicking in my ear. "Oh shit," he says.

His cock is still nestled deep in my hole, his arms around my waist, holding me tight, but we don't move. "It's Krieger," he barely mouths in my ear.

And sure enough, Derek Krieger has come within view of the slats in the closet door.

Oh shit, I'm thinking, not Derek. I'm feeling like he really *is* my school principal. That I'm in some serious trouble now.

Then a female comes into view. This is definitely not Susan Krieger.

Oh my God, I'm thinking.

At the same moment, Jack mouths in my ear, "Christ, it's Veronica."

Veronica is Jack's ex-lover. Another architectural drafter at the firm. She's even younger than me. One of those lithe, helpless-seeming blondes from Connecticut.

"You're late," Derek is saying to her. He sounds angry.

"I couldn't get a cab . . ."

"Bullshit," Derek replies, cutting her off.

I'm stunned by his abrupt tone. What does he care if Veronica is late to his party? It's not as if any of us are on the clock. It's only a party, for Christ's sake.

Veronica is plaintive. "I'm sorry, Mr Krieger."

Mr Krieger? Nobody calls him Mr Krieger – he's Derek.

"I absolutely couldn't help it. I couldn't get a cab."

"You should have thought ahead, young lady, and left earlier."

Derek's using quite an intimidating tone. Something here doesn't seem right. Then suddenly Jack's hand dips down furtively between my legs. His fingers deftly feel between my slick lips, looking for my clit. I can't believe he's trying to arouse me now, here, with this going on. But I'm too nervous to pull away, to make a sound. I'm still impaled on his cock.

In my ear, Jack says almost inaudibly, "I think he's going to spank her."

I'm incredulous. "What?" I try to say.

"I know Veronica," he tries to explain. "Krieger's going to spank her."

Well, I'm stunned again. But now I'm a lot more interested. These two are having some twisted affair! I'm trying to get a better view through the slats in the door without moving at all. If Veronica is going to get spanked by Mr Krieger, I definitely want to see.

Jack's cock is reviving inside me and his fingers have zeroed in on my clit. I can't believe any of this is happening. I'm so glad we decided to come to this party.

"But I gave you specific instructions," Derek is going on.

"I know, but . . ."

"And I expected you to follow them."

"I know." Veronica is practically whining.

"I'm too busy to be wasting my breath on someone as incompetent as you are. You're over an hour late."

"I know, but I . . ."

"Save it, Veronica. Save it for someone who has time to give a shit about your next lie."

"Oh yes," Jack agrees quietly. "I know that feeling. I hope she gets it good – with her panties pulled down."

Her panties pulled down? That hadn't occurred to me. I'm really on fire, overwhelmed by all the stimuli. But Jack's commentary is making me feel too crazy. I don't want to get caught here; I want the show to continue. I want to keep watching.

"Come here, Veronica."

He's good, I'm thinking. Very stern. I'm actually a little scared for her.

He sits down on the edge of the bed. She moves only slightly.

"Right here," he says. "You can see where I'm pointing, can't you?"

"Yes."

"You're not having any trouble hearing me?"

"No."

That answer was barely audible. And Veronica doesn't seem to be moving.

"Derek," she pleads suddenly. "Don't make me do this. Your wife is practically in the next room. All those people."

"What did you call me?"

"I'm sorry – Mr Krieger!"

Boy, he sounds menacing. Sitting on the edge of the bed like he is, I can easily see his face now and he looks deadly serious. I wonder if Veronica is really scared? She sounds it. I think I would be, too.

Jack is breathing heavily against the side of my neck, his cock working slowly inside me, methodically. He's soaking up every nuance of this scene, just like I am. I wonder how that must feel? Watching an ex-lover about to get disciplined? I wonder if they were into this spanking stuff when they were living together? Funny how much you don't suspect about people . . .

"Veronica, I'm waiting. The longer you put this off, the more you run the risk that my wife will come looking for me. Then how will we explain it? Not just to her, but to a roomful of party guests?"

The sound of Derek's commanding voice is electrifying my clit, while Jack is giving it just the right pressure at the same time. This spanking stuff is amazing. I need to have a serious talk with Jack about all this when we finally get out of this place.

A quick breath of lust is caught in Jack's throat. Immediately I see what it is he's lusting over. Veronica's hands are up under her skirt. She's pulling her panties down. She's really doing it. She's moved in front of Mr Krieger. We can see everything. With her skirt held high, Veronica lays herself across Mr Krieger's lap.

I'm thinking, that's some ass she's got there, white and so perfectly round. I'm also thinking, I never once dreamed I'd see Veronica's ass – for any reason at all, let alone because of this.

Jack's cock is swelling up inside my cunt. He's giving it to me slow but very hard. I clutch at his arms, needing to hang onto something. The lust is galloping through me now. I want to cry out.

The spanking is swift and sound. Veronica tries hard not to emit even a tiny peep. I know she's afraid of being discovered. Maybe that's part of her thrill, who knows? But how she manages to endure those well-aimed, decisive smacks on her bare ass without once giving out with a cry or a shout is beyond me. Mr Krieger is not playing. His strokes are severe. Veronica's ass is already bright red.

I'm too enchanted to breathe. Jack's steady fingers have tripped the tremors of orgasm in me and I have to endure the onslaught of pleasure in my clitoris without so much as making a move. He must know I'm coming. He's holding me very tight.

The spanking is over before I'm even through coming. Veronica is off Derek's lap, pulling her panties back in place. Derek is standing now, too. They kiss. They moan.

"Okay, kiddo," Derek says, giving her one last playful swat on the behind. "Let's get going."

They leave and suddenly the room is black again.

"My God," I say at last. "That was amazing."

Jack repositions himself to fuck me like crazy now. It feels so good but it doesn't take long for him to come.

"Come on," he says, pulling out of me and zipping up. "Let's get out of here. Let's go back to my place."

"My panties, Jack. Give me my panties."

"I'll give them to you when we get home."

He lets himself out of the closet and all I can do is follow. It isn't the first time I've gone off with him without my panties. I just straighten my skirt and hope for the best.

We're down the hall in a flash. In the foyer, however, Jack remembers the Ciroc. It cost us nearly sixty bucks. "Go get the vodka," he says. "I'll wait here."

I dash back to the kitchen, oblivious to everything around me. All I want now is my vodka and to get to Jack's bed as quickly as humanly possible.

In the kitchen, I run smack into Derek, alone. I'm thoroughly startled and painfully conscious of not wearing any panties. I'm not quite sure how to explain why I'm taking an expensive bottle of vodka out of his freezer.

"I put it there," I try lamely, smiling at Derek. Now I see him differently. Now he makes me incredibly nervous.

He looks at me and says nothing.

"It's my vodka," I keep explaining, feeling sweaty between my legs. "I'm going now."

He just stands there, offering nothing. Silence. Just staring at me.

"Thanks for the party, Mr Krieger." Jesus, why did I say that?

He raises an eyebrow. His eyes pierce me with the faintest hint of a questioning smile. "You're welcome, Alison. See you Monday."

Matt Thorne

Five Times

1

He always sends me a tape so I can see what he did to me. I've never seen him except on screen. I have to blindfold myself before I go into his room. I know what he looks like from all the videos but he never wants me to see him when he's doing it to me. He's dark: good-looking. He films me.

I was there two days ago. I took off my blouse in the hallway and he let me in. The first thing he did was touch my breasts. Then he forced me onto the floor, on my knees. I can see myself on the video, looking lost, not knowing where I am in the room. He is over by the window, opening the curtains. A yellow light shines in from a streetlight. He always does that so the neighbours can see.

He brings back a length of cord and ties my hands behind my back. I remember at that point hearing him unzip himself, and on the film I can see myself flinch. He tells me to open my mouth. I gagged instantly. I can see myself gagging on the film. He filled my mouth with his cock and started forcing it down my throat, and there was nothing I could do, because my hands were behind my back. I couldn't breathe but he kept fucking my mouth until he ejaculated and I almost choked on his come.

2

The more it hurts, the more he knows I love him. Sometimes I dream of ripping all his skin off, damaging all his flesh, so that he belongs to me totally. The feeling of his skin under my nails drives me in same, mainly when his cock is inside me, too far, too hard, in the wrong place. It has to be dark and it has to hurt. I bite him; his fist in my mouth, and I tear at his face. He holds me down, his whole weight on me, and if anyone was watching they would think he was raping me and I was trying to get away. But I'm attacking him because I need to. I want more of him, so I tear him to shreds. He wants me, so he fucks me till I bleed.

3

There was a swimming pool in the hotel. No one else was there, because of the bomb scare. We weren't afraid. It was our bomb scare.

He went first. He looked beautiful in the pool in the blue light, like he'd already drowned. I could see his cock hard under the water, and I slithered in. He smiled at me and went under, just falling back while I climbed on him and moved myself around until his cock was deep inside me. He stayed under and I stayed on top of him, until he came, and then he stopped breathing.

I managed to revive him a few minutes after he passed out. He vomited water on the concrete floor and asked if I thought he was brain-damaged. I laughed. Then it was my turn. I did a handstand under the water and he grabbed my legs and held them open. I let myself become weightless as he pulled me to him and penetrated me again. He said that after I passed out, my flesh felt like one of those stress relief toys; completely soft, but not elastic. When I came to, I was in the middle of an orgasm, and his fingers were inside me.

4

There's this guy across the road who's completely mad. These girls (who all look incredibly similar) come to his place all the time, and they do stuff with him, or rather for him. It's weird.

I met someone who actually knew him once. Apparently this person heard it was the same girl each time, although it can't be,

I'm sure, because he does something different with each of them. The stripper comes on a Tuesday night. She's small and pretty and this week she's wearing see-thru white: a shirt and a blouse and cerise underwear, which is completely visible through her thin clothes. She's eating ice cream, and getting some on her top. She always does something cute while she's stripping, like last week she popped bubble-gum the whole time, and the week before she did something with a skipping-rope.

She dances, looking cute, to some fucked-up music. It's really sleazy and smoky over there, and loud and dark, and there she is, eating ice cream in white, starting to strip for the guy. She licks at her ice-cream while she moves her butt around, dancing to the music. Every couple of seconds she pulls up her skirt a little and then giggles and pulls it down again, like she didn't mean to do it. Then after a while, the skirt slips off altogether, and she's standing there in her knickers, rubbing ice-cream onto her stomach, sticking her sticky white hands down her knickers. There's still some of the cone left, and she pulls her knickers to one side and penetrates herself with it. The guy says something to her, and she pulls her knickers back over the pointed end of the cone, leaving it stuck inside her, and starts pulling at her top.

He finishes as always, by walking over and taking her top off for her, pulling her breasts out of her bra and then closing his blinds.

That always makes me come.

5

Do you remember the time I stuck five candles in myself? It was this urge I had. Two in my cunt, two in my bum. Then I put one in my mouth and waited for you. When you saw me like that you smiled, took out your lighter and lit them all. You made yourself come looking at me like that, and then you watched as each candle burnt down. And just before they all burnt right to the end, you aimed your cock at me, and put them all out, one by one, with your piss.

Maestro

Rose B. Thorny

If an injury has to be done to a man it should be so severe that his vengeance need not be feared.
Niccolo Machiavelli (1469–1527)

Andrea watched transfixed by the ebony figurine bobbing between her splayed legs. It might have escaped to glide over her stomach towards her breasts but for her hands, which hovered over her hips trapping it. She paddled the bath water alternating her palms in rhythmic syncopation. The black wooden cylinder shifted sideways, but like a moored vessel, could not break free of the fleshy slip formed by her wet, pale thighs. Instead, it rocked towards her then back again mimicking a weak, incomplete, fucking motion.

Except for the colour, it reminded her of the way his cock had bobbed in front of her face the very first time she went down on the Maestro, though, back then, he was still just Aaron. It was her very first blow job ever and, in her opinion, she acquitted herself not too shabbily for only having read descriptions in cheap paperbacks.

He must have liked it; he convinced her to repeat the performance every time they were together, except for the last. That was back when "safe sex" simply meant not getting pregnant. Blow jobs were a sure bet in that direction.

The water was still hot and she slid further down so that her neck and the back of her head were immersed. She had to bend her knees at a sharper angle. This had the dual effect of displacing more water and bringing "The Boy" closer to eye level. In her mind, she played with the name of her favourite dildo. Right now "The Boy" was more like "The Buoy". She reached over her shoulder to start the jets again. There was a momentary grinding hum as the motor started then the eight spigots surged into action. Rapid streams of bubbles massaged her neck and shoulders, breasts, and thighs. She tingled from the steady spurts on the soles of her feet and toes.

Andrea no longer used her hands to impede the toy's progress, but the eddying patterns kept it suspended over the dark patch of pubic hair. She smiled. It looked like a dinghy floating over seaweed.

The mechanical rumbling became music lulling her, turning the tub into a whirlpool of warm, liquid sensation. She closed her eyes.

Aaron was so handsome. That he took notice of her at all was at once bewildering and thrilling. He, too, was still a student, but older by several years and well-known at the Conservatory. He was brilliant and well on his way to becoming *somebody*. He was often chosen to be a student lecturer and his articulate eloquence always drew crowds. Andrea, new to the school, felt a little foolish falling for his clichéd good looks; a tall, blond, blue-eyed Adonis. Female students, much more attractive and talented than she, fluttered about him like moths around a flame. Andrea noted that not a few of the male students were also drawn towards him. He basked in the adulation of both, but she was pleased to observe that the boys were consistently rebuffed after the fawning was done. She hovered outside the corona, but one day had a sincere question concerning one of his addresses in the lecture hall. It was late afternoon, the end of classes for the day. She always wondered if she had subconsciously orchestrated the scenario; hanging back as the other students filed out, waiting for a couple of them to chat with him then approaching him tentatively after all had departed.

She introduced herself and made some inane comment about how much she had enjoyed the talk. Before her mouth became any dryer and her quavering voice failed her completely, she asked, "Do you really think being a little crazy helps you to become a successful artist?" God, it sounded so lame to her ears.

He turned on a thousand-watt smile and said, "If you'd really like to talk more about this, we can do it over dinner." His voice was melodious. An image flashed onto the silver screen in her mind of her cello and the way it sang to her as she held it clasped between her legs. She forced the picture away.

She wasn't sure she'd heard right. "Dinner?"

"Well, yes, but if you don't want to. . ."

She hastened to correct any misunderstanding. "No, no. Dinner is fine. Dinner would be . . . um . . . really fine."

She wanted to smack her own mouth for stammering like an idiotic teenager. Well, she *was* still a teenager, if only for another year, but right now she wished more than anything that she were older and sophisticated like him. What could he possibly find attractive about her? She did not ponder the question long. It was enough that he wanted to dine with her. She was not about to pass up the golden opportunity. It was, as she came to believe, the start of life.

He was charming and witty. Everything about him exuded talent. Across the dinner table in a cosy booth of an almost empty, out-of-the-way restaurant, she watched him as he expounded on madness and the creative mind. She listened intently to his expressive discourse, though if asked, she would have been hard pressed to repeat what he said. She studied his hands, the hands of a conductor. The fluid motion of his long, slim fingers accompanied the music of his voice. She fixed her gaze upon his lips as they shaped themselves around his words. She wondered how those lips would feel against hers. How they might feel on other parts of her body. His self-confidence was overwhelming. Andrea had never met anyone so assured of his own genius.

Later, at his apartment, he stood godlike before her. She knelt, with her virgin mouth encircling his cock, and prayed she was doing it properly. Despite the misgivings she had about her ability to fellate with any degree of expertise, she elicited the desired response, a final choking thrust against the back of her throat and a gush of warmth that filled her mouth and her being. She never forgot the sensation of that first time. She gagged and swallowed, but the force of his orgasm caused some of the creamy froth to spurt around her tongue and out the corners of her mouth. She could hold only so much. She was embarrassed by that, thinking she may have done something wrong, but his moans and the way he stroked her hair, even as he softened within her, were reassuring.

Their subsequent trysts always concluded with this act of obeisance. Aaron's erect penis was Aaron; long and lean, firm and beautiful. She worshipped it as she worshipped him. She wondered a little at his apparent lack of desire to have actual intercourse with her and longed for him to make love to her. She never thought of it as fucking; that would have been too coarse a description. But she did not question him. He was the master and she the student. She interpreted his proclivity for oral sex as respect for her virginity. She interpreted his request to keep their affair quiet as respect for her honour. Despite his sensuality, he was a true gentleman.

Andrea found herself daydreaming much of the time when they were apart. She tried to feel sufficiently guilty about the growing disregard she had for her studies, but admitted to herself that she cared more about being with Aaron than she did about her music. She loved the music, but it couldn't touch her as Aaron did. He was alive, warm, and she was convinced of his devotion to her. She drifted though her classes and ignored first the mild comments then increasingly harsh criticisms from her teachers and fellow musicians. In her mind, she joked with them about giving up the cello and majoring in skin flute instead.

As spring blossomed, Andrea often sat for hours in her dorm room idly plucking at the strings of her cello, or bowing her way through the first few bars of a composition, then drifting into a fantasy involving Aaron and his magnificent member. In these flights of fancy, it satisfied all her senses. She adored the way it looked bobbing in front of her face, the way it smelled as her nose pressed into the golden curls of his belly once she had it in her and down her throat, the way it felt stuffed in her mouth, the tantalizing taste of pre-come on her tongue. And as his semen flooded her accommodating oral cavity, his agonized groans were all the music she ever cared to hear.

One day, after she had paid him her usual lip service, he remarked, for no apparent reason that he didn't really think she had the makings of a world class cellist, that if she were going to be successful at it, she would already be making a name for herself and, obviously, this was not happening. She felt a twinge of panic and, yes, anger, because it sounded *almost* as if he had lost respect for her as a musician and a person. Then she realized he was right. How could Aaron possibly be wrong? He was, after all, a genius. She truly was *not* cut out to be a musician, didn't really have that much talent, and wondered why she ever thought a career in music was part of her future.

Aaron was at the Conservatory, however, so she remained as well, going through the motions of being a student of music, but knowing it was all a sham. She wanted to be near him, but knew she needed to find another vocation.

Andrea greeted the news of Aaron's upcoming departure with fear and dismay. She knew it was coming, but kept denying it would happen. As arranged, she had met him at *their* restaurant. They sat in *their* booth. She glanced away from him for a moment, looked around, and wondered how this place ever stayed in business. There was one other couple in the opposite corner and one nondescript patron at the bar. She looked back at her lover. He had already finished his dinner. She merely picked despondently at hers, alternately using her fork to stab at bits of meat and shove morsels from one spot on the plate to another.

"I won't be gone that long," he said. "When I come back, it will be just the way it is now." He laughed and added, "Except I'll be famous."

She ignored the quip and watched him sip his wine. "Not that long? Two years in Berlin?" She felt sick to her stomach.

"Well, not two years solid. I'll be back to visit. Probably in six months or so. In the meantime, it will do both of us good to branch out a little."

She had no idea what he meant. Branch out from what?

"I have something for you. A goodbye gift so you won't forget me." He set an unwrapped black box on the table to one side of her plate. She had noticed it beside him on the bench seat, but had declined to ask about it. It might not have had anything to do with her and she didn't want him to think she was presumptuous or nosy.

She perked up slightly. A gift! He had never bought her anything before. "Oh, how could I ever forget you?"

The gleaming smile again. "Well, you're right there. I am rather memorable."

She laughed for the first time that evening. Aaron was delightfully arrogant. She envied him his self-confidence.

"Go ahead and open it."

Andrea stared for a moment at the box. It was covered by paper of a suede-like texture and she ran the fingers of her right hand over it tentatively. It was roughly ten inches long and four inches both wide and deep. She lifted the lid and set it aside then parted black tissue to reveal the object contained within the box. There was no way she was going to remove the item as long as there was a chance anyone else might see it.

Aaron, however, reached into the box, withdrew the ebony statue and placed it upright on the table between them. A furious blush spread over Andrea's face. She was hot with embarrassment.

It was a statue only inasmuch as it had the features of a human male carved into the surface of it. It tapered to a dull point, the top of the little man's head. The purpose of the sculpture was clear. In reality, it was an eight-inch tall dildo, two inches in diameter.

Andrea grasped the black toy and replaced it with amazing swiftness into the box, yet even in that brief moment of contact, she noted the weight of it and she felt a rippling quiver inside her. She shifted and wiggled in her seat.

"You don't like it?" he asked sounding surprised.

Andrea thought, for a fleeting moment, that he looked just a little hurt. She smiled to reassure him.

"I love it, but. . ."

"But?"

"Nothing. Just . . . wow." She was achingly aware of how much the figurine aroused her. Suddenly, she couldn't wait to get away from the restaurant and back to Aaron's apartment. Tonight would be the night. She knew it.

And she wasn't wrong.

As excited as she was, lying naked on Aaron's bed with him kneeling between her legs, Andrea was trembling. His cock, so familiar to her in one way, suddenly seemed considerably larger than usual. It was about to be used as the weapon in the assault on her virginity. She was afraid.

"It's okay," Aaron reassured her. "Just relax."

He reached over to the night table. The black box lay open and he retrieved the dildo. Andrea's eyes widened. She was having difficulty reconciling the fear with the intense arousal she felt at the sight of him holding the thick, heavy toy.

"It's okay," he repeated. He placed the tip of the wooden tool against the wet lips of her pussy then rubbed it along the length of her slit. She felt him wedging it with just a little more force between her lips. It felt huge.

Andrea breathed rapidly, shallowly, wondering what was about to happen. Surely he wouldn't use the dildo on her first. This was not how she imagined it would be. And it was too large anyway.

He pressed the head of the statue against her clit and she jumped.

He chuckled. "Think of me every time you use this little guy."

He tossed it aside and it rolled off the bed onto the floor with thump. He leaned over her and rubbed his cock along the same path the dildo had just traced.

Andrea looked into Aaron's blue angel eyes and held her breath. She flinched then gasped at the first sharp jab. Even though he seemed to be moving gently, it hurt more than she thought it would. Realizing her teeth were clenched, she tried to relax her jaw as well as the muscles Aaron was putting to the test. She could feel tears tracing twin paths along her temples into her hair. She would remember this moment all her life. She had just started to enjoy the rocking rhythm that developed when something changed. He stopped. The stretched discomfort Andrea felt was suddenly absent and she was totally confused. She might be inexperienced in actual intercourse, but she was sure he hadn't come. This definitely was not how she imagined it would be.

Aaron pulled out of her.

She looked up at him. "What? What's wrong?"

He appeared to be unfazed, which seemed somewhat bizarre to her.

"Nothing." He rolled off her and instead of lying down beside her, sat on the edge of the bed, leaned down to pick up the dildo and put it in the box. "I'm just not in the mood tonight."

He stood up, totally unselfconscious of his deflated penis, and looked down at her.

"Geez," he said, "you're bleeding all over the bed."

His words didn't register. *Not in the mood?*

He pulled out a wad of tissues from a box on the night table. He reached down between her legs and wiped along her wet, bloody gash. The action was neither gentle nor rough. It was . . . perfunctory. He tossed the tissues into the wastebasket beside the bed.

"I have an early appointment. I need to get some sleep."

A panicky sick feeling washed over Andrea. "Can't I stay?" she pleaded.

"I'm sorry, babe, I really need to sleep. You understand, don't you?"

Andrea sat up, nodding weakly, and saying, "Yeah. Yeah, I understand. I'm sorry. I shouldn't have . . ." She left the sentence unfinished. "You have a lot to do before you leave, too. I'll go. You still want me to drive you to the airport on Saturday, don't you?" She thought she sounded desperate. She retrieved more tissues, pressed them against herself as she stood, lest any more blood escape, and went into the bathroom.

"Yeah, if you don't mind."

Of course she didn't mind. She would do anything he asked. She dressed, ignoring the ache between her legs, as Aaron tore the fitted bottom sheet off the bed.

"I'm sorry," she said, "I should have done that. I'm sorry about the mess."

Aaron balled the sheet up and handed it to Andrea. "Throw it in the hamper, if you would. Thanks."

She obliged him then gathered her things together. She was about to leave, after they kissed goodnight, when he said, "Hey, don't forget your boy." He handed her the box with the lid covering "The Boy" once again.

Two days later, Andrea drove Aaron to the airport. They kissed goodbye in the departure lounge – airports and airplanes were still safe places back then – and she stayed to watch, with a curious empty feeling, as the Lufthansa jet faded into a gray, overcast sky.

Andrea opened her eyes. The water had become tepid. She shut the jets off and the swirling eddies ceased their sensual massage. She reached down and grasped the floating toy half tempted to play with him right now, but the water temperature was unpleasant. She sat up, lifted the chrome plug, and stood up shivering. She stepped out of the tub, listening to the gurgling of the water as it drained. She set the black dildo on end upon the vanity top and wrapped herself in a black terrycloth bath sheet. The Boy invited her gaze standing there upright, ready for action. She picked him up and dried him off lovingly. She placed the rounded tip against her lips and kissed it with a little sucking sound. He certainly had withstood the test of time. Twenty-five years of faithful service.

A string of boyfriends, some long-term, most of a shorter duration, all wealthy, often wondered at her great affection for the unique sex toy. Several bought her state-of-the-art vibrators or dildos of newer, and they thought better, materials. She let them use their purchases on her and if Oscars were handed out for best faked orgasms, she thought she'd be a shoe-in, very possibly beating out Meg Ryan. Though none ever guessed, no matter what any of her men did, no matter their fervent ardour, no matter how fancy the gizmos, she never came unless she used The Boy. Of course, her clients had never cared one way or another whether she came or not. It was irrelevant.

For a long time it didn't bother her, but lately she thought she might be missing something. She thought that perhaps she should broaden her horizons. Her epiphany coincided some months ago with finding the Maestro's North American tour schedule on-line. Tonight he was conducting in her city.

As Andrea dressed for the concert, she stopped and looked at the entertainment section of the newspaper lying on the neatly made bed. There was no mistaking the face even in the grainy black and white photo; older, of course, but he was as handsome as she remembered. And now he was a world-renowned maestro. He conducted, he lectured; aspiring brilliant students vied to study under him. He was everything he ever wanted to be. And why not? He was, after all, a genius.

She remembered the last time she saw Aaron.

He *had* come back from Europe in six months for a visit, as he said he would, though she heard of his return through the grapevine. She had attributed his complete lack of correspondence to his devotion to studies. It was something of a reunion party. Many of the students she'd known at the Conservatory were there. Some conversed with her politely, but most did not. She was no longer one of them. When he walked into the room, heads turned. Andrea's heart went into overdrive and she beamed at him even before he noticed her. She made her way to him and placed herself squarely in his path.

He seemed surprised to see her.

"Andrea, how nice to see you."

She frowned and looked at him quizzically. He sounded so formal. "How nice to see you?" she asked wryly. "How about a hug?" She smiled and moved in closer to him.

It was almost imperceptible to anyone else, but Andrea saw how he pulled back and her smile faded.

"Aaron?"

"Not now, Andrea. Later."

She was about to ask him what he meant, when a ravishing red-haired creature, with the air of a prima donna, strode up beside him. She linked her arm through his, a gesture of easy familiarity. Andrea was stunned to find herself thinking with cool detachment that they made a breathtaking couple.

"Aaron, my love, you must introduce me to all your friends. Who's this?" she asked smiling graciously at Andrea.

Andrea just stared at the woman as she tried to digest the scene. It was difficult to maintain her composure as the world tilted away from her. The sounds around her were muffled and she felt as if all the air had been sucked out of the room. Though it seemed an eternity, the disorientation was momentary. Her instinct to not look like a complete idiot took charge within seconds. She smiled at Aaron then at the redhead.

"I'm Andrea. I'm sure Aaron must have mentioned me."

Aaron jumped right in. "Andrea, this is Diane. Diane Moore."

Diane shook her head. "No, Aaron was remiss I'm afraid. I'm sure I would have remembered an Andrea. But nice to meet you, Andrea."

Andrea stood outside herself and watched as she made some small talk with the perfect couple then headed for the bar. The bartender, an amiable sort, chatted with Andrea as he poured her a glass of white wine. Andrea sensed Aaron's approach. She felt him standing there, but he did not touch her. She turned to look at him.

"What's going on?" she asked. "Why didn't you ever write back or call? What about *us*?"

He didn't look the slightest bit embarrassed about the situation and didn't seem to care that the bartender was listening. In fact, he did not acknowledge the existence of the fellow.

"Listen, Andrea. You read more into it than there ever was. There was no *us*. I mean we only went out, what . . . a half a dozen times or so? It was . . . an experiment. Something a little different for me. It was okay, but you're just not in the same league as I am. You need to find your own niche. You really need to get on with your life."

She remembered staring at the back of his head as he walked away from her and her stomach turned over and the blood pounded like timpani in her ears. She remembered the bartender asking, "Would you like something a little stronger?"

And she clearly recalled thinking, "It was nine. It was nine times. Don't you remember?"

Andrea finished dressing and studied her reflection in the full-length mirrors that were the sliding doors of her bedroom closet. They emphasized the now-Spartan expanse of the room around her. The stylish black velvet pants suit was most becoming. She stood at an angle and threw her shoulders back. Inhaling deeply she sucked in her slightly rounded tummy and smoothed the plush fabric over it. Forty had brought voluptuous with it. The jacket slid apart revealing a black satin blouse with a plunging V-neck. She smiled thinking of a line from a favourite funny movie: "*What knockers!*" The only jewellery that adorned her was a simple silver chain around her neck.

In response to the chilly weather, she wore boots instead of shoes. They were black patent leather that hugged her calves and rose to her knees under the pant legs. The heels added four inches to her height.

Her long hair was swept up and classically coiffed further enhancing the illusion of tallness. Until last week, it still had been mostly brown, but the grey streaks were becoming more pronounced of late. In honour of tonight's planned events, Andrea's crowning glory was now a warm auburn.

In the living room, she slipped into a long black trench coat – a recent acquisition – and gathered up her purse and tote bag. She opened the apartment door, turned back to survey the almost empty space then, satisfied that what remained was in order, she flicked the wall switch to extinguish the lights. She stepped across the threshold and pulled the door closed behind her. The solid, metallic *kachunk* of the deadlock echoed along the deserted corridor.

Andrea sat throughout the concert thinking about the many things she'd done since last she saw Aaron, and all the things she never did. She clutched her purse tightly in her lap; her tote bag was firmly wedged between her feet and partially under the seat.

She barely took her eyes off Aaron, though she kept the cellists in her peripheral view to the right. Tonight they were all male. She never tired of watching the way they held their violoncellos gently, but firmly, between their thighs, heads inclined toward the neck, cheek almost brushing it, as one would lean into a lover to whisper a seduction, one hand sliding confidently along the fingerboard, holding, executing the vibrato, the other gripping the bow, coaxing the long, melancholy notes from within the depths of both the varnished wood housing and their own souls. Andrea could *feel* the harmonic resonance inside her.

Aaron himself was a concert of fluid, poetic movement. The baton was a living extension of his lithe hand movements. The patterns could mesmerize the willing. It seemed somehow appropriate that his back should be turned to her for the duration of each selection. She watched him dispassionately even as she breathed with the cadence of the soaring music he conducted. She held her breath through each climax. During the quiet denouements, she glanced around to study the faces of the people watching him. The adoration was unmistakable. She, herself, was not one to deny his talent, which was self-evident, or his charisma. He had both . . . in spades.

He also had an ego the size of Mount Rushmore; equally impressive, but much less attractive. Andrea had felt it as an actual force of nature the moment he emerged from the wings. He crossed the stage, graciously shook the hand of the concert mistress, and mounted the podium.

She could also feel that it had grown. It overpowered the collective egos of the talented performers behind him. He had surveyed the sea of expectant faces as a monarch granting his subjects a glimpse of his magnificence. Even after a quarter of a century, she felt his familiar arrogance as it drowned out the applause. Recently, she wondered how she ever could have found that air of superiority appealing. Ah, well, no matter. That he still had it was to her advantage.

Getting backstage, after the initial crush of patrons had subsided, was not a problem. Aaron's people knew the type of fans he sought and to whom he granted an audience.

Carrying her coat over her arm, and hugging her tote bag and purse close to her body, Andrea made her way to him and dazzled him with the gleaming, perfect smile she had paid much to acquire. Her orthodontist had probably vacationed long and hard in some exotic locale thanks to the work he had performed on her mouth. She smiled ruefully to herself; pity the bills could not have been deducted as a business expense. She laughed nervously as she handed Aaron her programme and he perused it. His own face stared up at him.

"I feel like a silly schoolgirl asking for your autograph," she said with just a hint of self-deprecation. Her practised voice was mellow. She had learned to modulate the pitch and knew it sounded sexier and much different from the higher, more nasal tones of her youth.

He hesitated a moment, as if he thought he recognized her. Andrea forced herself not to look apprehensive even though her heart rate increased, but his pause was fleeting. Her eyes, tinted green by contact lenses and further camouflaged by non-prescription eyeglasses, were unfamiliar to him. He would remember brown eyes, if he remembered them at all. Perfect make-up further disguised the face he had only ever seen without cosmetics. Andrea had never worn her hair up when she was with him. There was no recognition, no remembrance. He returned the smile and nothing about his had changed.

He laughed and said, "Well, you may *look* like a school-girl, but I'm sure you're not silly." He scrawled his name on the programme absently, but did not relinquish his hold on it.

Andrea could not fake a blush, but she did incline her head down and glanced away shyly before tilting her face toward him again, staring directly into his heavenly blue eyes – she couldn't deny the magnetism – and saying deliberately, "The way you play the orchestra is breathtaking. They say you're a genius and . . . I believe it."

He was not abashed by the compliment in the slightest, accepting it as his due, but raised a brow. "Interesting turn of phrase . . . play the orchestra. Almost poetic."

Andrea inched out further along the limb. "I also heard you lecture once, a few years ago, but . . ." she offered up another anxious laugh, "this is going to sound foolish . . . I was too nervous to talk to you afterwards."

"Which lecture?" he asked, ignoring her little confession and apparent embarrassment.

Of course, she thought, *he doesn't care that I was nervous or why. He only wants to know the part about himself.*

"On the development of talent at a young age." Andrea paused momentarily, then added in a confident tone, "I think one of the reasons I was afraid to approach you afterward was because I wasn't sure I agreed with all your theories."

In for a penny, in for a pound, she thought then said with conviction, "I still don't."

As she spoke the last words, she stared at him unblinking. His demeanour altered perceptibly.

Hooked!

It was all she could do to keep from happy dancing and saying, "Yessss!" out loud. Instead, she fixed him with a cool stare, a subtle challenge.

Aaron glanced around at the small milling crowd then back at Andrea.

"Are you with anyone?" he asked.

"Um . . . no. Why?"

"Just a moment." He turned away from her, still clutching her programme she noted, and addressed a slight, young man hovering near him.

She heard him say, "Tony," then caught only a few whispered words, *not feeling well*, before the aide took immediate action. The fellow cleared his voice and offered sincere apologies, but declared that the Maestro would be unable to stay any longer as he was feeling the effects of a rigorous and unforgiving tour schedule. He politely asked everyone to please leave. He was rewarded with a murmured chorus of disappointment, but these were people who were too well-mannered to press further.

Aaron turned back and placed his hand on Andrea's arm as she feigned a motion to depart.

"Not you," he said quietly. "I know it's late, but would you have dinner with me?"

Andrea watched the others leave and Tony the aide following them out of the dressing room. She smiled and asked in her best incredulous tone, "You want to have dinner with *me*? Surely, you must have other things planned?"

Tony had closed the door behind himself. They were alone.

"You're a breath of fresh air. I know this may seem surprising, but it isn't all glamour and black tie parties. I don't have any commitments for tonight. All I was going to do was go back to an empty hotel room and order room service. I'd love to discuss that topic of young talent over dinner with you instead."

Andrea chuckled on the inside . . . *Yeah, right. You just can't stand that someone disagrees with you and I must be converted. You can't wait to tell me how right you are and how wrong I am.*

"Well, actually, um . . . I had dinner before I came here. I'm not really hungry. But if you'd like my company . . ."

"I would love the opportunity to talk with you and get to know you."

She laughed shortly and wondered if he wanted to get laid, or something, as well. "That could be a problem, the getting to know me part, I mean. I'm only in town for the night. I . . . um . . . I traveled here just to see you." She hastened to add, "I mean to see you conduct."

Playing the ingénue was having the desired effect. God, he lapped up the worship.

"What's your name?" he asked.

"Promise you won't laugh?"

"Why would I laugh?"

"Well, it's an unusual name. I don't have a drop of Greek blood in me, but my mother had an incredibly warped sense of humour. She was an entomologist of some note and specialized in arachnids . . . absolutely loved spiders. Doctor Letitia Webb. She named me . . . Arachnia. So, can you believe it? My name is Arachnia Webb." A suitably doubtful expression creased her forehead

He stopped and looked at her, studying her for a moment then nodded. "I like it. It's unusual. Truly unforgettable." He scrawled something on the programme above his signature and handed it back to her.

She read, "To Spiderwoman", and laughed out loud. "Well, I've been called that, but I've never seen it in writing." She timed her pause then said, "You know, even your signature looks somehow . . . musical."

"I don't suppose you know any good restaurants around here?" Aaron asked as he divested himself of the black tailcoat, throwing it carelessly over the back of a chair. It slid to the floor and he did not deign to retrieve it. He sat down in front a dressing table peering into the mirror and preened.

Andrea resisted the urge to pick up the jacket. She responded to the question, an opening for which she had dared not hope. Although she had set up a number of contingency plans, his invitation to dine was a gift.

"Well, I thought the restaurant at my hotel was more than acceptable, if you'd care to try it."

"Wonderful. I trust your judgment. We'll go there." He flashed his thousand-watt grin. "I'm really looking forward to this."

Andrea gave him her best Mona Lisa smile full of seductive promise. "So am I. Really."

Andrea's only concern, though not a major one, was the limousine driver. He would probably remember her and though it would make little difference, any complication needed to be considered. During the short drive to the hotel, all the while making introductory small talk about the evening's performance and the tour schedule – it was all about him – Andrea mulled over the best possibilities.

The doorman was already at the curb as the limousine coasted to a smooth stop in front of the hotel's main entrance. They got out of the car while he held the door open for them.

The chauffeur came around as well with a professional economy of movement. His words were clipped and quiet. "Shall I wait, sir?"

Before Aaron could say a word, Andrea squeezed his arm to gain full attention and looked directly into his eyes when he turned to her. She said softly, "It could be a long dinner and a very leisurely *discussion*. Perhaps he should come back . . . later?"

The expression on Aaron's face was all she hoped it would be. This was perfect. Andrea had a vision of herself holding a baton, weaving an elaborate invisible web in the air, conducting the ultimate symphony.

Once inside the hotel – the lobby was almost deserted at this late hour – Andrea first guided Aaron towards the dimly lit restaurant. Part way there, as they passed the elevators, she stopped and said, "Would you mind terribly if we went up to my room first? I really would like to freshen up a bit."

Aaron played his part as if he'd read the script. Andrea almost felt a twinge of disappointment that he was so predictable, but he looked as unsurprised by this overt come-on as she had anticipated. He expected adulation, and groupies were groupies. The high quality ones were a mainstay of his life.

"In fact," she continued, "we could order room service, have a lovely dinner, perhaps even some champagne, and enjoy some comfort and privacy up there. No reason our debate can't be *friendly*."

Aaron said nothing; he did not have to.

They stepped onto the elevator and watched the doors slide shut without a sound. Andrea linked her free arm through his. She felt the trembling vibrations of captive wings along invisible strands like the continuous bowing along a cello string.

Andrea stood over the king-sized bed gazing down at Aaron, who was partially reclining, pillows piled behind him against the cherry wood headboard. He was sipping from his champagne flute as he watched Andrea slowly stripping for him, teasing him.

He was slightly heavier than she remembered, perhaps a little prone to gustatory indulgence, but still trim enough. His genes had been almost as kind to him as Andrea's had been to her, though she suspected it was more his vanity that held him in close check. She felt no warmth at the thought, but it crossed her mind that they would have made a beautiful couple, the kind that would turn heads. Well, his loss.

Andrea's outer clothing was a black velvet pool on the deep pile, cream-coloured carpeting. She was down to just her black lace panties and lace top stockings; and the boots. The boots, she felt, added a little something to the overall effect. She reached up and unfastened the barrettes holding her hair in place, discarded them, and shook the lustrous mane. She stood tall and unashamed, with her shoulders thrust back, exhibiting her luscious, all-natural breasts.

Aaron's erection was a testament to her seductive display. He had good reason to thank his parents further for their contribution to his genetic superiority. Andrea, however, had little trouble reconciling her awe at his magnificent member with her resolve to deprive him of its use.

She had placed her tote bag casually beside the bed between the night table and the stand upon which the sterling ice bucket perched. The bottle of champagne nestled in the crushed ice was still half full. Andrea's glass stood empty on the night table.

She leaned over Aaron and curled her fingers around his rigid penis.

"Well, Maestro, you've certainly made your point," she said, giving him a little up-and-down stroke, "and I concede." She released him, wiggled out of her briefs, and climbed up on the bed to straddle him. She held her arms wide. "To the victor go the spoils."

Without taking his eyes off Andrea's tits, Aaron extended his arm and set his glass atop the matching night stand on the other side of the bed. He reached up and very lightly stroked the rounded curve of Andrea's left breast.

She closed her eyes and moaned deep in her throat. She knew it sounded genuine. It was easy enough to feel transported back in time, to recall the thrilling newness of her first sexual encounters. In the present, it was equally simple for her to feel the thrill of knowing she was composing her own concerto. How satisfying it was to know that for possibly the very first time, the Maestro was totally unfamiliar with the score.

Andrea swayed over top of Aaron, half opened her eyes, and with a sufficiently dreamy look, said, "You are so amazing. I can't wait to explore *all* your areas of expertise."

She leaned over him and deliberately brushed her nipples back and forth across his chest. Her lips curved in a coquettish smile and she bent close to his face, kissed him very lightly on the lips, and worked her way down his chin, his chest, his belly. She tickled him with the tip of her tongue. She explored then pretended to discover his sensitive spots. In fact, she remembered them clearly.

His responses were encouraging. The man's libido certainly seemed to have kept pace with his career.

Andrea slid her warm fingers over the gentle curve of Aaron's cock. Her nails were not too long, but well-shaped and painted in a favourite dark berry hue. She raked them, lightly over the velvet head and taut skin, following the line of a bulging vein. Beneath her touch, the beast pulsed and twitched, an entity in its own right.

Aaron groaned and reached down to twine his fingers through her hair, pressing her head with a gentle insistence. Andrea the actor had to force herself not to grin widely.

Andrea the observer watched with the satisfaction of those whose mastery of the baton produces the heart-pounding crescendos.

She submitted to his coercion and pressed her lips against his cockhead. Aaron had no idea just how in *her* area of expertise he was. She varied the use of her lips, her tongue, and her teeth in the cause of the desired effect, and employed her hands with the finesse of a concert musician. She made all the right sounds, moaning and whimpering, gagging audibly as he butted the back of her throat, the submissive willing to choke for the master's pleasure. She glanced up at him with just the right look of wanton lust and humble servitude to feed the hungry ego that could never be sated. She worshipped, with smoky eyes, the unsuspecting condemned man savouring his last meal.

When she knew he was approaching the point of no return, she stopped and moved sinuously up his body. He muttered an agonized protest at the cessation of her attention to his painfully rigid penis and tried to push her back towards it, but she did not relent.

She nuzzled his neck and murmured, "I have something very special that I can do for you. It isn't like anything you've ever felt before."

She slid off him and reached over the edge of the bed into her tote bag. Her fingers closed around the prepared object of her search and deftly obscuring it from his view, she kissed his mouth hungrily, distracting him. Over the past month, she had practiced her moves repeatedly on a life-sized, padded dummy until they were smooth and flawless.

With the same swiftness as a spider lunging at its captured prey lest it escape, she moved her hand towards him, held the needle point firmly against Aaron's neck, pierced the flesh, and pressed the plunger without pause, emptying the syringe.

She raised her head to watch as his eyelids flew open, and held him down fast feeling his body convulse against hers once in surprise then a second time in feeble protest. Within seconds she felt him fade.

Andrea was leaning over him when he regained consciousness. A satisfied smile spread across her face as she watched dawning comprehension.

"Oh, Aaron, if you could just see the look on your face." Andrea paused then said gaily, "Oh, wait, you can," then in a singsong voice, "Don't go away," as she headed to the bathroom. A moment later, she returned holding a large hand mirror.

She paused briefly standing beside the bed to watch him lying motionless. The shallow rise and fall of his chest and the terror-brightness of his blue eyes were the only visible signs of life.

Smiling she held the reflective surface over his face, adjusted it this way and that, and spoke conversationally.

"I know your whole face looks a little slack because that's what the stuff does. But the eyes are still *so* expressive. They really are windows into the soul, aren't they? Assuming one has a soul, of course. See the shock in yours . . . like this couldn't possibly be happening." She took the mirror away and set it on the bedside table. "But I assure you it is." She paused then stared into his eyes and said deliberately, "Oh yes, Aaron, it is *soooo* happening.

"You know what's really funny right now? I can actually *see* your mind racing. 'What's happening to me? What's she *doing* with me? Who *is* she?'

"Oh, yes. That last question is the kicker, isn't it? Who *am* I?"

Andrea casually caressed her breasts and toyed with her nipples closing her eyes and drifting away momentarily with the sensation, performing for her captive audience. She murmured a long *mmmmm*, inhaled deeply then sighed audibly.

Her reverie ended abruptly and she stared at him unblinking.

"Well, for starters . . . my name is *not* Arachnia Webb. I can't believe you actually bought that. Well . . . perhaps I can. After all, it is rather unusual and noteworthy and would certainly appeal to your sense of being entitled to all that is unique."

Andrea went over to the alcove beside the bathroom and hefted a large, black sport bag from the luggage bench. She dropped it with a thump beside the bed then sat down beside Aaron's inert form.

"Now you're probably also wondering just what that stuff was. Well, it's kind of a long story. I could make it shorter, I suppose, but what the hell? I do owe you something and we have." Andrea peered at the glowing green digital display on the clock radio. ". . . well, a bit of time yet. So, I'll give you more than just the little blurb you'd read in People magazine, but less than *War and Peace*. Think of this as the Reader's Digest version.

"The name is Andrea, my dear Maestro. Andrea. And once upon a time I played cello at the Royal Conservatory right here in this fair city."

She watched as the gears ground then saw comprehension anew.

"Ah-ha! There you go. Your reputation for being a genius remains untarnished. Total recall. You're just *so* fucking clever.

"You were right, you know, when you told me I would never be a world-class cellist. I don't know if I actually started out aspiring to *be* one. I just wanted to play the cello, but the thing is, after you enlightened me as to my woeful lack of talent, it never occurred to me, for years afterward, to be quite honest that being world-class wasn't the point. I wanted to play the cello. I know now that I'm responsible for my own actions, but back then . . . your opinion made all the difference. Do you have any idea at all how much your opinion of me counted? Well, probably not, but you will.

"The point is, my brilliant maestro, I really loved playing the cello, but you made me feel that I was wasting my time if I couldn't make it on the world stage, or be as perfect as you, or as perfect as you thought I ought to be. Certainly not as perfect as *Diane* was in her chosen field. I found out all there was to know about Diane and she was pretty good. Lovely soprano, but not exactly world-class either. For a while, I even followed her career, brief though it was. Shame when she did that accidental overdose, eh?"

Andrea saw Aaron's eyes go blank.

"Oh, God, you don't mean you don't remember her, either? Christ, Aaron, just how many women does a guy like you have to fuck over before their names and faces start disappearing into the mists of time? I guess being a genius means never having to remember who you've screwed.

"Well, I don't want to wax philosophic. Sands through the hour glass and all that. No, the fact is that I *do* owe you for a couple of things. First of all, a heartfelt *thank you* for enlightening me as to the nature of men. I really do enjoy them, you know, but so much more for knowing what makes them tick. And second, for letting me know up close and personal the one thing I *did* have a knack for.

"You once said I needed to find my own niche, and thanks to you, I did. What I discovered, much to the delight of my pragmatic and somewhat mercenary self, was that what you so enjoyed me giving you for free a lot of other men were more than willing to pay for. So instead of becoming simply a mediocre cellist, I became a world-class cocksucker . . . in the truest sense of that word. I'll tell you, Aaron, they paid a lot more for that than they would have paid to listen to a cello concert. So, in a sense, I owe my fame and fortune to you.

"Still, you were such a shit and, honestly, I do wonder how different my life would have been if I'd pursued music." Andrea sighed, bent down, and unzipped the bag. After a moment of theatrical rummaging, she withdrew a translucent white plastic container, snapped it open and set it on the bed beside Aaron. She carefully picked out another tiny syringe from the box and a small, dark brown bottle and held them up so Aaron could see them.

"You're probably wondering, or maybe not, but it doesn't really matter – I'll tell you anyway – you're probably wondering what I *did* do instead of keeping up with the cello . . . I mean besides starting up *Blow Jobs R Me*. After all, you can't suck cock twenty-four-seven, can you? Well, I guess you could, but it's hard on the jaw and would probably get a little tedious. Anyway, when I wasn't raking it in for paying lip service to a lot of rich guys, I dabbled. I ended up doing all kinds of stuff. I'll bet you never realized how bright I was. I just never was very focused . . . not like you at all."

With her right hand, she waggled the bottle in front of Aaron's face.

"This, Aaron, is a fascinating little substance consisting of neurotoxins and myotoxins. Do you know what those are? No? Well, isn't it nice to know you're not a well-rounded genius." She lowered her right hand. "In simple terms, they are the main ingredients in the venom most commonly found in poisonous snakes and almost all spiders. This is spider venom, of course. Only appropriate, I think. I whipped it up myself. I'm rather brilliant in this particular arena. You should know that. First I harvested it – and let me tell you, *that* wasn't easy – and processed it, distilled it to a highly concentrated form, refined it so it would do exactly what I want it to do, then diluted it to administer. I know you've always felt privileged and you should do now as well because I did this just for *you*. Now the shot I gave you was rather mild and mixed with just a wee drop of a potent little tranquilizer. You were actually out cold for about half an hour. I had some other stuff to get ready for you and no reason I shouldn't let you rest up for it.

"Oh, one thing I did while you nodded off . . . I wheeled the dinner cart into the hall and hung the 'Do Not Disturb' sign on the door, so you don't have to worry at all about us being interrupted. The rest of the night is ours.

"Anyhow, the signature attribute of these charming potions is muscle paralysis and the general destruction of organic tissue.

The toxins in the venom allow the female spider, once she has incapacitated her prey, to keeping it alive so she can suck the life out of it at her leisure. An evolutionary coup, don't you think?"

Andrea held the tiny syringe a little higher so Aaron could see it clearly. His eyes had taken on a wild cast.

"Shortly, I will inject this into you because the initial dose will start to wear off. I made the first one weak because I didn't know how much you weighed. By the way, you still *look* fabulous. But I'm sure you're also still a shit, so how you look doesn't really count for anything. I've prepared a few doses to last us for a spell. I have to be very careful, because too much at once could kill you and we wouldn't want that to happen too soon, would we?"

She replaced both the bottle and the syringe in the plastic case, but didn't close it. Shifting her position so she could access his crotch, Andrea fingered Aaron's now limp penis. She flip-flopped it back and forth playfully.

"How the mighty have fallen," she said yanking on it a few times then letting it plop down.

"You know, this thing is looking pretty pathetic. It just isn't right. To your credit, Aaron, although you *are* a first class prick, you also *have* a first class prick and you just don't look like yourself without a good, stiff hard-on."

She got off the bed and squatted beside the sport bag, rooting around in it once again. She stood erect and proudly help up "The Boy".

"Ta-daaaaa!"

She grinned broadly and said, "Remember this guy? Of course you do. You gave him to me so I wouldn't forget you while you were away. Something to remember you by. Well, I remember, Aaron. I remember all of it. Every . . . single . . . thing . . . even if you don't."

She leaned over him and pressed his legs together tightly. As expected, there was no resistance. She wedged the base end of the dildo between his thighs so the head pointed toward the ceiling. The ebony contrasted sharply against his pale skin and blond pubic hair.

She stood back and admired her handiwork.

"There. That's better. That's more like the real you; a prick with absolutely no feeling at all."

Sitting down on the bed, Andrea picked up the syringe again.

"I think we can give you a little more now. Don't want you getting up and walking out on me."

As she again stabbed him with the tiny needle and slowly pressed the clear liquid into his system, she chatted as would a nurse attending her patient.

"So, where was I? Oh, yes, dabbling. I've always liked entomology. Although I wasn't completely honest with you when I was pretending to be someone else, I was serious about my mother being an entomologist. Just an amateur of course . . . and not all bugs. She certainly didn't fancy spiders at all. She was a lepidopterist. Actually, she was a real bitch, too. I think that might be why she took such pleasure in catching butterflies, killing them, and pinning them to her little boards."

Andrea withdrew the needle from Aaron's neck and rested her arm on the pillow. She was looking at Aaron, but not seeing him. She gazed into some distant past.

"It was rather bizarre really. I caught her once – she didn't see me watching her – I caught her pinning a live one down. She was smiling. She watched it struggling, trying to beat its wings, legs flailing uselessly, and she just smiled. She enjoyed it you see, capturing this beautiful winged creature. It wasn't enough for her just to kill it and keep it as a trophy. She wanted it to know it was caught and would never fly free again . . . that it would die without ever soaring on the wind one last time. I'm not even sure how old I was . . . maybe ten or eleven. What I saw her doing horrified me. At that moment, I wished more than anything that I could go back, just a few minutes, and instead of stopping at her study, just passing right by it and doing something else, anything else. I have never wanted a do-over so badly in my life as I did that day. I left without her knowing I'd seen what she'd done. I went to my room and took out my cello and started playing, just playing and playing. I have no idea how long I kept at it. It could have been hours. Probably was. The room was light when I started. It was dark when I gave up. I played till my fingers bled. I started with Haydn and Dvorak then just made up stuff. Not anything you'd recognize, just notes and chords . . . and really loud. I just wanted the sound and the pain to drown out the vision. It never really did. I can still see that butterfly with its beautiful, useless wings and pawing the air with those spindly, weak legs in utter futility. And I can still see that smile, that satisfied smirk. Fuck, I hated it."

She fell silent, lost in the memory then jerked back to the present and said brightly, "Well, how's that for a little trip down memory lane? You never asked me much about myself. It was always about you. You and your genius intellect and your awesome talent and . . ." she gave his flaccid penis a kittenish bat with her free hand, "your formerly splendid cock."

She straightened, replaced the syringe in the plastic case, closed the case, and tucked it into the bag saying, "Won't need this for a little while."

Searching the bag once again, Andrea said, "But I do have something else in here that you're just going to love." She gripped the prize in her right hand.

She sat upright again and fixed him with a serene smile, keeping the occupied hand out of his line of vision. She adjusted her position then used her left hand to rake her nails lightly across his chest and down his belly to rest in his pubic hair. With a dreamy nonchalance, she twined and untwined a lock of the blond curls around her index finger with the help of her thumb. She pulled on them absently each time the strands were twisted.

"I really do love cocks, Aaron. Hate you, still love your cock."

With one smooth flourish, Andrea held up the Bowie knife in front of Aaron's face and laughed out loud when she saw the expression in his eyes.

"You know what I really hate these days? Package deals. Like those satellite dish packages. There's like, what, maybe ten channels you actually watch and enjoy and the other hundred-and-forty are basic shit that no one would pay for if they weren't included in the sixty bucks a month. And they won't let you do it *à la carte* either. It's all or nothing. You're almost like one of those package deals, Aaron. There's like *three* good pieces of programming with you and the rest is crap. You have this breathtaking musical talent, which I truly admire. I love music and what you do with it almost too much to take it away from the world prematurely. You also have that supreme gift of gab and I will be the first to compliment you on your riveting lectures."

"And you have . . . this," she said, pointing to his penis, just barely touching it with the tip of the gleaming seven-inch stainless steel blade. She heard him sucking air through gaping lips.

"That little anecdote about my dear mater? I told you that so you'd understand that I come by my love of bugs honestly. My preference is to study them live, though. Under natural conditions is nice, but under controlled conditions is my specialty. I wonder if bugs feel anything that equates to emotion. Love, hate or fear perhaps? It wouldn't seem so, but you never know. I realize I anthropomorphized with that butterfly, but who knows? Maybe it really *did* know what was happening to it. What do *you* think, Maestro? Love? Hate? Do you feel either of those emotions? God, I wish you'd speak up. You always had so much to say and now I can't get a word out of you.

"Well, I guess I'll never know about the love or hate. But I *do* see fear. You *are* a genius, Maestro, adding two and two and coming up with fear.

"I had a truly spectacular collection of bladed weapons. Sold it just recently for an obscene sum. This is the only one left. I have a great fondness for it because it was my first, just like your cock. Your cock was just the first blunt weapon in what turned out to be a very lucrative collection of blunt weapons. The blade collection, like the blunt objects, outlived its usefulness. Shortly, this blade, to which I have a sentimental attachment, will be retired." She smiled at her own unspoken conclusion. "I can't take it on the plane and don't want to chance it in the luggage either."

Andrea tapped the glossy black dildo with the steel.

"Well, at least that's good and hard . . . still plenty useful."

She drew the knifepoint along Aaron's thigh. She heard him gasp as she pressed the point into the meaty flesh.

"Entomology, biological toxins, bladed weaponry. Tip of the iceberg. I studied some basic anatomy and medicine, too.

"You know what you did to me, Aaron? With surgical precision, you excised my harmless little dream. That cello was all I had, it was all I knew how to do, and for no reason that I can think of, other than your need to inflate your own fucking huge ego, you pinned my wings to the board. You were such a prick. And then that last time before you left for Europe . . . you may as well have been smirking at me watching me floundering like some helpless bug. There I was giving you the only thing I had left to give and . . . you . . . weren't . . . in the *mood*?!"

Andrea bared her teeth, shoved the weapon harder and twisted it. Despite the chemical working its venomous magic, pain neurons sprang to life and Aaron's leg twitched. An agonized groan escaped him.

She relaxed as quickly as she had tensed to inflict the injury. Smiling once again, she said, "I can see what you're thinking." She chuckled. "Oh, don't worry, I'm not going to separate you from your baton . . . or your lovely little castanets. God's sake, Aaron, give me some credit for originality. That's been done to death."

Still gripping the knife, Andrea rose and looked down at him. She inhaled then heaved a theatrical sigh.

"Geez," she said, "you're bleeding all over the bed."

She snickered and turned away from him then went to the mirrored dresser. She laid the weapon down on the surface, opened up a small bag and took out a digital camera. A tiny beep sounded as she activated it then after making some adjustments, she pivoted to face the bed.

"These will make really terrific publicity shots, don't you think?"

She aimed and pressed the shutter button. She moved casually around the room angling the camera and taking pictures then paused and reviewed the shots squinting at the small window.

"I love the technology these days, don't you? I've found you on a few web sites just by punching in your name. You've carved out quite a niche for yourself, but you can never have too many fans, can you? I could post these with a link to your name and cultivate a whole new audience for you. Do you think these shots would do you justice? How about a few close-ups?"

Andrea stood over the bed and aimed the viewfinder at Aaron's genitals. "The Boy" stood out in stark relief and she snapped several shots.

"I think I'll call that one 'A Study in Contrasts,' or maybe, 'The Long and the Short of It.' God, I'm clever. I never used to believe I was a genius, not like you, but hey . . . think about it. I'm standing here taking shots of your limp dick and you're lying there like a crash test dummy. So who's the genius?"

She focused on his face to capture for posterity the essence of helpless dread.

"Love the look, Aaron. Still so lifelike." She went back to the dresser, set down the camera, and picked up the knife again.

Humming no identifiable tune and gripping the haft in her right hand, she returned to him.

She stared down and reached out with her left hand to caress the dildo. As she did so, she brought the knife back to the single wound. Only a thin trickle of red still seeped out.

"Hmmm. The flow seems to be drying up. It was hard to be exact with the procoagulant factor because I was working with others' research and computer models. I've never actually used this on a human, and the idea of trying it out on some helpless little animal, who never harmed me, seemed totally unjustified and unfair. So let's see what we can do about getting that flow going again."

Once more she retrieved the plastic container and took out another syringe.

"I may not have been a very good musician, Aaron, but I'm a world-class dabbler. I planned for this contingency."

Yet a third time, Andrea injected her prey with a clear fluid.

"I have several options here," she said, replacing the paraphernalia,

"I think, just for the poetic justice of it all, I should let you exsanguinate. That's the technical term for 'bleed to death,' but you must know that because you are, after all, a genius. Exsanguinate is forensically correct. It really doesn't sound like what it means, though, does it? It's such a lovely, melodious word. Musical." Andrea lowered her voice and, in the manner of an elocutionist using full, rounded tones, said, "Exsaaaaanguinate."

"Oh, does 'forensically' bother you? You're thinking that's the word they usually use when a corpse gets involved."

Andrea sighed. "Oh Aaron, Aaron, how can you be *sooo* creative in one area and so monumentally unimaginative in another? I hate having to nudge you, but . . ." She jabbed at the wound again going deeper and watched as the flow of blood resumed.

As she continued conversing, Andrea idly caressed herself with her free hand; stroked her breasts, pinched the nipples. Her fingers found their way to her pussy and she massaged absently.

"So where was I? Oh yes. I could let you . . . exsanguinate. You'd just get weaker and weaker and pass out. It really wouldn't be too exciting. Well, not for me at least. I imagine *your* frigid little heart would be all aflutter though . . . for a while, anyway. But bleeding to death is rather pedestrian, don't you think? Wouldn't make very good press either and no one would really make the connection between you shedding your blood for my pleasure the way I was willing to shed mine for yours. It's still an option, though, so let's not cross it off our list just yet.

"Option two represents the time and effort I put into dabbling in chemistry. I have two more vials in my little bag of tricks. One of them contains a simple saline solution with a sedative. The other is something totally different. It's something I concocted that would be rather fascinating to experiment with. A delicious little cocktail of toxins, but more like liqueur, highly concentrated. A super-venom combo that just shuts things down. Muscle tissue disintegrates and brain function ceases. Depending on the dosage, this could occur gradually or rapidly.

"That would probably be a little more stimulating than watching paint dry. You'd probably panic a little, which would be good; once-in-a-lifetime photo op for me. And you'd feel nauseous. That would be *very* good. I think you *should* feel sick like that. I think it would do you good, just once before you die, to feel your stomach heave like someone just punched you in the gut and kicked your balls at the same time. But I'd be a lot more honourable about it than you were, because I wouldn't turn my back on you. Nope, I'd stand here and watch the whole thing. You'd feel like shit for a while then you'd just suffocate because the muscles enabling you to breathe would just . . . pffft.

"Hmmm. Your breathing is getting a little raspy there, Maestro. That's just excitement and to be expected. I haven't given you a lethal dose, so no need to get too panicky just yet." Andrea reached with wet fingers to Aaron's mouth and smeared a light coating of her own juices across his lips. They glistened.

"Wouldn't do to have chapped lips, now, would it? Heh! Bet the forensics team would get a chuckle when they analyzed *that* lip balm."

Andrea stroked "The Boy".

"I really *do* like men, Aaron. Oh, not you, of course, but men in general. I have to tell you, though, there's a lot to be said for the fair sex, too. That's something else I dabbled in. Still do. Quite enjoy it. I was doing a remarkable business simply catering to men, who crave a woman on her knees sucking them off. Some of them get off on it even more, if I wear handcuffs and a collar, a few chains, the occasional blindfold. In my line of work, knowing how to accessorize is really important. And honestly . . . I do so love indulging them. Hell, I'd do it for free, but getting paid for it is icing on the cake and I say, 'find something you love to do and make money at it.' Well, you'd know that, wouldn't you? So I was doing that and one particularly adventurous evening, when I was still cultivating a loyal clientele, one of my wealthier patrons proved to me that three *is* a crowd, but a fun one. He presented the opportunity and, *bingo*, one more joy of sex.

"I *did* find that I lean more towards having the upper hand in those relationships and apparently I have a knack."

All helpless innocence, Andrea shrugged. "What can I say? The girls like me, too."

"Oh, stop looking so 'what's-she-on-about-now?' I'm getting to that."

Andrea checked the oozing wound in Aaron's thigh and gave it a little poke with the knife tip, testing the meat. The trickle increased.

"So anyway, not only do I indulge myself in the sheer pleasure of *playing* with pussy, I've formed some very rewarding friendships. And a few very sturdy bonds of something way beyond playing and far exceeding friendship. Three ladies in particular seem to think the sun rises and sets on me. Wow! I sound just like you used to. You probably still would if you could get your tongue to work and actually talk again.

"These three ladies are a blessing. Heh! A blessed trinity. I just thought that up. See how inspiring you can be even just lying there like a seemingly useless piece of crap. Anyway, I've worked with them for quite some time, trained them in many ways. They are a labour of love on a number of levels. Each on her own is a perfection and joy. The three of them in concert are a work of art, a masterpiece. In fact, I think of them as *my* concerto.

"Hey, you're not the only genius in this room, Maestro," she said elbowing him as a teammate would, sharing a gruff, intimate understanding of what it takes to succeed.

Andrea's demeanor transformed from playful to serious in a heartbeat.

"What I should tell you about my Concerto is that, unlike me, and despite the fact that they are able to put on a really good show of being cock-worshippers, they have no use for men.

None whatsoever. In fact, if I were a man, I wouldn't feel at all safe alone with any one of them. What you *need* to know, Aaron, what you *must* understand, as you may never have understood anything else in your life, is that these three ladies will do anything I ask them to do. *Anything*. I don't have to make it an order. I can just say, 'I would be *very* appreciative, if you would find a way for this fellow to suffer and die,' and any one of them will consider performing that act both a joy and a privilege. They're a little competitive amongst themselves, too, which is good because they try to outdo each other in pursuit of my happiness. They would vie for the opportunity not only to win my favour, but to satisfy their own rather perversely male-oriented homicidal lust.

"They are my third option. You're going to love the simplicity of this creation. Here's what I'm thinking.

"Other than what I've just told you about them, there is nothing else you will know about my little trio, except that one day you will meet one of them.

"She could be outstandingly, stunningly attractive, or just one-of-the-crowd ordinary. She could be blonde, brunette, redhead, raven-haired . . . even a little or a lot grey. Young, not so young, my age. Tall, short, thin, plump. Skin colour could be white, black, brown, creamy, olive. She could speak perfect English, or barely any, or with a foreign accent: French, German, Chinese, Australian, Italian. Take your pick. A southern belle, a Midwest farm girl, or a Boston socialite. She could be part of the audience sitting behind you, or one of the fans jostling to meet you backstage, after a performance, or an intense student hanging off every word in one of your lectures. She could present herself as artist or academician. She might approach you smoothly, but shyly, just like I did, or come across as a giggling groupie. She could be someone seemingly not paying the slightest attention to you, or a fawning acolyte. You could be seated beside her at some posh dinner party, or she could be someone totally anonymous sharing an otherwise empty elevator with you.

"The point is, Aaron, *Maestro*, you won't know. You will never know, for certain, who she is. Any woman you meet, ever again, could be the part of my Concerto who won the draw, earned the reward of taking you out of the picture. Any time there are unfamiliar women around you, you will search their faces and study their behaviour for clues that will be too well hidden for you to see. Every time you are alone with a woman, you'll need to ask yourself, 'Is this Andrea's slave?'"

She gazed at Aaron with an expression of serene superiority that she knew he had never before seen.

"The only other thing you need to know about option three is that you don't have to be a genius to understand I have the money, the power, and more than anything, the incentive, to exercise it."

She looked at the clock and said, "I have to get going."

She took off her boots, rose and gathered together her belongings. She put the knife and the used syringes in the sport bag, but left the open plastic case with the two vials of clear liquid on the night stand. She took three lengths of gold drapery cord out of the bag and tossed them on the bed.

After packing the velvet suit, the footwear, and the long black coat in her luggage, she dressed in stylish blue jeans and a white cotton shirt. She paused to check Aaron's pulse, nodding, satisfied that all was in order. She donned a pair of tan cowboy boots and a brown leather jacket then checked her grooming one more time in the mirror.

"I'll leave the goody bag here so that you can have everything analyzed if you want. A little additional proof for you, if any is needed, that I know exactly what I'm doing and that this wasn't all some elaborate practical joke."

Andrea stood over Aaron, reached out and patted his shrivelled penis then stroked the dildo.

"I'm going to leave 'The Boy' with you, too, something of substance to remember me by. I think I'll leave him right here like this. It'll make for an interesting tableau when they find you. And they *will* find you. I'll make a couple of phone calls just before take-off. I've been very diligent with the quantities, Aaron. The dosages I've given you won't kill you, although, sorry, but there may be some permanent muscle and nerve damage. Nothing too drastic . . . perhaps a slackness here and there.

"In any case, I don't want you getting mobile too soon. Wouldn't do to have you up and about before I'm safely in the air."

Andrea picked up one of the ropes, grabbed his left wrist, and secured it to the nearest bedpost then moved to the other side of the bed to repeat the procedure with his right arm. Finally, she bound his legs together just above the knees and adjusted "The Boy", who had slumped a little. Once again, it stood straight and tall.

"There. All snug. And I must say that you're looking much more erect than the last time we parted company.

"Okay, last but not least, I don't want you regaining the use of your vocal cords for a while. Don't want you making a whole lot of noise, waking everyone up at this ungodly hour and attracting a crowd too soon."

She stretched her hand towards the night table, then stopped short.

"Oh, shit!" she said.

She picked up first one vial, studied it then replaced it. She did the same with the other, then sighed.

"Now how the fuck did *that* happen? I could have sworn I marked the killer stuff."

Andrea shrugged. "Ah, well. I guess I'll just have to take my chances."

She frowned, said, "Eeny, meeny, miney, mo," then with no further hesitation, made her choice. One last time, she jabbed Aaron's neck and depressed the plunger.

"This will either put you to sleep for a few hours then you'll wake up, if not all bright-eyed and bushy tailed, at least alive, or very excruciatingly turn everything inside you to mush before you expire. Hope I picked the right one. I really would hate to deprive one of my little slaves of my pleasure."

Andrea bestowed a benevolent smile upon her subject noting with glee the stark terror in his blue angel eyes. She watched and waited. She listened to the panicked gasps ratcheting from his throat.

Andrea cackled. "Oh, relax, Aaron. That was just a little goodbye gotcha for old time's sake. Do you really think I'm airheaded enough to get my potions mixed up? You just don't get it, do you? She sighed and shook her head. "I *want* you to live . . . for now. I want my *Concerto* to be one of those tunes you just can't get out of your head." She patted his cock.

"Well, Maestro, I can't begin to tell you how much I've enjoyed our sweet reunion, but I have a plane to catch. I'm finally taking your advice and getting on with my life."

She turned and walked away from him. She could feel his eyes staring at the back of her head. Andrea grinned.

Serendipity

Tsaurah Litzky

I walk out the door of my father's building in the Serendipity Senior Housing Complex in which he lives. It is Yom Kippur morning and I've come down to Philadelphia from my Brooklyn home to spend the highest of the holy days with him.

I don't feel very holy. Sadly, ten minutes in my father's company has the same effect on me that it did when I was small. Then he was always comparing me to my cousin Marcia who got straight As in school and played with dolls like a little girl should; now he compares me to my dead mother who looked like a movie star and never, never burned his oatmeal like I did an hour ago. Whatever I do, I can't please my father; spending time with him makes me feel useless and sad.

I pause and survey the lovely pale blue cloudless sky. I enjoy the comforting feeling of the warm sun on my face. I feel useless and sad lately anyway. I miss my old boyfriend Robby. I miss his miraculous tongue. It's been almost a year since we broke up and in all that time I haven't had any of the old in-and-out except with my Blue Bunny vibrator.

Before I can ponder the sources of my melancholy further, I see Mr Tom. He is sitting on the bench beside the door. Three times a week he goes for radiation for liver cancer, but he still chain-smokes his brown Nat Shermans, lighting the new one off the butt of the last. He sits smoking cigarettes and holding court on this bench everyday except when it is raining or snowing or too cold. One of the neighbors has even donated an old stone spittoon that sits beside the bench for him. Mr Tom is a friend of my father's. They're both WW II vets in their eighties, though Mr Tom is older. On his good days, my father wheels outside to join Mr Tom and trade war stories. Mr Tom is genial and sharp; he always has a smile on his face.

"Hey, Girlie," Mr Tom calls out to me, "so you're visiting your Dad." He offers me his hand. I take it and sit down. His fingers are strong and firm as he grasps mine and draws me closer to him. He is freshly shaved and smells of Brut, the same aftershave Robby used. "Yes," I tell him, "I'm trying to be a better daughter."

"You're a good girl," Mr Tom says, "and good looking too. The first time I saw you, I said to myself, Tommy, there's a girl, who can break a man's back and look like a beauty queen while she does it." I'm taken aback at the turn the conversation has taken; maybe it's just his way of being courtly.

"Er, um, thank you," I say but I decide to change the subject. "How's Mrs Susie?" I ask. Mrs Susie is Tom's wife; she had a stroke three months ago and has been in a nursing home ever since.

"About the same," he says, shaking his head, "She won't be doing the old hootchie-kooch any time soon." I am conscious of the warmth of his thigh next to mine. He's always dressed impeccably. Today he's got on fine beige linen slacks and a creamy colored pullover. With his big blue eyes and leading man smile, Mr Tom is adorable. He continues to hold my left hand in his left hand. He puts his right arm along the back of the bench, encircling but not quite touching my shoulders. We sit like this as I watch a monarch butterfly flit about the geraniums in the flowerbed next to the bench. Mr Tom clears his throat.

"So," he says, "How is your love life, girlie? A good looker like you must have plenty of boyfriends." I tell him the truth, "Nah," I say. "There is a guy I've been going out with but he's holding back, all politeness and pecks on the cheek. I can't get him to make the move."

"Ha!" says Mr Tom. "Doesn't he know life is short? You wouldn't have any trouble getting me to make the move!" He starts rubbing my back, caressing my spine with sure, supple fingers. I can't believe this is happening, the butterfly continues to play in the flowerbed, the sun is still warm on my face, but suddenly my kundalini is being expertly elevated by a senior, senior citizen in expensive looking tasseled loafers. I feel the space between my legs part, the crevice between them moisten. In less than a minute he's got me wet. All the stored up juices inside me start to simmer.

"You wouldn't have any trouble getting me to make the move," Mr Tom murmurs again and then he just leans over and plants a big, juicy kiss right on my mouth. I can't help it, I respond. His lips are as firm and determined as his fingers and his mouth smells like tobacco. I haven't smoked a cigarette for fifteen years but the smell of tobacco still turns me on. I open my lips to Mr Tom. I feel his hot tongue slide between them, but then it hits me. This is crazy! I'm crazy, so crazy! What am I doing, canoodling in broad daylight with a lecherous octogenarian who is older than my father and on Yom Kippur no less?

I leap up as if it was a golem who was kissing me. Mr Tom is left with his mouth hanging open. He appears surprised but right away he gives me that big smile.

"That was lovely, Girlie," he says smoothly, nodding at me, his bald head pink as a baby's bottom.

I start to stutter, "C-c-c-c coffee, I came out for c-c-coffee."

"I bet you take it sweet," Mr Tom calls out after me as I turn and lurch away.

The next day I am sitting at my father's dining room table grading homework for the erotic writing class I teach. The student who wrote a story in which he keeps referring to his heroine's nipples as ripe strawberries gets a C. The student who refers to her heroine's twat as the Bat Cave gets an A.

My father glides in on his new motorized wheelchair. He rams into my mother's three-thousand-dollar mahogany china closet filled with her precious collection of Rose Medallion china. Miraculously, he doesn't break the glass or damage the china, but when he disengages the wheelchair there is a long scratch in the dark wood that is shaped like a scythe. Then, standing behind my father, the angel of death appears, his grey hooded burnoose stained with blood. With infinite care, he brings his scythe down towards my father's neck. I draw back, horrified, shutting my eyes tight. When I open them again the grim reaper is gone.

"You look just like your mother, honey," my father says. I have repeatedly asked him not to call me honey because that was what he always called my mother. He has repeatedly ignored me. "But," he goes on and his eyes stray to my breasts. I remember the day when he told me, a shy, scrawny teenager proud of my new tiny boobies, that I would have a good figure if only I had bigger breasts. I shudder, but when my father continues he surprises me, "You're even prettier than your mother."

Maybe he is mellowing because it is the New Year and this is the time that the Midrash says we must make amends to those we have slighted. Maybe he just wants love like me and everyone else.

I look at my father in the scooter. He's gotten so skinny but he has a big belly as if his once fine physique has melted down around his waist. He used to swim a mile a day. He is wearing a baseball cap as he always does to conceal the fact that all that that is left of his once thick, dark hair is a few silver strands. Today it is his Baltimore Orioles cap, a bright red flag above his pallid face. It must be so hard for him now, careening around these four rooms in his little cripple's cart, struggling to change his diapers.

"Hey, Dad," I ask, "You want to have tea and cookies? I need to take a break."

His face brightens. "Sure, honey," he says.

We sit together drinking tea and eating Oreos. My father starts to tell the story about how my mother wouldn't take off her nightgown on their wedding night. I don't want to hear this story, certainly not for the twentieth time. I recite *Kubla Khan* to myself and pretend to listen.

My father has stopped talking and is looking at me expectantly as if he is waiting for an answer. "I couldn't hear what you said, Dad," I tell him, "because I was chewing. What did you say?"

"Will you do something for me, honey?" my father asks. "Bring some books up to Mr Tom? He has some books for me."

My father and Mr Tom are both mystery fans, sharing a preference for the contemporary thrillers of Lawrence Block. They trade books back and forth. "Er, um, sure," I say.

"Thanks, honey," my father answers. "I'll call Mr Tom right up." My father drives off eagerly to the telephone in his bedroom. He soon calls in to me, "Tommy says come up in an hour."

I'm standing in front of Mr Tom's door holding three paperback books. The top one is *The Sins of Our Fathers*. As I knock on the door, I feel nervous. Mr Tom answers immediately. He is wearing a maroon satin smoking jacket with a white cravat. The smell of Brut surrounding him is very strong. I fight the impulse to run back into the elevator.

"Here, Mr Tom," I say as I hold the books out to him. 'If you'll just give me the books you have for my dad, I'll be on my way." He shakes his head, "Oh, no, no, you can't do that, you just can't. You must come in, you must. I have something special to show you. Please, please come in." He looks at me so imploringly that I cannot refuse.

"Okay," I say, "but only for a minute." I follow him into a spacious living room with fancy furniture in white and gold. A big white sofa dominates the room, a low gold coffee table in front of it. "Do me the honor of sitting down," says Mr Tom and I do.

"Take a look at this," he says, "I've made a little display for you." Standing on the coffee table, there are perhaps a dozen framed pictures of Mr Tom, a much younger Mr Tom, Mr Tom in uniform, Mr Tom the soldier. There is also an open cigar box filled with medals and brightly colored war ribbons. In the center of the table sits a pink porcelain candy dish piled with Hershey's kisses.

"These are the souvenirs of my military career," says Mr Tom. "I wanted you to see me when I was a young warrior fighting for my country. I enlisted again after the war. Now in this one, I'm in front of my plane, we were liberating Belgium, bet you didn't know Tommy was a pilot." He picks up a picture of a handsome young charmer with large, luminous eyes, his light hair combed into an old style pompadour. One by one he shows me the photos, recounts their histories. He was in Morocco standing under a palm tree. He was in Palermo sitting at the wheel of a jeep. "Those Italian lasses were saucy," says Mr Tom, "but they couldn't hold a candle to you." My father said when Mr Tom was diagnosed with cancer the doctor said he'd be dead in three months. Now a couple of years later, here he is, an aged Don Juan trying to seduce me with war pictures and medals attesting to his courage and valor.

"Will you join me in a cocktail?" Mr Tom asks. "I usually have one at this time of day."

I thought of Timothy Leary's last words. "Why not?" I say.

"I like an Old Fashioned," he tells me. "Would that be okay?" I tell him that would be fine. He vanishes into the other room, while I idly examine his Silver Star, his Purple Heart.

He is soon back with a tray holding a cocktail shaker and two highball glasses, the glasses already full. The old devil has planned this very carefully. The drink is deliciously sweet and powerful; just a few sips and my head is spinning.

"Hits the spot," I say to him.

"I like a woman who appreciates her liquor and I like you, Girlie," Mr Tom says. "Would you grant my wish? Would you permit me to use my Uncle Woody the way God intended at least one more time?" Even though he was trying to play on my sympathies, I am charmed by his ingenious attempt at seduction, his courage. Mr Tom has a pair as big as Sicily.

"Yes," I say.

"Oh, baby!" Mr Tom exclaims. He reaches into the pocket of the smoking jacket, pulls out two pleasure mesh Trojans in their purple packets and puts them on the table. I don't know what to do next so I gulp down the rest of my drink and ask for another. Mr Tom pours it for me and I take a big swallow. He slips off the smoking jacket and cravat to reveal he still has plenty of wiry white hair on his bony chest. His nipples are plump and pink like those of a much younger man. He puts his arms up like a body-builder and begins preening, flexing his biceps for me, showing me he still has some muscle. "I'm the boogie woogie bugle boy," he starts to sing; proving he can still carry a tune. He is so happy his bugle is already making a little tent inside his pants.

Mr Tom starts to kiss my face with his big lava lips. He moves on to my mouth, opening it with a wily tongue. He shows me he knows how to take his time as he slowly fucks my mouth. Once again he quickly gets my little jam pot simmering. I put my fingers up to tug languidly at his nipple and soon it hardens beneath my fingers. Matching the rhythm of my fingers to that of his tongue in my mouth, I pull it; milk it like it was a tiny cock. Our lower bodies start to work in tandem grinding against each other. The heavy package he presses against my vulva is so big, I wonder if he has a howitzer in his pants.

Mr Tom stops kissing me and starts to fumble with the bottom of my sweater. I let go of his nipple and help him pull my sweater and bra off over my head.

He surveys the terrain below. "You got tits like an angel," he says. He lowers his body on top of mine and we start smooching again, making out wildly like teenagers, our hips churning even faster. It was all so pleasurable and I felt those juices simmering between my legs heat up to a rolling boil.

"Are you ready?" Mr Tom asks.

"Proceed, soldier," I tell him.

He sits up on the edge of the couch and unzips his trousers. He picks up a condom packet and tears it open. I look away; I don't want to watch this part. I'm afraid I'll see a strange wizened appendage, wrinkled like a prune, but at the last minute, my curiosity gets the best of me. I glance over. I see Mr Tom slide the love sock onto a long meaty shaft that would make a twenty-year-old marine proud. He hovers over me again and pulls up my skirt. I spread my legs eagerly; I want that big thing inside me. I shut my eyes. I feel Mr Tom pull the crotch of my panties aside.

My sweet cunt stink floats out into the room, I hear Mr Tom take a hearty sniff, and then he slides right in, filling me completely. We begin our campaign and I hear troops, whole regiments, marching, stomping into battle. I hear rifle fire, artillery, cannons, mortars exploding. We come at exactly the same instant. It's a direct hit.

"Bombs away!" Mr Tom yells. For the first time in ages, I feel completely relaxed. I want to reach up; touch Mr Tom's cheek, his mouth. I open my eyes as he pulls out of me. His face is very red. Suddenly, he just keels over and falls off the couch with a big kerpunk, landing between the couch and coffee table. I'm frightened! Did he have a heart attack? Has he died in the saddle, my saddle? I make myself look down.

He is still breathing. His eyes are open. "Mr Tom," I ask. "Are you all right?"

He smiles up at me. "Yes, Girlie," he answers. "Guess I just got a little wobbly. How did I do?"

I am so relieved. "Victory on all fronts," I tell him.

We put our tops back on and straighten our clothes. We polish off the Old Fashioneds. Mr Tom gives me a couple of books for my father that had been on the floor next to the couch. As I get up to leave my eyes fall on the unused Trojan on the coffee table.

Mr Tom sees me looking. "For next time," he says.

My father is sitting in front of the TV in the living room watching Oprah when I return. "What took you so long? I was going to call up," my father asks.

"Mr Tom was showing me some of his war souvenirs," I tell him. "You're a sweet girl," my father replies. "Trying to make an old man happy, I'm proud of you," and this time he doesn't call me honey.

The Good Place

Ashley Lister

I've heard psychologists refer to "the good place".

It's not a specific location, or a town you can visit. It's a state of mind where – instead of being glum about your lack of prospects or miserable because you're lonely – you're content with life and all it has to offer. I was there once and I know it's a good place. It's a better place than where I am now. But, as I'm currently sitting on death row, Waverley, Virginia, with less than a week to go before execution, I think any other place might be considered better.

Not that I should be on death row.

I'm an innocent man.

And, while I did kill Katy and although I do hear voices in my head, I'm not one of your crazy murderers.

Have I just rushed ahead too fast? Should I slow this down a pace and start from the beginning?

I first fell in love with Katy's voice. She spoke with a throaty chuckle set deep into her Virginia drawl. There was the hint of mischief dripping from every word and the sultry promise of passion in each syllable. She breathed every sentence, speaking from the swell of her breasts and projecting with the competence of the finest opera singer. It would only take the simplest invitation: *Are you coming for dinner? Can I do anything special for you?* and the mere timbre of her suggestion had me besotted.

And she chose her vocabulary with a deliberation that was always delightful. She had a risqué way of phrasing every question or response, so you never knew if she was teasing, talking straight or deliberately flirting. When I fixed her dilapidated runabout, she gave me a kiss and told me she *"appreciated the services of a capable man."* Each time I saw her at the diner, where she faithfully waited tables, Katy would ask if she could *"try to satisfy my appetite."*

Not that it was just her voice or her wordplay that I loved.

She was a good person – kind-hearted, intelligent and fun – and the sexiest woman I've ever had the good fortune to encounter. Petite, brunette, perfectly formed and invariably dressed in shorts and a T-shirt: she was blessed with a figure to die for.

I guess that last observation is an irony.

I genuinely do regret killing her.

But it wasn't murder and . . .

I'm getting ahead of myself again, aren't I? Things didn't happen slowly between Katy and me. The sultry tone of her voice was enough to tempt me to her side and, as soon as we were alone together, I discovered another quality to her words aside from the rich accent or the clever wordplay. She could make the air crackle with the electric taste of promise. Using no more expression than a flutter of dark lashes over large eyes, she had me enlisted as a willing partner to her every sordid fantasy.

And, now that we're talking about Katy's fantasies, it's only fair to mention that she had more than a few. The first time we made love it happened on a balmy summer's evening. I found her sitting on the porch, with a V of sweat molding her T-shirt to her breasts and giving her sun-kissed skin a glossy luster. The fading light of the day caught auburn flecks in her brunette tresses. Beads of perspiration on her neck and collarbone glistened like diamonds.

"I'm hot," she breathed.

And there it was again. The casual inflection in her tone that said more than those two words should be able. It was a double entendre that was maddeningly appropriate regardless of which way I chose to interpret what she'd said. The day was sweltering, admittedly. But the glint in her eye, and that perplexing way she spoke, suggested that she wasn't discussing the clemency of the weather.

The electricity in the air made it hard for me to breath. I tried to shift my legs in case she was embarrassed about the effect her declaration had stirred in me. Not wanting to appear stupid, or incapable of matching her banter, I struggled to find a suitable retort. Swallowing thickly, nervous that such a specimen of feminine perfection could show an interest in a lummock like me, I observed, "Hot suits you."

"You don't think all this sweat makes my skin look clammy and unattractive?"

"Hell! No!"

"You don't think it makes my skin feel unattractive?"

I hesitated, aware that she was taking my hand, watching as she guided the tips of my fingers to the slick skin of her collarbone. The heel of my palm was mere millimeters above the thrust of one nipple. I had noticed they stood erect, their shapes defined through the fabric of the clinging T-shirt. The ghosts of her areolae were deliciously obvious beneath the flimsy material. Touching her body – and painfully aware of how close I was to properly touching her breasts – I came near to shivering in spite of the sweltering heat.

"Well?" Katy prompted. She stroked my hand back and forth over her chest. Her skin was moist velvet with perspiration lubricating my caress. The ball of my thumb glanced against her breast and I was sure I felt the nipple stiffen. "Do you think that feels unattractive?" she asked.

"I don't recall touching anything that ever felt better," I answered honestly.

Her questioning expression turned into a mischievous grin. She lowered my hand to one breast so I was cupping her through a film of damp cotton. In the stillness of that moment I could feel her pulse through the hard bead of flesh that sat at the center of my palm. "In that case," she whispered, "if perspiration suits me so much, why don't you see if you can make me sweat a little more?"

It was the beginning of a beautiful relationship.

Maybe there was something appropriate about the fact that it began at the end of the day? I don't know. I only know that, once we'd started, our passion quickly became boundless.

Perhaps I should have noticed there was something a little

kinky in her desire to excite me on the porch. The exhibitionism of what we were doing didn't cross my mind until afterwards, when I realized that any passing neighbor could have seen us and been shocked or offended by our intimacy. But at the time it simply felt natural to do everything Katy asked. I was content to bury myself deep inside her smoldering depths and bask in the cries of her encroaching orgasm. Once again it was her beautiful voice – that musical cadence and enchanting lilt – mesmerizing me and blinding me to everything except Katy. And, from that moment on, I was oblivious to everything except the pleasure that came from being with her.

But I only began to suspect that she had unusual appetites after a month of our relationship. We'd tried a million and one variations on the traditional themes of sex, going from her porch, to the bedroom, detouring via the kitchen/diner, and the stairs on the way there. She invited me into every recess of her body, welcoming me with her mouth, sex lips and other places. She worshipped my erection with caresses from her breasts, tongue, hair and hands and we took each other to climax after climax in a splendor of shared bliss. I spent endless, happy hours watching her tease herself. And I particularly adored the way she would trill her fingers against the beautiful split of her sex – parting the dense, dark curls that covered her labia – while she charmed me back to arousal with the whispered promises of what we would do next. Each step further in our relationship seemed more like a declaration of our love, rather than another jolt down on some descent toward a perverted conclusion.

We made love in semi-public places – under the stars and sometimes under the noon sun. We played power games and water sports, screwed while we were drunk, fucked while we were high, then made love when we were grounded and stone cold sober. We confessed our wildest fantasies, then endeavored to make them reality for the pleasure of each other. And, although I'm probably wrong with saying we did everything, it's true to say: *we did everything we wanted*.

Which is why I had no problems with the ropes Katy brought to the bedroom. The contrast of coarsely woven hemp against her dainty wrists was ugly, but somehow exciting. The vulnerability of her naked form, spread-eagled for me and available for the satisfaction of my every whim, was infuriatingly arousing. When I placed myself between her legs, then rode her helpless frame as she sobbed and moaned through a multiple orgasm, I could totally understand what those psychologists meant when they referred to "the good place". At those moments, when Katy was screaming with joy and her inner muscles convulsed around me in the throes of ecstasy, I knew we were both in the good place.

But, I suppose, good places were never meant to last and ours ended two nights after Katy first suggested we bring another rope into the bedroom. The term anoxia is cold and clinical – a million miles removed from the joy of Katy's last moments or the liberating release of her final climax – but it was bandied around a lot by my defense lawyers in court. It was usually lumped with a string of other fancy words and supported by dry accounts of the reported stimulation that comes from autoerotic asphyxiation.

The prosecution simply called me a strangler. The jurors were won over by their succinct use of words and, because I was convicted of first-degree murder with more than one of nine aggravating circumstances, I found myself a resident on death row.

Which, until last week, had been the total antithesis of the good place Katy and I had known. But, on the morning when I was ready to meet the attorney handling my final appeal, Katy decided to speak to me again. At first I thought I was dreaming – I hadn't properly climbed out of my bunk and was enjoying the sounds of the morning calls from bluejays and chickadees – when she whispered in my ear.

"What's a nice guy like you doing in a place like this?"

I could hear her voice as clearly as when she used to nibble on my lobe while we were locked in a post-coital embrace. It was that familiar Virginia drawl, deep set with a throaty chuckle of mischief. Death hadn't killed her sensuous way of speaking, nor had it stifled the effect she had on me. As my erection grew I began to wonder if I was either insane, or mistaken, or still asleep. Unable to stop myself, I spoke her name aloud. "Katy?"

"Do you like being inside?" she breathed.

And, in that moment, I knew it was her. I didn't know how she was talking to me. I didn't know why she was talking to me. But I knew my own imagination could never have supplied such a perfect Katy-esque innuendo. With that one question I was beyond being skeptical that the voice was the product of my own diminishing faculties. I knew that Katy was back by my side.

"I've missed you, lummock," she confided.

"I've missed you too," I admitted.

Her words were a balm, soothing and massaging away the tension I had suffered since incarceration. She hadn't said anything overtly sexual, yet already she had excited me to the point of full arousal. An appreciation of my responses told me that it would only take another couple of sentences and she would have me ejaculating like some over-excited schoolboy on his first real date.

I closed my eyes and easily pictured the way she had looked when she was speaking. The fullness of her lips was easy to recall, the sensuous pout of her mouth was invariably glossed each time she trailed the tip of her tongue across her Cupid's bow. When she had used her tongue on my length I always remembered the thrill of pleasure that came from hearing her words and feeling them reverberate through my shaft. On this occasion, when she first spoke to me from beyond the grave, the pleasure was every bit as intense as it had been during those fondly recollected times.

"I've come to help with your release," she giggled.

It was another of her double entendres and hearing that sly humor made me simultaneously excited, relieved and delighted that she was back in my life. I had missed her and I had quietly mourned her passing. But the pressing demands of death row and impending execution had urged my focus to slip away from such important things. "How can you help?" I asked. I wasn't doubting her ability: I was simply curious to know. "My lawyers are qualified and alive," I pointed out. "At the moment, you're neither."

She laughed. With my eyes closed I could picture the way her breasts always trembled with mirth and her entire body shook. If I kept my eyes closed I could have believed she was in the room with me. It was all too easy to imagine she was struggling to lie by my side in the cell's single bunk and squeezing her body close to mine. With only the effort of a little concentration I could feel her bare flesh pressing against me. She had one long, muscular leg curled around my waist, and her bare crotch kissed at my thigh. The scrub of her pubic bush scratched wickedly at the top of my leg and rekindled the eager thrust of my arousal.

"I've been talking to the state's governor," Katy explained. "He has the power of clemency – the right to say whether you live or die – so I thought it best to go to the man who makes those decisions. I made a special plea for him to personally consider your case."

The statement was too unexpected for me to comprehend. I was still being enchanted by the lull of her words and teased by the seductive lilt of her voice. The meaning behind what she said took a full minute to register. Disembodied, with no more presence than her voice, she was still able to excite me more fully than any other woman I had previously met. My body ached for her and the threat of climax throbbed in my groin. If she'd had a physical presence I knew I wouldn't have been able to resist. Passion would have overwhelmed me and we would have revisited the halcyon days of our brief time together. Because I was only listening to her sultry whispers I managed to contain my impulse – but it was still a challenge.

"You've spoken to the governor?" I repeated. "How did you manage that? You're dead."

Again, she laughed. I hadn't realized how much I had missed the sound of that merriment. As comforting as the sex, as exciting as the most daring of her propositions, Katy's laughter was almost enough to make me cry for what we had lost. "I know that I'm dead," she agreed. "But I spoke to the governor the same way I'm speaking to you now, you lummock: with words."

My mind glanced over the technicalities with a simple rationalization. If the disembodied voice of my lover could speak to me, why couldn't she also speak to the governor? "What did you tell him?" I asked. "Is my sentence being commuted? Are the charges being dropped? Or am I being released?"

Katy didn't get the chance to respond. The crashing of gates being thrown open, and the hollow stamp of boots from the corridor outside, announced the arrival of my attorney. I leapt from my bunk and pulled on my uniform of garish orange overalls. Judging from the heavy clomp of feet I could hear there were three of them. And, after Katy's revelation, I wasn't surprised to see my attorney and the guard were accompanied by the state's governor.

Our meeting was surprisingly swift.

The guard was dismissed.

My attorney started to speak.

Then the governor drove his fist into my nose. He called me a murdering son-of-a-bitch, turned around and left the cell before I had finished falling to the floor. On his way out I heard him say I was going to fry. Unnecessarily, he added: *and fucking soon.* Clearly startled, my attorney shrugged an apology and hurried off to pursue the chief executive.

"That went kind of well," Katy said guardedly.

"Yeah!" I had a hand over my nose, collecting a stream of blood while I struggled to decide whether I was angry, surprised or simply confused. All three emotions were vying for control of my reaction but sarcasm eventually won. "That went so well I think the governor's going to go and check the wiring on the electric chair so there's no danger of a mistake. What did you tell him, Katy? I thought you said you'd explained what happened on the night you died."

"I didn't stick to the truth," she mumbled. "I said you'd killed me in a vicious and deliberate attack. I mentioned that your diabolical assault has left me walking in limbo for all eternity. And I demanded that he avenge me, or else I'll haunt him forever." She laughed, the sound tinged with nervousness this time. "None of it is true," she said quickly. "But I didn't think it would matter if I lied a little on this occasion."

Closing my eyes, trying to show patience and restraint when all I could really feel were confusion, disappointment and betrayal, I asked, "Didn't you think that sort of statement would be likely to make him believe I was guilty? Didn't you think that sort of statement was likely to expedite my execution?"

"But that was my plan, lover," she whispered. "I thought you understood."

For the first time since Katy's death a smile stretched along my lips.

"You're going to get out of here," she promised. "And, this way, we'll be together again, where we should be."

As the understanding continued to dawn I realized exactly what she was telling me. I wasn't just going to get away from death row: I was going to be with Katy in the good place.

Dangerous Games
with Competent People

Kim Wright

The last thing you want when you're going to see your boy-friend's hooker is a helpful man. But this man is determined to help. He has the look – you know the look – he has the look of a helpful man. It's three o'clock in the afternoon. You're standing in the lobby of a surprisingly nice high-rise in a suburb of DC, typing numbers into a security pad, waiting for a woman to come on the line and tell you her apartment number. Her instructions were quite specific.

The money is in a plain white envelope inside your purse. She has instructions about this in the zip file too: "I never discuss payment in person, nor do I wish to see cash. Please place the envelope discreetly on the table as you enter." It strikes you as strange that a woman with such delicate sensibilities that she cannot bear the sight of money would be prepared to repeatedly bury her face in the genitals of strangers, but your boyfriend described her as "nice". Perhaps this is what he means.

You key in the numbers and wait for her voice. You get a busy signal. When you try it a few minutes later, you get the busy signal again. The man sitting behind the marble desk calls out pleasantly, "Who are you here to see?" That's the problem. You don't know her name or her apartment number, you only know that she calls herself *alexandriaandrea* and that your boyfriend is sleeping fitfully somewhere in Paris. *I'll be fine*, you tell the man. *My friend must be on the phone. I'll give her a minute and try again.*

But he wants to help. He waves you over to the desk. If you give him her code he can go into the computer and find her apartment number and ring you in himself. Which seems the opposite of what a security guard's job should be, but you know that everything about you – your age, your gender, the way you move and the way you dress – makes you unthreatening to other people. Makes you seem like a bastion of respectability. The wall behind the man is mirrored; you can see yourself, your long knit dress with the slits up the side to the knee, your strap sandals, the knockoff Gucci sunglasses pushed back on your head, your real Dooney and Bourke purse over your arm. There is no reason why a man like him shouldn't help a woman like you enter this building.

But her instructions said nothing about conversations with security men, nothing about struggling to think of a plausible explanation for why you are visiting a woman whose name you do not know. You smile at him, mutter something, go back to the intercom system, type in her code again and this time she answers. She gives you her apartment number and, shooting a smile at the security guard, you head toward the elevator.

When she opens the door she is prettier than you expect. Your age, close to fifty. Her hair is blonde, cropped in a stylish manner, longer in the front than the back, slightly damp from a shower. Andy has said she's a jock, so you're a bit surprised she has on full makeup, that you smell perfume, that she's teetering on bronze slingback heels. She is wearing a very tight slip, burgundy in color. She is about your height, she has a quick laugh, and she further surprises you by saying that you are pretty.

Your coloring, she says. *You have beautiful coloring. He didn't tell me you were pretty. He said you were smart.*

And although you are happy to see that she is pretty too, and pretty in a way that means she might be a friend to you, happy that no one would take notice if the two of you walked into a restaurant, even though you are relieved to see that she is much as he described her, something about it all throws you and you forget to leave the white envelope on her table. She has dressed to seduce you – as if you were a man. The cups of her slip thrust her breasts forward. When she raises her arms to brush back her hair, the slip slides up her thighs. Her legs are muscular, an athlete's legs, and indeed ropes and climbing shoes are all over her small apartment, as well as oars and a racing bike. Perhaps you tell her that she's beautiful. You think it. Perhaps you say it aloud.

Then there is nothing to do but to go on through the den into her bedroom and to lie down on her bed, to prop yourself up casually on one elbow and watch her as if you were a friend come over to help her get ready for a date. There is a bookcase beside the bed and full of travel guides . . . Tibet, Peru, Turkey. *Were you scared about coming?* she asks. *No,* you say, *not until a man down in the lobby tried to help me.* She laughs. She laughs easily. She has laughed a half dozen times since you entered her door.

You say something about her travel books but she isn't in the mood to chat. You've only hired her for an hour and she knows you didn't drive all this way to talk about Peru.

She begins to stroke your leg, stopping her hand just above your knee. She notes that you are not wearing any panties. This is not an affectation – you rarely wear panties – but she runs her hand farther up your thigh and whispers *Bad girl.* It's a bit like the high heels and the perfume, vaguely off in some way you can't define. She has undoubtedly called any number of DC lawyers and politicians and bankers "Bad boy." She has undoubtedly said this to your own boyfriend. You reach down and slip off her shoe, you cup the instep of her foot. You catch her eye and you both laugh for no particular reason and when you slide your hand up you find that she is pantyless too and you say, *You've got a lot of nerve calling me a bad girl.* It's easy to roll around with her on the bed. It's easy to nuzzle her neck and breathe in the perfume and ruffle the slightly wet hair. *I was a little nervous,* she tells you. *This is the first time I've had a woman by herself. But you, you're so pretty. I didn't expect you to be pretty.*

Truth be told, you're not all that pretty, but these things she says seem to be part of the deal and you're willing to go along with it. You run your index finger along her pussy lips and find she's wet and you push your finger into her, feeling the slight sucking quality of a woman, something half-forgotten that pulls you in. *But you've been with women? Sure*, she says, *but only in threesomes. Have you ever done a threesome?* You shake your head. Her breasts, you decide, are incredible, better than yours, and you reach into the burgundy slip and lift out one and then the other. It's all quite nasty, the way the lycra pushes them forward. You bend forward to suck her left nipple, feeling the puckered roughness on the flat of your tongue. She moans. You almost laugh. The moans are like the slingback shoes and the compliments – a little excessive. She wants to make sure you're getting Andy's money's worth.

This thing about the threesome is why you're here, isn't it? Or at least part of the reason. Andy found you, eight years ago on an airplane between Tucson and Dallas, and now he's found this girl, the only woman in his mountain climbing club, a group so demanding that she is the only woman who has met the criteria to join. It's been almost a year since he first mentioned her, since he lay across your own bed, 500 miles from here, and wondered idly what she did for a living, how this woman found so much time to train.

And then he asked her. Asked her one day as they were loading up after a climb what in the world she did for a living that would allow her to train every day. She said she had men, a few men, male friends who sponsored her athletic career. Just a few close male friends who were happy to help her. He didn't totally understand what she meant. Andy is an attorney, well aware of the myriad penalties when one person fails to understand another. Was she a hooker? He knew you were the person to ask. He finished loading up his equipment and retreated to his car and dialed as he drove home to his house in the Maryland suburbs. *Yeah*, you said, *she's probably a hooker. Nothing else makes any sense.*

You push your face into her breasts, feeling the softness as they separate on each side of your cheeks. She moans and you say, *You don't have to*, meaning that you are a woman too, you understand that it is too early in the process for such ostentatious moaning. Sex is a long drive, it's Maine to Florida and there is no sense in her carrying on like she's in Georgia when you know damn well this is Connecticut at best. Don't treat me like a man, you want to tell her. I'm not that dumb and it's only two hundred dollars and Andy's paying for it, after all. He wants us to like each other. She pulls away, as if she's read your mind, and you roll onto your back.

Here's the deal. He went to see her, he fucked her, and told her about you. She was very open to the idea of seeing a couple. She liked to do women – the only trouble was the women she saw were always dragged there by their husbands. They weren't really into it and things could get awkward. Two women putting on a show for the benefit of a man, who needed that? When he told you this, you said maybe it would make more sense for you to go see her first by yourself. There needed to be a spark between the two of you, otherwise, she was right, it was just a show. *By yourself?* Your offer clearly surprises him. He'd like to be there, but you know he's out of town all that week. She is going down on you now, she has pushed your legs apart and she's very direct. She doesn't do it like he does it, no moseying around, no circling, no lifting of the head to talk. She is very direct, her tongue pointed and focused, and involuntarily you glance at her bedside clock. You have been here ten minutes.

There are ropes around her bedroom, ropes and an ice ax, the accoutrements of her sport, and as she pushes through the layers and goes deeper you close your eyes. Your hands find a rope stretched across the headboard behind you, a rope she has probably tied there for just this purpose or one very like it, and you reach back and grasp it. She's good, she knows what she's doing: people need something to hang onto. Next week Andy will be back from France and he will fly down to see you. Over dinner the two of you will discuss his last climb. He has this friend Mike whom he adores. Mike is older, balding and chubby and unassuming, but a hell of a climber. Andy likes to lead the climbs. He feels nervous when someone else goes first and he has described the risks of his sport to you many times. How the lead man finds a ledge or a little toehold, drives a spike, threads through the rope, how the lead man is responsible for everyone below. He told you this the first time you met him, on the plane, told you how catastrophic it would be for the lead to fall. You sat in the airplane seat somewhere in the air between Tucson and Dallas and listened to him describe how the chain of people are attached – attached to each other for reasons of safety or maybe just for the promise that they won't, come the worst, die alone. *This*, he said, *this is what matters*. If the leader fell everyone else would follow suit, ripped from the rock, one by one.

But on this particular climb Mike was leading and that's okay. Andy trusts Mike. They were right on that edge where things were starting to get interesting. Mike had hoisted himself over a ledge and was watching as Andy followed, as he eased his way past that point where just for a moment you dangle. They were very high and very far from home. Mike had grinned down at him and said, *God, I love doing dangerous things with competent people*.

You're loud when you come. You make a noise – you suspect not a pretty noise – and your body goes rigid, pushing you away from her like a swimmer pushes off from a wall. You hold it for a minute, you say *my god*, more to yourself than to her. It was so sharp, so fast, it was on you without warning. She is crouched between your legs, resting her head, against your knee. Her hair is still damp. *But wasn't that a great thing for him to say – doing dangerous things with competent people?* Andy will ask you and he will nudge the last piece of calamari toward you as if you were in a scene from *Lady and the Tramp*. You run your hands under her slip. *You don't have to*, she says. What is it about this that she's not getting? *I want to do this*, you tell her. *Let me*.

He said she smelled good. She does. Your face falls forward and you're momentarily dizzy. You slide your elbows under her thighs and settle into a rhythm. She shudders – it seems real – and your mind wanders. Your mind always wanders when you're going down on someone, it's the only time in your life when you could honestly be called contemplative. *It's easy to fall into women*, you think, *It's easy to let go and fall into them. Women*, you think, *we are gravity personified*. You flash on an island where you once vacationed, a teacher you had in college, how much time is left in the parking meter downstairs. Once, at a Halloween fair at your kids' school a psychic told you that you'd been male in a past lifetime. A silly psychic – somebody's mother in a scarf – but she leaned toward you and whispered, *Last time through, you were a man. You still remember, don't you?* Silly as hell, but it would explain a lot. It would explain why you're willing to forgive them so much.

She doesn't come. This bothers you. You got the impression from Andy she was an easy come. Hell, got the impression from him she was coming all over the place. Does she like men better than women? Your mouth is between her legs as you're asking, you mumble the question into her crotch and suddenly the two of you are shrieking with laughter.

A funny time to ask, she says.

But no, you say, rising up, giving up. *I'm absolutely dead serious. What makes you come?*

I came a little bit when you did, she says.

Oh, come on. Please. Don't give me that shit. Don't talk to me like I'm a man. Show me. Show me what you do when you're alone.

She shakes her head. You've embarrassed her. She asks what she can do for you. She asks this over and over. You keep forgetting. There is $240 dollars – for you have insisted that Andy tip her – in an envelope in your purse. There's no need to make it reciprocal. *Show me*, you say again, more sharply, and she opens the top drawer of her bedside table and pulls out a small white vibrator, the cheap kind that takes AA batteries, and she clamps it between her legs.

What exactly does he want? He has a wife and girlfriend and a hooker, as well as some hunchback secretary from another floor who once blew him in the office parking deck and an Asian lady who jerks him off in a massage parlor out by the airport. He calls her the happy ending lady and he does a funny imitation of her voice. She rubs him the normal way and then she giggles and snorts and asks him, *You want happy ending?*

Andrea has pulled herself into fetal position, eyes clamped shut. She does not move or make a noise. Surely between the five of you he would be sated and yet you know people are never sated, neither women nor men, and your mind shifts briefly to your other boyfriend, the one in New York. You wonder what he would think of this, but it's not really his sort of thing, is it? No, he wants something else.

A simple convulsion, one single spasm, and she's done.

I liked watching, you tell her, and she says yeah, she likes watching too. She likes everything about sex. That all she wants is sex and time to climb and enough money for an apartment where she can see the river. *I don't want many things*, she tells you, *but the things I want, I want a lot.* She glances at the clock and offers to fuck you. *No*, you say, *I'm fine. I like to come once hard, and then just roll around. This is perfect for me.*

He wants to see me fuck you, she says. *That's part of what he wants, but I guess he told you that.*

Don't worry about it. When the time comes, he'll do whatever we say.

She shrugs. *I guess so. He seems like a nice enough guy.*

You're stunned by how quickly she's dismissed him. It's the last thing you expected her to say. This man has been the best lover you've ever had. You expected – what did you expect? You expected that she would congratulate you for having left no stone unturned, for having found this man among all the men who don't know what to do and who don't care that they don't know what to do. That fluttery thing with his tongue. My God, there are times even after eight years that you think your heart will stop. How can she say he seems like a nice guy?

You have a strange and sudden urge to weep. You're from a small town. Your mother was a second-grade teacher. The truth of the matter is you've been over your head for some time now. *I'm not used to all this*, you tell her but, *God*, she says, *who is?* She opens her arms, you roll toward her. Who among us was raised for this? She was born in Nebraska.

The next week you will confront him, in a restaurant miles from here, in an Asian restaurant in your hometown where you like the calamari. He will hand you that line about dangerous games with competent people and you will snap back at him *You didn't give her the full treatment.* The minute she said that he was a nice guy you knew it, that he'd gone down on her but he hadn't given her the full treatment. He didn't do the flutter thing.

I only do the flutter thing with you, he says.

You will walk back from the restaurant to your house holding hands. You'll talk about your jobs, your children. His daughter's volleyball team went to the state finals. She is fifteen, beautiful but very tall and he thinks the boys will stay away for several more years because of this. You call him sweetie and rub his head. He is a good father, in his way. When his girls leave home it will break his heart.

And so, she says, *we'll all get together?*

Of course, you say, *we'll get together.* You've already put the envelope on her table while she was peeing. She is barefoot now as she walks you to the door, slightly shorter than you as she hugs you goodbye.

On the drive back through Northern Virginia you dig through your purse for your cell phone. You call your friend, the one you're staying with tonight, the one you always stay with when you come to DC. She's married, she says it's good but a lot of work and she told you, just this morning over cereal, that she thinks you use sex to avoid intimacy. She answers on the first ring. You tell her the Monet exhibit was incredible and offer to stop at the grocery. Does she need anything, a bottle of wine perhaps?

No, she says, she has enough. She's doing tuna out on the grill because you liked it that way the last time. She is sweet like this. Whenever you come up she puts a terrycloth robe on your bed, she gets in your favorite green tea, even though it means driving to a second grocery. It is nice that you have called to offer to pick up something on the way in and it is nice that she already has everything she needs. The rituals of domesticity are so soothing. Men probably do this, you think, they probably call their wives on the way home from hookers.

You sing with the radio. An oldies station. Abba, Joni Mitchell, and then the Mamas and the Papas. You roll your neck from side to side, getting out the kinks. Your tongue is sore from licking her. Sore, right in the root and it will be sore all the next day. You're lifted, in the way that only sex can lift you. Chemicals have poured into your system, the adrenaline, the endorphins, the alcohol from the beer wedged between your thighs, and colors seem brighter and you know every word of every song that comes onto this radio station. You see, just for a moment, the inter-connectedness of everything, the delicate way we're all webbed together, and you send up a quick wordless prayer for your boyfriend's wife. Maybe you'll stop and get another bottle of wine after all, for who can say what is enough?

The traffic has come to a standstill as it often does on 1–95 just south of DC in the late afternoon. There is a man in a convertible beside you. He smiles, you smile. If you break down right here, if you have a flat tire or an overheated engine, this man and perhaps others will stop and offer to help you. Men like you. Men are nice to you. They will always stop and help, they will give you the last bite of calamari and pay other women to go down on you. That's your karma for this particular lifetime. It's very beautiful here, very safe. You're a safe woman, men can see that at a glance. They will let you into buildings where you have no business being. The man in the convertible edges slightly past you. It's hard to say what will happen next.

The Penis of My Beloved

Ian Watson & Roberto Quaglia

During my Beloved's lifetime his penis was of great importance to me – how could it be otherwise? Of course there was much more to my Beloved than his penis. For instance there was his tongue. I don't merely refer to his skill at licking, but also to all the words he said to me (except, obviously, while licking). Words are so important to a woman during love, just as they are in the everyday aspects of life. Also, there were his dark eyes, which spoke volumes of silent poetry. Also, there were his arms which held me. I need not enumerate more – there was all of Oliver. When my Beloved suddenly died of a heart attack, how desperately I craved to have him back again, alive.

This was possible due to advances in rapid cloning. However, a whole body cost a small fortune. Oliver and I had never given much thought to the morrow. Even by availing myself of a special offer from the Bodies'r'Us Clinic, and by paying on the instalment plan, the most I could afford was the cloning of a small part of Oliver.

Which part should it be? His right hand, sustained by an artificial blood supply and activated to a limited extent by a nerve impulse box with control buttons? Even a whole hand was out of my financial reach.

Should it be his tongue, likewise sustained by a costly blood supply?

Minus mouth and throat and vocal cords, a tongue could never say anything even if it wanted to, although it ought to be able to lick, for such is the nature of tongues. Body parts are aware of the role they play in the entirety of the body, consequently this memory lingers on even when they're amputated or dissected, or in this case cloned. Oh yes, his tongue ought to be able to lick, although the sensation might seem to me more like a warm slug than his robust tongue of yore.

How about one of his eyes, which spoke volumes? The eye could rest upon an eggcup and form an image of me. Before going to bed I could perform a striptease for his eye. Yet to be perfectly frank, what could his eye *do* for me? Also, although I had no intention of ever being unfaithful to my Beloved, a naked eyeball might seem like a spy camera keeping watch. This wasn't the kind of continuing intimacy I craved.

Really, my choice could only be the penis, especially as the cost was based upon the "normal" size when flaccid rather than erect. In this instance the money I would be paying in any event for the blood supply, so as to keep the part alive, would provide a special bonus benefit, namely erection when the penis was caressed. You couldn't say about any other cloned body part that your investment could grow ten-fold, as it were!

"You mightn't realize," the cloning salesman said to me, "that a penis becomes stiff not because of blood pumped actively into it by an excited body, but because certain penile muscles *relax*, which allows the blood to flow in and fill it. Normally the muscles are tense and inhibit the volume of blood – otherwise men would have permanent erections."

"So if you feel nervous and tense, you never get an erection?"

The salesman flushed, as though I had touched on a sore point. He was a young man with ginger hair and many freckles. The wallpaper of the consultation room was Klimt, so we were surrounded by hybrids of slender women and flowers.

"Madam, it's simply that you might be expecting too much. We can't absolutely guarantee erection, for that would be to alter the biology of the penis. In effect we would be providing you with a bio-dildo rather than with a genuine cloned organ – and we don't supply such things. Prostho-porn isn't our profession." This was spoken a shade tartly. The salesman may have been upset by my previous remark, supposing that it reflected upon his own virility.

I was sure that my Beloved's cloned penis would remember my own particular touch and wouldn't feel inhibited.

I made like a wide-eyed innocent. "Is 'prostho-porn' *anyone's* profession?"

"I've heard that in China . . ." The salesman lowered his voice. "Multiple cloned cunts of pop stars in pleasure parlours . . ." Now he seemed mollified and was all smiles again. "This won't be the case here! Your commission will be unique to you."

"I should hope so!"

It goes without saying that I'd arranged for sample cells from all of Oliver's important organs and limbs to be frozen in liquid nitrogen – which wasn't too expensive – before the majority of his dear chilled body finally entered the furnace at the crematorium. I'd read that in another few years it might be possible to coax a finger or a penis, say, to diversify and regenerate from itself an entire body, but apparently this was a speculative line of research pursued by only a handful of maverick scientists. Small wonder: it's much more common for a body to lose a penis than for a penis to lose a body. So I was skeptical of this possibility. In the meantime my dream of recreating the entirety of Oliver, to rejoin his penis, would remain a dream because of the cost.

"So that's the famous penis!" exclaimed my neighbour Andorra, who was short and who spoke her own mind. Andorra and I were best friends even before the sudden death of my Beloved, about which she was very consoling. Currently Andorra was working for the Blood Donor Service.

Her parents chose the name Andorra for her, to suggest that she would be adorable. Naming her after the tiniest independent state in Europe did prove prophetic as regards her stature and personality – she was short and assertive. Yet as regards adorability in the eyes of the opposite sex, the ploy failed. Andorra had only ever had one boyfriend, and he was a disaster. No-one else tried to get into bed with her, or courted her. I think Andorra trained as a nurse due to reading too many doctor/nurse romance novels, many of which still littered her apartment, next door to mine.

Next door to *our* apartment, I should say. Oliver's and mine; mine and that of his penis.

Andorra's dog Coochie sometimes chewed her romance novels or carried them around her apartment while awaiting her return from work, and a walk, and an emptying. Coochie was a yellowish Labrador.

"Famous?" I replied. "There's nothing famous about it except in my own eyes." And in my hand, of course.

"It's a bit small . . ." but then she quickly added, "at the moment." She eyed the apparatus to which the penis was attached by two long connecting tubes. "Will you pump some more blood into it?"

So that she could behold an actual erect penis in the flesh at last?

"That isn't why a penis stiffens. Don't you know anatomy? What's important is the receptive mood of the penis."

"Well, it would be more impressive . . ." She tailed off.

Did she hope that I would stimulate the penis of my Beloved for her benefit? I almost succumbed to her implied entreaty, if only to demonstrate Oliver's penis in full gory, I mean glory, but this was an intimate matter.

"I'm perfectly satisfied," I told her. Only as I spoke did I realize how this might imply smugly that Andorra herself remained unsatisfied. She had mentioned dissatisfaction with dildos. I might seem to be cock-crowing, lording it over my friend.

Andorra looked thoughtful.

Due to the length of the blood tubes it was easy to take the penis to bed with me so as to stroke it in just the way my Beloved had liked, then pleasure myself after it stiffened. It remembered me. Because only Oliver's penis was cloned, not his prostate and other attachments, inevitably there was no ejaculation, yet this was no disadvantage – on the contrary! I would hold the rubber grip-mount, shaped like a small plantpot, in which his penis (as it were) grew, and much prolonged joy was mine. I was blissful.

Sometimes after an orgasm I would take the penis out of me and talk to it, or use my mouth for a different purpose. I felt like a little girl: the penis of my Beloved, my lollipop.

But then came a problem with the blood supply – I don't mean the tubes and pump, but rather my finances. Bodies'r'Us strongly recommended renewing the blood each month to prevent degeneration of the penis. As part of the initial cost, I'd received five vouchers for replacement blood. Now I'd used those vouchers, and I discovered that in the meantime the cost of blood had risen by 25 percent.

Bodies'r'Us was a significant user and retailer of blood, needing to buy blood – good blood, too – from healthy sellers. Nobody would donate blood charitably so that some rich woman could maintain a clone of her dead poodle, or me a cloned penis. Andorra had complained to me that the Donor Service, which supplied hospitals, was suffering a bit of a blood drain because former donors were choosing to sell rather than donate, but luckily altruism and generosity still prevailed on society, not to mention donations by way of the vampire churches as part of their safe sex campaign.

At this point I consulted Andorra and she made me an offer . . .

. . . To smuggle blood from the Donor Service – providing that I let her use the penis of my Beloved privately one evening each week, say every Friday.

I was astonished and disconcerted.

"I'm your best friend," she pointed out.

"It won't respond to you," I said.

She pouted at me, full-lipped. "I'll find a way."

I should have refused. Yet if I refused, I might embitter Andorra. It must have cost her dear to make this request, this admission of craving for the real thing – or at least for the cloned and partial thing. Refusal might seem like a slap in the face. But also, of a sudden, I was curious as to whether my Beloved *would* respond to the touch of a stranger.

*   *   *

According to Andorra, the penis did react to her, and very satisfyingly, too. She might be fibbing so as to salve her pride, and I could hardly ask to be present while Andorra writhed on her bed. Besides, I wouldn't have wished to behold this personally. Consequently every Friday evening Andorra would carefully carry the pump and the penis along to her apartment and bring them back to me a couple of hours later. During this interval I would watch TV and try not to think about what might be happening. Once the penis was mine again, I would wash it, irrespective of whether Andorra had already done so. Washing excited the penis as much as caresses, since the actions were very similar. The penis seemed to be wishing to make up to me for what had occurred, even though it was I who owed the penis an apology.

I would kiss it. "Forgive me, my Beloved. You earned your blood, that's the main thing."

After some weeks I made a terrible discovery. When Andorra brought the penis back, Coochie was with her, pawing at her thigh and sniffing.

"Stay!" ordered Andorra, but Coochie pushed his way into my apartment. The dog's gaze was fixed on the now-floppy penis. He seemed to want it – not for a snack, which was my first fear, soon dispelled by a much worse realization: Coochie wanted the penis as a *penis*.

When I stared accusingly at Andorra, she broke down in tears of remorse.

"He's become addicted," she confessed.

"Do you mean . . . do you mean . . . you've been giving your dog *bestiality treats* with the penis of my Beloved?"

"He's an unusual dog! I love Coochie, and Coochie loves me, but I knew he was gay!"

"Gay? How did you know that?"

Andorra remained silent.

"Did Coochie bugger some other male dog while out walkies with you?"

More silence. My best friend couldn't tell me an outright lie. Suddenly I realized that if Andorra's discovery had *not* occurred during walkies then only one possibility remained . . .

"You used to try to get Coochie to fuck you! But no matter how you went about it, Coochie couldn't get it up because—"

"– Because Coochie's gay. It's the only explanation."

I felt sorry for Andorra. Yet I also had a persistent image in my mind . . . of Coochie, who was gallumphing around, his anus frequently visible. How degrading for the penis of my Beloved!

While performing that canine service, Oliver's penis must have been stiff! Was the penis utterly undiscriminating?

"Look," I told Andorra, "you must promise me, don't do it with Coochie again. That's unhygienic."

"I always did me *after* I did Coochie."

That would have cleaned the penis?

Resulting in Andorra's vagina smelling of male dog? In due course Coochie might learn to associate . . . Andorra had not given up hope.

"I'd be well within my rights to refuse you the penis ever again."

"And I to refuse you blood," she murmured.

She had a point. Consequently we didn't quarrel.

With some difficulty she hauled Coochie away. Alone once again, I eyed the wilted penis.

"Beloved, how could you do it with a dog?"

I tried to come to terms with what had happened by being objective and logical. The episode with Coochie was not my Beloved's fault.

The next week Andorra remarked, "Maybe the penis has erections in a Pavlovian way regardless of with whom or with what. Poor Oliver loves you, but he can't resist. You really ought to have more of him cloned."

How would I pay for that?

Oh, but she had the answer!

At the hospital where Andorra worked previously, she knew a junior anaesthetist who moonlighted as a stud in porn movies. Mark's rugged good looks and intelligence made him a desirable actor. As for his prowess, before each performance Mark would sniff a stimulant gas to keep himself stiff irrespective of ejaculation. Unfortunately Mark had recently been sacked for stealing gas from the hospital. Now he needed to rely full-time on porn to earn his living just at the time when he'd lost access to what boosted him.

What – suggested Andorra – if I were to offer the penis of my Beloved as a stand-in for Mark's penis while limp? With clever editing, viewers mightn't notice the temporary substitution, the tubes, the little plantpot clutched by Mark, or by whichever woman.

My Beloved's penis would be earning some money with which to recover more of himself for me.

"How is Coochie coping?" I asked.

"I lock him in the bathroom with a lot of cold turkey. He loves that. It takes his mind off the penis."

Andorra made arrangements. A couple of weeks later I watched a copy of the video in order to see with what sort of woman the penis was being unfaithful.

The poor editing hid little. It was obvious that part of the time a detached, hand-held penis was in use. Not a dildo, oh no, but a living penis which happened to lack a man attached to it.

What a dream for a woman, you may well say! And you would be right. Thanks to chat on the internet, word spread rapidly. The video became a wow among women. Few men bought it, maybe because of castration fears, but the producer was jubilant. Here at last was a porn video uniquely suited to females. Therefore we must make another video quickly – starring the detached living penis itself. Mark would play the role of a sex counsellor administering the penis as therapy to a patient. Not long after this second video was released, requests began arriving from dozens of sophisticated high society women requesting "private performances" – and offering to pay well.

Thus it was that at a private orgy, held in a woodland clearing on the outskirts of the city, the penis of my Beloved was mounted on the bonnet of a Jaguar car in place of the usual little model of a leaping jaguar. Several naked women wearing Venetian carnival masks took turns ascending the front of the car while friends cheered. This gave a new meaning to auto-eroticism.

Because of those private performances I was accumulating money fast. A down-payment on cloning all the rest of my Beloved looked possible, not least because the wife of one of the directors of Bodies'r'Us was one of those who had privately enjoyed the penis of my Beloved. She regarded my quest for the entirety of my Beloved as so romantic.

This woman, Natalie, made short art films as a hobby. She was convinced that a film made by her about my eventual reunion with my Beloved might win her a prestigious award given for short art movies featuring sexual themes, the Shiny Palm. This trophy took the form of a feminine hand, in polished metal, grasping an erect penis made of purple glass.

On account of the porn movie about the autonomous penis, Bodies'r'Us had gained new customers. Wives who had seen that movie, and whose husbands failed to satisfy them sufficiently, urged their spouses to have their penises cloned so as to support the men's performance in bed. An identical under-study, or penis double, would increase the women's pleasure and offer extra possibilities.

Excellent publicity for Bodies'r'Us! In Natalie's opinion an artistic movie would add true chic to the cloning of small body parts.

Not necessarily always penises, either! A lovely nose might be cloned and mounted on a plaque, like a small hunting trophy, the blood supply out of sight in a hidden compartment. A hand might be cloned, or a finger. Due to lack of auxiliary muscles, one couldn't expect the hand to flex its fingers dramatically, or the finger to bend much. A finger is not a penis. Probably penises would be most popular.

"Rivalry might even arise among men who have cloned penises," Natalie declared to me on the phone one day. "Those can be displayed on the wall as a talking point at a dinner party. You know how men boast – but it would be most unsuitable for a man actually to pull his own trousers down during a fashion-able dinner party! Besides, he mightn't rise to the occasion on account of too much alcohol or shyness. A cloned penis, which wouldn't imbibe, can represent him at his best. Wives will take pride in demonstrating the penis to their guests."

She speculated further: "Failure to mount your cloned penis on the wall might even give rise to suspicions as to the quality of the original penis. Too small? Too thin? Whatever! Maybe deficient men will buy more magnificent penises not cloned from themselves – provided by Third World companies without the scruples of Bodies'r'Us. On the other hand, the display of a less-than-splendid penis on the dining room wall might be a form of inverted boastfulness: 'It may not look much, but if only you knew what I can do with it, and for how long!' You do want your Beloved back, don't you, dear? If you let me make a film about your quest, I'm sure Bodies'r'Us will be very easy on the terms for a full Beloved. My film wouldn't be intrusive, just a few remote-control mini-cameras concealed in your apartment."

I was so excited I would have agreed to almost anything.

Bodies'r'Us must have exploited some of that research by those maverick scientists I mentioned. Instead of cloning a 100 percent new body complete with brand new penis, they *integrated* – as they put it – the already-cloned penis into the ensemble of all the rest of Oliver's cloned anatomy. The cloned penis, which I already knew was precious to me – it stood for continuity. I could hardly discard it, but it would be downright silly to maintain that autonomous penis unused, expensively keeping a blood pump working at the same time as the full Oliver maintained a blood supply to another cloned penis by natural means. It was only sensible that the original cloned penis should be coupled to the rest of the clone.

And so my Beloved came back to me.

Along with some cameras and microphones for my apartment.

In years gone by, scientists predicted that a duplicated brain shouldn't retain any of the memories of the brain that it's cloned from. According to past scientific wisdom, the new brain would only exhibit the same capacities and personality traits and tendencies as the original brain – for instance the tendency to fall in love with somebody looking much like me, or the ability to learn languages easily.

Now we know that a cloned brain actually inherits many of the typical *dreams* of its source brain. This is because dreams are deeply archetypal. The original brain and the cloned brain are genetically identical, so by morphic resonance the cloned brain acquires much of the dream experience of the original from out of the collective storehouse from which dreams emerge and into which they return. Thus my cloned Beloved couldn't remember any actual incidents of our waking life together, but he knew who I was in a dreamy way. And because dreams contain speech, he could speak, although in rather a dreamlike manner.

"You are an almond tree," he told me, shortly after Bodies'r'Us delivered him to the apartment. Was that because of the colour of my eyes? If so, this must be an endearment.

Yet to my horror I very quickly found that my Beloved was impotent with me! No matter what I did, or how I displayed myself, his penis remained limp – that very penis which had previously responded so enthusiastically! This shocked and chagrined me – and I regretted the cameras and microphones Natalie had installed.

We have all heard how the arm of the executed German mass-murderer, Sigmund Hammerfest, was grafted on to an amputee, Rolf Heinz, who'd lost his arm in a car crash – and how the murderer's arm subsequently made Herr Heinz homicidal. While Herr Heinz was making love to his wife one night, the arm broke Frau Heinz's neck. The organs and limbs of the body possess a kind of memory, as I've said.

Could it be that, rejoined to its body, the penis conveyed memories of its multiple infidelities to my Beloved's body? And the body, now powering the penis, developed *guilt*, which disabled the penis? Thus the memory of the penis was contaminating the true wishes of its owner.

Yet what really *were* the true wishes of my Beloved? Could it be that the penis had truly loved me, but that Oliver himself as a complete person hadn't been quite so devoted? Could it be that formerly the penis had been ordering my Beloved to love me and nobody else? That it was the desire of the penis, rather than true love, which had made Oliver want to fuck me? Yet I had permitted the penis to respond to anybody; in a sense I had trained it to do so. Consequently now I was no longer a unique focus of desire. My Beloved might call me an almond tree like some medieval Arabian poet, but those were just pretty words! This was very confusing.

Why, oh why, had I cloned all of Oliver at such cost when the penis had been my real lover all along! I had prostituted the penis, the only part of him that truly loved me. Now Oliver was inhibiting the penis from performing, and I might be discovering all too late that my Beloved's flowery sentiments were hypocritical!

I accused my Beloved.

His replies were hard to understand – unlike the formerly clear, if nonverbal, responses of the stiff penis.

"You didn't truly love me," I cried.

"Balloons bring roses," said Oliver. "Scent escapes from bursting balloons." Did this mean that love dies?

"It was your penis that loved me, not you!"

"The rubies of your nipples are so hard they could cut glass." Was he complaining about my nipples? In the old days of our passion, had they hurt his chest?

I was shouting at him in angry disappointment when a knock came at the door.

Andorra stood outside, Coochie on a leash.

The blood froze in my veins. Here was the moment I had been fearing.

"May we come in?" Andorra asked with a big, insincere smile. The dog wagged his tail, excited, probably foreseeing who knows which kind of filthy development.

No, no, no! I thought with all the power of my mind. However, I heard my voice answer politely: "Yes, of course, feel at home." Oh, the hypocrisy of etiquette. I could have bitten off my tongue. But there was no escaping from destiny.

Oliver remained expressionless as he met the gaze of Andorra, then of the dog. Andorra was observing Oliver inquisitively, as if to perceive a penis improbably hidden between his eyes. The gay dog was salivating, detecting the smell of a friendly penis that it knew . . . in the biblical sense. Coochie pushed close to Oliver and insolently sniffed his genitals through the trousers. Was the trace of an erection swelling in there? Oliver's forehead was knit. Did Coochie awake in him those dreams that I feared? Under no circumstances should I leave Oliver, and above all *my* penis, alone together with these two sexual jackals. As yet we were only in my hallway, which was quite large.

The doorbell rang again, and I turned to open the door once more. Etiquette!

Outside stood two mature women.

"We're from the Church for the Protection of Genital Organs," announced one of the ladies. "We'd like to interview you for our religious magazine."

This church had sprung up recently. Advances in plastic surgery were making it possible to have one's genitals exotically customized. Surely this insulted the sexual organs God designed for Adam and Eve and for all of us! Biblical believers had long since abandoned defending the sanctity of marriage as a lost cause; consequently they poured their piety into defending the sanctity of copulation as God intended, using the exact organs He provided, not pudenda reshaped into orchids or trumpets, or giant clitorises or bifurcated dicks.

As I later discovered, Bodies'r'Us – who approved of exact copies, not baroque variations – had given some money to the Church of PGO and encouraged them to interview me to make an interesting scene in the movie. Drawing the attention of the Church of PGO was a big mistake, as subsequent events proved. But meanwhile I got rid of the two women as quickly as possible, although not fast enough. When I turned back to my guests, they were not there anymore. Andorra and Coochie had vanished along with my Beloved and his/my penis!

Obviously they had gone into the lounge, but why then had they closed the door? Worry clutched at me. I gripped the door handle to follow them only to discover that the door was locked! With a shiver I imagined the spectators of the movie seeing my face turn pale at this point as the most horrible of scenes formed in my mind, of my beloved Oliver buggering the Labrador, who in turn was buggering Andorra, who, between moans, was sipping champagne from one of the crystal glasses my grandmother had left me in her will.

Was the artistic, romantic movie of reunion with the Oliver of my penis destined to turn into the usual bestiality porn reality show, the commonplace of television? I banged loudly on the door, but the only response was what sounded like a suffocated whine. Nobody came to let me in to my own lounge.

"Oliver!" I shouted. "Andorra!" For answer, just another whine.

This was too much. I fainted.

When I recovered, I was lying on the couch in the lounge. Andorra and Oliver were watching me with worried expressions. Coochie was sitting, looking sleepy.

"How long have I been unconscious?"

"A few minutes," replied Andorra, whether this was true or not.

"We heard a thump and found you behind the door. You ought to have the handle seen to. I don't think it works properly."

Was she sincere?

"Why did you close the door at all?"

"To be discreet. You had visitors." Oh, etiquette again. If I believed her.

I turned to Oliver. "What happened in here before you found me passed out?"

"What is passed or past is the turd of the Fall, come Springtime."

In other words, *No use crying over spilt milk*? By which he might mean spilled semen. Did *turd* allude to a dog's anus? To my mind those two items are always closely linked. Oliver was no help at all. I'd been getting along better with his, or rather *my* penis.

Ignoring the gaze of my Beloved, I looked lower, so as to distinguish within his pants my more beloved penis, probably the only part of Oliver which ever really loved me. That wasn't difficult – an evident protuberance seemed likely to perforate his pants at any moment. Obviously Oliver's penis was completely erect, the way I remembered it, the way I had long loved it. Hidden as it was by trousers, I couldn't actually see it, and this seemed unjust. Forgetting about the presence of Andorra and the hidden cameras, instinctively I reached out a hand sweetly to caress my beloved penis, which I hadn't seen – nor felt – in its full, majestic, generous erection for far too long. In the very moment when my hand grazed it, the penis imploded like a Hindenburg airship, deflating at once and evading my contact. Suddenly everything became atrociously clear beyond any doubt!

The penis itself could not know so quickly that it was me who touched it, because the trousers were a barrier to its sensitive nerve endings. Therefore the order to deflate must have come directly from the brain of Oliver. I became furious and shouted: "You treacherous fuckface prickhead, get out of my home! Get out, but leave my penis here!"

Seizing Oliver, I propelled him with all my strength out of the lounge, through the hall, to the front door. He didn't resist but let himself be thrown out, although of course he took my/his penis with him. Those two damn churchwomen were still loitering outside, index fingers scribbling on smartscreens nestling in their palms. Were they inventing a nonexistent interview? Aurora and Coochie hurried past me without a word or a woof, and I slammed the door behind them. Then I allowed myself the wisest feminine recourse in emergency circumstances: I began to cry.

Oliver took up residence in Andorra's flat. Some days later a man with the face of a mummified pig presented himself at my door.

"I'm the lawyer of the penis," he introduced himself.

I discovered that the Church for the Protection of Genital Organs had arrogated to itself the right to represent the interests of Oliver's penis. From Pigface I heard talk about the rights of genital organs to self-determination and about some Treaty of

Independence from the Bearer of the Organ. Oh the mysteries of jurisprudence! The ways that lawyers get rich!

Pigface explained to me that Oliver's penis had gained the status of an individual by virtue of having lived independently for a sufficient time before finding itself again attached to a human bearer. The Church for the Protection of Genital Organs was entitled to represent the penis because it was the first to claim that right, without the penis raising any objection.

"But the penis wouldn't be able to understand any of this!"

"Exactly. So it needed legal representation."

Later I learned how the judge at the court in question had become obsessed with making controversial landmark judgements in the hope of being retired soon with a knighthood or some other honour. The Church of PGO had been well aware of this.

In Andorra's flat there were no hidden cameras. Andorra had refused the TV company permission to install any cameras in her home – probably so as not to expose to the world her affair with the dog. For the TV company and for Bodies'r'Us this was unacceptable. On the other hand, the impotence Oliver's penis displayed toward me when it was attached to Oliver hardly made his return to my own home a very exciting prospect for Natalie and the other people involved in the production of the movie. The public doesn't much care for erotic dramas with impotent characters. Therefore the lawyers for Natalie and Bodies'r'Us were petitioning to have Oliver and his penis separated again, so that the penis could go back to performing in the role that had made it so famous: the penis without a man.

The penis without its Oliver had already become a star. A poll revealed that as an anonymous part of a normal person it wouldn't be so interesting to people.

The Church for the Protection of Genital Organs likewise wanted the penis to be separated from Oliver, yet not so that it could perform in porn movies or couple with me again, which they viewed as unnatural. Instead, they wanted it to retire to a Zen monastery. Oh, the moral obsessions of churches!

Thus there was conflict between the movie producers, with whom I had signed an agreement on behalf of the cloned Oliver, and the lawyers for the penis and the Church of PGO.

"We won't allow you to go on sexually exploiting that poor penis," Pigface told me at a deposition hearing.

"It's a sexual organ. It was born to be sexually exploited," I retorted.

"He's an individual with full rights, included the right of freely choosing the modality of his sexuality."

"It's a penis. If it becomes hard, that means it wants to fuck."

"Not at all! Diseases exist, such as priapism. Erection can be the symptom of a pathology."

I decided to change my strategy.

"It's a piece of meat without a brain. It's not compos mentis."

"Another reason to protect his dignity. We will never allow that poor penis to be forced into any more intercourses for which he didn't give written consent."

"How can a penis write anything?"

"If held properly, it can produce a DNA signature."

"Without a prostate it can't ejaculate, so where's the ink?"

"We can prepare all necessary documents *before* the separation."

Suits and countersuits were heard, and the lawyers were all very happy until at last no legal problems prohibited the penis being separated from Oliver. Final judgement was that since the penis was cloned *before* the body, *it* was the one who owned the other, and not the contrary. The penis owned the man, namely the cloned Oliver; Oliver did not own the penis. If it's legitimate for a man to cut off his own penis, provided that he isn't attempting suicide, logically the penis could decide to cut off its own man. The lawyer for the penis, as his legal representative, had full power to act in this regard – and to *steal* the penis of my Beloved, I was thinking in anger and frustration.

The judge duly retired and became a Lord.

⋆   ⋆   ⋆

However, we live in a strange and unpredictable world.

Under its various Patriot Acts, the USA had permitted itself to intervene in any part of the world in defense of its homeland security and its supplies of oil and cheap obesity fast food full of oil and sugar and additives. To signal to the world its rise as a rival superpower, China enacted the Salvation of Culture Law, by which the Chinese gave themselves the right to intervene anywhere to protect the interests of art. This was something that the American government found hard to understand, so they did not threaten the Chinese with thermonuclear war.

If the USA was the Global Cop, China would be the Global Curator. A popular US slogan was *Kick Ass America!* So Beijing declared *Save Art China!* – and why not, China being the oldest civilization on Earth? When Venice began to sink rapidly, swift intervention by Chinese technology had rescued the Italian city, preserving it in a dome to the applause of most nations. From then on, China could take great liberties in the defense of art.

Art included performance art, and one of the many ways of preserving art was Gor-Gon, a polymerizing nanotechnology inspired by Gunther Von Hagen's corpse plastination factory in the northeastern Chinese port city of Dalian. In just a few seconds, a jab of Gor-Gon administered by injection or by a dart fired from a gun could transform any living being into plastinated artwork, petrifying forever (though by no means as stiffly as stone) the target animal or person at that moment.

The penis had been quite a performer; and the legal case was by now notorious worldwide, as was the prospect of cloned penis and cloned person parting company. So Chinese art agents targeted Oliver. Already Chinese art agents had over-enthusiastically targeted several famous opera singers and actors for a Hall of Fame. Since the salvation of Venice the Chinese could do pretty much as they pleased, but plastinating artists suddenly while they were on stage caused demands for ticket refunds, arguments about civil rights, and also poorer performances by many divas and stars who didn't wish to be plastinated; which was all very regrettable and counterproductive. So this was made illegal. But according to Chinese law plastinating a clone was just as acceptable as plastinating a criminal for export to medical schools . . .

I'm so lucky. At the moment of petrification, the penis of my former Beloved was fully erect – he had to be slid out of Andorra by the Chinese agents who invaded her flat. So now I live in China, inside a big transparent cube. I couple with the penis attached to Oliver whenever I want. Plastination keeps the penis stiff, yet soft and comfortable to use. Of course plastinated Oliver never says a thing, nor moves, although I arrange him artistically just as I please.

Outside the cube every day crowds of visiting art lovers and connoisseurs admire us and shoot holographic movies, so that we never feel alone. Inside the cube, the air is always fresh and rich in happy-making hormones. The Chinese takeaway meals supplied to me free are so varied and delicious. Life is beautiful! Or maybe life is simply too complex to understand.

Cherry Bottom

Shanna Germain

"You okay, babe?" Andrew's voice above me was half sexual rasp, half concerned. His warm, oiled hands had moved from the outside curves of my ass to the inside of my thighs, and they were resting there, not pulling or teasing, just resting against my skin. I kept my eyes and mouth closed like I was supposed to and tried not to think about my naked ass in the air. I nodded against the pillow.

"She'll tell you if she's not," Miss Suzanne voice came from the other side of me. "Won't you, Cate?" I nodded again, the rasp of the pillow filling my ear. Miss Suzanne pressed her cool, slim fingers next to Andrew's, higher up on the inside of my thigh. The hot and cold of their hands made my ass break out in goose bumps. "See, Andrew? She'll tell you. So stop stalling."

Miss Suzanne's fingers left my skin. Her heels click-clicked away, presumably to another one of the six couples whose husband was also stalling.

Andrew's hands didn't move. I waited, head on my hands, belly and thighs resting on the prop-up pillow, ass in the air. My bare body was still in goose bumps, although the room was warm enough. Some of it was anticipation. But most of it was fear – Miss Suzanne's anal sex class was our last resort. If we couldn't get Andrew over his fear of anal sex here, I was afraid it was never going to happen.

It had been difficult enough to ask for it – the way I was brought up, girls aren't supposed to like any sex. And they definitely aren't supposed to like it the way I liked it. And poor Andrew – he wanted so badly to please me, but couldn't get over his fear of hurting me. No matter how many times I told him, no matter how much I begged for it. We'd tried videos and books. I'd even bought the smallest butt-plug at the store. Straw-sized, really, but still, he couldn't bring himself to put anything inside me. Not even just a little bit. Bad experience, was all he'd say. But this class had been his gift to me, and I knew he wanted to please me that way, even if he was too afraid. So, now, here we were, being taught anal sex by Miss Suzanne Saunders, southern belle turned sex therapist. Our first two classes had been lecture and book-learning. Today was hands-on. Today was our last chance.

I concentrated on letting my muscles go loose, on breathing in through my nose. We'd just spent ten minutes playing, getting warmed up. A little strange, to share foreplay with a dozen other people in the room, but every time I looked up, they were all concentrating on their own space, their own bodies. It was like a yoga class in the nude. And despite his fears about anal, Andrew didn't seem to have any fears about public sex. He just ran his tongue up and down between my thighs, reached up and ran his wet thumb over and over my nipple until I could only lean back and try to keep my moans quiet.

I wanted this so badly, I could already feel him inside me, the fullness of him, the weight. The way his balls would slap against me. Jesus, it had been so long, I could barely remember how it felt. I took a deep breath, tried to think of something else for a minute, to be calm so that Andrew would be calm.

Andrew's fingers held steady at the inside of my thigh, one second, two. Then he ran them up through the crack between my cheeks. With one hand, he spread my ass cheeks open. With the other, he circled the skin around my asshole. Part of our class had been learning the anatomy of the asshole, getting used to its pink pucker, its hairless expanse of skin. Knowing that Andrew was looking at me like that, that he was studying me, made my pussy ache for his fingers. My asshole too. I wanted to reach my fingers underneath me, to ease the ache in my clit, but we weren't supposed to move, so I squeezed my eyes tighter and tried to enjoy the ache. Maybe I could learn something too.

Andrew's finger went around and around, tighter and tighter circles toward my asshole. The tip of his finger against it and I could barely breath. I wanted him, any part of him inside me so bad. He held his finger there, not moving it in or out . . . just resting his finger against it like it was a button he was deciding whether or not to press.

Miss Suzanne's heels click-clicked toward the front of the room. "Okay, boys, I want you to get your fingers really well lubed, the way we talked about earlier. We're going in."

The class broke into nervous giggles. I was glad to hear Andrew's snort, the same one he gave at the comic strips at home. But his finger at my ass didn't move. Against my legs, his thigh muscles tightened.

C'mon, baby. C'mon . . . mental telepathy, the only encouragement I could offer him. I hoped he could hear. That he could hear me begging, could hear how much I wanted him like this.

Miss Suzanne and her heels again, right at our table. "Can I help, Andrew?" she asked. He must have said yes, because then her cool fingers were at my ass cheeks again, spreading them for him. My asshole puckered up against the cold. My tightening nipples crinkled the paper sheet beneath me.

Andrew's fingers left my body, came back oiled and warm.

"It's like playing pool," Miss Suzanne said, her thin fingers still in place. "It's all about speed and angles."

Andrew's finger was back against me, pressing, pressing. I fought the desire to lean back onto the tip of his finger, to force him inside me once and for all. But part of our class promise had been to let our partner do all the work, go at his own pace, let him do only what he was ready for.

He increased the pressure, opening my asshole, careful to use the flat of his fingertip. "Go," Miss Suzanne whispered, and then Andrew pushed his way inside me. Just a little, just the tip so I could barely feel it, but oh Jesus, there he was.

"More," Miss Suzanne said. Andrew pushed his finger farther into my asshole. Farther, until I was sure he had to be at the first joint. Having him in there like that made my pussy ache with that special emptiness that I loved. Andrew entered me to the knuckle. I imagined what he looked like behind me –

starting to sweat beneath his glasses out of fear and excitement, his finger disappearing into my asshole.

"All the way in," Miss Suzanne said. And then he pushed and his finger was inside me, tearing through me with that certain pain that is mostly pleasure. I bit down on the pillow, but most of the moan came out anyway.

"See?" Miss Suzanne said. "She likes it. You're doing a great job."

"Jesus," Andrew whispered. "Oh fuck." Awe and arousal deepened his voice to a husky whisper. Hearing that voice – no fear in there – almost made me come.

Miss Suzanne raised her voice. "Okay, class, is everyone in? Foxes all in the holes?" I'm sure the class laughed, but I couldn't even concentrate to hear all the answers. All I could feel was Andrew's finger in my ass, the way he held it there, so still, the way it filled me and at the same time made me ache for something more, something bigger.

"Great," she said. "Now I just want you to wiggle your fingers in there a little bit. Not a lot, just enough to feel the room, to see what kind of reaction you get."

This time, Andrew didn't hesitate. As soon as she said wiggle, his finger started moving, up and down, up and down, inside me.

"Okay?" Andrew asked. But this time he wasn't asking if I was okay. He was asking if it felt good, if he was doing the right thing in there.

My voice was all whisper and the pressure of not fucking his finger. "Yes," I said. "Yes, please don't stop."

Miss Suzanne click-clicked back to the front of the room, apparently trusting that Andrew had gotten the hang of things.

After a few minutes she said, "Ladies, now it's your turn to help out. Gentlemen, your job is just to hold yourself still. Maybe for the first time ever, your ladies are going to fuck you."

Andrew's finger stopped moving in my ass. Lightheaded, I pushed myself backwards onto Andrew's finger, so far back his other curled knuckles rubbed against my skin. I let myself fuck him, showing him how much I wanted him like this, how much I wanted him inside me.

With each thrust, Andrew's breathing quickened. His finger burnt and rubbed the inside of me in pain and pleasure. I was so full back there that the rest of me ached, empty and untouched. With one hand, I reached beneath me and fingered my slippery clit, letting everything build inside me. The fullness and the empty. The sweet burn of Andrew's finger in my ass, the soft roll of pleasure through my clit. And the best part was Andrew behind me, bracing himself against the table, letting me fuck him, I hoped, without fear for the first time. Seeing there was no pain, that there was only pleasure.

I was close to coming, but I wasn't sure if we were supposed to, if we'd been given the go-ahead, or if there was more I was supposed to do. And then Andrew moved his finger inside me, up and down, just enough to hit that spot and it didn't matter if I was supposed to or not, it was happening. Everything sliding through me from Andrew's finger out to my toes, up into my head. I cried out, and heard Andrew do the same.

I pulled forward, off of Andrew's finger, and let my head hang on the pillow. "Holy shit," I said. I had no idea where anyone else was at in the room, or if there was even anyone else in the room any more. And then I heard Miss Suzanne's heels click-click up. "Once you two have washed up, meet in the front room to debrief and get your assignments for next week." She put her hand, still cool as ever, against my shoulder. "Nice job, you two."

When I sat up, Andrew's face was pink and flushed. But he had the biggest grin on his face. Just seeing him like that, aroused and confident, made me wet all over again. He leaned down and kissed the lobe of my ear. "That," he whispered, "was awesome. I can't wait to see what our new assignment is."

I thought of his cock, the tip of it entering me, the way it would feel when he finally pushed inside of me. "I can't either."

Mindy's Pheromones

Jeremy Edwards

Mindy made me sex-obsessed in a way I hadn't been since eighth grade.

Here I was, a well-adjusted, experienced man of thirty-two. Throughout my adult life I had studied with women, worked with women, socialized with women, seduced and been seduced by women, formed strong bonds with women, built complicated relationships with women, and had one-night stands with women. I had been fraternally friendly with them, professionally proper with them, uproariously ribald with them . . . and gloriously, so gloriously, intimate with them. I respected women, I admired women, I learned from women, I sympathized with women, I adored women.

In the course of all this, I'd experienced captivating sexual obsession – but always in the sophisticated manner of a man of the world. These were grown-up obsessions explored on moonlit beaches furnished with champagne, or in boutique hotel rooms with their inevitably inviting beds and bathtubs, or at 1 a.m. rooftop parties for two.

And suddenly one humdrum Tuesday, a woman whose face, though pleasant, I would never have picked out of a crowd . . . and whose interests had little or no overlap with my own . . . and whose personality, though undoubtedly agreeable, didn't really grab me . . . was assigned the cubicle next to mine. And just as suddenly, I became, for all practical purposes, a 13-year-old again.

It must have been pheromones, I kept telling myself. I must have been responding to her on an unconscious, olfactory-driven level that made my chemicals boil and my sexual intellect regress. No matter how blatantly I failed to connect with her, her femaleness screamed itself to me in a primal way.

Mindy is sitting in the cubicle next to mine. Mindy, who is female, is in the cubicle next to mine. Mindy, who has breasts and slender fingers and wears dresses and skirts, is in the cubicle next to mine. Mindy, who shaves her legs and whose underpants have no fly and who inserts fingers into herself to masturbate, is in the cubicle next to mine. Such were the endless, compulsive trains of thought that displaced my priorities as a skilled graphic designer facing a precarious stack of deadlines.

Meanwhile, Mindy had hair that was a color I thought of as "nondescript" and an hourglass figure that struck me as "predictable" and a tone of voice that reminded me of my sister's. Her eyes glazed over on the few occasions I tried to talk to her about Art Nouveau or exotic beetles, while her rapturous discussion of car trends left me in neutral.

After I had somehow managed to complete the most urgent of my assignments with Mindy's chemicals simmering next door, I took a couple of personal days. I thought if I didn't go near her from Wednesday night until Monday morning, I might shake this obsession. But all I did from Wednesday night until Monday morning – to the extent my body was up to it – was fondle and shake myself to absurd orgasms, while thinking about how Mindy had a vagina and small feet and a hairless ass. The mindset may have been eighth-grade, but the orgasms were industrial-strength. What was driving me? Could I somehow, unconsciously, smell her even from home? Ridiculous. Unless . . .

It was a natural conversation for me to start on Monday morning.

"How was your weekend?"

"Good, thanks," she replied. "Yours?"

"Long and absorbing," I answered truthfully. "I mostly just did things at home."

"Yeah, I was mostly home, too," she stated matter-of-factly.

This was the opening I'd wanted. "What neighborhood do you live in?"

"I have an apartment near the Symphony. I've lived there about a year now."

Aha! But I realized there must be hundreds of apartments, in dozens of buildings "near the Symphony". It would be audacious to assume that she lived in one of the few studios beside, above or below mine that could plausibly be within smelling distance.

"Yep," she continued, "near the Symphony." And then she tossed off the address. My address.

And yet if she'd been living in my immediate vicinity all this time, exuding her potent pheromones, then why had I never been affected by them before we became co-workers? Had sitting a mere cubicle away from her somehow triggered something – akin to an allergic reaction – which could now be rekindled by a weaker, more distant version of the same stimulus? For lack of a better theory, I accepted this premise that close exposure to Mindy's chemicals had made me hypersensitive to her.

"It's kind of funny that I ended up in that area," Mindy was saying, "since I'm totally uninterested in music – of any kind."

More evidence, of course, that we had nothing in common. I could not even imagine living without music. I appeared to be a thoroughly unsuitable match for Mindy.

Mindy, whose legs converge in a neat, feminine juncture instead of a collage of male genitalia like my own. Mindy who has a smooth neck and a high voice and would sing soprano, if she didn't hate music. Mindy who keeps her knees together when sitting on the bench in front of the elevator in our lobby. Mindy who walks nonchalantly through a door marked WOMEN when it's time to wash up for lunch.

Mindy's computer crashed a minute later. "Argh!" she said from her cubicle. Argh. I wondered if she said "Ngh" when she approached orgasm. I had fucked three or four women in my time who said "Ngh" as they ramped up to climax, and I wanted desperately to know if Mindy said "Ngh."

Mindy couldn't have cared less about the food I liked or the authors I treasured. She loved camping and skiing, which I couldn't stand. She never laughed at my jokes. Nevertheless, I spent my first morning back at work pondering whether she said "Ngh" in bed.

We had two single-occupant, unisex bathrooms in our office. That afternoon, as I was heading for the restroom nearest our department, Mindy came out of it. I had heard her on the phone just a minute or two earlier, so she'd obviously just gone for a quick pee – or maybe simply to glance in the mirror.

As I closed the door, it became obvious that Mindy had indeed pulled her tight little jeans down in this room. The aroma of her femaleness was as overwhelming as it was immediate. No unconscious senses were required to detect her this time. Though my intention in sequestering myself here had been to take a piss, I found myself stroking my cock as I stood at the toilet, gazing down on the seat that had hosted her bare ass moments before, her sex diffusing into the small room's atmosphere. *Mindy is female. She sits down to urinate and makes the bathroom smell like cunt. Her cunt.* In seconds, I was ejaculating into a palmful of bleach-white toilet paper.

Over the next few days, my sense of smell finally seduced my other senses. Now I could not look at Mindy without admiring the subtle grace of her features; I could not listen to her talk without feeling tremors. How, I marveled, could I ever have found her looks to be bland and her voice to be ordinary? I began to see my previous unresponsiveness to her physical charms as a reflection on my own shortcomings.

Even more, her personality began to fascinate me. Her lack of interest in the things I cared about somehow became an *intriguing* lack of interest. Her enthusiasm over subjects which bored me became enchanting enthusiasm. I was infatuated with everything about this woman, even though I knew it was ultimately just the result of mischievous molecules from her vagina tickling my horny nose, day in and day out. I didn't care. I just wanted to fuck her all night, every night, and really get to know her during the intervening days.

On Friday, the day she wore the soft white jeans with the pocket-buttons, I couldn't hold back any longer. You know the sort of pants I mean – with cute little button-down pockets on the ass, impractical as pockets but intoxicating as textures, ornamenting pert cheeks the way that nipples ornament breasts. When Mindy was standing at the photocopier with her back to me, I found I could not take my eyes off those little buttons. All I wanted to do was unbutton each pocket in turn and caress her ass.

I had three deadline-sensitive projects on my desk. But the only projects I worked on that morning consisted of various fantasies that each involved (a) unbuttoning those pockets and (b) fondling Mindy's bottom through the thin layer of fabric inside them. (For the purposes of these fantasies, I took the liberty of presuming Mindy to be wearing a thong.) By lunch-time, I had already masturbated my head off in the john three times.

"Hey, do you have plans this weekend?" Any reservations I might once have had about asking this question were by now comfortably submerged beneath my consuming desire to touch Mindy's body.

She smiled. "I was going to ask you the same thing."

So dinner that night it was, at a restaurant near our building. It was a curry place – one of the few cuisines on which we agreed. It seemed appropriate that we were going somewhere enticingly fragrant.

"They don't serve alcohol," she warned me. Mindy liked beer; I liked wine.

"No worries," I ventured in reply. "I've got stuff at my place, so we can go up for a drink afterwards."

"Perfect."

Dinner conversation involved a predictable assortment of dead ends. And yet there was a level of comfort there, a rapport. We had come a long way in two weeks of cubicle-bumping.

After dinner, we very naturally slid onto opposite ends of the convertible couch in my pad, drinks in hand. We raised our glasses in a casual, unspoken toast.

"You realize we have nothing in common," said Mindy after a sip of beer.

"Oh, yes," I replied.

"But you're cute," she stated, as if this were a fact. "That's why I wanted to go out to dinner with you . . . and everything."

She blushed. I couldn't remember the last time I'd spent an evening with a woman who blushed. "How about you?"

"You mean, why did I want to go out to dinner – and everything?"

"Yes. Even though we—"

"I know, I know. Even though we have nothing in common." We laughed together, perhaps for the first time, united by a shared awareness of our irreconcilable differences.

Mindy's candor inspired my own. "Don't take this the wrong way, but – believe it or not – I wanted to go out with you because . . ." I hesitated and made a quick detour. "Now, I think you're cute, too, and I like you. I like you more with each moment, in fact." I cleared my throat. "But I really wanted to go out with you because . . . I can unconsciously smell your cunt all day long, and it's driving me wild."

Her mouth dropped open. Was it shock? Incredulity? I thought I saw her eyes tearing up.

"Wow," she said softly, her soprano pitch suddenly husky.

With great delicacy she placed her beer on the coffee table, next to my glass of wine.

Then she pounced on me, and I was enveloped in arms and legs and breath and liquid kisses, my head spinning in the strongest dose yet of Mindy's aroma. Of all the times I had fantasized about Mindy, it had never occurred to me that she might go even wilder than I would, that she would fling herself onto me and fuck me like she'd been waiting for it all her life.

I don't remember how, or when, our clothes came off. But I'll never forget the way she rode me, her thighs trembling while she guided herself up and down my pole, juicing every ounce of pleasure from the machine of our genitals. She smelled like home, like dinner, like laughter and dessert . . . and, of course, like cunt.

"Ngh," she said, her face a grimace of hard-earned bliss. "Ngh," she reiterated, and reiterated, with shorter and shorter interludes between iterations. When she'd taken us as high as we could go, I clutched her butt cheeks for my own ninety eternal seconds of free-fall.

Afterward, she rolled into the crook of the loveseat. I dropped to the floor, preparing to make a proper meal of her. But her ass was facing out, and I couldn't ignore it. I had to kiss every inch of this ass – this ass I had once dismissed as "ordinary" – before going near her pussy, potent though the pussy's olfactory beckoning was.

When I had kissed cheeks and crack so comprehensively that Mindy's bottom was jiggling in my face like it had its own motor, I moved at last to the heart of the matter. Tonguing and kissing every possible place between her legs, I felt drunk on her essence. It was the oxygen my lungs had craved since I met her. And though Mindy claimed not to have a musical bone in her body, her soprano trills were tonally perfect every time she hit a climax. "Ngh" for fucking and trills for being eaten, I noted, having always been a devoted student of languages – unlike Mindy, who could rattle off sports stats but had flunked out of Spanish.

"I have to pee," she said after I'd finally exhausted her.

My couch smelled like Mindy's cunt. My body smelled like Mindy's cunt. My bathroom would soon smell like Mindy's cunt. And I knew I would do my best to make sure that Mindy returned again and again, so that her delicious scent could never dissipate and leave me deprived.

Mindy the delightful. Mindy the compelling and enchanting. Mindy who, at that very moment, was making her splendid, fluid, utterly naked way toward my bathroom. Mindy who was, and always would be . . . Mindy.

Underneath

Kevin Mullins & Marcelle Perks

They coughed between kisses, sucking in mould-ridden air as sex-lust quickened their needs. The man leant down to enter her mouth, his body mimicking the curve of the ceiling. His hand pushed and slid to part her as the metal gods roared their approval. In, tight and holding, both thrilled further by the vibrations of the tunnels around them. The searing singing! Ah, so good! Just a wall beyond there were people chatting about West End shows, something about Britney Spears. They were going home, easing the day away. But the real underground was here where life was deadened. It was sealed disharmony, a jerking cock-in-the-mouth, a secret world where fugitives took a mystery trip to the unconscious.

Chris thinks he looks dead ordinary in his London Underground Oranges. Sometimes, when he dons the illuminated vest, punters ask him about trains and tickets. As if! But he's meant to blend in, don't want nobody to know. See, it's been happening a bit too often. They keep jumping, don't they? Two a week or more, no let up. Sometimes they're lucky and they get pushed into suicide pits, hollow ovals designed to displace a man-made corpse from the thrust of the engine wall, but there's always the blade's breath of the rails and the resulting severed limbs; artery overload with its blood spill; bone drop-out, giant skin tags.

If he's unlucky the body gets drag-pushed the entire run to the mouth of the tunnel, greasing and falling out the whole stretch. Although it's filthy down there anyway and rats will pick-eat the carnage, the carriage has to be uncoupled, everything taken out of service. The whole thing pulled out to a lone siding, rubbed down, strip-searched. He collects all the evidence: bones, earrings, jewellery, teeth, scalp fragments. Often a photo from the morgue is sent to him, so he can fill in the gaps. His official title is Search and Recovery. You wouldn't believe how far a pinky finger can fly! Scrape and wipe, that's his job description, a position they could never advertise. And it's demanding, takes a genius to work out where everything is, the possibilities for fall-out, the angle of the blood. A hard job, but someone's got to do it. Gossamer webbing forms between his gloved fingers as he delicately fingers stumps and seared flesh.

Rhonda gasped at the chill of the wall on her back. The rounded gloom looked congenial, but moist speckles drizzled onto her hair. It was damp down here. She'd chosen him for his perfectly spaced, open blue eyes. There had been a spark between them, a subtle movement of breath. And now they were here there was less need for talk, far easier to just feel and press his penis. He had a nice hefty cock that felt heavier the more she sucked on it. Good energy, pulsating all the way down to the base. It was sexier in the dark. They were like mime figures in ancient Greece, shuddering shapes moaning in darkness. Down here her senses were heightened, her nipples never harder, insides leaking out with longing; all the pinky skin screaming out for flesh, a good hard shaft.

It was so unreal, it almost didn't count, this milking of men in forgotten shadows. And this one too, already she could taste the pre-come droplets on her tongue, imagine this stranger's entire body cued up to deliver a last extra-hardened jerk of orgasm. It would come like a wave of electricity, pulsating all over her. Vital, alive. This one she would engulf raw, until every bit of him had fizzled inside her. Here, their heartbeats were magnified, body movements in extreme close up and heat. His hand pushed into her slippery slit, the finger tickling the edges of her labia, the panty edge useless, now being breached. Look how the bitch wants it! They could smell each other over everything else, the scent enflaming them. Kissing like pigs, nonsense noises loud now. Sitting on it, riding it, deep deep into the spot! Hah! Agggh!

Sliding underneath now. Have to get the body out first before they can do anything. And this one was a splatterer. Fat ones were always the worst, some of the shits that came out of them! And their body fat, even uglier unpeeled, its consistency of chip fat and liver nearly gagging him every time. The work load here is overwhelming, all chore. He's now tired of this. Needs something else to keep him busy. Maybe the latest closed circuit video passed around among the crew.

Inside her, the chemical reaction. Millions of live sperm cells in chase, needling and reacting to her. He was still shuddering, penis limping down now. She'd be bumping and jerking off for hours. Probably get Chris to milk her velvet insides too, even if he's not that fertile, at least his lovable cock could push this sperm around her even deeper in. Manual insemination. What he didn't know couldn't hurt him, not when he was being hurt by his failure already. Her legs were damp like the weeping walls. She felt malleable, but the station would be a hive of activity after the last train had gone and they had to go a while before they reached the abandoned interchange to the other line. She reached down to pick up her keys. He stammered something, but she only put a finger to her lips, gently pushed his chest, easing him towards the concealed exit. It was powerful, this primal guiding instinct. A fantasy woman had snatched him and fucked him underground. There was only the moment. For her two fertile days she had to work fast.

Chris was used to death, to scraping it matter-of-fact off rails and trains. What he had problems with was life, creating it. Since the clinic had told him he had a low sperm count, it was like his penis had died. When she looked to it for sex, he pushed her away and she had to dry-hump his leg to get off. (Funny, he thought, that she now got off with him on one of the parts that was routinely cut off on the lines.) It was cool that he was kinky (they'd found each other at the Scala screening of *Nekromantik*) but not enough. Twisted things gave her pussy ache, but sometimes a hard cock and a soft cunt were the only language she needed.

"The smell is stronger tonight," she said, ruffling his dark, almost black hair. Repeated exposure to death permeates, you can't simply wash it away. Aggressively, she pressed her semen-imprinted body in front of his. Nothing. He didn't resist, just started whining.

"Another fat guy, you know how they stink. Make more mess. Overtime for a week long, though." He looked tired, his hands were shaking. He saw her looking at his faded eyes.

"Why can't it be the cool goth chicks that jump the trains?" he joked feebly, he was still exhausted, head down.

She smiled, kissing him, knowing already that female bones are less likely to fragment, and thinner mortals stay more intact, are easier to dispose of. Tonight, he was tired. Let him watch fucking TV then. Like there was nothing else going on. He still didn't want to talk about it. She hid the pregnancy testing kit she'd bought safely in a drawer. If he couldn't guess the date, then fuck him. When it was positive she'd show him. Low didn't mean zero.

Underneath the very streets everyone walked on was something old and sacred, scarred into the city's shape, listless but fertile in the dusky dirt. London breathes resonance that tugs at the subconscious. Is it the pagan gods, or the Greek ones, or the apostles of Lucifer that haunt its medieval-formed alleyways? She could imagine her forefathers worshipping in dank caves, pushing out winter, hunger, unmedicated pain. The chanting faces mixed with hope and sorrow. Oh yes, *then*.

Now the awe had left the people. Everybody was the same and nothing. London on the surface was a bubble palace, all flash lights and gab. A sprawl of unmatched buildings, most of it old and shady. Everybody rich-poor and raging. But underneath, there were oh so many undercuts and passageways, in this most undermined city in the world. And all along the stretches and sprawls of commerce and laid back-to-back housing, the arteries of the city flexed its nerves. Hundreds of trains teemed in, out and around the tunnels, feeding ever more strangers all the way, forcing them into darkness and decay. But under the neon lights, if you looked them carefully in the eye, you could see a tremor of hesitation, on dark nights it looked like fear.

Maps didn't really help. The old stuff wasn't built logically. The plans were still secret, freemason's mischief, whiffs of occult magick. There were platforms that joined in the shape of a figure 8, a double track constructed that was never used, the abandoned stations left whole and rotting to slug up the city's heartbeat. And this was Chris's world, the dungeon behind the tiled façade.

The first time he'd taken her to an abandoned tube station she'd nearly pissed her pants. It was that scary, all the fear that she'd ever felt before was like nothing in front of it. He'd shown her the key, made her lick it before they scurried through the discreet door. Then down a decrepit, still dirty staircase to the now disused platform; just yards from the hub of the main station, but here was deserted, fading posters still on the walls.

He'd leaned her against the hush and eased down her panties as images of mummified corpses flashed on the wall behind them. A surprise film show for her, something his bosses were trying to sell as a concept. Somebody laughed, a horrid cackle in the background. There were a few workmen in the tunnel, enjoying the show, the screen crackling as they watched. Each image had a shadow cloud of filth as the moving dust spots squeezed the dead station into life. That was good, the first time he'd touched her inside, the hesitating but unstoppable fingers. Her skirt, as always, was short and provoking. She looked past her lust at the flickers of the moving screen.

It was uncensored footage from the Bodyworlds exhibition, real corpses plasticined and exhibited for the public. It was bizarre. At one point they stepped in front of the projector and the footage played on their frantic bodies. It was an experiment, maybe they would use the disused Aldwych to pander to film premières. The underground was a treasure trove of such decay. A stripped away horseman on screen grinned at her thrashing pleasure. And passion swept over all like a blackout. A lust that tunnelled her into nothing.

It seemed to take ages for them to get to have sex. Oddly, he was old-fashioned, sometimes unbearably courteous. But after their first time, a heavy blanket of lust had dropped over them. They couldn't seem to stop, yet had little lasting satisfaction.

Nightly they'd made love, all the positions, mutual masturbation, all to heat and exhaustion. Sometimes, it was four a.m. when the bed stopped heaving. And even after they had come the fourth, fifth time, it was never enough. Even after they were married. For all their sex, still nothing happened. The stirring of life they planned, failed to bud. Then came the consultations with doctors, strange pills that made them feel listless. The encroaching silences. She had become desperate to revive her dark prince. And where better than in his kingdom, the womb-like tunnels of his private underground – the forgotten stations – to court and milk her donors? What happened there wasn't real. It was passion and adventure, secrets and darkness. And the underground was so much a part of Chris anyway, like the caverns behind his eyes. She took copies of his keys and found the best locations. Cruised from work's end when she was hot and ticking. There were risks of course, but she targeted the one-time thrill seekers, hunted for the surprised look. She wanted a result. In the midst of life we are in the midst of death. And Chris was so down, he needed it.

After four weeks of cruising, she felt a flush of expectancy. Her eyes shone brighter, breasts pointed higher north. Something was in the air. At the same time, she had seen even less of Chris, who had dealt with nine deaths below: an unusually high number – 56 percent of attempts were unsuccessful. They were like Hades and Persephone, he to quench life, she to bring it forth. She thought of this as they curled up on quiet evenings. But something was stretching out, far and away. They were drifting apart, long tunnels separated by empty static. They sat in the evenings caught in the TV's glow, a still life of sadness.

The walls were stark, meant to be white. But it was impossible to judge colour down here. The grain of the breezeblock chewed into her hands as the man who she often saw at Holborn thrust into her from behind. Funny, although he looked a capable guy, he had the angle all wrong, and it was hurting a little too much on the left hand side. She tried to manoeuvre, but, ooh, everything goddamned scraped the skin here. The entrance this time had been a bugger to find. Odd that people had actually lived here once.

Yeah darling, come over from Jamaica and get a nice job with London Transport with a free flat. Well, a codenamed hell known as The Hostel; it had been a revamped bomb shelter from the Second World War. Must have seemed like they'd left the sunshine and gone to hell. Roll fifty years, still she's keeping up the fucking spirit in platform 6. I bet those guys (usually they were guys) had brought some gals down here. Yeah, just like she was giving this some fizz.

He couldn't get a full rhythm going because the corridor was too narrow. But his cock was hard and it was inside her. The usual mashing rhythm. She let go, fell forward, her breasts scraped against the rough painted surface. If she closed her eyes she could have been pressed against the roughness of a cave or tree. He was mauling her with his greedy hands everywhere. She decided to moan, give him some satisfaction. Aggh. His finger pushed hard up her anus. Unexpected. Extra kinky! Her stomach tightened.

"Harder!" she gasped. She could feel the poke of his finger span deepen. Yeah, come darling, before I leave you here to wank by yourself. She'd thought an older guy, one with silver streaks in his hair, might at least be proficient. Up for it. Maybe she wouldn't let this one come inside her. His sperm wasn't good enough for Chris!

She stood proudly looking at herself in the mirror. She looked back at her shining eyes and lustrous hair, something was up. Why didn't he notice the change in her? He was bathing again with the door shut. They always used to do it together, drinking lashings of wine with the water. Should she pop into the bathroom, show him her breasts? No, his bag was here. She just had time to steal a cigarette. Her hand reached down right between a file. Shit, it was photos, perhaps she'd creased one. Quickly, she pulled the file out. He was bringing his work home again. Photographs dotted with unique codes. All corpses vaguely swollen or mangled, rendered fantastic through the extent of their injuries. It was their vagueness that got her in the throat:

"AA456G T. 17 pieces + fluids. 8 Stone." The picture was of a teenage girl without clothes, both her arms had been crudely severed. The pressure in Rhonda's head tightened, a flash headache was forming at the base of her neck. Still, she was somehow unable to draw her eyes away. More of them, too many. A fat woman in a flowery dress, the cloth surprisingly more intact than her body; a punk rocker whose head had been badly mangled. Was it really human? The gent with the snarled body, as if a dragon had breathed fire and cut him to pieces. His silver hair all that was normal. The curious way after everything it still looked so neat and dapper. Her fingers throbbed just looking at it. It could have been that guy from the other night, the one who didn't know where her vagina was positioned and had made her sore. She pushed the photos back into the file. She couldn't face this shit now.

The man wiped his hand with a neatly folded white handkerchief. Another stranger. Underneath he looked gnome-like, pig ugly. He looked ruefully at the smears of red and brown on her underwear. Sometimes she got carried away. She inspected the scratches on her breasts and stomach, thinking ahead to how she could conceal them. Sometimes she felt weary doing it, it was just like another job.

It took minutes of silent readjustment before they were ready to re-enter normal life. From the open platform side the doorway looked like a storage cupboard, so it was difficult to go in or come out without it looking odd. Timing was everything. She listened for a long time whilst her donor shuffled impatiently behind her.

When the coast seemed clear she edged open the door, checked that there was no one visible and swung through. The man bundled after her. A moment after she'd looked up, a thin-faced black woman in LT uniform turned the corner and faced them. She seemed horribly familiar, somehow. The woman gave them a quick hard glance then turned away. Perhaps the security cameras had picked something up. Normally she got the man to take the first train, but they were both too eager to escape for that protocol to be even suggested. They separated with an awkward touch two stops down. She felt she could feel the ticking of her body as she eventually climbed a thousand steps onto a train. Yes! Surely this was it! How then to break it to Chris?

When she'd said she wanted to do something special, she'd meant dinner, candles. The local Italian round the corner maybe. But tonight he was the old Chris again, dressed in gothic clothes he hadn't worn in two years, a daub of kohl around his eyes.

"Hey babe," he reached for her and pulled her lips hungrily to his mouth as she came in. "I gotta see a man about a dog, know what I mean." She stared at him quizzically; it was their codename of old.

"You mean you got another way in? Another dungeon for us to explore?"

"Yes, babes, this one's the best. We've gotta travel with my mate on the 8.15 from Finsbury Park, right behind him in the cab, then when we get there, a little tap and he'll let us out at the old Brompton Road station. And on the last train, he'll pick us up just before he goes to the depot. You wanna come?" He held out his arms for her.

"Oh, Chris, you are fabby!" She jumped into his arms and ran to change into her army trousers and dockers. Time to go underground again. What better setting than the disused Brompton Road station, which they had never explored, to proclaim her pregnancy?

When they caught the bus to Finsbury Park station, darkness was falling. It was a cold Autumn night, the trees slowly dying in the battered streets. They made an odd couple. Chris painfully tall, his skin so white it looked grey. He was wearing his work clothes just in case; it was easier if there were any awkward questions. Rhonda wore her own uniform of slick black over her trim short frame, with the familiar orange waistcoat over it; a fake LT Visitor badge completed the deception.

They spent a long time on the platform, nervously waiting for Pete to turn up and give them a lift. The other passengers, perhaps thinking they were checking tickets, avoided them like the plague. They stood near the mouth of the tunnel, talked without looking at each other. Going to these disused stations had always been something they did together, now she felt guilty after her own private forays into this domain. Near the watching eye of the CCTV camera, she felt like an insect in an open glass. If they waited much longer, someone on station control would get suspicious.

The sound of bumping, painful searing, the gears of a large train slowing, caught their attention. They craned their necks looking. Was it him? The window of the driver's cab was smeared with something, but Pete's cheery face came into view. His warm brown eyes and laughing smile were a real charmer. He opened the door with a flourish, "Come on, love birds, get yourself in. You wouldn't want to miss this extra special experience now, would you?"

It was really too small inside for three. Chris wedged himself on the floor by the controls, and she stood by the shaking door. The train gave a little wheeze and teetered backwards for a fraction before rushing forwards into the darkened tunnel.

"Wow," said Rhonda, her eyes wide with shock. "In here it looks so different. I can't believe I go this way every day! Is there anything to see down here?"

"Not much," said Pete airily, "That's why we get so bored. You see the odd rat scurrying off the tracks, once I thought I saw a fox, but nah, there's just lots of rubbish that gets blown through the system. Sometimes you get to thinking you see things though!"

Chris was no longer smiling; his voice, when it came out, didn't sound like him at all,

"It's the people who do the weird shit. You should see some of the CCTV footage, fucking, shitting, you name it." For half a second, her heart jumped in her mouth. But he couldn't, could he?

His flat voice continued, "All golden boys and girls all must, like chimney sweepers turn to dust."

"Yeah," said Pete, "and after doing a double shift again, I'm half way there!" It was an old joke; working underground was akin to being buried alive in the heart of the city. She'd heard that some of the workers felt weirder on the surface when they scurried home.

The endless enclosure of the tunnel distracted them. It was an eternal penis that stretched for miles. The train bucked along at a pace, eating up the stations one by one: Piccadilly Circus,

Green Park, Hyde Park Corner, familiar London just metres above. At Knightsbridge, Chris said, "Get ready, babe." His voice was still uneven, as if he needed to wash out his throat. Normally he was high now, anticipation dancing in his veins. But she would show him. The train slowed down, through the window the colours of the tiles changed. Pete, hand on the brake stick, said, "On the count of three."

She had the door in her hand and it was half open before the train had even come to a halt. Heart racing, she jumped out into blackness, careful to keep away from the rail. She pointed her torch at a recent wall that had been built over the old platform and cut her hands trying to clamber over it. Ouch! There was something sharp on its edges, some barrier trying to keep them out. Behind her the train door was slamming, just seconds to get out of the way before being seen by one of the punters. The train groaned onwards.

"Chris?" she shone her torch at the empty space where the train had been. Impossible, surely?

For some reason, she'd been left alone in the dark.

At first she sat and waited, indignation filling her with hate energy. She felt hot and stupid, panicking in the dust. Why had he done this? The idiot, dumb fuck! She'd kill him when she saw him. The remains of the platform were indistinct, half re-built with a raised area, the rest in disarray. Now she was here, it didn't feel real. She'd always descended below with another man, first Chris, then the others. Alone it had a different feel, the only thing she longed for was to be out of there.

The strangest thing was, it wasn't pitch black. Although it hadn't been used as a station since 1934, the lights were on, although their colour was dusty, sepia-like. The curve of the walls seemed about to fall and engulf her. Torchlight was more romantic, you didn't get to notice the asbestos dust from the brake linings, the rat droppings and oozing mildew. An ancient track plate remained in place. If she ignored the abandoned building project that cluttered the platform, she could imagine she really was waiting for a train, and not for Chris to reclaim her. Perhaps she should start counting the passing trains that galloped dangerously close, buffeting her hair with their passage of air. The noise, like the trains, would come and go. She could have been here minutes or hours.

How many trains had gone by? Ten? Twelve? Noise travels differently underground, already she was disorientated. It was hard to breathe the musty old air. Her eyes were aching with the dust. Her mask, water, mobile, and extra provisions were all in Chris's rucksack. And there was no exit now. The MOD and Territorial Army had locked shut all access to the entrance above. If Chris didn't come back, she was trapped. She'd punch him when he turned up. In the gloom, her mind worked overtime, trying to work out the meaning of his voice in the cab. Lately, they'd grown apart. She was no longer sure she could trust her instincts about him. But he was a bastard to do this! Her seething temper kept her company for a while, but as her anger cooled, and she could feel the station's dampness entering into her throat, she started to feel the first chill fingers of fear.

And then the sounds started. Up there, right above her! A clank, like an iron pail being hit with a hammer. The air seemed to get even thicker. Now a scraping, quick footsteps, but who could it be? The walls crouched over her, thick, impenetrable. Something trickled over her fingers. A spider? She jumped to her feet, not sure in which direction to run. Along the half renovated platform a series of wooden, rotting partitions afforded a multitude of hiding places. She could still see the tiles, with their familiar brown, green and cream paint, but underfoot, the dust was so thick it felt like wading through sand.

She started running, breathing as quietly as she could, and shone her torch into each partition. Nothing but dust. Wasn't that what Chris had said? What was it, "All golden girls and boys all must, like chimney sweepers turn to dust?" Could it be Chris, somehow having a laugh? Secretly filming her panic? She stood pensively, shining her torch on the corridor ahead. Abandoned rooms gaped empty from off the corridor, each entrance painted a familiar green. Chris had told her the military had taken over this complex during the war. She moved towards the first room, noting how inside here the dust was thicker. A sharp smell assailed her senses.

It was like a museum piece. Old strategy maps hung on the walls. Coloured pins still clung to ancient boards. Why had they left it? Somewhere outside there was a clunk as if something had fallen. She froze, felt prickles forming on the back of her neck. She crouched by a table. Louder now, a sound like dragging steps. Was she imagining it? Perhaps this place was haunted. She'd heard that in the wartime, lots of accidents had happened, the details of which had been suppressed. There were rumours that some of the stations had been deliberately built through plague pits. And of course there were the suicide victims. But, surely the noise was getting louder?

Wasn't that a man's voice, talking to a woman? And another conversation, there in the corner, and there from the other room. All around her now, there was a searing singing, she could hear bubbles of noise, as if a crowd of people were talking all at once. She caught a few syllables here and there, but nothing distinct. It was as if the station was a hive of underground operation again, and she was stuck in time with her wires crossed. She crouched under the desk. If she made herself as small as possible, perhaps they wouldn't find her.

The sounds were louder now. They sounded like fireworks, way off distant. Perhaps it was bombs like in the blitz. After each crash of sound, the silence that followed it seemed louder. The room seemed to vibrate, there was an perceptible energy in the room that frightened her. A red heat seemed to be peeling her scalp away. Her eardrums recoiled, her breaths came out ragged and harsh. Her mind was racing, like a bicycle being pedalled by a demon. Abstractly, she thought about having a cigarette and inhaling all the fumes along with the nicotine. Quick as a flash, she recalled her hands slinking into Chris's bag, taking out the photographs. She was suddenly sure that the last corpse had been her donor with the silver streaks. He'd said his name was Jimmy. And now Jimmy was dead.

The air was getting heavier, she could feel her lungs struggling to cope. These rooms hadn't been ventilated properly for decades. Scrambling out on her hands and knees, she stood up and looked around the room again. Strangely, although it was the same, its colour and edges had become indistinct, and it was the shadows that pulled her eyes in. In front of her, the brown was becoming muddied, as if the very clay behind the façade of the walls was glowing. She fancied she could see shapes writhing within, taking form. Up above now, the booming resumed. She ran, choking as she went, trying not to fall over old bricks and planks of wood. Now she was really afraid, the platform stretched out even more, its uneven surface treacherous. Ugh! Something had got to her, she was spiralling out of control in the air. The pain lit her adrenalin for an instant, making it burn brighter, before her head hit the corner of a wall. A thin trickle of blood slid out of her nose.

When she came to, she thought she'd woken in the wrong house. Her head was burning and an insane thirst coursed through her body. She pushed herself roughly to her knees. The realization hit her like a brick. She was still trapped. Alive but underground. She wandered along to the edge of the platform. She could see in the dust her footprints where she had climbed over the wall. A peculiar silence hung in the air. They must have turned off the rails by now. She stopped, made herself count to 240. Every few minutes, a train leaves on the Piccadilly line. If she counted to 240, and no train went past, then it was safe to proceed down the tunnel.

"A hundred and one, a hundred and two."

Now she didn't care who heard. She had to get out of here. When she shone her torch at the mouth of the tunnel, it stared back at her. It would be like walking into a lion's mouth, the most dangerous thing that she had ever done. Her dry tongue tried to suck some moisture from the gaps between her teeth. She'd run the whole length, shining her torch the whole way. It could only be three minutes to South Kensington, two and a half if she went really fast. She could press the station alarm button once she got there. Say she got drunk and must have got out at the wrong stop.

Silence. Only the settling of the dust seemed audible. Most of London must be asleep. She had to go before the first train started, otherwise she'd be trapped here for another day. And she couldn't bear that. Having counted all the way, she wanted to wait a moment, perform another ritual. But there was nothing safe to cling to, the only thing to do was run.

The first thing she noticed was that it was hard to move quickly through the tunnel. The going was tricky, she had to take care not to trip on the rail. Anyway her head hurt and she felt sick. The scorch of burnt engine oil had soaked into the roof above her, and the air was acrid to breathe. She picked her way forward, steadier now, she'd got into a rhythm, forcing herself to move quicker. Now the tunnel was sloping sharply down, if she didn't keep her balance she might fall. Funny, it was harder going downhill than on the straight. A drip of water startled her from overhead. Could it be a leak? No, she had to keep going, she was not so desperate yet that she had to drink where that had come from. At the start, she'd thought she could see the end of the tunnel, but now it was stretching on, winding round corners, it felt like she would never get to the end of it. But it was too late to go back. Had to keep going. It was hard work though, her breathing was more precarious. If only she could breathe some real air, get the edge of fear out of her nerves. She was trotting like a pony, pumping her arms up and down, until at last she could see the end, the proverbial light at the end of the tunnel. Faster now, only another ten metres, it was getting light and easier to breathe every step.

She feels it before she hears it. The sound of a train galloping in the distance. Is it in front or behind? Doesn't know, runs on. The whole tunnel vibrates, as if in orgasm, as her sweating, dirt-encrusted figure struggles, makes a break for it.

Why haven't all those attempted suicides told anyone how loud it was by the track's edge? Her head will explode before her heart does. She almost dives through the edge of the tunnel, a dusty, demented thing. Instinctively, she heads into the welcoming air and light. The last Piccadilly train rushes to greet her.

To the last few waiting passengers, it seemed that she'd lain in wait to do this all along. "Suicide dive", the papers called it. A new and growing menace. The driver was suspended until further notice, owing to reports that an unidentified friend had accompanied him on that fatal night. A friend who had laughed hysterically as Rhonda's blood splattered the cab from underneath.

NB Brompton Road Station really exists. To find out more about the abandoned stations of the London Underground, check out this site: http://www.starfury.demon.co.uk/uground/index.html

The Courtyard

Robert Buckley

Arnold stepped back to inspect his mirror image. He still liked to dress, no occasion necessary. It was a matter of style and class, concepts long-faded from the modern world, he thought. A neatly pressed, summer-weight ivory suit and a crisp white shirt, silk embroidered vest, and a hat trained just right to complement the suit. His shoes gleamed with a high polish; he polished them himself, though at his age he lamented the passing of the neighborhood cobbler with shoe-shine service.

He smiled at himself, still a straight-backed six-foot-one, not stooped like many men his age. He touched the brim of his hat with the silver-tipped walking stick as a way of salute. Then he frowned as the weather report came over the radio. It would become humid later in the day, and he tended to perspire heavily. He decided he would take a cab to the cemetery rather than make the round-trip via public transportation. He envisioned himself wrinkled and wilting on the way home and sighed.

He called for the cab, then he stepped into the hallway, turning to lock his door. Sunlight poured through the cathedral windows at one end of the hall and reflected off the polished floor creating an ethereal gleam. He squinted into the glare as a figure made its way through the illumination. It was Ricker.

He reached up and pinched the edge of his hat brim as a gesture of greeting, but old Ricker just sneered and tottered by. Arnold caught an intense whiff of body odor as the man passed, his faded brown fabric shoes shuffling with each step. He winced at the yellowed, short-sleeve shirt Ricker wore and the trousers, which were a nondescript brown, cuffs high above his scrawny ankles, and the waist pulled high, almost up to his armpits.

Arnold shrugged and continued toward the elevator, but when Ricker entered it he decided to ascend the stairs. The box was too close to spend any time inside with a man who had sworn off deodorant since the death of his wife.

Ricker was already in the lobby when Arnold emerged to await his taxi. He caught the hushed conversation of the fretting retirees who gathered with him. Ricker, of course, was leading the chorus of doom.

"They'll put us all out, that's what they'll do."

"But they just can't put us out," Mrs Califani replied. "Not if we're paying our rents."

"Rents? The rents are going to go up. None of us will be able to afford to stay here. They got rid of rent control last year."

Mr Poole, his voice barely more than a whisper, said "Well, maybe we're grandfathered."

"Yeah," Pekins added. "Hey, why don't we ask Mr Arnold; he's a lawyer."

"Forget him," Ricker hissed. "That shyster would probably charge you just for asking. You know you can't trust that guy."

"But," Pekins demurred, "he seems like a nice fella. I've talked to him before."

"Pekins," Ricker yipped, "you'd be better off trying to move in with that son of yours that you're always bragging about, the one in Georgia."

Pekins shrugged. "Well, Josh and Mary would be glad to have me, but they don't have much space, you know, with the two boys and a baby on the way."

"Yeah, just as I thought. Kids don't got much use for you when you live too long."

Arnold continued to let on he hadn't heard them, and gazed past the lobby door. He recalled some weeks after settling his dad into elderly housing so many years before.

"Dad, so how do you like the place?"

"Aw, the place is all right, but I can't stand these old bastards."

Arnold had laughed at the time. "But Dad, you're an old bastard."

His father had chuckled wryly. "Yeah, well these people are miserable old bastards, and they didn't get that way just on account of they got old, they were mean and miserable all their lives."

Now Arnold smiled. Dad would have loved Mr Ricker.

The taxi pulled up and honked. He stepped through the door, leaving his neighbors to ponder their future.

Mount Auburn was as close as the rich and famous could come to taking it all with them. It was filled with ostentatious monuments to ostentatious lives. The tombstones and monuments read like a Who's Who, and the place was more like a private park than a cemetery. He had the cabbie leave him at the main gate. He didn't bother checking with the office, but strode into the magnificently landscaped necropolis with nothing but a clipping from the old *Herald Traveler* to guide him.

The Major's funeral had been covered by the newspapers of the day. The *Traveler*'s article included a photo of the tomb. It resembled the entrance to a small stadium, or perhaps the bow of a ship.

Arnold continued to walk the grounds, stopping to enjoy a pair of hovering hummingbirds sipping at honeysuckle. Then he spotted it. He didn't approach for some moments as he pondered why he had come. He hadn't gone to her funeral because he wasn't welcomed, and he certainly hadn't attended the Major's because he had no use for him. He'd never visited her grave before; he was not one for visiting graves anyway. What was there, after all? Grass and sod? Bones beneath?

But he had dreamt of her these past few months – frequently and vividly. He walked slowly, but deliberately toward the monument. A bronze statue of the Major stood at the front. It was smaller than he had imagined. Walter Jansen Peckering looked like a sour, wizened, old man. Arnold couldn't help but grin. He inspected the statue for the artist's signature, but he found none. Too bad, if he were still alive he would have sent him a note complimenting him; he'd captured the essence of the man.

Behind the statue set into the wall were bronze initials.

Arnold turned and faced the statue. "You egotistical bastard. Couldn't you afford more of a tribute to your own children than a set of initials?"

His eyes scanned the sets of letters from left to right. JFP had a small weathered flag set into a hole in the granite. That must be her brother Jay, the one who was killed in Korea. LKP had to be her brother Laurence, the one who "disappeared" somewhere in the Chilean Andes. She always suspected he just ran away from the old man. KMP also had a flag set next to it. That was Knowlton. His demise was a mystery, but it was believed it had something to do with his work with the CIA during the Missile Crisis.

Finally his eyes settled on ASP. He smiled at what her initials spelled. A bit of Cleopatra, he thought, if Cleopatra had wheat-blonde hair and pale blue eyes. Then his smile faded and a tight knot of sorrow twisted in his chest. He looked toward a distant fountain and was transported to that early summer day when she first gave herself to him.

She was driving him to Groton where her father was being honored for donating a pile of money he'd never miss. Whatever they were going to name for him, he would insist it be the Major Walter Peckering . . . Hall? Auditorium? Dormitory? Privy? Whatever. "Major", for a man who'd never been in the service. It was an honorary title he acquired by virtue of his membership in the Ancient and Honorable Artillery Company.

They got lost, probably around Ashby or Ashburnham, driving aimlessly from one country road onto another until she had thrown up her hands and said, "Enough! I'm hot."

He had been enjoying the ride in her convertible, watching her, her hair all blonde streamers in the wind. But she pulled off the road and gleefully pointed toward a pond within a grassy meadow. She hopped out and ran down the bank stopping just long enough to reach behind her and unbutton the green and yellow print sundress. She let it fall off her shoulders; she then dispatched the bra and pushed her panties down her pale legs.

He stood astonished, his eyes darting to all sides looking for anyone who might be nearby. But there was not another soul in that rural eden.

"C'mon, what're you waiting for?" She beckoned him with her arm, her small breasts lifting and jiggling with the motion, then she turned and her pale behind like a beacon enticed him to strip and follow her.

She plunged into the water and he, less gracefully, tumbled after her.

They swam, splashed and played in the warm waters as he grabbed her limbs and she tried to escape. Touching her naked flesh had given him an aching hard-on. And he blushed furiously when she clasped her arms around him and pulled him close to kiss him; her thighs captured his rampant cock between them.

"Oh, dear," she laughed. "I think I caught a fish . . . a very long, very firm fish."

He could barely speak. "For the love of . . ."

"Hmm, feels like a swordfish. I wonder what it would be like to be skewered by such a creature."

"Skewered?"

She took his hand and led him to the bank. They emerged from the pond like the first lovers on earth. She lay on the grass, her body glistening in the sunlight. She lifted her hands and curled her fingers, beckoning him to lie on top of her. Her legs spread as he trailed kisses over her breasts and shoulders. She reached beneath him and grasped his cock, guiding it toward the gate of her cunt.

"I can't wait," she pleaded. "Please."

He slid into her wet depths, pushing slowly until he could push no more and his balls jostled against her anus. Together they found a rhythm as he thrust and she met each thrust, then she crossed her legs behind his thighs and pulled him more deeply into her.

He didn't want it to end; he would gladly die inside her. In that moment he knew she was all he wanted or would ever want.

"I love you," he cried, then grunted.

"No-no, shhh . . . don't love me . . . just fuck me."

Fuck? Then it was an ugly word, but the way she said it, with a sigh and a whimper, it sounded as if it had slipped from the lips of an angel.

Then his thrusts became more desperate and he felt the roiling in his balls. She cried out and raked her nails down his back, and he launched his fluids into her, one spasm after another until he had emptied himself.

He rolled off her and she cuddled against him. Together they dozed in the warm sun. When they woke they were surrounded by indifferent cows.

They were in no hurry to get dressed. Groton was a write-off and the day was not one to waste. He had her lie on her tummy while he licked her thighs and nibbled her behind, and trailed kisses up her spine.

She mewed under his attentions. "Ohhh, yes, Mr B. Andrew Arnold . . . my ravisher . . . you've turned me into quite the content harlot."

"Hmm, not a strumpet?"

"Strumpet! Oh, I love that word, I love being your strumpet, Mr Arnold. I'm naked and at your mercy and I'm feeling so, so wicked."

He laid his hand across her ass – a gentle slap.

"Oww, and did I mention what a brute you are? Now that I've surrendered my maidenhead, cruel sir, the least you could do is tell me your first name."

"It's B."

"It is not . . . tell me. If you do I'll tell you anything you want to know, all my darkest secrets."

"Okay, it's Benedict."

"Oh, my gosh . . . Benedict Arnold?"

"It would seem my parents hadn't thought that one through."

She laughed, then wiggled her behind for more attention.

"Now, tell me the truth . . . why did you tell me not to say I love you?" he asked.

She shrugged and tugged a blade of grass. "I don't know . . . I don't want to hurt you."

"You don't love me?"

"Yes . . . I do . . . but . . ."

"But what? I want you; I want to make a life with you."

"Marriage? Babies?"

"If that's what you want . . . just tell me you'll spend your life with me."

She rolled over to face him and he couldn't help but take one of her nipples in his mouth. She moaned as he released the bud and looked into her eyes.

"My father . . ."

"What about your father?"

She shrugged again. "He's lost all his sons. I'm all he has left. He wants the firm to continue after he's gone . . . it's to be his legacy."

"Legacy to whom?"

"I can't let him down. We have to wait, darling. Just a few years, once everything is settled and my father knows he can – he can die and know it will go on."

"I've never wanted anyone before. I want you so much."

"A few years . . . I promise."

He hadn't thought to bring flowers. With difficulty he knelt, kissed the tips of his fingers, then touched them to her initials.

He stood and turned toward the gate. He boarded the track-less trolley that took him to Harvard Square, and then the subway back into the city.

The walk from the station was hot and beads of sweat dripped from his brow. He could feel his clothes become clingy and damp. But his thoughts again turned to her, and her final days.

She had agreed to move in with him by then, but she still would not marry him. It didn't matter to him as long as they shared their lives. He worked for a smaller law firm but the work was steady and the rewards more than adequate. She had taken the helm of her father's brokerage firm as he had wished her to do.

The illness came upon her quickly and it was unrelenting. The Major was cursed to live to see all his children die, but it was a curse that cut Arnold more deeply.

He was inconsolable, but pulled himself together to attend the wake. The funeral parlor was packed with political and financial power, and it was in front of that audience that the Major confronted him.

"You have no standing here!"

Arnold was so taken aback he could not speak at first.

"I know what you want. You want to steal what's mine – what I built. You fouled my only daughter with that aim, and I will not let you – damned lawyer! Vulture!"

After the Major's tirade, one could have heard a feather hit the carpet.

Finally, Arnold found his voice. "You miserable son of a bitch. I came here to mourn your daughter, but you, you selfish bastard, all you can do is whine about losing another heir. Damn you. I hope you live a long time – long enough to see it crumble."

He turned and strode away. The Major croaked the last word: "Ruthless!"

The irony was that the old man's epithet became his reputation. He was sought after as a relentless legal competitor; the man who almost finagled the Peckering financial empire out from under the Major himself. It was bullshit, of course. But the legend brought him clients and wealth.

He never got to see her in her casket, and he thought that was a good thing. He didn't want to remember her like that. When he did think of her, it was always of that day, by that pond, surrounded by those dumb cows.

He was withering in the humidity as he approached the building. He craved an ice tea, or perhaps a gin and tonic. A white pick-up peeled up to the curb beside him. He glanced at the advertising on the door: Urban Edens – Specialty Contractors.

A young woman hopped out from the driver side, stepped around the truck and into his path without giving him any notice. His breath caught as she walked toward the front door. It was her legs that grabbed his attention first, long and lean and tanned. They rose from a pair of tan work boots to the frayed edge of denim cut-off shorts that revealed the half-moons of her ass cheeks, winking at him with each cant of her hips. She wore a white hard hat but two wispy fringes of hair trailing down her neck revealed her as a brunette. A white, sleeveless tee was partly tucked into her shorts and partly hanging over one hip.

He thought to call to her, but she disappeared through the oak and glass door into the foyer. He made his own way to the door and stepped inside. She afforded him a glance and just a hint of smile, and then turned her attention to the rows of buttons and names of tenants. Her finger hovered over one and pressed.

His eyes fell to her breasts, which jostled freely beneath her tee. Their pale crescents peeked through the armhole.

"He's not home," he said.

She turned, and her lips curved into a perfect "O" before she said, "Excuse me?"

"Arnold – he's not home."

"Oh? Well do you know . . .?"

"I'm Arnold."

"Oh . . . well, good to meet you." She held out a hand.

He took it and said, "You're with P. L. Darby?"

"I am P. L. Darby. You can call me Lauren."

Her head cocked slightly. "Is there a problem, Mr Arnold? I can give you references."

"No, none at all. You're just . . . so young. But very highly recommended."

"I'm 27, Mr. Arnold. I learned the job from my Dad, who did it nearly forty years. I've been in business for five years."

"No need to sell me on your abilities or the quality of your work, Miss . . ."

"Lauren."

"Yes, Lauren. Anyway, come with me and I'll show you what I have in mind."

He held the door to the lobby and gestured to her to enter. Ricker was still holding court with several of the other tenants. Arnold wondered if he had been yammering all the time he was gone. They hushed as he escorted the girl to the elevator.

She was a few steps ahead of him when he heard a woman's raspy whisper: "Look at that girl – why her behind is practically falling out of those shorts."

"Never mind her behind, her boobs are showing," another said.

"Must be a call girl," Ricker hissed. "And a man his age – guess he thinks he can buy anything."

Arnold winced and hoped the girl hadn't heard. But when she reached the elevator she turned and a wry smile curled her lips.

"I'm sorry," he said. "They're a bunch of old farts without anything else to do."

Lauren shrugged. "Doesn't bother me, if it doesn't bother you. I like to be comfortable when I work. Do you think I look like a call girl?"

Arnold cleared his throat and looked down and to the side. He felt the heat rise in his cheeks and amazed himself that she made him blush.

He poked at the button to call the elevator. He turned when he felt a feathery tap on his shoulder.

"Mr Arnold?"

"Mrs Ginty. What can I do for you, dear?"

"Mr Ricker . . . well he's been saying the new owners will want to put us out, raise our rents. He said they won't let me keep my cat – use it as an excuse to evict me. You're a lawyer, could they do that? I can't lose my cat, he keeps the loneliness away, you know, since my Danny died. They won't let me have him in the public housing . . . I just don't know what . . ."

"There, there, Mrs Ginty." He took her hands and patted them. "No one is going to force you to give up your cat, or hike your rent."

"But . . . how do you know? Mr Ricker . . ."

"Mr Ricker likes all the attention you folks give him, and the only way he can get you to pay attention to him is to tell you all sorts of gloom and doom stories. He, frankly, doesn't know what he's talking about. Now, you listen to me, you have nothing to worry about."

The elderly woman seemed to take comfort in his assurances. "But, Mr Arnold, how do you know?"

"My dear, I'm a cunning old lawyer." He patted her hand again and then turned just as the elevator opened. He took Lauren's arm and guided her inside.

When the door closed and the car began to rise, Lauren said, "You sure are smooth, Mr Arnold. You haven't told those people that you bought the building?"

"I did it through a trust. I want to remain anonymous."

"Was it true, what you told that lady?"

He looked at her and frowned, one eyebrow cocked high. "By today all the tenants will receive letters from the trust. They'll be told there will be no rent increases during their tenancy. In some cases, such as Mrs Ginty, their rent will be cut substantially. And she will certainly be allowed to keep her cat."

"How about that old crab there . . . Mr. Ricker?"

"He too . . . especially him."

"Why? I have the feeling you don't like him much."

"Just to shut him up." He turned to her and grinned, a perfect devilish grin.

Lauren laughed out loud.

The car stopped and the doors opened. He led her down the hall to his apartment. Again he held the door for her.

She noted the sparse furnishings, a large sound system but no television. He led her to a table covered with blueprints and plans.

"Here . . . you see? This building was supposed to be a premier residence, but the Depression hit before the developers could realize their plan. They had planned for an elegant garden courtyard, with a fountain, shade trees."

"It looks more like a cocktail patio. I could recreate it, or rather, construct what they had in mind. Or . . ."

"Or what?"

"Create something unique."

"Such as?"

"My company is called Urban Edens, Mr Arnold."

"Eden, eh? I'll be satisfied with a cool place to enjoy a summer day."

She drew her finger across the top of one of the blueprints. "What does this mean?"

"It's what I intend to name the building."

"You want to give the building a name?"

"All buildings had names at one time. Back when a building

was an individual creation, and not a prefabricated box you set into the ground. This building was supposed to be called the Briarwood, but I have another in mind for it."

"Anstis? I've never heard that name before. It's – unusual. Almost as unusual as Phoebe, but way sexier."

"It's a very old name. You don't see it much anymore . . . except in cemeteries."

Then he looked at her and a crooked smile creased his face. "P. L. Darby – Phoebe Lauren?"

This time he made her blush. "Oh, you are smooth. I can't believe I gave away my deepest darkest secret. Well, if I agree to take this job, you'll have to tell me what the B in B. Andrew Arnold stands for."

"Will you take the job?"

"It won't be cheap. I'm selling something special."

"The price is no object."

"Then I'll take it. What's your first name, Mr Arnold?"

"Benedict."

"Benedict Arnold? Wasn't he a traitor?"

"He crippled himself for a cause, and got nothing but contempt for his sacrifice."

"So, I guess that means I can trust you?"

"You have my word. And in a day you'll have my name on a contract."

They shook hands. He showed her downstairs to the front door and they shook hands again. He smiled as the pale rounds of her ass winked at him again as she turned to leave.

At precisely 7:30 a.m. the buzzer rang in his apartment. He put the percolator on the stove and shuffled in slippered feet to the intercom.

"Yes? Hello?"

"It's Lauren. I need to see that courtyard of yours."

"I'll buzz you in. Wait for me in the lobby."

He dressed quickly and hurried toward the door, stopping to return to the stove and kill the flame beneath the percolator.

As the elevator doors parted he saw her. She'd modified her outfit somewhat: khaki shorts that didn't reveal more than her thighs just above her knees. The work boots were the same, but the tank top had been replaced by a pale blue denim shirt that tied just below her breasts, leaving her midriff bare. Her belly button? He wondered if he dropped a pebble into it how long it would be before he heard it hit bottom. The thought caused him to grin.

"Hi," she said. "Do I look funny or something?"

"Huh? Oh, no, I was . . . just thinking of something."

"This is Paulo."

A tall, lanky man stepped from behind him. He hadn't noticed him when he stepped off the elevator, despite the fact he was over six feet. His skin was a deep, roast coffee color.

"Paulo's going to take some measurements."

"Oh, of course." He shook the man's hand but felt vaguely annoyed at his presence.

"So," Lauren said. "Lead the way."

"Yes, come with me."

He led them through a door and a narrow corridor that ended with another door. He fumbled for a key, then tried to push it into the lock, which stubbornly refused to be penetrated. Lauren's companion tapped his shoulder and then produced a small can of WD-40 seemingly out of thin air. He took the key from Arnold and sprayed it, then sprayed the lock. He nodded as if to suggest he try it again.

Arnold slid the key in with no difficulty. "These doors are not used often. No reason to."

They stepped into harsh sunlight that reflected off a rectangular expanse of concrete.

"Ouch, this sure is ugly." Lauren squinted. "Any access for vehicles?"

"There is a driveway." He pointed toward an arch.

"Might be just high enough to get our equipment in here. Eventually we'll need a crane, though."

"A crane?"

"For the trees," she said.

Paulo went about measuring the area with a simple tape. As he did sounds jumbled from his lips.

"What's he saying?"

"I dunno, I don't speak Portuguese."

It took him no more than five minutes, then Lauren punched a button on her cell phone and handed it to him. Another rush of Portuguese, then he handed the phone back to Lauren.

"Hi, Rita. Yeah . . . yeah . . . okay."

Lauren put the phone away and took a block of note paper from a pocket in her shorts. She wrote a figure on it and handed it to Arnold. "Still want to do it?"

"How soon can you start?"

"You're sure? That's a pretty hefty figure. In fact, I think it's more than I ever estimated for a single job."

"Tomorrow?"

"Okay, you got a deal."

"I'll put that figure in the contract. You can fill out the details. I'll have already signed it."

The worry warts had already gathered when he led them back through the lobby. Ricker was holding center court as usual.

"It's a damned trick. We can't believe what's in these letters. I ain't signing mine."

"Well, I'm signing mine," Mrs Ginty said. "They cut my rent by $400 and they said I could keep my cat. How did they know I have a cat?"

"Me, too," Pekins added. "I mean, about the rent. And it says I can live here with no increase for as long as I want."

"I think it's wonderful," said Mrs Califani. "And I'm not going to look a gift horse in the mouth."

Arnold could hear the grumble in old Ricker's gut. He had nothing to say. He'd been shut up.

Arnold grinned; so did Lauren.

"Gee, no remarks about your call girl this time. I'm disappointed."

Paulo had already exited. Arnold held the door for Lauren. "See you tomorrow."

"The jackhammers will start at 8. You better warn the folks."

Arnold returned to his apartment, relit the flame beneath the percolator, and pondered how to fill the rest of his day. Perhaps a visit to the Museum of Fine Arts, or the Gardner.

He poured a cup of coffee and sat in his favorite chair, idly stirring the brew.

His mind wandered, and then he envisaged Lauren. She stood with her back to him, then slowly, sensuously, she slid her shorts off her hips. Her behind was a pair of pale globes, but her legs and back were tanned to a nut brown. She crossed her arms in front of her and lifted her top over her head.

Arnold shook the vision from his head. "Damn! What the hell is the matter with you? She's . . . she's young enough to be your . . . *granddaughter*."

But the vision had changed. Instead of Lauren's tanned skin, he saw – felt – a pale, peaches-and-cream back and derrière. His hands slid around her waist then up to caress two small breasts. He sat like that a moment, clutching thin air.

Then he did something he hadn't done in a long time. He unzipped his pants and closed his hand around his cock.

She stood naked for him, just behind his eyelids, up to her knees in the pond. He began to stroke himself slowly; he wanted it to last.

All the sensations of loving her came back in a rush. When the euphoria passed and he came back to reality, come oozed over his fist, and a tear trickled from his eye.

That evening he posted notices throughout the building about the construction. In the morning the building sounded like a war zone replete with automatic weapons fire. The jackhammers pulverized the concrete relentlessly throughout the morning. Finally the workers broke for lunch. The silence was palpable.

He peeked into the area and saw Lauren inspecting the chunks of concrete scattered about like a bomb had been dropped dead center. She wore green shorts, cut very close to her groin and a bright pink tank. No sign of a bra. Arnold took note of the workers' smiles and leers as they devoured their boss with their eyes. If Lauren was aware of their lascivious looks, she didn't appear to care.

Just as the men returned to their work, she bent over and took a can of soda from a cooler. She lifted it under her tank and rubbed it over her belly and then her breasts. The men's jaws dropped all at once, so did Arnold's.

Finally she touched the can to her cheeks, let her head fall back and took a long, slow swig.

Once Arnold shook off his reverie it occurred to him that a piano could have fallen off the roof and neither he nor the workmen would have noticed.

Lauren turned to her men. "Hey, what's everyone standing around for? Am I paying you guys, or what?"

It was a gentle, playful admonition and the men responded in kind with grins and chuckles before resuming their work.

Well, she knows how to handle men, he thought. *But how can they keep their minds on their work?*

He smiled, shaking his head, and then headed back to the lobby.

The tenants had gathered again, animated, talking. But Ricker stood off from the others, his head down holding a paper in his hands. Arnold walked past him toward the elevator.

"I don't get it," he heard Ricker say, as if to no one in particular.

"Excuse me?"

"I don't get it. Says here my rent has been reduced."

"Well, Sir, rather than wonder why, why not just accept the bit of good fortune that's come your way." Arnold turned and pressed the button to call the elevator.

"No one's ever done anything for me, never got any kind of break. When my wife got sick, why couldn't someone come along then and pay for the treatment she needed? Medicare didn't cover it; the lousy insurance I got when I retired didn't cover it. She died because I couldn't pay to keep her alive. Why the hell didn't someone come along then and say, 'Hey, Ricker, tell you what, we'll pick up the tab, and you won't have to lose your wife'? I don't need a break on my rent, I need my wife back."

The old man's chin trembled. "I guess they got no use for me, now," he said, gesturing to the others. "They all think I'm full of shit."

Arnold had an urge to put his arm around the old crab. "I . . . I'm sorry about your wife, Mr Ricker. I guess we all get bad breaks . . . nothing we can do about that. But, maybe we should take the ones we do get and make the most of them."

He gave in and gave the old man a gentle pat on the shoulder. Ricker nodded; he even managed a smile.

His surge of sympathy for Ricker surprised Arnold. Perhaps it was the old man's lament that good fortune meant little if the timing was off. Arnold had pondered that conundrum himself. By any measure he had led a successful life, with a long career that provided him wealth beyond his needs. But he was bereft without her. Finality has no remedy.

Inside his apartment he tried to put his mind to work. After Lauren and her crew departed another contractor would clean and sandblast the façade and repair the copper cornice and gutters. If only she could see it, his tribute to her.

A soft knock on his door became more urgent. He opened it to find Lauren in the hall.

"Hi, could I ask you a favor – I'm really sorry to impose, but . . ."

"Anything."

"A shower?"

"A . . . shower?"

"I have a date in a couple of hours; I'll never make it if I go home. I brought a change of clothes," she said and held up a fabric gym bag.

The word *date* struck him with a shallow thud. "Well, I suppose . . . sure."

"Thanks," she said and walked past him. "Where . . .?

"End of the hall."

"I really appreciate this. Damned concrete dust gets in my hair, and everywhere else."

"You'll find plenty of towels, help yourself."

"Okay . . . I should make it on time – gonna take my Dad for a steak dinner."

"Your Dad?"

"Yeah, he lives in one of those assisted living places in Brighton. Likes to get away from the old folks once in a while." She giggled, then disappeared into his bathroom.

She hadn't closed the door. "Wow, great old tub. Wish I could take a bath."

He smiled and sat back down at the table with his building plans, but he could not concentrate on them. Instead he listened to the water splash and Lauren hum a tune he didn't recognize.

The water stopped and the quiet became disquieting. Then Lauren stepped into the room holding the corner of a bath towel just above her breasts with one hand, and rubbing the wet out of her hair with a smaller towel in the other.

Arnold froze. The towel draped haphazardly over her barely shielding breasts, its opposite end trailed along the floor. Her hips were exposed and remained so even after she casually flopped into a chair. Still patting the moisture from her hair she said, "God, that feels good. Hope I didn't clog the pipes with all the grit."

When she looked at him their eyes locked. Self-consciously, now, she arranged the towel so it covered more of her.

"Oh, gosh. What you must be thinking."

Arnold shared her momentary embarrassment. "Um . . . what would I be thinking?"

She shrugged. "I'm used to going home and peeling everything off; I usually spend the rest of the night in the buff. Well, I might pull on a pair of fluffy socks. But, you see, I'm not much for wearing clothes."

"Oh," he nodded.

"Yeah, even when I was a little kid. I remember, dead of winter, and we'd get a snowstorm, and I must have been about five years old and I ran out in my all-togethers and made snow angels in the yard. It felt wonderful. Drove my mom nuts though, especially since I was still doing it when I was 14."

"I noticed you are rather . . . *nonchalant*, about exposing . . . um . . . skin. Your men . . . I don't suppose . . . um . . ."

She looked down at her knees and her voice became soft. "I know they look at me. But, hey, I figure it's just another perk for working for P. L. Darby."

He chuckled.

"Hey," she looked up, her grin flashing across her face. "I like my body. I don't have many what you'd call girlfriends, cause I get tired of hearing women piss and moan about their ass or their tits, or whatever. I like my body; it's a great body. I mean . . ."

She stood up. "Look at these legs, and I got a great ass and my boobs are really cute. So why should I worry about showing them off? I know I'm not the prettiest girl."

"Excuse me?"

She plopped back down in her chair. The towel poured off her thighs, but shielded her sex.

"Well, look at my nose," she said, tapping it with one finger.

"What about it?"

"Can't you see? It's crooked. It veers to the left. And my eyes . . ."

He strained to make out the defect.

"Oh, c'mon, can't you see? One's lower than the other. I swear, someone stepped on my face when I was a baby."

He shook his head and laughed. A clock chimed behind him.

"Oh, nuts," she said. "I'm wasting time. I need to dress."

"My bedroom . . . on the right. Feel free to close the door."

She stood and winked. "I don't think I need to. You're a gentleman, Ben . . . a real, old-styled gentleman – you won't peek."

"Old-styled, huh?"

"Oh, you know what I mean." She picked up her bag and retreated down the hall.

He exhaled a long sigh. What was he thinking when she said she had a date? Did he actually feel a pang of jealousy?

"What the hell were you thinking?" he whispered to himself.

She appeared again, a little black dress poured over her figure. She shook her still moist hair out, but she didn't seem to have put on any makeup. She didn't need it, he decided.

"Hey, Ben?"

No one had ever called him Ben. It made him smile. "Yes, Phoebe?"

"Cut that out. I was wondering, that picture on your dresser, the handsome guy leaning against the old Pontiac convertible – that's you, isn't it?"

"A lot of years ago."

"Hey, you're still handsome. Who's the girl? She's pretty."

He worked to keep the smile on his face, but he already sensed himself slipping into the shadow.

"Well, c'mon, she's a girlfriend, right? Did you two ever . . ."

"No!" he said abruptly.

"Well, she had a name, didn't she?"

He saw the darkness in his own features reflected in her eyes.

"Oh, Christ . . . Ben, I'm sorry, I'm just being nosy. I didn't mean . . ."

Something emerged from deep in his soul; he pushed the darkness away. "It's okay . . . really."

"I'm really sorry." Her voice was soft again, and tentative as a timid child's.

"It's just . . . she died."

"I'm sorry. She was . . . very special, wasn't she?"

"Yes . . . yes, she was."

"I didn't mean to pry, please . . ."

"And her name was . . . Anstis."

There was something in her eyes – a benediction. It dissolved the darkness.

"This building – what you're doing for the people who live here – it's for her."

"A poor tribute, but yes."

"You're a good man, Ben."

He tried to swallow down the thickness in his throat.

"Young lady, there's a very lucky gentleman awaiting your company."

"Yup." She stood and turned toward the door.

He stepped around her and opened it for her. Then he took her hand and kissed it behind her knuckles. "Lauren, I think you are very . . . very pretty."

"Oh, you are smooth. Thank you, Ben."

"I hope you find your father well. Have a good evening."

She winked and stepped into the hall.

He spent much of the rest of the evening looking out his window over the avenue toward the Fenway, enjoying a peace he hadn't felt in a long time.

*   *   *

Spring yielded to impatient summer. The days grew warmer and Lauren matched the rising temperature with her scant work attire. The courtyard was just a crater now as teams of men worked to install piping in the pit.

Lauren continued to wear shorts cut close to her groin – boy shorts, she had called them, but Arnold decided there was nothing boyish about them. She had taken to wrapping her breasts in little more than a kerchief, and her body turned a deep brown as the days and the work went on.

The tenants had become curious and frequently wandered into the worksite. Lauren would gently shoo them away for their own safety, but not before she'd exchanged pleasantries. They had become quite fond of her, though mildly disapproving at her lack of coverage.

The building would become eerily quiet whenever the crews broke for lunch. Arnold would inspect the progress then. Frequently he would find Lauren with one or more of the tenants chatting and enthusiastically explaining the job.

Then there was the Monday afternoon he found Mrs Califani smoothing sun block over Lauren's back.

"A tan is fine, young lady, but you don't want your skin to look like shoe leather before you're even 30, do you?"

"No, ma'am," Lauren answered like an obedient school girl.

"And you really shouldn't be teasing these boys like you do."

"Teasing, ma'am?"

"In my day, ladies didn't show so much . . . well, so much of themselves."

"But, ma'am, it gets so hot . . ."

"Hot's the word. Now, if you were my daughter . . ."

"I'd be a very lucky girl."

Mrs Califani stopped smoothing the lotion over Lauren's shoulders. Her hand went to her throat, and Arnold thought he saw her chin tremble.

"Why . . . thank you, dear." She took Lauren's face between her hands and kissed her forehead. "Well, I better go see about my pasta sauce . . . I left it simmering."

The old woman nodded to Arnold as she hurried past, her eyes wet, but a smile spreading over her face.

Lauren's eyes met Arnold's. "She's a nice lady."

"She's certainly taken a shine to you," he offered.

"Wish my mom was as nice as Mrs Califani." Lauren stood and stretched, sunlight glaring off her newly lotioned skin.

"How's the work going?"

"The piping will be completed today."

"For the fountain?"

"The pond."

"No fountain?"

"I was thinking more of a waterfall. Hey, you told me not to show you the plans; you wanted it to be a surprise. You still trust me, don't you?"

"Implicitly. A waterfall, huh?"

"A little one."

She rallied her men back to work. They still devoured her with their eyes, but there was obvious respect too for a boss who knew her craft.

"A goddess with a hard hat," Arnold mused.

The following day a dump truck was painstakingly guided beneath the arch with barely an inch to spare. It unloaded rich, dark earth into the crater and returned three more times. Another crew arrived to smooth out the soil and place stones to mark off where trees would be planted.

It was quieter work than had gone on the previous two weeks. Arnold came by late in the afternoon as the workers were breaking for the day. He was surprised to find Lauren and Ricker chatting in the one area of the courtyard where a shadow had formed shade from the unrelenting sun. Her voice was hushed, but he could make it out clearly. She spoke to Ricker in an instructive tone.

"Just try it," she said. "And don't be a shy guy. Oh, and don't forget . . ." She took something out of a plastic bag and tossed it to Ricker who fumbled it and finally clasped it to his chest.

Ricker nodded and turned toward Arnold; he tottered past with a huge grin.

"What was that about? What did you give him?"

"Seems Alvin is sweet on Emmeline."

"Alvin? Emmeline?"

"Mr Ricker and Mrs Ginty."

"Go on!"

"It's true. He was asking me how he should ask her for a date."

"Ricker? So what did you toss to him?"

"Deodorant." She laughed.

"Thank God."

"Hey, Ben, can I ask you another big favor?"

"Name it."

"Can I take a bath in that big old tub of yours? I feel like the dirtiest woman on the planet and I've been dreaming of a good soak ever since I saw it. I brought a change of clothes."

"Of course."

"Good, I already picked up some bubble bath." She grinned as she held up the same plastic bag from which she had retrieved Ricker's deodorant.

Arnold led her to the lobby and the elevator. The tenants who passed through all made it a point to greet her and exchange small talk. A young woman who had been known among the tenants as "the single girl with the two babies" got off the elevator.

"Hi, Maria. We still on for Thursday?"

"Lauren, yes, thank you. Then just two more classes and I get my certificate."

"Cool."

They stepped onto the elevator.

"What was that about?" Arnold asked, one brow raised.

"Oh, Maria's a nice girl. She was asking me if I might have some work for her. I said I'd teach her landscaping, but she's going to school to be a vet tech or something. Anyway, I told her I'd sit her kids Thursday. She usually has to haul them across town to her mom's. It's no big deal."

"You're babysitting?"

Lauren shrugged then stepped into the hallway as the doors opened. Arnold stepped ahead of her and opened his apartment door.

"Yuck! Can't wait to get into that tub." He watched her stride down the corridor as if she lived there. She tugged at the knot binding the fabric around her breasts. It fell to the floor.

"I'll get that," she said, as he watched her bare back disappear into his bathroom.

He sat looking out his bay windows listening to the water fill the tub. Then it stopped and he heard Lauren's long, heartfelt "Ooooooo!" as she settled into the water. He smiled at the sounds of gentle splashing and thought that he would miss her when the job was done.

He wasn't prepared for the sadness that welled up inside his chest. Perhaps they could keep in touch. He would like to take her to the city's museums, symphony, show her its hidden treasures. But no, she was a young woman; she had to have a life beyond this temporary meeting at life's crossroads. There had to be a young man somewhere in the picture.

"Hey, Ben! Where'd you go?"

"I'm right here . . . do you need something?"

"No . . . you just got awfully quiet. C'mere and keep me company."

"Young lady, I don't think that would be proper."

"Oh, c'mon, I'm covered in bubble stuff. Besides, I want to talk to you about the job."

He got up and walked the short corridor to the bathroom, took a breath and stepped through the opened door. He put the cover down on the toilet and sat. *So dignified*, he thought.

Lauren was indeed shielded by the thick layer of foam up to her collarbones. But then she raised one leg out of the water. The suds slid down her limb and she moaned, "Oh, this feels so good."

"Um, you said you wanted to talk about the job."

"Yeah, well, we're all set for the trees, but we'll need to bring in a crane to lift them over the building."

"My God, how large are these trees you're bringing in?"

"Well, pretty big . . . and tall. We won't be able to back them through that arch. The dump trucks barely fit. Anyway, I have to clear permits with the city so we won't start that phase until next week."

"Oh."

She noticed his frown. "Um, I have a couple of other jobs I have to get started too, so . . ."

Already he was going to miss her being around, if only for a few days. "I – of course, I understand."

Lauren sat up and he couldn't avoid noticing her brown nipples, pixilated through the translucent suds.

"Ooops." She slid back beneath the foam. "Sorry . . . don't mean to make you feel uncomfortable. I just . . . forget."

"Hmm, well, I never knew a young woman who was so casual about . . . well about . . ."

"Letting a man catch me naked?"

"Yes, well, you explained your . . . um . . . predilections."

"Ha! My Mom would have used another word. She just knew I was bound for Hell."

"Maybe she was just being protective."

"Mrs Califani, she's protective. She scolds me for – what did she call it? – running around like a bollicky bambina. But my Mom, well, see . . . she found religion."

"Oh?"

"Yeah. I guess it happened right after I was born. Dad wanted to have more kids, but he said something happened to Mom; she got all weirded-out about sex. Then she kinda fell in with some local church. Before he knew it, she's telling him she's getting a divorce. It really hit my Dad hard, you know? He really loved her – at least, he loved the girl he married, the one she used to be.

"Anyway, Mom was determined to *save* me. She got custody and took me out west, hooked up with some congregation of fundamentalists. I had to go to church school. That was hell. It was beautiful country though, so every chance I'd get I'd shed my clothes and go wandering through the woods. Got caught, got punished. I don't know how I held out so long. I just lived for my 18th birthday, especially after I got caught playing doctor with a boy."

"Well, young kids are curious about each other."

"I was sixteen."

"Oh."

"Yeah, well, after that my Mom told me I was going to marry

some kid in the congregation just as soon as I reached legal age. And that I better learn to be obedient and all this other crap. Can you imagine? Like it was the Middle Ages or something. The morning of my 18th birthday I packed some stuff, grabbed the money I managed to save and took a bus all the way back to the East Coast. I moved in with my Dad, and we've been together ever since – well, until he moved into the assisted living place."

"I take it your Dad is more . . . tolerant of your proclivities."

"He loves his little girl." She smiled. "He let me be me, let me find my own way. I went to law school, you know."

"No."

"Yeah, but I loved the work I did with my Dad and wanted to keep the business going when he retired. I wasn't much for the lawyer gig anyway – no offense, of course."

"None taken," he chuckled.

"I remember, though, discussing a case in class – Remy vs. Halloran Industries."

Arnold's back stiffened.

"Halloran's lawyer had pretty much torn the plaintiff's case to shreds. Everyone expected him to seek a directed verdict of dismissal. But then they settled – it was one of the largest settlements up until that time. I wondered why – until I met the great B. Andrew Arnold."

Arnold's eyes were fixed to his knees, but then he looked straight into hers. "A good lawyer has to do what's in the best interest of his client. Children were injured. And Mr Halloran was a decent man. If he had walked away with a judgment, he would not have been able to live with himself. It would have eaten him alive."

"Yeah . . . that's kinda what I thought. Here, help me up." She reached up her hand.

He took it and she stood, the soapy foam clothed her nakedness momentarily until gravity began to undress her. "I'll need to shower now."

"Yes . . . of course." He left her and began to reach for the door to close it. Then he shrugged and left it open. The sound of spraying water followed him back to his living room.

Later she emerged, her hair still damp. She was dressed in a modest top and faded jeans.

"Ben, that courtyard of yours – I'm going to make something very special for you." She smiled and then stepped through his door.

Arnold occupied himself with other matters, different contractors and crews of workmen. He scheduled a cleaning of the façade, and brought in specialists to restore the lobby and install new lighting. But it was otherwise quiet throughout the building, and the tenants behaved like a bunch of kids moping around at the end of summer vacation. They missed her too, and the gentle, rejuvenating electricity she brought to the place.

Several had stopped him in the lobby or hallways and asked him if she would be back. He assured them she would; there was still more work to do on the courtyard.

"But, what is it going to be?" Mrs Riley asked him.

"An oasis, dear, a nice cool and shady place to enjoy the summer days. And Miss Darby assures me it will be completed in time to enjoy most of the rest of the season."

"Oh, that sounds wonderful. She's such a sweet girl – and so capable. Doesn't wear a lot of clothes, have you noticed?"

"Yes, Mrs Riley, I've noticed."

In the evening he sat looking out his window beyond the rooftops. The ballpark lights glared in the distance. He thought of the few ballgames they had attended, and while he was a casual fan, she was indeed a fanatic. He remembered how her hair shone golden in the bleachers, and how many a head had turned in her direction, and how even the pitchers in the bullpen vied to get her attention.

His memories of her had become so vivid, so filled with sunshine and bright colors.

The knock at his door startled him. He groaned as he pushed himself out of the seat he'd occupied for more than an hour, and shuffled toward the door.

The knock came again as he turned the doorknob and swung it open.

"Hi."

"Lauren? What . . ."

"Babysitting, remember? It's Thursday – Maria just got home. I need to ask you something, Ben."

"Sure, come in." He noted her attire, modest for Lauren: jeans and a sleeveless tee, under which her breasts jostled unhindered.

"Gee, did I wake you up? Where are the lights?"

"I like it dark. There, flick on a lamp."

Lauren clicked the switch on a small end table lamp. It didn't do much to illuminate the room. She sat on the small couch and crossed her legs.

"What's on your mind?"

"Maria – she's not a tenant."

"What do you mean? I've seen her around the building – well, it must be two years."

"No – I mean, she just kinda moved in. See, she used to know someone who lived here and when that person moved out, she moved into his flat."

"A squatter?"

"I guess. Ben, she had to move out of her mom's place because she got into trouble with some people in her neighborhood – dangerous people. The poor kid doesn't really have a dime; she's trying to get through school so she can support her kids. Now she's afraid, with the ownership change, that they're going to find out she's been here all this time not paying rent."

Arnold laughed out loud and grabbed his sides. "Jesus! What a bunch of boobs. How the hell did the managers miss her? Didn't they realize they had a vacant apartment?"

"The thing is, Ben, she kinda had to do favors for the former super."

"Favors? You mean Carlos? He disappeared before the sale." Then his brow furrowed and his eyes narrowed. "What kind of favors?"

"I don't think I need to draw you a picture. In exchange he fixed it so the management company didn't know."

"I always had a feeling about that . . . what a slimy bastard."

"Ben, she did what she had to do, but now she's scared, she's . . ."

"Tell her to sign up for the Section 8 housing aid at the public assistance office. That'll cover her rent. Tell her it's okay."

"Thanks . . . I knew you'd . . . I mean, I just knew . . ."

"Forget it. Just another lost lamb amongst the flock."

She lifted a brown paper package onto her lap. He hadn't noticed it before.

"This was downstairs. It's addressed to you."

"Oh?"

"Can I open it? I love opening packages."

"I . . . well, what is it?"

She shrugged and began to tear at the brown wrapping. She lifted an object shielded in protective wrap. She gingerly peeled it away.

"Oh, my gosh, it's like a miniature portrait. It's . . . Anstis."

Arnold reached and Lauren stood to give him the portrait that was about as large as a dinner plate. She stood to his side and peered over his shoulder as he held it.

"I . . . I almost forgot. I'd seen this listed in an estate auction. I couldn't believe it. That was months ago."

The girl in the portrait sat on a boulder in a meadow. She was clad in blue jeans, holes in the knees, which she hugged together. She wore a loose flannel shirt, one shoulder covered with a spray of blond hair.

"May I?" Lauren reached for a typed index card taped to the frame. " 'Portrait of Anstis Sally Peckering – artist unknown.' God, she was pretty. You must have loved her so much."

He didn't say anything. Lauren touched his shoulder, then returned to the couch.

Finally he looked up from the portrait, but he looked past Lauren.

"Old Ricker was right – timing is everything. That's what I've had, a lot of time. I think – I think you can just live too long. All that time – all so meaningless."

His eyes focused on Lauren. "Her father – oh, he was a piece of work. He thought his immortality was vested in a company, a bloodless, soulless thing that couldn't love you back if you wanted it to. She wasted what time she had – what time we had – so his company would go on. Well, it didn't – I'd be surprised if anyone even remembers it. So, he made his mark? Plenty of people make their mark – you know what, they still end up in the graveyard, and that mark fades real fast."

Lauren had drawn up her knees and hugged them to her chest. Her hair spilled over one shoulder.

"I wish . . . I wish my Mom and I could have gotten together one more time. I wrote to her after I left and got settled in with Dad, but she never wrote back. We only got word last year that she'd died. I was always sorry for that. She was my Mom, after all, and I guess . . . I guess I loved her. I just wish we could have said that to each other, never mind we'd never see eye-to-eye about other stuff. But it never happened. I'm sorry for that, but I'm not – that is, I couldn't do anything about that, you know what I mean?"

He sighed. "It's just the finality of it."

He lifted the portrait. "She was my wife. She never took my name; we never had words spoken to that effect, or a piece of paper to certify it. But she was my wife."

Lauren stood up and then stepped in front of him. She gently tugged at the portrait. "Can I borrow this for a little while? I promise I'll bring it back safe and sound."

"I . . . suppose."

She leaned down and kissed him on the forehead. "You're a good person, Ben, but I think . . . well, it seems like you're always beating yourself up, and I can't figure out why."

She patted his shoulder. "I gotta get going. Have to drive to the Cape tomorrow to scout out another job. See you Monday. And, thanks again – about Maria."

He nodded, then watched her go.

It rained that weekend and the gloom penetrated to the building's corridors. It seemed as if everyone had locked themselves away in their apartments. But Monday dawn broke clear and cooler than it had been.

Arnold bolted up in bed at the sound of sirens from the street below. He hurried to the window and looked down to see two police cruisers shepherding an immense crane truck along the avenue. It stopped in front of the building.

He hurriedly dressed and went downstairs. Some of the other tenants had gathered there.

"I thought they were fire trucks," Mrs Ginty said.

"We would have heard the alarms, dear," Ricker assured her.

Dear? Arnold smiled. He went out to the street where Lauren gestured to the crane operator. She wore gray boy shorts and a cropped T-shirt, and as she stretched he knew it was just a matter of millimeters before the crescent swells of her breasts would be revealed. A detail cop's mouth hung open as he watched her impromptu choreography.

A flatbed truck hauling a large pine tree pulled next to the crane, restricting the avenue. The cop reluctantly peeled his eyes off Lauren and set about directing traffic. Arnold stayed back, deciding it was best not to distract her. A crowd had gathered and as the crane began to lift the pine above the truck they became more vocal.

Other workmen on the roof calculated the distance needed to clear the building and signaled the crane operator. The big pine was swung out of sight as the crowd broke into applause. The truck pulled away and another took its place. This one carried several smaller, deciduous trees. They too were lifted over the building, then another pulled up – another pine. It took all of the morning and most of the afternoon before the operation was completed. The cruisers then guided the crane up the avenue.

Teams of men pounded stakes through the root balls of the larger trees as Lauren supervised. Arnold's curiosity overwhelmed him and he tapped her shoulder.

"What are they doing?"

"Trees this big – you just don't plant them like a pansy. You gotta make sure their roots are stable. You don't need one of these things toppling over onto your roof."

By late afternoon a small forest had appeared in the barren courtyard. An entirely different landscaping team had taken over, nearly all young women, who had set about installing smaller trees and shrubs and rolling out carpets of grass. Green hardhats, khaki shorts and white tees stained with dirt and perspiration made up the uniform worn by these busy sirens. Whether tall or petite, black or white or Asian, the crew of a dozen young women, their bodies lean and taut and shimmering in rivulets of sweat, had drawn a crowd of admirers among the bachelor tenants.

Arnold took note of the blissful smiles and dubbed them the lazy lechers. He approached Lauren again. "Hey, you want me to move these guys along?"

"Aw, let them stay and enjoy the view. The girls are getting a kick out of it. But, for the next few days, I'm going to have to insist on everyone staying clear of the site. When it's done I want it to be a surprise, okay?"

"Okay – if you say so."

He took another look at the lecher bench and a few signaled him to join them.

"Go ahead," Lauren said and winked.

For the next few nights Lauren worked with a small team of men and women. They would emerge and then disappear from the now wooded oasis like ants coming and going from their anthill.

Arnold checked by around 8:30 as Lauren had just dismissed her crew. She doffed her hard had and let her dark hair fall in tangles over her shoulder. She was streaked with dirt, her skin moist.

A heady aroma of perspiration and foliage wafted from her. She sniffed at one armpit and winced. "God, I stink!"

Stink? Arnold was awash in her scent of raw femininity and earth. He thought of how it would feel to hold her naked in his arms. He shook the thought from his mind.

"Shower?" he offered

"Yes, please."

As she stepped past him he took a long sniff. It was almost a shame to wash it off.

Lauren emerged from the shower as usual, giddy and girlish, and haphazard about covering herself with the bath towel.

"Could I interest you in a light repast?" Arnold said, bowing slightly.

"Ben – are you asking me out?"

"A coffee, a sandwich, and some conversation: whadya say? I

know a place close by; they're open late and they sell these amazing pastries."

"Okay – it's a date. Soon as I get dressed."

Would she be just as comfortable strolling the city streets naked? He wondered.

She took his arm as they walked the block and a half to Hank's. There he was greeted at the entrance by a large woman with a dazzling grin.

"Andy! Child, where you been? Haven't seen you since . . . well, it's been a long time."

"Hello, Hank. I know, it's been a while. I missed your turnovers, though. Missed your muffins too, but . . ." He patted his stomach.

Hank reached over and patted it too. "Hmm, well I see I got my work cut out for me. And, who's this pretty child?"

"My friend, Lauren."

"C'mon in honey. Like as not he'll break your heart too, but it sure be worth the ride."

Lauren cast a quizzical glance at Arnold as Hank showed them to a table. They each ordered a sandwich and coffee, but Hank insisted on a pastry tray. "A sampler," she called it.

"Hmm, what is this? Raspberry and . . . something else." Lauren closed her eyes as she munched the flaky pastry.

"Amazing, isn't it? I had to stop coming in here before I weighed three hundred pounds."

She brushed a flake off her lips. "So, I take it from what Hank says you've brought other dates here. A real ladies' man, huh?"

He sipped his coffee. "A few. A man . . . well, there are needs, urges . . ." He shook his head and a smile crossed his face. But she thought it was a sad one.

"Ben, I hope . . . I hope I didn't make you feel bad. It's not like I thought you were being – I dunno – disloyal to Anstis. She'd understand, I know she would."

He nodded and his smile widened. "I know she would too. It's okay. But . . ."

"But?"

"How about you? There has to be some young man in your life – some poor, bewitched, enchanted young man."

She shrugged, smiled, and looked down at her cup. "Sure, there have been a few – well, maybe more than a few. But they were mostly for, you know, like you said, scratching an itch."

"Oh?"

"I, uh, like sex. Truth is, I really like sex. I like to play in bed. I like to play with guys. I gotta be careful, though. Guys can be so . . . oh, possessive isn't quite the right word. Maybe – yeah, serious, that's it. Some guys can be just too serious about sex, you know? Like, they get all worried about whether they were as good as the last guy I was with, like they were in some competition. Jeesh, just have sex, have fun, live in the moment. Just play."

"Hmm, I suspect a lot of the men who work for you would be all too willing to . . ."

"No-no-no! Never have sex with an employee. That's an iron-clad rule. Of course, it sure would be easier to get dates."

"Never ever?"

"Well . . ." Her eyes focused past him. "There was one guy."

"Uh-huh."

"He wasn't technically an employee. The job was over and he was moving to Florida. But . . ."

"That's a heavy-duty sigh, my dear. Who was this Lothario?"

"Aw, he was just a kid."

"A kid?"

"Nineteen. Jeesh, I was 25, older vamp robbing the cradle. But Arkady – he was from Russia – I knew he had a huge crush on me. He was tall and blond, and he was so sweet and shy, and on his last day he gave me flowers and told me he'd never forget me . . . well, I invited him home."

"Sounds pretty slick to me."

"Oh, no he was not. In fact . . ." she grinned. "He was a virgin. God, I had to show him just about everything. But he learned fast. Oh, and he was just so . . . sweet and fumbling and . . . God, I screwed his brains out."

Arnold felt a pang of jealousy, but at the same time a grin spread across his face. "Broke him in, eh?"

"Yeah. You know, I liked that, knowing I was his first. He went to work for some cousins in Florida right after that. I like to think he's a big stud down there, all on account of me."

"Yeah, getting more tail than a toilet seat."

Lauren almost spit her coffee across the table. "That's awful!" she laughed.

He laughed with her, but the shadow reappeared.

"I – I wish you could have known her."

"Anstis?"

"You two would have really gotten along – you're a lot alike, and then . . . you're different. Ah!" He slapped his hands on the table. "I wish . . . I just wish I could . . ."

She reached over and took his hand.

"Getting late," he said finally. "Better send you home, and get these old bones to bed."

Arnold stirred from his slumber and lifted one heavy eyelid to peer at a pink morning sky beyond his window.

"Another day . . . still breathing." He could never return to sleep once he had awakened, so he slung his legs over the edge of the bed and forced himself to stand. He stumbled toward the bathroom, then emerged to perform his morning ritual with the percolator.

The courtyard would be finished soon. Probably by that night. Lauren had not permitted anyone to enter the wooded rectangle that now graced the area that had been barren concrete.

But she would be gone, and he felt that familiar hollowness assert itself again, like a part of him was missing.

He drank his coffee and dressed casually in khaki pants and a short sleeve shirt. He retrieved a straw panama hat from a closet shelf and stepped into the hallway. Before he reached the elevator, its door opened and Maria emerged. She grinned when she saw him, and her pace increased as she approached him. She flung her arms around him and her head thudded against his chest.

"*Gracias, tio . . . muchas.*"

"Huh?"

"Lauren told me you would speak with the owners for me. I can stay."

"Well, of course you can stay, dear. Did you get approved for the Section 8 voucher?"

"Yes, and this letter . . . it says it covers my rent."

"Fine, fine. Well, I guess you can complete school."

"Yes, thank you."

He gently pried her arms off him, though she was reluctant to let go. Finally he patted her hands, and said, "You're most welcome, dear. Now, I have to get along."

Minutes later in the lobby, Mrs Califani stopped and hugged him too.

"That's wonderful what you did for poor Maria."

"Well, I really didn't . . ."

"Oh, don't be modest, Mr Arnold. We all know you work for the new owners. But, who are they? They must be wonderful people."

"They prefer to remain anonymous, dear. Now, I need to check the progress on the courtyard."

He smiled and tipped his hat as he turned.

"He's such a gentleman," he heard Mrs Riley say as he strode toward the courtyard entry.

He found Lauren conferring with a petite Asian girl and stood back until they'd finished. The Asian girl then hefted a small pallet of flowers and disappeared behind the trees.

Lauren's face brightened into a wide grin when she saw him. "Hey, Ben, tonight's the night."

"Huh?"

"I'm going to give you a sneak preview before tomorrow's dedication."

"Dedication?"

"Sure, there has to be a dedication. Tonight at around 9 p.m. I want you to come down here and just follow the path. But, don't stray off it . . . you might get lost."

"Lost?"

"Well, maybe a little disoriented. Oh, Ben, you're going to love it. I gotta go help Li now. Remember, 9 tonight."

She disappeared behind the trees like a wood gnome. He stood back and gazed up at the trees. They were so tall, like they'd been there a lifetime. She had created a miniature forest.

He did not see her the rest of the day, but instead was busy fielding inquiries from tenants who had evidently determined he was an agent of the new owners. Who were they? Why had they cut their rents and promised them tenancies for life?

"Are they aliens?" old Mr Wilkie had asked.

He was disarmingly evasive, a talent he had polished in courtrooms, but at last he had to retreat to his apartment. He dozed, but came awake with a start. It was already 9 o'clock. He hurried downstairs and out to the courtyard. A bright crescent moon hung almost directly overhead and a star tumbled off its lower tip. The sky was a deep velvet blue and the air was sweet with floral scents carried on a gentle breeze.

He stepped onto the path and entered Lauren's wooded realm. Garden lights illuminated the way dimly, but curiosity led him into the trees. It was as lush as any forest, and as he continued he was startled at the sensation that he was falling deeper into the woods.

He thought he should have already emerged at the other side, but he continued to stumble and feel his way between the dark arboreal sentries.

"This – this can't be happening. My God, I think I'm lost." The woods just didn't end.

"It's just a courtyard," he said to himself, but an unsettling disorientation had come over him. He looked up to the crowns of the trees and fixed his eye on the star dangling off the moon. He followed its course, but found he had to readjust his progress each time he stepped around a tree or shrub.

At last he found the path again, and in the distance – distance? – he heard running water, and the sounds of a human being playing in that water.

He came into a little clearing with a small grotto. Benches ringed the area. A ribbon of a waterfall fed the pond where Lauren was doing lazy backstrokes, her bare nipples pointing toward heaven. Arnold was transfixed at the sight.

Then she waved and stood up to her waist, naked and shimmering in silver rivulets of reflected moonlight.

"Well, what do you think?"

"My, God, girl. How . . . I mean . . . I feel like I'm in the middle of a forest. I got lost . . ."

"Lost? Ben, I told you not to wander off the path . . . not until you get used to it."

"Used to it? But, how . . .?"

"It's like an optical illusion, except that I suppose it's a full three-D illusion. It's just the way we arranged the trees and shrubs. You can't walk in a straight line so you think you're walking forever."

"But, when I heard you – it sounded like you were far off."

"Acoustics – it's just how the sound travels through the trees."

He stepped back and sat down heavily on a bench. "My God. You did create an eden."

"You like it, then?"

"It's more than I could have imagined. But Lauren, I can't have people getting lost."

She laughed. "The effect isn't as strong in daylight."

He breathed in the scents of the flowers and heard birds sing overhead.

"Night birds," she said, as she stepped out of the pond without any regard to her nakedness. "It doesn't take them long to settle in once they find to a place like this in the city."

Arnold looked at her as if he were appreciating a work of art. His eyes caressed every curve, every shadow and nuance of her taut body.

"Young lady, this is worth so much more than what I paid you."

"It was my pleasure. I–I never wanted a job to be as perfect as this one. I wanted to do it for you, Ben."

She strolled slowly toward him, and then she knelt.

"You're such a good person, Ben. But you're so sad. You don't deserve to be sad."

"No one does, Lauren. But in the end, it doesn't matter, and deserving has nothing to do with anything. Good person, bad person, you can get the ground yanked out from underneath you and lose everything you ever cared about. Nothing lasts – neither good deeds nor bad, it all ends the same."

"I can't believe that."

Her fingers fumbled with the button on his fly. He pushed her hands away.

"No. No, Lauren."

"Yes."

"I – I won't have it. You're a young girl, a beautiful woman."

"You're a wonderful man. Let me . . ." Her hands slid up his thighs.

"No, please. That's one indignity I would never inflict on you."

"Indignity? Ben, I want to do something for you . . ."

"Not this . . ."

She had opened his fly and inserted one hand inside his boxers.

"Let me – just tonight – let me be Anstis for you."

He looked into her eyes, unable to speak.

"And maybe . . . for her too."

Her hand had found his cock and as she freed it from its confines it stiffened in her hand. Gently and steadily she stroked him.

"Tell me about her, Ben. Tell me about Anstis. How she felt, how she tasted."

His head lolled back and he exhaled a long sigh.

"Her skin," he rasped. "I miss the feel of her skin."

Lauren let go of his cock and placed his hands on her hips. "Like this?"

His hands reached around her back as he pulled her to his chest. His eyes closed as he imagined Anstis, her hair falling over his belly, and the supple feel of her skin as he explored her soft places and her firmer places.

"I'm with you, sweetheart," she said. "I'm always with you."

Anstis straddled his lap and guided his yearning cock into her flowing cunt, then clasped her legs around his back to draw him even deeper inside her. She was in his arms again, at long last. And she rode his cock, pressing her breasts against his chest as her hair spilled over his shoulders.

"I won't let go of you," he vowed. "I'll never let go of you again."

She giggled as she bounced, up and down, her cunt clenching his cock as she gently raked her fingernails across his back.

"I love you!" he cried.

"Then fuck me . . . fuck me forever, don't stop . . . don't stop."

He tried desperately to hold back his orgasm, pleading to whatever gods not to let him come. But his fluids erupted inside her lush body just as an angel cried in his ear.

His mind emerged from a warm, moist fog. Then his eyes cleared and focused on the moon overhead.

Lauren, still on her knees, smiled at him, and the evidence of his orgasm dribbled off her hand.

Was that all it was, a hand job? He smiled. But what a wonderful hand job.

"Are you okay, Ben?"

"Yes . . . thank you, Lauren."

"You looked like you were far away for a while."

"I was, my dear. I was."

"She's with you, Ben. She's always with you."

Lauren wiped her hand on the grass, then stood. "Don't forget to follow the path."

Then she was gone.

Arnold remained on the bench, listening to the birds and the falling water, until dawn.

Arnold was startled awake by a pounding on his door.

"Mr Arnold? You're gonna miss the dedication." It was Ricker.

He pulled on a robe and stumbled to the door. "Huh?"

"Well, it's almost 2 o'clock. Everyone's waiting for you."

He tried to shake off his confusion. "Okay, tell them I'll be there in 15 minutes."

He closed the door before Ricker even replied.

He stumbled into the bathroom and showered quickly. Now a bit more awake, he dressed and set off downstairs.

Outside a crowd that included tenants but also scores of other people pressed against the wooded rectangle. Photographers took pictures of Lauren's little forest.

An arm curved around his. Lauren pressed her cheek to his shoulder. "We're being covered by three of the country's biggest landscaping magazines."

"Oh?"

"Yeah, but we're just about ready for the unveiling."

"Huh?"

"You'll see."

She led him through the crowd until he stood in front of a wrought-iron gate partially covered with a cloth. She gestured to the crowd to quiet, then she announced:

"Ladies and gentlemen, it is my pleasure to welcome you to The Oasis." She tugged the cloth off the gate and revealed a plaque, and in full-color relief, a reproduction of the portrait of Anstis.

"And it is dedicated to the memory of Anstis Sally . . . Arnold."

There was a smattering of applause, but the tenants as a group pressed near the gate to gaze at the plaque. Then, one by one, they turned to Arnold, and noted the tears falling freely over his cheeks.

Ricker patted his shoulder and Mrs Califani and Mrs Ginty each held one of his hands.

"We had no idea, dear. You're the new owner." Mrs Califani squeezed his arm.

"Your wife, Mr Arnold," Mrs Ginty said. "My, she was a pretty girl." She stood on her toes to kiss his cheek.

Then they all pressed around him, offering hugs and pats. And he couldn't speak. All he could do was look back over his shoulder at Lauren, and mouth the words: "Thank you."

Grave Circumstance

Cameo Sunset Brown

There's something uniquely trashy about having sex with a girl in a cemetery. Then again, there's always been something uniquely trashy about Betsy, so it's a propos. Don't get me wrong, I love her – in a way that's totally unimaginable to most ordinary guys. Betsy's white trash, without a doubt. That makes me, I guess, a white-trash lover. And I take my job very seriously.

"Most guys would think fucking me here is gross or creepy." Betsy swoons, buck naked and spread-legged against a tombstone, "But you like it! You like fucking me here, don't you, Oliver?" Then she lets her hand nestle in her thick damp curls, their silkiness dully reflecting the dim yellow glow of the security lanterns blazing nearby. I can't tell whether she means fucking her in a cemetery or in her hot pussy, because my brain is on fire with thoughts of porking her good. Porking her *real* good.

"And here, too," she clarifies. She slides a finger between her thighs and giggles. Her sudden gasp at the shock of her own stimulation makes my prick so hard that I could cut diamonds with it. God, she's a tease.

We've made love just about everywhere – car trunks, chapels, under tables, on top of bleachers, on sandy beaches . . . even at funerals. That's where Betsy got the cemetery idea: her Aunt Noreen's funeral, of all places. But considering Aunt Noreen had five kids by four different guys, what did I expect? Count me out, I thought at first. Too Poe. Who needs to roll around in freshly dug dirt, pale ass humping in the moonlight while screech owls rate your performance every five minutes with a bone-shattering caterwauling that makes you want to shit your pants?

And the goddamn flowers aren't even yours, either, but some other poor schmuck's who's lying under you, decomposing and wondering what the hell all the noise is up there. So at first I said – unequivocally, mind you, and with my flaccid penis showing nothing but the most sincere moral support – I said *No*.

But I'd do anything to be with my Betsy. Who can resist those tits, that soft curve of belly, the golden brown curls that dangle happily around her heart-shaped face, those pale blue eyes, and most of all, that mouth? I love Betsy's mouth. Kissing it, fucking it. Just touching her lips gets me hard. Always the sexual tactician, she brazenly does that thing she does where her lips lightly caress my cock, leaving a trail of her fuck-me red lipstick on my member, and my resulting erection nearly knocks her off her feet.

Of course, being an opportunist, I pushed her all the way down and, without even a thought as to whether her sweet cunt could take it, plunged right into her moist opening. Deep.

She groaned and spread her legs wide, giving me access and pulling me in. Her hips bucked wildly, meeting my thrusts, and I rode her, her yells and yips and yahoos (told you she was white trash) cheering me on even as I worried my dick would disintegrate from the friction. Too soon, earth-shattering waves of release reverberated from my cock through my body, and I collapsed in a heap on top of her – spent, wet and happy.

I had no idea whether Betsy got off or not, so to be on the safe side, with the last of my energy I slid my dick out and slipped my fingers in.

Betsy's an index-and-middle-finger-type girl, so I, being skilled in the arts of Betsy-fucking, started stroking her immediately – in and out, in and out. I kept the pressure going through the middle finger, just like she likes it, with my index there just to fill her up a little more. Harder and harder. Stroke, stroke, stroke. Then I did a little up and down, and she grabbed my hand and pumped against it. Betsy loves those fingerblasts.

Next on the agenda would have been my tongue on her hard clit to send her over the edge, but her time had come, and so had she. Glorious Betsy-goo doused my fingers in its richness, and I took the opportunity to kiss my way up from snatch to navel to tits to neck to those glorious red lips that started it all. The satisfaction in her grin did not escape my attention – she'd tricked me again in that slutty way of hers – and so I couldn't escape playing a little graveyard *Hide the Wienie*.

So we did, indeed, fuck in the cemetery. And it became a habit – a useful habit, as it turns out.

Tonight she wants me to take her from behind while she bends over poor old Mrs Wannamaker's granite marker. I used to feel sorry for the old lady and Mr Wannamaker, being as their tombstones suggested they had been simple folk in life, unassuming and definitely not sexually active. Their bearing witness to our sexual displays seemed almost blasphemous until I noticed Betsy's legs were spread wide over Mr Wannamaker's side of the plot. Do you know what people would pay for a money shot like that? Necrotic voyeur bastard.

Anyway, here we are, Betsy in that pink number she always wears and me with my jeans down around my ankles, dick at attention, heart pounding. She pulls up her dress, bunching it around her hips so I can get a look at the goods by the eerie glow of the lanterns.

I've been through this before, but my cock still throbs at the rank smell of Betsy's excitement. One of my hands slips around her pale belly, massaging its way toward her soft mound. I rub Mr Dong – yeah, I named my own dick – against her wet slit (which is surprisingly hot) spreading her lips just a little with my girth. She kisses me over her shoulder, breathless. She whimpers as I pull Mr Dong away to help her position her hands just so on Mrs Wannamaker's marker. Then I slide one hand down between her thighs, letting my thumb gently slip inside. Betsy presses down, trying to ride it, and I can tell she wants to be fucked. Bad.

I spread her legs enough to achieve the perfect balance, one that will keep her on her feet as she accepts me from behind while providing her with maximum penetration. We don't want any toppling over on the Wannamakers, do we? Their tombstone is the perfect height. I wonder how they like the Mr-Dong-Does-Betsy-Wetsy-in-the-Graveyard Show down there tonight?

And Betsy *is* wet. She wiggles her round ass, impatient for my AWOL cock. Mr Dong stands rock-hard and ready, so I grab her hip and guide Mr Dong to her heat. I've lubed him up with her goo – God, there's a lot tonight – and placed the tip at my very own doorway to Heaven, right here in the graveyard. She tenses for the sweet invasion.

I push my length all the way in. She's tight. She's always tight, and I fight to keep control as sensation overwhelms me. But I finally plunge Mr Dong into her as deep as I can.

Betsy likes it deep. She throws her head back and moans.

Then I do her even better. I start in and out, real slow, enjoying it she begs for more. I give her more. Hell, I give her all I have. I love this girl, my white trash Betsy-Wetsy doll, my graveyard chick. Nothing can keep us apart.

I drive harder and faster now, and she's lovin' it. She likes to yell, and here in the cemetery no one seems to care. So I make her yell into the dense night, my strokes coming faster and my finger doing her clit. She's about to explode, and so am I. Jeez – right now would be a really bad time for a security guard to show up.

I want to feel Betsy's delicious tits, to suck her nipples, but that will have to wait for next time. Tonight's all about below the waist. I'm coming like a freight train, yelling myself, but all I hear is her panted encouragement and the roar of blood in my ears.

Everything goes white as orgasm grips me. Sensations override my system. I hump wildly to keep it going, wanting the pure bliss of our coupling to never end. I'm vaguely aware that Betsy's riding me for all she's worth, her hands reaching back, trying to grab at my ass, trying to balance herself so as not to plunge headfirst onto the headstone. She's panting, begging, singing my praises. Ever her hero, I keep thrusting and fingering her nub, even as my own release fades. My valor is rewarded. Betsy tenses and comes, screaming into the thick air as she rides my cock furiously, then slows to an easy rhythm.

Gradually, we both still. I pull her up to face me, and her dress falls down to where it should be. Now my Betsy looks just like any other girl, though she's not.

She presses against me, and I sweep her into my arms. Wisely, I kick off my pants with great effort, and once free, I carry Betsy to a plot just three away from the Wannamakers. I lay her down on the soft earth and cuddle up beside her, pantsless and happy. We lie there quietly for a long time before she stretches and pokes me.

"Hey, time to go, Ollie," she says. I love it when she calls me that. I love her name, too. I reach up and touch the stone above our heads, tracing the letters with my fingers . . . E-L-I-Z-A-B-E-T-H.

Her hand stops me before I get to the last name. This is always the hardest part, the saying good-bye. But she grabs my hand and kisses the palm, sending ripples through me just as she has always done, even after the accident.

Then she blows me a kiss and I pretend to catch it and tuck it in my shirt pocket. I grin, and she leans down to plant a kiss on Mr Dong. The seduction never ends with this girl.

Suddenly, she pulls her head out of my crotch and sits up with a cry, grabbing her nose.

She looks mortified as a worm pops out of her nostril and lands on the soft earth in front of her. It's a wiggly little thing. I pretend to pick it up and eat it. A small gesture of comfort for my baby, but necessary when you consider ol' Wannamaker over there just waiting for his chance at some young puss. I don't let Betsy ever forget how much I love her. Just in case.

We watch the worm slip into the soft ground.

Betsy will soon follow. Both of us burst into laughter. She kisses me once more, on the lips this time, and lies back, legs together, urges satisfied. Then, as grey morning dawns across a pink-streaked sky, my Betsy sinks away into the soft earth, heading back to her resting place, smiling and waving until she's out of sight.

I sigh and sit up. I trace the letters of her last name – which is my last name, too: W-I-L-L-O-U-G-H-B-Y. Oh, I know people are shocked that we're hitched. They probably wonder how two such people can keep hot sex going. Not possible, they say? Well, buckaroo, anything is possible when you love someone enough. We're living proof of that, no pun intended. Sort of.

I ponder Poe, him and his Annabel Lee and their "sepulcher down by the sea." He was a pussy. A whiner, too, but mainly a pussy.

I'm a doer, and as I sit here on my wife's grave, freshly fucked, picking leaves off Mr Dong, I reaffirm that, yes, indeed, Poe was just a whiny pussy. Because when it comes to loving my white trash Betsy-Wetsy, nothing – and I mean *nothing* – can keep us apart.

In the Middle of Nowhere

Gwen Masters

I took another sip of my beer and watched the stars. I was lying on the porch at our summer cabin in the middle of nowhere, out where earthly lights didn't compete with the heavenly ones. I was sure the stars were always up there, but I had never seen so many. I watched as one of them lost its anchor and fell in a gentle arc, crossing the horizon before blinking out.

"Cheers," I said aloud, and lifted my beer in salute.

This was exactly where I needed to be. Relaxation was long overdue, and besides that, I needed some serious time to think since my life had turned itself upside-down and inside-out.

Keith and I had been together for long enough to read each other's moods. We understood one another in the ways that only a couple who has been completely open and honest can. That's why he didn't hesitate to tell me about his fantasies.

"I have always wanted to see my woman with another man," Keith announced one night as he lay in bed beside me. He was still trying to catch his breath.

The thought of two men was always a fantasy of mine, too. My body instantly responded again, even though I had just been satisfied over and over.

"Why?" I asked.

"I want to see a woman of mine take all the pleasure she can possibly stand," he said. "I guess it helps that I don't have a jealous streak. As long as you're doing it in front of me, it's not cheating, and I don't mind whatever you might want to do. I like being able to let you fulfill all your fantasies, and not have to worry about you going elsewhere to do that."

That was not what I expected to hear. I sat up and looked at him in the near-darkness. I knew Keith was always very laid-back when we were around his friends or mine, even the male friends who liked to flirt from time to time. But I always chalked that up to him simply trusting me, not to his very nature.

"You don't get jealous?" I asked. "At all?"

"Never have, no."

"Even if your woman was with someone else, it doesn't bother you?"

"It would bother me if you did it with someone else and I wasn't included. I think that would be cheating. But if you can do it right in front of me, that's not cheating, right?"

"I guess so."

"So I would like to see you do it."

"But what if I like him more than I like you?"

Keith shrugged in the darkness. "That's the chance I have to take."

"So you mean you would be willing to take a chance that I might leave you?"

"If you're going to leave, you're going to leave. There's nothing I can do to stop you."

"But you don't have to bring it on by allowing me to be with other men, right?"

Keith sighed. "You don't understand that kind of lifestyle," he said quietly.

"What? An open relationship?"

"No. It's not exactly open. It's more like swinging. Doing it together."

"What if you choose to have another woman involved?"

"Would that bother you?"

"You're damn right it would!" I was on the verge of furious at the thought. Keith looked at me in the darkness. I could make out the outline of his jaw but I couldn't see his eyes. I flicked on the bedside lamp and he immediately threw an arm across his face.

"Shit!"

"Do you want another woman?"

"No! I never said anything about that. You were the one who brought it up."

"So you would be okay with me being with another man."

"Yes," he said with strained patience.

"But you wouldn't be jealous."

"No."

"Why not?"

Keith threw his hand down and glared at me. "Because I'm not the jealous type. I already told you that. What is this, selective hearing?"

I glared right back at him.

"Well?" he asked.

"Well, what?"

"Do you want to do something like that?"

I flopped back down on the bed. Now Keith was the one who sat up to study me. "I don't know," I said softly. "It's a good fantasy. But what I need in real life is much more important."

"What do you need?"

"I need a man who will give a damn if I'm with someone else. I want a man who will barely restrain himself from kicking the ass of the guy at the bar who dares to hit on me while I'm with him. I want a man who will deliver that ass-kicking if the guy dares to hit on me twice. I want a man who will proudly tell everybody I'm his girl and that is that, period, end of story. I want to feel protected."

"You want a man to be jealous?"

"Not jealous," I said, thinking hard. "Possessive, maybe."

"So now you're an object. A possession. Great."

I rolled away from him and faced the wall. "You don't understand."

"Honey," Keith said, touching my shoulder. "It's not that I'm not proud of you. I'm happy to call you mine. I think we make a great team. I love you with all my heart. I just don't see the jealousy bit. I've never been the jealous type. If you want to be with another man, fine. Do it right in front of me, so we can both enjoy it. Just don't do it behind my back. That's all I ask."

"I would never," I said vehemently, and Keith cut me off.
"I know. I trust you."
"I don't think I can do it in front of you, either."
"We can try," he suggested.
"How?"
"I have a friend," he said. "His name is Jake."

The moment I laid eyes on Jake, I knew I was in big trouble.

Jake was tall and lean, with an athlete's body and beautiful green eyes. His hair was far too long, almost shaggy, but looked soft as a baby's locks. He had a great tan and a smile that showed perfect teeth. His laugh was infectious and he moved with a grace that belied his rough-and-tumble attitude.

Perhaps if Keith had never mentioned Jake's name, I never would have looked at him as a potential lover. But he had, and for many nights the idea of this man had been in my head. Now that I was seeing him in the flesh, my body was already responding in certain ways that were inappropriate – or appropriate, depending on how I looked at the situation.

Keith and Jake embraced there in the parking lot of the coliseum. Inside, the crowd was rowdy and loud – the show had just started. We had tickets, but it had taken us a bit too long to find each other in the many parking lots around the venue. Out among the many cars, the scene was quiet. The two men clapped each other on the back and talked about the usual things – how's that truck holding up, how is your Momma doing, would you like to meet my girlfriend?

Jake turned to me. He gave me a quick once-over, but that was enough. His eyes met mine and the appreciation in them was evident. I blushed as he looked at me.

"The pleasure is all mine," he said, and I blushed harder.

Keith looked at me, then at Jake. He sized up the situation and cast a knowing grin in my direction.

"Let's ditch the show and go out to dinner," he said.

Dinner was at a bistro just outside of town, where the locals rarely bothered to venture and the out-of-towners seemed to have missed in favor of the concert going on down the street.

We were practically alone in the restaurant. I twirled my fork through the spaghetti and listened as the two men talked about football and travel and music and everything in between. I occasionally spoke, but mostly I was just quiet, taking it all in while the two of them caught up on what life had brought them in the six months since they had last seen each other.

"I've missed you," Keith said once, and Jake smiled at him. The look that passed between them was that of two old friends who are closer than brothers, who have spent their lives looking after one another. Watching them together made me feel warm from the inside out.

"I missed you too," Jake said.

Keith excused himself from the table shortly after that, and Jake turned to me.

"You've been quiet all night," he said.

"I've been listening."

"Do you always do that?"

"Do what?"

"Listen so intently? You don't miss much. You seem comfortable as an observer. Either that, or you have something serious weighing on your mind."

I looked at him in surprise. "You read people very well," I murmured.

Jake smiled at me and took a sip of wine. "Sometimes."

"There's nothing on my mind," I said. We both knew I was lying. Jake didn't say a word – he simply sat back in his chair and swirled the wine in his glass, staring straight at me.

I tried not to squirm under his gaze. It was impossible.

"I've got a few things on my mind," I admitted.

"I know how Keith is," he said, and I looked at him in surprise. Jake went on. "I know why he wanted us to meet. I know what's on his mind, so I'm pretty sure what's on yours."

I took a big drink of my own wine. "So he's done this before?"

Jake shrugged. "I don't think so, no. But I know he's always wanted to."

"Why me?" I said, almost to myself.

"Because you were open enough to consider it."

"But I'm not."

"You're not?"

"I can't get past the lack of jealousy."

Jake shifted in his chair. His eyes dropped to his wineglass. "Some people just aren't jealous. I know it's hard to believe, but Keith really is one of those people. It must be hard to adjust."

"Did other women find it hard to adjust?"

Jake smiled and answered carefully, "I think they just weren't right for Keith."

"That's a diplomatic answer."

"I'm a diplomatic kind of guy."

"Are you a jealous kind of guy?" The question came out of nowhere. I hadn't even known I would ask it until the question was already out in the open. Jake raised an eyebrow. He blushed and for once, looked as though he didn't have an answer. He looked over my shoulder.

"Hey, look who's back," he said, and refused to meet my eyes for the rest of the meal.

That night in bed, Keith asked me what I thought of Jake.

"He's a very nice man," I said honestly. "I like his manner. And he's very talkative but he doesn't monopolize the conversation until you start talking about sports."

Keith laughed. "He's the sports fanatic, definitely."

"I like him," I said.

"How much do you like him?"

It was very odd to hear that question from Keith, knowing there was no jealousy behind it. There wasn't even a hint of it in his tone. He was simply curious as to how I felt, and of course, there might be an agenda behind that curiosity.

"A lot," I said frankly. Keith cuddled me closer to his side.

"Really?"

"Yeah."

"Enough to like him as more than a friend?"

I bit my lip. This was the strangest conversation I had ever had with anyone. "If I were not with you, maybe. But I'm a one-man kind of woman. You know that. I'm not going to look elsewhere. Even if you encourage me to do so."

Keith sat up in bed. I thought he was reaching for something on the nightstand, but he was actually reaching for his robe. He shrugged it on and walked out of the room. The door slammed behind him.

I lay there for a moment, completely stunned. I didn't know how to react. I couldn't see the situation the same way he did. I couldn't imagine doing what he wanted me to do, even though the fantasy was huge in the back of my mind. Sometimes I fantasized about more than two men – sometimes my fantasies involved gang-bangs, strings of men who wanted only one thing and took it, over and over and over. But could I actually do those things? The fantasies stopped at the point where the reality began. The fantasy was great but the reality might not be.

But maybe that wasn't what was really bothering me. Maybe it was the fact that Keith wanted the fantasy so badly, he wasn't willing to see my point of view. I simply wasn't comfortable with being with anyone else. Why couldn't he accept that?

Everything else about him was perfect. Why was I so intent on having a jealous man?

I lay there for a very long time before Keith came back to the bedroom.

"I'm sorry," he said as he crawled in beside me.

I didn't answer. Soon his breathing was deep and even, but I was awake for hours before I could finally join him in sleep.

Keith awoke the next morning in a very pensive mood. We hung around the house and said little to each other during those hours when he was thinking things through. Finally he came to me and wrapped his arms around my shoulders.

"If you aren't comfortable with it," he said, "I won't bring it up again."

I was startled by his change in attitude. I had a surprise for him, too.

"I thought about it last night," I admitted. "And I decided that I would try it."

Keith and I looked at each other, neither of us knowing how to respond. Finally Keith cleared his throat and kissed my forehead.

"Seems we love each other enough to compromise," he said.

I took him down to the kitchen floor right then and there and had my way with him. Our lunch burned on the stove. I was making love to Keith, but Jake was in the back of my mind.

The next night Jake came over for dinner.

I had a whole spread for us – chicken with mushroom sauce, asparagus steamed to perfection, mashed potatoes and carrots that were golden with brown sugar. Fresh bread cooled on the sideboard. A good bottle of wine was chilling in the cooler. Jake walked up behind me in the kitchen and kissed me on the cheek.

"It's good to see you," he said.

We sat down to dinner and I watched the men talk. Keith kept looking at me, more animated than he had been in a long time. Jake was drinking the wine like it was going out of style. Keith watched him with growing concern.

"Are you all right?" he asked once, and Jake glanced at me before he answered.

"Of course I'm fine."

I was puzzled at Jake's attitude. He had said he knew how Keith was, and he had agreed to have dinner at our home – surely he knew the kind of things Keith and I had discussed since the first time we had dinner. He kept looking at me as though he wanted to say something, but he couldn't find the proper words or the proper time.

As I was cleaning the kitchen, Keith went out onto the porch. Jake leaned on the counter and looked at me.

"You're not okay with this," he said bluntly.

I didn't play dumb. "I told him I was okay with it."

"That doesn't mean you are."

I turned to Jake. His green eyes were bright with too much alcohol. He looked at me with a very guarded expression, but his body told a story he couldn't hide. He was tense from head to toe. He drained the wine. I watched as he set the glass on the counter. He picked up the bottle and tipped it in my direction.

"I think I'll just drink from the well," he said, and turned it up. I watched his throat move as he drank the wine. He sighed and looked at me, then motioned with the bottle.

"Want some?"

I stepped forward. Now that I was so close to him I could smell his cologne, something deep and woodsy and masculine. Jake moved the bottle away from between us, giving me even more opportunity to come closer. His free hand came around to the small of my back. The first touch was electric, almost frightening, and I suddenly knew that I wasn't ready for this after all.

Keith walked into the room. Jake put more pressure on my back and pulled me closer. I looked at Keith as he sank down into one of the kitchen chairs. I watched his eyes for any trace of jealousy, any sign that he was uncomfortable, but there was none. He looked at us with something that could only be approval.

I stared at him. Minutes ticked by on the clock. Keith watched us closely. His eyes took in everything, from our toes to our hair and then back down. Jake tipped up the bottle again, and that was the only time Keith looked concerned about what was happening right in front of him in his kitchen.

"You're drinking fast," Keith commented, and Jake looked at me.

"I'm not drinking fast enough," he said. The expression in his eyes was unreadable. He pulled me tight against him, hard enough that I could feel what the wine and the tension had done to him. His cock was hard as a rock. His whole body was tense. Jake didn't take his eyes away from mine.

I was very aware of Keith. He sat there and watched his friend pull me tight against him. He knew what was coming, and he wasn't about to protest. I knew he wouldn't. My body leaped at the thought of having Jake. My heart fell at the fact that I actually could.

I twined my fingers through Jake's hair and pulled him down for a kiss.

Jake moaned lightly as soon as my lips touched his. His tongue found mine. He tasted like wine. I kissed him slowly. I took my time and explored every inch of his mouth. Jake's arm came around me as he kissed me back. I was wrapped up in his arms, wrapped up in his scent, wrapped up in what he was making me feel – a deep and low trembling, right between my thighs.

Jake uttered a curse against my lips. He pushed me back against the counter. He kissed me harder, all doubts forgotten. The fire that raged in me was obviously in him, too – he kissed me with what was almost desperation. I twined both hands into his hair as he settled himself firmly against me. My breath was harsh. His heart was beating even harder than mine was.

It was only when I opened my eyes and pulled away to catch my breath that I remembered Keith was in the room. He sat on the chair at the other end of the kitchen. His eyes were bright with something I recognized. Keith was horny as hell.

My face flooded with heat. Jake kissed his way down the side of my neck and then back up. He found my ear and the gentle stroke of his tongue made me shiver. I stared at Keith while Jake worked magic that made my nipples hard and my body wet. Keith stared right back. Jake thrust up against me, one time only, and whispered into my ear.

"I would never let another man do this to you."

My heart and my body were plunged into confusion. Anger swamped me. Part of me wanted to pull Jake closer and another part of me wanted to push him away. Guilt was a violent tempest within my head. I closed my eyes so I didn't have to see Keith.

But I couldn't shake the fact that I wanted Jake.

Jake was the one who stopped. He ran his fingers through my hair, kissed me hard and then slowly took a step back. He looked right at me while he spoke to Keith.

"I can't do this."

Keith looked from Jake to me. He didn't seem surprised at all. Jake was breathing hard. He closed his eyes and rested his forehead against mine for a long moment.

"I'm the jealous kind," Jake said.

Keith did look surprised then. The edge of anger surfaced in his eyes. Though he buried it quickly, the quick blush on his face said he knew I saw it. Jake stepped away from me and handed me the wine. The bottle was cool but where his hand had been was almost slippery with warmth. He shook his head once, slowly, then turned and walked out of the kitchen. He went out the front door.

"He's too drunk to drive," I told Keith. He didn't meet my eyes.

"He will be fine."

I ran to the front door. Jake was pulling out of the driveway. He gunned the engine and tore down the road without looking back. There was no way I could have stopped him.

I turned to see Keith standing there behind me.

"Is that what you wanted to see?" I almost hissed.

"Yes."

I threw myself at him like a wildcat. Keith caught my arms and we both tumbled to the floor, right there in the open doorway. The wine bottle thumped on the floor and then rolled across the hardwood, spilling drops of wine as it went. Keith yanked my shirt open. I pulled his jeans down. Within seconds he was buried inside me, thrusting hard into the wetness Jake had created.

It was the best fuck of my life.

I could not get Jake off my mind. Keith called a few times but Jake never answered his phone, and didn't return the messages. Days went by and Keith and I settled back into our routine. We rarely mentioned Jake and we never mentioned what had happened that night. It sat between us like the elephant in the room that nobody mentions, but that nobody can ignore.

It was a few days later when Keith came into the bedroom and saw me packing the smallest of my suitcases.

"Where are you going?" he asked.

I was quiet as I pushed in a pair of sandals. "I'm taking a few days up at the cabin," I said. "I need time to think."

Keith glared at me. He went from calm and collected to furious in the time it took me to answer him.

"Like hell you are," he said. "Like hell you do."

I wasn't expecting that. Keith had taken my silence in stride these last few days. Surely he knew what was going through my head? Did he really think everything would continue as it had been?

"I feel as though I have done something horrible," I said to him, and I was chagrined at the tears that pricked my eyes. I had sworn that I wouldn't cry over this. I took a deep breath. "I feel as though I have betrayed you, and myself, and even Jake. I need time to sort things out in my head and I can't do that here with you."

Keith grabbed my wrist as I reached to close the suitcase. He shoved it off the bed. Clothes went everywhere. I didn't move as he stood over me.

"You said you were okay with what you did," Keith said. "You were okay with it. What if Jake hadn't stopped? You would have fucked him just like you fucked me as soon as he left."

My face flooded with heat.

"I thought that was what you wanted," I said to him.

"I didn't want to lose you over him!" Keith hollered.

"That's what I warned you might happen!" I hollered right back. "I told you I wasn't comfortable with it! I told you I was a one-man woman! I told you those things and you kept insisting. You were so certain I would like it that you pushed and pushed and pushed and now this is how I feel and I can't help it. I don't know what to think or what to do or what to want anymore!"

Keith stared at me with wide eyes. For the first time, I saw fear in them.

"Your lack of jealousy is not something I can handle," I said softly. "You show your love in so many ways. But if you really loved me, wouldn't you want me to be with you, and nobody else?"

"If I really loved you," Keith countered, "it seems to me I would want you to have as much pleasure as possible."

I took a deep breath. "In this whole situation," I said, "the one thing you haven't taken into account is that maybe being with you and nobody else – being your girlfriend, and not being touched by any man but you – is the most pleasurable thing I can imagine."

Keith sank down on the bed. He let go of my wrist. My hand throbbed, and I rubbed it while Keith watched me.

"I'm sorry I hurt you," he said.

"It's all right. I know you didn't mean it."

"I don't mean just your wrist. I'm sorry for all of this."

Keith and I looked at each other. Finally he looked down at the suitcase, but not before I caught the tears in his eyes.

"I think we both need time to think," I said, and Keith nodded.

"You're right."

I should have been happy that he agreed with me, but instead I felt as though I had lost something very special in return for winning the argument. I sat down on his lap and wrapped my arms around his shoulders. Keith buried his face against my neck. We sat there like that until the sun started to fall from the sky.

I watched the stars and thought about the last few weeks. I knew I couldn't handle making that fantasy a reality. If kissing Jake in the kitchen had caused so much turmoil, there was no way that I could handle doing anything more. But pleasing a man was so important to me, and I wanted to give Keith the fantasies he longed to fulfill. He had trusted me enough to share them, and this was how I rewarded him?

It seemed we were at an impasse, with no compromise possible.

I laid there on the deck and watched the stars twinkle. I listened to the crickets and night birds. I watched a plane glide across the sky, its lights flashing red in the midst of black and white. I studied the Milky Way. I tried to count stars, a fruitless exercise in frustration, but it kept me from thinking about other things.

I heard the sound of tires on gravel while the vehicle was still miles away. I listened to it with less than a quarter of my attention, sure it would pull into a driveway long before it reached me. I was surprised when I heard the whine of the tires come up the hill to the cabin. I sat up and watched the headlights make their way through the trees. A startled raccoon fled through the light, ran through the underbrush and scampered up a tree, where it disappeared into the leaves.

The truck pulled into the drive. I took another sip of my beer.

I was surprised when the lights flickered off. I was even more surprised when a man stepped out of the truck and walked toward me. It was only when he stepped through a shaft of moonlight that I realized who he was.

I should have known.

"Keith told me you might be out here," Jake said.

I held out the beer. He took it and drank the rest in one long swallow. We sat side by side on the porch and looked out at the silhouettes of the trees.

"How is he?" I asked.

Jake picked at a spot on his jeans. "He's all right. He knows everybody handled the situation badly."

"I don't blame him. I don't blame anybody."

Jake chuckled ruefully. "That's the problem with things like this. There is nobody to blame. It's easier if there is someone who can be held accountable."

I got up to get another beer. I pulled two longnecks out of the cooler and handed one to Jake. We twisted off the tops and sat in companionable silence, watching the night close in around us.

"Why are you here?" I asked.

"I don't know."

I nodded, grateful for his honesty. "Keith knows you are here?"

"Yeah. He invited me to come out here. He said you might want some company."

I looked at Jake. He looked at me.

"I didn't ask," he said softly. "I just took it for what it was."

I looked away, unsure of what to say. Anger and sadness warred for top billing. What the hell was happening here? I needed time to think, not time to spend with anyone else.

"I'm still his girlfriend," I said. "Does he know that?"

"Are you?" Jake asked bluntly.

I looked up at the stars. "I don't know. I don't know who belongs where anymore."

"I think he's already made up his mind," Jake said, so softly I could barely hear him. I pretended not to hear him at all, even as my heart beat a tattoo of fear in my chest. After a time the fear was replaced with a quick flash of anger, then with the same sadness I had felt for days and days.

"How long are you here?" I asked.

Jake took a long drink of his beer. "That depends on you."

I stood up on the porch and offered my hand. He held it a little too long after he stood up. We looked at each other and the electricity between us was still there. The only thing missing was Keith. I pulled my hand away.

"I'm too drunk to drive," I said. "So you get to do the honors."

Jake grinned.

The karaoke bar was loud and rowdy. There were no parking spaces, so Jake parked the truck on the side of the road. The night air was muggy out here by the lake. Each time the door opened, the music blared. A woman was singing a very bad rendition of a Gretchen Wilson tune. Men were lined up at the bar, holding down stools while they eyed the women walking back and forth. Waitresses slid bottles of beer across tables and flirted with customers. The DJ was drinking just as fast as he was playing songs.

We slid into a table at the corner next to the stage. The speaker was right in front of us and so talking was virtually impossible. I called for Bud Lights and the waitress slid them down to us like the professional she was. Jake watched me the whole time he drank his. I knew he was looking, and so I carefully kept my eyes on the singer.

A Toby Keith song came next. Jake slid his hand across my thigh. My eyes met his, but he didn't move his hand.

By the time I had finished the beer, caution had disappeared. I took his hand and led him to the dance floor. The grace I had first seen in him was evident out there among the two-steppers. He spun me effortlessly. Every time he pulled me back toward him, we were a little closer. By the time the song was over, we were in each other's arms.

The next song was a slow one. Jake and I didn't notice the singer at all. We were too busy enjoying the way it felt to be so close to one another. We moved in a slow waltz. Jake kissed my neck and trailed his lips along my collarbone. His lips found my ear and stayed there for a long while, kissing and singing softly along with the music. Before the song was over, his lips were on mine and I was kissing him right back.

The next number was a fast dance track. We stood back and looked at each other as the dance floor filled up. By silent agreement, we went back to the table and held hands while we watched everyone else. I occasionally looked at him, and every time I did I caught him studying me.

Another beer and I was brave enough to sing. Jake watched me as I sang, a smile on his lips. He was the one who clapped the loudest, even though I was sure I sounded just as drunk as I felt. I was surprised when Jake came up to the stage right after me. His voice was deeper than I had imagined it would be, and he was a hit with the bar, especially the ladies. I watched as they crowded around the front of the stage and looked at him with lustful eyes.

When Jake came down off the stage, he kissed me quickly on the lips.

"I'm jealous," I admitted, and he looked at me for a long time.

"Let's go home," he finally said.

I stumbled up onto the porch, laughing. I wasn't drunk enough to forget things, but I was definitely feeling good. Jake was right behind me. His laugh was genuine, hard and deep, from the belly up. He twirled me onto the wide porch and caught me right before I fell.

I wrapped my arms around his shoulders and kissed him. Jake kissed me right back, until we were both breathing hard, until my head spun from something other than the alcohol.

He asked me only one question.

"Where's the bed?"

I took him into the house. We left the door open and our clothes on the floor. I fell into the bed and Jake was immediately there beside me. His hands were everywhere. Discovering his body was like a different kind of liquor. I was drunk on him.

"My God," he breathed. "Look at you . . ."

Jake settled above me and kissed my throat. The heat of his arousal was insistent against my thigh, but he didn't let me have it. He held himself just out of reach. I touched him everywhere and kissed every inch my lips could find. I reached for him with my hips. He chuckled against my mouth. Then he was chuckling, and humming and murmuring against my nipples as I held them up to him, pushed them together so he could take both into his mouth at once.

He slid an inch of himself into me, just enough to give me a taste of what he might feel like. I tried to get him deeper but he braced himself above me. He watched as I moved under him.

"That's gorgeous," he said. "I love the way you try to get me inside you."

I slid my hands down his back and grabbed his hips. He gave me that wicked smile. I pushed hard and thrust up at the same time, and was rewarded with another few inches of him. Jake laughed out loud, and I laughed right along with him.

"Please, baby," I murmured. "Please?"

He slowly pushed forward. It seemed to take an eternity before he was completely inside me. Our bodies pressed tightly together. I lay very still and enjoyed the feeling of being filled by him. Jake closed his eyes and didn't move for the longest time.

"I have wanted this since the moment I saw you," he said.

Jake started to move. I gasped with the thrill of that first gliding thrust. Hard and fast or slow and easy, it seemed everything he wanted was exactly what I wanted, too. I was wetter than I had been in recent memory, and Jake appreciated it by moving harder into me. Our hips slammed into each other. His hands tightened in my hair. I scraped my nails down his back and he cursed sweetly through gritted teeth.

Soon all the foreplay was over and we were in the middle of an all-out, hardcore fuck.

He drove me up the bed with his thrusts. I arched right back against him. The harder he gave it to me, the harder he got it. His kiss bruised my lips. I nipped at his. He pulled out and shoved me onto my belly, and was instantly on top of me, his hands in my hair as he yanked my head back. He slammed into me from behind and I could hardly catch my breath.

"You're a good fuck," he growled into my ear.

"You're getting there," I answered.

Jake paused in mid-stroke. He laughed out loud. "Oh, you're going to pay for that."

"Good. I haven't seen your best yet."

The next thrust almost knocked me into the headboard. I braced myself hard on the mattress and pushed back against him. He thrust so hard that my elbows gave way, and I had to grab onto the headboard to keep from hitting it. Pain flashed though me as he hit bottom again and again. My legs trembled. Those finally gave way too, and he pinned me down to the bed with his weight. He thrust hard into me, driving right into that certain spot that drove me wild.

I came with a satisfied howl, but Jake didn't let up. He didn't even slow down.

"Jesus, Jake!"

"Had enough yet?"

I bit my lip. No way was I going to be the one to cry uncle. Jake slammed me hard. Surely he had to get tired soon – surely. I grabbed handfuls of the quilt under me and yelled at him, taunted him, and drove his passion to an even higher pitch.

"Is that the best you got, Jake?"

Jake rolled me over onto my back. I almost toppled off the edge of the bed. He yanked me back by one leg. He lifted my legs over his shoulders and then pushed them even farther back. His hands were spread wide on my thighs as he pushed my knees up to my shoulders.

Jake slammed in with one hard thrust. He pushed so deep, I could almost taste him. The pain flashed through me and I screamed aloud in surprise.

"That's what I wanted," he growled. "I wanted to make you fucking scream."

He did it again. And again. Over and over, while I clawed at his back and begged him to stop, begged him to keep going, begged him to come as deep inside me as he could.

Jake finally began to lose control. His arms trembled on

either side of me. Sweat ran down his body. He threw his head back and cried out loud as he shoved as deep as he could. He throbbed inside me. The heat of him flooded me. I rocked against him. He held himself deep, until the thrill of the orgasm had passed.

Jake collapsed over me, breathing hard.

"Is that good enough?" he asked, as soon as he caught his breath.

I smiled against his skin. "I'm going to hurt so bad tomorrow."

"Do you mind?"

"No."

Jake carefully rolled off of me. He pulled me against him, even though we were both overheated and covered in a fine sheen of sweat. He kissed my forehead.

"Sleep with me," he said.

"I just did."

Jake laughed weakly. He closed his eyes. I watched him for a moment before I closed mine, too.

The next day, the phone rang. I was sitting on the couch, eating oatmeal, trying not to think and nursing the aches and pains of a body that had been roughly used. Jake was sitting in the recliner and reading the newspaper. We looked at each other through the space of two rings.

"It's him," Jake said.

"What do I say?"

"You be honest. He knows I'm here. He probably knows what we did, too."

I blushed. Jake smiled and looked down at the newspaper, but I knew his whole attention was focused on the phone call. I answered and Keith's voice came over the line.

"Did you two have fun?" he asked, and I was silent for one beat too long. I started to say something, but Keith cut me off. "It's all right. I sent him there."

I closed my eyes. "Why did you do that?"

Keith sighed. "Because I realized after you left that we really had reached a crossroads. I realized you and I had found something that we might never be able to compromise on. But I knew that you and Jake thought along the same lines."

There was actual pain in my chest as I listened to the sadness in Keith's words.

"We're over?" I asked, though I already knew.

"I think we are," Keith said gently.

I started to cry. "I'm sorry, Keith. It's not about you. It's about me, I think."

I could hear Keith's smile. "Don't cry over guilt, baby. You haven't done anything wrong. You can't make a heart feel what it just doesn't feel, you know?"

"I love you, Keith."

"I know. And I love you, too. That's what makes this so hard."

We sat in silence for a few moments. Jake had put down the newspaper and was watching me intently, but he didn't make any move to get up and come to me. He wasn't going to interfere.

"I have it easier than you," Keith said suddenly.

"What do you mean?"

"It's easier for me, because I know Jake will take care of you."

That was why he had sent Jake. He knew this was coming, and he wanted me to be okay once it did. Suddenly I realized that he really did mean what he said – that it wasn't about not caring. It was about caring so much that he wanted the best things for me, no matter what those things might be.

"I wish you had someone there with you," I said slowly, realizing that I really did mean it. "You deserve someone. I would give anything to know you would be okay."

Keith cleared his throat. "I will be okay. I promise you that. I've never broken a promise to you, have I?"

I smiled. "Never."

"Now listen to me, baby. I think there's a man around there somewhere who needs some attention. I'm willing to bet he's scared to death right now, but he's trying hard not to show it. You need to let him know I'm not a threat. You understand?"

That set off a fresh round of tears. Had I ever known someone so selfless?

"Yes."

"I'll see you both when you come back to town."

"Will you?"

Keith laughed, and though I could hear the tears, I knew it was genuine. "Absolutely."

I said goodbye and hung up the phone. Jake looked at me from the recliner. He hadn't moved and he looked calm, but a storm was brewing in his eyes. I stood up and walked slowly to him. I took his hand in mine, and he squeezed hard enough to hurt.

"Is he all right?" Jake asked.

"He will be."

"Are you okay?" he asked, though we both knew I wasn't. I looked into his eyes and offered the one thing that I knew would make us both feel better.

"Take me to bed," I said, and Jake smiled.

Disciplinary Action

Thomas S. Roche

Carrie comes up behind me and peers into my cubicle. I'm so entranced by the pictures on the screen that I don't even hear her until she clears her throat. I jump, and go to switch the windows on my computer. My hands are shaking so badly that I fumble with the mouse and the image stays there: a woman's rosy cheeks, with a feminine hand, long-nailed, resting on them. The woman was spanked so hard just a moment before the picture was snapped that hand-prints are still evident. I finally get the window closed and swivel on my office chair.

"Juliette," she says. "Could you come see me in my office, please?"

I get a sick feeling. It's over. I've been caught. I'm in big trouble; I might even be fired.

I'm still on probation. I can be fired at the drop of the hat. And I really, really need this job. Brent really needs me to keep this job, so he can do his art.

"Sure," I mumble, and start to get up from my chair, quickly jiggling my mouse to see if there's anything else I should close out before leaving the computer.

"There's no need for that," Carrie says crisply. "I've already seen it."

My head spins. I've already lost the job. I'm going to be fired. I can already hear my phone ringing with credit card collection calls.

I follow Carrie into her corner office with the enormous windows. She sits behind her desk and turns to her computer.

"Please close the door," she says absently, absorbed in what she's doing on the screen.

Now I know I'm in for it. I obey, the quiet thunk of the door like the fall of the guillotine.

"And turn the blinds, please," says Carrie, still sounding distracted and uninterested.

My God, this is really going to be humiliating. I've seen her fire people before – for much less than I was doing a moment ago. I can feel the tears welling up in my eyes as I pull the chain that closes the blinds. What will I do? Beg? Plead? Tell her I won't do it again? Tell her I really need the job?

"Have a seat," Carrie tells me, and when I do I see that she's turned her flat-panel monitor so that we can both see it.

There it is on the screen: Spanked Sluts. The website I was just looking at, the website that I've looked at many times in my three weeks here. The website that always makes me wet enough to soak my seat. I sit nervously in the chair facing Carrie's desk.

"I can explain," I begin, my voice sounding squeaky.

"I don't think so," Carrie says. "Or, rather, you don't need to. You're looking at porn at work. You know our company rules state that computers are not to be used for personal business."

I open my mouth to speak, struggling for an excuse as to why I *had* to look at Spanked Sluts, why it was an integral part of my job. I can't find one. I can feel my face going hot.

"I'm sorry," I say. "It's just that it's been so slow, and –"

Carrie clicks her mouse, changing windows. On the screen is Red-Cheeked Girls, another of my favorite websites. Another click, and it's Over The Knee. Punished Tarts. Red-Cheeked Schoolgirls. Slave Girrls Spanked. Forced To Bend Over. And my very favorite: Youvebeenaverybadgirl.com.

"I know you don't know this," says Carrie. "But with the monitoring system this company has in place, I can see everything you're doing on your computer. I've seen how much company time you devote to your extracurricular activities."

The tears brim over my eyes, and I try not to sniffle.

"I'm sorry," I tell her.

"No, I don't think you are sorry. I think if I give you half a chance to get away with it, you'll keep looking at these filthy websites on company time. Juliette, you seem like a nice girl. You even have a fiancé, you told me. What attracts you to this kind of filth?"

Now I can't stop them, the tears rolling out of my eyes, the sobs coming quickly. I try to suppress them as I say: "I don't know, Carrie. I just . . . can't stop myself."

"From looking at them on company time, I know. But do you look at them at home, too?"

The answer is too humiliating: I don't have to. Brent looks at them all the time, the raunchiest of the spanking sites – Spanked Sluts in particular. He finds the best images, bookmarks them, and sends them to my web-based email address, Spanked-Slut69.

And when I get home later, he does everything I've seen on the screen to me, and more. He draws pictures about it later, my face rendered in a cartoon frame based on the pictures he's bookmarked, my face twisted in pain and dismay as I writhe over the laps of faceless men and women.

"Yes," I finally tell her. "I look at them at home."

"Does your fiancé know?"

"Yes," I say meekly.

"And he likes it."

"He . . . he started it."

"Did he? So none of this is your fault, then?"

I search for the words. How can I tell her? How can I admit that Brent is the one who gives me the command to look at these sites while I am at work, that every morning he puts me over his lap, spanks me, slips his hands between my legs, fingers me until I'm right on the edge of an intense orgasm and then leaves me, panting and sweaty with my clit throbbing, and sends me off to work on trembling legs? That throughout the day I receive emails from him with links he orders me to look at – and that an order from my fiancé is an order I can't refuse? That by the time I get home each night, I'm so frenzied that I'll do anything – *anything* – he demands if he'll just put me over his lap, spank me again, and finger me until I come, sobbing with pleasure?

And that each night I do anything – *anything* – he orders me to, just to get him to do that?

"It's my fault," I say. "I know it's my fault."

"I see. Do you see yourself as the spanked or the spankee?" Her lips are curled with contempt, as if she already knows the answer. I know that she does: sometimes I feel like people can see it in my eyes. How could anyone look at me and not know what I want?

My voice is shaking.

"I'm . . . I'm submissive," I blurt out, surprised to hear myself say the words.

"That's what I thought." She glances over to the computer. "I see you like to be spanked by men," she says. "But also women. Many of these are lesbian sites," she says. "Girls punishing other girls."

I nod, my head spinning.

"What's your fiancé's name?"

"Brent," I say. "Brent Martinsen. He's an artist."

"Yes," says Carrie brusquely. "I know all about Brent Martinsen's filthy art. Is Brent your Master, or does he just spank you? Or do you just do everything he says?"

"He's – I–I do everything he says."

"So it's just that he thinks women should be bossed around and disciplined by men, is that right?"

"Um," I say. "He . . . he thinks *I* should."

"But some women boss other women around, don't they?" says Carrie icily.

Perhaps she can see me shiver; maybe she sees the flicker in my eyes, the heat that pulses between my legs.

"Yes," I say. "Some women are . . . some women are bosses."

"And some women discipline other women, don't they?"

My head is swimming, my thoughts disordered.

"Yes," I say softly.

"And what do you think about that?"

I'm so turned on I can barely speak. I was already turned on from the porn sites, but being forced to confess my lifestyle to my boss is more than I can take. My nipples are very hard. They show right through my silk top. I have to push my thighs together to prevent myself from dripping on Carrie's chair, especially since Brent doesn't allow me to wear panties.

"Yes," I say. "Sometimes women punish other women."

Carrie looks satisfied.

"I think what you did on company time certainly merits punishment, doesn't it?" Her eyes narrow. "It warrants disciplinary action."

I look up at her, the humiliation washing over me.

"Yes," I tell her.

She leans back in her chair. "Why don't you lock the door."

My eyes are wide; this can't be happening. I've only been here for three weeks.

I get up and do it, locking the door to Carrie's office and turning back to her, standing nervously on my high-heeled shoes. I've never gotten the hang of wearing the shoes that Brent insists on; I like the way I look, but I'm always stumbling and tripping like an idiot.

Carrie makes a gesture with her hand.

"Go ahead," she says. "Take them off."

"I'm sorry?" I ask.

"Your clothes," she says. "All of them."

"I–I can't do that," I says. "He —"

"Do you want me to call his cell phone?" asks Carrie. "And tell him you're about to lose your job if you don't take all your clothes off right now?"

My heart pounds. I can't believe this is happening. It's like a dream; maybe that's why I'm able to do it. I unbutton my shirt and slip it off, ashamed of the way my large breasts are peaked by hard nipples that show my arousal right through the transparent mesh bra. My nipples are dark circles, aching against the thin mesh.

My hands hang limp at my sides.

"All of them," she says.

I drape my blouse over the arm of the chair and unclasp my bra. My breasts feel sweaty, cooling in the breeze from the air conditioner. Again, I hesitate.

"I said *all* of them," growls Carrie.

My hands shaking, I unzip my short skirt. I slide it down my legs and it pools on the floor around my ankles. I step out of it, tottering more uncomfortably than ever on my four-inch heels now that I'm otherwise naked.

Carrie leans forward and peers at my body.

"Come around," she says, leaning back.

My face goes red hot. She's seen it. I am so humiliated I can barely walk. But I manage to come around the side of Carrie's desk and stand there while she inspects me, her eyes focusing on the place just above my sex, where my pubic hair would be if I wasn't shaved.

"You lied to me," she says sternly.

"I – I know."

"He's your Master, isn't he?"

I nod. "Yes."

"You should have told me straight off," says Carrie. "Now that we've gone this far, you're going to be in quite a bit of trouble if I spank you, aren't you?"

I take a deep breath. "I – I don't know."

Carrie leans forward a bit more, her finger coming to rest on the tattoo just above my sex. She traces the single word there, in ornate script: *SLAVE*.

"Well, that's not my concern," says Carrie. She leans back again, pushing the chair forward so that her legs, smooth with nude-colored stockings, brush against mine. "Get over my knee."

Fear strikes me. Brent would never allow me to be spanked by another woman – to *play* with another woman, it's called euphemistically enough – without his permission. I can't let Carrie take me over her knee. I just *can't*.

"Please," I blurt out, but Carrie snaps her fingers.

"I have the power to fire you right now, Juliette," she says. "Would you rather I do that?"

I shake my head, then nervously drape myself over Carrie's lap. Her office chair is a big leather one, with arms, so I have to perch myself precariously to maintain the position. It feels suddenly comfortable, familiar – I've draped myself over Brent's lap in this position, anticipating this same result. Many times – almost every night.

Her hand comes to rest on my bare bottom, her long finger-nails scratching it gently. I shiver and whimper a little.

"Does he spank you often enough?"

"Yes," I murmur. "Usually."

"But a girl like you," sighs Carrie, "can always be spanked a lot more than she is. You could be spanked 24/7 and it still wouldn't be enough, would it?"

I squirm in her lap.

"No, Ma'am," I moan.

"Your ass is very pink," she says. "Did he spank you last night?"

"This morning," I tell her, breathless. "Just before work."

Her hand slides between my slightly spread legs. Her fingers stroke my pussy, and I let out a plaintive cry of humiliation.

"Fingered you too while he was at it, it would seem. You're nice and wet. Or is that just from the pictures?"

"He fingered me," I bleat miserably.

"Does he always finger you when he spanks you?"

"Usually," I whimper. "Unless he's very angry with me."

"I'm very angry with you, Juliette."

"I know," I moan softly. "I'm sorry."

"Spread your legs wider," says Carrie.

I fall into the command, reacting exactly as I would if Brent had given it. It does not feel strange; I have submitted to many men before Brent. Never a woman, though, and that frightens me.

She touches my sex with a firmer pressure. I let out a tortured moan as her thumb finds my clit. She grasps my hair with her free hand. The feeling of pressure sends a surge of excitement through me. Brent always pulls my hair when he wants to get me going. I can feel my nipples, which are so very hard against the wool of her business suit. They feel only a little different than they feel against Brent's jeans when he spanks me. But what feels totally different is that there's no lump in her crotch, nothing pushing against my body to tell me that I'm pleasing her.

Her hand comes away from my sex, flicking droplets of my juice over my thighs. She spanks me, hard, making me yelp. I feel a rush of shame – the walls are paper-thin around here. People in the hall can surely hear.

Her hand comes down again, hard, and my naked body shudders as the blow meets my cheeks. With Carrie, there is no warm-up, no gentle spanks to get me started – much as with Brent. She spanks me again, and again, faster and faster as I writhe in her lap. My arousal mounts as the pain increases. The blows send hard thudding sensations into my cunt – I know I can come if I can just bring my thighs together a little bit. . . .

"Spread them!" she snaps. "Spread them wide!"

"Y – yes," I gasp. "Yes, um . . ."

"Don't call me Mistress," she barks. "You've already got a Master. I'm not his fucking girlfriend."

"Yes, Carrie," I whimper.

Her hand comes down fast, this time, harder than before. But she is not spanking my ass now – her open palm connects with my cunt, again, again, again, and the stinging blow wrenches great moans out of me. The pain makes me rise up on my hands and knees, makes me perch over her precariously in a vain attempt to get away. She puts her hand on my ass and shoves me down into her lap, hard, then begins spanking my cunt in earnest. I moan wildly, no longer caring if people outside Carrie's office can hear. I moan wildly because I'm going to come.

She knows it, too – she spanks my sex harder so that it hurts, and hurts bad, when I finally reach the peak and climax uncontrollably.

White-hot waves of pleasure course through my naked body. I want to say "I'm sorry" – Brent always makes me ask before I come, and I'm punished if I don't. But Carrie doesn't give a damn. And she doesn't stop spanking my cunt – not until long after I've come, when my sensitive pussy is so pained I can feel it swelling with the force of her blows. It's hot, now, and I know I won't be able to sit still for days.

I'm sobbing when she's finally satisfied. She tips herself up slightly, dumping me painfully onto the floor.

I curl into a ball, my body still pulsing with the sensations of orgasm. My sobs slowly dwindle as I look up at her through eyes blurry with tears. Carrie has lifted her prim pencil-skirt, tucking it under her ass.

She's not wearing panties underneath. Her sex is naked, framed by the angled lines of her garters between her spread legs. She's tucked her ass forward so that it's on the edge of the chair, and her trimmed pussy is open, glistening in the fluorescent lights.

"Well?" she says.

It hurts for me to move. My ass and cunt are so sore I can barely get myself onto my hands and knees again. Looking up at her, I nervously lower my face between her thighs. I am so used to giving head that the position feels perfectly right, but the scent is unfamiliar. And when I touch my mouth to her close-cropped sex, the taste is even more exotic.

"That's a good girl," she sighs as I let my tongue laze out and begin to lick her clit. "Get all of it, dear. The lips. The hole. I want you to taste it. I'm sure Brent wants you to taste it, too."

Carrie is so wet that her juices flow onto my tongue as I lick between her lips, swirling the tip of my tongue around her entrance. The flavor is tangy, musky, salty and a little bit sweet. I feel my pained cunt responding as I service her. Her thighs close slightly around my head, as if to hold me in place. Her breath comes quickly.

"Now back to the clit," she murmurs.

I return my attentions to her clit. I begin to tongue her rhythmically, the way I liked it when men used to go down on me. Before I was the one always doing the servicing. Before I became a slave.

"Very good. A little more pressure, Juliette. Just a little more."

Carrie's voice is rich with arousal. Her hand drifts to my head; first one hand, then both hands tangle in my hair. She begins to grind her hips against the chair in time with the thrusts of my tongue. She's getting close, I can tell. That knowledge makes me lick her more firmly, my own sex responding in kind, moisture dripping down my inner thighs.

"Don't stop!" she growls, and then she comes. I continue licking her as her body bucks and pumps against me, driving her clit more powerfully onto my tongue. She grips my hair hard now, pulling it, shoving my face between her legs.

Then, an instant later, she is finished. With both hands still gripping my hair, she yanks my head from her crotch and shoves me back. I spill backwards and land on my tortured ass, gasping as the sore mounds reach the rough industrial carpet. I sit there looking up at her, my cheeks stained with tears, Carrie's juices running down my chin.

Carrie lifts her ass off the chair, pulls down her skirt, and returns her attention to her computer.

"I'll be sending you some websites," says Carrie. "Please be sure that you only look at them when the phones are slow. Don't forget to put your clothes on, Juliette. And you might want to fix your makeup."

I take a great shuddering gasp of relief and rise painfully to my feet. I put my clothes on with shaking hands, glancing over to see if Carrie is watching me.

She is not; I have been disregarded.

As I button my blouse, I blurt out: "Thank you, C—!"

I stop. The name sounds wrong on my lips, still covered with the juices of Carrie's pussy.

"Thank you, Ma'am," I say.

"What will happen when you tell your Master about this?" asks Carrie, without looking up from the computer.

I feel a wave of dread.

"He'll spank me," I say. "For . . . for letting you do this."

"Good," she tells me. "He'll be spanking you a lot more for that in the future."

I take a deep breath. "Yes, Ma'am," I say softly.

"You missed a button," she says, without looking up.

I look down at my blouse; it is buttoned unevenly. I fix it quickly and unlock the door.

I pause with my hand on the knob.

"Thank you for not firing me," I say. "Ma'am."

"Don't be sure I won't," Carrie says. "You'll still have to convince me."

I nod. "Yes, Ma'am," I say, and leave her office.

Nothing But This

Kristina Lloyd

I call him the Boy although he isn't. He's skinny enough, it's true – as skinny as the kids who do backflips in the square – and there's not a single hair on his flat brown chest. But his age is in his eyes, eyes as green as a cat's, and when I look right at him, though we're meant to be ignoring him, I see eyes that might be a thousand years old.

He's been following us for half an hour, weaving among the crowds, his flip-flops slap-slapping in the dust of the souk. "Hey, mister! Hey, lady!" he keeps calling. "You wanna buy carpet? Teapot? Saffron? You wanna buy incense? Come, come! Come to meet my uncle."

His urge to "come, come" sounds grubby and erotic and the refrain pulses in my head like some dark drumbeat, weird enough for me to wonder if it's going to bring on one of my migraines.

"Lady, you wanna buy handbag? Real leather! The best! Hey, mister, nice wallet for you! Look this way! You are my guest. Come!" The Boy averts his eyes, head down and spinning, and the whole song and dance routine seems a pastiche of the real hustlers, an empty act he can turn off at will. No wonder he can't look at us: we'd see right through him.

"I feel like David bloody Niven," mutters Tom.

Tom's posh as fuck, so self-assured and confident you don't even notice it. He's relaxed and ironic. A bit on the prim side, it has to be said, but I adore every hot salty inch of him. I like to draw him, standing, sitting, lying, sprawling, my futile bid to capture him in charcoal and pencils. In evening class, I learnt to draw not just the object but the space around it. I learnt to see absence. "What's not there is as important as what is," said our tutor, although personally I'd contest that with Tom. I'm quite a fan of what's there. Naked, he's pale and softly muscled with strong swimmer's shoulders and thighs like hams. Sometimes I sketch his cock, big and randy or just lolling on his thigh, framed in dark curls, and when I show him the end result he'll invariably wince. "Oh God," he drawls, looking away and sounding slightly camp. "You're so *vulgar*." But he can't help smiling and I know deep down he likes it.

"Pssst!"

It's the Boy. I can't see him, only hear him. The medina is crammed with noise, its maze of tiny streets choked with the scents of paraffin, leather, spit-roast meats, sour sweat, baked earth and strong rough tobacco. Here and there, the souk opens out, exposing its squinting stall-holders to a livid blue sky. But for now we're in the thick of it, two clueless pink-skins in an ancient labyrinth, lost among beggars, hawkers, shoppers, mopeds, donkey carts and big wire cages squawking with heaps of angry hens. The Boy's hiss slices through the chaos, clean as a whistle, but I can't spot him anywhere.

I'm disappointed. I'm supposed to be relieved because the official line is he's been annoying us from the off, prancing around like some mad imp of consumerism, urging us to buy this, buy that, buy the other. The thing is, we do want to buy a carpet, a nice Berber runner for the hallway, but he's probably on commission and, besides, we'd rather do it in peace.

My disappointment tempers the arousal I'm half-ashamed to acknowledge. At first, I couldn't be sure it was sexual although I suspected it was. Heck, it usually is with me. And then I knew damn well it was when my groin flickered its need and I grew aware of my inner thighs, filmy with sweat, sliding wetly as I walked, my sarong flapping around my ankles. But it's a weird kind of sexual. It's not as if I fancy him, this slip of a lad with the calm, creepy eyes, but I'm drawn to him in a way I can't identify. He keeps dropping back from us to sidle among the crowd or prowl at a distance, elegant and stealthy, stalking us like prey. My money's in a belt. I must have checked it a dozen times. I don't think he's a thief though.

I don't know what he is. All I know is he's sparked off in me some intrigue, some furtive hunger that makes me not quite trust myself. We keep walking, Tom and I, and within the humid fabric of my knickers, I'm as sticky and swollen as a Barbary fig.

"Pssst!"

His call sounds so close I actually look over my shoulder, expecting him right there, but no sign. It's as if he's invisible, some mythical djinni up to no good or a golem from the old Jewish quarter, laughing to himself as I pat my money belt once again.

"Seem to have shaken him off, the little shit," Tom says mildly as he unscrews his water bottle.

I realise Tom's not hearing what I hear, making me question my senses. The heat in this place stupefies me and I haven't been sleeping well either. At night, after an evening of jugglers, magicians, fire-eaters and snake-charmers, the bedsheets tangle themselves around my legs, cobras for the pipe-player, and my mind whirls with madness and enchantments. To soothe me, I think of the stillness beyond the town: snow-capped mountains, endless deserts and a black velvet night sprayed with silver stars. But I sleep fitfully, slipping in and out of dreamscapes, grotesque and lewd, and I wake each morning sloppy with desire. When I sink onto Tom's cock, drowsy and heavy, I feel fucked already, post-coitally limp, as if I've been possessed by an incubus, a gleeful demon who screwed me senseless as I slept. My limbs seem to liquefy as I ride Tom, awash with vagueness, remembering feral creatures, how they pawed at my flesh, and priapic monsters with gas-mask faces, rutting in steamy swamps.

I don't imagine we'll buy a carpet today. I'm not really in the mood. Feeling a tad psychotic, to tell the truth. But I hide it well. I'm probably just premenstrual.

A few minutes later and the Boy's with us again. I don't see him but I smell him, a pungent sexual whiff as we pass stalls selling metalware, shards of sunlight glancing off pewter, copper and brass. Then, in the shadows behind, I see two green beads peering out from the gloom, points of luminescence, freakishly bright. My heart pumps faster. Among so many brown-eyed folk, those eyes are hauntingly strange, non-human almost. He doesn't belong to these people, I think. An outsider, perhaps; a man who leaps across gullies high in the Atlas mountains, surviving on thin air.

"Oh, God, there's that smell again," complains Tom.

A few yards ahead, the Boy darts beneath a tatty awning. He's wearing filthy, calf-length shorts and his legs, I notice, are dark with hair. He's a youth, I think, and then some. Old enough, I'm quite sure, to go snuffling under my sarong.

"It's foul," says Tom. "Really fucking rank."

I think he's talking about the Boy. I think he's smelled his appetite and is repulsed. Then it dawns on me he's talking about the tannery. When we were last here, I was about ready to retch with the stink of it but now the tannery's just a backnote and it's the Boy's odour I'm getting. It's as if my senses are tuning in to him, to the sound, smell and sight of him, and everything else recedes. The whole thing's starting to make me nervous.

Tom offers me the water before taking a swig himself. He has beautiful manners, partly because he's from Surrey but stemming too from a naturally submissive streak he doesn't fully acknowledge. He's no pushover, believe me, but his gentle manner, combined with a curious intellect, makes him tend to the deferential or at least a fascinated passivity. Give him a good book and he's lost for hours. Give him a good woman – or better still a bad one – and he's lost for months. I took him away from someone else. Well, he left her for me at any rate. Two years down the line and we're still in love, half-daft and quite besotted.

But I'm no fool. I know damn well if some other woman caught his heart he'd be gone in a flash, leaving me spitting with rage. I like Tom a lot. I want to hang on to him. I want to keep him mine. But all I can do is hope for the best. And meanwhile, I try to catch him as I can, all those impossible charcoals and pencils, all that seductive permanent ink.

My favourite sketches are the ones I do in bed at night, Tom lying there with his mouth agape, dreaming eyeballs quivering beneath his lids. I love him so much when he's fast asleep, when he doesn't even know he exists. Tom doesn't realise I do this. I keep the sketches well hidden, my treasured possessions, proof of all the hours I stole from him while I watched him sleep. I have bouts of insomnia, you see. It's not only out here.

"Half a mo'. Batteries," says Tom. He edges past slow, swathed people, and I wait for him by a spice stall. Black strips of tamarind and threaded figs hang like jungle vegetation over sacks heaped with nuts, dried fruit, tea leaves and herbs. SNORING CURE NEVER FAIL! says a sign and APHRODISIAC FOR THE KING! proclaims another. The air is powder-dry and colours catch in my throat, scarlet, copper, ochre and rust, an earthy rainbow of seasonings that makes me cough like a hag. "I have medicine! Never fail!" cries a djellaba-hooded man, and I protest my health, realising there's some seriously dodgy shit for sale here: a turtle strapped to the canopy's scaffold, bunches of goats' feet, dried hedgehogs, chameleons, snake skins and live lizards flicking around in giant-sized jars.

"Pssst! Lady!"

His voice goes straight to my cunt. The sensation's so strong he might have tongued me there. My senses reel and I turn, catching a glimpse of sharp brown shoulder blades before he's swallowed up by the crowd. Across the way, Tom's holding a pack of batteries, appealing to a stallholder who looks out with a half-blind gaze, his eyes veiled with cataracts. A woman with a wispy beard jostles me. Instinctively, I check my money-belt and I see the Boy just feet away, throwing a backwards glance, an invitation to follow. I cannot refuse him. I don't even question my options. I just go.

As I move, Tom turns. He catches my eye, nodding acknowledgment of my direction. It's fine, he's cool. He rarely makes a fuss. And, should we lose each other, we've both got our phones. An image comes to me of my mobile trilling away, whiskery rats nosing the screen where the words "Tom calling . . ." glow for no one. I push the image away. It's not important. But the Boy is.

Anxious not to lose him, I squirm through the crowds, keeping his shorn head in my sights. A man with a monkey distracts me briefly and for a terrible moment I think I've lost him. Frantic, I whirl around, a vortex of faces blurring past me, colours racing. He's gone, he's gone. But seconds later, I have him again. I watch as he vanishes into an archway so narrow that at first I think he's ghost-walked through a wall. Panicking, I hurry, elbowing people aside. Somebody curses me but I don't care. I'm high with fear. I don't know why I'm following him. I only know I can't stop. Dark eyes flash around me, and my cunt's pumping nearly as hard as my heart. I'm in the grip of something scary, my juices are hot, and I try to remember if I've eaten something funny. Maybe I stood too close to those desiccated hedgehogs. God knows what they were for. God knows what I'm doing.

In the alley, I pause to catch my breath. I've got the Boy in view again. The alley's cool and whitewashed, not much wider than a person, and a few feet in, the racket of the souk goes dead. There's no one around but us. Suddenly, it is so still. So silent. My own breath surrounds me, a whispering rush like a seashell to my ear. I walk on and yet I don't think I move. I just pant. The sun doesn't fall here, but the alley seems to shine with its own light, the white walls reflecting each other in a numinous glow, and I wonder if this is it. I wonder if I'm dying on an operating table, my soul sailing up to enter the kingdom of heaven, or to at least try tapping on its door. I want to look back to see where I've come from but my head's far too heavy. I can't turn.

There is nothing but this: me, my breath and the Boy. It's as if I've slipped into a chink in the world.

Several yards ahead, half-crouched, he creeps along with cautious grace. His slender torso is sweet and supple, the rack of his ribs visible beneath grimy fudge-brown skin. The scent of him drifts in his wake, pheromonal and ripe. Civet, perhaps, or musk. How pliant his body must be, I think. How smooth his skin, how eager his hands, how tireless those beautiful, plum-coloured lips.

I follow, both of us keeping a steady pace, then the Boy stops, poised low. His arched spine protrudes in a knobbly ridge and the stubble of his hair prickles with light. I freeze, feeling I ought to, and realise I'm barely breathing. Then, slowly, the Boy swivels his head around to face me. And that's when I nearly keel over. Because the eyes that look into mine belong to no man on earth. For several stunned seconds, I stare back. They are cat's eyes: green as gooseberries with black slit pupils.

Fear thumps me in the gut but I cannot scream. I cannot move either. I can't do anything. I just gawp, rooted to the spot.

He smirks and turns away. I think I must be in one of my dreams. Soon, I tell myself, I'll wake at the hotel and I'll straddle Tom's cock in a trance of remembering. I'll rock back and forth, head swimming with a post-human dystopia, a stinking medieval market peopled with DNA freaks or inter-species offspring. Look around and they all seem perfectly normal till you spot their webbed feet, forked tongues, folded wings or dog-fang teeth. And I'll climax and so will Tom. Then we'll get up, have breakfast, take a bus to a town with tiled palaces, koi carp and orange trees, and we'll buy something lovely in Spanish leather or cedar wood and everything will be all right.

The Boy creeps forwards. I'm so scared and I'm so wet. But wet is winning. I follow, turning a corner then another until he ducks into a small archway in the wall. Moments later, I'm there too, head down and heart hammering as I descend three worn white steps.

In front of me, a cool cavernous chamber opens out. Hung with tapestries and oil lamps, its edges are banked with stacks of carpets, and in a far corner stands a cluster of earthenware jugs alongside sacks of grain. Sunbeams, soft and fuzzed with dust, slant down from high plaster-work arches, a tranquil light for prayer. It smells of straw and mice.

I catch a glimpse of the Boy as he flits from one stone pillar to another then stays there, hiding. Sitting cross-legged on a tall pile of carpets is a bald, muscular man with dark skin and heavy brows, his jawline shadowed with bristles. He's bare-chested, whorls of black hair clouding his pecs and making a seam over his neatly rounded paunch. He looks like a cross between the Buddha and a thug. It's not a look I'm familiar with but I do like it. He has a small, neat smile, and he's observing me steadily, chin propped on his fist. I get the feeling he's been expecting me.

"Hi," I say, trying to sound brave.

I walk deeper into the chamber, across the flagstone floor, shoulders back. I know this man is going to fuck me and, frankly, I'm ready for it.

No one replies. The man keeps watching me, smiling. Though I'm still scared, I have an inkling of a new confidence. I'm starting to feel powerful and ageless, like some whore of the Old Testament. The Boy emerges from behind his pillar to lean against it, arms folded and smirking. His attitude's changed. He has the jaded, haughty air of a rent boy, hard faced and sleazy. It's attractive in a sick kind of way. His eyes are normal too. Well, relatively speaking. They are the most astonishing sea-green – *National Geographic* eyes – but they are normal in that they are human. I must have been seeing things earlier, a trick of the light, nothing more.

They both watch me as I sashay forwards. I feel deliciously easy. I'm a harlot, houri, concubine, slave. I could dance like Salome, seduce them with a strip show, except I don't have seven veils, just sarong, vest and Birkenstocks.

Besides, my guess is, these guys really don't need seducing.

"You chose well," says the man, addressing the Boy.

Now hang on, I think. Didn't I just walk here myself of my own free will? Then I correct myself. Who am I trying to kid? I've been picked up, haven't I?

"My uncle," says the Boy, grinning and nodding at the man.

Uncle tips up his chin in a curt greeting. "Show her to me," he says to the Boy.

Barefoot, the Boy saunters forwards. He parts my sarong, exposing my legs, and presses his hand between my thigh. All the weight of my body is suddenly in my cunt, resting in that skinny hand. My gusset is damp and he paddles his fingers there, grinning at me before latching on to my clit. He rubs through the fabric, judging my expression. I want to appear impassive but the smell and touch of him makes me dizzy with longing. Truly, I can't remember ever feeling so horny. I guess I don't manage to pull off the cool, composed look because the

Boy chuckles softly. In a whisper, he says, "Ah, you like that, don't you? Hot little bitch."

Well, you got me there, I think.

"She's OK, Uncle," announces the Boy. "Nice and wet." He tucks the gusset aside then pushes two fingers up inside me. My knees nearly buckle. "Really wet," he adds, stirring his two fingers around. In the silence, I hear my juices clicking.

"Excellent," says Uncle in a thick, languid voice. "We have a willing woman."

"A willing slut," says the Boy, "who wants to get fucked." He seems to be relishing the words, testing their strangeness like an adolescent keen to rid himself of innocence.

I'm relishing them too. I like being objectified. It takes the heat off having to be yourself.

The Boy, still working me with his fingers, slips his other hand up my top. He strokes me through my bra before pushing up the cups to squeeze and massage. My nipples are crinkled tight and he flicks and rocks them, bringing my nerve endings to seething life. Then, just as I start to feel I'm losing myself, falling open to ecstasy, the Boy pulls away and crosses the floor to Uncle.

It's a cruel, desolate moment. I'm about to protest but before I can utter a word, the Boy has sprung up onto the carpets, leaping from a standstill like a mighty ballet dancer. On his haunches, he straddles Uncle who reclines, mouth parted, to suck on the Boy's fingers, offered like dangling grapes. The Boy cups the man's shiny head, supporting it, and Uncle goes slack with surrender, eyes closed in bliss, as he slurps and snuffles on a sample of my snatch.

Now, I'm not averse to a spot of guy-on-guy action but I've only just arrived and I'm feeling a touch neglected. So I walk towards them because, dammit, I want to play too. As I near, they stop their weird feeding and, holding the pose, look down at me with benign curiosity, blinking heavily. It's as if they've never seen me before. Jesus, it's creepy. Without smiling, they continue to stare and blink for what seems like an age. A pair of green eyes and a pair of bright brown ones.

Then Uncle perks up, his expression changing to a villainous leer. He looks seriously gorgeous, like he ought to be behind bars. Sneering, he sits straight, swinging his legs over the edge of the carpet-pile, and delves into the crotch of his baggy pants. His pants are slate-blue silk, and a materialistic impulse asserts itself because that's just the shade I want in the hallway. I consider asking for a thread so I can choose a carpet with a matching weave but the moment passes. I have a different object of desire, other needs to gratify.

"Suck my dick for me," says the man, grinning. He releases a big fat erection, wanking it gently, the muscles of his beefy arm flexing under dark skin. It's a beautiful brute of a cock, arrogant and obscenely large.

"Dirty bitch," adds the Boy. He still sounds like a kid trying out rude words. "Suck the man's dick."

I'm happy to oblige. The stack of carpets are almost shoulder height and all I need do is lower my head to engulf him. His pubes tickle my nose and, butting deep within my mouth, he's superbly stout and powerful. My head bobs between his thighs and I'm getting weaker and wetter as I dream how it'll be when this beast slides into me. The Boy drops to the floor and I feel him at my feet, nuzzling my ankles then crawling under my sarong. I spread my legs for him and feel him rising, the heat of him on my skin, his shorn, silky head, his tongue trailing a path up my inner thighs. He pulls down my knickers and I feel him between my legs, his hot breath on my cunt before his tongue, so delicate and perfect, dances over my clit and squirms into my folds.

Oh, my. That tongue has truly been places. Like his eyes, it could be a thousand years old, a tongue that's pleasured geisha girls, ladyboys and Babylonian whores. Fingers fill my cunt, a thumb rubs my arsehole and moments later I'm coming hard, gasping around Uncle's cock, Uncle clutching my head, keeping me steady for fear I neglect his pleasure in favour of my own.

"She's a slippery little bitch, isn't she, huh?"

Uncle's voice is loud enough to carry across the chamber. He's talking to someone else; not to the Boy, and certainly not to me. I pull back and turn, wiping saliva from my mouth.

Tom, of course. Hell's teeth, I'd forgotten him. He's standing within the white stone archway, looking somewhat dazed. Really, I'd completely forgotten him, forgotten the man I love. Well, I guess fresh meat can do that to a girl.

Tom stares, mouth sagging dumbly. I worry for a moment, fearing my blue-eyed boy is going to be appalled, but I can see he's interested, absorbing the scene. It's that fascinated passivity again. "My God," I can almost hear him say. "You're so *vulgar*."

"Come, come," cries Uncle, jumping down from the carpets. "Welcome, my brother!" He pumps Tom's hand and claps him on the shoulder as if they're the best of mates. "You want her to suck your dick too, huh?" Pleased with himself, Uncle laughs over-loudly.

I think Tom's had a hit of whatever I've had, the scent of dried hedgehog or something. He smiles. I know exactly what he's going to say. He's going to say, "*I* don't mind" in that sing-song way he does when I say, "Shall we have coffee here or there? Rice for dinner or pasta?" It can get a bit annoying, to tell the truth. He looks at me; his smile's ironic. "*I* don't mind," he says, and I realise he knew that I knew he was going to say that, and his tongue's in his cheek because he knows all that knowing will amuse me. Long-term relationships can be so nice.

The Boy, on his hands and knees, peeps out from under my sarong to edge a cautious pace forwards. Then he's motionless, watching as Uncle leads Tom to a low bank of carpets, stacked at three levels like a shallow flight of steps. A hazy shaft of sunlight falls across them, revealing tiny squalls of dust as the men clamber and sprawl across this wool-woven stage. Uncle sits on the higher level, legs akimbo, and Tom lolls within his silk-clad thighs, head resting there as he yields to an off-centre shoulder massage. Uncle bows forwards, murmurs in Tom's ear, and Tom smiles gently, stretching his spine in a discreet arch, his pleasure private and contained, as the man kneads with big oafish hands.

I stand there, entranced, hardly able to believe what I'm seeing. The Boy edges closer, moving gingerly as if wary of disturbing them. Sitting back on his heels, he watches intently as Tom relaxes deeper in to the massage, occasionally grunting.

When Tom and I fuck, a glazed expression sometimes settles on his face. His eyes close, his mouth drops open, and he looks completely gone, blanked out with bliss as I move on top. He's got that slightly dead quality about him now, and when Uncle reaches forward to remove his T-shirt, Tom acquiesces, raising his arms, as docile and obliging as a sleepy child. He doesn't even protest when the Boy pads forwards to nuzzle his pale chest. All he does is smile fondly and, like a basking chimp, he stretches his arms back, exposing their white undersides, tendons taut, his dark patches of armpit hair attracting the Boy who tentatively sniffs, a hand sweeping broad caresses over Tom's flexing body. Tom is clearly loving it.

Well, you sly old tart, I think.

I can't take my eyes off him. I wonder if they've drugged him. And then I'm clearly not thinking straight myself because soon I'm wondering whether it actually *is* Tom. Perhaps someone – or something – has got inside his body because I've never seen him like this before. Tom likes to size up situations, to tread carefully, to fret unnecessarily; and he's never shown even the slightest interest in men. And now look at him, pushing the boundaries of his experience as if it were a walk in the park. I start to fear I may never get him back.

But then I notice his smile fading and he moistens his lips, a small moment of nervous desire. It's exquisite, so tender and Tom-like, and I feel I know who he is again. I see his Adam's apple bob in his throat and, in his neck, a hint of tension, as he tests the air for a kiss. The Boy bends over him, their lips meet, and lust flares in my groin. I watch a knot of muscle shifting in the Boy's jaw, movement in Tom's neck, and I'm all eyes as, without breaking the kiss, the Boy reaches down to unzip Tom's fly. Tom's erection springs out, weighty and lascivious.

I don't know what I want to do most: watch or join in.

Then Uncle grins at me, rummaging around in his silky blue crotch. He exposes his cock and moves it against Tom's face, tipping it back and forth like a wind-screen wiper. "Come here," Uncle says to me. "Bring us titties."

He's dead right: I want to join in. So I cross to them, whipping off my top half as I do so. Greedy and urgent, I scramble up onto the carpets and Uncle welcomes me by holding out a brawny arm. He opens his mouth and I fill it immediately with soft pink breast, pressing a hand to his crisp chest hair, my body pushing against the bulk of his belly. His tongue lashes my nipple and he delves under my sarong, searching eagerly for my hole. With a force that makes me gasp, he plugs my wetness with thick, crude fingers. Grinning up at me, he holds my nipple between his teeth and gently pulls on it, stretching my flesh. I hold his gaze, daring him to keep right on going.

For the first time, I notice how stunning his eyes are. They're a hard amber brown, sparkling like topaz. But this is no time to be romanticising, because the guy's moving us into position, my sarong and belt are off, and I'm utterly naked, poised above that prodigious cock, buttocks split in his big rough hands, cunt wide open. With heavy luxury, I sink down on him, groaning all the way until I'm stretched and stuffed to capacity.

Truly, it's a beautiful moment, made more beautiful by the fact that beside me is Tom, being sucked off by the Boy. They're both naked too, Tom with his knees apart, the Boy's shorn head bobbing in his crotch, his pert little butt stuck up in the air. Sprawled against the carpets, Tom has an arm flung wide, eyes closed, mouth open. I've never seen him looking quite so dead. I wonder if his expression's the same when I go down on him. My guess is not. All the same, I try and commit that face to memory, thinking maybe I can reproduce it some time in charcoal and pencil.

Tom must sense me looking because as I start to slide on Uncle's cock, he reaches out with a blind hand to stroke my arse. In that tiny affectionate gesture, I feel such a connection with him, such warmth. And I feel free to fuck like there's no tomorrow, knowing Tom and I are united, mutual support in mutual depravity; for richer, for poorer; for better, for worse.

Uncle clasps my hips, bouncing me up and down, and I'm as light as a doll in his hands. This man can do what he wants with me, I think. And I don't mind if he does. It's a while since I've been overpowered. The two of us mash and grind, silk hissing beneath me, sweat forming on my back where sunlight heats my skin.

"Hey, brother," calls Uncle, addressing Tom, "does she like it in her ass? Huh? A big prick in her tiny little asshole?"

Tom's too zonked to reply immediately. He just sprawls there, half-dead, before his head rolls sideways, eyes still closed. When he finally speaks, it sounds as if it's costing him an enormous effort. "Probably," he croaks.

The Boy pulls away from him. Tom groans in despair.

"Dirty little slut," says the Boy excitedly. His cock is ramrod stiff, its ruddy tip gleaming, and against his scrawny frame it looks grotesquely large. He springs off the carpets, takes a small copper can from near an Aladdin's lamp, and pours thick clear liquid into the palm of his hand. "Uncle," he says, "you in her pussy, me in her ass. Bam, bam, bam. We fuck her hard, yes?"

Uncle laughs lightly.

"No," I whisper. Then louder: "Yes. God, yes."

The Boy leaps back onto the carpets, lubricating his cock with lamp oil. Tom groans again. I reach out, feeling sorry for him, and Uncle, gent that he is, shuffles us closer. I lean over to kiss Tom and he responds eagerly, our tongues lashing awkwardly as Uncle pounds into me. Sweat dribbles down my back into the crack of my buttocks and I feel the Boy's greasy fingers press against my arsehole. He wriggles a finger past my entrance and I'm groaning into Tom's mouth as the Boy opens me out, forcing the ring of my muscles wider, making me slick and ready.

"Keep her still," urges the Boy, and Uncle obliges, his cock lodged high.

"Lean over," orders the Boy and I obey. His knob nudges my arsehole and pushes into my resistance. I think I'm going to be too small for him, my other hole too full, and that it's all going to hurt like hell. I make a feeble cry of protest.

"Don't pretend," snaps the Boy. He grasps my hips then there's a flash of pain and, with a sudden slippery rush, he's fully inside me, and I'm swamped by dark, fierce pleasure. Uncle calls out triumphantly. I feel I'm on the brink of collapse, the intensity of having both holes packed so solidly taking me to a place I didn't know existed. I gasp into Tom's mouth, quite beyond kisses now, as the two men start to drive into me. Bam, bam, bam, as the Boy said. I have to pull away from Tom. I need air. I need to groan and wail.

Beneath me, Uncle's face is flushed with exertion. He spots me looking at him and he grins, meeting my eye with a deliberate gaze. There's the weirdest kind of friction going on inside me, the two men jostling my body as they fuck. And then I know I've lost it. I know pleasure has reduced me to lunacy because I see something wild in Uncle's eyes. His pupils contract and, for a moment, they are like the Boy's: bright with black, slit pupils.

It's the light, I tell myself, the light, the light. And I can't bear to look. I flop forward onto Tom, seeking a kiss, wanting the reassurance of his mouth, his nose, his face. I'm close to coming and so is Tom because the Boy, gorgeous greedy creature, is sucking him off again. As the two cocks shove fast and hard inside me, I nudge my clit and then gasp into Tom's mouth, our lips so hot, so wet and loose: "I'm coming, I'm coming." That sets him off and he groans and pants, his body twitching as he peaks. My orgasm rolls on and on, and Tom is still gasping into my mouth, still coming. It feels sublime, orgasm-without-end. Our lips slide and smear, and nothing else can touch us. It's as if we're melting into each other at every breath. And I am him and he is me, and we are all ecstasy, all delirium, all gone.

Sex, I think, will never be the same again.

We didn't buy a carpet for the hallway that holiday. But sometimes it's like that. You go out hoping to buy one thing and come home with something totally different. I've stopped drawing Tom in the middle of the night as well. I don't feel the need any more. I don't have that yearning to capture him. Because I have my Tom, I have him entirely, from now until the end of time. And if I ever start to doubt it, I just need to picture his face, glazed with rapture at the point of climax. He doesn't know what he looks like. I don't know what I look like either. People don't, generally speaking, do they?

All I know is that he'll never look at another woman like that; he'll never be able to. Because when he comes, something shifts in his eyes. He rides the wave, annihilated with bliss, the two of us breathing so hard and so deep. And when he looks at me, his beautiful blue eyes have black, slit pupils. And I am him and he is me. And I know we are possessed.

Betty Came

M. Christian

She remembered the first time that Betty came. Sitting in her
tiny kitchen, beams of warm sunlight painting it with brilliant
yellow stripes, it was so easy to think of Betty as being there,
next to her. It had been one of Audrey's all-night parties.
Another of the ex-boy's "No other reason" Friday night dancing and drinking bashes. June had gotten pretty toasted early
on – washing down the stubborn truth that she and Wendy had
broken up the month before – and was quite satisfied to sit in a
corner of the hideously cluttered apartment and get lost in the
Pussy Tourrette album blasting from Audrey's frankensteined
sound system.

Didn't know the tiny black girl's name, didn't even see who
she'd come with. One second June was belting back her fifth
Red Rock and the next the room exploded with a billion
flashbulbs when she had walked in.

But Wendy was still a dull ache and the one thing you don't
think about when you have that "no one loves me any more"
pang is that someone, suddenly, would.

Somehow, intros were made and June found herself fighting
that fifth Red Rock to be on her best behavior. Chat. Joke.
Smile. Flirt. Smile some more. Bat those eyelashes. Flirt. Chat.

While the sexy heat of the sparkling little girl was something
that made all of June's clouds blow away, the beers (and a bitchy
week at work) had started to take their toll on her. Even against
the searchlight brilliance of the girl's smile, incredible cheekbones, and humming eyes, June's own face started to feel
haggard, drawn, and – yawn!

She remembered saying something like: "Sorry. Luckily I live right around the corner."

"I'll walk you," the dream had said, smiling a sunrise at her.

Her place was a mess, of course. Isn't it always? Some kind of universal law: bring trick (or love of your life) home and the first thing they see when they walk in the door is a pair of stained panties tossed on the floor.

"Wouldn't want you to be too clean," the lovely charcoal sketch had said, leaning in close enough so that June could slip an arm around her.

A cup of coffee had sounded good. June prattled some kind of empty dialogue, pretty much to herself, as she had ground the beans and tried to find the sugar. She was pretty sure she had said something about what she did for a living (messenger), what she liked to do (theater), what she liked (pecan pie and sleeping in), and what she wanted (someone special). Now, sitting in the same kitchen, June wasn't sure if she'd mentioned Wendy. She hoped she hadn't.

Sometime during the beans and the milk and the water and all the talk, talk, talk (that mostly June did), she found herself next to her again, found herself with one arm stroking her T-shirt-covered back, feeling the strong planes of her shoulders, and the thick warmth of her dark skin. She remembered, strongly, perfectly, the girl looking up at her and smiling a glowing smile. June had kissed her.

It seemed to last forever, that first kiss (well, don't most first kisses? Another universal law). June felt herself catch fire from head to toe. To the background sounds of the percolating Senior Coffee, she had let her hands fall to the girl's shoulders, arms, and then her perfectly shaped titties.

The T-shirt came off quickly and she had stood up. Holding her close, June stroked and kneaded her arms, sides and even her tiny little pot belly. They had sighed and moaned and groaned together as they both touched (her hands on June's own big biceps and almost non-existent tits) and kissed. Some-where, June lost her flannel shirt and the black girl had lost her jeans and shoes.

She had circled her big, hard nipples with hot kisses as she squeezed June's cunt through her own jeans like a trick fondling a John. June couldn't keep the hissing moan in, so she had let it out into the girl's mouth – feeling it echo through her as her own hand cupped a shaved and slippery cunt.

With Wendy it had been walking on eggs. Her first real lover, June had treated Wendy like she was priceless, fragile – even though Wendy was five years older than June's 26. June had barricaded them in June's tiny place against her being alone again and tried to do whatever it would take to keep Wendy there. If Wendy liked something, June did it. If Wendy didn't like it . . . it never happened again

After a point, June followed Wendy everywhere. Never led. Tried not to want, desire, anything.

But then, there, in the kitchen that night something different was happening – it was June and her. No top, no bottom, no give, no take. Just kissing and tits and cunts and heat.

The girl had sat down in one of June's battered old wooden chairs and spread her legs as if to let some of the heat escape. June had sat down herself, surprised into almost squealing by how cold the linoleum floor was on her bare ass (lost her own pants and shoes somewhere). Since she was down there already (yeah, right) she kissed the girl's thighs; that delicious, all-but-invisible belly; and then rummaged in her hot, hot slit with her nose: playful rooting and tickling like a frisky puppy.

She had sighed and spread her legs wider.

June gently brought one hand up and pulled her cunt lips apart, spying with almost childish delight a pink clit the size of a marble in a sculpture of black and pink lips, almost smoking in the cool air of the kitchen. Of course she had licked. Of course she sucked and kissed and stroked it with her tongue.

June had forgotten her name almost the instant it had been told her. She called her Betty because she looked kind of like a black Betty Page.

In the same, now empty, kitchen: Betty came.

Now empty. June got up and wandered back into the rest of her apartment. Not the same, but the same kind – pair of slightly yellowed panties on the hardwood floor next to her stack of Bay Times newspapers. The same old, barely working

Mac Classic her father had bought her. Same old futon on the floor. Same Pier One rattan blinds. Same sketch Fish had done of her at the Folsom Street Fair. Same tiny stack of playbills with her name on it.

It kind of scared June when people reminded her that they were only together for two months. It seemed longer. Lots longer. Betty was the kind of girlfriend she thought she always needed. Looking at the futon, with its discolorations, stains and lumps, it was too easy to feel her again. Standing, as she always seemed to, so that she was just touching June's hip or arm.

June sat and absently flashed through the newspapers, trying not to think about the bed. Betty.

Lots of luck.

One night – oh, boy – that night: it was their second week together so, naturally, Betty had hauled over most of her stuff. They had gone long into the night prowling through her records, books, tapes, clothes, sharing stories about them or June's similars – when this thing of plastic and nylon webbing had come out of one box.

"Haven't you ever?" Betty had said, digging in another box for the main part of it.

June hadn't. Wendy had been a kind of old-world dyke. Plastic or meat it was still a cock and she wouldn't have wanted any part of it. June had actually been interested for a long time but never had the opportunity – and after Wendy had left she had pretty much lost interest in much of anything.

Betty found her cock – a pretty, stylized blue thing that looked more like a gizmo from a science fiction movie than a penis. Maybe that's what made it easier for June. As Wendy protested in the back of June's mind she kept telling the phantom: have you seen a cock like this?

Buckle, snap, synch. Condom, lube . . . "Bend over, dear."

"Waitaminute," June had said, feeling out of control, "who wears the pants around here?"

"You do," Betty had said, stroking her penis, "but I have the cock. Now bend over, or do I have to call you bitch?"

"No, sir!" June snapped in sarcasm, but added in a much smaller voice: "Take it easy with that thing; I'm a virgin."

"Now this is going to be a novel experience," Betty had said, all smiles with enthusiasm, "I've never deflowered a virgin before—"

June had suddenly been aware of a different part of her: a part that wanted the cock and Betty behind it, sure, but wanted it because of Betty. She instantly knew what it was all about, the surprising desire to feel the plastic penis in her cunt. It wasn't just hornyness. It was love. She wanted to be wanted by her

It almost made her cry. It was something she thought she'd left when Wendy had left to find someone even more subservient. Having it back was almost too much for her to handle: the fear that it could go again.

Slowly, June had stood up on the lumpy futon, unbuttoned her jeans, and then, teasingly, dropped her panties. She did it slowly because while it seemed that all she and Betty did was fuck, the magic of their bodies hadn't rubbed off yet. She had loved to get naked in front of Betty, watching her eyes dance and hunger for her.

It was a little chilly in the apartment, so June left her T-shirt on.

"Make like a doggie, love," Betty had said, "It's easier that way."

Slowly, kind of scared, June had: she got down on the futon, first on her hands and knees and then – 'cause her arms started to ache – leaning down on a pillow.

"So pretty," Betty said from behind her.

The kiss was kind of a shock. June had been so psyched to receive the brilliantly blue silicone dildo that the one thing she hadn't expected was the butterfly kiss of Betty's lips on her cunt lips.

Slowly, worshipfully, Betty kissed her again and again: on the cheeks of her ass, on the little knot of her asshole, on her puffy outer lips, and then, with a little skillful positioning, on the little dent where her cunt lips started and where her clit lay hidden.

"So very pretty," Betty had said, massaging June's cunt with a smooth, slightly cool hand – rubbing her mons and lips and thus her clit in its folds and valleys of very warm skin (and getting warmer). It was the kind of touch that June loved even more than a hard, driving jerking off; having her tits really worked on; nipple sucking and biting . . . it was a kind of gentle, worshipping touch that was almost unfamiliar. Wendy had done it, very early on in their relationship, then tossed it aside as she got bored.

June had missed it.

Betty had been so gentle, so tender with her touches and kisses that June almost didn't realize that the cock was entering her. It was warm, not too big, and definitely not persistent. It had felt, in fact, like Betty had just sort of parked its condom-covered plastic head just outside her cunt and was just sort of letting it be there as Betty stroked and gingerly touched June's back, thighs and ass.

June had been so caught up in the gentleness of something she had always considered harsh and probably painful . . . fucking . . . she almost didn't notice, didn't pick up, that Betty was talking.

"Such a beautiful woman. Such a gorgeous woman. Oh, God, I look at you and I get all wet. Yeah, my pussy, too, but me, inside, too. I get all warm and squishy when I look at you and touch you and . . . God . . . I get all gold inside, all sunlight and hot and tingly—"

The cock had slowly started to ease inside June, to make its way very slowly and very sedately into her cunt. In some way it reminded June of taking a dump – backwards: the sense of being filled, or being stretched by something warm and slightly resident. It wasn't an unfavourable feeling but it was . . . different: fucking and sex before had always just been quick and flickering things like tongues and fingers – not big solid things like plastic cocks.

It was unique, but something, June knew, there on her lumpy old futon, that she could grow to like. A lot.

She was filled, she was empty, she was filled, she was empty – the transition from just being occupied by Betty's cock to being fucked by Betty's cock was so smooth that, at first, June really didn't know what was going on. The sensation was warm and rhythmic, like her whole ass and cunt were breathing with the dildo – like she was expanding and contracting with each thrust.

Heavy, warm surges ran through her and she had found herself panting into the pillow she was resting on. Her legs started to ache.

She must have said something, because Betty had taken a few careful moments to adjust her – putting a pillow under her tummy and moving her legs so she was more flat-out – before easing her cock back into June's cunt.

It was like floating in a boat, June had decided as Betty fucked her. Gentle, warm waves on a lightly moving sea. She liked it. She wasn't going to come – no way – but it was like a kind of internal massage.

"Try rubbing your cunt," Betty had said in a voice laced with a kind of aerobics pant.

Thoroughly committed, June had done exactly that. She snaked her right hand down to her clit and found it delightfully hard and wonderfully wet from the juice and lube that had dripped down from her slurping cunt. Since she loved it usually when she jerked off, her left also went to her left nipple where she found it, also, incredibly hard. As Betty fucked her she started to really get down and nasty with her clit as she rubbed and pulled at her nipple.

Oh, boy – she remembered thinking as the first of five deep and rumbling comes surged through her. She also remembered the leg cramps and the embarrassing huge wet mark on the pillow where she had been drooling in excitement.

Slowly, cautiously, because of her raging leg cramps, she had turned over and hugged Betty. A delightful surprise awaited her as she did so: in her arms, Betty had her own hand down between the harness and the plastic cock, and was furiously working her own clit.

Holding her, feeling her fiery heat, Betty came.

That was then. June got up from the futon and her old newspapers and tried to think without thinking of Betty. Even though the tiny black girl had been pretty thorough about taking everything of hers it was still painfully hard not to try and think of her. Every room brought back flashes of wonderful times: tea and talk, tears and hugs, and comes – lots and lots of comes.

Even the fucking bathroom, June thought with a sudden flash of anger, remembering that one morning: cold tiles under her back as Betty lowered herself onto her face. It was an odd scene, one she, again, would never have thought of. She also remembered that they hadn't talked. It had just sort of happened the same way that first time in the kitchen had happened. June had been taking a piss. Betty had just stepped out of the shower. Betty walked over to her and asked June to towel her off. June had, then kissed her lips and then the younger girl's nipples. There was such joy in Betty – like it all was just a game of come and come again. She didn't seem to worry like Wendy had, about right and wrong things to do and enjoy. Betty had just drifted from one fun thing to another.

The fun, for instance, in hauling June down to the cold tiles and carefully lowering her sweet little cunt down onto June's face. It was kind of scary – to have someone, no matter how tiny, hovering over your eyes and nose and mouth and tongue. But then it started to kick in for June, and she felt an explosion of pure, crazed hornyness: Betty was using her, shoving herself down onto June's tongue and eagerness.

In the hall, looking into the now dark bathroom, June didn't even have to close her eyes to experience the taste of Betty's cunt – the heady perfume of her excitement. She remembered waking up many mornings to that smell on her lips and fingers, permeating even the time she spent away from her.

She remembered the bathroom, the gentle weight of Betty on her face. She recalled the giggles and the sighs that eased and surged out of the little dark-haired black girl as June licked and nibbled and sucked at her cunt and clit.

Sweet music—

Betty's hands, always busy, always hunting for June's tits, ass or cunt, had fluttered on the tight skin of June's thighs, forced then apart with the crazed energy of the very, very excited, and then had started to work on June's pussy. Betty had been surprisingly deft, considering the feverish licking June had been giving her, and soon June was staring down into the white light of a brilliant come.

Together, they went there. June came from Betty's fingers. Above her, Betty came.

June found herself in the hall. Down the stairs was the front door. Probably the one place where they hadn't played, where Betty hadn't come. She'd gone, though.

What she said, what Betty said, was pretty well gone. All June could remember was a bad week – bad work, bad parents, bad city – and a fight about . . . something. Maybe she had talked about Wendy. She hoped not.

Betty had gone.

Now, five days later: the little apartment was cold and empty. It was dark and quiet. June, and June alone, slept on the lumpy futon, made coffee in the morning and read her newspapers. No calls came in, and she didn't feel like making any.

Except one. Now, in the quiet dark.

June's fingers felt numb. It was hard to admit that she wanted Betty, wanted her back. It was hard to say she wanted anything. It was a scary place – as dark as the apartment was: What if she said no?

But would it be any worse?

Audrey answered on the second ring, her surprisingly deep voice: "Speak your peace."

"Is Betty there, Audrey?"

"Just a minute, you heartbreaker—"

"Yes?"

"Come. Please come. I want you."

Betty came.

Undercover

Nikki Magennis

I was half-drunk with lack of sleep, standing in the hot white buzz of Central Station while hordes of commuters bumped past me with their sharp suits and shoulder pads and brief cases. I stood there blinking and yawning. What the hell was I doing up at this hour?

The answer, of course, was Sam.

I growled at the thought of his stubbornness, at the selfish way he'd announced he was leaving to make his fortune. Hotfooting it to London like a carefree bird. Not for a second had he stopped to think of how it would screw up our relationship – four hundred miles between us was a serious blow. The salvation of our bickering, up-and-down love affair was the Olympic sex we indulged in most mornings, afternoons and evenings. We could hammer away for hours, and he took me places I'd never thought possible, body twisted into breathtaking positions, him so deep inside me it felt like blasphemy. After he left, my sex life became a sudden blank. I was left gasping with shock, reeling from the terrible aching loss of his body.

I missed the bastard.

Despite my rage at his pig-headed arrogance, I couldn't resist his sneaky allure. One twitch of his eyebrows and I was hot to trot. I spent my nights dreaming of his hot and swollen cock, of his roving hands. Our late night phone calls left me wound up like a clockwork toy.

I'd woken at the crack of dawn because I couldn't stand another day in the desert of celibacy. Almost against my will I found myself in the station, ready to travel all the way across the country for a good fuck.

The train finally boarded at six a.m. and I settled in for the long journey. The only upside to the hours sitting on a bristly nylon seat was the anticipation of seeing Sam. My body was so sensitized that even the feel of my clothes against my skin made my heart do a drum roll. I had butterflies about turning up unannounced on his doorstep, but half of them were excitement at the thought of holding him again, feeling his body against mine. How I'd melt when he touched me.

I'd dressed with that in mind: my kinkiest underwear, the extreme-cleavage bra, and the split-crotch panties. They cut into me, cantilevered my tits and exposed my ass when I bent over; when I wore that get-up I felt like a concubine primed to fuck.

The outfit was horny as hell, but definitely impractical for traveling. The clever little slit up the front of the panties left my softest skin exposed, and the rough denim of my jeans rubbed against me. I wriggled in my seat. I had another four hours before I'd arrive in Euston, and more hours after that before I'd get to take them off.

Outside, the countryside rolled past in a green blur. I looked round the carriage. Most of the other passengers were businessmen. The man across the aisle, a fat, gristly guy in shiny shoes, was clattering away on his laptop, taking big gulps from a tiny plastic coffee cup. Our eyes met. His were pink-rimmed and baggy, hard little eyes like a bully's. I caught the leer as he looked me over, that licking-the-lips sleaze that makes me squirm. Nothing for it but to turn my back on him and try to lose myself in sleep.

I half-woke with the noise of the train still humming around me, warm sun on my face. The carriage was now the temperature of a hot oven; I felt parched with thirst and cramped from sleeping in the hard, upright seat. When I tried to stretch out, I found my legs trapped. I struggled to open my eyes. Across from me was a young couple. They must have got on at Newcastle while I was asleep. The man, tall and blonde, was stretched out lazily in his seat, his long legs on either side of mine. I'd obviously just kicked him, but he gave me a wide smile.

"Sorry," I muttered, still fuzzy with sleep.

"S'okay," he replied, in a deep American drawl. "We're kinda crammed in here, aren't we?" His mouth curled in another lopsided grin, and I saw a flash of square white teeth.

The girl watched the countryside pass by with a bored look on her face. Also tall and long-limbed, she had the dark complexion that seemed southern European. She curled like a cat across her boyfriend, long brown hair spilling over her shoulders and a thin cotton summer dress barely covering her figure. From the corner of my eye I could see the top of her tanned breasts, full and heavy against the gauzy flowered fabric of the dress. Her nipples were darker shadows through the patterned cloth. The tight pressure of my jeans was cutting into me, and I shifted in my seat, my leg grazing the American's. I wished I'd worn something loose fitting and cool. The underwear was agitating me.

"You goin' to London?" the man asked, his voice lazy and low.

I nodded, aware that my heart was starting to thump in my chest. As if reading my thoughts, he let his gaze meander down my body, though he was looking at my tits rather than my beating heart. I felt my nipples stiffen as though they had been stroked. Under the table, I felt his leg press my knee. I shot a look at the girl, but she seemed oblivious to her lover's little game. His knee was now rubbing insistently against my thigh.

Around us, businessmen read newspapers and talked on mobiles, occupied with the real world. I felt my cheeks getting hot. The American leaned forward as if to look closely at something he'd seen out the window. I felt a hand on my leg. He brushed the inside of my thigh with the back of his hand, casually, as though we were lovers who had known each other for ages. He rested his chin on his other hand.

"All tickets please." The conductor was barging up the aisle, checking each table for new faces. The boy pulled back, searching his pockets.

I exhaled, the tension broken, half-relieved and half-disappointed. I had a brief vision of the girlfriend throwing a Continental tantrum in the middle of the train and a catfight in the aisles, the two of us rolling around pulling each other's hair. But the man had turned me on. Perpetually horny from Sam's absence, it didn't take much to get me going.

To distract myself, I opened the newspaper and scanned the headlines. On the periphery of my vision, I could see the two sweethearts opposite me nuzzling each other. I tried to ignore their display of affection, feeling even more frustrated and uncomfortable. Under the noise of the train, I could make out the man whispering in his girlfriend's ear. She giggled.

"Can I sit next to you?"

I looked up. The girl was standing, looking right at me with wide brown eyes.

"I don't like going backwards." There was the hint of a French accent in her voice.

"Yes. Yes, of course," I said, feeling as though I should apologise to her for sitting on this side of the train, and guilty because her lover had just made a sly pass at me under the table.

She smiled as she slid into the seat next to me. I shifted the newspaper to make room. She wriggled into the seat and leaned into me, looking over the stories, her arm against mine. I could feel her breath on my neck and instantly was surrounded by the heavy fragrance of her perfume. She had the generous confidence of Europeans, and their unconscious intimate way of sitting too close.

"You like this picture?" she asked, pointing to a shot of Madonna onstage at a concert. "Sexy woman, no?" The girl drew her hand back, running her fingers along my arm. Slowly, so it was clearly not an accident.

The atmosphere suddenly crackled with heat, my heart booming in my ears and the train sounds beating in time with it. I looked across at the man. He was leaning back, watching the two of us, grinning that grin of his. I felt like a deer caught between two predators. Trapped in my seat, I felt the touch of her hand linger on my skin and spread over my body. My breasts ached. I could feel my heart beating all the way to the tips of my nipples. In my tight jeans, between my hot thighs, I felt myself melting.

She put her mouth to my ear. "We would both like to fuck you," she breathed, making my head swim and my pussy throb.

Her boyfriend leaned forward to slowly rub the insides of my thighs with his agile fingers. I sat stock still and let him manipulate me, frozen with confusion. Under the cover of the newspaper he pulled at the fly of my jeans, popping the buttons one by one. I felt the cool air rush against my pussy, exposed by the slit in my panties. God, I wanted his fingers inside me. I thought desperately of the other passengers – the carriage was full. Drunk with desire, I turned to the girl. She leant in to press her tits against me.

She was still perusing the open newspaper on my lap as though reading a story, while rubbing her nipples against the bare flesh of my arm. If we'd been alone I would have reached out to touch her, but I was terrified of drawing attention to our little threesome.

The passengers chattered. The wheels clicked over the rails. Under the cover of the paper, her lover was working his way inside my knickers. I felt his finger strum me, felt ripples of warm pleasure through my body. To onlookers we were just two girls reading a paper and a man looking out the window. Below the surface, though, a thrilling game of hide and seek was going on.

He kept playing with me, his long fingers pushing further inside, building up an irresistible rhythm that moved in time with the train. I thought, briefly, of Sam, and what his face would look like if he could see me now. And with a vicious rush of pleasure, I turned to the girl, looking straight into her laughing brown eyes. I let her see the flush on my cheeks, the wild, urgent look in my eyes that meant I wanted to kiss her. I licked my lips, watching her mouth as she leaned in again to whisper, "How do you like train travel?" The huskiness of her voice betrayed her arousal. I was caught between her dark amusement and her boyfriend's fingers.

I felt my orgasm rushing towards me with an intensity so blinding that I was scared I would scream when I came. Silently

I begged for the pressure of his hand to bring me off, all my consciousness concentrated in that white-hot spot of arousal so it was only his smooth fingertip rubbing lightly over the bud of my clit that connected me to the world. Such a slight, circling pressure from his outstretched hand; the glint in the girl's eyes, the feel of her warm flesh against my arm, the underwear cutting into me and the rustle of the newspaper as I spread my legs wider, dying to peak.

And then it came – an orgasm that shook me so hard I thought I might pass out, cheeks burning, heart thudding, breath spasming in a gasp I couldn't hold back. Waves of pleasure moved through me, overtaking all my fears. The noise of the train receded and I surfed on blissful oblivion.

. . . and then the awareness of where I was flooded back into consciousness, my awkward perch on the edge of the seat suddenly feeling strange, my flushed face feeling like a flag of guilt. I was gripped with panic that the other passengers had heard me, that I was naked and exposed with a stranger's hand between my legs, and an even greater panic that I had committed a treacherous betrayal of Sam.

But then I turned to the girl.

Her eyes locked on mine. She smiled as though we'd shared something dark and delicious, a secret encounter that could happen only between destinations. As though the fact her lover had just brought me off was simply a *divertissement*, an act of friendliness between fellow travelers.

Winking, she settled back into her seat, satisfied. Her boyfriend withdrew his hand and carefully buttoned me up again, his movements as tender as if I were a precious gift he was wrapping.

I wondered: would Sam notice that I'd already been opened?

Boys and Girls Come Out to Play

Barry Baldwin

One day, sensational news hit the village. A Canadian girl had come to stay. The gang met that night in emergency session under the yellow sodium street lamp by the school playground to discuss this intelligence.

"I don't believe it," somebody said. "Why would a Canadian come here?"

This was my question as well, but I had no standing in the gang as an authority on anything, let alone Canadian girls, so I had waited for another member to ask it.

"Perhaps she's learning English."

"Don't be daft, they speak English in Canada."

"Not proper English, they don't."

"I heard she's here to be a nanny for Mrs Grover at The Grange."

"Who cares why she's here?" This was our leader, Frank Blunt, who predictably took over the debate and bulldozed it towards his favourite topic. "I bet you I'm up her in a week. Those Yank bints are sex-mad."

The first speaker tried to object that Canadians and Americans weren't the same thing, but he didn't stand a chance. Frank Blunt's status as sexual know-it-all was long established. That's not to say we necessarily believed all his claims about doing girls, which in turn is not to say that we didn't want to. Some of the other members also made their own more modest boasts. These usually involved "titting" a girl at the pictures or behind the cricket pavilion. There were two levels of success: a touch of breast outside or inside her clothes. One or two hopefuls tried to persuade us they had progressed to the point of getting their hand right inside and down to the knicker elastic frontier but, led by Frank Blunt who was determined to preserve his supremacy in the minge stakes, we always shouted them down.

"You know what," Frank Blunt went on, "those bints will let you do them without a Durex on."

"What if they have a baby?" asked the lad who'd tried to distinguish Canadians from Americans.

"They know how not to," Frank Blunt replied, without explanation. Since no one contradicted this, he moved into more advanced territory. "And what's more, they'll let you put your thing in their mouth."

A couple of the knicker elastic brigade nodded in silent support of this allegation. One added they knew for a fact that Helen Rowe, the village bike, did this as well. I privately thought the idea both disgusting and frightening. Fancy anyone putting their mouth where you pissed out of. And what if they bit through it like a stick of liquorice?

"I'm telling you straight," insisted Frank Blunt, as though he had read my mind. "And what's more, they'll even let you stick it up their backside."

For once, he had gone too far. It was obvious from people's faces that nobody was willing to credit such an idea. I myself, with the confidence that only ignorance can give, felt sure it would be physically impossible, even if you wanted to do it. Moreover, there was nothing about this activity in Hank Janson's *Baby Don't Dare Squeal* which was currently circulating under our desk lids at school. One member even called, "Get out of it," though he did not identify himself when challenged by Frank Blunt to do so. "Well, anyway," summed up a boy who generally contributed even less to gang debates than I did, "I expect she's got one in the middle and two at the front like the rest of them." On this thoughtful note, the meeting broke up.

I left resolved never to so much as speak to this Canadian, always assuming she existed. But she did, and I did, once. The very next day, in fact. I had gone into the village shop for a bag of Tidman's gob-stoppers and there at the counter was this strange girl trying to buy all sorts of things old Ma Pocock had never heard of. Finally, to save face, she stonewalled one request with, "I could have it in the back, I'll go and see," and the two of us were left alone.

Already impressed by the way she'd got Ma Pocock running around in a way none of us ever had, I swallowed my surprise when she spoke to me first and did not even lower my eyes, my standard practice when dealing with girls. It was obvious from the greeting "Hi" that she must be the Canadian. I knew enough to know they used this short form of our "Hey Up". What I couldn't fathom was how she came to be on the small side with dark hair and no lipstick and as far as I could tell no tits, when everybody knew all lasses from over there had blonde hair and dollops of make-up and whacking big ones in front. Still, she did have bright white teeth which no girl I knew in the village did, so there couldn't be any mistake. The only other people I'd met with gnashers like that were blokes old enough to have been given a full extraction and new set for their twenty-first birthday, as used to be the custom.

For some reason, she made me feel like I was speaking to a grown-up, so instead of "Hey Up" I answered with "Hello".

"I'm Gina," she continued, her teeth flashing so much that I would have taken my sunglasses out of my pocket and put them on, that is if I'd actually had them on me and always supposing I had the wit to do so. I didn't say anything back. Who cared what she was called? And we didn't give out our names as easily as that. I was saved by the return of Ma Pocock who had unsurprisingly failed to find what she hadn't looked for. "Must have run out," she said aggressively, feeling the need to restore her shopkeeper's authority. Gina shrugged her not very big shoulders, paid from the largest handbag I'd ever seen for the few things Ma Pocock had managed to come up with, and left.

However, when I'd got my gob-stoppers and come out of the shop, she was waiting there.

"Hi, again."

This deserved no reply.

"Do you live here?"

"What, in this shop?"

"No, I can see you don't do that. I meant, in this village."

"I suppose so."

"I don't know. They told me England was a funny place, but I never figured it would be like this."

I felt I should spring to the defence of my country against this foreigner throwing her weight around, but the only thing that came to mind was a limp "Like what?"

Gina, though, was in no mood for an England versus Canada argument. "Can you tell me where the church is?"

I was dumbfounded. No one I knew, of any age or sex, ever went to church except at the proper time: Christmas or weddings or funerals. And if Frank Blunt was right, what would a Canadian bint who let you put your thing in her mouth or up her arse want with a church?

"No." I couldn't think of a smart answer, so salvaged as much pride as I could with this rude lie.

"Okay, if that's the way you want it," was Gina's curious reply. Showing absolutely no sign of being upset, she swung herself on to a brand new girl's bike, provided by Mrs Grover at The Grange I supposed, thinking of the rusty hand-me-down which was what I had, and pedalled off.

I saw Gina quite a lot after this, either wheeling a big pram containing the Grover twins or heaving a lawn mower around their garden or just biking in the village on her own. She always shouted "Hi, there" and every time her stupid teeth looked even whiter. Of course, I never answered.

Interest in her soon died away, being replaced by more important things like football. After one or two further sessions under the street lamp, she ceased to feature in gang discussion. Naturally, Frank Blunt got in a claim to have had her behind the pavilion, adding the standard details about minge size and greasiness but nothing about mouths or backsides. Nobody disputed him, either believing because they wanted to, since if he had got it, "it" remained a possibility for them as well, or because if they showed too open a disbelief, they would find his fist in their face or boot up the goolies.

I kept my trap shut as well. Partly because I too liked minge stories, partly because he was bigger than me, and partly because I had seen him duck down behind a wall to avoid Gina when he spotted her coming down the street towards him.

It wasn't long after the arrival of this Canadian, not that she had anything to do with it, that I lost two of my virginities, within hours of each other. In neither case could I claim any credit for taking the initiative. I didn't score, I was scored against. And although for obvious reasons I was never exactly the same afterwards, neither loss did anything to change my life.

One Saturday afternoon, I and some other lads biked over to the next village to support our football team in a semi-final. City were away, it was decent weather, and there was nothing better to do.

The boys I went with seemed all right. I didn't know them that well, most were a bit older, and none were in our gang. My real comrades weren't there. They had either been taken by their fathers to follow City on the away game or were doing something else with their families. Frank Blunt said he had a date at the pictures with some "pushover" or other.

We stood on the squiggly whitewashed touchline for the first half, cheering our team and exchanging insults and the odd push-and-shove with lads from the other village. All routine stuff, nothing serious. At half-time, there was no score. We hung around our players for the break, partly to make sure they knew we were there, which might help get us into the team in a few years, partly to grab our share of the lemonade and orange slices that were being passed round.

About ten minutes into the second half, the other team broke away and three of their forwards came steaming down the pitch towards our end. Apart from the goalie, who was jumping up and down on his line calling to the defenders to get back to where they effing well should be, only our centre-half was anywhere near. He was a big bugger called Ray Oxby, though to us he was commonly known as Mighty Joe Young, a tribute to his size and hairiness inspired by the gorilla of that name in a King Kong kind of film we had all recently seen at the village hall.

You know that bit from the Bible on the Lyle's Golden Syrup tin? "Out of the strong came forth sweetness." Well, it didn't apply to Mighty Joe Young. He was a nasty piece of work. But you couldn't say he didn't get stuck in. He put on a good turn of speed and went in feet first against their pack of forwards. There was a loud cracking noise, followed by a great bellow from Mighty Joe Young: "Christ, I've broken my bloody leg!"

He had, as well. It was too big a job for our trainer with his bucket of water and magic sponge. While the other team clustered around the stricken Mighty Joe Young, our lot stood or sat in little groups or nipped back to the touchline for more lemonade. One or two made a big show of getting cigarettes from their wives or girl friends and lighting up. The referee came off and bullied one of the locals into biking to the nearest phone to call for an ambulance from the city hospital.

We were obviously in for a long wait. To pass the time, and to avoid going on the pitch to express any sympathy for Mighty Joe Young, I joined with the others, first in a scratch football game against the lads from the rival village, then when we got tired of that, in some aimless wrestling and chasing around.

For no particular reason, I ended up through the hedge and into the next field with a boy from our side called Roy Seager. He wasn't as tall as me, which was saying something, but he was stocky and keen, and in the general scuffling had proved as good as anyone else. We eyed each other, not saying anything. All of a sudden, this Roy Seager bent down, picked up a stone, threw it at me, and galloped off across the field. More surprised by the running than the throwing, I hesitated for a minute before setting out in pursuit. The stone had sailed harmlessly by me. I bore no grudge for this attack; I would have done the same, had I spotted a stone first.

By the time I caught up with him, Roy Seager had reached a patch of long grass and cow parsley in front of a ditch. He was sitting in it, looking puffed out. I stood over him and was trying to decide just where to kick him when he reached up, pulled me down, and thumped me in the solar plexus. I lay there winded.

When I got my breath back, I became aware of him unbuttoning my trousers and sticking his hand into my fly and dragging out my thing.

"Hey, stop it," I objected automatically, more out of surprise than anything. "What are you up to?"

Roy Seager didn't answer. By now, he was sitting flat on my chest with his back to me. I couldn't move. Once he had my thing pulled through the tangle of underpants and flies, he started to jerk it. I shouted at him to stop, it was hurting, especially when he began to peel the foreskin back from the tip. He took no notice and carried on, himself making no noise of any kind. Then, without being aware of any change of action on his part or reaction on mine, I realised that it wasn't hurting any more, in fact it was feeling all right in a way I couldn't have described, though this pleasure was mixed with a new sensation of alarm as I understood that my thing had doubled in size. So as not to give anything away, I continued to tell him to stop it. He did, but only after a final tweak that made me feel like I was bursting open.

Roy Seager released me and got off. I sat up and anxiously examined my thing. It was red from all the jerking, and there was a trail of bubbly white running down from the tip. I wasn't going to give him the satisfaction of either complaint or thanks, and there didn't seem anything else to say, so without a word we walked back to see if the match had started again. It turned out that the ambulance still hadn't come. After another twenty minutes or so, the referee blew his Acme Thunderer whistle three times and announced with great self-importance that the game would have to be abandoned. Everybody started to drift away, the players more quickly than the spectators. Mighty Joe Young lay where he had fallen, alone now except for the referee and the trainer who was still flapping around uselessly with his bucket and sponge.

I hung about until everyone else had set off. I wanted to bike home by myself. Despite my surprise at what had taken place in the long grass and the way it had been done, I knew what it was all about. Although backwards in sexual experience, especially compared to those lads who had sisters, I was, thanks to Frank

Blunt and the gang elite, well aware of the basics, above all about tossing off. It was simply something that I hadn't got around to trying for myself. While I couldn't help noticing that I had grown hair "down there", regular checks with the tape measure from my granny's sewing basket had convinced me, even using millimetres instead of inches, that I wasn't yet ready to blast off. Now, although the tossee not the tosser, I had joined the facts of life, at least in a small way. As I biked back, a little stiffly, I was thinking that, with the details suitably changed, I would have my first starring role in the gang's next session on this subject.

I expected to be in trouble when I got home. I lived with my grandparents: my mother was dead and my father had vanished so long ago that for all practical purposes he was as well. My granny wouldn't want to be hanging around making late teas. Saturday night meant the whist drive for her, brown ale and dominoes at the British Legion for my grandad. But for some reason she was in a good mood, so instead of a bollocking a big plate of egg, chips, and beans was set in front of me with even an enquiry about how the match had gone. She then hurried off to her whist drive. Grandad had already gone to the Legion, so I was left to eat my tea in peace. Normally, I would have dawdled over it with a comic. Instead, I wolfed it down in record time and didn't even consider raiding the larder for any cake that might be going begging.

As soon as I had finished, I got as far away from the window as possible, pulled down my trousers, and started to jerk away for dear life. Nothing happened: no nice feelings, no increase in size, not a drop. After about ten minutes, since it was hurting and I had got a bit of a belly-ache as well, from doing it too soon after tea I supposed, I packed it in. I had no idea why it hadn't worked. Perhaps I could contrive to get Frank Blunt to explain the problem without seeming to be asking.

What was I going to do next? There was no prospect of a gang meeting, and my pocket money was already spent. I decided to wander around the village. There were usually a few lads outside the pub waiting for their grown-ups. Or a game of kicking-in under a street lamp. But I was out of luck. There were not even any cats or dogs to throw stones at.

I was on the point of jacking it in and going home, when I found myself walking past the cricket field. It occurred to me that I had lost my penknife somewhere there the other day, so I thought I'd go and see if I could find it. Fat chance at night, you might say, but the village council had put up quite a big light next to the pavilion to discourage people like me from vandalising it, so it wasn't entirely a waste of time.

As I approached the pavilion, a wooden affair with a verandah and four steps leading up, I thought I heard some sort of noise coming from it. Good-o, I said to myself, maybe there are some lads having a crafty smoke in there. But just as I was going to put my foot on the first step, the door opened and somebody came out. Not any lad I knew, in fact not any lad at all, but a girl.

And not any old girl. It was Helen Rowe, the village bike, who was said to give anything in trousers a ride. The grown-ups said she "got it" from her mother who'd farmed Helen out to some relative early in the war and gone off to join the Woman's Land Army, whose motto was Backs To The Soil. There was a lot of guesswork about who her father was. The official one had gone missing in action and was presumed dead, but my granny was not the only person to say he was more likely buried in the Tomb of the Unknown Quantity.

There was a Helen Rowe in every village. The sort of girl that gets buried in a Y-shaped coffin. It had very little to do with the way they looked. Faces didn't count. It was common knowledge that you didn't look at the mantlepiece when you were poking the fire. What mattered was that they had the experience and the know-how to take you in hand and get things started.

Our Helen was not actually all that bad, if you didn't mind a girl on the tall side with slender legs and frizzy red hair wearing a mohair jumper over average bazookas and a knee-length tartan skirt. The snag about the skirt was that where it stopped emphasised the knobbliness of her knees. No one in the entire world has nice knees, in my opinion. As always, her face was lathered in make-up; this was one of the biggest things about her in the eyes of the village. Lots of black mascara and bright orange lipstick which under the pavilion light looked all smudgy.

The thing about Helen, though, was not so much what she looked like, or even the things she was supposed to do, but the way she behaved in general. She talked like a boy, swore like a boy, and seemed to think she was as good as a boy. She even smoked, Woodbines at that, not cork-tipped. As my granny was fond of saying about my grandad, she smoked like a chimney. I had heard Frank Blunt remark that Helen Rowe didn't have red changes like other girls, she just had a fall of soot once a month.

"Baldy," she said in that off-putting tone she had, halfway between "hello" and "bugger off". It was typical of her to launch right in with the nickname I hated but which anyone called Baldwin is bound to have at that age. "Christ, look what the wind's blown in," she went on, her voice going up almost to a shout. Did she think I'd been struck deaf? "What brings you here on a Saturday night? Looking for something?" Her voice went down again on this, for no reason I could fathom. But how did she know why I was there?

"I was just looking for my penknife," I replied, feeling quite proud of myself for not stuttering.

"He's looking for his penknife," she echoed, loudly again, as if there were somebody else there. Then she went on in her normal voice with a funny sort of smile that got you even worse, "Looking for your penknife, are you? At this time of night? Don't tell me you've got to get a stone out of your horse's hoof?"

Our penknives were always judged in terms of the number of gadgets they had attached, chief of which was the one that was supposed to be for hooves and stones, although that wasn't so daft in those days; there were still plenty of dray horses around. What got me, apart from the voice and smile, was how this girl came out with the sort of line you associated with the comedians on the wireless.

"No, it's just that I lost it here a few days ago and I was walking past so I thought I'd have a look."

"He thought he'd have a look," said Helen, reverting to the invisible third person. Then back to the low tone and smile,

"You've come to the right place for a look, I can tell you. Bugger your penknife, aren't I sharp enough for you?"

"You what? Come on, let me look for it. I won't be a minute."

"No, I bet you wouldn't be," she replied mysteriously. "All right, let's find this shitting knife of yours. Where is it?"

I suppose Helen would have thought more of me if I'd made the answer she'd set me up for: if I knew where it was, it wouldn't be lost, would it? But I wasn't up to that level of repartee. So I just said, if it's here, it must be down in the grass somewhere.

"Hark at clever clogs. You ought to be on Paul Temple." Yes, I thought, but daren't say, and if you were Steve, the wireless sleuth's wife and helper, he wouldn't get a word in edgeways. Instead, I mumbled, "I don't think I'll bother, after all. I'll come back tomorrow when it's properly light."

"Don't be mardy, you've only just come. Look, I'll help you." She promptly got down on her knees, contriving without seeming to do anything to let her skirt fly up high enough for me to see her knickers.

And not just any old knickers. Not for Helen the usual girl's brown ones with elastic at the waist, the ones Frank Blunt called Harvest Festivals because everything is safely gathered in. Hers were black. Real black, I mean, not dirty. Black knickers! This was real Jane of the *Daily Mirror* stuff.

"Come on," she ordered, not turning her head. "What are you gizzhawking at, as if I didn't know?"

"Nothing." I was still hypnotised by the sight.

Helen was back up as quickly as she had gone down.

"Did you like my knickers, then?"

"They were all right."

"Drop dead, Errol Flynn. All right, were they? How about this, then? Have a proper gleg." She stood close to me, pulling the tartan skirt up high. I knew I was going to mess myself if I wasn't careful. I also knew that the front seat view I was getting beat anything we had ever seen in the Tuesday Night pictures at the village hall. It crossed my mind that the little blotches which stood out on her thighs might be the knicker burn which Frank Blunt said happened to girls who dropped them like lightning;

but they were only freckles. I heard myself saying, "I have to be off", then, making myself sound even more like a soppy-cake, "I'll get into trouble if I'm not home."

"Diddums do it to him, then?" she jeered, twanging her knickers like Shirley Abicair doing the Third Man theme on her zither, though there was no sign of any elastic. "Don't be such a twerp. I bet you toss off every night thinking about this. Here's your big chance. Come on, I won't hurt you."

"Yes, come on, you prat," a third voice suddenly boomed out. "Get stuck in." I was even more petrified at this, and when the owner of the voice came out of the pavilion into the light, my bowels almost went into my boots. It was Gonge.

This Gonge was a figure of unique fascination in our world. None of us knew his real name. He lived just beyond the end of the main street in a tumbledown cottage, lower on the social scale than even the council houses and the worst yards. Gonge must have been several years older than the rest of us, though as far as we could tell, he didn't read or write. At least, he was never seen with so much as a comic. Although he was a great lummox of a lad, it was his fierce eyes that most intimidated us, along with his Sod You way of walking and his conversation. Well, conversation isn't the right word for it. He had this knack of looming up on us at street corners or as we were walking home from the bus stop or waiting to bat at cricket and launching straight into a monologue about minge. Unlike Frank Blunt, though, he specialized in lurid descriptions of "breaking girls in" or how he did it to them when they had their jammy rags on. The blood and the hurting were what was most important to Gonge: he never seemed to mention the pleasure side. There were rumours in the village that he had put at least two of his many sisters in the pudding club, tales which the grown-ups themselves believed, making him seem even more formidable. Of course, I ooh-ed and ah-ed over his reports like everyone else, though privately and not out of any sympathy for the girls I was more than a bit put off by all the stuff about blood and hurting.

Incidentally, if you're hoping Gonge came to a bad end, you're in for a disappointment. The last I knew before leaving the village for good was that he had followed contentedly into his father's idling and poaching footsteps and was married, with no kids which ruled out the obvious reason, to a girl from the posh end, a girl so plain and prissy that not even in my most wankful moments had I honoured her with a wet fantasy.

"Get stuck in," Gonge urged again. "Do you want me to show you how?" He seemed more het up than Helen over the proceedings.

"Hold hard, you've had your lot," Helen interrupted. She might have been arguing over who should have the last chocolate from a box of Milk Tray.

To my amazement, Gonge seemed almost as in awe of Helen as I was. "I was only trying to help poor old Baldy here. He's not got the first idea . . ."

"Don't bother, I'll be teacher. Fuck off, Gonge."

Not even Frank Blunt had ever been heard to say a word of disagreement to Gonge, let alone "fuck off," the ultimate deterrent, not one you heard a lot of adults use in those days, at least not in front of us. Yet here was Helen, a girl, telling Gonge of all people to do it, and not even shouting. And he did, there and then, with a tame "Best of British, Baldy, you'll shagging well need it."

"You don't want to take any notice of Gonge," observed Helen mildly. "He thinks he's it, but he's shit."

I didn't say anything. Mentally, though, I was storing up this phrase for future use at gang meetings.

As she spoke, Helen moved right up to me. I fumbled at her knickers, first with one hand, then both. I didn't get far, what with nerves and having my eyes closed. I would have done anything rather than meet her gaze, except have a gleg at what was inside the knickers. There's nothing worse for a lad than having his sexual dream come true. Why wasn't I at home reading the *Adventure*?

"Here, let me do it," chafed Helen. "There, they're off. Do you reckon you could manage the rest by yourself?"

I hesitantly lowered myself to the ground, hoping there were no nettles, and lay on the grass waiting for her to join me. But this was wrong as well.

"Now what are you up to?"

"Getting ready. Isn't this right?"

"What about your precautions?"

"Precautions . .?"

"A Durex, cloth ears."

"A Durex?"

"No, of course you haven't. I bet a bob you've never even seen one. Look, if you don't have a Durex, you've got to do it standing up. That way, I don't get put up the spout. I thought everybody knew that."

Miserably, I levered myself back up to my feet, helped on by a sharpish kick from Helen. "Get your trousers down, then," she ordered, adding in her third person voice, "Christ on a crutch, he's still wearing braces."

There was no point in trying to explain that I did wear a belt these days, but had mislaid it at home, and only had the one. I eased down the offending braces and stood shuffling about with the trousers round my ankles. I knew what was expected of me. How I was going to do it was another matter, but I wasn't going to risk another explosion from Helen by asking. I got my arms around her, more for balance than anything, and started a vague prodding at her lower parts with mine. Helen pulled me as close as she could, then put both hands on my arse and tried to manoeuvre me into position for a better aim. She was strong for a girl. So strong, in fact, that she knocked me off balance and in the flailing panic that followed we ended up on the ground, her on top of me.

"This is no shitting good. I tell you what, I'll stand on the top step and lean on the verandah post. You get on the next step down and work from there."

Battle stations. This must be what the minge experts called a knee-trembler. I could see why. My knees were trembling, all right. The trouble was, the part of me that needed to be, wasn't. I heaved away at her for ages without getting anywhere.

"Sod it, we'll be here all night at this rate."

Taking this to be my dismissal, I backed down a step before she could change her mind, dragged up my trousers, and was about to escape when she said, "Where do you think you're off to, then?"

"Er, home. I thought you'd had enough."

"Had enough? Haven't had any yet, have I? You want to eat your greens, get some lead in your pencil. Any road, get back up here. Nothing wrong with your hands as well, is there?"

"Hands? No . . ."

Helen took tight hold of me again, grabbed my right hand, and guided it down to her middle. I could feel a sort of rounded area, covered in bristles and sticky, a bit like an old cricket ball in a cowpat. "Don't muck around there. Get your fingers down in and keep them moving till I say different.

"Come on, duck," she added in her quiet voice.

I did as I was told, relieved that here was something I could apparently do to her satisfaction. I went on with it, my eyes glued to the ground, until after some squirming about and a funny noise, she said I could stop. I risked a quick look at her face. Just for a second, she seemed different. I had an idea of what it was all about, though couldn't have put a name to it. That was the other thing about village bikes: they liked it as much as the lad, maybe more.

Not that Helen was letting on. She replaced her knickers in an impatient sort of way, then pulled out a packet of Woodbines from a pocket in her skirt and lit up, not offering me one. I suppose I was looking up at her like a puppy wanting approval. "Never mind, Baldy. You know more than you did an hour ago, don't you?"

As I left, I was vaguely wondering how many reserves Helen might have lined up inside the pavilion. She didn't seem very surprised or even that much bothered by my failure to perform. "Sling your hook, you useless article," were her parting words, but they were said in her mildest tone.

Wouldn't you know it, the moment I got clear of the field and Helen, my balls started bouncing as though they'd been invented by Barnes Wallis and my thing shot straight up and wouldn't go down until I went under a tree and scratted it a few times and got the second ration that day out of it. Then I took myself off home and went to bed. Or would have, but there was a big rumpus going on over something between my granny and grandad and I got clouted by both of them for being there, so it was a good while before I could get myself bedded down.

Even though I hadn't gone all the way, I had had my first go with girls and boys. In fact, it was the most versatile day of my life in that regard. But thinking about it kept me awake for five minutes at the most, and it played no part at all in my dreams which were routine ones about playing for England and scoring the winning goal in the last second.

I never had another crack at Helen. God knows what became of her. Perhaps she took a lorry ride to shame, as the Sunday papers used to say. Or else turned into a nun. Who cares? Well, perhaps I should. Helen was a sport in her way. She didn't let on to anybody about me missing my big chance. At least, no one ever taunted me about it, not even Frank Blunt who would have if he'd known and, whatever the truth about him and Gina, there could be no doubt that he had Helen a good few times. And Gonge himself did no more than loom over me a few days later outside Ma Pocock's and say, "You didn't get lost, then. You could get a horse and cart up it, couldn't you?" I was thrilled at this unexpected and never to be repeated chance to feel on an equal footing with the great Gonge.

Gina left the village after three or four months. Everybody remarked that she was going away a good deal bigger than when she came. Since it was unthinkable that someone from Canada could have fattened up on our austerity food, tongues wagged. The gang members started to look at Frank Blunt with renewed respect, and there was talk about Gonge as well, until Mr Grover suddenly left The Grange with his suitcases, never to return.

Gina herself went very soon after, a more subdued departure on the Boat Train that stopped at the village station once a week. It was reported that the only person to see her off on the platform was Helen Rowe. I was the only one not to be surprised, because that pair had already surprised me before when I spotted them down a lane where I'd been sent on some errand kissing each other in the way men and women did in

American films. That puzzled me for a long time, but I never did bring it forward as a topic for debate under the street lamp, even if they'd have believed me it somehow didn't seem right, and I doubt even Frank Blunt could have come up with an explanation for it.

Tight Spots

Debra Hyde

If an interviewer ever asked sex writer Delta Faragate where her ideas came from, she'd have to look the person square in the eye and admit, "Honey, I do my best thinking sucking cock." That answer might go down just fine in the pages of *Playboy* or *Hustler* but it'd be cause for scandal in any "family" paper or periodical. But Delta wasn't fantasizing about fame or notoriety. She was busy puzzling out the topic of her next column – and voraciously working her boyfriend's meat in the process.

She had it just right, too: matching the right force of suction to his rhythmic pumping, pressing her tongue to that one spot on his dick that made him swell towards orgasm, giving him a sensual extra by cupping his balls. His breath was ragged; his moans barely escaping his lips. She knew it was only a matter of moments.

When she heard that certain firecracker gasp of his, she knew he was there, and his dick surged and shot forth the fruits of their shared labor into her waiting mouth.

After Robert came, Delta tended to his retiring tool with gentle licks. And, when he recovered from his explosion, he chuckled and asked, "So what'd you come up with this time?"

Robert, the dear soul of a beau, was in on her dirty little trade secret. And he loved these working meetings of hers.

Delta mumbled something unintelligible. Robert grabbed her hair, tilted her head up towards him, and reminded her, "It's impolite to talk with your mouth full. Swallow."

Swallow, she did, tasting sweet jizz upon her tongue. *He's still drinking OJ*, she thought.

"Well," she resumed in a more polite fashion. "Think about this: with visions of long hair and love beads dancing in their heads, America's oldest boomers turn sixty this year."

She paused, rose from the floor and joined Robert on the couch.

"I want to write about one particular symbol of hippiedom and sexual liberation."

"The peace sign?" Robert posed.

"No. The VW Beetle. Pneumatic made mobile."

"Huh?"

"Remember the first time you encountered the word pneumatic?"

"Yeah. In an engineering class."

Delta laughed. "OK, so my literary reference might be lost on you slide-ruler types. I first saw it in a modern lit course – *Brave New World*, where a woman's sexual value was measured by her innate 'pneumatic' ability. When I think of the VW bug, pneumatic comes to mind. And pneumatic makes me think *Brave New World* and *Brave New World* reminds me of youthful freedom and discovery, coming into your own, and the no-turning-back of the sexual revolution."

"But," Robert countered. "The revolution kind of fizzled, you know."

Delta scoffed. "You think today's sixty-year-olds are hanging up their spurs? I bet lube is selling better than ever in their demographic."

Robert smiled at Delta. She had a point.

"Why not drum up some nostalgia?" she asked. "I mean, remember the backseat? What it was like to fuck in glorious and cramped abandon?"

"I remember the cramped part."

A sly smile crept across Delta's face. "Let's test drive a Beetle. Let's do a backseat assessment."

"Too cramped. Let's try the PT Cruiser instead."

"That's a guy car. Only guys had jalopies. The bug was a car of its time, owned and adored by all – freedom, liberation, equality! Besides, be thankful I'm not hankering for that Mini-Cooper. Remember what I told you about them?"

Robert remembered. Delta's USAF father had brought a Cooper back from England in the 1950s and driving it stateside brought vocal ridicule, namely "What's it going to be when it grows up?" From guys driving jalopies.

"Call the dealer," Robert relented. "I'll take time off from work."

Sometimes, it didn't pay to be a known sex writer. Often, people didn't want to see Delta coming their way – sin by association, she called it – and trying to jump-start the Volkswagen story was a case study of people fleeing in the face of Delta's notoriety. Dealers throughout the greater metro region begged off Delta's brand of automotive review. Oh sure, they wished her well and why not? Risk nothing and if her column created a buzz, they'd reap the benefits. But help her directly? No way.

The entire situation made Delta roll her eyes and shake her head in facetious disgust.

To run with her story, Delta had had to dig into the Volkswagen underground, networking her way among Beetle hobbyists to find a car geek who owned Beetles both old and new *and* had a sense of adventure. That geek turned out to be one Paul Clotsman; middle-aged, glasses, receding hairline, and a swallowing tic. He owned a fleet of Beetles, one for each decade of its North American existence, and he was both open- and dirty-minded. In negotiating the terms of acceptance, his only request was that he got to stand guard over his new bug as they did the deed.

"Don't trust us?" Delta asked.

"It's not that. I'm a big fan of yours, actually." Paul's swallow ticked three times between sentences. "Umm, I'd like to watch."

Delta rolled her eyes as Paul, having risked it all, shuffled from foot to foot, awaiting her answer. The last time something like this happened, she recalled, was at an SF convention and it involved Klingon mating practices. Then, she had declined the offer but, this time, with her deadline looming, Delta didn't have time to fuss the details. She eyed Paul and, as he squirmed under her scrutiny, she deemed him harmless compared to that wannabe Klingon.

"Done," she decided.

Paul's swallow was working overtime when he met Delta and Robert outside his garage. He pushed open one of two rolling doors and admitted his guests to his own private little heaven, a long and deep barn in which Volkswagen Beetles sat, lined up in formation.

It wasn't difficult to pick out the new Beetle among the old. A vibrant blue, it was rounder in the front, blunt in the rear, and shaped wider overall. Paul opened the driver's side door and, Delta looking to Robert, she motioned him to get in. "We might as well do this like a date out of the 70s," she said as she made her way to the passenger side and slipped in.

Robert put his seat back as far as it would go and smiled conspiratorially at Delta. She slid her seat back and returned his grin in kind. They reached for each other and started kissing. Action underway, Paul shut the driver's door and went to a neighboring car where he sat on its hood and watched.

Robert and Delta let their kisses lead to necking and necking to groping. They shared the hurried passion of a mutual agenda and in no time, his pants were open, her skirt hiked up, and their first complaints came in unison. Presenting herself sprawled and spread to Robert, she yelped as the door handle pressed into her back; Robert as he attempted to straddle her.

"Damn stick shift," he complained, defeatedly plopping back into his seat.

"So much for a well-planned lay," Delta observed. Struggling, she returned her legs to her side of the car. "Let's try some lap action." She dove onto Robert's cock mouth-first and started working him in earnest. She licked and sucked him, teased that sweet spot which had inspired this entire lark, and bobbed along until she muttered a second "ouch!" This time, the gearshift was against her shoulder.

How did we do it back then? she wondered, rising from Robert's prick and apologizing. He shrugged. "It wasn't quite the right angle anyway."

"Yeah," Delta agreed, "Kind of hard to give you a satisfying hummer from the side."

"Guess you need a hummer for that," Robert quipped.

"Ha. Ha," Delta said in sarcasm unmistakable.

"Lean back and put your legs up," Robert suggested. "Let's see if oral works in the other direction."

As she raised one leg to the dashboard and the other to the head rest of Robert's seat, Delta felt positively porno with her strappy little red shoes pointed heels on high. She braced her hands against the car's floor and car seat to resist placing all her weight on the door handle and Robert angled himself to reach her rich lap of luxury where he would place the talents of his tongue. She shivered as he touched her there, his tongue lapping and circling her clit. Delta sank into the pleasure of arousal and, eyes closed, wandered through several imaginary scenes of lust before watching her legs bounce in synch with Robert's hearty efforts.

Looking around, she spied Paul spying her. Standing, he peered over the hood, taking an occasional drag on a cigarette.

He reminded Delta of a long-ago beau who didn't have a car. Or rather, of his best friend, who drove them around and put up with their backseat antics. Occasionally, he would park the car and they would kick him out so they could grab a hot quickie.

Paul blushed and turned away, returning to the nearby hood like a neighbor who had outstayed his visit.

Just like her beau's friend had done. Only Delta didn't remember the high school friend peeking quite so openly at them.

Delta shifted her focus to Robert's tongue, which was moving downward to her slit and trying to pry its way in. He lapped and poked and made some headway, but again the angle wasn't right. Delta knew her chances for an orgasm were evaporating in the process.

Just as well, really. Her hands were giving out, the door handle again was against her back, and Robert's tolerance was giving out as well. Rising up from her, he stretched and straightened, then reached a hand to the back of his neck and rotated it left, right, then left again. It cracked twice, knuckle-like.

"How'd we do this when we were young?" he asked, baffled.

"Backseat," Delta answered by way of order.

They slid their seats as far forward as possible and stumbled from the front to the back. They didn't even try to go over the seats; at their age, one of them might twist an ankle – or break a hip – trying.

They settled into place and sought out the same position. Delta hiked her legs and, grinning like a Cheshire cat in heat, raised her skirt up, slowly revealing her sweet thighs and the womanly cleft between them. Robert watched as she displayed herself and, when all was in plain sight, he let out a teasing "yummy!"

"You're all swollen down there," he remarked, placing fingers on her clit, her slit, massaging them into renewed excitement. "You look like you could come."

Delta's grin waned into a sly smile. "Maybe I will if you do it right," she coaxed.

Robert took the challenge, slipped a finger into her slick depth, and unbuttoned her blouse with his other hand. He laid her breasts bare and nuzzled his way to her nipples, sucking and tonguing and nibbling her into readiness. Delta gave into the mounting pleasures he offered her, growing aroused enough to grind against his busy hand. She clasped his head in her hands and urged him to nibble more exuberantly. Her breath quickened, matching the heat that grew between her legs, a heat so intense, it cried out for cock. Delta pulled Robert away from her tits and cooed, "Get up here and get that big prick of yours in me."

Robert struggled to lower his pants and fully free his hard length. The metallic sounds of pocket change and his belt buckle jangled as his cock came into view, bobbing eagerly. Delta grabbed it and guided it to her. She felt its tip at her slit and she rose to meet it, contorting herself as she moved. Robert grunted, not out of passion but because he couldn't decide whether to scrunch into a rounded hump or lay flat. And no matter how Delta tilted herself, they succeeded in achieving only the slightest of penetration.

The Beetle's backseat was not ergonomically designed for pelvic assignations.

"You've got to be on top," Robert finally declared, exasperated.

They keystone-kopped their way around each other until Robert was on his back, one leg resting on the seat, the other stretched across the floor, with Delta spread over him, her knees competing with him for whatever seat space they could claim. Again, she had him by his length and, this time, she took aim. Lowering herself, she moved slowly, sinuously, drawing him into her and making him slick with her wet glee.

Robert reached for her breasts and kneaded them. "Great globes," he muttered. He tweaked a nipple here and there, adding as much sensation as possible to Delta's sensual fucking. "You look like something out of a porn movie," he claimed.

"Oh, baby," she moaned in mock dialog, "Fuck my pussy. Fuck it." She punctuated her words with movement. "Come on, baby, ram that big cock up my hole."

Delta giggled and looked down at Robert. Fuck-addled, he could only smile while he absent-mindedly worked her breasts. "You're tight," was all he could manage to say.

But his hips did push upwards. His generous length and girth plumbed her depths at the pace she commanded, plunging into her and satisfying her need to be filled. Robert pulled out almost entirely, dragging her rippling labia as he did; touched her rich spots of desire and pleasure, ground about in her, stabbed her and pierced her – and fucked her good.

Delta was there, ready. Fingers to her clit, she took him fast, slamming and banging her way to orgasm. Clenching her legs to his side, she grew rigid, held her breath, and focused entirely on the tightening, swirling sensation until it seized her and shook her and took all she had.

When she slowed – afterglow fucking, she'd call it in her column – she noticed Paul, watching. This time, she played to him, opening her blouse and flashing him. She toyed with her nipples and licked her lips and gave him a memorable moment.

Robert, though, had other plans. He pulled himself from her, grabbed his cock and began to stroke himself. Delta slid from him and, as he pumped himself more fiercely than she had fucked him, she settled into the gully of the backseat, watching and waiting. She pulled her blouse open, gathered her tits in her hands, and pressed them together. Positively porno all over again, she beckoned to Robert, "Come on, baby, give it to me right here." She leaned forward and brushed her breasts against his hand.

It was just what Robert needed. He gasped and, in swift strokes, came, his cock a fountain that gushed over Delta's tits in several powerful surges.

Soon in repose, Robert surveyed his pro bono money shot as it dripped from the rise of Delta's breasts. "Too bad it's so cramped in here," Delta teased, "I'd love to have you lick my titties clean." Instead, she rubbed his juices into her skin, massaging her breasts so sensuously that, had Robert been a younger man, he probably would've achieved an instant, second-chance hard-on.

A knock on the passenger-side window sounded. Paul. Delta smiled as she looked up at the man's geeky, peering face. Impulsively, she shimmied over Robert and out the backseat. She went to her host and shook his hand so vigorously that her still-exposed tits bounced and jiggled in an unabashed and retro T&A fashion. The way she figured it, Delta owed Paul.

As she and Robert departed, Delta buttoned her blouse and gloated over her final exploit. "If that doesn't make him masturbate the minute we leave, I don't know what will."

Robert threw her a sidelong smile and drove on. Life with Delta, he had decided long ago, would always be exciting, so much so that he'd likely wake up retired one day and discover that he forgot to have a mid-life crisis. But, hell, who needs a red sports car and a twenty-something trophy babe when your Significant Other brought Delta's kind of work home from the office?

Field research completed, Delta hunkered down to the task of writing her column. She wrote that the pneumatic appeal of the Beetle reborn was offset by its cramped quarters. She wrote about cracking joints and fading flexibility, how the older age body couldn't contort the way the teen body could. She wondered if the middle-aged need for generous, backseat legroom prompted some kind of subliminal or subconscious response in boomers who bought SUVs. And she pondered whether small cars made for outdoor sex, speculating that perhaps the Brits were so into dogging now was because their cars were forever small.

Delta even pondered the possibility that Volkswagen might, as more and more boomers aged, bring back its once-hip van – perhaps as a hybrid or a green machine – and if it did, she vowed to assess its shock absorbers and cargo space. Horizontally, of course.

"Don't come a-knocking!" she proclaimed out loud as she finished her column. Then she cocked her head thoughtfully and added, "Unless you're Paul."

Deadline met, Delta leaned back in her chair and considered treating herself to a long, hearty lunch. But first she picked up a notepad, scribbled on it, and tossed it onto her desk.

Call Robert, it said.

Story ideas, Delta needed more story ideas. And a really intense brainstorming session to boot.

The Man from Albuquerque

Julie Saget

The first time I heard about him, where was it exactly? The man from Albuquerque . . . His real name was never uttered, perhaps no one knew it; that was what he was called: the man from Albuquerque.

Yes, the first time, where was it exactly?

Surely in a city with a harbor, those are the only ones he visits. What he looks for he finds on the wharves, along the docks; inland towns don't interest him, he keeps to the edges of the continents; from there it's easier to escape, to vanish.

That is what I was told: he disembarked one beautiful day – in Valparaiso or Liverpool, Tampico or Hamburg – and no one even knew he had landed, for he was only a shadow haunting the ports. And then someone boasted of having seen him, and the news spread; it was the only thing people talked about. On the gangways of the cargo ships berthed at the quay, his name, like a rumor, passed from mouth to mouth, and along the counters, too, in the bars for sailors, which smell of sour beer and men's sweat. They spoke of the man from Albuquerque with dread, admiration, disgust, and envy. I can still hear all those voices talking about him. I started to look for him, and what each voice revealed pushed me forward to meet him.

That's what I remember from the first time: it was in Barcelona, in that hotel room with a rancid smell, where I had been dragged by two Russian sailors from Novorossisk, who were wandering, like me, in the alleyways of the Barrio Chino. We had drunk too much, as if each of us wanted to lose some of our life in that bad drunken state. We made love, the three of us. They rode me, shot all over me, soiled me with sperm and piss. Dawn surprised us, limbs entwined, in sheets soaked with urine. My teeth were chattering, my lips and tongue swollen from far too many bites, a taste of salt and ashes in my mouth, too much sperm swallowed. I was shaking.

It was at that precise time, in that bleak light of early morning, the time for ultimate confessions, that one of the sailors mentioned the man from Albuquerque. I realized immediately that I had to find him. That now my life had meaning. I had to reach him, the elusive man, whatever the cost. He was a cloud pushed by the wind, a stench; he brushed against the black walls of warehouses, a vague silhouette in the fog drowning the pier, barely alive, barely real. We were the same, he and I.

I wasn't always like that. I was married to a powerful man, wealthy, very wealthy and influential. I was an ornament in his house, I was refused nothing. In exchange I had an obligation: to know how to behave, to spare my husband the least scandal. I loved another man. It was a passion approaching madness. Under the pretext of being looked after, I demanded to be split up. In reality, it was to be even closer to the object of my desire. That lover taught me the mysteries of my body, he pulled my body apart, he offered me to others, he fucked me alive and dead. I came for him, in front of him, I came because of him, he crucified me in anticipation of his goodwill . . . Then death took him away from me. For days and nights I howled like an animal for its food – my lover's flesh, which I would never taste again. My husband offered to help me. I started to hate him. I bought my freedom for the price of my silence and total disappearance. As a result of his upbringing, if not fear that I would prostitute myself in order to survive, his ruthless generosity forced him to provide for my needs. I accepted that condition, for I was free then to take all the men I wanted without thinking about money. I would give my bush, my tuft to eat to anybody I fancied, and if I felt the desire, I would pay – with the money of the man whose name I bear – rough men who, however, don't ask for anything other than fucking the woman who offers herself asking nothing in return. At the beginning I sought those men at the gates

*of factories, the men who worked by night. I waited for them in the
early morning, I chose one at random. Some were frightened by my
offer. The money scared them, they feared a devious trick. Others,
fortunately, agreed to make the most of that godsend. They allowed
me to slip my hand into their fly, forage around until I pulled out
their naked penis, which I masturbated until it went stiff. Standing
against the factory wall, I let them work me, but none managed to
calm my fury. Like a crazy bitch, from my throat sprang the growls
of a trapped animal. I ordered: "Deeper, deeper, smash me!"
Then, with a nasty laugh: "Are you scared? Are you scared I'll
swallow you and your prick, and your balls, and all your shit?
Scared I will gulp you down, drain you of your blood, drain you of
your life? Fuck you! Go deeper, deeper than that! Do as I say!"
They did their best. I could see in their eyes desire mixed with fear
in the face of such rage. In the end I found those men too servile;
they stank of machine grease and obedience. I was aiming for
something else. Men of another consistency – but their bodies
always had to be dirty and their cocks had to stink – men whose
language I would not understand and who would not hear my
words, men coming from the four corners of the earth, with no home,
no homeland, like myself. I knew I would find them in ports.
Makeshift crews, they arrive from every part of the world, all races
mixed, embarked for a mere pittance of a wage on tankers so
decrepit that no repairs can save those floating monstrosities from
disaster. Indians, Malaysians, Yemenites, they feed on spicy stews
and raw onions; they have foul breath and their sweat reeks. It's
them I want, them I need.*

So I left. Gibraltar, Tangier, Alexandria and then, as I said,
Barcelona and the two sailors from Novorossisk . . .

I went up north, ready to scour all the ports on the Baltic. I
ended up in Hamburg. In the evening, I wandered in Sankt
Pauli. Girls in their windows, boxed in tackiness, with an air of
decent housewives displaying their asses. Not one worth fucking, but men were there, strolling about, eyeing them. My God,
they looked like first communicants walking slowly to the altar
to receive the host! Monumental hard-ons because that one
shakes her tits under their noses and they imagine themselves

stuffing their pricks in the holy of holies! You bet they haven't grown one inch since the time when, as adolescents, they shut themselves in the toilet to jerk off out of sight of their mommy's eyes! Men's desire disgusts me.

It was certainly not in those alleyways with no dark corners, where the gaudy pink neons filter, that I was going to meet the man from Albuquerque. It was down to the wharves I had to go . . . I hung about between the angular shadows of the container stacks waiting to be loaded. I moved toward the ship I thought was the most rotten, an old tub with the look of a rusty scrap heap. I took the gangway that hadn't been lifted, a useless precaution anyway. Where could they go, the crew, those poor guys with no papers, with no money? I hadn't walked three steps onto the deck when a voice came out of the shadows to stop me.

"What the hell are you doing here?"

I answered:

"I'm looking for men."

"Men. What for?"

"For fucking."

I heard him sneer and saw him come toward me. I thought he must be the captain.

"You're in the wrong place. Do you know what the men down there look like? For three weeks, since we berthed, their wages haven't arrived. There's nothing to take here, fuck off!"

"You've got it wrong. I'm the one who pays."

He grabbed me by the sleeve, and there I was, in what must have been the steward's room. He and I sat in front of a glass of bad whiskey.

"So then, you are the one who pays? Tell me more."

I told the captain the woman I had been before, before knowing myself, before knowing who I was. I talked about the deceased lover who had taught me to understand who I was. I told him about my taste for filth and abjection. That what would seem a descent to hell in the eyes of the uninitiated was for me the path to the absolute. That I was not crazy. That I had chosen and that I had to go all the way, till the end of what I had

decided to accomplish. And that it was for that reason I was
looking for the man from Albuquerque.

The captain remained silent for a moment before blurting
out:

"Port Sudan, in a month's time."

He showed me how to gain access to the holds. As I went in, I
had difficulty discerning the dozen men sleeping on the bare
floor. I slipped between them. The heat was stifling. The first
body my hand encountered was half-naked and sweaty. I
touched the damp torso and the sleeper woke up, muttering
in an incomprehensible tongue. I quieted him by placing my
mouth on his. His breath was repugnant and my tongue
plunged into a cesspool. At the same time I undressed and
lay down on top of him. I became an undulating reptile. My
belly rubbed against his and when I felt the hard swollen penis,
I undid the man's sarong and, opening my thighs, I violently
forced his penis inside me. There was a long moan, like a
powerful note on the barely audible chords of the breath of
the other sleeping sailors. My movements became more rapid,
more violent, to make the man cry louder and wake up his
companions. The first to wake up lit a hurricane lamp and
moved closer. I beckoned him to come even closer. I undid the
belt that held up his rough cotton trousers, I took his penis in
my mouth. I started to suck him as if I was going to draw out the
substance in his balls. The one I was riding let out an anguished
rattle and I felt he was coming with all the power of a male
deprived of women for ages. All the others were now crowding
around the three of us. Each wanted his turn, now. I gave
myself to all. I offered them my cunt, my lips, the furrow
between my breasts, my armpits, my hair, all the places in my
body where their come could pour out. I think they were
laughing and crying at the same time. It lasted quite a while.
Dawn was already breaking. Each part of my flesh was pain and
pleasure at the same time, as if I had just gone up the Via
Dolorosa on my knees with a crown of thorns on my forehead
and the weight of the cross on my back. Transfiguration
through abasement, with voluntary suffering. Before coming
out into the open air, I threw them a bundle of banknotes,

which the men rushed for, with the greediness of famished dogs.

As I walked down the wharf where the first dockers were already at work, I heard the voice of the captain shouting:

"You're really going there?"

I nodded. He added:

"Perhaps we'll see each other again!"

We were too far apart for him to hear my reply:

"I doubt it very much."

He must have seen, though, that I was smiling at him. I knew that was the image he would keep of me.

Port Sudan. When I disembarked, I was challenged immediately by a native in uniform who was probably acting as harbormaster, customs officer, and commissioner, the symbol of all authorities. He was fat and sweating heavily under his cap. The air was a furnace, no relief to be expected from the sea, no sea breeze, earth and water an inferno. I followed the representative of the law into a shack used as an office, where the blades of a decrepit fan stirred the fire, no more. He wanted to know the purpose of my visit.

"I've come to wait for a friend."

He appraised me suspiciously, the same way he had examined my papers earlier.

"I keep your passport," he stated in bad English. "You come get it when friend here."

Used to all sorts of traffic, he was calculating what gains he could obtain for himself from my presence. It was he who found me a place to stay. In a rickety jeep driven at breakneck speed, he took me to an old woman who spoke only Dinka. The house comprised two rooms. I would occupy the one at the back, the old woman's bedroom.

I lay down, naked, on what was nothing more than a litter stinking of rags and the sour smell of old people. I was exhausted, like someone who has just accomplished the final stage of a race. Sleep! . . . Between my half-closed eyelids, I caught sight of a hand pulling the curtain that was supposed to give some intimacy to my room. I saw the eyes of my landlady,

full of curiosity, a black and greedy look whose only intelligence
was that of an animal, the eyes of a rat. She came closer,
attracted by my nudity, and her bony hand traced the whole
surface of my skin. I was too shattered to push that hand away.
The caress was soothing, in a way. The fingers lingered on the
fleece of my pubis, appreciating its abundance and thickness,
then they plunged inside me, digging into my depths, exploring
both orifices. It was the hand of an expert who knew what it was
to finger a woman, and pleasure rose in me until the combustion
of orgasm. The old woman lifted her fingers to her nostrils,
sniffing the traces of her exploration. She looked like she was
inhaling a delicious perfume whose fragrance she had herself
lost a long time ago.

How long did I sleep? When I woke up night had fallen. The
old woman and I shared a stew she had prepared. Then,
through a series of signs, she explained that she was going
out, that she would be back soon, and that I should wait for her.
I stood on the doorstep. The sky was nothing but a huge, jet
black cavity dotted with stars, an oppressive cover imprisoning
each portion of that godforsaken place. I realized that if there
was a place where I could find the man from Albuquerque, it
was Port Sudan, and nowhere else. One only lands here to run
aground or die a slow death. Here everything is wrecked: men
and ships.

The old woman came back, as she'd said she would. She
had brought with her an adolescent boy whose eyes were lined
with kohl – the eyes of a gazelle – a mouth with thick lips, and
the skin of a girl. I said to the old woman, no, I was not
interested. But she got upset, took me by force back to my
room. She threw herself backward onto the bed, lifted her
skirt, and, legs spread wide, opened the edges of her cunt and
forced me to look. In place of the clitoris there was a long scar,
the mark of excision. No need to speak Dinka to catch what
the old woman told me:

"You're lucky, my girl, to possess that bit of flesh that
provides woman with a pleasure even more intense than the
one given by the bludgeons of men. It's your pleasure, not that
of the male, so enjoy it!"

I let the ephebe with painted eyes put his head between my legs. His tongue came to get me, first pointed and wriggling like a lizard's tail, then wide and flabby – the tongue of a licker savoring his favorite dish with wet lapping noises. Finally the thick-lipped mouth caught me, sucked me in. I felt my clitoris swelling, my whole body condensed into that single growth, there where the alpha and omega of my woman's desire resided. I became dizzy. I grabbed the frizzy hair with both hands to make sure he wouldn't escape, his mouth wouldn't leave me before I fell back disheveled and shattered. The orgasm left me burning and unsatisfied. I wanted the penis of my lover, I made signs that he should penetrate me. That was when the old woman burst into laughter and lifted the young man's *gandoura*, showing me that he had been emasculated. They both laughed, the madame and the ephebe, as if they had played a trick on me in their own way. Afterward, they asked me to pay them, as was only right.

On the third evening the commissioner came to fetch me.

"I think your friend arrived. You want I take you to him?"

I didn't even ask how he knew that it was precisely that man I was waiting for. I climbed into the jeep and we drove in the direction of the port. The moon was full and its light, a phosphorescent lactation, radiated the sea, changing it to mercury. At the far end of the docks, a few warehouses still stood, the last remnants of a time when Port Sudan had countless fleets mooring there. The jeep stopped in front of the last shed. A man was there. He walked toward me. At first I saw only his teeth, gleaming like snow, brightened by the whiteness of the moon. The face had no outlines. It was as if he wanted to melt in what was still blurred, in that nocturnal part that the reflections of the moon hadn't been able to reach. The deep voice made me bet the man was handsome. One couldn't imagine ugliness associated with that voice.

"I know you're looking for me. In fact I was told a while ago, and I was wondering where we would finally meet."

As he pronounced those last words with an ironic smile I saw his teeth, so white in his carnassial mouth. He took his time, pulled a cigarillo from his shirt pocket, and lit it. The acrid smell of tobacco suited him. His voice grew louder:

"I know you're looking for me. But what I don't know is why."

I answered simply:

"Snuff movies."

"You're a client? You need that to come?"

"It's not what you think."

The voice spoke with a falsely innocent tone. It was a way to make fun of me.

"But I don't think anything! And I don't care what others think! It's none of my business."

"I'm not a client. I just want to be the next."

There was silence. The man threw down his cigarillo. He took his time to crush the stump.

"I never do it with women. A question of principles. I work with men perfectly aware of what to expect. Most have no more than six months to live. Tuberculosis or that type of shit . . . Their life is not worth more than that of a dead dog. They think that with all the dough they're going to earn, they can provide their family with a living, back here. You see, those men agree. It's a proper contract. I don't know what you are looking for exactly."

I explained what I was looking for. The stigmata on my body, which were nothing but purification, the come of all those men I had taken and who had come on my belly, breasts, and face, and which was like spit on Christ's face. Redemption, redemption! The martyr had to reach her end, like Christ crucified. Then I would finally be freed, liberated from the weight of my organs, saved from suffering. I wanted that ultimate orgasm and I wanted him to obtain it for me.

"Go home! I'll come tomorrow night and let you know."

All the next day I waited like a fiancée on the eve of her wedding. The next night he was there. He came into the bedroom. I undressed, and, once naked, I undressed him. His skin was like amber, smooth and golden. I ran my tongue over his torso to get the taste of that skin. He took my breasts in his hands to hold me captive. I knew that this first approach sealed the pact and that he had accepted what I had asked of him. I knelt in front of him, religiously, for my mouth to take his penis. I didn't want to hurry anything. I wanted that night to become a bountiful eternity.

With incredible slowness I swallowed the man! He had taken my head in his hands to transmit the rhythm he wanted to my movements. There was no impatience in our gestures. With infinite gentleness I came out to the tip, for it was the most vulnerable spot – there, the envelope is so thin that the flesh appears in all its transparency.

"Come here," he murmured.

He hauled me up. I wound my legs around his loins, my arms around his neck, and he plunged inside. For him I weighed no more than a small child. Again he set the pace of the ebb and flow. So strong, so manly, yet so attentive to my pleasure, as if it was the only thing that was important to him. When he realized, from the paleness of my face and the violence of my moans, that I was about to reach orgasm . . . he allowed himself to ejaculate, so that we came together.

Rolled into a ball, I remained gasping on the floor while he got dressed. He wrapped me in the old woman's sheet and carried me out to the jeep. I knew where he was taking me. Still in his arms I crossed the threshold of the shed, like a bride. Was it not the case after all, tonight, of celebrating a barbaric wedding?

In the shed, a big lamp was lit, making a luminous halo, a circle of crude light defining the stage. I saw a pulley there, suspended, where chains could slide. He tied me to them, my arms stretched toward the ceiling, as high as possible. My feet just touched the ground.

Two men in hoods appeared. I recognized one of them as the commissioner. They whipped, burned, lacerated, and mutilated me. They dug into my insides with their blades. My blood flowed abundantly. They had taken precautions to cover the ground with sawdust. Don't worry: only the first gashes really hurt. Afterward, the pain becomes so intense that one no longer feels it. The spirit escapes from the matter to float in an elsewhere where nothing can touch you.

I'm almost certain that the fat commissioner had an erection like a donkey. But not the man from Albuquerque. His eye was riveted to the camera, filming my agony. He was just doing his job.

The angel of death.

He spread his wings – that was my last vision – and, taking me once again in his arms, lifted me up and took me away. I was finally in flight.

Her last thought was that she had made him promise to send a copy of the film to her husband. He would not hesitate to pay dearly to recover the original and destroy it.

"Thanks to me," she had said to the angel, "you'll have a lot of money. Perhaps you can even stop."

The angel had placed his lips on hers (a good-bye kiss, gentle like the down of a fledgling) and, with a smile, replied:

"It's my life, you know!"

She had smiled back at the angel. And that was how she departed.

The Four Elements

Claude Lalumière

Air (Hiding)

The gloves are designed to look like a hand. Pink, with a subtle tint of olive; fingernails painted blue.

A blonde wig lies next to them on the floor: shoulder length, with a bounce that stops short of a curl. High-heeled shoes. Blouse. Skirt. Tights. Bra. Cotton panties. More pseudoskin: a one-piece mold that mimics her features, and then spreads to the neck, the chest, the shoulders, below the nape.

She's in a playful mood.

I pick up the panties and slip on the blindfold that I keep in my pocket for games like these.

I bury my nose in her panties. Cotton is so much better at absorbing her odour than silk or lace. Her smell is heady, powerful: she's at most a day or two from her period.

I drop the panties and start my search. Step by step I cover the entire house. I open every closet. I palpate every nook and cranny. The whole time I'm sniffing. Sniffing her pussy. That smell! It's everywhere I go. My balls tingle with anticipation.

Is she even here? Maybe I shouldn't have rubbed my face in her panties. Maybe that's all I'm smelling.

"Darling . . .?"

Someone rams into me and knocks me down.

"Silly! I followed you the whole time – you couldn't win."

She yanks off my blindfold, but there's nothing to see.

My fly is zipped open, my cock pulled out. Moist warmth envelops my erection.

Her smell is overpowering. I open my mouth and stick out my tongue. She presses her pussy against it. I manage to find her hips and tilt her so my nose slides into her juices.

When I come, I see the faint milky outline of her tongue, her palate, her teeth, her cheeks – the insides of her mouth. My invisible woman.

Fire (Metamorphosis)

Her footprints are seared into the tarmac, leading to the woods bordering the road. I follow the trail of burnt leaves, burnt wood – that rich blend: subtly fruity, pungently ashy.

There she is: sitting on a boulder, naked. Her face tells me she's confused, scared – like the others I've tracked down.

She doesn't notice me. The symptoms are too overwhelming. Coarse, ragged breathing. Dizzy, sweating, and shivering all at once from the heat, nausea, and weakness.

Gently, I say, "I can help you."

She tenses, panicked. Perspiration runs down her skin. Then fire bursts from her pores, enveloping her. When the flames subside, she balls up into herself, crying.

I say, "No. It's beautiful. Exciting. Fantastic."

"Beautiful?"

"Yes. Reach between your legs."

She hesitates. But she opens her thighs and places her fingers on her sex.

"Touch yourself. Focus the heat."

She does. She moans, closing her eyes. I take off my clothes. I masturbate, too, relishing what will soon happen.

"You should celebrate these changes in your body. These hot flashes, they're not the end: they're a beginning."

Her breathing intensifies. She's close.

I say: "Let me join you."

Her gaze lingers briefly on my hand stroking my cock. She nods.

I pick her up in my arms. She's burning – scorching – hot, but her fire cannot consume flesh. I lay her down on the ground.

The leaves and twigs under her burn and sizzle, releasing that delicious aroma.

I touch her face, admiring the beauty of the lines etched by age and time.

I enter her. We move together. I whisper into her ear, and she comes. Flames enfold us both. My skin tingles with pleasure so intense it is almost pain. Her heat rushes into me. When I come, for a moment, I too am fire.

Earth (Nephesh)

She hears them leave. Still, she waits. Hiding. She hears the clatter of rain. Some time later, she emerges from her hole in the ground, her well-concealed cellar. The sun hurts her eyes.

The stink of death hits her. Blood. Shit. Piss. Rot. A brew of odours she will never forget.

She thinks: Words carry power.

Yirah. Fear.

Sawnay. Hate.

Met. Death.

Pogrom.

Everyone she's ever known: dead. Slaughtered. Mutilated.

It is too much for tears, she thinks. But she is crying. In silence, lest she be heard.

She leaves the village. She walks aimlessly until she collapses in the drying mud.

She rubs the mud on her face. She inhales its earthy odours. They scrape at the stink of death lodged inside her.

Her hands work the mud and the soil. She kneads the earth. Molds it.

Words carry power, she thinks again.

Emet. Truth.

No. A more appropriate word occurs to her.

She looks down at her handiwork. The shape of a man. A man with broad, strong shoulders. With a powerful, heavy chest. Endowed with an enormous *zayin*, created erect under her hands.

She touches between her legs. Her time has come. Her blood. Not the blood of death, but the blood of life. She squats on her creation's mouth and lets her menses flow into it.

Life. *Nephesh.*

With a bloody finger she carves the word on its forehead, then whispers it in its ear.

The creature stirs.

She impales her wetness on its *zayin*.

For a time, while they squirm together in the mud, while she loses herself in the smells of the earth and the sensation of the massive *zayin* grinding inside her, she desperately thinks of life.

Later, she will think of the death her golem will visit upon her enemies.

Water (Scars)

He closes his eyes. He takes a deep breath. A melancholy smile spreads across his face.

I love to look at him: his square jaw, his dimpled chin, his thick eyebrows, his mane of golden hair.

He's smelling the sea. They say smell is the sense most strongly linked to memory. A lifetime ago, the sea was his.

I touch his face. My lips brush his lips, and then his ear. "Watch me. And wait for me."

Basking in his gaze, I take off my shirt, slip out of my shorts and underwear.

I walk towards the waves and plunge into the ocean.

When I emerge, my fists are carrying seaweed.

Rejoining him, I hand over the seaweed, and then I lie on the sand. On my back, my legs spread.

He decorates my body with the strips of seaweed.

He removes his clothes. His cock is huge and dripping. For me.

I moan.

He rubs the seaweed into my wet skin: my face, my neck, my arms, my breasts, my stomach, my legs, my toes. He runs his face against my naked body. I hear him breathe me in, smelling the ocean on me.

I'm so eager for him.

One last strip of seaweed he brushes against my cunt.

He buries his face between my legs, pushes open my labia with his tongue. He takes a deep breath of my smells mingled with the sea's, and then releases his hot breath over my clit.

I gasp.

He moves up to kiss me. As his salty tongue finds mine, his cock spears me.

He nuzzles my neck, sniffing furiously. His thrusts are strong, savage. I come, pulling at his hair.

After his orgasm, I tenderly kiss the scars on his neck, the remnants of his gills.

Bethany Barefoot

Tara Alton

I hated weddings. Nothing good for me has ever come of them. For example, the last wedding I went to, I ended up alone at a table with my great-aunt while all the couples swooned about on the dance floor. Their closely pressed bodies seemed to be saying aren't we the lucky ones as the white paper streamers delicately fluttered on the ceiling.

Meanwhile, my great-aunt was going on about some freaking tea party she claimed she had for me in Florida when I was four years old. I don't remember Florida. I don't remember her, except for meeting her in the receiving line two hours ago. What did I get from attending this blissful event? A paper cut from my place card, a cranky buzz from cheap champagne and a regretful comment I slurred to my great-aunt at the end of the night.

"I won't be you," I called out in her direction. I didn't know what that meant, because I hardly knew her. I think it was directed more at what she represented, an old crone sitting alone at a wedding banquet table with her odd great-niece.

I would rather do these things instead of going to a wedding. Get a tetanus shot, which always gives me a huge bruise because I tense up. Go for a gynecology exam, with a student doctor in tow, who would do a second far more clumsy and embarrassing exam than the original doctor would. Finally, clean up cat puke.

I know you're asking why all the fuss. It's because I have to go to my sister's wedding. Actually, it's her second time around, but she still wants all the drama and fuss because she likes to show off how clever and stylish she is. She was so taken with her first wedding that she actually wrote and self published a *How to be a Bride* book. She tried to sell it in the back of bridal magazines and lost thousands of dollars in advertising. Not one order came in. Occasionally, she threatens to dust it off and send it to a real publisher, but she never has the time, not with her new budding career as a newscaster.

I've been in such denial about this wedding that I've made myself late. I've missed the wedding ceremony, and now I'm struck rigid with fear in the reception hall parking lot. Things are not looking good. I bought her a crappy, last-minute, hastily wrapped gift. It was a silver frame from a greeting card store that anyone off the street could buy. What makes this worse is that I've agreed to live with her and her new husband for a few weeks until I can get on my feet.

In addition, I have a confession to make. The other reason I'm late is because of a self-inflicted finger fuck. I got all excited writing porn. I know I should say erotica or even better literary erotica, but this was the down and dirty. I wrote about butt cheeks and short hairs bobbing all over the page until I had to do something about it. I mean, why not. This could be the last time I get off before moving in with my sister.

If my sister truly comprehended what I wrote about, she would have a massive shit. Once upon a time, I did hint about my choice of subject matter, but she didn't get it.

"What is there to write about?" she asked. "There are only a couple positions."

I felt sorry for her last husband and her new one if that was her way of thinking. Wanting to avoid any further elaboration about my writing career, I told her I write literary stories and submit them to publications with names like *Coffee* and *Mudhouse*.

Meanwhile, I'm working on collecting writing credits as Bethany Barefoot in magazines who use body parts for names. I would like some non-body part credits, but I haven't been accepted yet in any high-crust anthologies with intelligent themes. If only something nice would happen to me and put my raunchy imagination to sleep for a while. Have you ever fantasized about something for so long that you wore it out, and now you had to add something new every time to get some zing? Well, I've been adding too much for too long.

How was anything nice going to happen to me while I sat in my car wearing a cut-off, floral print bridesmaid dress? I couldn't wear my black sexy dress because I discovered an hour before I was supposed to leave that it had become a litter box in the back of my ex-roommate's closet.

Forcing myself out of my car, I grabbed my sister's present and headed for the entrance.

Leave it to my sister to book the trendiest, upscale chapel with a banquet hall attached. I felt my knees almost knocking together with nerves as I noticed the glimmering lights on potted trees and elaborate bows on white chair covers through the windows. I didn't see any Jordan Almonds or after-dinner mints nestled in little white paper cups, which was a shame because I liked after dinner mints.

I prayed everyone was already soused enough not to notice me slipping in. I stood in the doorway, trapped by fear. I didn't recognize anybody. Was I at the wrong place? Did I get the date wrong? For a second, I was giddy with relief, but then I noticed the bride's table was curiously empty. Oh, God. The receiving line had started, and there was my sister.

Slinking over to the gift table, I squeezed my present onto the edge, thinking I should have rethought the wrapping. Although I had managed to buy a gift and a card, I hadn't remembered to buy wrapping paper. Therefore, I had dug out bright green parrot paper from a drawer at home. Now, the present screamed its jungle theme from the bland sea of cream and beige.

My nerves were so bad that I grabbed a glass of champagne from a nearby table, received a dirty look from its owner, and gratefully inhaled half of it. The bubbles went straight up my nose. It burned. Blinking back the tears, I considered a hasty retreat to the bathroom, thinking I could avoid the receiving line from hell all together, but I had to do this. I was moving in with her tomorrow. Where was all this dread coming from anyway? I loved her, for Pete's sake. She was my sister. I just wasn't convinced how much I liked her.

Chugging down the rest of the champagne, I put down the glass, plastered a smile on my face and got in line.

"Bride's sister," I said, with a firm handshake to the first person.

The parent spot for us was empty. Our mom was locked away in a nut house. Our dad was dead.

I was getting dangerously near the bridesmaids. Who were these girls? I recognized Crystal, the weather girl from Lisa's station. She was wearing her plastic TV smile, and she looked at me as if I was a freak.

"So what is the forecast for today?" I asked, thinking it would be an icebreaker.

She gave me a murderous look. Jeez. Couldn't she take a joke? Why was my sister even friends with her? She seemed like such a fake person, and yet she was the one standing next to my sibling.

I looked away. I was a stranger here. I should go. I should leave.

"There you are," said Lisa.

In my panic, I had let the line propel me forward.

Lisa hugged me.

"You look incredible," I said, staring amazed at her manufactured cleavage. She was too squeamish to get fake boobs so it had to be a push up bra.

"You should have come earlier," she said in my ear. "I had a corsage for you."

Our gazes met. I saw the crazy look in her eyes that mom used to have. We called it Mom's crazy fish eye. Why had I been kidding myself? The shrill Lisa who could hold a grudge for months was still alive and well.

I had been so wrapped up in Lisa that I hadn't even noticed the groom. I was shocked. I had expected another version of henpecked Simon, and I vaguely remembered Lisa saying he was a construction foreman, but I never imagined this. This guy was oozing masculinity with his intense, smoldering eyes and fantastic build.

"Jeremy, this is my sister," Lisa said.

Lisa went on to embrace the next person, leaving us facing each other.

I stuck out my hand. He took it, pulled me forward and planted one on my mouth, dead on. I felt a spark, a little firecracker of zing between us. I saw the surprise in his eyes.

As I finished the rest of the line, I barely registered the other introductions. The groom had flummoxed me. I kept glancing at him. He kept watching me.

Free at last, I headed to the bar where I asked for two glasses of champagne.

"No. Make it three," I said.

The waiter looked as if he didn't want to give it to me.

"I'm the bride's sister," I said.

With my three glasses in an awkward hold, I replaced the one I had stolen and went to find my table. I started looking near the front where I would assume Lisa would put her family. Maybe I would be sitting with her in-laws. Amazingly, I didn't find my name. Still searching, I reached the rear of the room where I found it. I was seated at the last table near the restroom with my cousins. I was at the reject table. I knew this because I had helped her plan her first seating arrangement, and that was what she called it. Trying to conceal my disappointment, I smiled at the people who loosely called themselves my relatives.

"How is everyone?" I asked. "Where are the kids?"

"It's a kid-free reception," said my cousin Helen.

"Are you kidding?"

Helen nodded. I glanced around. I hadn't even noticed my nephews were missing.

They started to serve dinner. The choices were chicken breast or a T-bone steak. Everyone had a plate but me. Finally, a lone dish came trailing out. It was cold pasta with sun-dried tomatoes. Lisa had remembered my fear of bones. I hadn't eaten meat since I cut the top of my middle finger off when I was twelve. Now every time I saw a bone I felt sick.

If the pasta had been served when it was made a week ago, I might have managed to choke it down, but it was inedible. I arranged my tomatoes in the middle with the dry lifeless noodles around them. A waiter stopped in front of me to take my plate. He saw what I'd done.

"I'm artistic," I said.

He whisked it away.

I was starving, and I was buzzed from the second glass of champagne. A little thought danced in the back of my head. What had Lisa said about a dessert? She had chosen a lovely mousse. Of course, it had to be chocolate. They brought it out. Why was my chocolate mousse pink? It was strawberry. It was like ordering a diet cola and getting a fully leaded one. I couldn't eat it.

Nibbling on the vanilla wafer on top, I watched my sister. She was having the time of her life, and I needed a cigarette like a vampire needed blood.

Excusing myself, I found a side door near the kitchen. The fresh air was liberating, and the familiar click of my lighter was like a kitten getting its mother's milk. I inhaled deeply and looked around. There was another waiter having a cigarette like me. I thought he wasn't bad looking in a swarthy, Greek sort of way. I liked the cut of his crisp white cotton shirt and the sleekness of his black pants.

"I bet you're having a better time than I am," I said.

He smiled and came over to me.

"You must be having an awful time if that is true," he said.

I paused, thinking about it.

"It is true. I'm having an awful time."

"Why don't you go home?" he asked.

I laughed.

"Easier said than done," I said. "Have you ever been at a family event where you feel lonelier than you do alone?"

He shook his head.

"Your family seems nice," he said.

"So it seems. The photo op bride is my sister. I'm the proverbial bad seed, who writes smut and has to go live with her because I can't support myself."

I looked closer at him.

"I should be a waiter," I said. "Because I'm always waiting for something to happen."

"You write smut?"

"You were listening," I said.

"Why wouldn't I?" he asked.

"Because I'm a slightly drunk guest prattling on about her personal problems," I said.

There was a pause. It didn't feel like a bad one, just interesting.

"You are easy to talk to," I said.

"The smut?" he asked.

"I write for one-hand glossy whack-off mags. You know, the kind you get in party stores behind the counter. Are you shocked?"

I looked into his eyes to see the surprise. I didn't see any.

"No," he said. "Someone has to write them. Why not someone as pretty and sexy as you?"

"You think I'm sexy," I said.

I looked him up and down, feeling frisky.

"Are you on break?" I asked.

I guess I was horny, because one moment we were standing there, innocently smoking our cigarettes, and the next moment, we were behind the building, doing it in the shrubs. We were standing up like a couple of horny kids, who couldn't keep their hands off each other. I came so loudly that he had to clap his hand over my mouth to keep me from being heard.

As we straightened our clothes, I gave him a sly smile.

"I've had a one-night stand before, but I wasn't actually standing," I said.

He smiled back and gave me his phone number. His name was Dominic.

Feeling flushed and happy, I turned. I should go before anything ruined this mood.

I found my sister in a cluster of bridesmaids. Jeremy was standing nearby with two glasses of champagne.

"I'm here to tell Lisa I'm leaving," I said to him.

He looked at me.

"You have the most amazing glow," he said.

"I just had sex with a waiter outside," I blurted out.

Shock paralyzed his face. Oops. Had I actually said that? I panicked.

"Don't tell Lisa," I said.

Without saying good-bye to her, I left the hall. I felt weird, appalled and tramp-like. It was amazing what three glasses of champagne and a lack of food could do to my reasoning. I needed food soon.

On the way to the hotel, I stopped at a grimy little grocery store, the kind Lisa would hate on sight, and I bought bananas, peanut butter and sprinkles. She had made me a reservation for the night at a motel, the kind that felt like a prison cell inside. Hardly any cars were there. I grabbed a box of my clothes and checked in.

I decided to take a bath, because I didn't have the energy to stand in the shower. Normally, I hated baths, especially shaving in them. There was something about those little hairs floating in the water. It gave me the creeps, but tonight, I soaked, eating my bananas dunked in the peanut butter and topped with sprinkles.

In the morning, I woke to find myself sprawled naked on the bed with a huge stomach ache, no doubt from the bananas. My head was pounding. I touched my scalp, realizing my hair had dried weirdly as well. Rolling over to see what time it was, I noticed the front curtain of the motel room was partway open. Who knew who had been standing out there, getting a glimpse of my bare ass!

I tugged on a robe and looked outside to see if there was any incriminating evidence on the brick wall. Only a porn writer would even think of this. Jeez. This would make a good story.

Finding a scrap of paper inside my room, I started scribbling about a luscious brunette in a motel room with an open curtain and a lust-filled admirer. Wait a minute. I was writing trash again. Hadn't I said if something nice happened to me I could write better things? Something had happened. I had met Dominic. Had it been a good thing, though? It was certainly sexy and tawdry.

I needed coffee, like a gallon of it. On my way to Lisa's, I stopped at a donut shop. It was mostly filled with regulars, old men who were smoking, reading the paper and staring at the walls. I wanted to tell them that I had sex with a Greek waiter last night, but I decided not to. My gaze fell on the donut counter. A glistening chocolate donut with sprinkles gazed back at me. Ugh. I thought, remembering the bananas, but it wasn't their fault. The sprinkles, I meant. I couldn't hold it against them.

With the coffee and the donut, I left.

I was wired by the time I got to Lisa's house. The donut had given me a high, glossy, sweet buzz, and the caffeine was challenging the sluggishness in my veins with an ultra kick.

Lisa had one of those houses that made you wonder who could afford to live there. I had heard tales of house-poor people. They were home owners, had a nice house, but they didn't have enough money to furnish all the rooms. They never went out to dinner or the movies either. They didn't do anything but sit in their big, but poorly furnished house. I could tell Lisa didn't fit in this category. She had cement lions on her front porch.

One of my nephews answered the front door. He'd grown. I couldn't remember when I'd seen him last. He looked at me as if he had never seen me before. Kids always knew I didn't have the mom gene. I had no idea what to say to them.

"Can I see Lisa?" I asked.

Lisa came and got me. You would have never thought she got married last night. Her hair and makeup were perfect. Even her casual clothes were pressed. Her sparkling two-carat diamond ring was the only giveaway.

"I was worried about coming too early," I said. It was eleven a.m.

"I've been up for hours. Someone had too much to drink last night," she said.

Me, I thought, but I realized she meant Jeremy.

"How was the hotel?" she asked.

"Fine," I said.

"You should have stayed longer."

"I had cramps."

"Jeremy liked you," she said.

My heart fluttered. The waiter thing. Had he said anything? Apparently not or Lisa wouldn't be this relaxed.

"Your house is amazing," I said, changing the topic.

There was a big pause. This one was bad. Neither of us knew what to say next.

"Why did you seat me at the reject table?" I demanded.

"Is that why you left so early?"

"I had cramps."

"I didn't intentionally put you back there. Besides, I thought you'd want to see our cousins."

I nodded. Seeing them more than once every ten years was more than enough.

"Why the kid-free thing?" I asked.

"The network executives were invited. I wanted it to be an adult party."

Jeremy came into the room. Oh, baby. He was only wearing pajama bottoms. I inventoried his six-pack abs, great arms and shoulders, tousled hair and sexy stubble in two seconds flat.

"Look who just woke up," Lisa said. "You could have worn a robe or something."

"I'm sure your sister has seen a man's chest before," he said and looked at me.

"Morning, Madison," he said.

"It's Maddy. No one calls me Madison but Lisa."

How could my sister have even gotten out of bed with him? I would be bending him like a pretzel and licking the salt off the good parts.

"Don't you think the waiters at the hall did a good job last night?" he asked.

I glared at him.

"Marvelous," I said.

"Very attentive," he said.

"Yes."

"Why are we talking about the waiters?" Lisa asked.

Jeremy shrugged.

There was a knock at the door.

"Who could that be?" Lisa asked.

"Probably the man about the Jacuzzi," Jeremy said.

He went to answer it. I was relieved. Please, no more bloody talk about waiters, I thought. Lisa offered me a cup of coffee. I accepted. Men's voices filled the foyer. When I turned to see who he was bringing into the kitchen, my jaw dropped.

There stood Dominic, the sexy waiter from last night. He was looking as surprised to see me as I was to see him. Without his waiter clothes, he didn't look half as sexy as Jeremy did. I tried not to remember him pounding into me up against the wall, my dress pushed up to my hips, my foot cramping from holding it in the air. What was he doing here?

"Madison, have you met Dominic?" Lisa asked. "He is Jeremy's best friend, and he was one of the groomsmen last night."

I was rendered mute from fear. Lisa didn't notice.

"Now we've got his wedding to do," she said. "He's marrying Crystal, the weather forecaster from my station."

I raised an eyebrow. Not the horrible weather girl in the receiving line. I felt sick. I'd screwed a groomsman and a weather girl's fiancé. This was becoming a nightmare. How could I escape?

"Mom," one of Lisa's kids called out.

"We're in the kitchen," she replied.

The one who answered the door wandered in. He was carrying a piece of paper.

"What's aniligus?" he asked.

"What?" Lisa screeched.

She snatched the piece of paper from his hand. In horror, I realized it was the piece of paper I had scribbled on about the brunette at the motel. It must have fallen out of my car.

Lisa's face turned an odd color as she scanned the offensive piece of paper. Jeremy looked over his shoulder, his face amused in comparison.

"Oh, my God. Where did this come from?" she asked in a high pitch voice.

"It was on the ground. Between Dominic's and the lady's car," her son said.

I'm your aunt, you half-wit, I wanted to say.

"Get out of here. Go to your room. Take your brother. Now!" she cried.

He fled, screaming his brother's name.

"Horrible. Perverted. Disgusting," Lisa said, her voice trembling as badly as her hands. "My child will never be the same."

She took a huge swig of black coffee.

"Where did this come from?" she asked.

"The wind may have blown it in the driveway," Jeremy offered.

Lisa looked at him as if he was crazy.

"It's mine," Dominic said.

I stared at him in shock.

"What? Why?" Lisa asked.

"I'm writing pornography for extra money for the wedding," he said.

"Does Crystal know?" Lisa asked.

She grabbed a cell phone and hit speed dial. As much as I disliked Crystal, I couldn't let Dominic break up his engagement. If Crystal was as half as uptight as Lisa, she would implode. Sure the entertainment value was high, and I really didn't like her, and I was appalled that he would be with her, but I couldn't let this happen.

"It's mine," I said. "Dominic was lying to protect me."

Lisa steadied herself on the kitchen counter.

"How does he know this?" Lisa asked.

"Last night, we spoke."

"Why would you tell him something like this?" Lisa asked.

"I thought he was a waiter."

"You're the waiter?" Jeremy asked. "Madison told me she had sex with a waiter, but it was you."

"You screwed him at my wedding!" Lisa shrieked.

Dominic covered his face with his hands.

"Thanks, Jeremy," I said.

"No problem," he said. I could have sworn he looked pleased with himself.

"And you wrote this?" she shrilled.

Looking at my sister, who was ready to have a stroke over a casual screw and a not even truly perverted piece of porn, I realized this was a moment of truth. The self I was presenting to her and the self who I really was could no longer exist together any longer. One of them had to go.

"Yes, I wrote it. I'm a pornographer. I sleep around with men indiscriminately," I said. "Dominic and I hooked up outside the hall last night."

Suddenly, there was screaming from the cell phone. Crystal had to be on the other end. The phone seemed to vibrate with her cries. Lisa handed it to Dominic. He slunk off with it.

I looked back at Lisa. I saw it in her eyes, the good old crazy Lisa who would hold a grudge for years. This could go on for a lifetime though, never to be forgotten, but not today.

Without warning, she lunged for me. Suddenly, we were back in our room as kids. Fur flying. Screaming. Slapping. Crying. Kicking. Yanking. Shoving.

Jeremy tried to separate us. His hands were like warm, blurry buzzes on my skin. I did the only thing I could think of to get Lisa off me. I had done it several times before when she had got like this. You would have thought she'd learned by now. I kneed her in the crotch.

I heard her breath suck in. She let of me, staggered by the pain of my kneecap on her pubic bone.

Taking a huge breath of air myself, I hurried from the house, my body hurting in several places, as well as my brain. I was hot and dizzy, staggering with the exertion of the fight. Not until I was in my car could I even breathe or think straight. Then one thing occurred to me like a cold hand on back of my flushed neck.

My story. I wanted it back.

Determinedly, I stomped back to the door. I knocked. Looking as if she had been in a Royal Rumble, Lisa answered the door.

"My story. I need it back," I said.

From behind her back, she held it up and tore it up before I could grab it back. The pieces fluttered to the foyer floor. A guttural cry escaped my throat. She slammed the door in my face.

"How very mature," I called out.

For a moment, I considered knocking over her lion statues, but I would be stooping to her level. Instead, I got back in my car and found another piece of paper. She couldn't take my story away. It was still in my head. Furiously writing, I tried to get the down major points when I heard a knock on the passenger side window. I steeled my nerves, thinking it was Lisa coming back for another round.

I looked up. It wasn't her, nor was it Dominic. It was Jeremy. He had the pieces of my story and a roll of tape. He was still wearing no shirt. I let him in my car.

"I thought you might like this," he said.

"Thank you," I said.

I took the pieces from him.

He sighed and closed his eyes. It seemed as if a huge tension drained from his body, and he looked so vulnerable. Tearing my gaze away from him, I matched up the first pieces of my torn story.

"She can be appalling," he said. "I can't imagine why I married her."

My throat felt tight. Should he be telling me this? He was her husband.

"Why did you then?" I asked.

"I was so flattered that she liked me, and then this momentum took over everything," he said. "I woke up this morning and realized I was married to someone I didn't even love."

He opened his eyes and gazed at me.

"It's like a nightmare," he said.

Amazingly, Lisa had ripped the word anilingus directly in half.

"That's why you aren't close with her, because of who she is," he said.

I nodded. Another section of my story came together. My brunette had her full figure and sexy legs back, thanks to the tape.

"That is quite the story," he said.

"Thank you."

He turned sideways so he could look at me better. Why did he have to be so damn sexy?

"Did you feel something last night when I kissed you?" he asked.

I froze. I couldn't believe he was asking me this. Would it be so awful to admit it? Suddenly taping my story together didn't feel important. The car was suddenly stifling. He was so close. Despite my better judgment, I nodded.

"I would rather get to know a pornographer than stay in this newscaster, psycho Lisa world," he said.

"Feeling something in a receiving line kiss does not a relationship make," I countered.

"I have kissed Lisa a hundred times, and I have not felt anything even close to what I felt last night when I kissed you," he said. "When you said you had sex with that waiter, I wanted to go beat the crap out of him."

"Really?" I asked, flattered.

I heard a door slam. Lisa was standing on the porch, glaring at us. She was holding my parrot-paper-wrapped frame from the card shop. It was another nail in my coffin. Now her husband was in my car. Did I dare?

"Do you want to go get some donuts with sprinkles?" I asked him.

His answer was his kiss. He planted one full on my mouth. Our tongues touched. The fireworks returned, sending a searing flame through my body and setting my panties on fire. I felt my story slip away to the floor. Something hit the windshield. I knew it was the frame, but I kissed him back with all my soul. A new story leapt into my brain, with flowers and orchards and star-crossed lovers caressing each other in the moonlight, birds chirping.

The Stars Fell Down

Kristina Wright

The accidental brush of a hand. A knowing look across a room. The tilt of a head toward the door. Signals shared between spouses at a party? I suppose. In this case, they were signals shared between lovers whose spouses were oblivious.

William was drunk. It wasn't apparent in his demeanor, but I knew the signs. He brushed by me on his way through the kitchen and his hand touched my ass. Lingered there for a good minute as he blocked the path of two other guests trying to get by.

I glared at him, knowing it didn't matter. "Had too much to drink?"

"Not too much. Enough to know what I want," he said. He leaned close, stirring the hair on my neck as he whispered, "We're leaving soon. Meet me."

I didn't have a chance to say no or, rather, ask where and when, because my husband came toward us. As if sensing that his territory had been encroached upon, he wrapped his hand around my waist and gave me a little squeeze. William's hand moved from my ass at about the same moment and I wondered if the two had touched in between.

"How's everything, sweetheart?" Brad asked. He kissed me on the cheek, but he only had eyes for William. "Everyone seems to be having a good time."

My parties are legend. I am the hostess extraordinaire, making sure everyone has enough food, enough drink, a good time. I smiled at Brad, ignoring the set of William's jaw. "Everything's great. I think we're running low on wine, though."

"I can go get more."

I could practically feel William tensing, though he was no longer touching me. "Oh, no," I said quickly. "We'll be fine."

"Well, let me know," Brad said, releasing me to make the rounds once more.

"Nice," William murmured. "I was starting to think you didn't want to be with me tonight."

I didn't have time to respond. Rachel, William's wife, appeared at his side. I wondered if she'd heard what he said. One look at her bland, expressionless face told me she hadn't.

"I need to go home," she said to William, ignoring me. It wasn't that she suspected anything, Rachel simply didn't like parties. She let William drag her to these get-togethers, only to stand off to the side, hardly speaking, and demanding to leave shortly after arriving. It was, to my way of thinking, quite irritating. To William, it was convenient.

I watched as he pulled her close and brushed her hair aside to lay a kiss on her neck. I shivered, knowing what that felt like. Wanting it.

"I guess we'll be going," William said, genuinely sounding disappointed. "Tell Brad thanks."

I saw them to the door, hugging Rachel first, then William. His touch was polite, distant. His words in my ear were another matter. "The university parking lot in an hour," he breathed so softly I wouldn't have heard him if his lips hadn't been touching my ear. "I need to fuck you."

I clung to the doorframe as I closed the door behind them. Weak-kneed with desire, I had the fleeting thought to refuse his request, to simply not show up. I checked my makeup in the mirror by the door, noting the flush in my cheeks, the way my eyes sparkled. He did this to me, so easily.

I would go. I would think of an excuse to be gone for a bit and I would leave my party to fuck my lover. I smiled at my reflection, but it didn't quite reach my eyes.

The minutes dragged on. Ever the hostess, I served finger foods and poured glasses of wine and made small talk about how Bobby was doing in Little League and whether our subdivision needed stricter covenants. Finally, I slipped away. I told my best friend Theresa to tell Brad I'd gone for wine. Theresa doesn't know about my affair with William, but she suspects something, I'm sure.

"I won't tell him until he asks," she said. Theresa is a good friend.

It was a short drive, no more than fifteen minutes, but the lights worked against me and my frustration level was near to breaking when I finally pulled into the parking lot. I slowed the car, realizing I had been driving well in excess of the speed limit. I needed to see William and nothing, not traffic lights or speed signs or twenty-five people at my house would stop me.

William teaches at the university. He is a professor of philosophy and ethics, the irony of which doesn't escape him – or me. His car was there, parked in the shadow of the arts and letters building. I saw his silhouette in the driver's seat, could see the movement of his fingers as he drummed the steering wheel. William is an impatient man, especially where I'm concerned. The knowledge made me smile.

I parked my car next to his and got out. The passenger door was unlocked and I slipped inside. "Hi. Miss me?" I could hear how breathless my voice sounded and I hated it.

"Took you long enough," he said, fisting his hand in my hair.

"I'm having a party, William. It's not easy to get away." I was, in fact, ten minutes early. "But I'm here now."

"Yes, you are."

He leaned across the center console and kissed me. Hard. His mouth tasted of tequila and I sucked his bottom lip between mine, biting it gently. Finally, he released me and I leaned back in the seat.

"You shouldn't drink so much at my house. It's not safe to drive," I said. "It's not safe to be around me, either."

He watched me, his eyes heavy-lidded, but not with sleep. "I can't help it. All I want to do is touch you and I can't. So I drink."

It was a familiar argument. A familiar situation. I kept coming back for more, unwilling to lose this feeling. "Be careful next time," I admonished. "Brad wasn't too happy to have you pawing at me."

"Poor Brad," he said. "Maybe if he wasn't fucking his assistant he'd notice you're in love with me."

I wished I had never told William about Brad's infatuation with his paralegal. I couldn't prove they were sleeping together, but the truth was I didn't much care. As long as I had William, Brad's extracurricular activities held no power over me.

"What about you?" I taunted. "How would you feel if Rachel was with someone else right now, knowing you'll be home any minute and so hot to get fucked she's willing to risk it?"

His eyes widened. "It would never happen."

"What if it did?"

"I'd leave her."

I shook my head, closing my eyes. "Hypocrite. You can fuck other people and she can't?"

He reached for my hand, lacing my fingers with his. "I don't fuck other people. I'm in love with you."

"You fuck me."

"Yes. And you love it."

I opened my eyes and started at him. "Hypocrite," I said again.

"But you love me."

It was true. I did love him. I just didn't like him very much.

"Kiss me," he said.

I obeyed because I wanted to, leaning across the console once more to wrap my hands around his neck and kiss him. We sat like that, separated from the waist down, kissing and touching each other until the windows fogged and I was squirming in my seat.

"You are so beautiful," he said. He stroked my hair, trailing his fingers down the collar of my blouse to the swell of my breasts. "I need you."

I reached for his belt, half leaning across the seat as I undid the buckle, then unfastened his pants. He leaned back, letting me unzip him, pulling his erection free of his pants. He was rigid, thick, ready. I whimpered softly as I leaned over him and sucked the head of his cock between my lips. I licked him gently, tasting his arousal, that familiar salty-sweet taste unlike any other man I'd ever been with. I dreamed of that taste, looked for it in things I ate and drank, longing for it like a craving, a thirst I couldn't sate.

He twisted his fingers in my hair, guiding me slowly up and down the length of his cock. I sucked him greedily, hungrily, taking him as far as I could without gagging, then forcing a little more of him into my throat until I did gag and had to come back up. I sucked him the way I knew he liked, the way Rachel never did, the way it took to make him come.

He dragged me off his cock by my hair, the slight jolt of pain making me whimper with need. "I need to fuck you," he said, his breath coming in rapid pants.

"I don't have time," I said. "Let me taste you. Please."

His grip in my hair tightened. "I need to be inside you," he said. "Get out of the car."

He didn't give me time to respond. He was out of the car and around to the passenger door before I could take a deep breath. He opened the door and reached for me. I let him take my hand and pull me from the car. I felt exposed, vulnerable, the night air chilled compared to the intimate heat of the car.

"William," I protested as he leaned me against the car and unfastened my pants. "We can't. Really. We're going to get caught."

"I don't give a damn," he muttered as he tugged my pants and panties down in one motion. "I need you. Now."

I let him turn me around and bend me over. I braced my hands on the hood of his car, my legs still pinned together by my pants around my ankles. I didn't protest as I felt his fingers between my legs, slipping inside my wet, wet cunt, gliding forward over the ridge of my clit. I didn't complain when he drove his thick cock into me in one quick stroke, burying himself inside me so hard it was almost painful. I didn't tell him to stop, I didn't worry about getting caught, I didn't care about anything except the moment, his cock and the way he made me feel.

He held onto my hips as he fucked me, driving his cock into me hard and fast, over and over again. My arms buckled and I was face down on his car, the metal cool against my fevered cheek. I cried out as he went deep, hearing my whimpers echoing off the walls of the buildings and bouncing back on me, sounding like the cries of a woman in pain. A woman in agony.

I bit my lip to quiet myself, but William seemed intent on wringing every sound from me that he could. He wrapped my long hair around his hand and pulled my head up, leaning forward to bite my exposed neck. I whimpered and my cunt clenched around his cock.

"Oh God, fuck me," I moaned. I was beyond caring if someone heard me. I needed William to fuck me, fuck me hard and make me forget where we were and who was at my house – and who was waiting for him.

I tried to brace myself on the hood, but the slope prevented me from keeping my balance. "Wait," I gasped. I reached back, putting my hand on his hip and pushing him away. He slid out of me and my body felt empty, bereft.

"What?"

I turned around, facing him. "I can't stand up. If we're going to do this, we might as well do it right."

I leaned down to free myself of my pants twisted around my ankles. Then I sat on the edge of the car, braced my hands behind me and spread my legs. "Fuck me," I whispered. "Fuck me, William."

He put his hands on my hips and I reached down to guide him into me. I wanted to tease him, to stroke my clit with the broad head of his cock, to hold him until he begged to be inside of me, but I was too far gone to tease him or myself. I pulled him into me and wrapped my legs around his waist to hold him close.

My soft whimpers and moans were the only sounds in the still night air. William was silent and stoic as a sentry, fucking me senseless, fucking me into oblivion

I opened my eyes and looked up at him. His face was just a shadowy spot above me, blending into the endless night sky. I blinked, staring at him, willing myself to see his features, but all I saw was darkness. Then, instead of seeing him more clearly, I saw the stars. The night sky, devoid of a moon, was filled with stars. I stared up at William as he fucked me, his face obscured by darkness and surrounded by twinkling stars that seemed close enough to touch.

"You want it?" I could just make out the movement of his lips. He leaned closer, brushing his mouth against my neck. "You want to suck me?"

"When I come," I whispered, fearing he would pull away before I could finish. "When I come."

I wasn't sure he heard me, but he fucked me harder, his thrusts more shallow and at just the right angle to stroke my G-spot. I strained forward, pushing my hips at him, propping myself up on my arms to get closer, to pull him deeper. I came in a gush of fluid, my entire body wrapped around him as my cunt tightened and rippled around his thick cock inside me.

"Yes, yes, yes," I screamed, the echo of my voice ringing in my ears. "Fuck me!"

"Now, take it, now," he said, pulling me off the car by my hair and pushing me to my knees.

I opened my mouth wide, wanting to taste him, take him, even while my body still throbbed in orgasm. William guided his cock into my mouth, thrusting his hips forward so that it slid across my tongue and hit the back of my throat. I gagged, but instead of pushing him away, I grabbed his hips and pulled him closer, relaxing my throat and swallowing as he started to come.

Finally, William moaned. William who was always so quiet, moaned loudly as I took his cock deep into my mouth and swallowed everything he could give me. He relaxed his grip on my hair, but I didn't move away. I sucked him gently, lingering over him until my knees ached from kneeling on the hard ground. Finally, slowly, I released his cock and he helped me stand.

William held me, both of us naked from the waist down, and the incongruity of it made me want to laugh and cry at the same time. The moment was over before I could make sense of my feelings and he was pulling up his pants and handing me mine. We got dressed silently, without looking at each other. Finally, while I was trying to detangle my hair, William put his hand on my cheek.

"Thank you," he said. "I love you."

"I love you, too." There was no emotion in my voice. "Be careful going home."

When I made no move to get into my car, he hesitated. "I need to get home before Rachel starts worrying. Are you okay?"

"Fine." I nodded, as if that decisive movement would convince him. "I'm just going to stand here for a minute and catch my breath." I gave him a wry smile. "I don't want Brad to wonder what I've been up to."

"Okay." He didn't move. "Are you sure you're all right?"

I looked up at the night sky, filled with more stars than I had ever seen in my life. They seemed so close, as if they were falling on top of me. Tears filled my eyes and the stars twinkled. "I'm fine. Just go, William."

He went. I didn't watch him leave, I never could. Instead, I watched the stars fall down and wondered when I would see him again.

It's All Right, Ma
(I'm Only Bleeding)

Mitzi Szereto

Lay, lady, lay . . .

Oh, God, not again! That horrible nasal whine. Sounds like the man should blow his nose.

Lay across my . . .

I'll give you brass beds. Maybe a nice brass bedpost to smash your head in with. Oh, bliss. Oh, silence.

"HON-ey, did you pick up my blue suit from the cleaners yet?"

She sighs. Yet another thing she's forgotten. Like the Kellogg's Frosted Flakes for the kids. She'll catch hell tomorrow morning at breakfast. She can see their matching blue eyes, glaring at her in accusation. "*M-a-a-a-h-h!*"

A lawnmower starts up next door. Christ, it's not even 8 a.m. Well, at least it helps drown out those Bob Dylan CDs Richard puts on every morning while he's getting ready for work. Not to mention every night before going to bed. CD player in the living room. CD player in the bedroom. CD player in the bathroom. She can hardly wait for him to get out of the house so she can have some quiet. She wishes they had CDs with silence on them.

Her dumb luck his office moved out of the city and into the suburbs. His early-morning train is now a quick ten-minute drive to the industrial park at the edge of town. Richard couldn't have been happier. It meant he could get in a quickie before work. That, and playing his goddamned Dylan. A yawn, a poke, a fart – then off to the shower. Not the sort of sex she reads about in *Cosmo*. But maybe *Cosmo* girls aren't married to Richard. Could be she's too old for *Cosmo* these days anyway. Might be time for *Reader's Digest*.

Middle-aged. OK, *late* middle-aged, if you want to get technical. When will her husband realize it's time to put away the love beads, the anti-war slogans? He can't seem to disconnect his late middle-age self from his hippie teenaged self. Well, pseudo hippie. They were both raised in Hartsdale, New York, not exactly a bastion of poverty and underprivilege. So they both ran away to Woodstock in high school. Big deal. That didn't qualify them as hippies. Hell, they couldn't even get near a stage to see the performers. Hendrix was in a purple haze, all right. It was just a sea of mud, people OD-ing, backed-up port-a-potties. But talk to Richard and he'll go on and on about how great it was, like the second coming. She came home with tetanus. You call that great?

It wasn't so bad before, but something seems to have gone off in his head – a time bomb that's driving him to regain his lost youth. It started with the *Grecian Formula*. So what's wrong with a few gray hairs? She's got some herself. Yet every time she says they make him look distinguished, he drives off in a huff to the Costco to pick up a super-sized bottle of the stuff. Why doesn't he do something about his spreading gut? After all, he's not exactly Richard Gere in the buff. Not that she's ever actually *seen* Richard Gere in the buff, but she can draw a good enough picture from his movies. Next was the new car. Here she's stuck driving their wheezing 10-year-old Chevy with its seats sticky with melted candy and old chewing gum, and Richard's flitting around in a shiny red Japanese model with a spoiler on the back. "I need it for work," he says. *Work?* It sits in the parking lot all day! Then came the prescription for Viagra. "But honey, isn't that for old men suffering from impotence?" she asked, later thinking it might've been more PC to use the term Erectile Dysfunction. After all, Bob Dole didn't mind letting the entire country know he couldn't get his pecker up. Well, Richard set her straight on that one. She still wonders whether the kids heard them in the bedroom, what with the headboard slamming against the wall and Richard's Tarzan yodels. They did look at her with more contempt than usual the next morning at breakfast. OK, so she might manage to put up with a few annoyances when it came to her husband. But now, to top it off, they have the resurrection of Bob Dylan. Christ, it's like he's in bed with them! It might work as an aphrodisiac for Richard, but not for her. Give her soft music, some candles . . . She can dream, can't she?

Maybe she should get one of those vibrator things. There was an article about them in last month's *Cosmo*. (Not that she ever has the nerve to buy a copy; she reads them at the library, always tucked discreetly inside a copy of *Good Housekeeping*. After all, you never know who you might run into.) They actually have the kind you can carry with you in your hand-bag. She can see it now: get all hot and bothered over the zucchini at the supermarket and off you buzz! Obviously if she bought one, she wouldn't be able to tell Richard. She knows how he'll react – all hurt and offended. "But I'm your husband. *I* should be pleasing you, not some inanimate piece of plastic." Yes, dear, but that inanimate piece of plastic has three speeds! Oh, what's the use? She'll never get one. Looks like it'll be Richard's inept fumbling to the nasal warbling of Mr Dylan till they draw their last dying breath. With any luck, maybe Richard'll kick off first. Statistically men do die before their wives.

Oh, what's she saying? She loves Richard. They've been married nearly fifteen years. Of course they lived together for eons before that. When they first met, *no one* got married. It was too old-fashioned. Not the thing to do. But years later when she got pregnant with Sammy (who absolutely *hates* being called Samantha), the parental pressure to make it legal became too much and they finally took the plunge. Good thing too, since Tyler (who prefers to be known as "T") came along a year later. God, what a terror he was. *Is*. Those horrible baggy jeans he wears. How he can walk in them is beyond her. They hang so low the waistband of his Fruit-of-the-Looms sticks out a good four inches. And the way he speaks – she can't understand a word he says anymore. Plus he's always making these jerky hand gestures like some kid from the ghetto. Not that she's ever actually *been* to the ghetto, but she does watch television. Unfortunately Sammy's no better. Barely fourteen and she's wearing black lipstick and drawing weird symbols on her arm with a ballpoint pen since they told her she's way too young to get a tattoo. She was such a pretty little girl. Always Daddy's girl. These days Richard can hardly stand to look at her.

The thing is, she really does love Richard. He's a good husband, a good provider. Their little family never lacks for anything. The kids go to camp every summer, she and Richard always take a nice vacation when he gets his requisite two weeks off work. Last year they even made it to Europe. London, Paris, Rome. The weather was sweltering and it rained a lot, but who cared? They were in Europe! She's never had to work. It was her choice. Just as it was her choice to stay at home with the kids. She happily gave up her career in pharmaceutical sales to be a Stay-At-Home Mom. It felt like the right thing to do at the time, and no, she's never regretted it. Of course now that the kids are older there's the question of what she'll do with the rest of her life. No more kids, that's for sure! The hot flashes have already started to kick in; she's going to have to get one of those HRT patches soon before she goes nuts. Besides which, the risk for Down Syndrome is so much higher at her age. It'd been risky enough when she got pregnant with Tyler. Sorry. *T.* Thirty-five's the cut-off year, according to the articles. Which means she was playing Russian roulette with both Sammy *and* T. On the one hand they tell women to have careers. Then when you do and wait till you're older to have kids, they go and tell you you're risking giving birth to a Mongoloid. Horrible word. Her mother always used it whenever she saw a child with Down Syndrome. Always an embarrassment, her mother.

She's been thinking of going back to school for a Master's degree in business management. The local university has it where you can attend classes at night. That would be perfect.

She could still be there when the kids came home from school and Richard from work. They could still eat dinner together as a family, though it would need to be just a little bit earlier than usual for her to make a 7 p.m. class. She thought Richard would be thrilled for her. The night she finally made up her mind to do her Master's she had the brochure from the university all ready for him to look at. They were lying in bed, watching Jay Leno on television and listening to Dylan, when she reached into the bedside drawer and pulled out the color brochure. The cover had all these happy smiling faces of men and women, black, white, Hispanic, Oriental, many of them her age. She felt certain she was making the right decision. She set it on Richard's lap like a prize.

Silence.

"*Wel-l-l-l-l?* What do you think?" she asked.

Richard cleared his throat. It sounded like something had gotten stuck in it. She hoped it wasn't those expensive lamb chops from New Zealand she'd cooked for dinner. She knew she should have bought another bottle of mint sauce to go along with it. The kids used up the whole thing, then didn't even bother to eat it, just let the pink juice from the meat leach into the jellified green, turning it a bloody purple. God, how they waste food. Finally her husband spoke. "You know, there are plenty of women out there who find me attractive. *Young* women."

Before she could grasp the meaning behind his words, Dylan was knocking on heaven's door, and Richard was doing likewise in a Viagra-induced frenzy.

She was sore for a week.

It took her another week to get up the nerve to ask him what he'd meant by his *women* comment. "I was just saying, that's all."

"Richard, are you seeing another woman?"

"No, I'm not seeing another woman. Don't be ridiculous! I love you. I love the kids. Why would I do anything to jeopardize that?"

That night a hard rain fell. At this rate she was going to have to get over to the Costco to pick up a super-sized tube of K-Y.

Cosmo doesn't have articles about women whose husbands are experiencing what Richard seems to be experiencing. Sure, there's plenty of those *how to get a man* things, all of which pertain to scx. Oral sex. Anal sex. You have to do both these days in order to be competitive. Yikes! Just the thought of Richard putting his whatsit up her whatsit – it doesn't bear thinking about! Some things are best left for what God intended them for. Where do people come up with such crazy ideas? Aren't vaginas fashionable anymore? Maybe Dylan really was a prophet. *For the times they are a-changin'*.

Because it was only a matter of time before Richard caught on to the latest fad. "Let's do it the other way," he cooed one night, Leno flickering on the TV screen, Dylan wheezing and whining in the background. *Something's Burning, Baby*. She grimaced. By then she'd already bought the super-sized tube of K-Y, and he discovered it in the bedside drawer along with her forgotten brochure from the university. Before she could stop him, he'd flipped her onto her belly, stuffed a pillow under her pelvis, and took off at a gallop. By the time he rolled off her, Dylan was nasal-warbling *It's All Over Now, Baby Blue*. She noticed the bottle of Viagra lying on the carpet beside the bed. It was empty.

"C'mon, hon, it's no more painful than taking a shit," Richard told her the next morning when he wanted to go at it again before work.

Ragged and Dirty was playing on the CD player. That's pretty much how she felt.

And angry. *Really* angry.

Later that morning she went down to the university to speak to a post-graduate advisor.

That evening dinner consisted of KFC. There would be no more lamb chops, no more mint sauce. The days of the perfect wife were over.

Now she's in her first semester as a graduate student. She thought she wouldn't fit in, but it's been no problem. There are plenty of people her age, including this one man – a funny little fellow – with an Eastern European accent and a mustache. He always smells of pickles. She probably shouldn't say anything,

but he's sort of been coming on to her. Not that she takes it
seriously. Just a little flattery. She knows she's no hot potato.
Not that she ever *was* a hot potato. Of course she's still a woman.
It's nice to be made to feel attractive, even if you're not. She
can't remember the last time Richard gave her a compliment,
though he did bring her some ragged-looking red roses on her
birthday. For some reason she thought he'd recycled them from
work, some discarded gift to one of the office girls for Secre-
taries Day. They did smell of coffee grounds, as if he'd taken
them out of the trash.

Ever since she started school, Richard has developed a
hostility toward her. OK, so she never made good on her
pledge to step down from Perfect Wife status. She still keeps
up with the nice meals, the clean house. And yes, she still
keeps up with – or should she say *puts up with* – the Dylan.
But the other stuff, that's got to stop already. Richard has to
realize she's not some piece of meat to be used and abused,
some porn image come to life for him to act out his twisted
fantasies on. Oh, yeah, did she mention about the porn? Now
Richard's into that too. She found out by accident when she
was doing some research on the Web. She needed to find a
home page she'd visited a few days before, so she checked for
it in the History folder. Well, it was there all right. And so
were a lot of other home pages. At first she suspected Tyler.
You know teenage boys and their hormones! Of course it was
disconcerting to think that her sweet little boy would be
viewing such disgusting smut. The things that were there
– she never would have imagined women allowing themselves
to be used like that. Why, they didn't even look like human
beings anymore. It was just so heartbreaking that her young
son's budding sexuality should be developing in this way. She
was so upset she decided to discuss it with Richard. After all,
it's a father's responsibility to discuss sex with his son, not a
mother's. Well, did she ever get a surprise when Richard
broke into laughter, then admitted it had been he who was the
purveyor of extreme Internet porn. She couldn't decide
whether she was relieved or horrified that it was her husband,
not her son, who was the sicko.

She probably shouldn't have been surprised when one evening Richard came home from work with a camcorder. "I thought it'd be kinda fun to film ourselves while we're doing it," he said, setting the thing up on a tripod. Christ, she didn't even know they *owned* a tripod. "Lots of couples do it," he added by way of comfort.

That's when the proverbial penny dropped. She remembered one of the websites – it had featured real couples having sex, particularly kinky sex. Was this what he had in mind? To broadcast their crude couplings to the entire world? And to the nasally soundtrack of Bob Dylan? What if someone they knew actually saw it? Not that she could imagine anyone in their social circle visiting such a website. Then again, Richard probably came across as pretty innocuous to friends and colleagues. Guess you can never tell about people.

Richard was determined to go through with it. She was determined not to.

He had it all planned, even marking it on the calendar by circling the date in red. A Saturday night. The kids would be weekending with friends. It would be just the two of them, a bottle of Viagra, and Dylan.

Oh, and the new camcorder.

D Day arrives. The day she's been dreading.

Richard announces that he's going to take a bath for the event. How mighty big of him, she thinks, hoping he runs out of hot water. No sooner does he turn on the taps than the CD player in the bathroom begins wheezing and warbling with Dylan. *It's All Right Ma* . . .

She goes into the kitchen to get a stiff drink. She never drinks. Well, maybe the occasional glass of white wine with dinner, but not the hard stuff. But tonight she chugs down three shots of J&B as if they're Coke. Her stomach roils as she hears her husband singing along with Dylan. She can't decide which of them sounds worse.

All day Richard's been leering at her. It makes her flesh crawl. She never understood what that meant before, but she can feel her skin writhing over her bones in some Edgar Allan

Poe-esque frenzy. She catches her reflection in the kitchen window. It looks reptilian.

Splash. She can see him soaping his genitals with the bath-sized bar of Ivory soap. Not a pretty sight as she envisions his shrunken penis and furry balls bobbing and billowing in the sudsy water. "Hon?" he shouts from upstairs. "You about ready?"

She swallows one more shot of scotch, feeling the burn going down, way down. It matches the burn she's been experiencing in her hind end courtesy of her loving husband. Isn't there some kind of law against what he's been doing to her? She knows some states still have anti-sodomy laws in their books, although they were generally aimed toward homosexuals. How do they do it, she wonders, setting down her glass? How do they take it up the ass all the time?

Ever so slowly she mounts the Berber-carpeted stairs, Dylan's voice growing louder with each footfall, his every nasal whine mounting in intensity. The splashing sounds are becoming more furious. What the hell's Richard doing in there, jerking off? Then suddenly she realizes this is exactly what he must be doing. If he comes now, he'll last longer for when he's got the camera trained on them. Christ, it's gonna be a long night.

She reaches the bathroom. The door's wide open, and she can see Richard's right arm moving frantically in the tub. She steps all the way inside, receiving a big smile for her efforts. Dylan's voice is in full nasal throttle now; it's like being locked inside a bomb shelter with Felix Unger.

"Hey! 'Bout time," Richard scolds good-naturedly, grabbing his erect penis and waving it at her, as if this is sufficient to inflame her passion. "Hand me that towel, will you? . . . *Or* would you like to get in here with me?"

Her eyes drift to the CD player. It rests on a wicker shelf beside the tub, the electrical cord plugging into the socket directly behind it. They're lucky to have so many outlets in the bathroom; there's another one by the sink, where Richard can plug in his electric razor and she her hair dryer.

"So Miss Roberts, are you ready for your film debut?"

Miss Roberts. By that he means Julia Roberts. She's his favorite. It's her large mouth, you see. Richard has fantasies of – well, never mind. You can probably guess.

She moves nearer. Richard's penis bulges obscenely in his fist. It looks as if it's being strangled.

"Hon, have you been drinking? I swear I can smell booze on you."

"Just a little scotch."

"Scotch? But you hate scotch!"

She shrugs. She doesn't hate it any more. She likes the numbness it gives her. Maybe she should've taken it up earlier. Guess it's never too late to make new friends.

Richard slides downward in the bath, his freckled shoulders disappearing as his knobbly knees crook up. "Did you shave?"

"Huh?"

"*You* know. SHAVE."

Oh, yeah. He's asked her to shave her whatsit so she'll be more exposed for the camera. She forgot all about it.

"You forgot, didn't you?" Splish-splash. "Want me to do it for you?"

Dylan's whine is unbearable now. It's as if someone's turned up the volume to full blast. She stares hatefully at the CD player, willing it to be quiet. The J&B has given her a headache. Or perhaps it's Dylan.

"C'mon, jump in. I'll take care of business." Richard holds up the pink razor she uses for her legs and underarms, his smile broadening. What an idiotic expression he has. It reminds her of President Bush. She feels an overwhelming desire to tell him this, knowing it would be the ultimate insult.

Her head's really beginning to pound now. It's like all the air's being sucked out of the small room. The steam from the bathwater has fallen over her eyes, clouding her vision. Richard's goony expression has gone hazy, as if she's viewing him through a Vaseline-smeared lens. His lips are moving, but she can't hear anything coming out. All she can hear is the Dylan.

I'm only bleeding . . .

Her hands grab hold of both sides of the CD player. It's lighter than it looks, she thinks, as she drops it into the bathtub.

Richard's lips stop moving.

The bathroom light flickers.

Silence.

Kissable Cleavage

O'Neil De Noux

As I enter Etienne's Ladies Shoe Store, shortly before noon of another steamy New Orleans day during the sizzling summer of 1948, a tall brunette in a low-cut, red dress steps up to me and says, "What do you think of these?"

My gaze lowers to her plunging neckline and she laughs.

"No, silly. The shoes."

I look down and see she's wearing black, patent-leather high heels. She turns and walks away to give me a better look. I checked out her sleek legs and nice round hips and wipe my sweaty brow with the back of my hand.

As she approaches my old war buddy, Freddie, sitting on one of those stools, the woman turns back to me and says, "Well, Mr Caye. Do you like them?"

She *knows* me?

Freddie rolls his eyes as the woman sits in the chair in front of his stool.

"Y'all know each other?" Freddie asks.

I step up to them as the woman pulls her tight dress up past her knees and raises her left knee to put her foot up on the stool. When she leans back, I can see the front of her sheer, white panties.

Freddie's already staring between her legs as he slips off the black high heel.

"I'm sorry," I say as I look up at the woman's blue eyes. "Do I know you?"

"We met last week." She smiles as Freddie slips a red high heel on her left foot. Dropping her left leg, she raises her right knee, exposing even more of her panties as her dress rises.

I look at her face again and it hits me. She's the woman who just moved into my apartment building. She has a husband, little guy, looks like a jockey.

She must see the recognition in my eyes and extends her right hand and says, "Evelyn Bates."

"Lucien Caye." I shake her soft hand and she holds mine for an extra second before letting go. I wonder if she knows I'm already sporting a helluva hard-on.

She stands and walks back to the front of the store in the red heels, her hips moving nice and languidly. Returning, she's shaking her head. She moves around Freddie and I have to step back out of the way. I catch a whiff of Chanel.

She sits with her hands on her knees, which are pressed together, nice and proper now. Leaning forward, she reaches down for the shoes and the top of her plunging neckline falls open to give us a nice long look at her round breasts inside her lacy, low-cut bra.

She says she can't decide. Freddie tells her he doesn't get off until five. Evelyn says she might come back. He helps her out of the red high heels and into her own heels.

Rising, she extends her hand to me and we shake again.

"See 'ya around, Sport." With that, she pivots in her toes and walks away.

As she reaches the door, a burly man in a rumpled brown suit enters and glares at her on his way in. Freddie introduces the man as his boss.

"Come on," Freddie says. "Let's get a bite." He grabs his hat on our way out.

"No extended lunch break," his boss calls out as we reach the door.

Stepping out on narrow Royal Street, I look up and down but don't spot Evelyn.

"She'll be back around five," Freddie tells me as he leads the way down Royal toward Canal Street. He puts on his hat. The bright sun is hot on my head, but I never wear hats. Don't like to mess up my hair.

Freddie is exactly my age and height. Thirty. Six feet. Only he's balding already and soft, with a little pot belly. He's grown a pencil-thin moustache since we got out of the army. I'm clean-shaven, as always. My half-Spanish, half-Mediterranean French complexion is a couple shades darker than freckle-faced Freddie with his Irish red hair.

"Who was that? Etienne?" I ask.

"His name's Ernie Zumiga. He figured *Etienne* sounds like a shop you'd find in the French Quarter."

As we approach Iberville Street, I feel a slight breeze from the river and smell crawfish boiling. One of the little restaurants along here has its crawfish boiler directly beneath its exhaust fan. My stomach grumbles.

"Zumiga doesn't like women."

"You mean he's . . ."

"Naw. He's no fruit. Just doesn't like waiting on women, who can be picky as hell with shoes." Freddie chuckles. "In the wrong business. Now that *last* woman. She'll come back around five. Probably without panties."

We turn on Iberville and make for the rear entrance of D. H. Holmes Department Store.

"No panties?" I ask as we cross the street in front of a yellow cab who punches his horn because we made him take his lazy foot off the accelerator.

"No panties," Freddie repeats. "Happens all the time."

We enter the store and head for the Holmes Café. It's much cooler inside. Typically, Freddie doesn't bother lowering his voice as he explains how he's got it down to an art, looking up skirts. Even the longer skirts. The women don't think he can see, so they throw their legs all over the place and his face is right there at knee level.

"If you noticed, I push my stool up close so they have to lift their knees extra high."

We sit at a table next to the windows and I can't help wonder why I'm having lunch with this lunatic. OK, so he saved my life. That was four years ago, May '44, on that dusty hill outside Monte Cassino. Freddie kept me from bleeding to death after a goddamn Nazi with a Mauser slammed a round into my left arm, knocking me on my ass.

I order a chicken salad sandwich and coffee. So does Freddie. He doesn't have to tell me how good the chicken salad with the poppy seed dressing is here, but he does anyway.

"The Babe died today," I tell Freddie when he finally pauses to catch his breath.

"Babe Ruth?"

As if there's another fuckin' Babe.

"Heard it on the radio."

Our waiter drops off our iced teas.

"Man-o-man. The Sultan of Swat." Freddie shakes his head. "Seven hundred, fourteen home runs. Nobody'll ever break that record."

I don't remind him records are made to be broken. I just look at his comical face and smile. Son-of-a-bitch saved my ass with bullets ricocheting around us, when no one else, including the medics, would come forward to help me. Buying an occasional lunch for this man, who decided New Orleans was warmer than his home town of Moose River, Maine, is the least I could do.

"What's so funny?" Freddie asks.

"You."

"What? Lookin' up skirts. You didn't look at Evelyn's lily-white panties? You didn't see her pubic hair right through the fabric?"

Thankfully our waiter arrives with our sandwiches.

Freddie takes a quick bite and talks with his mouth full. "Maybe I'll get lucky. Screw her in the back room."

The chicken salad is nice and cool, the poppy seed dressing sweet and tangy.

"I screwed a woman in the back room last week. We got a couch back there."

"Did Porky watch?"

"Naw. Zumiga leaves at four. On the dot."

I wait until I finish what's in my mouth before telling Freddie, in a low voice, "Evelyn's got a husband."

"Good. I don't wanna marry her." Freddie's voice echoes. "Just screw her."

A blue-haired woman with a black hat that looks like a

tarantula, gives us a haughty look as she throws down her money and leaves the table next to us.

"Freddie," I say as I pick up my sandwich.

"Yeah?" He wipes his mouth with his shirt sleeve.

"Glad you asked me to lunch." I grin at him. "I can always use a laugh." "Well," Freddie says. "You wanna come by the store 'round five to see what happens?"

I shake my head. Hell, my hard-on is just going away now.

Sitting in my high-back chair, behind the beat-up mahogany desk I bought at a used furniture store on Magazine Street (it would be an *antique* if I'd bought it in the Quarter), I look through the open Venetian blinds of my office windows at the commotion going on outside.

Two mockingbirds are dive-bombing a hapless alley cat across the street in Cabrini Playground. The cat races to this side of the street to hide under my prewar, gray DeSoto, parked against the curb. A mockingbird lands on my car's roof and squawks so loud I hear it through the windows.

I flip the switch to "high" on the small, black revolving fan, perched on the edge of my desk and turn back to my typewriter to continue pecking out my report on the Choppel Case. The sooner it's done, the sooner I get paid. My old Corona is one of those big models and works well, except the "e" gets stuck once in a while.

Living in the low-rent, lower end of the French Quarter has its advantages, besides being in the center of town. Clients can easily find Barracks Street and the parking's no problem. So what if most of the buildings are decaying.

I hear footsteps in the hall outside my smoky-glass door. My electric clock reads four-thirty. Is it a pantyless Evelyn on her way back to Etienne's? The outer door of my building opens and I see the old Englishman who lives across the hall from my upstairs apartment. He walks leisurely up the sidewalk next to my windows. Turning my way, he waves.

It's hard to concentrate on typing my report while I'm thinking of Evelyn Bates and her round, kissable cleavage. I adjust my dick and continue typing. No, I'm not going to knock on Evelyn's door, casual-like. Just passing, I could say and wondering how your breasts are hanging, if they need adjusting or re-alignment. I used to be a bra fitter, I'd tell her. She'd invite me in, of course and I'd slip my arm around her waist, pull her close and start nibbling her neck . . .

Damn! Now I'm getting another hard-on.

I'll never get this fuckin' report done!

As I'm shaving the next morning, my phone rings. It's Freddie.

"Can you meet me for a cup o' Joe?" he asks.

"What's up?"

"I'll tell you over coffee." There's a catch in his voice.

"She came back?"

"You want details, meet me at Morning Call. Half hour."

I climb into my light blue seersucker suit and new brown-and-white Florsheims, matching brown belt of course. Stepping into the bright, morning, I'm taken aback. Something's wrong. The humidity is gone. It isn't cool, but the insufferable combination of heat and steamy air is gone. Guess some sort of autumn front has breezed through the city.

I walk down to Decatur Street, past Creole brick cottages with their upstairs dormers and pastel colored houses with louvered shutters covering their windows and doorways. I turn right on Decatur before reaching the French Market where I smell the fresh fruit and vegetables – bell peppers, garlic, onions, apples and oranges.

Freddie is unshaven, in a wrinkled white shirt and equally wrinkled black pants. Seated at the long, marble counter of the coffee stand, he's looking at his reflection in the mirror that runs the length of the counter. There's a bruise on his jaw and his left eye is swollen and will be a regular black eye by this afternoon.

A waiter, clad in all white, including a ridiculous white, paper hat similar to the cunt caps we wore in the army, asks my pleasure before I sit.

"Two coffees."

"Beignets?"

I tap Freddie on the shoulder. "You want beignets?"

Freddie shakes his head so we pass on the French pastries –

donuts actually with no holes, generously sprinkled with powdered sugar. The place reeks of sugar as several customers
pound on tin shakers, inundating their beignets with even more
sugar.

As I sit on the stool next to Freddie, our waiter returns with
our coffees in thick, off-white cups and matching saucers. I
pour a teaspoon of sugar into the strong café-au-lait mixture
and take a sip.

"So, what's up?" I ask.

Freddie starts laughing and can't stop. Pointing at himself in
the mirror, he laughs so hard he almost falls off his stool. I drink
most of my coffee before he recovers and tells me, between
chuckles how Evelyn Bates came back, but still had on her
panties. It didn't take Freddie long to get her out of them and
into the back room where they went at it, "like rabbits."

An elderly couple at the closest table are listening, the man
grinning, the woman's eyes glaring at Freddie as if he just
pinched her ass.

Taking my friend's shoulder I tell him to lower his voice.

He leans close and says, "Just before I get a nut, her goddamn
husband comes in." Freddie rolls his eyes. "He musta been
following her."

Freddie notices his coffee, dumps two spoons of sugar in it
and takes a hit. I finished mine and wave to the waiter for
another.

"Short bastard's like a bantam rooster," Freddie goes on.
"He tore into me with those little, pointy fists and there we are,
shoe boxes falling all over the fuckin' place, me with my pants
around my ankles. I finally shoved him into the store room to
get away. Only I ran into my damn boss, who was supposed be
gone, and he fired me on the spot."

The old couple gets up and the woman pulls her husband out
the door.

Freddie rubs his jaw and speculates that Mr Bates might have
been a boxer once.

"So what are *you* doing today?" Freddie asks as he picks up
his cup.

"Have to see a lawyer. Get paid for a case."

The waiter brings my second cup.

"He didn't hit Evelyn, did he?"

"Nope. Just me."

I wonder if she's all right.

"Well, I'll let you know when I get another job." Freddie finishes his coffee and reaches into his pocket. I tell him it's on me. He thanks me and says he's on his way to pick up his last check from good ole generous Ernie Zumiga.

"Before you go looking for another job," I tell him. "Take a shower and change."

He laughs and walks out, rubbing his jaw.

Back on Barracks Street, I spot Evelyn and her husband standing in Cabrini Playground. She's in a white dress, one of those loose-fitting cotton dresses New Orleans women wear to fend off the heat. Her husband, in a black tee-shirt and black pants, is a head shorter. His black hair is slicked back and he has a two day growth of beard on his face. He's got his hands in his pockets as he digs the toe of his shoe into the grass. They're talking.

They don't notice me as I pass along the brick and wrought iron fence alongside the playground. I cross the street to our building, glancing over my shoulder to see they're still talking.

I go over my report one last time, proofreading my typing. It's only nine a.m., so I have plenty time before my one o'clock appointment with the attorney who hired me.

A good twenty minutes later a movement outside catches my eye. Evelyn and her husband come out of the playground and cross the street. With the sun behind her, I can see the outline of her body, the curves and the dark spot between her legs. When they reach my side of the street, I can almost see her nipples through the dress.

Evelyn looks in and waves at me.

I wave back, hesitantly.

The outer door opens and I see their shadows through my smoky-glass door. The husband continues toward the stairs. Evelyn taps on my door and opens it, leaning in to smile at me.

"Are you busy?"

"Nope." I stand.

"I'll only be a second," she says as she steps in. She's unbuttoned the top two buttons of her dress. Her cleavage, like a deep, inviting chasm seems to dare me to stare, to leer, to want to kiss . . .

I look up at Evelyn's face. At least she isn't beat up.

"How's your friend?" she asks.

"He'll live."

She sighs and asks me to tell Freddie she's sorry. Those penetrating, blue eyes stare at me for a long moment before she turns and leaves.

Three minutes later, I see her husband out on the sidewalk. A tool box in hand, he raises the hood of their black, '47 Buick sedan, which is parked behind my DeSoto. Although only a two-door, the Buick's much bigger and swankier with its wide, chrome grill. He starts working under the hood.

I finish my proofreading, deciding I need to re-type only three pages.

Putting a pot of coffee on the small stove in the tiny kitchen at the rear of my office, I go to work. It takes me nearly an hour and three cups of coffee before the report's acceptable to me. I carefully file away the carbon copy and slip the original into a manila folder. Rechecking the invoice, I have to smile. Haven't made this kind of money in a long time.

Finally, I get to sit back with the morning paper to check what's new with the world. Today the big news is Truman calling the House Un-American Activities Committee more Un-American than anyone they're investigating. Man's got a point. I turn to the sport section to read about the Babe.

At eleven-thirty, I put away the paper, wash up and head out for lunch.

Just as I step out of my building, a black prowl car pulls up, along with a black and white marked police car, both stopping in the middle of Barracks Street. A squat man with stubby arms and a regretfully familiar face, jumps out of the passenger side of the prowl car and heads for Mr Bates.

Flashing his silver star-and-crescent NOPD badge, Detective Jimmy Hays snarls, "You Billy Bates?"

"Yeah." Billy pulls his head from under the hood.

Hays grabs Billy's right arm as two uniformed officers I don't know chip in to cuff my startled neighbor. Hays shoves Billy toward the prowl car. I hear someone behind me and Evelyn steps out.

"What's happening?"

Hays notices me for the first time and freezes. I lift my left hand and wave slowly, my face remaining expressionless.

"You Mrs Bates?" Hays snaps.

Evelyn rushes forward, "What are you doing with my husband?"

The two uniforms move around Evelyn and take her by the elbows. She stiffens and asks again what's going on.

"We'll tell you at the precinct," Hays says. Taking two steps toward me, he points a finger at my face and growls, "What the fuck are *you* doing here?"

I stick my tongue out at him. His partner, still sitting in the prowl car, starts laughing. He's an old timer named Frank Lemon.

Hays takes another menacing step toward me, narrowing his dull gray eyes, as if that'll scare me. "What were you just doing with the man's wife?"

"Fuck you!"

Hays doesn't take the bait. I'm braced and ready to drop him, as I did before when we were both in uniform, rookies right out of the academy, back before the war. He shot a dog that had knocked over the garbage can outside the Third Precinct Station. I decked him with one punch. Glass jaw.

A jack-o-lantern smile comes to the face as Hays says, "Your pal Freddie O'Hara should be over at the coroner's office 'bout now."

I feel a hollowness deep in my belly.

"And *I'm* the one who caught his killer." Hays pulls on the lapels of his ill-fitting brown suit, backs into the prowl car and continues eye-fucking me as the cars pull away.

I drop off the Choppel report with my client's secretary on my way to the morgue. Parking on South White Street, next to the gray, cement Criminal Courts Building, I walk up the steps of the building's side entrance to the Coroner's Office.

Immediately, I smell the putrid scents from the morgue downstairs – formaldehyde, ammonia, human waste. A large black man behind the counter looks up as I ask if any of the coroner's investigators are in.

He waves me to my right and I go down the hall to a narrow office with ancient wooden desks and wall-to-wall filing cabinets. Behind one of the desks sits Sean Harrigan, a burly man pushing sixty with a receding hairline and droopy brown eyes. He recognizes me and waves me in. I ask about Freddie.

"We won't post him until morning," Sean tells me on our way down the narrow stairs to the morgue.

Freddie is in the first cooler. Eyes half open in that dull look of death, my friend still wears the same wrinkled white shirt and pants. I take a long look at him, reach over and touch his hand, already cold now and stiff.

I have a flashback of that dusty hilltop and Freddie's grinning face as he drags me away from the line of fire. Guess I always suspected Freddie wasn't long for this world. My throat tightens and my heart stammers as I pat Freddie's hand and back away from the drawer.

"Cause of death?" I ask Sean in a voice I have trouble controlling.

"Blow to the back of the head. Blunt object."

"When was he brought in?"

Sean closes the drawer, shoving Freddie back into the cooler.

"Eleven o'clock. Cops found him around ten this morning." Sean wipes his hand on his black pants as he leads me away. "He was lying in Exchange Alley between Bienville and Conti."

Jesus!

"Did he have a check on him?"

"Personal effects are upstairs."

There's no check, just a wallet, keys, Sin-Sin breath mints, a pack of Lucky Strikes, Zippo lighter and seven dollars and fifty-three cents.

I pick up the phone and dial the operator who puts me through to the operator in Bangor, Maine. Three minutes later

I hear the scratchy voice of Freddie's uncle with the unforgettable name Harry O'Hara of Moose River, Maine. He gotta be pushing eighty, a veteran of the First World War, he was middle-aged back then.

It takes a minute for my message to sink in.

"Freddie's folks have passed away," Uncle Harry tells me. I tell him I know and ask about Freddie's sister who lives in one of the Dakotas.

"Yes. Priscilla. I'll have to look up her number."

Uncle Harry thanks me for calling and tells me he'll contact Priscilla himself. "Aren't you the friend in New Orleans Freddie talks about?"

"Yes, I am."

"Good that you're there for him."

Yeah. Fat lot of good.

I pass the phone to Sean Harrigan who wants to get mailing information for Freddie's personal effects.

When I leave ten minutes later, I stop at the bottom of the steps. Taking in deep breaths of fresh air, my face lifted to the sun, my eyes closed, I fight it as best I can. My heart aches and my stomach feels like marbles are rolling around inside. But I can't let it get to me. Not now.

I've got a killer to catch.

Billy Bates didn't kill Freddie.

Fuckin' Hays arrested the wrong man.

Parking on Conti Street, within view of the Third Precinct Building on Chartres Street, where they're holding Billy and Evelyn, I walk into Exchange Alley. The uneven bricks cause my ankles to turn as I move through the alley that's as wide as our narrow French Quarter Streets, which were built for horse and buggies.

Ancient wrought iron light posts dot the center of the alley, which services the rear of the small shops and eateries of Royal and Chartres Streets. Long ago, young blades practiced here. The small buildings of Exchange Alley once housed the finer fencing schools, where Creole Frenchmen and Spaniards learned the art of dueling.

I find a man emptying garbage into a large bin. He saw nothing this morning. Neither did any of the other people I speak with as I move up and down the alley. A nervous antique shop owner admits she saw police in the alley, but nothing else.

Since the alley's only two blocks from Etienne's Ladies Shoe Store, I pay Ernie Zumiga a visit. He's finishing a sale. A silver-haired woman with an umbrella figure, an opened umbrella, snorts as she counts her change and leaves.

Zumiga doesn't seem to recognize me, so I play it like this –

"I have some follow-up questions about Freddie O'Hara."

His dull brown eyes reveal nothing. He wipes sweat from his brown with the sleeve of the same rumpled brown suit coat he wore yesterday.

"I thought y'all already arrested that Bates lunatic." Zumiga moves through the store, repacking several pairs of shoes the umbrella woman must have gone through before making her big decision.

"We have information that Freddie O'Hara was heading here to collect his last check around the time he was killed."

Zumiga turns and glares at me.

"I gave him his check." The brown eyes widen as he says, "Hey, ain't you Freddie's pal?" He takes a menacing step toward me, a vicious-looking pair of brown mules dangling from his fingers.

I stand my ground and tell him the check wasn't on Freddie.

"Where's your checkbook?" I ask casually. "We'll need the check number so whoever took it doesn't cash it."

Zumiga steps right up to me, fists balled up against his hips, mules dangling from his hands.

"Let me see ya' badge."

I look at his eyes and tell him I turned mine in.

"Then get the fuck outta here!" He makes the mistake of moving forward but quickly sees I'm not moving backward so he does a little dance before falling back a step.

"I'll call the real cops," he says on the way around the counter.

"Good," I tell him as I step up to the counter. "Then we can all check out your checkbook."

The door opens and three women breeze in, middle-aged ladies in nice outfits. Wives out shopping. One smiles shyly at me as I step out of their way.

Zumiga grabs a black checkbook from next to the cash register. He opens it on the counter for me, then steps around to help the women. He tells me to knock myself out.

It's right there, two checks back. In the name of Freddie O'Hara for forty-two dollars and seventeen cents.

Zumiga has his back to me and doesn't turn around as I close the checkbook and leave it there on my way out.

It's four o'clock by the time I step back into my building. There's a note taped to my office door. It's from Evelyn, asking me to come see her, if I can.

She doesn't answer her doorbell until the third ring. Breathless, she leans out and says, "Oh, Mr Caye. Thanks for coming." She opens the door wider and I step in.

Evelyn is in a shortie, blue silk robe with lots of bare legs showing. She also wears blue pumps as she stands there, staring at me, hands behind her back. Her face is made-up as if she's going out tonight, her hair freshly washed and curled, hanging to her shoulders. Only thing that's out of place is her eyes. Red-rimmed and ovaled, she bats them at me, so innocently.

"Where's Billy?" I ask as I force myself to look away from those legs. Her apartment has the same layout as mine, only everything's on the opposite side. We have the same light green curtains, but her sofa's dark green and there's a matching loveseat and a desk and bar with plenty of liquor stacked atop. The place smells faintly of pine oil.

"They're still holding him," she answers.

"They won't for long."

She tilts her head to the side, the way a puppy does when you make a funny noise. Her brow furrows in confusion. So I tell her I'm Billy's alibi. No way he could have killed anyone.

"I had coffee with Freddie this morning until eight forty-five. Came back and y'all were out in the park. We both how know Billy came right down to work on his car and he was there until the cops came."

Her eyes become wet as she tells me she told that to the police, but they didn't believe her.

"They'll have to believe me," I say. "I'm good on the witness stand."

She wipes a tear from her left eye as I tell her that I used to be the police and used to testifying in court. They won't shake me. Billy has a good alibi because Freddie was my friend and I know Billy didn't do it.

"You have a lawyer?" I ask.

She shakes her head.

"I know a couple." I point to the door behind her. "Down in my office. I have their numbers and can make a call for you."

"Let me slip into something," she says as she moves past me quickly toward the master bedroom. She doesn't close the door, but I don't peek. I call out, reminding her we need to call right away. Lawyers are nine to fivers.

She hurries out carrying a pair of brown high heels, a tan blouse and brown skirt draped across her arm. She drops them on the sofa next to me and pulls off her robe and I can't help staring at her lacy, white bra and semi-sheer white panties.

"You've seen my panties before," she says in a husky voice. "When you looked up my skirt at Etienne's."

I watch her pull on her blouse and oouch into the tight skirt. She puts a hand on my shoulder as she pulls on each shoe. I catch a whiff of Chanel as she finishes, looks up and pulls her hair away from her face, which is only inches from mine.

She smiles and thanks me, then leans up and brushes her lips across mine. I have trouble rushing downstairs with the lumber between my legs. We have to catch the lawyer who hired me for the Choppel Case before he leaves for the day. He agrees to see us and I can pick up my check at the same time.

"He might be a little expensive," I warn Evelyn on our way back out of my office. "But he's very good."

"That's what we need."

She takes my hand and squeezes it and doesn't let go until she climbs into my car.

*   *   *

Unlocking her door just before seven that night, Evelyn looks back at me and says, "Don't be silly. The least I can do is fix you supper."

She moves to her small kitchen and puts a pot of water on the stove. Reaching into her refrigerator, she pulls out left-over spaghetti and meat balls. As she warms them, she offers me a drink.

"Beer will be fine."

She passes me a Schlitz on her way to the sofa where she kicks off her shoes and climbs out of her clothes and puts on the robe. Only she doesn't bother tying it shut. I'm about to get lucky, I guess. If she isn't a little fuckist, I'm a goddamn bomber pilot, instead of an ex-infantryman.

We have dinner at her small Formica table, her robe open the entire time. I watch her breasts rise and fall, rise and fall as she breathes, as she talks to me about how she and Billy met. They met cute, him helping her fix a flat along Gentilly Boulevard.

"But he's tiny," she says, finishing off her spaghetti.

I know where she's going with this.

"Everything's tiny." She stands and drops her robe on her chair, picks up her plate and goes back into the kitchen, bending over to scrape off her plate in the trash can, pointing that round ass at me.

She comes back and pulls her bra straps off her shoulders. She reaches around and starts to unfasten it, but hesitates, waiting for something from me. In the long seconds that follows, I know it's time to decide. Get out now or listen to the beat of the hard-on throbbing between my legs.

"Let me help you with that," I say as I stand, readjusting my dick.

She smiles seductively, opening her arms.

I step over and reach behind her to unsnap her bra in one smooth movement. It falls to the floor and I stare at her full breasts, at her pink areolae and small, pointed nipples.

My hands move to her hips as I lean down and kiss each nipple softly, then run my teeth over them. She gasps and pulls my mouth up to hers. We French kiss, our tongues rolling, our arms wrapping around each other tightly. The kiss continues as my hands slip down to her ass. I squeeze and she tightens her arms around me.

I kiss my way down her throat back to her breasts, cupping them in my hands, kneading them as I suck each nipple. I continue massaging her breasts as I kiss my way down to her panties.

I lick the front of her silky panties, momentarily sucking at her crotch. Her breath comes fast and she moans and spreads her feet apart. I yank her panties down and bury my face in her bush, my tongue working its way inside her. She's already nice and wet.

She cries out and rolls her hips to my tonguing. I continue and she grinds her hips against my tongue. She tugs at my hair, but I won't stop. Moaning louder, she grabs my ears. I keep licking. She pulls harder until my ears hurt. I flick my tongue against her clit.

She yanks on my ears, pulling me up to her mouth.

We barely make it to the sofa, her tugging at my pants, me trying not to fall. She lays back on her sofa, legs spread and guides my dick into her. As I slide in, she cries out and freezes, then starts gyrating and we fuck there on her sofa.

It's frenzied. It's hot. It's a ball slamming fuck. Trying to hold back isn't an option and she lets out a high-pitched cry as I come in her in long spurts. We catch our breath and kiss softly before I climb off.

Evelyn takes my hand and leads me into her bedroom, to her brass bed for a long, smooth, deep penetrating second fuck. And as I'm on top of her, looking down at her lovely face in the dim light, seeing those bright blue eyes looking up at me, eyes filled with passion, I think of Freddie, lying in the morgue.

I don't lose my stroke. I keep grinding her, and think of Freddie and her husband, illegally in jail, and here I am nailing this gorgeous woman.

I know – a hard-on has no conscience.

For a moment I almost waiver, but only for a moment. I catch my stride again and continue fucking her in long, deep strokes. I do it because we both want it. I do it because she's beautiful. I do it because Freddie didn't get a nut and I'm about to get my second one in her.

I'm finishing what my friend only got to start.

If there's one thing I know about Freddie – he'd want me to.

Something wakes me and it takes a few seconds for me to realize I'm in Evelyn's bed, alone. The curtain from the French doors of her bedroom swirl in on the night's breeze and I see her standing beneath a dim yellow light out on the rear balcony of her bedroom.

I get up and slip out on the balcony behind her, my hand caressing her naked ass for a moment. She turns and kisses me.

"That feels so nice," she whispers in my ear. "Don't be obvious," she continues whispering. "See the window across the courtyard, on the first floor?"

I nod.

"There's an old man sitting inside watching me."

She turns her naked body toward the old man, raises her arms and stretches. Her breasts rise as she arches her back.

Craning her neck back to me, she whispers how the old man is there every night, watching her. She comes out naked like this every night for him.

"He probably hasn't seen anything like this in a long time," she says.

"Maybe never."

"That's sad."

Evelyn reaches back for my dick, which is already semi-hard. She hardens it, leans her ass against me and bends over, spreading her legs. She guides the tip of my dick to her pussy lips and we fuck on the balcony, Evelyn holding on to the railing, those luscious breasts bouncing back and forth as I screw her while the old man watches.

It takes less than a day to solve my friend's murder.

A visit to the coroner's office confirms Freddie died of a skull fracture. One blow to the back of the head.

At nine-thirty, I'm in Exchange Alley looking for people who were there the same time yesterday. Several kids are tossing pennies against a warehouse wall.

I pick out the boy who appears to be the leader and talk to him man-to-man. He's about ten, tall and skinny with cocoa skin and black hair. Of the seven kids there, three are white. The leader tells me he's Michael. I lose a few pennies to them, then pull out some bills to loosen their tongues. It still takes a good half hour.

Eddie, the smallest in the crowd, a boy with skin so dark it has a blue hue, saw it. He saw Freddie bopping into the alley, saw the fat man come in behind him, saw Freddie turn. They argued. Over money. Freddie cursed the fat man and turned to walk away. The fat man pulled a pipe from his coat pocket and hit Freddie across the back of the head.

"Got a good look at the fat man?"

Eddie nods and points across the alley to a restaurant worker cleaning stainless steel trays. "He saw too."

I walk over to the young man. He's reluctant to talk at first. He gives in after I point to the Holy Cross ring on his finger. We went to the same high school, although he's a lot younger. His name is Charlie Parker and works part-time at the restaurant, before his afternoon classes at Loyola.

We get permission from his boss to take a walk. I ask the kids to come along.

"I'll give each of you another buck to take a walk with me."

They make me pay first and we all go around to Royal Street to Etienne's Ladies Shoe Store where Ernie Zumiga is just opening up.

Eddie points through the front window at Zumiga and says, "That's him!"

Charlie confirms it and follows me in. Zumiga stops straightening stools and stands there with a queer look on his face as I go around the counter, pick up his phone and call the Third Precinct. As I hang up, I spot a metal pipe under the counter. I think I see a strand of red hair clinging to the end of the pipe.

We wait. Zumiga sees Charlie and sits heavily in one of his chairs and closes his eyes. He shakes his head and says, "They arrested *Bates!*"

When Jimmy Hays rushes in, snarling, "What the fuck is this?" I ignore him. I turn to his partner and lay it out methodically to Frank Lemon.

"But what happened to the check?" Hays growls.

"Probably in the trash can." I point to one under the cash register.

When Frank Lemon pulls out the crumpled check, Zumiga starts shaking, his lower lip quivering, liquid pooling around his shoes.

I can't help thinking of the old police cliché – *thank God criminals are stupid.*

The day after the newspaper runs the story of Ernie Zumiga's arrest by two of New Orleans' finest, I'm sitting in my high-back chair, my brown and white Florsheims propped up on the corner of my desk.

The heat and humidity have returned with a withering vengeance so I'm dressed casually today in a tan and white shirt and brown pants as I read the sports section of the morning paper. There's a tribute to the Babe. I didn't know he broke into the major with Baltimore in 1914, didn't know he tossed a record twenty-nine consecutive scoreless innings in a World Series. How he was sold to the Yankees by Boston, I knew. How Boston's never won much since, even with Ted Williams . . .

Someone taps at my office door and I can see, through the smoky glass who it is before the door opens. Evelyn slinks in. She's in navy blue today, another low cut dress that's too tight around the hips. She stops in front of my desk and folds her arms beneath those luscious breasts.

"I just came from that lawyer's office." The little fuckist licks her crimson lips. "Now I'm here to pay you."

"For what? I solved my friend's murder."

"My husband was released this morning." Evelyn reaches back and starts unzipping her dress. I shake my head and smile, pull my feet down as she works the top of her dress down to her waist, then starts working it the rest of the way down.

Evelyn unsnaps her bra and drops it on my desk. I realize the blinds are open and move over to shut them. When I turn back, Evelyn's naked. She does a slow pirouette for me.

I move back behind my desk and readjust my dick as I sit.

Evelyn comes around and reaches for my belt.

"Look, um . . ." is the only intelligent thing I can think of, taking in a deep breath as Evelyn runs her fingers across my erection. I reach for those breasts hovering in front of me, softly squeezing them, pinching her nipples.

Evelyn unbuckles my belt and pants and unzips me. She pulls out my dick and squeezes it. She sinks her mouth on mine and we French kiss as she climbs on me. I instinctively grab her ass. Rising, she guides my dick to her pussy and sinks on it.

We fuck right there on my chair, Evelyn riding my dick, bouncing and groaning.

"Fuck me!" She moans. "Yes. Oh. Oh. *Oh!*"

She's hotter than ever and wetter than ever and I pounding her when I think I hear my door open. I shove my face around and Billy's there, wearing all black, glaring at us like a bull terrier.

I lift Evelyn and she wails passionately. I put her ass up on my desk as Billy comes forward, fast, fists rising, face contorted in anger.

"Wait!" I gasp.

"No!" Evelyn cries back. "Fuck me, you big bastard!"

I try to pull away, but she's got her arms around my neck like a vice.

Billy runs around the desk and tries to punch my face, but I duck forward and his fist bounces off the back of my neck.

Evelyn sees him and cries out.

Billy punches me again, on the side of the head as I disentangle myself from his panting wife who's up on my desk now, legs aspread.

Billy howls and lunges at me with both fists and I block his blows as I fall back. I shove the high-back chair at him and hobble around my desk, trying to kick my pants off.

He comes at me, face red with rage. Screaming, he rushes right into the left jab I throw at him in self-defense. It slams against his nose and he screams. He bounces back and runs his left hand under his nostrils, then looks at it for blood.

"Hey," I call out. "This is enough."

There's no blood and Billy leaps at me again. I block his punches with both arms.

"Stop!" I shout. "Quit hitting me!"

Billy tries a roundhouse right, but I back away. Stumbling, he tries to come back with a left, but I catch him with my own left hook, right on the temple and he tumbles against the bookcase.

"Let's stop," I try but Billy keeps coming, swinging wildly.

I slam another left to the side of his head and the little man goes down.

"Don't get up!" I back away but Billy jumps up again and I block his shots with my left. Damn little fists hurt like hell.

He pivots to his left and runs smack into the right cross I throw. It lifts him off his feet momentarily. His knees buckle and he goes straight down.

Evelyn hovers over him, rolling him on his back.

He seems to be breathing OK.

I pull up my boxers and pants and fasten them quickly.

Satisfied her husband's not hurt badly, Evelyn gets up and moves back to me with that hungry look in those blue eyes.

She tries to put her arms around my neck, but I grab her wrists.

"What the fuck?"

She smiles and leans forward to peck my lips.

"Watching me get fucked gets Billy juiced."

I let go of her wrists and she kisses me, tonguing me as she grabs my stiff dick again. I try. I really try to resist, but I'm only human. Evelyn yanks down my pants and drawers and we do it on my desk, right on top of the Sports Section, her unconscious husband on the floor.

Our mouths fish each other, tongues rolling together. I come up for air, not missing a stroke and ask, "Why did he hit me?"

She gasps and says I'm pretty naive for a detective.

"Watching me like this gets Billy hot and his blood boils, so he wants to hit you. Then he'll screw the hell out of me later." She grunts with my grinding. "Actually, he'll try. Get his little dick wet. But I get my pussy reamed by you, big boy. Come on!"

She closes her eyes and bounces under me, nearly lifting me.

"What . . . are . . . you . . . com . . . plaining . . . about?" Her voice is husky with passion. "You get to do this with me!"

Jesus! These are my neighbors.

I feel myself close to coming and try to hold back. Evelyn wants no part of that and bucks me wildly.

"We're . . . going . . . to have . . . lots . . . of fun . . . this summer!" Her eyes are closed and this gorgeous woman is flushed with passion. I come in her, jamming my dick in her, making her cry out in pleasure.

Just as we finish, I see her husband stirring.

Here come the little fists again.

This is what I get for thinking with the wrong head.

Again.

Watching Lois Perform

Saskia Walker

"Trust me, Lois." Jack's arm shot out, blocking the doorway to her office. "I know what you need." His shirt sleeve was rolled up, revealing a strong forearm dusted with black hair, his fist sure and large against the door frame. Halted in her steps, she took a deep breath. Her glance moved to meet his. "Trust me, Jack, you don't." Steeling herself, she pushed his arm aside, ignoring his knowing look, ignoring those dark eyes filled with suggestion and the tangible wall of testosterone he exuded.

She headed for her desk, her stiletto heels clicking over the polished wood floor. The skin on her back prickled with awareness, awareness brought about by his presence. He'd done it again. He'd made her curious, responsive. She didn't take any nonsense from the men she worked with, but Jack Fulton had unsettled her. Counting to five, she put her laptop down on the desk and turned to face him, ready to challenge his comment. The door was ajar, the space empty. He was gone.

She shook her head. "Typical." Grabbing her bag and coat, she left the building.

The pavement outside was growing crowded with commuters; the Friday evening London rush hour was under way. She stepped into the crush, leaving the office behind, hurrying to the tube station and descending the escalator at a pace. The display board told her it was four minutes until her train was due. She strode up and down the platform, her body wired. She was always like this after delivering a successful presentation. It had gone well, and she'd easily dealt with the put-downs issued by the men who defied her female power. She thrived on her success, but now she longed to throw off her city suit and heels.

The crowd thickened on the platform behind her, noisy and restless. Wind funneled down the tunnel, a distant train rumbled. She glanced across the tracks. Her breath caught in her throat when she saw Jack standing opposite her, still as a predator about to pounce. A barely perceptible smile lifted the corners of his mouth. Even across the rail tracks she could see the intense look in his eyes.

She swallowed. What was it about Jack Fulton? The way he looked at her did powerful things to her, sexual things. They'd worked together for just a few months, but he was one of the few men who didn't challenge her. Instead he sat back with a secret smile, watching as she defended herself at board meetings, where she proved over and again that she had earned her right to be in this male-dominated world. But it was more than that. His dark sexuality was evident in the way he carried himself and the way he scrutinized her. He made her self-aware in the extreme, her underwear soon growing damp when his gaze followed her with that knowing look in his eyes. *The knowing look he had on right now.*

He inclined his head in greeting. She nodded back and then glanced away, fidgeting with the strap of her shoulder bag. One minute until her train would arrive. His earlier comment echoed through her mind: *I know what you need.* Her curiosity was growing. Her instant denial had been because of the controversy at the meeting, where she'd been giving the research stats for a proposal to change power source in the company's major manufacturing plant. Men were always telling her they knew better than her, even though it was her field of expertise. As soon as she'd rebuffed Jack's comment about knowing what she needed, she'd realized he meant something other than work. Something more intimate. She wanted to know more. And he'd gone.

Glancing back, she saw that his train was approaching. He never took his eyes off her. She craned her neck when her view was obscured by the moving carriages. The shift of the crowd into the train made it impossible to pick him out. Then it was gone. The platform was empty. She stared at the place where he had stood until her train pulled in. She moved to the far side of the carriage, where she could stand out her journey, and turned on her heel just in time to see Jack close in behind her.

"Your place it is then." His eyes glittered with anticipation, with certainty.

Her heart thudded in her chest. Her lips parted, but this time no retort emerged. Between her thighs, a pulse throbbed with need. She closed her mouth, snatching at the overhead hand-hold for support.

His smile was triumphant.

Later, in her flat, he threw her by rejecting a comfortable, relaxed seat on the sofa. Instead he pulled out a dining chair, indicating that she do the same and sit facing him.

He'd teased her all the way home, innuendo in his every word, keeping her wired. And now, despite the fact they were in her home, he took charge immediately. Not in an aggressive way, but with a relaxed sense of surety that was disarming. She put her wineglass down on the table and took her seat, noting how exposed the setup made her feel.

He lounged back over his chair, one leg folded, his ankle resting on the opposite knee, his hand loosely on the juncture. His looks were rugged but suave. He was dangerously attractive.

She tried to look as relaxed as he appeared, but she was far from it.

"I enjoyed watching you deal with that moron Laybourne at today's meeting."

She gave a breathy laugh, releasing some of the tension he had aroused in her. "He's just an arrogant little prick with very little real knowledge."

"You're so right." He gave a deep and genuine laugh. "He's jealous of your abilities though, and he's lusting after your body. The two vying motivations confuse him. Lust for a competitor can screw with a guy's mind." He looked at her with deliberation.

Her heart raced. "It can?"

"If he lets it." His gaze moved over her body, slowly.

"And are you jealous of my skills?" She crossed her legs high on the thigh, crushing the pounding pulse in her clit.

"No, I admire them immensely. I'm not threatened by you."

Then for a moment silence hung heavy in the atmosphere.

He raised one eyebrow. "I notice you didn't ask if I lusted after you."

"I don't think you came here with the sole purpose of analyzing today's meeting."

He tipped his glass at her. "Indeed. And you did let me come home with you."

She couldn't deny it. "So I did."

Silent acknowledgment raced between them. *We are going to fuck.*

He took a sip of his wine, eyeing her as she crossed and uncrossed her legs.

"It's not easy for you, is it? Blonde, pretty, extraordinarily intelligent."

Something akin to relief hit her. "No, it isn't." She smiled, genuinely appreciating his words. He really had been observing her.

"What do you usually do, when you bring a man home for sex?" He said it as if he was discussing the weather, and glanced around the open-plan living area, as if the furniture could tell tales.

"Oh, fast, dirty sex, nothing prolonged in terms of involvement. I don't have time." She pushed her heavy hair back from her face, watching for his response. It was the truth. What would he think of her?

"That doesn't surprise me."

"Really?"

"Perhaps you should make time."

"Perhaps I should." *Where was he going with this?*

"How many times do you reach orgasm, when you have 'fast, dirty sex'?"

It felt as if the temperature had risen dramatically. "That's a rather intimate question."

"I mean to be intimate with you, Lois."

He wasn't kidding. His provocative questioning had her entire skin prickling. "Once, mostly," she replied eventually.

He nodded. "I'd like to see you come more than once. You deserve better than that."

If he'd wanted to grab her attention, he'd certainly found the way. Up until that moment she could have turned away, asked him to leave. Not now. Not anymore.

"There's a determination about you that fascinates me," he continued. "You stalk after everything. If we were living in a primitive world, you would be a powerful huntress."

She smiled at the image, loving it. "Very amusing, but what's your point?"

"My point is that even powerful women can learn by pacing themselves." He ran one finger around the rim of his wineglass. "You might benefit from restraint."

Her sex clenched. The nape of her neck felt damp. "You're suggesting bondage?" She let her gaze wander over his body: bulky with muscle, his expensive clothing barely concealed his obvious strength. Being under him would be quite something.

He shook his head. "No. I'm talking about a different kind of restraint altogether. *Will power.* I enjoy seeing you battle with your energies, using and controlling your power in the workplace. Whether it's in the boardroom or elsewhere, your desires are only just harnessed. You're a powerful woman, but it's as if you're always on the edge of losing control. And that is such a turn-on."

Breathing had become difficult. More than that, his words about willpower struck a note with her, and she recognized herself in what he said. She had never thought about it that way, but *yes.* He was right.

He smiled and it was filled with dangerous charm. "I'm enjoying watching you now; you're racked with sexual tension. I can almost touch it." He moved his hand, as if he was touching her from where he sat. "Your eyes are dilated, slightly glazed. Your body is restless, your movements self-conscious, jumpy; your skin is flushed. Your nipples are hard."

She took a gulp of wine. The way he described her was sending her cunt into overdrive.

He loosened his tie. "You've been squirming on that seat for the last five minutes. I'd put money on your underwear being very, very damp."

Her skin raced with sensation, the thrill of his words touching her every inch of skin, inside and out. She wanted to fuck. *Now.* But he was making her sit there and listen, controlling her with his intimate, knowing words.

His glance dropped to her cleavage. She realized her fingers were toying with the button there. She clutched it tight, stilling her hand, and bit her lip.

"Be careful, you'll draw blood."

He didn't miss a thing.

"How wet are you, Lois?"

She squirmed on her chair, desperate for contact, her eyes closing as she replied. "Wet, very wet." She stifled a whimper.

Silence hung heavy between them again while she looked up at him for his response. He was still as a bird of prey, his chin resting on one hand. A large bulge showed in his expensive Armani pants. She wanted it badly, wanted it inside her where her body was begging to be filled.

He lifted one finger, gesturing at her crotch. "Open your legs, show me."

Swearing under her breath, she followed his instruction, dragging her short skirt up and over her hips, her eyes never leaving his. As she opened her legs, pivoting out on her stacked heels, his eyes darkened.

"Oh yes, you are wet." His lips remained apart as he stared at her. She sensed his breathing had grown quicker. "Touch yourself, through your panties," he instructed.

She rested her hand over her pussy and groaned aloud. Her clit leapt, her hips wriggling into her hand for more.

"Enough." He smiled. "Stand and take your underwear off."

Her heart thudded so hard she thought she might crack. She took a deep breath and stood up, rested her thumbs in the lacy waistband and paused.

With one finger, he gestured downward.

She rolled them over her hip bones, growling quietly when she found herself exposed under his gaze. Dropping the panties to the floor, she stepped out of them. Her skirt was wedged around her waist, her pussy exposed. She rested her hands on her hips in an attempt to feel less awkward.

"How delicious. I can see your clit poking out. It's very swollen, isn't it?"

She nodded, her feet shuffling, her face on fire.

He gestured at her abandoned panties. "Pick them up and bring them here."

His instruction hit her like a left hook. He wanted her damp underwear. She steadied herself. Bending to snatch them up, she looked at the floor, counted to five. *He also wanted her to move closer.* Standing, barely in touch with her equilibrium, she swayed on her heels. When she stepped forward, she had the panties clutched against her chest.

He gestured with his hand.

She held them out.

He leaned forward, took the wispy garment. Slowly, he opened the crotch out, holding it up to the light. "Poor Lois, you were finding this hard, weren't you?" A damp patch reminiscent of a Rorschach inkblot spanned the fabric. He breathed in appreciatively, his eyelids lowering. "Delicious."

A combination of embarrassment and nagging lust burned her up inside. Her juices were now marking the insides of her thighs. "Do you get off on making women hot," she blurted, "and then leaving them hanging?"

He rested the panties on the table, next to his wine glass, and put his hand over the bulge in his pants. "I'm a slave to this as much as you are."

"Hardly." He was so controlled. She felt as if she was about to lose it and beg. *Was that what he wanted her to do?*

He moved his hand, unzipping his pants and letting his cock spring free. Moisture dribbled from its tip. With one hand, he rode it up and down, slowly and deliberately, watching her reaction. It was long and thick, a prize specimen, and it was as ready for action as she was. When she glanced back up at his face, she saw it all; saw a mirror of where she was at, wrestling with her inner desires, barely controlling them.

"Hard, isn't it?" His mouth moved in an ironic smile.

"Please. Jack, please?" Her hand had found its way into her pussy.

He watched her hand moving. "What is it that you want?"

"That." She nodded down at his cock, her hand latched over her clit, pressing and squeezing. "Inside me."

"Show me how much you want it."

She stared at him, panting with need, then dropped to a crouch, moving in between his knees to kneel at his feet. She opened her shirt, pulled the cups of her bra down so that her tits pushed out. She plucked at her rigid nipples. "I want it so much," she whispered, looking up at him pleadingly. She licked his cock from where his fist was braced around its base up to the tip and over.

His eyes gleamed with pleasure, his lips parted.

She took the swollen head into her mouth, riding it against the roof of her mouth. When he groaned, she took him deeper, rising and falling, sucking him hard. His hand loosened, his balls rode high. She drew back.

He looked down at her, his eyes glazed. Still he made no move. Her hips swung behind her, her arse in the air, her cunt begging to be filled. "Please, please fuck me. Jack, I'm dying for you to fuck me."

It was as if she'd tripped a switch. Undoing his belt, he stood up, shoving his pants and jockeys to his ankles. He hauled her to her feet, kissed her fiercely, his tongue claiming her lips, her mouth. Between them, one hand moved on his cock, the other stroked her pussy, squeezing it in his hand, sending her clit wild. She whimpered, entirely locked to his actions.

He grabbed her by the shoulders and turned her round, bending her over the dining table, pressing her down onto it, his hands roaming over her exposed buttocks as if, suddenly, he couldn't get enough of it. He kneaded her flesh, hauling her buttocks apart, his cock nudging into her swollen pussy. He grunted with primitive pleasure when her hungry cunt quickly gave way, sucking him in. He bent over her, sliding in, filling her to the hilt.

"Oh, yes." She shuddered with sensation, her hands clawing for the far edge of the table.

"Good?" he murmured against her back. When she moaned agreement, he thrust again, crushing her cervix, circling his hips as if he was testing her for ripeness. "You're so swollen, so sensitive; your cunt is like a hot fist on my cock."

He wasn't kidding. She was already close to coming.

He thrust hard. "Wasn't that worth waiting for?"

She nodded again, awash with sensation, her thighs spreading, her belly flat to the table.

"Ready to be well and truly fucked?"

She opened her mouth to retort, to say she thought she was being fucked already, then she noticed the extent of the tension at her back, like a loaded gun. *He hasn't even started*. She bit her lip, braced her arms, and nodded, her head hanging down.

With the precision of a well-oiled machine, he started to move, grinding into her, holding her hips as he drove his cock in and out. She pressed back, meeting each thrust with a low cry, pleasure spilling from her core. He filled her completely. She felt wild, yet tethered. She came fast and hot, her cunt in spasm.

"Nice one; feels good, Lois," he panted. "Ready for more?" He stroked her hair, but he didn't break his stride.

She was his, a rag doll to his will, her body riding the table as he fucked her. Her inner thighs were slick with juices. Her feet were off the floor, heels in the air. Her tits and clit were crushed onto the table, fast growing painful with the push and shove on the hard surface.

And then he thrust harder, swearing when he felt the hot clutch of her body on his. His fists grabbed at her buttocks, manhandling her back against his hips, anchoring her on his cock. He was so deep, wedged against her cervix; she felt his cock grow larger still. It lurched, spurting. She wriggled and flexed, on the verge of coming again. He squeezed her buttocks, as if milking himself off with her body. Acute sensation roared through her, spiraling out until every part of her was vibrating. She gave a long, low moan, her body convulsing.

Against her back, Jack breathed hard. She put her hand over his where it rested on her hip, gratitude welling inside her. She'd never had it this hot before, she'd never taken the time.

He reached for her and kissed her cheek, lifting her and

sliding her to her feet, supporting her in his arms. "I'm not done with you yet, Lois. I want to see you perform some more."

She gave a breathy laugh, leaning back against him. "Is that a threat or a promise?"

"Consider it a bit of both."

At the end of her presentation, Lois turned to the gathering and smiled, ready to take questions. Most of the board nodded in agreement. Tim Laybourne rapped his pen on the table, swiveling his gangly head from side to side as he raised the pen in the air to make a point.

Here we go, let's see if Jack's right. She leaned forward and put both hands on the table, flashing her cleavage at him. "Tim, you had a question?" She glanced past him, at Jack, who winked.

Tim coughed uncomfortably, flushing from the top of his collar to the roots of his hair. "I remain unconvinced about the financing of this project." He didn't even sound convinced of his own words. Jack was right; he had the hots, severely.

She eased onto the table, facing in his direction and resting on one hip, her short skirt growing even shorter. She lifted the finance sheet. "The figures don't make sense?" She gave him a gently enquiring smile.

Laybourne stared at her thigh, open mouthed and speechless.

"If I might interject?" It was Jack and his expression indicated his restrained humor. "Why don't you just run through that last part again? I'd certainly appreciate a repeat performance." He lifted one eyebrow suggestively.

The tone of his voice and the way he looked at her assured her he wasn't just talking about a run-through on the sums. He reached for her again, invisibly nurturing her strengths. She'd always thrived on her role in the workplace, but under his knowing gaze she reveled in it. Since their encounter the week before, everything he'd said to her at work had been laden with suggestion of the sexual kind, keeping their affair on rapid simmer. And right now the tug of his call pulled on her, from cunt to mouth. She was salivating for more of what he'd given her.

"Of course not, Jack. I'm quite sure it would benefit everybody involved."

Jack nodded, his eyes gleaming with affirmation. Then he sat back in his chair and watched Lois perform, just like he would watch her perform again that night, with measured willpower and the perfect level of restraint, leading to the ultimate mutual reward.

Back by the Weekend

Jacqueline Applebee

My boyfriend sleeps with other women. Sometimes he sleeps with other men too.

Bring them on, I say. I'm a big enough woman to handle it.

You see, Liam has a heart that's so big it would be selfish to try to keep it all to myself. Big heart, big cobalt-blue eyes, and I must say, a cock that's pretty impressive too. We got into the whole sharing thing innocently enough. We were getting ready for work one quite ordinary morning, when out of the blue he asked me if he could sleep with Andy, the computing technician in his office.

I was shocked for all of five seconds . . . and then I came round.

Andy was leaving soon; his going-away party would be Thursday, then he would be flying off to look after his elderly parents on the Isle of Man, one of the few places in Europe where being gay is still illegal. I think Liam wanted to give Andy something special before he left. They were good friends; they had known each other for more than three years. Andy had taken Liam to the hospital after he'd sliced his arm whilst moving furniture to a new office.

I said it seemed like a good idea, but I made Liam promise to tell me all the naughty details afterwards. It was as simple as that. By the time we caught the train to Liverpool Street station that ordinary morning, our relationship had evolved in a most interesting way.

The two men spent a passion-filled night together and when Liam told me everything they had done, I ripped his clothes off and we devoured each other.

I'm not jealous. Actually, I'm strangely happy. And the only requirement I have is that whenever Liam spends time with someone else, I want him to make sure he's back by the weekend. That's our special time.

One Sunday morning a few weeks later, Liam was in a fine mood. "Babe?" he looked up at me coyly from between my open legs, where he had lain his pale shaved head. I was blissful and receptive after the altogether satisfying licking he had just given me.

"Umm?" I looked down, enjoying the contrast between my dark skin and Liam's paleness: I often went the colour of rosewood after sex, changing from rich brown to a glowing reddish.

"There's a new receptionist." He spoke the muffled words into my warm thighs, still wet with his saliva.

"*Another* one?"

"Her name is Joysna. She's delicious. Shy as you please."

I smiled and stroked his scalp affectionately.

"You don't have to ask my permission."

"Yes, I do. I don't want to do anything without letting you know first."

"What is it you want to do?" I asked as he raised himself up and then collapsed on my shoulder. I leant my head against his scrubby beard – only a few days' growth, but already prickly as hell. "Do you want to eat her up or eat her out?" I drawled with a fake sultry-sexy voice. It didn't quite work, though, with my Cockney accent.

Liam stifled a chuckle and snuggled closer.

"She says she doesn't mess with married men."

"We're not married. Does she know that we're not married?"

"I think she meant it figuratively."

"I'll have to set her straight then."

And that was that.

A few days later I was loitering in the Princess Louise pub at 6:00 p.m.; it was the nearest watering hole to Liam's workplace in Holborn, and on a warm Wednesday evening it was packed with staff from the neighbouring offices.

I spotted Joysna easily; Liam had described her to a tee: a tall, deliciously juicy Indian woman, with hot honey skin and long wavy black hair. I sidled up to her as she waited to be served at the bar and introduced myself. "Hi, you don't know me, but I'm Liam's girlfriend. Can we talk?"

She looked mildly freaked as I held out my hand and smiled politely at her.

We found some low plush seats at the back of the bar and sipped our drinks whilst Joysna fiddled with the hem of her floral skirt, distracting me with the sight of her ripe thighs peeking out from beneath the fabric.

Liam has very good taste.

"Liam likes you. He's told me how lovely you are and that you have reservations about being with him."

She stared into her glass in silence.

"Is this some kind of set-up?" she asked quietly. Her timid voice held a note of wariness, but she looked so edible! Her pouting lips were way too glossy and inviting for their own good. The thought of "eating her up" suddenly came to mind.

"You have every right to be suspicious," I reassured her, "but no, this isn't a set-up, or some evil plan to take advantage of you."

"Then why are you doing this?" Now she was staring at me with earnest inquiry.

"Like I said, Liam would like to get to know you better. He sees other people, but he doesn't fool about, or take things lightly. Liam respects himself and everyone he's with."

"How many others are there?" she blurted out in a suddenly strong Northern accent that surprised me. She looked about the bar and whispered lower: "I don't want to be the 'other woman' in your relationship." Her accent was weaker now, as she relaxed, with just a bit of a Bradford lilt to it.

I laughed at that and she smiled back, looking more at ease.

"Look, I'm not going to force you or anything like that, but I do want you to know that you don't have to be afraid. You're not hurting anyone."

With that she slumped back in her plush seat, blowing out a

resigned puff of air. Her skirt rode up a little more. I gazed discreetly at the scrumptious butterscotch of her flesh.

"I want him to have a good time, with good people – hot safer sex and lots of fun," I explained, leaving out the 'back by the weekend' bit. I thought it best to not overwhelm her right then.

"I'm not used to being invited to sleep with someone else's partner, but I do like Liam." She hesitated before adding, "He's been so kind to me since I started at the Institute."

"He's a good guy and a very considerate lover. You'll have a great time." I felt like a saleswoman all of a sudden, but my words were true – Liam was very special.

"I suppose we could get together . . . but I have a condition." She suddenly leaned forward and smiled dangerously at me. Every single hair on my body stood on end.

I gazed at this strange woman, trying for cool. "What's the condition?" I asked breezily, straightening my tunic top; the multicoloured African fabric was suddenly too bright to look at.

"That you stay with us whilst we . . ." She paused shyly. "Whilst we do it." She emphasised the "it" and wiggled her chest.

I choked on my orange juice, spluttering it all over my top and our small table. Several other patrons turned and looked at me with grins on their faces.

"I thought you were shy. Liam said you were shy!" I managed to croak the words, dabbing at my clothes.

"You've inspired me to be bolder," she said, shrugging her shoulders and flashing that hazardous smile once more.

"Bolder? No, bold would be you and me getting it on in the toilets. This condition of yours, my friend – this is a whole other world." I couldn't believe the little slut! I brushed my hand through my tight-cropped afro exasperatedly.

She stared me up and down. I waited for whatever she was going to say next. "Okay, then, I'm game." She grinned. "If you're too scared to watch your fella and me do the business, then you and I can just take ourselves off to the loos right now."

I wasn't quite sure how things had turned around so quickly.

* * *

Five minutes later, I found myself squeezing into a small cubicle, with Joysna inching herself in after me.

I had to laugh at what we were actually doing. Even if we didn't have sex, we would certainly get to know each other a whole lot better. I was determined to call her bluff – and I was sure it was a bluff: no one goes from timid to wanton in the space of a few seconds.

There were certainly worse places to try this; at least the pub had decent facilities that weren't dirty or smelly.

Just as I was thinking that, Joysna elbowed me in the ribcage as she finally popped into the stall, the jolt making me topple backwards onto the plastic toilet seat. Joysna had a fit of giggles as she landed on me heavily, her breasts jiggling in her low-cut white work blouse.

Her weight was making me pant.

"How do men manage this?" She squeaked out the words between hiccupping laughter.

"Beats me," I gasped.

The sight of her heaving tits had instantly eclipsed the pain I felt. I wanted to get into her cleavage so badly, I was practically salivating. I grabbed two generous handfuls of flesh and pulled her to my face, burying myself in her, breathing her in.

Her perfumed skin was softer than I could have imagined, creamy smooth, a sweet rich dessert just waiting to be eaten up. She tasted delicious, too, like heady cardamom and scented mangoes.

I was in heaven.

Joysna straddled my large thighs, rubbing herself against the denim of my baggy jeans. She kissed me hungrily, her wide fat tongue reaching out to meet mine. Our teeth clashed as she bore down, sucking my tongue into her mouth with force. This was no shy, inexperienced girl. Joysna was wild.

"Liam told me about you, too," she whispered against my ear once she came up for air. "You sounded really nice."

I silently thanked Liam and proceeded to lift her round, caramel-coloured globes out of the black underwired bra she was wearing. Her mocha nipples stood erect, inviting me down.

I bit them greedily, chewing and sucking until she moaned against my neck.

She rose up and wiggled out of her blouse and bra, knocking her shoulders and elbows against the sides of the stall.

Whilst she was still standing, I took the opportunity to sneak beneath her skirt, feeling like a naughty schoolgirl as I pulled and tugged her knickers down until they pooled about her ankles. She jiggled like crazy as I snaked a hand around to her backside, gripping a hot, round cheek and massaging it, firmly but sensuously. The whole cubicle smelt of sex-sweat and Joysna's delicious scent, our perfumes trapped by the confined space.

She went very still as my inquiring fingertip investigated her ass, circling the heated sensitive flesh there. She looked down at me strangely, and then slowly closed her dark eyes and let out a loud, long sigh. As the sound left her, tension seemed to leach out of her system. She relaxed against my touch, melting like molten brown sugar before my eyes, swallowing my finger into her syrupy depths.

I soon realised I had a decision to make: stop what I was doing so I could reach into my bag and get my ever-present gloves and lubricant, or stay where I was, knowing that I wouldn't take this any further without protection. Easy decision! With lightning speed, I grabbed my bag from the tiled floor. Joysna whined and gyrated, urging me to be quick.

When my finger returned to her darling backside, she gasped and smiled. Her breasts moved rhythmically as she ground against my hand, hypnotising me with their swinging bounce: two juicy bonbons hanging just out of reach of my hungry lips.

I tore myself away from the sight; there was so much more that I could do if she was facing the other way. I wanted her to feel everything. "Turn around," I whispered hoarsely and she twirled about, stepping out of her underwear to brace against the toilet door, curling her fingers over the top of the wood. I struggled up and stood behind her, cupping a free breast. She really had fantastic tits.

Now that we were both standing, I was free to plunge my gooey fingers deeper inside her – two to start with, and then three sticky digits, twisting and pushing into her heat. She grunted earthily with my every movement and shoved her hips back against me, impaling herself on me.

I wanted to pound my whole body into her. I found myself wedging a knee against her open thighs, rubbing the rough fabric of my jeans against her soft, sweaty skin for extra leverage. I promised myself that if there were ever a next time, I would break out the biggest black dildo I owned. I wanted to see Joysna on her hands and knees as she took inch after inch of that tool deep into her ass. I wanted to stretch her, fill her up and slam her until she screamed.

My own breath was ragged and halting. I could screw this gorgeous woman for hours; just the feel of her against me was driving me crazy with desire. My clit throbbed angrily between my legs, desperate, ravenous, hot and hard.

She started to shudder when I added more lube. She was close, approaching her peak. I helped her along as best as I could, reaching forward to pinch and pull on her lovely nipples.

She twisted her neck to kiss me and then rested her forehead against the door, her long, jet hair falling around her shoulders in disarray. She shook and juddered. Joysna was a human bracelet. I longed to have her hot around my slippery wrist.

She came with a jolt, clenching hard, bucking against me, almost throwing me against the back wall of the cubicle, making so much noise that I was sure that we would be discovered.

The words she cried out were alien – I couldn't tell Hindi from Urdu if I tried – but it sounded positive.

I think she had fun.

Getting out of the toilet cubicle was tricky. Joysna needed to pee so we danced past each other in the confined space, edging around in a sticky sweaty mess. She pulled me down and kissed me again as she peed, hard enough to hurt my teeth.

That night Liam asked me how things had gone and I told him everything.

He ripped off my clothes and we devoured each other.

Stuck Inside the Uh-Ohs With the Red State Blues Again

Susannah Indigo

*"What if the hokey pokey really **is** what it's all about?"*

I. You Put Your Left Foot In

The first time you see Cassidy Wheat-Thin, she's dancing on top of a trash bin on the corner of Colfax and Pearl Streets. Black jeans, a long pink sweater belted at the waist, deep auburn hair that flows wildly beyond her shoulders, and that smile. Not a smile really, more of a silent laugh as she dances. Someone has set up music and loudspeakers down the block from a small protest at Civic Center Park, and at least a dozen people are dancing – not in a way you usually see anyone dance on the street – not to show off, but more to spread happiness and celebrate being alive and make you pay attention. It's like she's in the middle of an old Grateful Dead show and you're the one who can't even see the band.

You could keep walking; maybe you should. You're just an overworked guy trying to get out of his building and get some lunch. But you're mesmerized by her, and want to laugh with her. She's not a young girl, probably about your age, maybe around thirty-five – not your usual attraction – chasing barely-legals always makes you feel shallow, but at least it makes a man feel alive, one night at a time. But you want exactly what she has on this Tuesday afternoon in Denver. We're halfway through this first decade of the millennium that some smartass has named the "Uh-Ohs", and everything in the world is going downhill, one damn disaster after another, with everybody afraid to look around the corner. When you live in a country that is pro-torture but anti-porn, where you can put someone on a leash as long as they're not enjoying it in a sexual kind of way, laughter becomes a necessity.

You wait, you watch. You compliment her on her dancing when she jumps down.

"I was born in the year of the snake," she says with a shrug, as if to explain something. You don't even know your own Chinese New Year's animal – that might require some kind of focus, or belief in anything mystical – but it will turn out later you were born in the year of the pig.

"Take me home with you." It's not exactly your normal bar pickup line, but it seems like the right thing to say to her.

She pulls off her pink sweater to get cool and stands there in her black sports bra, sizing you up while you size her up.

"Why?" she finally asks, reaching up and unknotting your tie, with a glint in her eye.

"Because I want to dance with you." Every girl you've ever known is laughing somewhere in the universe, since dancing is not exactly your thing. At 6ft 4in you never quite got over the too-tall gawky high school thing. But you say it with a straight face. A straight face that's counting the tattoos on her arms and chest while you speak. A Chinese symbol on her toned right arm. A sparkling fountain on the other. A band of flowers on her wrist. And on her beautiful, breathtaking, freckled chest, at least two tattoos that are unidentifiable without ripping her sports bra off to see the complete drawings, which is exactly what you want to do. You're suddenly jealous of the tattoo artist who got to touch her for so long, and you know you're heading for trouble, but the phrase "uh oh" somehow never reaches your brain.

"Cassidy Wheat-Thin," she says as way of introduction. "But I have roommates." She gives you a light kiss on the check. She smells like jazz and sweat and cinnamon and you're ready to marry her right there in front of the trash bin. But still, you have to repeat her name in a questioning manner – you're a factual guy, and you've never yet had any luck in accepting the mysteries in life just as they are.

She laughs, even though you imagine she's been asked a million times. Your tie is off now and hung around her neck as she takes your arm and starts for a cab. "It's my porn name," she explains. "No one ever forgets it."

II. You Put Both Hands In

The past is not always prologue. You wonder who said that. You could look it up, except that you're sitting on the big brass bed in your loft with your hands tied together in front of you with your own tie. She said this was to help you focus, and you vaguely recall saying okay. But the past – it's gone. You're going to be a new man now, the focused and soulful kind, the kind who dances in the middle of the day. People can change. This is your new belief – new beliefs are easier to come by when you can't move your hands and a beautiful woman named after a cracker is starting to strip in front of you. She doesn't exactly dance like a stripper, though your loft does have a nice pole you hope she might wrap her legs around soon.

She's still wholesome looking, even now, with her jeans sliding down over her curvy ass – she can't possibly be a porn star, you think, that must have been a joke. *Was that a joke?* She made a big deal out of your recycling bins when she came in, while she was explaining how her Dance Mob group was trying to change the world one song at a time. *Do porn stars recycle?* You can't be sure. All dancing is revolutionary, she explained to you, and she added that there are two primary cultures at odds in America – one of them is inclined to dance, the other is not.

You are still fully-clothed, but your cock is almost hurting, it's so hard pressed up against your pants. You're regressing to sixteen years old when you could never quite get laid, and in spite of your best efforts all you usually had to show at the end of a long night was a wet spot on the front of your jeans. These days lots of girls seem to like you because you moved here from Manhattan and you're tall and look like you might have some money, but none of them have brought you anything resembling happiness for very long.

Janis Joplin is singing in the background about Bobby McGee and freedom being something you can't lose, or should lose, or never had or maybe wanted in the first place. Cassidy Wheat-Thin had her own CDs in her pack, of course, and is offering you a new soundtrack for your life – she's twirling, and her jeans are starting to come down, and while you think maybe you saw a glimpse of a thong, there seems to be nothing underneath. She's touching herself and she's talking to you while she does, but you keep staring back and forth between the tease of the sports bra with the hidden tattoo and the jeans removal – she might be saying something about recycling, or the whales, or the starving children . . . stopping the war . . . saving the trees . . . but you can't really see the trees for the . . . forest. There it is – her jeans are off, no panties at all, and she has something you can't recall seeing since high school. Full, lush pubic hair. Deep auburn-colored lush curly pubic hair. There are tiny hummingbirds tattooed flying across her lower belly, surrounded by miniature leaves – you want to be Hansel to their Gretel and enter her forest and never return. Her hips are full, her legs strong, and on the top of her left foot is another tattoo, a Hawaiian flower design in reds and oranges that curls up and around her ankle. She's dancing about a foot away from you now, almost touching but not quite, laughing, talking, and then kneeling, taking off her sports bra, releasing her full breasts. She has tiny gold rings pierced through her nipples, and a delicate complex blue drawing of a large fantasy butterfly floats between her breasts, swirling and dipping and almost touching the rings, and you're about to come just from looking.

You're staring, you can't really speak as she lifts her breasts and dances them in front of you – *that's the stuff you've got to watch* . . . she sings along with the song now playing. And you do.

She's raw and naked and touching herself. You're ready for the lap dance of the century, but she stays on her knees, keeping a small distance, leaning back like she's doing the limbo, with her full bush waving and curling like some natural grass right in front of you. Her fingers are walking through that forest and spreading her lips and entering, opening and entering, *come in, come in* – you're thinking you'll stand up and maybe just fall on her and fuck her even *without* the use of your hands, but she keeps telling you to just *pay attention and watch*.

You watch and you watch until she sinks three fingers deep inside herself and keeps her thumb vibrating on her clit, and then she's coming, and coming, and so are you, right in your pants . . . *uh oh* . . . without her touch . . . *uh o* . . . *uh o* . . . *uh O*.

She sees and she knows, and she's laughing and telling you that you have to do something before you see her next time, before you can actually touch her. You're trying to speak and take some control, but words are coming out only in teenage boy fashion – *God you're hot God you're amazing* – and then she's getting dressed and talking again about revolution and empowerment and making a difference and you have no idea why she's doing this, but just before she leaves she finally unties your hands, pulls a card out of her pocket, and drops it right on the wet spot over your cock.

III. She Puts Her Backside In

Cassidy, child of countless trees, Cassidy, child of boundless seas, Cassidy, child of . . . Greenpeace? That's what the card says, the next day when you've recovered enough to look at it, having slept forever and then called in sick. There are words on the back of the card in pencil, but no extra phone number, so you ignore them . . .

. . . until you try to call her at Greenpeace, where of course they only laugh when you ask for Cassidy Wheat-Thin. You still ignore the back of the card while you walk the streets for a week looking for her, or for dancers on trash bins, or for anything at all that makes you laugh. You've Googled her – *try different keywords, dummy* – you've looked up all the tree-hugging groups in the area, you've checked your voice messages incessantly, but, *nada*.

So you get out your checkbook and follow the damned instructions on the back of the card, feeling like a sucker who was just born yesterday – did she write this down just for you, or does she hook every guy this way? You join Greenpeace – the "monthly giving plan", generously, as requested. You join Amnesty International, and then the ACLU, both of them as "patrons", a synonym for "more money". Finally, PETA – you're now a proud member of the "Animal Savings Club". You notice on the Web there is another site calling itself PETA – "People Eating Tasty Animals," which sounds more like you. At least the old you. The new improved you will make sure to save any animal that comes your way, and *never* call them dinner – if only the one human animal you desperately need will come back.

Two days later she's at your door at 10 p.m. "Hi, you said you wanted to dance with me?"

Your suspicions are lost in the swirl of her short skirt, the twirly kind that makes you want to hold a girl upside down and spin her around. She's wearing sexy boots, some kind of leggings, and a glittery spaghetti strap top, but it's her face, and her eyes, she's so damned happy. How could anyone trying to save the world be so happy?

You wrap your arms around her like she's your long lost love, and at that moment you realize you'd do anything for her, even if you have to go out and plant a tree every single time you have sex.

"How did you know I did those things on the card?"

"It took you a while," she responds, "but it's good for you – you should always use your money, and your sexuality, to save the world. Let's dance."

And just like that she's coming in and she fills up your entire loft, and your life, with her energy.

It's not easy to do the hokey-pokey with a hard-on. That's what she starts you with, the kids' dance, laughing, putting one of her CDs on your stereo, and you'll do anything she wants. You've stripped each other down and you're completely nude and vulnerable and she's putting nipples in and then taking them out, fingers in, then out, hers, and yours, and then you're moving on to the kind of dancing you always meant to do – from the tango to dirty dancing. She talks a lot through it all, but tonight she's not talking about trees, she's talking about *you*, about sex, about bodies, about how other girls might know what you want, but *she* knows what you need. There's touching and massaging, and kissing, so much kissing – she seems to be insatiable, and there's nothing she won't do. You're dancing, you're on the bed, you're on the floor, she's bent over your kitchen bar in your favorite position . . . then you're in the shower, back in the bed . . . and when you surface for a five minute break to get a drink of water, you feel like you've fallen into a really good porn movie.

She's bright and funny and hot and open, and she's shining on you like the sun, the moon, the stars, and every inch of her is yours, and you want it all, you want to crawl up inside of her and own her and travel with her through every one of her days. At about five in the morning it occurs to you to ask the question you usually get to long before you're sucking on a girl's toes.

"So, Cassidy . . . what do you do for a living?"

She laughs and pulls you closer to her. "I'm sort of a nature-girl. I save trees. And animals. And people. Some people say I'm a kind of a dream-sweeper. I work at the Butterfly Bar & Tattoo Shop over by Coors Field, sometimes. And then, I fuck for freedom."

So maybe she's a *little* loony – you don't think there's a Butterfly Bar in Denver – but in the dark of the night it sounds like a pretty good life.

"In fact," she continues, "I have a shoot tomorrow night, so I should really leave soon and get some sleep."

"A shoot? Can I come? Can I come?" You really don't care *what* she's shooting. Probably not animals. You'll *never* tell her about your macho-guy hunting trip in Grand Lake last fall.

"Can you *come?*" This cracks her up, and you suppose it *is* a redundant question, considering that she's just made you come at least three more times than any guy your age normally does.

She says to meet her in front of the Hotel Monaco at six Thursday evening, and that you can go with her, but only this once.

In the middle of the kindness and laughter and kisses that send her home into the dawn, you realize you're feeling rather Johnny Appleseed-ish in your non-meat-brain-parts, and when you watch her skirt twirl out the door there is not a single *uh oh* in your mind, not a single concern that you forgot to even get her phone number – there is nothing but a sense of rising joy you didn't even know you owned, and a resounding echo from the repetition of the word *yes*.

IV. You Put Your Whole Self In

Cassidy, child of countless trees, Cassidy, child of boundless seas, Cassidy, child of . . . porn? Maybe it's true. Or maybe it will just be one of those boring art-installation type videos that people pretend to like so much. But she certainly *fucks* like a porn-star. She said to wear your sexiest clothes, but you keep it simple and put on black jeans and a black T-shirt, attempting a young Brando-look. You leave your boxers off underneath, possibly for the first time in your life.

There's an old dilapidated-looking bus in front of the hotel, and a small group of artsy-looking people standing around near it, and then there's Cassidy, and you're blinded by her light and can see nothing else. Her hair is in pigtails, little-girl style; she wears a short pink sundress and sandals that lace up to her knees. It's an unusually warm September evening, so you're pretty sure she's wearing nothing else underneath and that one swift breeze would share her beauty with every man in sight.

She hugs and kisses you, whispering, "We're going where it's dark enough to see the stars . . . but you'll have to do everything I say."

The guy who seems to be in charge is waving some papers at you, but not smiling. "You're either on the bus or off the bus," this long-haired guy says to you, and you're signing your name. Did he really say that, or did you summon it up from some sixties movie? But no matter what he said, you're definitely on *this* bus.

The long-haired guy is performing some weird poetry during

the ride while somebody else strums a guitar, but there's lots of pot floating around, and then you're so busy making out in the back of the bus like teenagers that you have no idea what he says. After while he comes back and greets Cassidy and kisses her, long and hard – *uh oh* – and says something about her being a fountain of laughter in the shape of a girl. You think that you want to either kill him or thank him, but she catches your look and says, "Let it be," and then goes back to kissing just you.

When the bus stops and you finally get out, you can see the lights of Red Rocks Amphitheater in the distance below you, and nothing but trees and mountainsides rising all around you, and it flashes on you that this is *it*. You begin to remember – *this* is why you came to Colorado and *this* is why you imagined a more peaceful place, and *this* is why you were put here on this earth, to love and to kiss and to romp in the forest.

Then it all begins. Lights, cameras, action. In your little clearing in the woods, the director says you'll shoot two videos tonight – the first for *fuckforforests*, a scene with a little girl lost in the woods.

Fuckforforests? Cassidy looks at your face and laughs. "Yes, there's several groups – *fuckforforests, shagthewhales, globalwarmingscrew* – it's what we call environmental porn. Every dollar we make – and we make a *lot* of money, 24/7 – goes to environmental causes."

You're sure you've never seen this kind of porn at Miss Kitty's Adult Emporium and you tell her so. "Oh, no," she says, "that's old-school. We go live on the Web – fuck locally, stream globally, that's our motto."

Streaming – you like the idea, that somewhere amidst all that porn-crap on the Web, somebody's fucking for the forests. And then there is a real stream, and you're wading around it, and there you are, trying to be Brando-like, chasing a girl with red pigtails and sexy laced-up sandals who suddenly turns and becomes some kind of new-age-bushy-sweet-dominatrix, lifting her skirt and dancing over you, ready to hump you on a log, and you feel like there's a log in your pants – *no fluffers needed for me!* you think wildly. You're in the moment, you've never *been* so in the moment, you're on the bus to never-imagined-land, you're on the log, you're stripped of your jeans and you're a grown man lying in the forest with just a tight black T-shirt on and pigtailed, nude Cassidy Wheat-Thin is climbing up on top of you and sliding down, and there are fish jumping in the stream in the background and between her *ohs and ahs* and *oh baby you're like a redwood tree inside of me, save me, save me,* she's whispering to you – *don't come yet, not yet, think of the starving children in Africa* . . .

. . . and then you lose all thought, and you've pulled out and you're coming exactly where she says to, all over her freckled butterfly chest. You had no idea you had so much come in you. You had no idea the things you could do.

There's a break, a lot of chit-chat and laughter, and amidst it all you know *one thing* that is true as you're sitting there in the wilderness with bright stars above you, ecstatically riding your own kind of Rocky Mountain high. Just *one thing* you know is true, after all your years of searching around. You are absolutely sure that you have found your new career.

This is it. Time for a new name, a new life. You could maybe be . . . Mr Nabisco? Yes, you'll be Mr Nabisco and you'll fuck Cassidy Wheat-Thin from here to eternity and save the earth at the same time. Why didn't you think of this before in all your boring days and nights?

By the time they're ready for the second shoot you're hard as a rock again. This time she's let her gorgeous red hair down and they've painted her body like a tiger. Several others are being painted to match her. Tigers, someone tells you, are an endangered species. You wonder if this is true – surely nobody eats tigers? "No," Cassidy chimes in. "It's trophy hunting, tiger rugs, tiger coats – and then some people think that tiger genitalia is a kind of aphrodisiac, so they poach for that."

Maybe you're glad you're not going to be a tiger after all. You can still *feel* like a tiger. But then they tell you to put your black jeans back on and hand you a whip. You're going to be the villain – *Snidely Bush*.

"No!" you cry out in your newly found activist voice. "No, I can't hurt an animal!" But Cassidy's cuddling up next to you and telling you to do it for her – and hey, it's just *acting*, and it will still raise money to save the world.

There's a rope cage, and you have to capture Cassidy's naked tiger body while she twists and turns and masturbates herself – *wait, would a tiger do that? no wonder they're endangered* – and then the long-haired director/auteur gets to jump in with his own tiger makeup on to save her. He ties you up with your own whip and leaves you in the dirt to watch.

The tigers rejoice. *Snidely Bush* has been vanquished, and they begin to pet each other. There's four of them, and they're all petting each other, growling, jumping around, batting at each other, rolling in the dirt, and you can't even move. The long-haired tiger-guy is on Cassidy, from behind, holding her long red hair back like a rein, riding her hard, facing her directly at you, and at the camera, and it's real and it's hot and you're insanely jealous in your meat-brain but still, she's looking right at you and she makes you smile, and in between her growls and whimpers she's whispering – *the tigers, the zoo, notice the color blue* – or at least that's what you *think* she's saying, and then she's coming and the other tigers are joining in and they're all tiger-daisy chaining and licking and fucking and pouncing – *it's like a tiger orgy, do tigers have orgies?* – and then they humbly let you go free if you promise to never be *snidely* to the animals again. You're a convert right there in front of the camera, and then four tiger girls and boys are undressing you and licking your cock like it's a hunk of meat, and when Cassidy dances down over your face and plants her luscious tiger bush on your lips, you put every single part of yourself into eating her like she was the last meal on earth.

V. And You Shake It All About

Three weeks later you haven't heard or seen Ms Wheat-Thin, nor can you find the enviro-porn guys anywhere. You can't have imagined the whole thing. You could look it up – and you do. Some of the sites she mentioned do indeed exist, and some don't. You search, and search, and even admit to yourself some

days that you're searching for your own dick on the Web, but
you never find your scenes. You've joined the few enviro-porn
sites you can find as a full-fledged member, and there are some
hot natural girls, but no Cassidy. You've sent emails to everyone possible. None of the sites has much detail – the servers are
all offshore, of course, in more enlightened lands.

It's all 50/50 in your spinning mind – your meat-brain half
says she's on to her next convert and she just used you, left you
to die sexually without her, not to mention to star somewhere in
cyberspace as a villain with a whip trying to kill tigers. Your
vegan/new age/good guy brain keeps shouting that maybe you
forgot something, maybe she gave you something to do, maybe
you were so drunk on sex that night in the forest that you've
forgotten – was there a card? a script? a hint? *Pay attention. Pay
attention.*

The zoo. She said something about the zoo. What did it
mean? Meet her at the zoo? Donate to the zoo? Free the tigers at
the zoo? You go there – the tigers look okay to you, they're
roaming freely around a wilderness-space area, not doing much.
You can't free them, where would you put them?

You find out there is no Butterfly Bar in Denver. You place a
permanent folded note on your door for her in case she comes
by and you're not there. You wonder if you should place a
personal ad somewhere – "Mr Nabisco desperately seeking
porn-cracker."

Walking down Colfax by the park for the millionth time,
peering around trash bins for dancers like a crazy man, it
suddenly hits you. You have to take some real action. That's
what an activist does – *acts*. And then, you could also do something besides think about yourself all the time. It's a concept.

You quit your job the next day. Maybe that's what she wants
you to do. You'll start a new enviro-porn group. Maybe that's
what *you* really want to do. You want to live in this world
wrapped in a cocoon of sexuality and laughter and caring.
That's all there is.

You throw away all your boxers and stuffy ties, saving just a
few for the headboard. You register a couple of Web site names
– *dicksfordecency; endangeredorgasms; spankforafrica* – if you

build them you're sure she will come, and then you will come, and then . . . no, back to saving the world – you're an investments kind of guy, you know how to make money. You'll expand the concept to Miss Kitty's Adult Emporium – they'll carry *Cassidy Comes for Charity* right next to *Debbie Does Dallas*. People will understand, people will become fans and speak out. Enviro-porn will not only save the environment, but change the rest of the world too. Pick a cause – porn will save it, because what are the best feelings in the world, what does everyone truly want in the dark of night? To get laid, and to do some good. Maybe you can expand this idea all the way to Walmart with a hard R-rated version – red state folks will shift toward blue, a purple haze of freedom will frolic through the land – all of this makes you giddy, even without Cassidy, and you think, *my God, no wonder she's so happy*.

And then you're walking down the street early one morning in your new permanent uniform of sexy black T-shirt and jeans, and you hear that thin, that wild mercury sound. It's metallic and bright gold – it might be just the sound of the street, that ethereal morning light, or maybe the light at the end of your tunnel. It's the sound of bells and distant railroad trains and arguments in apartments and lovers making up and the clinking of silverware, and you know that if you can keep walking straight through this crazy world right inside this sound, any minute you will turn yourself around and Cassidy Wheat-Thin will be twirling into your arms and telling you, *yes*, this is *exactly* what it's all about.

Sharing the Perfect Cock

Rachel Kramer Bussel

My boyfriend, Kyle, has the perfect cock. Really – if there were cock models, the way there are hand and feet models, I bet he'd be making a fortune off his pecker. It's tall and poised and beautiful, sleek and strong, with light brown hairs curling at the base, as if proud statue were rising from a vineyard. The first time I saw it I almost wept, but I resisted – and quickly got down on my knees. I've worshipped his dick, literally, since day (or rather, night) one and am just as smitten with the member as the man even ten years down the road. Don't worry, he's equally as enthralled with my pussy, and together we've had countless sexual adventures. But lately, I've come to the conclusion that his package really is too perfect not to share. I mean, what kind of selfish, spoiled brat would I be if I kept such a gorgeous cock all to myself?

Okay, you've got me. I'm the consummate selfish, spoiled brat, and I want to share his dick because I want to watch. I've been going wild picturing another girl's lips wrapped around that luscious fat head, her saliva dripping down his dick as she opens wide and takes him inside while he looks on proudly, brushing her hair from her face. I want to see everything I don't get to see when I'm lying on my stomach, ass in the air, taking a pounding from him as his cock smoothly dives inside me, my G-spot rushing toward him, my hips undulating beneath him, my body his for the taking; everything I don't get to see when his cock's all the way down my throat and I'm in blow-job heaven. Just thinking about his cock makes me horny, but usually I have it buried inside me, somewhere, swelling to fit my entire mouth, cunt or ass, his hard length leaving me little room to think or look, I must simply feel him grinding against my sensitive flesh until he wrings me dry – or wet.

I haven't told him yet, but I've been on a mission, a hunt. Every hot girl who passes my way, whether it's the waitress at our local vegetarian joint, with her long braided pigtails and ripped denim skirt and camouflage shirt that just hints at the curves underneath, or my boss's slamming secretary who I swear could make a killing as a stripper. She has flaming red hair, perfectly pink lips that she keeps natural or just hinting of gloss, and she wears these business suits that manage to be sexier than a bikini, her tits and ass practically popping out of their pinstripes. She gets away with her wild collection of stockings, in various hues with patterns and designs that could make even this confirmed straight girl lean down and worship my way from her feet on up. One time she even came back from a trip to England with black tights emblazoned with the Fab Four on them. Thankfully, our ad agency is pretty open to experimental dressers. She's never been anything but efficient and friendly, yet sometimes I detect a glimmer of something deeper, a womanly, sensual swirl to her hips; a gleam in her eyes that tells me she'd be perfect splayed across our bed with Kyle's cock spearing her over and over. But I know how badly that could go, so I move on.

In the end, Carrie, the girl who will grant me a front-row seat at my very own private sex show starring my boyfriend's dick and a beautiful babe, finds me. We meet at the gym, where she beckons me over so I can help her lift those last five pounds of a monstrous weight that I'm shocked her tiny body can handle. When she gets up, panting and exerted, instead of sticking out her hand for me to shake, she flexes her bicep, showing me just how strong – and sexy – she really is. Then she grants me a dazzling grin, showing off not just perfect even white teeth, but that the feeling is genuine, lighting up her whole face. I'd follow her anywhere if she'd give me another smile like that, and I know Kyle would too. We spend the rest of our workout time in close proximity, and I grunt extra hard as I push the weights with my legs, in part because my pussy is throbbing from my thinking about her sliding all over my boyfriend, brushing her breasts against his chest, her pussy hovering over his cock or his mouth, teasing him until he begs for mercy.

I know it might sound weird to you, but I don't want a threesome. While fun for other people, they've always seemed to me like too much work without enough reward – exciting, but not nearly as much so as watching this gorgeous woman devour every inch of Kyle. I want to watch him as I've never gotten to see him, his cock standing tall, his body at its most vulnerable as he strains toward her. I don't waste much time before bringing up the topic – unlike the rest of the gym-goers, who huddle around the juice bar for a dark green kale-filled smoothie, we head to a real bar, and over massive margaritas, I start to gush about my sexy man. I even whip out my favorite photo of him wearing just shorts on the beach in Hawaii, his skin tan and gleaming, his erection faintly visible, if you're looking. She licks the salt around the rim of her glass, then brings her tiny tongue back into her mouth and sucks. "He's quite the hunk – you're a lucky girl, Sarah," she says.

"You know, you could be lucky too," I say, taking a big sip from the light green slush.

"I don't seem to meet guys like that, no matter how hard I try," she replies, her voice slightly wistful as her eyes focus on something far away, or far behind.

"No, I mean . . ." I trail off, putting one hand on her leg, lightly, as the words come to me. "You can share his cock with me." I look away for a minute, my cheeks burning even as I'm determined to share my fantasy with her. "I have this thing where I want to watch him with another girl. He's the hottest guy I've ever been with, and I just feel like his dick is too perfect to keep all to myself. We've been together, and faithful, for ten years. Believe me, he doesn't even know about this naughty little fantasy of mine, though I'm pretty sure he'll agree to it in a snap – especially if you're involved. What's not to like? He'll get to fuck a beautiful girl, you'll get to enjoy what truly is the finest cock I've ever seen, and I'll get . . . well, I'll get to watch." I say "watch" like I'm winning the lottery or diving into an ocean of chocolate, like watching her and him together will be the pinnacle of my life thus far – and I mean it.

She drains her glass, her eyes seeking mine, making sure I'm for real. "But . . . why?" she asks, more confused than disdainful.

"I don't even really know. It's not like it just occurred to me today. I've been having dreams where I'm lying in bed and he's on his back and some beautiful girl is moving all around him, exactly the same way I do. I start telling her how he likes his dick sucked, but then I realize she's got it under control." I pause, searching her face. "I know, most women would die of jealousy if their guy so much as kissed another girl, but I'm freaky like that. You can't have him, but I'd love it if you borrowed him for a night," I finish, not sure what she'll say.

"Can I see it?" she asks finally, after a silence during which I try to look anywhere but at her. The bartender refreshes our glasses, and I fill my mouth with the icy drink before replying.

"His cock? Sure – I'll email you a photo when I get home." I lean in close, pushing her hair back as I let my lips brush lightly against her ear, getting a bit of a shock as I do so. "Your mouth's going to water when you see it, I promise."

Carrie looks like she's trying to figure out what to say as she licks the newly salted rim of her glass. "Girl, I have to tell you, I think you're a little bit crazy. But so am I, and he looks so fine, I feel like I'd be kicking myself if I refused. He really doesn't know a thing about this yet?" she asks, her voice lilting upward.

"Not yet, but he will," I say, slipping her my card as she scrawls her information on a napkin.

We finish our drinks, but every time her tongue pokes out to lick the glass, I can't help picturing it winding its way along his cock. I'm ready to race home, and I do – right after she leaves, right after I sneak off to the bar's bathroom and bring myself to a quick, rousing orgasm as my fingers flick at my wet clit while my other hand muffles my moans.

When I get home, I find Kyle on the couch in front of a football game. I smile and say, "Hey, baby," but when he puts his arms out to welcome me, I instead reach down and grab his cock, sinking to my knees. I pull down the layers of his shorts and boxers to unveil a dick that's already half-hard and getting harder by the minute as I hold it. I lean forward and ever-so-lightly suck the head into my mouth, then sit back and let my tongue toy with the veins traveling up and down his shaft before pulling back to look up at him. I'm gratified to see his eyes glued on my face.

"To what do I owe this honor?" he asks, his face lined with sexy stubble, his light brown eyes glinting as he tries not to break out into a grin.

"To a girl – Carrie," I say, then go right back for another lick. He moans as I inch my lips downward, taking half of his length into my mouth, but knowing he's not done growing. "I'm going to show her how to do this," I tell him, breaking my mouth's grip momentarily before plunging back down in one smooth movement, my lips wrapped around my teeth as I feel his cock travel all the way down my throat. I keep his full length inside me for as long as I can, breathing in his manly scent, feeling every bit of him pressing against my lips, my cheeks, surrounded by cock, cock, and more cock. Finally I slide slowly, reluctantly upward, my cheeks already aching with that glorious effort my blow jobs entail.

"What?" he asks, his voice husky, his eyes slightly cloudy as I stand and then straddle him, his naked cock bouncing back against him, then getting flattened between us as I rub my pussy along his hardness.

"I'm going to give her a little show and tell, and then she's gonna fuck you and suck your cock while I watch. I'm gonna make sure she does it perfectly," I say, then quickly plant my mouth back on his pole, tasting my own heady juices. The whole scenario, from the feel of his hot penis in my mouth to picturing Carrie doing the very same thing, to his strangled moans has me soaking wet. When he pulls me up toward him, turning me around so my hips are hovering over his face, then starts to devour me as I swallow him, I relent, even though normally I prefer to do one thing at a time, fully savoring each sensation. As his tongue parts my lower lips, diving into my swollen, dripping sex, I shudder all over, my hard nipples mashed against his torso, my mouth slackening involuntarily as he pushes deeper inside. His hot tongue swirls in mesmerizing circles as I sink my lips down, down, down, until they meet the base of his cock, the head easing around the bend in my throat. His fingers ply my clit, parting the hood and massaging the hard button beneath as his tongue probes me, his lips and teeth and fingers making me rumble. I ease up on his cock, barely able to breathe, barely wanting to. When he adds a finger inside me alongside his tongue, I'm a goner, my entire lower half tightening and then sparking, my legs clamped around his head as I suck the crown of his dick for all I'm worth, rewarded by the hot spurts of come that erupt from him.

He kisses me between my legs a few more times and then we finally turn around, and I taste myself, this time on his lips. Kyle looks into my eyes, smoothing my hair off my sweaty forehead, his fingers tracing my brows. "I'll give you anything you want, but I have to tell you, I don't think any girl out there can suck my cock the way you do," he finally says.

"Just wait," I tease, my previously sated body already perking up again at the thought of Carrie grinding herself against my man. I move aside, looking up and down at the man I consider my personal male model, my own private piece of eye candy others may sometimes get to borrow as their eyes drink their fill while we walk down the street, but who I get to take home every night. Feeling him against me is still a thrill, a prize, a treasure, but sharing him is going to take things to a whole new level.

I just hope Carrie is as excited as I am. When I call her the next day, she tells me she had a dream about him, about us. "I was lying on my back, my hands above my head, and his dick was coming at me, so big and hard and powerful. I spread my legs at the same time I opened my lips and he entered me in one fast motion. I gripped the headboard, and pulled against it, and then you shackled me to it so I really couldn't move, and while he fucked my face I watched his cock as it moved in and out. Then I saw you, naked, with your fingers between your legs, and I tried to focus on sucking his dick while memorizing the way you were touching yourself so I could do it later." Her words spill out in one big outpouring, racing ahead of one another, tripping over themselves in her eagerness to share her fantasy with me. The more she talks, the wetter I get, picturing exactly what she's described.

"I guess that means you're in," I tease her, knowing that I'd have a fight on my hands if I tried to refuse her at this point.

After that, everything else moves at warp speed. For the next few days, all I can think about is watching Kyle and Carrie, directing them in my own little play, and the very idea of her naked along with him, in a scene that I'd created but ultimately would only be a bit player in, has the part of my stomach closest to my pussy doing somersaults, dropping as far as it does when I ride a roller coaster. My body literally aches, and the night before we're to meet, when Kyle slides a simple finger inside me, I pitch forward, burying my face in his shoulder as I clutch him, my eyes tight as I squirm. "You're thinking about me with her, aren't you, Sarah? I know you are, and damn it, now I am too. You've made me want to fuck another woman, and even though I'm doing it for you," he says, his voice rough, almost growling, as his finger surrenders to my cunt's entreaties, pushing as far as it can go while the flat of his hand mashes my clit. "I'm gonna enjoy it. I'm gonna shove my tongue so deep inside her cunt that she'll scream." I reach for his cock through the haze, each of us alternating a fantasy web with our dream girl.

But as many scenarios as we've played out the night before, none of them could have prepared us for how hungry Carrie is for him. Any reservations she may have had have clearly vanished, because she pounces on my man immediately, as if they've been the ones conducting the secret affair, negotiating this night under cover of darkness, not her and me. I'm wearing a silky sheer black camisole and the tiniest scrap of black lace panties, which are soaked practically from the moment I put them on. I've kept them on me, though, letting my scent permeate the room, dipping my fingers inside to offer Kyle a taste of my juices as we wait. Then, all too soon, she's here, looking even hotter than she did when we met, *au naturel* in a slinky red dress that seems molded to her body. We converge in the living room where she greets me with a full body hug, her hands traveling from my shoulders on down, and then I hear her say, "And you must be Kyle." Unconsciously, I slip away, letting them get to know each other. I head to the kitchen to make cocktails, eavesdropping the whole while.

"Hi, Carrie," he says, his voice deep and husky. "I've heard all about what a naughty girl you are," and that's the last thing I hear as I fumble with the ice cubes. I pour us all sodas, nixing the alcohol, and quickly hurry back. I almost drop the glasses when I see them kissing, his denim-clad leg thrust between her thighs, pressing upward as she pushes downward. He suckles her lower lip, tugging it between his teeth. I set the glasses down on coasters, and he looks over and gives me a little smile. "You have good eyes, my dear, very good eyes," he says, and pulls back enough so we can both see how swollen his cock is. There's no need for small talk, awkward or otherwise, and things are moving along even faster than I'd anticipated. I follow them up the stairs, watch his hand on her back pushing her up, and I have a feeling he's going to spank her from that slight show of dominance. When she starts to go right instead of left, his other hand lashes out, pulling her close, while the hand that was guiding her back slides easily into her blonde tresses, tugging her head backward to expose her neck. "I'll show you where to go," he says, and she moans in response, giving me a glimpse of hard nipples pressed against the fabric of her dress. I realize she must not be wearing a bra and I feel a gush of moisture fall against my panties.

We reach the bedroom, his hand still tangled in her hair while his other hand immediately goes to his zipper. I step back, giving them a little room to explore but keeping them in my sight. I can see the tendons in her neck straining, her silent swallows as she looks up at him adoringly. She's caught the magic, the fever; that special ability he has to make powerful, sexy women quiver before him, eager to do his bidding. He lets go of her hair so he can push down his pants to reveal his hard, strong cock. He lets the jeans drop to the ground, then sits on the edge of the bed. "Down," he says, pointing, the single word enough to have her instantly on her knees.

This is the moment I've been waiting for, the one I can hardly believe is actually happening. She reaches for his cock with her hand, but he pushes it back and then leans over her, shoving his cock against her cheek as he fixes her wrists behind her back, her hands dangling down just above the end of her spine, right above her ass. "Keep them there. I just want your sweet little mouth," he says, the naughty words making me plunge my fingers into my wet panties for some much-needed relief. I try my best to stay silent, biting my lip as she kisses his cock reverently then licks her way in one long motion from his balls on up to the crown before taking him between her lips. I don't get to see the glory of his cock anymore, but watching her strain to wrap her lips around him more than compensates, maybe because I've been there countless times; maybe because I can hear her heavy breathing in the otherwise silent room, her snorts and gurgles as she swallows him. I peek around and see her rocking slightly, her ass bobbing along with her head, and know she's getting as wet as I always do. I give myself a mental pat on the back for having chosen such a perfect slut as Carrie, as my fingers dive inside my slit. It's hard to tell who'll be offended and who'll be turned on by the chance to bang your boyfriend, you know.

She's got his entire cock shoved down her throat, and her eyes gaze up at him, waiting for his next instruction. She keeps her mouth there, nudging the base, her lower lip flush with his ball sac, until she needs air, and then she slowly rises upward, unveiling his glistening cock for me. I add another finger, and feel my own breath shoot harshly out of my nose, my nostrils surely flared like a horse's, my noises of arousal joining hers.

Carrie starts writhing up and down, faster and faster; and Kyle, who's been trying to maintain a stoic expression, can't help but part his lips, his eyes starting to glaze. She's moaning now, her fingers twitching at their imposed exile from her pussy, when he pulls her up again. "You're a fabulous cock-sucker, Carrie. I hope you get lots of practice because clearly you just need cock as often as you can get it," he says, his voice husky, not giving away any sense of just how much he's enjoyed her skills. "I think that made you very wet, didn't it?" he asks. He's not talking to me, and yet it feels like he is. I've orchestrated this little game, but they've run with it. They're not putting on a show for me, I just happen to be their audience I realize as he sits up on the bed, propping his back against the headboard and lifting her dress off to reveal her smooth, naked backside. He hasn't looked at me once, his eyes fixed on her perfect ass curving across his lap. It doesn't matter though, whether they're trying to show off or not. Watching him do all the things he usually does to me, and seeing her react, has my eyes tearing with arousal, the way they do when I give him a really brilliant blow job. I wouldn't call them tears of joy, exactly; more like tears of overwhelming desire, my body's natural reaction to feeling like I might shatter, exploding in a fiery orgasm right there on the carpet. I dare to step closer and perch on a corner of the bed, so I feel it bounce as he lifts his hand and brings it down with a resounding smack on her ass. Her hands have automatically settled above her head, perfectly subservient, and now I see her bring her arm toward her mouth, so she can muffle her own cries as he does the same thing to her other cheek.

Handprints, large and pink, immediately flower on her pale skin, but he just keeps on going until her ass is totally his, marked by his smacks. I note the way her body moves slightly, her legs widening, her ass arching higher to make the most of his smacks. Soon even her arm can't muffle her sounds. He's had his hand pressed against her lower back, keeping her still so she can fully absorb his smacks, but at her cries, he moves to shove four fat fingers into her mouth. She immediately starts suckling them, as if starved, her face rocking against his invading fingers. This is all way too much for me, and I get up and grab my favorite vibrator. I briefly wish it were one of those small, silent ones, but those have never really done the trick for me. This is a dual-action powerhouse, and I lay it in front of me and hump it, sliding it inside me so I'm pretty much sitting on it before I let it start buzzing. As Carrie sucks and gets spanked, I let the toy whir against my clit and tumble inside my pussy, bringing me to a powerful climax in moments. Carrie turns her head and watches me, her eyes glossed over as he keeps on spanking her. Finally, he pauses, and the lack of noise suffuses the air. I'm spent, and I turn the vibe off. He slides his fingers out of her mouth, but when she whimpers, Kyle offers her his thumb, and she sucks it like a child.

He rubs his hand along her hot skin, then looks up at me, beckoning me forward. I inch closer, so I'm sitting on my knees, which are just grazing her hip. He reaches for my hand, and lets me feel just how warm he's made her ass. I rest my hand there, gently curving my fingers into her sore flesh, while he dips lower, bringing two fingers into her hole. I stare blatantly, so close up, as they emerge covered in her juices, and I hear her sucking on his thumb, gurgling almost as his fingers torment her pussy. He adds a third finger and she cries out. "I think Carrie's ready for my cock, don't you, Sarah?" he asks me, though it's largely rhetorical – if he wants to fuck her right now, he will, and all three of us know it. When he says this, she buckles against him, and he pushes deeper, twisting his fingers around, making her come while I feel her body tremble below me.

Usually he likes to be on top, doggy-style being his favorite, so I assume it's as a favor to me that he lies back against the pillows, sinking down so he's flat on the bed, and turns her around so she's on top of him. He pushes her up so she's straddling him, her hips near his, then nods toward me. I scurry to get a condom, then hand it to her, watching as he holds the base of his cock and she rolls the latex sheath along his bulging length. Her face is serious, full of concentration as she unrolls it. I'm back in the corner of the bed, my body heating up again as she completes her mission and climbs on top of him. I watch from behind, see her reddened ass as it rises up and down along his cock. I let my fingers drift to my cunt, but the urgency isn't there anymore. My fingers lazily part my lips, simply feeling the blood gently swirling below as he keeps his hands on her hips and guides her.

They're not too loud, so all I hear is the slapping as their bodies rub together. I'm suddenly wiped out, exhausted in a way only orgasm can make me, and I lie down next to Kyle, my head on an adjacent pillow, as Carrie smiles at me, her perfect breasts bobbing along with the rest of her. When his hands move around to cup her ass, squeezing it firmly and then pulling her cheeks apart, she pitches forward, tumbling on top of him and smothering my boyfriend with her blonde hair. A few strands land on me, tickling until she lifts her head and shakes them behind her. They kiss; a slow, passionate meeting of the lips as they grind together. I shut my eyes for a moment and find the image of them seared into my mind, captured indelibly. I purr without meaning to, open my eyes to find him sitting up, pushing her onto her back, and sliding out. He takes off the condom, tossing it to the ground as he now climbs on top of her. I don't know what he's doing at first until I see her hold her breasts together, and he slides between them. He spits into his hand to lube up his cock, then puts it back into her titty tunnel, and she pushes them tightly together. "Come on my tits," she says, her gaze fixed on his swollen head riding ever closer to her mouth as he thrusts in and out of her. She doesn't have to do much to get him to spurt, and when he does, I watch his hot lava arc over her body, then land all along her chest, leaving her covered in his white mess. He grunts, then jerks the last few droplets out of his dick before getting up to wash off.

Kyle's never much of a talker right after he's come. I'm still absorbing all of what's happened, my mind adrift as Carrie stares back at me lazily. I'm about to ask what she thought when she says, simply, "You were right. It's perfect," then smears his cream all over her.

I guess if there's any lesson to be learned it's that you shouldn't gloat over your prized possessions, be they a mansion in Malibu, a sleek sports car, or your boyfriend's killer cock. The best things in life, the ones that truly matter, aren't meant to be hoarded, they're meant to be shared. I'll probably lease out Kyle's cock again, maybe for our anniversary, but for now, I'm gonna spend some time savoring his perfect cock all by myself.

Making Do

W. S. Cross

Married men are easy to seduce. And being a secretary has made it even easier. I get to know them, and no matter how much they love their wives there's always a restlessness, an ego that needs stroking. That's what has been so damnably frustrating about you, Will. I've tried everything, but to no avail. You're not my boss, but being married to my boss has made the campaign all the more tempting and galling.

"I'm not interested in cheating on Carolyn, Trisha."

Your words, each time I've tried to win you over, aren't always the same, but your meaning is: "You know I find you attractive, but I can't do that to her." I see you fight the yearning if I brush against you. And that time I kissed you hard on the mouth in the kitchen last year while Carolyn was charming everyone at the dinner table? Your mouth told me all I needed to know. But I don't try any of that cheap shit any more. You won't give in to me.

I had no other choice than to get to you by seducing Carolyn.

I wasn't sure I'd be able to. You both had given me clues by joking about your "wild days" in college. I couldn't be sure Carolyn would yield to me, or if I could pull it off. I'd had a few experiences with other women, but never actually gotten off with a woman.

"You're too voluptuous to be gay!" It was another one of their dinner parties. The three of us were joking in the kitchen while you cut up luscious red peppers for the shish kebab. I had said I was thinking about giving up men (not adding "if you don't sleep with me"). You weren't buying any of it: "Men always buzz around your magnificent tits; you don't need a woman."

After you made it clear you'd never cheat, you and I became great friends, almost brother and sister, and so casual that Carolyn never shows any jealousy. She not only invites me to your house (for dinner, in groups), she and I talk about you at work. You telephone me; we instant message at home and at the office (I make sure your screen name is different from the one you use with her). There's nothing we can't tell the other, and nothing we haven't. I even quizzed you about her past sexual experiences or inclinations to women. You couldn't realize I had a plan, and that all your confidences were duly noted and filed away. Hers as well.

"So you like my tits?" It was my turn to skewer you like those peppers.

"How can you call them tits?" Carolyn objected from beside you where she was putting the frosting on a red velvet cake. I felt touched – and surprised – by her coming to my defense. Her smoldering displeasure with you made me see in yet another way why you were so in love with her you'd turned me down flat.

I knew she'd be a tough assignment. Beautiful, in a quiet way. Easy to see how you're so in love with her long after the "seven-year itch" has passed. At first I thought being ten years younger than both of you would be an advantage, but I was up against her easy conversation, her confidence and poise. She's so much my opposite: dark hair cut to the nape of her neck, smallish breasts that look firm and shapely in whatever she wears.

It's her poise I can never match. Not just the boss/secretary thing (she never lords that over me). We're not girlfriends exactly, but we laugh way too much for unequals. And the longer I know you both, the more I feel like a rookie in matters of love. You two are special, still holding hands in public and stealing kisses at dinner parties.

I don't mean it to sound conceited, but there's no point in false modesty. I've had pretty much any man I've ever wanted. God knows, I've been lucky, with all the assets men want: large breasts; good, shapely legs and a closet full of minis, along with a drawer full of stockings and garters. A little-girl voice that turns men into stammering children and makes women hate me. I'd trade that voice for a news anchor's in a heartbeat, but the boys like it fine.

Some features I've enhanced, including hair that I let cascade down to my ass and lightened to the color of honey. And I make sure of enough sun to keep the legs tan and the tits golden. The *pièce de résistance*, though, is my pubic hair, shaved to an inch-wide landing strip pointing to the goal. I modeled for, and shared, some nude photos just to make sure you both knew about that.

Carolyn thought the pictures were marvelous – and even purchased a couple to hang in your den. Oh, they were artfully done, the kind of thing she could show dinner guests and tease you with.

"Will's particularly fond of this one," she'd say, pointing to the one of me with my back arched, face hidden by shadows.

"You have such good taste in art," one of the guests would always insist.

"Trisha here is the model."

The first time she did that, I thought I'd die. Not from embarrassment, but because I'd seriously underestimated her as a rival. The first few times she shone that spotlight on me, I'd just smile. Finally I asked Carolyn to stop telling people.

But as my intentions shifted from stealing (or at least borrowing) you to getting at you through her, I waited for the right opportunity. Tonight.

"That's me in the photo," I offered unprompted to a couple who was admiring my attractively lit black and white breasts displayed on a Victorian fainting couch. Carolyn turned to me with real surprise. I felt a bit of shame for being so scheming, but finally besting her at this made me quickly forget my scruples.

"You're so sophisticated," I whispered to her later in the bathroom.

"What makes you say that?" She blushed.

"You're everything I wish I could be: successful, beautiful, smart."

"Trisha! You're so much younger and sexier than I am."

"I'd change places with you in a minute."

She dismissed me out-of-hand, saying she was the one who wished she was me. We hugged. I couldn't tell if I wanted to slap her or if the heat in my cheeks was something more than simple jealousy.

"So, Will," I asked later, finding you alone in the kitchen washing up plates. The night was turning into nightcaps; most of the guests had left. My date was drunk in the living room, probably because I'd ignored him the whole evening. "You're telling me you never want to fuck another woman?"

Your answer surprised me. "Wanting to fuck someone and wanting to make love are not the same thing." My question had been said in a light-hearted way, but you got all quiet and sober. "I'm still young enough to feel attracted to a good-looking woman, but I know that cheating isn't something I'd like to do. Ever."

"You're getting serious on me." Joking is one of the least-understood aspects of flirting. But then I shifted: "What about swinging?" My heart was pounding; it took real effort to keep my voice off-hand and quiet.

"No, we tried that years ago."

"Really?"

"First of all, none of the women were half as good-looking as Carolyn. And the men seemed sleazy. But the real reason was that without an emotional connection, the sex wasn't very good."

"Funny how love ruins everything." I tried, I swear I tried not to let my bitterness come out like that. You said nothing. Maybe you felt awkward at the sexual turn the conversation had taken?

To ease the strain, you smiled. "I should check on the other guests." You headed into the living room.

"Is Will boring you with stories about our wild and crazy days?"

Carolyn was suddenly behind me, with her hand on my shoulder. Was it the wine? Or did I just throw my usual caution out the window? I don't know, but I turned around and kissed her on the mouth. She was shocked, gave off a little "mmmph" of surprise – but then put her arms around me. The kiss went from soft and gentle to firmer pressure . . . to something more like what happens between a man and a woman.

"Excuse me, ladies." We broke our clench and turned in the direction of your voice. I could see surprise, discomfort and amusement in your half-smile.

"Can't a girl get a drink in this place?" Hoarse from the passion I could feel building inside me, I could barely manage a whisper. Carolyn turned without saying a thing and walked out of the room. *Shit.* I never let myself go like that, and now look what happened. I wanted to bolt and head home, but it turned out my "date" wasn't so drunk he hadn't managed to slip away, leaving me stranded.

"Can you drive me home?" The last couple was saying good-bye to Carolyn at the door. "It seems my date and I, well, it didn't work out, and I'm a damsel in distress, and—"

Carolyn interrupted. "You can stay here tonight."

"I'll drive her home," you called as you picked up dirty plates. I felt like a piece of discarded pastry, without a say in the matter.

"Will, you've been drinking." Carolyn was insistent in the easy, firm way that always gets her what she wants. "I want her to stay over. I won't sleep if either of you leave tonight."

There was no point in pretending any longer: I'd set my trap for her, and she was willingly walking into it. Putting my arms around her waist, I began by nibbling her neck. Her shudder of desire caused her to drop the half-full wineglass she'd been taking to the kitchen; it shattered on the hallway marble. Neither of us made a move for it. My lips made their way up her neck and onto her soft, yielding mouth.

We kissed, and kissed some more, my hands gradually moving from her waist to her breasts. No bra, I discovered, just a camisole underneath her silk shirt, her tits hard under my rubbing. Her tongue was thrusting into my mouth with an eagerness I hadn't expected. I fumbled with her buttons, but she simply pulled them apart, several popping onto the glass fragments at our feet. The blouse open, I bent down and pulled up the camisole, exposing nipples already dark and hard.

As I sucked each breast, I could feel my cunt sliding in my panties from the growing wetness. I could have wondered if you were watching, but I was too intent on the work at hand. I led her into the bedroom – the bedroom I had fantasized about so many nights as I masturbated before sleep, but about being taken by you.

On the way, we giggled like best friends from school, but once in the bedroom pulled off our clothes like whores ready for business. I pushed her onto the bed, heading straight for her pussy. It was shaved into a Brazilian, like mine! Her own idea, or from seeing my photos?

No matter, my tongue was in her wetness. Within seconds she was moaning, grasping my hair, pulling my face into her cunt.

My experiences with other women had been furtive, both of us too awkward and inexperienced to do things properly. Carolyn clearly felt no awkwardness, and her orgasms emboldened me. I tried one finger, then two, then three, and with each, her intensity went through the roof of the one before.

My own cunt was dripping – hurting. I needed to fill it soon. I discovered you sitting in a chair by the bed, fully dressed, watching us. I couldn't read your expression, and for a fleeting second I worried that even this wouldn't break down your wall of virtue.

Carolyn saw me look over at you. She sat up and dove on top of me.

"Roll over!" she commanded in that forceful way that makes her so good in everything she does. The instant my back hit the bed, she grabbed my thighs and parted them. Her tongue plunged in with no hesitation and in the same moment an orgasm sucked the breath right out of my lungs. It was the first time I'd ever come with a woman.

No time for reflection. Carolyn tongued my labia, then switched to fingers, moving her tongue to my clit. My thighs began to shake as surges of pleasure short-circuited my brain.

"God, Carolyn."

"I'm going to fuck you, Trisha. Fuck you hard." And she did.

When it was over, I lay there spent. Then I felt you sit down on the bed, naked. Carolyn began kissing you, hard. I was jealous. How lucky! A thorough girl-fuck, and now she gets you.

"I think our guest should be first," she whispered in your ear, the flush of orgasm still on her cheeks. The words made my heart pound in my chest.

Your touch was superb, as if we'd done this a thousand times. Was it how you make love to Carolyn? I felt no jealousy asking myself that question; it was intensely arousing to think I might be trading places, even for a few moments, with the woman you love. Your hands slid around my waist and glanced across my belly. I spasmed when you kissed me hard.

I yielded totally to your touch. I could feel your hard cock pulsing against my thigh, its pre-come dripping onto my skin. I broke from your embrace and pushed my mouth onto it, your groan of pleasure the only sound in the room. Was Carolyn watching? Would she object? I saw her massaging her clit, her eyes threatening to roll back into her head.

How long had I dreamed of having your cock in every opening of my body? I ran my tongue along its ridges, feeling your excitement. Pre-come leaked from it in a steady salty stream. I twirled my hands, bobbing my head up and down.

I might get only one shot at you. On my back or on top? You were on your back as I sucked you, so the choice was easy: I slipped my thigh over you, pushing your cock inside my open pussy. Your wide cock perfectly filled my cunt, and the first few thrusts brought me to orgasm again. Sitting, I could control the thrusts, regulate the rhythm. I rested my hands on your shoulders, angling my cunt just right: G-spot, clit, labia . . every inch of my pussy was being rubbed. It was the perfect complement to the fingering and tonguing I'd received from your wife.

But wait! Why was I thinking about Carolyn at the very moment when I'd finally gotten to you?

"Shouldn't I put on a rubber?" you asked.

"I want you bareback," I croaked, barely able to speak.

Your thrusts were gaining force. I knew you were about to come, and in that moment your cock contracted like a hand making a fist, and a stream of hot come burst inside me. Oh God, it was like I'd never felt another man before. The room began to spin, and I collapsed on your chest, kissing you furiously.

After a while, I remembered where I was. Carolyn slid her right arm under the small of my back, kissed me hard on the mouth, and then thrust her left hand deep into my pussy. No sooner did her fingers slide in, sticky with the mix of your come and mine, than I was climaxing again.

When I couldn't come any more, she swung her hips over my face and ate me again. I worked on her with my mouth and fingers while she lapped my cunt like a happy cat enjoying the milk you and I made. Soon she could no longer lick me at all. Instead she grabbed my legs and held on for dear life. Orgasms flooded over her in waves, and I felt as if I were at the beach surfing her sexuality. She called my name before she melted into shrieks of passion.

When finally her body could take no more, she pulled herself off and lay beside me, clutching my legs like she was about to be washed overboard.

"That was wonderful."

At first I thought it was Carolyn, but then I realized it was your voice.

After that, I watched the two of you. It wasn't the first time I'd seen a married couple fuck, but it was the first time I'd seen this kind of love. I'd thought I might feel jealous as I watched you kissing her lips, whispering in her ear, "Oh, Carolyn, I love you so much," or "You're so beautiful tonight, so exciting when you come." Instead I felt only longing. I wanted to carry away a few crumbs of what you feel for her.

Carolyn remained quiet the whole time, but I saw her body reach one last height of passion as she wrapped her legs around your beautiful ass, shuddering as you climaxed inside her. At the moment you spurted inside her, I watched you raise yourself up on your hands, watching with strange fascination as your beloved came again, her head whipping side to side as your body released its last drops of love and lust.

As guests go, I'd made out pretty well. It was better than I could've hoped for, and certainly more satisfying than if you and I had rented a motel some afternoon. I drifted into sleep content that things had begun so well.

The sun was up and the room bright when pitiful weeping somewhere outside the bedroom woke me. I found Carolyn in the living room with her head in her hands, weeping like someone had died.

"What's the matter, sweetie? What is it?" I sat beside her on the couch. As I put my arms around her shoulders, she turned and hid her face in my breasts. The hot tears tingled my nipples.

"I can't," she sobbed, "I can't share."

I was stone sober now, the intoxicating night evaporating in her words. My heart felt as if it would crack like cold iron plunged into boiling water. I had gotten all that I had wanted and more, but now it was slipping out of my grasp.

"Hey, no big deal." I tried sounding casual and light, but the words were struggling to escape a quicksand of panic. "We just fell into it. I know he's your husband and all—"

"No, Trisha," she wailed, "it's not Will. It's you I can't share." The tears dripped down her face in a steady, wretched stream. "I love you."

That sort of shit would send me screaming from the room with a man. And in another circumstance, it might have with anyone else. I only had a few seconds, or I'd blow it all. So I did the only thing I could: I let myself go.

"I love you, too."

Our kisses roused our cunts to superwoman sacrifices. Later, when you walked in on us, the cuddling you saw was only the smoke from spent fires. I'm sure you thought we looked "cute" or "adorable" or one of the other things men say about two naked women lying in each other's arms.

And so we never slept with you again.

Carolyn tells me that sex with you is still wonderful, though different now because of me. Oh, I mention from time to time how nice it would be to bring you into our bed. But her response is always the same: that look of pitiful vulnerability that makes me hate her. I know without Carolyn saying it that if I stop sleeping with her, she would probably turn her fury on me. I'd never see you again. The sex between us is still hot, especially if I imagine that her fingers in my pussy are your fingers, her tongue is your cock.

It's hard. What other word would suffice to say how it is being around you now that I've felt your touch, tasted your cock, felt its thrusts inside me? I still masturbate thinking about that night.

This is a letter to you that I can never send. It helps writing it, though. I'm not looking for sympathy. Each time I part her pussy and thrust my tongue in where that cock of yours goes, each time I kiss that mouth where yours still plants passionate kisses, I realize that sometimes a girl has to make do with what life hands her.

Poppet

Elspeth Potter

I snuck the poppet into the hospital like it was contraband. Probably, no one would care, but I didn't want to argue with any idiot administrators. It wouldn't interfere with any medical equipment; it was less hazardous than a cell phone. I had sealed it safely into a silver case with molded neoprene lining. If I opened the case, one would see only a silvery humanoid shape about the size of a Ken doll cut off at the knees. Come to think of it, I could say the poppet was merely a toy.

I wasn't supposed to have it out of the lab but, in my mind, James and I *were* the lab, and I was going to visit James. My snug, low-necked top and flowing skirt proclaimed that. I had never been one to wear such blatantly feminine clothing, but I had begun to notice, since he'd been in the hospital, where his eyes focused most often and with the most interest. At the moment, I could do little enough else for him.

I was also wearing his favorite pair of purple panties.

The nurse at the burn ward desk looked up as I passed. "Morning, Jessamine," she said. "Come to see Dr Lincoln again?"

"Yes," I said, hoping I didn't sound surly. She never called me *Dr Farlow*, and it was useless to be irritated over a friendly greeting. I was annoyed anyway, by everything that morning. I'd been up until four, trying to brainstorm ways to save the poppet project now that James' continued absence was making things difficult. I was the brains behind linking the poppets to an individual's control, but James had invented protean plastic and constructed the poppets themselves. Without him to provide a good supply of them for testing, we would soon have to stop the research. The protean plastic didn't retain its malleability and shape-memory for more than a few months of use. At least, not yet. James would solve that. I had not a doubt in the world. But until then, we needed some use for the few we had, something that would make a large quantity of money quickly; neither of us wanted to consider selling the patents.

I felt, perhaps irrationally, that our future as a couple depended on the poppets' success, just as our initial meeting had resulted from our early work on the project, when we'd discovered our mutual compatibility was physical as well as intellectual. I'd often thought James was more attracted to my brain than to my body. We talked to each other about science while eating, while walking to and from the lab, while having sex. He'd solved the first hurdle of the protean plastic while inside me, my legs hooked over his shoulders: one minute, furious thrusting, the next, I lay gasping on the bed while he scribbled formulae on the sheet. If he'd stopped for anything less, it's true, I would have strangled him with my thighs, but I cared about the breakthrough as much as he did. We returned to business once he'd recorded his idea, and we finished up on the carpet so as to avoid smearing his notes.

James' mind was a large part of what attracted me to him, as well – not so much that he was brilliant, but because he most valued in me the same thing that I most valued in myself. That and, well, I had to admit the sex was really hot. And so was our constant exchange of ideas. James pursued one as fervidly as the other, so that watching him in the lab could make me horny.

There would be no sex for us for a long while, though, and little conversation. James lay, as he had for two weeks, immobilized by pain. Ironically, the burns covering his legs from feet to mid-thigh, and searing his hands, were the result of an accident in the lab where he manufactured the poppets. The melted plastic had caused pain that no drug could sufficiently ameliorate, especially if he tried to move. His entertainment was therefore limited to visits from me and the video screen set into the ceiling. He had found himself unable to work, his second-favorite entertainment; sometimes being drugged out of his mind prevented him, and the rest of the time he was too exhausted. Worse, because of the steam and chemical smoke he'd inhaled, his doctor had recommended he not speak until he was completely healed inside. After the first awful days, we'd resorted to his using an eyeblink register so he could type, laboriously, on a pocket screen. I'd asked him how he occupied his mind, and he'd spelled out, in his usual laconic way, "Fntsy." His eyes, a changeable pale hazel in his dark face, told what sort of fantasies they were. I hoped they helped.

I slipped into James' room unnoticed by any of the inhabitants: James on his bed and his doctor and two nurses. I winced; I knew the signs. Another debridement to remove dead skin from his legs. I'd asked how that felt and he'd slowly blinked out three filthy words I had never heard him speak.

I took a chair by the window, where James could see me if he looked away from the doctor. I unsealed the poppet's case. I'd brought it to cheer him up and remind him of all he'd accomplished. Perhaps I could distract him with it, even now.

This poppet was his. I'd keyed it to the chip that lived beneath the skin of James' neck, and after I manipulated the poppet between my hands for a few moments, the link activated and he knew it was there; I could tell by the way the protean plastic softened and warmed, James' brainwaves activating the power cell hidden inside the poppet's flesh. It was strangely like holding *him* between my palms, as if I was connected to his brain as well. Or, I thought, blushing, as if I held not his brain but his cock.

Obviously, deprivation was getting to me.

Hoping my facial expression hadn't given me away, I glanced over at the bed again. I couldn't see James at all except for a bit of his arm and chest. The doctor and nurses still didn't seem to have noticed my presence, or perhaps they were so used to me being there that it didn't matter. I was, after all, listed as his next-of-kin.

The silvery poppet wriggled free of my hands. Such directed action meant it was under James' conscious control. He was now focusing more on the poppet than his pain. Good. I watched with amusement as the poppet clambered upright on my knee and waved its little arms, silently expostulating. I guessed what he wanted to say: "Oww!" I swirled a finger over its knoblike head. It felt smooth and silky, like the most delicate of human skin, heightening my sense of handling *James* and not the poppet. If he experienced what I normally did with a poppet, he would feel my touch on it like a paintbrush against his body, except that the sensation would be all in his mind. It was better than nothing, better than not touching him at all.

The poppet responded to my touch with a rude gesture. I grinned and stroked the poppet again, wishing I could go over and do the same for James. Surely they would at least let me caress his hair while they worked on him, or hold his uninjured hand. He didn't really like me to see him while he was in pain, but his resistance was wearing down as the days passed. The more I visited, the less he protested.

The poppet leaned against me, gradually softening against my stomach like a contented cat. Perhaps I should tell James to build in a purring function. I found the poppet's fingerless hand and pressed into it with my fingertip. The hand reacted, clasping my finger in a suctioning kiss. Abruptly, I remembered James sucking my finger into his mouth, his expression seemingly blank except for his eyes, darkly intent on my face.

Involuntarily, I glanced over at him. I could see only his jaw in profile, clenched hard, before one of the nurses blocked my view.

I was unprepared for the poppet to suddenly struggle upright again and burrow underneath my blouse.

I clapped my hands down on my shirt's hem, a reflex response, as if to prevent the poppet from escaping. As if it couldn't crawl out the shirt's open collar, or around the back, or out a sleeve. I glanced at the group gathered around James' bed. None of them seemed to have noticed a thing, though the poppet was squirming like a bizarre alien pregnancy. Had he lost control of it?

The poppet poked me beneath my arm, and I writhed. No, he was in control. He knew exactly where I was ticklish, the bastard. And I'd been feeling sorry for him. He could at least have waited until we were alone before beginning this little game. I clapped a hand over the poppet, but it wriggled free easily, inching upwards until it clamped over my left breast, giving me the look of a silicone implant gone horridly wrong. I was about to reach beneath my shirt to try and pry the poppet loose when it applied suction to my nipple.

Even through my bra, it was exquisite, softer than human lips. My breath came short and my belly went hollow with arousal. For a few moments, I forgot I was sitting in a hospital room; I was thrown back in time to a darkened hotel bedroom, the revelry of a scientific conference pounding through the door in sharp contrast to the gentle pulling of James' lips. He'd slid one finger along my clit, lightly, so lightly. His eyes had gleamed in the semi-darkness, watching me.

We couldn't be caught doing this. Besides simple embarrass-ment, if the scientific agencies learned we'd been using the poppets so frivolously, the little funding we'd achieved could be cut off, the project ended, both of us unemployed. Recklessly, I surrendered to it anyway. Really, who would notice, or care? Here, James was just another patient, and I was just his girlfriend.

In moments, I was trying hard not to pant audibly. All I wanted was more, more, harder, and also for the other nipple to be sucked. I got my wishes, as if James could read my mind.

When the suckling stopped, at first I didn't even notice. My whole body gently throbbed, breasts down to toes. Gradually I began to wonder where the poppet had gone. The squashy, weighty lump of it had vanished – no, not vanished. Its body shape had flattened, spreading warmth over my chest and belly, like the glorious moment when two naked bodies first come into full contact. The poppet was a more subtle warmth, though, a gentle pulsation that rippled slowly downwards like a tentative hand on a first date, sliding down my belly, slipping beneath my waistband, and down beneath my skirt.

I dared a glance at the bed. One of the nurses had left. What had he seen, on his way out of the room? I flushed even hotter, thinking of it. The doctor and the other nurse blocked my view of James and were oblivious to my presence. I hoped. Or did I hope that?

I barely breathed. Faint sounds of a body moving against sheets – James – registered as pleasure, not pain. Perhaps it was. I would ask him later, after I'd told him he was a bastard. I would ask him if concentrating on the poppet had helped him with pain management. But the scientific aspect of the poppet was far from the center of my attention at the moment, as a sensation like a giant hand rippled and pressed over my abdomen, causing sympathetic ripples inside like precursors of orgasm. And the poppet was easing down between my legs.

It was pressing itself against me. The first time he saw them, James had laughed at the satiny purple panties I was wearing, before he became fascinated as I grew wet and the patch of fabric between my legs darkened in color and bloomed with musky scent. Now, the fabric felt hot.

Spread thin, the poppet rippled along my lower lips. I let my thighs fall ever-so-slightly apart to allow more access. James took advantage, fluttering the poppet like strokes of his tongue. Where had he achieved such control? He'd not had it before. Then I knew. Here. Hours to wait and nothing but fantasy, time he'd spent thinking. Thinking of me.

I looked down and saw the poppet coalescing again, pressing harder. I didn't think it would manage to enter me; that sort of delicate manipulation would be difficult; but the thought and its possibilities made my heart pound. The poppet pressed warmly against my clit, sucking, sucking. It didn't take much. Inexorably, my body tightened – only a moment longer – then released in waves, through which I felt the poppet clinging, all the touch James could give me.

When I could concentrate on my surroundings again, the room looked as if nothing had changed. Hurriedly, I tugged the poppet free of my shirt and concealed it between my hands. The protean plastic had cooled and was beginning to toughen. We'd used it up with all that enthusiastic subtle movement.

We'd have to work on that. James would be glad to have a project with which he could experiment while recuperating. I would be glad to help out, I thought, dreamily, as the nurse exited and the doctor made some encouraging comments to James.

It might not help our credibility to sell a poppet as a sex toy, but then we needn't call it that. Toy would be enough. Another way for the disabled to interact with their environment, distract themselves from pain, all sorts of things like that. We could garner publicity and more funding, I was sure of it, and continue to explore the wondrous possibilities. Our future was secure.

Just Words

Donna George Storey

I told him words wouldn't do it.

Not X-rated e-mails.

Or sizzling phone sex.

Or "You know how much I love you, babe."

And certainly not "I'm sorry I have to give up three weeks of great sex with you to go to Europe to kiss client ass for my fat boss who will pocket all the profit and maybe if I'm lucky give me a measly bonus at the end of the fiscal year" – although a little honesty about what's really going on here with his new job would be a step in the right direction.

What I needed was flesh. Heat. The music of his moans in my ear. His sturdy hands stroking my breasts. His finger teasing my asshole. His cock buried so deep inside my red, grasping mouth of a cunt, I didn't feel hungry anymore.

He couldn't take me there with just words.

To his credit, he did deliver the goods the evening before he left for London. It was just like the early days, when we spent whole weekends tangled together in the sheets, staggering out of bed only to get another bottle of wine or pay the pizza delivery guy. He made me come five times, twice riding his cock, twice on his tongue and once as he pinched my nipples and spanked my ass while I "secretly" rubbed my pussy against the mattress. I treated him to a postprandial crème de menthe blow job, along with my usual repertory of tricks to tease his tender parts. I liked the way he groaned and called out my name, but I really hoped our fuckfest would make him say other words.

Such as: "Fuck *them*, I'm staying with you."

Instead, he stumbled off to the airport, with a bleary-eyed wink and a promise he'd e-mail every morning and night, and we'd have a nice long phone call – on the company's dollar – every Saturday afternoon.

Still floating in the afterglow, I convinced myself that it was enough, that we could make it through three weeks apart with just words.

Until I got his first e-mail.

He wrote that he was really looking forward to our "date" on Saturday, but in the meantime he wanted me to refrain from any self-pleasuring activity – he actually used that lady-librarian expression – for the rest of the week. To make it all the hotter when he finally brought me off over the phone.

Yeah, right.

I gave a nasty little laugh, pulled my nightgown up to my waist, and jilled off right in front of the computer. Now and then I'd take a break and type a few more sentences of my reply.

Hey, lover boy. I think it's time for a little confession. When you're gone I keep myself plenty satisfied with the help of two tireless lovers. At night they take turns: One strokes my nipples into hard little points, while the other goes down to do the slip-slide in my wet pussy. Every morning, I wake up with a tight ache between my legs – don't kid yourself, girls don't rise at dawn, it's just hidden away inside. So me and my fuck buddies do it then, too, and I'm feeling so sexy from my morning quickie I put on a short skirt and boots, or the jeans that push right up in my crotch to go to work at the bookstore. You'd never let me out of the apartment dressed that way, but you aren't here to stop me, are you? I get so itchy I can't help but shake my butt when I guide the grey-haired married men over to the finance section. And I always make sure the cute young guys need a book from the lowest shelf, so I can bend over and give them an eyeful of ass or cleavage, depending on the angle. Yesterday, I snuck off to the alcove by the poetry journals, where I let lover number one climb under my skirt, while number two yanked my sweater over my tits and tweaked and pinched them until I came so hard my head

practically blew off. Moments after I straightened my clothes,
a really hot guy – one of those ponytailed literary types –
walked in and gave me a long, knowing look. I'm sure he knew
what I'd been doing. He could probably smell me, too. The
idea got me so turned on I had another encounter in the ladies'
room. But maybe next time I'll just fuck the guy against the
bookshelf. The truth is, I'm having such a wild time I don't
miss you at all. Why would I give up all this fun for an hour
of yakety-yak phone sex with you?

Think again, buddy.

I clicked the Send icon, spread my legs wider around the chair,
and climaxed right then and there on my dancing finger.
Loudly.

Sure, maybe I was taunting him, but it served him right.
Besides, a lot of what I wrote was true. I did get turned on when
I was working at the bookstore. I wouldn't admit it to him, but
it wasn't so much the customers as the words that excited me,
especially when they were packaged between the covers of a new
book. I loved to stroke its crisp pages, then spread it open wide
and bend to breathe in the perfume of fresh paper and ink. I
rarely started reading it at the beginning – I wanted to take a
book by surprise, slip right inside its soft middle. The good ones
always got under my skin to lift me, transport me, to another
time, another place, another body. A steamy sex scene would
always send me straight to the staff ladies' room for relief.

And when he was away, I usually did soothe myself to sleep
with some action between my legs, then woke up horny and took
the necessary steps to quench that fire, too. But busy as they
were, my hands never quite stilled the longing deep in my belly
the way he could do with his fingers, tongue, and cock.

And so, I had to admit, the last part of the e-mail was a bald-
faced lie. I did miss him. Bad.

When I saw his reply in my in-box the next morning, I felt a
twinge of worry that I'd gone too far with the insatiable-slut
revenge fantasy. But he didn't seem mad. In fact he apologized
and agreed he had no right to put limits on my private activities,

especially since he couldn't help jacking off after he read the part about me playing with myself in the poetry annex. While he stroked his cock, he imagined he'd been the one to catch me with my hand up my skirt and pictured all the ways he'd "punish" me for it.

But, he suggested again with all due respect, for my own enjoyment I might consider abstaining on Friday night and Saturday morning. He'd come up with some new ideas for our date, and he was pretty sure I'd agree they were worth waiting for. He promised to send instructions on how to prepare myself by Saturday morning.

I had to laugh again. While he'd certainly picked up on my intention to make him jealous with the public masturbation scene, he was apparently slow to grasp my broader message of female autonomy.

Still, I had to admit the word *instructions* made me tingle a little *down there*. I even took a little vacation from tickling the clam as the weekend drew near.

Of course, I got up extra early to check my e-mail Saturday morning. As promised, my instructions were waiting:

I'll call you at noon on Saturday, your time. Exactly ten minutes beforehand, I want you to do the following:
1. *Take off all your clothes and put on the Hello Kitty thong I brought from Japan last month. If you're cold, you may cover yourself with your bathrobe, but nothing else.*
2. *Place your hairbrush and hand mirror in the middle of the bed.*
3. *Lie down beside them and wait, hands at your side, until the phone rings. Then you may answer it.*

That was it. A bossy to-do list. No loving endearments. No "can't wait to hear your sexy voice." None of the things a truly caring lover should say to his long-suffering and very horny girlfriend.

So why was my heart going pitter-patter in my chest?

Of course, I told myself, no man gave *me* "instructions." I'd play along because I had nothing better to do – for the moment.

At the appointed time, I stripped and put on the thong, a black silk triangle on a string with a silly, beribboned kitty face on the front. I'd gotten a giggle out of it when he gave it to me after his last trip, but I hadn't worn it yet. It was a wise choice for overseas foreplay – definitely snug in all the right places.

But the mirror and the brush stumped me. Was he planning some kind of weird naked makeover session? I suddenly remembered some amateur porn pictures I'd seen on the Internet of a woman stroking her pubic hair with her hair-brush. She had this dreamy expression as if it were the most fascinating activity on earth, although at the time I suspected she was faking it for the photographer boyfriend.

Curious, I picked up the brush – screw the "wait with hands at your side" order – pushed down the thong, and ran it gently through my bush. No, I didn't blast off into orgasmic orbit at the first touch, but the sensation was interesting. Soft but rough at the same time, like the strokes of a cat's tongue.

The phone rang.

I jumped and tossed away the brush, as if he could somehow see me breaking the rules. It probably didn't help that I gulped, guiltily, in the middle of my "hello".

"Hey there, hot stuff, did you do everything on the list?" His voice was deeper than I remembered. And cocky. Too cocky.

"And what if I didn't?"

He laughed, warm and slow. "Then I guess I'll have to make you do as you're told."

"Sweetie, in case you didn't notice, you're thousands of miles away. How will you make me do anything? Not with words."

He paused. "We'll see about that."

In spite of myself, my cunt muscles fluttered, as if a secret butterfly was tickling me inside with its soft wings. But I didn't have to admit that to him.

"So, Part-time Lover, what am I supposed to do with the grooming implements?" I asked in my brattiest tone.

He laughed again, but this time he seemed embarrassed, as if he'd been the one caught with his hands down his pants.

"Well, I got inspired after I read that first e-mail. But I don't want to give away the surprise yet."

"Isn't it just like you to keep me waiting a long time for the good stuff?"

"Enough about me and my shortcomings, okay? I'd rather talk about you. Are you wearing the thong?"

"Uh-huh," I said, but with a healthy dash of defiance.

"Is it pulled up high so it presses between your pussy lips?"

That shouldn't have taken me by surprise, but it did, as a little zing of lust darted between my legs. "Somewhat."

"Pull it up a little higher. So that you can't think of anything else but that pressure against your clit."

I was about to refuse, on principle, but my hands seemed to reach down of their own accord and tug the sides another inch farther over my hips. An involuntary sigh of pleasure escaped my lips.

"See, that feels nice, doesn't it? Can you feel it rubbing against your sensitive pink asshole, too?"

His voice was so sweet it slipped into my ear like hot fudge sauce gliding over ice cream. Already my face was hot, partly because those dirty words were making me blush, partly because they were really turning me on.

"You didn't answer me," he scolded.

"Yeah."

"Yeah, what?"

"Yeah, it's rubbing up against my asshole," I murmured.

"Good. Now, I want you to open your robe and hold the mirror in front of your gorgeous breasts."

As I reached for the mirror, I noticed my hand was trembling. What would he tell me to do next? And would I continue to obey this easily, like a pliant little sex slave with no will of her own?

"Tell me, is your chest flushed and red, like it gets when you're all turned on?"

My "yes" slipped out before I could manage a lie.

"And your nipples? Are they hard yet?"

"Not really. The room's pretty warm."

"We'll have to do something about that. I want you to try a new trick. I want you to rub the mirror against your nipple very gently."

An unusual idea, but I figured it was worth a try.

I gasped as the cold, smooth surface brushed my areola.

"Does it feel good?" His voice had a hopeful lilt.

"Great," I sighed as I moved the mirror in slow circles over one nipple, then the other. "It's cold at first, but then it feels hot. And then it feels like your fingers are touching me there." Not to mention that the sensation of fire and ice was shooting straight to my pussy and making my hips do a twitching dance against the mattress.

Through the receiver I heard a little "hmph" of victory. "I'm glad it's working out so well. But I want you to stop now."

He couldn't mean it. This mirror trick definitely called for further exploration. "You're kidding, right?"

"I'm afraid not. But remember, all good things come to her who waits. I want you to move the mirror lower. To the kitty picture on your underwear."

I considered mutiny, but I had to admit that following orders thus far was bringing unexpected benefits.

"Okay, for this next part we have to get you wet. Very wet. But that shouldn't be a problem. I know how much you like to touch yourself."

"Yeah, and how about you?" I fired back.

"Guilty as charged, though I don't have nearly as many opportunities as you do, especially on the job. But right now I'm feeling fine – lying on my bed with my cock in my hand, a little lotion for lube, and a hot babe on the phone who sounds like she's getting hotter by the minute."

I frowned. For the first time he'd struck the wrong note. I couldn't help but picture him stretched out on a hotel bed, a blandly tasteful picture hanging on the wall beside him, pay-per-view porn on the TV. And the woman of his dreams on the other end of the phone was so far away, so insubstantial, she could be anyone willing to read the lines.

"Wait a minute, lover boy, before we proceed, what's your credit card number? Phone sex services always make you traveling businessmen pay up front to play out your fantasies, don't they?"

He was silent for a moment. "You are making me pay, babe, don't doubt it for a minute." The satiny seducer was gone. He was himself again. Lonely and a little sad.

"Hey, I'm sorry. I know I'm being a bitch, but it's tough for me."

"Yeah, I know. It's not easy for me either. Listen, I want to make you happy. Can you let me try? I know it's just words."

I felt another twinge, but higher this time, near my heart. He was trying, I could tell. In bed, in the flesh, he was more a man of action than words, but his new tongue technique was surprisingly effective. "It is making me happy. Really. Now where were we? I believe you were about to order me to masturbate."

His laugh was mixed with a sigh of relief. "That's exactly what I was about to do."

"I need very specific instructions, though. I promise to be a good girl and do everything you say."

"Hey, if that's what the lady wants. So, why don't you spread your legs for me? But just a little. Now I want you to touch yourself through the thong. Rub your clit until you make a nice wet spot on the kitty."

The hot-fudge voice was back, pouring down my spine, pooling warm between my thighs. My finger pushed the silky cloth of the thong back and forth over my sweet spot so deliciously I moaned into the telephone.

"Are you watching yourself in the mirror?"

I gazed down at the reflection of my finger wiggling away. Through my lust-fogged eyes, it looked like a stranger's hand, as if another woman were making love to me. The thought made my breath come faster. "Yes, I am watching."

"It's the best sight in the world, isn't it? A horny girl touching her pussy. But you have to take your hand away now."

I wailed in frustration. "Not again. Come on, I was just getting into it."

"Trust me," he cooed. "You're going to like this next part. I want you to give your clit a spanking. Not too hard. Just a few slaps to teach it a lesson for being so ravenous."

With a soft cry of shame, I covered my face with my hand. I suddenly felt so exposed, as if he'd reached through the phone and pulled me open to discover something darker and more secret than naked flesh. As if he heard that little voice deep inside me whispering, *Yes, you do deserve a spanking for being so hungry for sex. You love it when he makes you do bad things, so you can do just what the teacher wants and be good and bad at the same time.*

"It sounds like you're ready to begin. Shall we?"

Panting, I brought my flattened fingers down against my mons, once, twice, three times, groaning as the sharp jolt on my clit rolled through my whole body in waves.

"Again," he commanded.

I slapped myself once more, whimpering until the hot prickling pleasure faded.

"Very good. Now, we've got one more thing to try. I want you to pick up the brush, push the thong to the side, and press the end of the handle gently against your vagina."

I caught my breath.

"Um, I'm not so sure I can do that." My voice squeaked out, small and scared.

"What's the matter?" he asked, confused. "Don't you ever put hard things inside when you play with yourself?"

Should I tell him the truth? That, sure, I could talk like a crazed nympho, but when it came to push and shove, I was a pedestrian masturbator. Too chicken even to put my own fingers inside. "Actually, I don't."

"Hmm, I wouldn't have guessed that. Could you be a brave girl and try? For me?"

It really was magic the way he made his voice so warm and soft it sank under my skin to melt every muscle in my body. Including my tongue, which babbled out the answer I wasn't sure I wanted to give: "Yeah, sure. You know I'll do anything for you."

With a shaking hand and the help of the mirror, I guided the handle of the brush to my pussy lips. It probably helped that my only companions were his words, whispering inside me like the echo of my own lust. I don't think I could have done it if he'd really been watching.

I pushed the end of the brush slowly inside. My swollen lips parted with a faint, welcoming smack. He had made me wet

with his talk. Very wet. I pushed deeper. The handle slipped all
the way up to the point where the brush flared into bristles. It
looked silly, but it felt nice. And very naughty.

"It's in."

"Good girl. You don't know how jealous I am of that lucky
brush. But now we get to put everything together for the grand
finale. Do you think you can come around the brush if I let you
play with your clit and rub the mirror on your nipples?"

A rhetorical question if there ever was one. I was certainly
willing to try. I had to clench my legs together to keep the brush
in place, but the rest was easy. He was right, too, it was magic
how it all came together. The mirror was his one hand, twisting
and tugging my nipples. The thong was his other, teasing the
groove of my ass. The brush was his cock, so hard, so *there*.

And all around were sounds, moans and rhythmic grunts
racing at the speed of light under the Atlantic, the squish of a
lubed-up palm on his cock, the click of my finger finally snaking
under the thong to bare, slick flesh.

"Tell me when you're going to come. I want you to come
now," he barked.

"Yes, now," I called out, just as his guttural cries shot back
through the phone.

I could hear it was as good for him as it was for me.

Afterward, he told me how much he missed me and asked,
uncertainly, if I missed him, too.

I touched my fingers to my belly. I was a little sore down
there, deliciously tender and used. As if he had just been inside
me, as if he still was there, filling me with his voice, his cock, his
love. I wanted to tell him I didn't miss him at all, because he was
with me.

All it took was words.

Poker Night

Lisabet Sarai

It was just an ordinary door. Solid core, Yale lock, standard peephole, identical to all the other doors on the fourth floor of this unexceptional building on the corner of West 14th and B Street.

So why was he sweating and trembling as though he stood before the gates of hell? No, that wasn't quite right. He knew the door led through damnation, to salvation. He craved the peace, needed to be redeemed. But he was, as always, afraid to take that first step.

His cock was already an iron bar in his worn jeans. His heart jack-hammered against his ribs. Don't be a pussy, he told himself. Get on with it. His work-reddened knuckles hesitated, inches from the door.

Without warning, it swung open. His heartbeat raced into overdrive. He could hardly breath.

" 'Evening, Jack. I thought I heard you shuffling around out in the hall. Come on in, before I shock all my neighbors.'

She was decent enough, with her miniskirt and the black lace bra that cradled her ample breasts. But Jack scurried into the apartment. He didn't want to be seen, though everyone else in the apartment building was probably parked in front of the tube.

Helen stood with her back to the closed door, surveying him. He blushed and stared down at his work boots.

"It's been a while, Jack. I was beginning to think you didn't want to see me any more."

"Seven weeks, Ma'am. I tried – tried to stay away. But I

couldn't stand it." He was appalled to feel tears pricking the corners of his eyes. "I needed to see you."

Perceptive as always, she saw his distress. "Hey, don't cry!" She enfolded him in a brawny embrace, burying his face in her bosom. "It's OK. I understand." She smelled of Ivory soap and talcum powder. His swollen cock throbbed painfully, and for a moment he thought he'd come right there.

She released him in the nick of time. He stepped away from her, head bowed in embarrassment.

"How's Maude?"

"Fine," he mumbled.

"Does she know you're here?"

He gazed at his mistress, eyes full of pain. "Of course not. She thinks I'm over at the Moose Club, playing poker with the boys. Hey, I was, for more than two hours, before I came here." He stared at his hands, fighting the guilt. "I don't like to lie to her."

"Why don't you tell her the truth?"

"I can't. She wouldn't understand. She's the church organist, for heaven's sake. She teaches Sunday school."

"You told me that she likes sex."

"Sure she does, but only normal sex. Healthy, ordinary sex, insert tab A into slot B. You know what I mean."

"There's nothing unhealthy about what you and I do."

"Yeah, right." He gave a bitter laugh. "Well, I suppose there's no law against it. It's not like I'm a homo or anything."

"Nothing unhealthy about that either."

"Look, I don't want to talk about it. Ok? Let's just get on with it." Jack dug his wallet out of his pocket with difficulty, wincing as the denim stimulated his bulging prick. He pulled out a wad of bills and laid them on the television table. "Here. I was lucky tonight. Won more than a hundred bucks."

Helen looked at him, some unreadable expression on her broad features. Then she rearranged her face into a mask of authority. He could see it happen, the shift to her professional mode. He could hear it in her voice.

"All right, then. Into the dungeon, little boy."

She opened the door into what would have been the kids'

bedroom, if Helen had kids. The non-traditional decor, familiar as it was, still shocked him.

Heavy black curtains hid the walls and cloaked the one window, which faced onto the alley running between B and C streets. The yards of fabric muffled noise, making the room into a dark cocoon. The light was indirect and soothing, coming from several track fixtures installed in the ceiling.

The furnishings were home-made, but effective enough. In the center of the room was a punishment bench fashioned from two heavy-duty sawhorses – he knew the brand, popular with local contractors – and a plank padded with gardener's foam knee pads.

Opposite the door stood a bondage rack made of steel conduit. In one corner was a sturdy old armchair she must have picked up from Salvation Army, augmented by leather wrist and ankle restraints.

Arrayed on the pegboard along the left wall (just like the one in his garage, where he stored his tools) were coils of hemp and cotton rope, clamps and turnbuckles, a rattan cane, several paddles of wood and rubber, and a vicious bullwhip.

He knew that it was vicious. From experience.

The plastic storage bins under the pegboard, spray-painted black to fit in with the decor, held more implements and supplies.

Jack hovered on the threshold of the dungeon, temporarily paralyzed by fear and excitement. She gave him a little push.

"Get going. Or I'll send you home to Maude."

He stumbled in and stood, slightly dizzy, in the middle of the room. Helen went over to rummage in the storage boxes.

"Strip, boy," she called over her shoulder. "Now."

Jack kicked off his boots and unzipped his jeans. His heart was pounding again, so hard that it hurt. His cock surged as he dragged his pants off. His fingers fumbled at the buttons on his flannel shirt.

He was down to his underwear when she turned back to him, her arms full of paraphernalia.

"What? Not naked yet? Get a move on, boy!"

Hurriedly, he pulled the undershirt over his head, exposing

his broad, hairy torso. The stretchy cotton undershorts snagged on his swollen prick as he wrestled them off.

"Get over to the rack." Her palm landed on his pale butt cheek with a resounding smack. That single hot, sharp blow nearly sent him off. He tightened his muscles in alarm, struggling for control. If he shot his wad without her permission, she'd beat him till he couldn't sit for days. That always made Maude suspicious.

Helen secured his wrists to the upper crossbar, but left his ankles free. She circled his stretched body, appraising his state of arousal, making her plans.

"So, you were playing poker tonight?"

"Yes, Ma'am."

"Did you drink a lot of beer?" He knew right then what her nasty game was going to be. His cheeks burned with the understanding.

"Some, Ma'am."

"How much, boy?"

"Three cans of Bud, Ma'am."

"Not enough. Drink this." She poured a big glass of water and held it to his lips. He realized that he actually was parched, and drank greedily.

She refilled the glass. "Again."

He could feel the liquid settling in his gut. "I can't . . ."

"What did you say, boy? Why are you here, if you're not going to obey me?" Her anger melted him, then brought him to a boil. He drank two more glasses.

"Good. Now, my little boy, I know that sometimes you can't control yourself. But I have what you need."

She picked up something white. It was an old-fashioned cloth diaper, but on a giant scale, big enough to fit a six-footer like Jack. He wondered briefly where she had found it. Unlike most of her equipment, this wasn't something they sold at Home Depot.

"Spread your legs, baby." The soft cotton caressed his rigid prick, making him moan. Her fingers were cool on his sweating flesh as she pinned the thing at each hip.

She stood back to admire her handiwork. He blushed again,

aware that he must look ridiculous, embarrassed to realize that this simply made him hornier. "Very good. But I'll need something pretty strong, won't I, for you to feel it through that thick diaper?"

She retrieved the cane from the wall. "This should do the trick." The flexible rattan rod whistled through the air as she warmed up. The hair at the back of his neck stood on end at the sound. His balls tightened into aching knots.

"Open your thighs wider. And bend over so the fabric's stretched tight across your butt. That's good."

Jack trembled, off-balance, waiting for the first stroke. Leaning forward, he found that the padded cuffs around his wrists supported most of his weight. Then again, he felt as though the lump of granite jutting from his crotch would be heavy enough to drag him to the floor.

He had been hard half an hour before he left the game, knowing that this would be his final destination. He hoped nobody had noticed his hard-on when he got up to leave. Early delivery at the store, he had told them. Need to get my sleep.

All the last week he'd been harried by anxious dreams, but he'd sleep soundly tonight. He always did, after a session.

"Ready, baby?"

"Yes, Ma'am," he murmured. Still the pain surprised, biting into his flesh as though his ass was totally bare. "Ow!" he yelled. He had time for two deep breaths before she slashed at him again. His cock jerked against the cotton that bound it against his belly, threatening to explode. The cane left tracks of fire burning across his buttocks. The agony spread and mutated, merging with the awful pressure in his bladder.

Each searing stroke hurt more than the last. He was shaking, near tears, from the excruciating pain and the effort of staying in control. Yet, when she paused to get her breath, he craved another stroke. The pain was almost unbearable, but its loss was worse still.

She might have read his mind.

"Enough, baby?"

Jack was silent, overwhelmed with shame. He didn't want to admit it, his weakness, his sickness.

"Answer me, boy. Have you had enough of my cane? Or do you want more?"

The authority in her voice sent a delicious chill up his spine. Did it even matter what he wanted? He was in her power. Everything was up to her.

"No answer. I guess that means you're done, that you can't take any more . . ."

"No . . . more . . ." The croaking voice seemed to belong to someone else.

"What was that?"

"More. Please, Ma'am. Give me more."

Her mocking laugh shriveled him. It hurt more than the cane. Yet strangely, even though his erection sagged, he was still excited. His balls were still tight. His bladder was as swollen as his cock had been, and somehow that turned him on, too.

"It's hard to admit that you're such a kinky little baby, isn't it? That you like it when I beat you. But it's OK. That's what I'm here for, to give you what you're afraid to ask for from anyone else.

"Let's check your marks. See if I think you can take any more. We can't send you back to Maude with your butt looking like barbecued chicken."

The mention of his wife's name made him squirm. She knew that, Helen did. It was all part of the performance.

Just because he understood didn't mean that he failed to react.

She stood behind him, close to his suspended bulk. He could feel the heat coming off her body, smell her talc and a hint of oceany woman-scent. She barely touched the edge of the diaper covering his ass. The welts on his butt screamed as the cloth moved against them.

He sucked in his breath, struggling once again for control. The urge to pee was unbearable. Gently, Helen peeled the cotton away from his wounded skin.

"Hmm. Very dramatic. I know you're a tough guy, but I think you've had enough for tonight."

Jack was about to protest, to swear that he could endure

another dozen strokes. She cupped his butt cheeks in her cool palms, and squeezed lightly.

Echoes of the cane's agony raced through him. He screamed. His back arched. His legs turned to rubber. For a moment, he forgot to tighten the muscles controlling his bladder.

The pungent odor of urine filled the dungeon. Jack began to cry.

He flinched as Helen landed a vicious slap on his lacerated ass. "Oh, you naughty baby! You've wet yourself again. Naughty, naughty! Now I'm going to have to change you. Then, I'm going to punish you."

She unbuckled the wrist restraints and massaged his shoulders to stimulate the blood flow. Her touch brought the blood back to his cock as well. The soaked cloth clung to the growing bulk of his erection, a guilty pleasure that made him harder still.

"But for now, I'm going to let you stand there in your wet diaper and think about what a bad baby you are."

Helen stepped out of her skirt and unfastened her bra. She wore no panties. Jack watched from under lowered eyelids, admiring her fair, freckled skin and ripe body. A bushy tangle of red-gold curls decorated the place where her solid thighs met. Fat, juicy-looking nipples crowned her pendulous breasts.

She seated herself in the armchair, spreading her thighs a bit. Subtle musk mingled with the sharp stink of his pee.

"Come here, boy," she ordered.

He was at her feet in a moment. After fumbling with the safety pins for a while, she gave up and yanked the soaked diaper down to his knees. He groaned as the cloth rasped over his welts. His cock sprang out, fully hard again.

Helen reached out to pinch the purple skin stretched over the knob with her lacquered fingernails. "What a nasty boy you are! Well, I know how to handle nasty boys." She patted her thighs. "Over my knee. Now."

Trying to hide his eagerness, Jack draped himself across her lap. Helen was a big woman. His feet reached the floor, but just barely. He spread his legs to brace himself, and she trapped his erection between her thighs.

"Like that, do you? Well, let's see whether you like this."

Her cupped palm landed solidly on his ass, directly on top of one of his stripes. He yelled and jerked his hips away. His captured cock rubbed against the silky skin of her inner thighs. Pain and pleasure twisted together, racing through his body, and leaving him helpless.

"Breathe," murmured Helen. "This is going to hurt."

She spanked him, hard, first with one hand, then the other. The sting of her slaps was bad enough, but she deliberately aimed her strokes so that they'd reawaken the agony of his caning. Jack writhed against her, trying without success to escape the pain. She gripped him around his waist and rained furious blows on the tenderized skin of his butt cheeks.

"You should see your ass, boy," she gasped, breathless from her exertion. "You're red as a lobster. Can't even see the marks of the cane anymore. Everything's a nice, even scarlet." She aimed a few more slaps at his punished flesh, then stopped. She was clearly getting tired.

His skin burned and his muscles ached, but to be free from her blows was still a blissful relief. He lay in her lap, panting, more and more concious of his swollen cock poking between her thighs. He moved a little, stealthily trying to increase the contact with her firm body, and was rewarded with another slap.

"Oh, you evil little boy! Trying to get off, are you?"

"Yes, Ma'am." He couldn't hide anything from Helen. She knew him, better than anyone did.

"Get up. Let me see you." Awkwardly, he worked his bulk backwards, off her lap, gritting his teeth as his cock repeatedly brushed against her body. Finally he was kneeling at her side, his rigid prick swaying and pointing up at the ceiling.

She reached down and squeezed it, hard. He closed his eyes and held his breath, struggling for control.

"Well, you've managed to hold on through some heavy stuff. Maybe you deserve to come. Would you like that?"

He didn't dare raise his eyes, but he knew she could see his smile. "Oh, yes, Ma'am. Please, let me come."

"OK, you can come. But you have to jerk yourself off using your wet diaper."

"Oh, no, please, Ma'am! Not that! I can't! That's disgusting!" Disgusting or not, his cock ratcheted up another few degrees toward the vertical at the thought.

"It's that, or I'll send you and that proud erection home right now."

It was no good pleading. He knew that.

"Come on, Jack." Her voice held a new hint of intimacy and complicity. "Don't disappoint me. We both know you want it."

He crawled on over to the crumpled pile of fabric that lay near her feet. The smell was strong. He raised himself onto his knees, spreading his thighs for balance. Mastering his revulsion, he grabbed the diaper and wrapped it around his cock.

The damp cloth clung to his flesh, cool against his fevered skin. He took a deep breath, trying to ignore the odor and all the shameful memories that it awakened, and gripped his cock in strong fingers.

The diaper wouldn't slide. There was too much friction. It hardly mattered. Helen was watching him, leaning forward eagerly, lips parted, nipples taut, thighs open. One more squeeze was all it took.

Pleasure, untainted by pain, overwhelmed him. His whole body convulsed. Milky fluid spurted from his spasming cock, showering Helen's toes. He closed his eyes and felt all the tension, the rage, the fear, the shame, the self-disgust, flow out of him, leaving him empty and at peace.

"Clean me off." Helen's voice, gentle despite its message of command, broke his reverie. As though in a trance, he bent and began to lick his come off her white feet. He didn't mind the bitter taste. Long after he had consumed every drop, he continued to lap at her warm, fragrant flesh, dipping his tongue into the crevices between her toes, tracing the smooth arch of her instep.

"Enough." Helen raised him up until his face was level with hers. "Enough." She bent and kissed him with closed lips. "Get dressed. I'll wait in the living room."

Then she was gone. Jack groaned as he clambered to his feet and looked around for his clothes. The muscles in his thighs and shoulders were sore. His buttocks were on fire. He couldn't stand the tightness of his undershorts, though the rough denim created its own special agony against his punished flesh. Every step reminded him of Helen and his own degradation.

He smiled when he saw her, sitting in front of the TV watching the late news. She had put on a flowered housecoat, exactly like something Maude would wear. His heart swelled with something, something that actually felt quite a bit like love.

He fished another twenty out of his pocket and added it to the pile of cash. "Thank you, Helen. I really appreciate it."

She laughed. "Wait till tomorrow, Jack, when the pain really kicks in and you might not be so grateful!"

"No," he said softly. "I will."

She stood up to see him to the door. She patted his shoulder and kissed his cheek. "So, Jack. What will you tell Maude?"

A smile lit his middle-aged features, making him suddenly handsome.

"I'll just tell her that I had a lucky night."

All About the Ratings

Sophie Mouette

It all started when he came backstage during her cooking show and stomped around. The walls were thin. The vibrations carried.

Caroline had been making a soufflé in front of a live studio audience.

Okay, the audience hadn't been more than ten people – fifteen, tops – and had included her grandmother, her aunt, five desperately single men, and three women she'd gone to high school with. But it was still embarrassing, and she was still certain that Drew had done it on purpose.

And then, to make matters worse, he started stealing her ratings.

Hers had been the highest-ranked cooking show on WPVL, Peaveyville's cable channel, until he'd come along. On her show she'd emphasized simple but elegant meals, the type that you could serve on good china and light candles for, but that didn't involve complex recipes or hours of preparation.

Drew had breezed into town and offered up his own take: grilling, barbecuing, and good old-fashioned home cooking. The station manager, desperate to fill a sudden scheduling hole left when septuagenarian Etta of *Etta's Gardening* had fallen in love (at her age!) and up and moved to Florida, had hired Drew, despite the fact that both he and Caroline had similar shows.

Cooking with Caroline had had a wide audience. Busy career women recorded it. Stay-at-home moms swore by it. The local lesbians tuned in, and she suspected their interest wasn't always in the garnishing tips. She also had a variety of male viewers, both straight (for the same reason as the lesbians) and gay.

When *Warning: Man Cooking* came on the air, Caroline lost the gay men and a fair number of the straight women right off the bat. Fact was, Caroline could see why those segments of her audience had defected. Drew had a cheeky grin, a lock of black hair that tended to flop endearingly onto his forehead, and an ass you could bounce quarters off of. Plus he eschewed the traditional chef's jacket and baggy pants, preferring form-fitting T-shirts that showed off his biceps and faded, tight jeans that showed off his impressive package.

Some of the hetero men switched to *Warning: Man Cooking*, too, because Drew was a non-threatening guy's guy who gave it to you straight.

Curse him!

Caroline had to rebuild her audience base. She had to grab back her ratings. And she was willing to do whatever it took.

Lee Remini, the station manager, called her into his office after she taped her latest show (shrimp kebobs, Thai noodles, and cabbage salad). She'd had time to change into her usual outfit of mid-thigh, swishy skirt and high heels. Her one regret was that the cooking counter blocked view of her legs, which she considered her best features.

She was dismayed to find Drew already in Lee's office, lounging in a chair as if he owned the place, long jean-clad legs stretched out in front of him.

The problem – the biggest, nastiest, most annoying facet of this whole rotten situation – was that Drew Benjamin made her panties wet.

Trying to ignore him, she slid into the other chair, searching Lee's face for some hint of what was to come. It couldn't be good.

Lee burbled about the popularity of both their shows and how grateful he was about having them at his station. Caroline only half-listened. She was intensely aware of Drew next to her. She could smell his aftershave, musky and no doubt filled with illegal pheromones that people could smell through their TV screens. She was aware when he shifted in his seat, aware of his strong, long-fingered hand resting easily on the arm of the chair.

There were times, late at night, when the one thing that would bring her off was the thought of those hands on her body, tweaking her aching nipples, plunging into her wet sex until her hips rose off the bed and she panted out his name and . . .

"*Iron Chef*," Lee said.

"What?" Caroline said at the same time Drew did. They glanced at each other, startled.

She saw his glance travel further down, consideringly, along the length of her bare legs.

Hmm . . .

"Hugely popular show," Lee said. "We want to try something similar here. Only it'll be an all-day thing. A team thing. Teams pitted against one another. A cook-off. Ratings through the roof."

Drew leaned forward, resting his elbows on his knees. "You want us to compete?" he asked.

"Yes," Lee said. "No. Competition, yes. But not against each other."

"Separately?" Caroline asked. Sometimes it was hard to get Lee to express a full idea, and you had to coax it out of him. She'd learned what kind of questions to ask to get a successful response. Mostly.

"No."

This time when Caroline glanced at Drew, both their expressions conveyed their dismay. Then his changed to something more considering. His eyes narrowed thoughtfully.

This couldn't be good.

She uncrossed and re-crossed her legs. Drew's gaze was riveted.

"As a team," Lee said. "You two against an amateur team. Found a couple, husband and wife. Real whizzes in the kitchen."

"You want us to cook with amateurs?" Drew asked, breaking out of his reverie, obviously having missed part of the plan.

"Not with them. Against them. Two teams, competing."

"I understand the idea of a competition, Lee," Caroline said in her most placating voice, "but wouldn't it make more sense to put us on opposing teams?"

Lee shook his balding head. "Pros against amateurs. Plus demographics indicate viewers want to see both of you. Team thing. *Survivor*."

Caroline doubted Lee had ever seen a single episode of *Survivor*. But she understood what he was getting at. Teams, but with the members still clashing.

Who would get voted out of the kitchen?

Drew muttered an invective under his breath, so low that Lee couldn't hear it. Caroline could, though, and for the briefest flashes of moments, they were synchronized, in complete agreement.

It wouldn't last.

Soon, Caroline had a plan. It was a good plan, it was an evil plan, and if she pulled it off, she'd have her ratings back.

She put the plan into action the day before the actual show. Although they were going for an *Iron Chef* feel, with a studio-supplied surprise ingredient for each course, the teams were allowed to meet in advance to plan what other ingredients to bring.

Drew had suggested meeting at a café, but she'd proposed her apartment instead.

Her living room was already decorated with exotic, Middle Eastern-looking furnishings, plump pillows covered with soft sari silks, and lush, jewel-toned fabrics covering the walls. She made the room even more seductive for the occasion with scented candles and a bouquet of hypnotically perfumed Stargazer lilies. Some low, sultry Middle-Eastern music murmured and flowed through hidden speakers.

She dressed to suit the mood, in a silk camisole embroidered with shisha mirrors and bright patterns, a short black velvet skirt and stilettos. Not that she planned to seduce him, oh no. She just wanted him to start thinking about the possibility.

As soon as he showed up at her door, though, she realized the plan's fatal flaw: namely, she couldn't stop thinking about the possibilities either.

Drew seemed to fill the space. Every time she turned around, his long legs seemed to be in her way. His smell – not just aftershave but the underlying warm smell that was uniquely his – was inescapable. The candle flickering on a side table cast a shadowed light that accented his cheekbones and eyes.

Did she want to win or did she want to drag him to bed?

It was a shame it had to be an either-or question, but the parts of her that were voting for jumping him – and why bother getting as far as the bed – weren't the ones Caroline trusted to guide her career. There were always other men (although, as her body hastened to remind her, none recently that had the visceral appeal of Drew Benjamin). But there was only one cable station in Peaveyville.

And room for only one cooking show.

"Cucumbers," she said suddenly, hoping to catch him off-base. Judging from his expression, she succeeded. "As one of our ingredients, I mean. I saw the most gorgeous cucumbers at the farmer's market today. Thick, firm, perfectly straight. I had to pick some up – just couldn't resist." She gave what she hoped was a catlike smile.

"I've never been sure what to do with cukes." Drew realized what he was saying just too late to catch it. "Other than pickles or salad," he continued, evidently hoping that if he rooted the conversation firmly in recipes, he'd regain control. "You can't grill them."

Perfect. "Leave the cucumbers to me, Drew. I know exactly what to do with a cucumber." She leaned forward as she said that, giving him a glimpse down the shadowy front of her camisole and a whiff of her warm amber perfume. "I'll leave the figs to you."

"Figs?" he echoed, his eyes fixed on the shadowed curves under the silk.

She pitched her voice at a purr. "Don't you ever go anywhere but the meat market? It's fig season and I got us a case of soft . . . plump . . . juicy ones." If he only knew how closely that described the condition of her own "fig", they'd never get through the conversation.

As it was, he was leaning closer to her, looking like he was considering a kiss.

If Caroline let him, she'd lose everything. She sat back, crossing her ankles decorously in an attempt to remind herself to behave. "I bet you could grill figs and make a relish with them," she suggested. "Maybe Middle Eastern spices and Aleppo pepper."

They both thought of the implications of hot, spicy figs at the same moment and looked away from each other.

Maybe this plan wasn't foolproof.

Drew stood up and stretched. She could see his muscles rippling under his tight T-shirt. Once the play of muscles stopped distracting her, Caroline could see why he was restless. The fly of his jeans looked uncomfortably tight, and she liked the look of what was outlined against the straining fabric.

Definitely not a foolproof plan, but if she could keep her cool while making him lose his, it could still work.

It had to work. This was war, not sex.

"Yeah," he said too quickly, "fig relish. And melons are in season too. I saw some nice casabas . . ."

He looked at her cleavage again, turned red, and looked away. Caroline would be the first to admit her breasts were more the size of peaches, but the old joke was inescapable.

"Leave the meat to me," he muttered. "I can handle meat."

"So can I," she riposted.

Another long, breathless pause.

"Dessert?" he asked.

Oh, the places they could go with that thought! "Peach tart." She smiled as she said it. "With cream."

She couldn't be sure in the flickering candlelight, but it looked like he flushed.

The thick silence that followed that was broken by Drew adding, "I think we've got a good start. I've got stuff to get into marinade, so, uh, maybe I should go."

Oh, he was definitely riled up, all right. Caroline fell back on the overstuffed cushions and let out a long breath in her suddenly empty-feeling apartment.

The problem was, no matter how hard she tried to focus on

saving her show, she kept coming around to the same issue: She was riled up, too.

Curse him!

Caroline arrived at the studio early the next morning dressed to kill. Her bright turquoise knit dress was short enough that anyone with blood flowing in their veins would wonder what colour her underwear was – or if she were wearing any. (She was, but the lace low cut bikini did more to accent her ass than hide it.) The dress's halter top bared her shoulders, but was otherwise quite decorous – from the front.

The back view was another story. Her back was exposed to below the waist, low enough that if she moved just right, she flashed a hint of butt cleavage.

She always kept her strawberry-blonde hair pulled back in the kitchen. Usually she wore it in a ponytail, but today she'd gone for an updo, sophisticated, but with soft curls falling artfully out.

The viewers wouldn't see that it revealed the dragonflies tattooed on the back of her neck. At first glance, the tattoo was innocuous enough, pretty, delicate insects in shades of blue and green.

On second glance, you realized they were mating.

The audience couldn't see them . . . but Drew would.

Her only regret was the shoes. Stilettos weren't practical when she was going to be on her feet all day. The flat Indian-style sandals decorated with turquoise and coral went well with the outfit, but they didn't work nearly as well as weaponry.

When she sashayed into the kitchen, though, it was pretty clear no one was looking at her shoes.

Drew leaned forward for a closer look as she walked past him.

Their amateur opponents seemed just as fascinated. Ally and Stephen Jarvis could best be described as cute geeks: she was tall and angular, not conventionally pretty, but blessed with a charming smile and a perfect cocoa complexion. He was white, about six inches shorter and heavyset, with the air and fashion sense of someone who did something obscure with software. And both of them seemed to like what they were seeing, a lot.

Good. Drew was her real concern here, not the amateurs, but distracting them was a bonus. If she and Drew won the contest *and* she made Drew look like a fool, all the better.

At 9:45 a.m., the opponents shook hands and took their places at opposite sides of the kitchen. Except her real opponent was on her side.

At 10 a.m., the cameras began to roll and a studio employee came in with the secret ingredient for the appetizer course: asparagus.

While the amateurs consulted frantically, Drew said, "Prosciutto, asparagus, melon and figs. Classic. Only we grill the asparagus and figs."

"I like my asparagus . . . raw." Caroline picked up a stalk and began toying at the tip with her tongue, staring into his eyes.

"Are you trying to kill me?" he demanded sotto voce.

"What's that French expression? *La petite morte?*" She plunged the asparagus deep into her mouth, pursing her lips around it, then retrieved it, intact.

"Stop teasing me," he said, and then raised his voice to add, "Start splitting the figs. The other's team's already cooking."

"I bet I could get you cooking in no time, Drew," she whispered. But one glance at the Jarvises confirmed that it was time to get to work.

Nevertheless, she made a point of applying walnut oil (to protect the fruit on the grill) with her fingers instead of a brush, leaving the pink flesh moist, shiny, and more suggestive than ever.

This cost them half a fig. When the camera was trained on the Jarvises' frantic preparations, Drew picked up one of the fruit halves and ran his tongue along it, his gaze never leaving hers.

Caroline clenched inside, imagining him doing that to her.

Dammit. Not only was he on to her game, he was playing back with her – and rather effectively. That would make things a bit more difficult, but she could handle it.

She could handle it. Think about *Cooking With Caroline*. Think about not being usurped.

Somehow, they managed to finish their appetizer course without too many more incidents, although they seemed to brush against each other a lot. Caroline was doing it on purpose, but after a while she questioned whether she was doing it to distract Drew (who was fumbling the food quite a bit, although to his credit he hadn't yet dropped anything) or to enjoy the jolt of desire that zinged her whenever she touched him.

Purely an added benefit, that zing. She refused—refused! – to let it distract her.

The Jarvises had made an asparagus frittata. The judges pronounced it tasty, but it lost to the pros' offering partly on the grounds of visual appeal. The asparagus stalks were arranged poking into tunnels of pink proscuitto or laid out on top of gleaming, darker pink figs with heat-blackened skins, the plate accented with thin crescent moons of pale-green melon.

"Very sensual," one judge proclaimed, winking at Caroline.

Lee grabbed Caroline before they headed back for the next segment. "The phones are ringing off the hook!" he proclaimed gleefully.

"Who's winning?"

"It's weird. No one wants to pick a winner. Everyone's saying they love watching you and Drew interact. Well, except for the old guy who said you were both disgusting."

She chuckled and headed back to the set, swaying her hips so Drew, who was behind her, got an eyeful.

The secret ingredient for the next round was shrimp. "Predictable!" they heard Stephen Jarvis pooh-pooh. The couple's consultation was hushed, but Caroline thought she overheard an argument ensuing about the merits of garlic.

"We could do your shrimp kebabs," Drew suggested. "That's a great recipe. Or something Cajun or Southwestern. I can whip up a dry rub in no time."

She shook her head, in part to dispel images implanted by *whip* and *rub*. "Talk about predictable! That's exactly what the judges will expect from us. We have to think of something different."

"Japanese. A cold noodle dish with shrimp and seaweed and . . . something else. I'm not the Asian fusion expert – what do you think?" He bowed gallantly. Oh, oh, look at him trying to sway the audience to his side. Bastard!

"Cucumbers!"

Suddenly Drew looked less enthusiastic about his idea. "Not cucumbers, Caroline. Please, not cucumbers."

The studio audience tittered.

"But they're a classic Japanese ingredient. And wait until you see my way with a cuke, gorgeous!"

He tried to look away when she held up two cucumbers, both perfect specimens. Okay, he was going to play it that way? Fine.

She turned to the audience, leaning on the work counter that separated the stage from the seating area, and held up both cucumbers. Batting her eyes, she asked, "What do *you* think: short and thick or long and slender?"

The audience hooted and applauded, and she laughed along with them. That's right, get 'em on her side.

What the viewers saw was her being friendly and charming.

What Drew saw was her arching her back and presenting herself as if asking to be taken from behind.

She bit back a grin of triumph when Drew's voice cracked. "I'll get the rice noodles soaking while you, uh, work on those."

He moved behind her. To the viewers, it looked like he was just reaching around to grab the bag of thick rice noodles on the counter, maybe being a little playful, standing a little too close to get her back for the cucumber jokes.

They wouldn't know that that he whispered in her ear, "How about long *and* thick?" or that he pressed against her, pushing his cock into the crack of her ass.

From what she could tell, "long and thick" was an apt description.

And it would be so, so very easy for him to slip it deep inside her. All he'd have to do was unzip, raise her minuscule skirt, nudge her drenched panties aside. He could reach around and toy with her nipples through the dress. He'd start slow, with long, even strokes that would nudge her higher, then he'd gradually increase the speed until he was diving into her, filling her . . .

. . . and getting them both fired and probably banned from TV anywhere in the country except certain pay-per-view channels.

Caroline took a deep breath and a determined step to the right. Thank God nobody could see how her legs trembled as she did. She began carving cucumber flowers, first cautiously, not trusting her fingers. But as she pulled herself together, she wielded the knife with a certain vengeful glee.

She really couldn't say how they got through making the cold noodle dish. Every time she tried to focus on the preparations, her mind wandered back to the feel of Drew's cock pressed up against her – and her body followed right along, rewarding her with more deep, aching shivers.

It probably wasn't a factor, but this time, although the judges had good things to say about the Japanese dish, the Jarvises' Spanish-style shrimp, hot peppers, and garlic in olive oil got the nod.

"Remember, everyone," the announcer said, "This is an all-Saturday marathon. We need to give our talented chefs a short break, though, so for the next half hour we'll be showing highlights from your favourite episodes of *Cooking With Caroline* and *Warning: Man Cooking*, as voted on by you, the viewing audience."

"I *have* to get some fresh air," Ally Jarvis proclaimed, and the geek couple wandered off hand in hand.

Caroline got herself a bottle of water from the tiny fridge backstage. "Want one?" she asked Drew, who'd followed her.

"Thanks," he said with a nod, and she tossed the bottle at him.

She proceeded to do a series of yoga stretches to work out the kinks in her back from the marathon session of standing.

Drew spilled water down his front. Which was probably a good thing for him, since the bulge in his jeans could use an icing-down.

Dammit. The mental picture lodged in her mind of her wielding a pastry bag, drawing curlicues on his erect penis and then following the swirls with her tongue, tasting sweet powdered sugar and salty precome.

A taste sensation not found on any menu.

That was it. She had to hide in the bathroom, bring herself

off. Clutching her water, she turned to flee, and nearly slammed into Lee.

"Both of you. Here," the station manager said.

For a flecting moment, in her aroused, fanciful state, she thought Lee meant she and Drew should do it right there. Luckily she figured out he simply meant he wanted to talk to both of them.

"Phones are ringing off the hook," Lee said. "Audience is loving this. Real chemistry between you two. Who knew? Bonuses for you both. Now, back to work."

Caroline bit back a groan as he shooed them back towards the soundstage. No quickie masturbation in the bathroom for her. At this rate, by the end of the show she'd have to wring out her panties.

"Yeah, who knew?" Drew whispered in her ear, his breath fluttering the loose tendrils of hair.

The lights went up on stage, and she had no chance to reply.

They settled into their places in the kitchen, standing far closer to one another than was really necessary.

Caroline tried to concentrate, focus on making an amazing dessert that would be a feast for all the senses. But the heat of Drew's body so close to her own and the way her insides felt as hot and sweet as molten chocolate whenever he brushed against her – and he was doing so a lot – blanked every recipe she knew from her mind.

The announcer came on. "Because our chefs have been performing at such a high level, we're throwing out a special challenge. There are two secret ingredients for the dessert round: raspberries and rosewater. And sorry, you're not allowed to sprinkle the berries with the rosewater and call it a day!"

Caroline turned to Drew and smiled. "I know we'd been talking about a . . ." she paused to give the words extra significance ". . . peach tart with whipped cream." She winked at the audience, admitting they were in on the joke. "But it looks like we need to be flexible." She hoped the word would call to mind her yoga poses. "Do you have any ideas about the best way to handle raspberries?"

"Delicately. Very delicately. More often than not, I like to nibble them plain." He slurred a bit, so nibble sounded almost like nipple, but not so much so that it would get him in trouble with Lee. "But I bet we could do something with them to give the peaches a lovely rosy colour."

Then he gave her a searing smile. Her nipples felt as red and plump and tender as the berries heaped in a basket on their counter. She didn't dare to glance down, but she suspected they were popping out through the fabric of her dress, clearly visible to anyone in the studio and probably to the TV audience.

What she wouldn't give to have Drew's sensuous mouth closed around one of those ripe peaks now, suckling at her, drawing out her arousal until she was dizzied and begging for more.

Breathe. Remember to breathe – and to make sure Drew, too, was distracted. "Maybe use some of them for a glaze," she said breathily. "Nothing makes a peach look prettier than a little moist sheen. And for a topping, how about a nice, warm crème anglaise?" She let the words sink in, watched Drew's eyes widen and darken.

She'd take his "crème anglaise" in her "peach" any day and she could tell he was thinking something similar.

The whir of a food processor brought her back to reality. The Jarvises were already at work, grinding nuts from the sound of it. (A linzertorte variation with fresh fruit? She should have been paying more attention to them, dammit!)

"Flavour it with rosewater," Drew added. His voice sounded a little shaky. "Sounds good."

"You start on the peaches and raspberries, Drew. I'll get to work stirring up the crème. It takes a little time for it to . . . thicken."

As she passed him, heading to the refrigerator for cream and eggs, she cupped his ass briefly under the cover of the counter, just long enough to feel it was as firm and delicious as she'd suspected.

His sigh wasn't loud enough for the microphones to pick up, but she heard it.

He got her back, though, as he started to split the peaches. "This peach is absolutely perfect," he sighed. "So juicy and succulent, with just the slightest hint of fuzz. I wish I could eat it right now!"

Even if she hadn't been sensitised already, that remark, in that tone of voice, would have zinged directly between her legs and gotten her speculating. As it was, she almost spilled heavy cream onto the floor, lost in a vision of Drew's tongue deftly playing over her slick lower lips and swirling in on the throbbing spot where she needed it most.

Then she glanced over at their opponents. The Jarvises, lacking such distractions, were hard at work and their dessert looked well underway. Time to focus!

As they busied themselves with making the rich, rosewater-infused custard sauce, turning some of the raspberries into a delicate red glaze and basting it over the split peaches before sticking them under the broiler, the banter and surreptitious touches continued. A brush here. An innuendo there. Eye contact that lasted longer than was strictly necessary.

By the time the peaches came out from the broiler looking perfect enough for a glossy food magazine, Caroline's legs felt weak from frustrated desire.

Caroline carefully spooned the crème anglaise into the hollow of each peach.

Drew, not to be outdone, took one intact raspberry and placed it strategically on each peach, placing himself between the dessert and the camera so the results wouldn't immediately go out to the viewers.

They looked at the dessert and then at each other. "Too much," Caroline mouthed, trying not to burst into obvious laughter.

Before the camera could focus on the erotic creation, Drew sprinkled the remaining raspberries more casually over the plate and Caroline swirled the creamy sauce. Now it might classify as food-porn, but it was no longer porn made from food.

Both of them still stifling chuckles and giving each other amused, but heated glances, they presented their dish to the judges.

"Ladies and gentlemen, we have . . . a tie!" the announcer said. "The judges are evenly divided between both teams. We didn't make provisions for a sudden-death round, so we're going to turn it over to you, the home viewers. Call the station and vote for your favourite team and their recipes. One call per viewer, please. We'll show you some more top highlights from *Cooking with Caroline* and *Warning: Man Cooking*, and we'll return in fifteen minutes with a verdict. Get those dialling fingers going!"

The station was so small that there was only one dressing room, a tiny box of a space with just enough room for a short couch, clothing rack, and vanity table and stool. Caroline made a beeline for it.

Not fast enough. She didn't get the door all the way closed before Drew pushed it open, and shut it behind him.

If the room had seemed small before, now it was downright tight. Drew's lanky frame took up a lot of space – and Caroline's libido filled in the cracks.

"Here's the thing," Drew said. "I know that you've been coming on to me to distract me, to mess me up."

Her mother had always told her she was too competitive. "Boys won't like you if you always have to win," she said.

Well, the boys had liked Caroline just fine, although admittedly they all got along better when the boys weren't trying to get the same things Caroline wanted – like the top cooking show on WPVL.

Her mother could be right about many things, but she'd been as wrong about boys as she was about cooking. Her idea of tacos included Velveeta "cheese", and she'd layered her lasagne with cottage cheese rather than ricotta. A healthy self-preservation instinct had driven Caroline to learn how to cook.

"Fact is, I respect that," Drew continued. "It was a slick move. It almost worked. Maybe it did work. But here's the thing."

He stepped closer to her.

That same self-preservation instinct was failing her now. She backed up until her knees hit the arm of the sofa. She caught herself before she fell – but, oh, she wanted to fall, and pull him down on top of her.

"What I need to know is if you're feeling what I'm feeling," Drew said, his voice husky. "If the audience is right and the chemistry is real. Because as much as I like cooking against you, right now I'd rather be cooking with you. Figs and asparagus and cucumbers and peaches . . . Licking and sucking and—"

The hell with it. They weren't on stage any more. The cook-off was over.

Caroline grabbed the front of Drew's T-shirt and dragged him down for a kiss.

There was no time for subtleties, and no need for them, either. They'd been enjoying foreplay for hours already. Even as they kissed, his hands were behind her neck, unhooking the halter top. He dragged the front of her dress down and filled his large hands with her breasts, catching her peaked nipples between his fingers and rolling them, lightly pinching them, murmuring something about raspberries, until her thighs turned to jelly.

She might have slid bonelessly to the ground if he hadn't insinuated his hand between her thighs and caught her in a most intimate way. His eyes widened, no doubt because he'd discovered how drenched her panties were. He hiked her dress up and she tugged the French-cut lace briefs down and he pulled them the rest of the way and she kicked out of them.

She popped the buttons on his jeans. No underwear for him. His cock was smooth and curved. She swiped her thumb across the bead of moisture at its tip, and brought it to her mouth.

He groaned.

She thought they'd make good use of the sofa, but instead he spun her around to face the dressing table. She was stunned by her reflection in the mirror, tumbling-down hair and dilated pupils and well-kissed, swollen lips.

"I've been dying to do this all day, ever since you leaned over the damn counter," he growled in her ear.

She spread her legs and wiggled her hips, and he needed no further invitation. He sank into her easily, her inner walls plump and slick with her own juices.

Oh, God, so good to be filled! Her eyes fluttered shut.

"No," Drew said. "Open your eyes. Watch what happens when I fuck you."

She tried, she really did. But with every thrust he sank deeper and she pushed back harder, and an orgasm began to build, an ache deep inside her that expanded and grew and burned until it threatened to incinerate her. Bracing herself against the vanity with one hand, she reached between her legs with the other. His cock slid across her knuckles as she found her clit.

The fire flashed and consumed her. She gritted her teeth to keep herself from screaming as she came. The walls were thin enough that they would have heard her on stage. As she keened deep in her throat, she heard him gasp her name, a short thrust for each syllable as he found his own release.

In the mirror, they both looked rather stunned.

He toyed with her breasts. "Casabas melons, indeed," he murmured.

She chuckled, enjoying the feel of him twitching inside her as she moved.

"Caroline? Drew?"

It was Lee.

"Where the hell did you go? We're on air in thirty seconds!"

She'd never heard Lee speak in sentences that long or panicked. In a flurry of motion, she and Drew separated. He tucked his still-wet, still-half-hard cock back into his jeans. She grabbed a towel and swiped between her legs.

"Where are my panties?"

"Who knows?"

They raced for the stage. His shirt was untucked, and her hair wild. The audience roared their approval, clapping and whistling and stamping their feet.

Stephen Jarvis glared. Ally Jarvis did, too, although she also looked a little longingly at Drew. Or maybe Caroline.

The announcer tried to spread out the results, but the audience was having none of it. They started yelling all over again when they heard Caroline and Drew had won.

* * *

And oh, how they'd won.

Once they were able to escape from the studio, they ran the only stop sign in town on the way to Caroline's house, where they spent the rest of the night playing with food. In bed.

On Monday, Lee called them both into his office and laid out a proposal for a new show: *In the Kitchen with Drew and Caroline*.

"With Caroline and Drew," Caroline countered.

"*Hot in the Kitchen*," Drew suggested.

"Yes!" Lee said.

A month later, the show was syndicated.

Some episodes could not be aired in the Bible Belt.

The Magician

Andrea Miller

The Magician stood in front of his makeshift table, three silver cups on its surface. And he held up a red bead, rolling it between his thumb and index finger. Then he slipped it under the cup on the right. "Keep track of the bead," he told the crowd of gray men doling out their francs.

The Magician moved the three cups, switching their positions again and again but slowly enough that I knew – that everyone knew – the bead was under the cup that was now in the middle. He touched that cup, bringing it to the exact center of the table. "Is the bead under here?" he asked rhetorically. "Or is it under this one or this?" he continued, touching the other cups.

The first to play was a man with a thick mustache and he, of course, picked up the middle cup. "A winner," the Magician declared, giving him his winnings, but after that the players were not so lucky. Yes, after that, the Magician always won and so at the end of every round he raised his shirttails (un-tucked) and stuffed the pockets of his jeans with dirty bills. And in this way I caught a glimpse of his belt – green-tinted snake skin that matched both his cowboy boots and his eyes. Gorgeous eyes. Yes, the Magician was handsome, or perhaps beautiful would be the better word. But there was something strange and ambiguous about his looks. He had broad shoulders, a sprinkle of stubble, full sensual lips and breasts like rosebuds under his shirt. And I didn't doubt that he knew real magic. After all, when the police officer came around the corner, he made his table, his cups and his customers disappear without a trace.

Now we were alone, even the click of cop boots was receding. The Magician leaned against the brick wall behind him and looked me up and down. I came closer. "Are you a man or a woman?" I demanded. But he shrugged. "I'm beyond all that. Are you playing or what?"

"That last trick was shoddy. Don't you have anything else up your sleeve?"

"Oh, I know lots of tricks." The Magician smiled, confident and sly. "Follow me."

We walked one block over broken glass on a cracked sidewalk and we went into a hotel where one has a choice of how to pay: by the night or by the hour. Then in the room the Magician shed his clothes – shed them like a snake sheds his skin, like he never again intended to cover himself. And, though I was fully dressed, he just stood there in all his unusual splendor: his skinny colt-like legs, his slender throat, his cock rising out of his slit.

"You're a hermaphrodite," I breathed, feeling my own slit cream.

"Intersexual," he corrected. "But are you gonna suck my magic wand or what?"

I knelt in front of him and put the whole of his rod in my mouth. Yes, he was small like a ten-year-old boy so it was easy to have my lips wrapped around his tiny balls and circled around the root of him while at the same time his piss hole tickled at my throat. And I sucked him savagely – like I was going to bite his prick off and consume it – but I also sucked with adoration, veneration. "You have the most beautiful cock," I murmured, my mouth full. "You have the most lovely cunt."

The Magician's cunt hole was shallow and tight – half formed by usual standards yet perfect in its way. I jammed my baby finger in and felt his slick pussy walls clamp down on my knuckle. He was getting close now. I could feel it in the way he thrust his hips up into my face, how he was shoving his tiny cock as far down my throat as he could. I shook with anticipation, I wanted so badly to see him come. Yes, *see*. I spit him out and gripped his little rod between the pads of my thumb and two fingers. "Come for me," I urged, yanking on him. One stroke, two, three. And then come he did. His jizm flew from him like a dove and fell to the ground like rain. Yes, he came torrents.

Most people, in moments like this, flush or pant like a dog but the Magician just smiled. A pearly spurt had landed on my cheek and he seemed to like me dripping with him, being a dirty girl for him. With his hand, he wiped my face and then slowly, as if he were thinking of something else, he rubbed his hands together until the jizm sank into his skin. And when he finally opened his hands, I saw that cradled in his palm he now had a knife. The Magician winked.

Perhaps, mesmerized, I was following his silent orders. Or perhaps, after I saw that glint of metal, I laid myself on the bed because that's what my cunt wanted more than anything else. But I do know I felt dazed – like I was in a thick enchanted stupor, like I was deliciously helpless as the Magician lopped off every button of my blouse and sliced through the crotch of my loose pants. Yes, he even cut open my panties.

There were mirrors on the ceiling and in their reflection it seemed my pussy grinned, then grinned wider as the Magician stroked its lips – his fingers cool and slender. I tipped my cunt up to invite him deeper and he obliged, sinking his hand into my hole, though so slowly and in such a way that I just wanted more. With his other hand, the Magician rolled my clit like he had earlier rolled the red bead and my clit turned red like that, hard as glass like that. I bucked my hips, and came so close to coming, but the Magician reined me in by pausing, by ignoring the strangled gasp that came from somewhere deeper than my throat. Yes, he paused and he pulled a coin out of my pussy – a coin warm and covered with my juice as if it had always been buried in me. Like this wasn't a trick. Then he dipped back in and pulled out another.

"Clean it with your tongue," he demanded. And I did. Until it gleamed.

Coyote Blues

Susan DiPlacido

Pedal-steel guitars and dusty windshields on heavy-duty pick-ups that're actually used for work and not just for cruising to look big and cool. Days of wind and sun and arid sand so thick you could drown in it. Washed out skies and cracking desert – everywhere you look is another variation on the colors of rust stretching out in gaping hunger. It's a sight that makes words like "forever" seem nearly comprehensible. A forever of crimson, umber, and amber. But it's not a muddied landscape. Mud would imply water, but there's not much of that. Least, not that you can see, or dive into, or ever really clean off with. Soon as you're out of the shower, the inescapable dust starts to cling before you're even toweled off.

Or so it seems to me.

Instead of blue or crystal clear, the liquids round here match the earthen, sun-drenched hues of the land. Brown whiskey, yellow beer, and gold tequila. And it's sucked down and sweated out by men in bootleg Levi's and Wranglers. Not stonewashed or sandblasted or otherwise altered from the factory. No – just the heavy deep indigo and red tabs from the factory that wash out and settle down on their own. They stride with loose, loping gaits – easy and deliberate. Big belt buckles, bigger hats, straight backs, leathered faces, sinewy arms and slow drawls. And the boots on all of 'em. Lord, the boots. And the way those men squint. They squint even past sundown, if they're looking up at the impossible night-time sky.

I don't blame 'em for squinting up at that darkness.

That black yawning chasm that would seem unbearably dreadful if it wasn't broken up with the litter of glittering stars. I'd never seen anything like it before. The vision was always framed or broken in some manner so that evidence of mankind would cut into the awesome, intimidating arena overhead. But that doesn't happen out here. You look up and it stretches beyond you, around you. That's when you realize it's a vastness that goes forever – encircling, encompassing. Encroaching. Infinity, looping around and looming tight.

That's when the eerie howls are most welcome. Now they are, at least. That spine-tingling, hair-raising, bad-mojo, lonesome wail connects somehow – pierces through the magnitude of the impossible illusion of it all.

First time I heard it, I sat up and shivered. I was scared enough about the scorpions and rattlesnakes. Now here was a bigger, bloodthirsty predator. I whispered, "Wolves."

Wes corrected me. "Coyotes," he said. "Don't got wolves 'round here, darlin'." He didn't laugh at my mistake.

I wasn't settled. Different name, same matted fur, same drooling fangs.

"Won't harm people none," he told me.

"But . . . the horses?"

"Them neither. Make 'em skittish, that's about all. Reckon we might lose coupla heads o' sheep tonight though." Then he smiled, but I knew he wasn't joking. That was his way of soothing. It worked. Same as everything else he did worked, even though it shouldn't have. If it didn't, I wouldn't have been there that night. Or any of the nights.

He didn't exactly sweep me off my feet. Nevertheless, it was the same night I met him that my Manolos were kicked off and sprawled next to his Tony Lamas. That was in the city. That was before I knew that he was the real deal. He and a friend strode up to a blackjack table I was playing on. I was working, deep in concentration on the count, had it in my favor. That's what I'm good at – Watching cards, figuring odds, and keeping counts to make money. I had the table to myself, just how I like it. He sidled up beside me, his friend next him. Even in my tunnel-vision absorption, I noticed him. Tall, dark, rugged. Handsome. Serene.

I ignored him and focused on the cards. I doubled my bet because I knew the pretty ten cards were headed my way. His friend played and fumbled by trying to pick up the cards. I didn't reprimand him – the dealer took care of that. I just swept my eyes across the table and did the math, satisfied as I looked at his hard seventeen, my hard nineteen, and the dealer's hard fifteen. But then Wes's pal fucked it up with a rookie mistake. He took a hit on his seventeen. He pulled a jack, which busted him. Worse, the dealer pulled a six to beat me. I cursed as the dealer took my chips. Disgusted, I got up to leave. That's when Wes caught my eye again. He was just placidly watching me.

"Where you goin', ma'am?" his friend asked me.

"Don't need tourists fucking up my game," I told him. A thousand bucks – that's what his mistake had cost me.

"Well, it's just a game," his friend said. I later found out he was a ranch hand of Wes's. They were out here for his bachelor party. Cliché, yes. Such is Vegas.

"It's a game involving money," I told him. "And you just cost me a bunch of it with that bonehead move. If you hadn't hit that seventeen, the dealer would've busted and we'd have both won."

"You got the disposition of a rattlesnake, don't you, miss? I didn't mean any harm to you. I apologize, but you don't have to be so nasty."

I was unnerved. Not only by the kid's gosh-shucks, contrite demeanor and my own embarrassing bitchiness, but mostly because of how Wes just sat there. Not slack-jawed stupid, and not awe-struck lascivious either. Just smoldering . . . Smoldering.

Finally, he spoke. He was talking to his buddy, but he fixed his eyes on me. "Don't think she's nasty so much as spirited, Ben."

It extorted an apology from me. "Sorry. You're right, it's not your fault. Enjoy the table."

Then Wes stood up and in his soft drawl and husky voice introduced himself and insisted on making it up to me.

I declined.

A half-hour later, I was still teaching them how to play blackjack. And, four hours after that, my shoes were getting acquainted with Wes's boots. And, a week after that, I was shivering and listening to coyotes howl deep into the night. In the morning, I woke to the sound of a gunshot. I'd never heard that before either, but I was pretty sure of what it was.

I'd heard six more rounds go off by the time I ran outside and found Wes with a shotgun. When he handed it to me, I nearly dropped it. I'd never held any gun before, let alone a shotgun. They didn't look so heavy in movies. Wes had a chew in, which I didn't mind 'cause he didn't hassle me about smoking. He spat, and just said, "Don't pull the trigger. Squeeze it." Then he nodded to some empty bottles of Cuervo about twenty yards away.

"The hell is all this about?" I asked him.

"Coyotes," is all he said.

"You're gonna go shoot coyotes?"

"I'd be teachin' you to shoot if I was fixin' to do it?"

"Wes. Shit. You want 'em gone, you shoot 'em," I told him.

"Rita. Shiiit," he drawled and spat. "I wasn't the one up all night."

"They really don't bother you?"

"They're a nuisance I tolerate."

"Oh. It's legal? To kill 'em, I mean?"

"You really care?"

"Wes . . ."

"It's legal."

I listened, did as he said, and then squeezed. Ready as I thought I was, I still stumbled from the kickback and the butt cracked into my shoulder. The reverbs stung my ears. And I'd missed, by a lot. I put the gun down. That night, I kept my eyes closed and stayed still when the howling started.

It was only four nights after that that the howls stopped, or at least I stopped hearing them. That was the night after Wes brought in the new stallion. For me. He said I needed a horse to get around and explore on my own. I said I'd be happy using his Jeep. He smiled silently, smoldering. There was nothing else to do around there anyhow, so I hung by the fence as the stallion grazed and freaked out. Grazed and freaked out. No one went near him. Wes laughed every time I ran away from the fence when the horse'd go on a bucking jag. At that time, he was letting me ride other horses around. I knew he had plenty of horses I could ride anytime I wanted. This was more about him showing off to me than anything else, so I indulged him.

After four days of that nonsense, Wes saddled him, or tried to. That mustang damn near kicked him in the head, and I damn near picked up that shotgun again I was so scared. Those were long days. Wes seemed amused. I was impressed. He was unfazed by the braying and struggling, content to let the ruddy dust settle in the slight crevices of his face. He kept egging me nearer, somehow convincing me to do more and get closer while the sun sizzled down on us. But those nights were quiet. I didn't hear the intimidating stomp of hooves or the whinnies of objection. I didn't hear those longing howls. I'd only hear Wes's heavy breaths in my ear and feel his wet kisses as he'd do things to my body the same way he did everything else – easy and deliberate. I told myself that's why I was here, only because the way he rode horses was nothing compared to how he rode me. Then, after, I'd just close my eyes, remember to forget about the awful, limitless sky overhead, and let my sore body go to sleep.

In the mornings, I'd wake up stiff and exhausted – feeling dusty, desiccated, and beaten before even climbing out of bed. But that only drove me harder. And, after a couple weeks, I got on that new mustang for a real ride. Wes'd been breaking him himself – getting on, getting thrown off. The horse was yielding – he was manageable for Wes now – he didn't get thrown anymore. I was scared, but Wes told me to stop being so full of shit and get up there. He threw me, of course, the horse did. But not right away. And it wasn't as bad as I expected. Wes was proud, I could tell. I named him that day. Loki. And that horse broke before I did. It wasn't a sudden change – took another couple weeks, actually. The bucks started to feel like undulations and his anger seemed to give way to spirit. Then he kept getting calmer and spooking less often until he stopped bucking altogether. And then he was mine.

A few nights after that, the coyotes came back, and I woke up to them. With Wes asleep, I went out to the stalls and found my boy Loki sleeping soundly, not the least bit bothered by the haunting calls.

I went back inside and nudged Wes awake. Didn't matter how sunworn, sore, or sleepy he was, he always woke up and obliged me, and that night was no exception. I couldn't tell right away if instead of pleasure it was out of pride or a feeling of obligation on his part. He wasn't moving quickly, his hands were barely roaming, and his kisses weren't devouring.

He just lay there, sprawled on his back, one hard-calloused hand brushing the hair off my neck and lazily rubbing my shoulder as I leaned over to him. Teasing kisses, I pulled my body on top of his but didn't straddle him, waiting to see if he was going to catch fire or not. He was hard already, but that wasn't unusual, and it wasn't all that telling. I wouldn't touch him there. Instead I kept my hands on his sides with our naked chests pressed together. I kissed him deeply, and he sighed. That's when I was pretty sure it wasn't out of pride or responsibility that he was obliging me.

I kissed a while longer but finally put my head down on his shoulder and nudged myself to his side. Just to make sure, I guess. It didn't take long. I was hoping it wouldn't. I was buzzing all over already, and if he'd've gone back to sleep and let it go, I probably would've had to wake him up again.

But he didn't roll over and go to sleep. Instead, he took hold of my wrists and rolled himself on top of me. Deep and hungry kisses right away, he hummed as our mouths met and before long that buzzing that I'd been feeling sparked and I was flush and fevered for him. I longed to touch his body all over. His lean stomach brushing against mine, all those sinewy muscles in his arms. But he kept my hands locked down near my head while he did the work with his body and mouth. He was teasing. Pressing his chest into mine, then undulating, rising up while pressing his hips into mine. He was rock hard, I was wet. And I was certain this was about a lot more than pride or feeling obligated. And probably about even more than pleasure. I didn't care. I wanted him.

I spread my legs and wrapped them around his waist, tried to force him down into me. I got him close, but not inside. Instead he was careful and controlled. Still holding my wrists, he kissed me deeply and slid his erection between my lips, gliding across my hot spot. Repeatedly. Repeatedly.

Lord, all that kissing, his hot breath. And that gliding, the rubbing of his dick against my clit. Friction and pressure and deliciously taunting rhythm. Wasn't long before I was panting and bucking. He obliged then and sped up, and when the pleasure got too intense and I started to shudder and come, that's when he shifted and plunged deep inside me. I was the one howling then.

I couldn't escape it. It was nearly overwhelmingly intense, I thought my heart was going to beat right out of my ribcage as I bucked wildly. Wes took it easy then. He stayed inside, still hard, still throbbing, but mercifully stopped thrusting. He still didn't release my wrists, but he did let me settle.

Once I'd calmed, he started again. The kissing stopped when the panting started and it wasn't long before we were all-out fucking. We usually moved a lot, but not that night. He kept my hands clamped down by my head and he stayed on top. When I tried to wiggle or thrust, Wes was having none of it. He set the pace, and he set it well. I didn't care – I was getting high again, getting close. The way he was driving into me I don't know how he was holding out so long. But I was starting to get an idea of exactly what this was really about.

That's when he released my hands and put his arms around me. Instinct, I guess it was, I put my arms around his neck and held him close. As high and hot as I was, I could still feel the details, like his sweat dripping down onto my neck, the rough stubble of his cheek scraping against mine, moist hot breath in my ear, the heat and silken steel of his chest pressed against my breasts, the muscles of his shoulders working and contracting under my hands, and that glorious frenzied fucking going on.

Everything I thought I knew about us changed when I gripped him tight inside, felt the start of another orgasm overtaking me and heard him whisper in my ear. Breathy and low. Urgent. Just my name. "Rita."

It pushed me over the edge.

He didn't stop calling my name and we didn't stop fucking. He called it louder, I shuddered, he thrust very fast, very hard.

And I said his name, called it out loud. "Wes."

He came too. I was clenched so tight around him I felt every spasm through his body, every spurt deep inside.

The day after that, I left for the first time.

I was out in the searing sun too long maybe. Or just pissed off about all the dirt everywhere, I got worried it was going to keep traveling up my sinuses and start to scratch into my brain. Maybe I needed a break from everything being a variation on the color of rust. Or, most likely, I had a jones for vodka instead of tequila. Maybe all that tequila was making me crazy. I never really cared for people before, but now I missed them. Or something. Then again, maybe those lonesome howls were just getting to be too much.

Whatever it was, when Wes came in for the evening, I told him I had to go.

"All right." He nodded.

Let me tell you, that really pissed me off. Honestly. I was geared for a fight anyhow, but I figured the son of a bitch would at least have the balls or pride to try and stop me.

But he didn't.

I went home. I went back to car-congested streets and high-reaching, tight-woven buildings built to the hilt to wash away the sand and natural dirty dust. To oscillating neon lights that bounce off hard concrete, all advertising and promoting. Selling and promoting money and sex. The home of money and sex. America's true heartland – Las Vegas. The aberration in the desert. The power of greed, nowadays, Incorporated. It's one big trick and mirage in this desert, and the illusion will never die because even though it's a paradise of sin, it's all shrouded in the most basic human grace. Hope.

These are the things I understand. Vices and logic. Sex and money.

The honks and clinks and shouts were a welcome relief. The sun pounded down, but man kept the balance with manufactured lakes and swimming pools. Clear and cool and blue, ready to dive in and able to wash away the last lingering remnants of dust. The closest I got to a cowboy was a fifty-foot tall neon one named Vegas Vic.

I gambled – that's my job. Sometimes high stakes, sometimes not. What mattered is that it had order, same as always. All I had to do was watch the cards come down, keep the running count, and then I knew what was likely to be coming next. I courted the tables, drank the vodka, and slept with the men. Normal men. Tourists I wouldn't have to see again. Men who'd yell back if I picked a fight. Men who'd lean close and crowd my space at the bar. Men who walked fast and spoke even faster. Men who couldn't fuck their way out of a paper bag.

And, deep in the coolest hours of the morning, when I was alone, the only sound I'd hear was the whir and hum of the air conditioner.

Eventually, I went back only because I felt guilty. I swear it's true. In those quiet hours before drifting off into numbness, I'd think of Wes and how lonely he had to be out there. The guilt gnawed until I went back to throw him a conciliatory break-up fuck. When I got back, he greeted me with a nod and just said, "Rita." Like he'd been expecting me for dinner. He opened the door and asked, "Comin' inside for a while?"

He didn't look heartbroken. He looked fine. He didn't need me. "No," I told him.

It was four weeks after that that I heard the coyotes for the first time during the day. Wes was out somewhere doing something. Work. He'd maybe tell me a few words about it later when he got home. I assumed it had something to do with hammering fences or rustling things around, or maybe even hog-tying a few things. Wasn't quite sure though. Anyhow, that's generally how the days had been going for the past month

– him off working during the day, while I'd been keeping busy cleaning up the ever-accumulating dust and cooking dinner. That was easy. Barbecue. Oh, I shit you not. Barbecue fucking ribs (short ribs, baby-back, beef, you name the rib, it got barbecued), barbecue chicken, grilled steaks, barbecue shrimp. I was happily rebelling against the feminist notions that it was exactly what I shouldn't be doing. To feel less girly, I'd go out and shoot some then. I got to the point where I shattered beyond recognition a dozen Cuervo bottles. Then I'd sometimes take a ride around the far perimeter of the house on Loki, the mustang I'd broken before I left. Or I'd try to get a tan, thinking I was getting darker only to realize it was just the dirt caking onto my skin. But I'd lay there in the thin breeze nonetheless, watching the sun turn the browns into brilliant oranges, then the orange into blazing red, then finally settle into a pink in the sky even more electric than the neon on Las Vegas Boulevard.

I was lying there, just like that, flat out in the midst of that great expanse, when I first heard the mournful call during the day. I chilled in the intense heat. I saw Loki freeze. I grabbed the shotgun, jumped on him, and rode home at a gallop.

That night, I asked Wes if he doesn't get lonely out here.

"No," is all he said.

"Never?" I pried.

"That's what I got you for," he said, smiled, and took a slug of beer.

"You don't *have* me," I informed him, pissed off.

"Okay, Rita," is all he said.

That night, when we went for a walk outside, I gazed up at the stars and swore I could almost see them crushing down around me. That great expanse of black smothering and cloaking all around us. I had to pull my hand away from his just to get enough space to breathe. I tried to calm myself by counting them. But I couldn't. That's what I do best in life – keep a count to create order, but I couldn't add up all them stars. Mercifully, later, when Wes fell asleep, the coyotes' call cut through the night. A temporal loop of beastly familiarity slicing through the inky dark.

I held on for a couple more weeks.

But then day got as bad as night. The dirt filled my nose and the lack of color glazed my eyes. The open, sun-bleached days wore away at me. Wes sensed the noose tightening, I guess. He took me out a couple times. I got to drink vodka in the saloons and honky-tonks. But all I heard was the whining slide guitar, or the crying pedal steel. Stetson hats and snakeskin boots were the dress clothes. Bolero ties. Big belt buckles. Everything was made of wood, which I just didn't understand. There weren't many damn trees around. I'd feel like a moron when my spike heels caught between the slats of the floor when we'd dance. I looked around at the other women. Sequined T-shirts and permed hair – with bangs and scrunchies to tie it back. Hats and boots.

A few other nights, we'd play poker with some of the guys, alternating between stud and hold-'em games. The only illumination was the nearby crackling glow of a bonfire, citronella candles, and the lonely neon of a bug zapper. But I always won, and I didn't take much joy or pride in it. Winning Ben's paycheck or Walt's drinking money didn't particularly hold a lot of satisfaction.

So, on a moonless night when I was having trouble breathing from the dirt clogged up in my sinuses, I sat up listening to the howls closing in and looked down at Wes stretched out next to me. I couldn't take those devilish howls any more. I pushed him 'til he woke up. He was not annoyed. Instead, he reached up and started soothing me. But I'd had enough of that, so I pushed him off and said, "I'm leaving, Wes."

Reedy-voiced, he went, "I figured that was comin'."

"I mean, I'm leaving now. Right now."

"All right then," was all he said.

"Don't you even wanna know why?" I was a little miffed he was so cavalier about this.

"I know why, Rita. Do what you need."

"You do not know why," I snapped. "If you knew why, you'd be more upset."

"So go on then, tell me why if you want."

"I'm leaving you," I explained, "because I have inner demons."

Wes laughed pretty good at that. I shit you not, I was furious. "The hell you laughin' at, Wes?"

"Horseshit," is all he said, still laughing.

"'Scuse me? You're saying my deep and tragic personal inner demons are horseshit?"

"No, Rita. I'm saying you're too full o' horseshit to have any room left for inner demons."

Well. I never. Honestly. "You used to say I was full of spirit, Wes. Now that things aren't going your way, I'm full of horseshit."

"That's right," he answered, still sort of laughing. "It's the same thing, darlin'. It's spirit when I find it appealing. Other times, when it's not so attractive, it's just plain horseshit."

In retrospect, I suppose I'm woman enough to admit that I was so furious because I knew he was right. Nevertheless, I left in quite a huff.

So I'm back in the city.

The clatter of coins in trays and hard-edged music and fast-walking people are all around. Exhaust fumes waft through the air, and Calvin Klein perfume as a woman brushes my arm as she clicks by in her Jimmy Choos. Hai Karate cologne – yes, really – on the valet. But at least there are valets. Valets and waiters and chefs and bartenders and dealers and other hustlers. The lights are bright and the buildings are big. Imported marble and polished brass, and so many different colors of lights to keep track of. But, within minutes, I have the total nailed at fifty-six. Now, somehow, these manufactured mono-liths seem dwarfed.

They're not as big.

And they're even closer. Pushing in and pushing down all around. And all they want is money.

After a couple weeks, I start to notice other things. That's a lie. I'm not noticing, I'm hyper-aware.

The drinks are watered, the chips are plastic, and people crowd very close even as they rush by in their frenzied state of hopeful inebriation. People talk fast and talk a lot, but now I realize that they rarely say anything.

I try. Lord, in my confusion I try. And I curse for doing this to myself.

A man I meet tells me I have a lovely little drawl in my voice, and it makes me want to punch him. I say, "Horseshit, I do not." So I let the guy fuck me, I suppose to prove everyone wrong. But he goes too fast, comes too quick, and I don't get any enjoyment out of it at all. I recall this wasn't uncommon.

I could lie again and say it's guilt that drives me back to Wes. But I know damn well why suddenly this illusion seems so much less illustrious.

On the drive back out to the ranch, the air gets thinner. The honey sand mixes and changes – soft butter in direct sunlight, bleeding to a rich mocha as the sun goes down. The sky above catches fire, streaky fuchsia fades and settles in the twilight, eventually yielding to the deep, comforting sapphire that'll reveal millions of glittering diamond stars. Way too many of them to count.

There's a distant, familiar howl as I walk up the path. Wes is alone, his lanky frame stretched out on a single chair outside. He's slugging tequila harder than I've ever seen him do. Not even a beer chaser in sight. "What're you doin' up?" I ask him.

He squints up at me. "Couldn't sleep through all the howling."

"Thought it didn't bother you."

"Never said that," he looks away. "I said I tolerate it, that's all."

He lets me pull the bottle from his hand and I take a long pull off it. I ease down on the ground, lean my back against his shins and take another pull.

Above me, he says, "Loki missed you."

"Yeah? He mope around?"

"Little bit, yeah."

Looking up to the sky, the last trace of blue has bled away, the infinite inky black has settled all around. I take a deep breath, then another hit off the bottle. "Wes," I say, "You better decide now, because I'm not like Loki. You will never tame me."

He reaches around and takes back the bottle. I expect him to laugh and call me on my horseshit. Instead, steely voiced, he answers me. "Well, Rita, my darlin'. Just so's you know. You won't ever break me."

In the close distance, a coyote unleashes a long, mournful howl.

Virgin of the Sands

Holly Phillips

Graham came out of the desert leaving most of his men dead behind him. He debriefed, he bathed, he dressed in a borrowed uniform, and without food, without rest, though he needed both, he went to see the girl.

The army had found her rooms in a shambling mud-brick compound shaded by palms. She was young, God knew, too young, but powerful: her rooms had a private entrance, and there was no guard to watch who came and went. Graham left the motor-pool driver at the east side of the market and walked through the labyrinth of goats, cotton, chickens, dates, and oranges to her door. The afternoon was amber with heat, the air a stinking resin caught with flies. Nothing like the dry furnace blast of the wadi where his squad had been ambushed and killed. He knocked, stupid with thirst, and wondered if she was home.

She was.

Tentative, always, their first touch: her fingertips on his bare arm, her mouth as heavy with grief as with desire. She knew, then. He bent his face to hers and felt the dampness of a recent bath. She smelled of well water and ancient spice. They hung a moment, barely touching, only their breath mingling and her fingers brushing his skin, and then he took her mouth, and drank.

"I'm sorry," she said, after.

He lay across her bed, bound to exhaustion, awaiting release. "We walked right into them," he said, eyes closed. "Walked right into their guns."

"I'm sorry."

She sounded so unhappy. He reached for her with a blind hand. "Not your fault. The dead can't tell you everything."

She laid her palm across his, her touch still cool despite the sweat that soaked her sheets. "I know."

"They expect too much of you." By *they* he meant the generals.

When she said nothing he turned his head and looked at her. She knelt beside him on the bed, barred with light from the rattan blind. Her dark hair was loose around her face, her dark eyes shadowed with worry. So young she broke his heart. He said, "You expect too much of yourself."

She covered his eyes with her free hand. "Sleep."

"You can only work with what we bring you. If we don't bring you the men who know . . . who knew . . ." The darkness of her touch seeped through him.

"Sleep."

"Will you still be here?"

"Yes. Now sleep."

Three times told, he slept.

She had to be pure to work her craft, a virgin in the heart of army intelligence. He never knew if this loving would compromise her with her superiors. She swore it would not touch her power, and he did not ask her more. He just took her with his hands, his tongue, his skin, and if sometimes the forbidden depth of her had him aching with need, that only made the moment when she slid her mouth around him more potent, explosive as a shell bursting in the bore of a gun. And he laughed sometimes when she twisted against him, growling, her teeth sharp on his neck: virgin. He laughed – and forgot for a time the smell of long-dead men.

"Finest military intelligence in the world," Colonel Tibbit-Noyse said, "and we can't find their blasted army from one day to the next." His black moustache was crisp in the wilting heat of the briefing room.

Graham sat with half a dozen officers scribbling in notebooks balanced on their knees. Like the others, he let his pencil rest when the colonel began his familiar tirade.

"We know the führer's entrail-readers are prone to inaccuracy and internal strife. We know who his spies are and have been feeding them tripe for months." (There was a dutiful chuckle.) "We know the desert tribesmen who have been guiding his armoured divisions are weary almost to death with the Superior Man. For God's sake, our desert johnnies have been meeting them for tea among the dunes! So why the *hell* –" the colonel's hand slashed at a passing fly "– can't we find them before they drop their bloody shells into our bloody laps?"

Two captains and three lieutenants, all the company officers not in the field, tapped pencil ends on their notebooks and thumbed the sweat from their brows. Major Healy, sitting behind the map table, coughed into his hand. Graham, eyes fixed on the wall over the major's shoulder, heard again the rattle of gunfire, saw again the carnage shaded by vulture wings. His notebook slid through his fingers to the floor. The small sound in the colonel's silence made everyone jump. He bent to pick it up.

"Now, I have dared to suggest," Tibbit-Noyse continued, "that the fault may not lie with our intel at all, but rather with the use to which it has been put. This little notion of mine has not been greeted with enthusiasm." (Again, a dry chuckle from the men.) "In fact, I'm afraid the general got rather testy about the quantity and quality of fodder we've scavenged for his necromancer in recent weeks. Therefore –" The colonel sighed. His voice was subdued when he continued. "Therefore, all squads will henceforth make it their sole mission to find and retrieve enemy dead, be they abandoned or buried, with an urgent priority on those of officer rank. I'm afraid this will entail a fair bit of dodging about on the wrong side of the battle line, but you'll be delighted to know that the general has agreed to an increase in leave time between missions from two days to four." He looked at Graham. "Beginning immediately, captain, so you have another three days' rest coming to you."

"I'm fit to go tomorrow, sir," Graham said.

Tibbit-Noyse gave him a bleak smile. "Take your time, captain. There's plenty of death to go 'round."

There was another moment of silence, this one long enough for the men to start fidgeting. Healy coughed. Graham sketched the outlines of birds. Then the colonel went on with his briefing.

She had duties during the day, and in any event he could not spend all his leave in her company. He had learned from the nomads not to drink until he must. So he found a café not too near headquarters, one with an awning and a boy to whisk the flies, and drank small cups of syrupy coffee until his heart raced and sleep no longer tempted him.

A large body dropped into the seat opposite him. "Christ. How can you drink coffee in this heat?"

Graham blinked the other's face into focus: Montrose, a second-string journalist with beefy cheeks and a bloodhound's eyes. The boy brought the reporter a bottle of lemon squash, half of which he poured down his throat without seeming to swallow. "Whew!"

"We have orders," Graham said, his voice neutral, "not to speak with the press."

"Look at you, you bastard. Not even sweating." Montrose had a flat Australian accent and salt-rimmed patches of sweat underneath his arms. "Or have you just had the juice scared out of you?"

Graham gave a thin smile and brushed flies away from the rim of his cup.

"Listen." Montrose hunkered over the table. "There've been rumours of a major cock-up. Somebody let some secrets slip into the wrong ears. Somebody in intelligence. Somebody high up. Ring any bells?"

Graham covered a yawn. He didn't have to fake one. The coastal heat was a blanket that could smother even the caffeine. He drank the last swallow, leaving a sludge of sugar in the bottom of the cup, and flagged the boy.

"According to this rumour," Montrose said, undaunted, "at least one of the secrets had to do with the field manoeuvres of

the Dead Squad – pardon me – the Special Desert Reconnaissance Group. Which, come to think of it, is your outfit, isn't it,
Graham?" Montrose blinked with false concern. "Didn't have
any trouble your last time out, did you, mate? No unpleasant
surprises? No nasty Jerries hiding among the dunes?"

The boy came back, set a fresh coffee down by Graham's
elbow, gave him a fleeting glance from thickly-lashed eyes.
Graham dropped a couple of coins on the tray.

"How's your wife?" Graham said.

Montrose sighed and leaned back to finish his lemonade.
"God knows. Jerries went and sank the mail ship, didn't they?
She could be dead, and I'd never even know."

"You could be dead," Graham said, "and she would never
know. Isn't that a bit more likely given your relative circumstances?"

Montrose grunted in morose agreement and whistled for the
boy.

He stalled as long as he could, through the afternoon and into
the cookfire haze of dusk, and even so he waited nearly an hour.
When she came home, limp and pale, she gave him a weary
smile and unlocked her door. He knew better than to touch her
before she'd had a chance to bathe. He followed her through the
stuffy entrance hall to the airier gloom of her room. She stepped
out of her shoes on her way into the bathroom. He heard water
splat in the empty tub. Then she came back and began to take
off her clothes.

He said, "I have three more days' leave."

She unbuttoned her blouse and peeled it off. "I heard." She
tossed the blouse into a hamper by the bathroom door. "I'm
glad."

He sat in a creaking wicker chair, set his cap on the floor.
"There's a rumour going around about some misplaced intel."

She frowned slightly as she unfastened her skirt. "I haven't
heard about that."

"I had it from a reporter. Not the most reliable source."

The skirt followed the blouse, then her slip, her brassiere, her
underpants. Naked, she lifted her arms to take down her hair.

Shadows defined her ribs, her taut belly, the divide of her loins. She walked over to drop hairpins into his hand.

"Who is supposed to have said what to whom?"

"There were no characters in the drama," he said. "But if it's true . . ."

"If it's true, then your men never had a chance."

This close she smelled of woman-sweat and death. His throat tightened. "They had no chance, regardless. Neither do the men in the field now. They've sent the whole damn company out chasing dead men." He dropped his head against the chair and closed his eyes. "This bloody war."

"It's probably just a rumour," she said, and he heard her move away. The rumble from the bathroom tap stopped. Water sloshed as she stepped into the tub. Graham rolled her hairpins against his palm.

Her scent faded with the last of the light.

He wished she had a name he could call her by. Like her intact hymen, her namelessness was meant to protect her from the forces she wrestled in her work, but it seemed a grievous thing. She was so specific a woman, so unique, so much herself; he knew so intimately her looks, her textures, her voice; he could even guess, sometimes, at her thoughts; and yet she was anonymous. The general's necromancer. The witch. The girl. His endearments came unravelled in the empty space where her name should be, so he took refuge in silence, wishing, as much for his sake as for hers, that she had not been born and raised to her grisly vocation. From childhood she had known nothing other than death.

"How can you bear it?" he asked her once.

"How can you?" A glance of mockery. "But maybe no one told you. We all live with death."

He had a vision of himself dead and in her hands, and understood it for a strange desire. He did not put it into words, but he knew her intimacy with the dead, with death, went beyond this mere closeness of flesh. Skin slick with sweat-salt, speechless tongues and hands that sought the vulnerable centre of being, touch dangerous and tender and never allowed inside the heart, the womb. He pressed her in the darkness, strove against her as if they fought, as if one or both might be consumed in this act without hope of consummation. She clung to him, spilled over with the liquor of desire, and still he drank, his thirst for her unslaked, unslakeable until she, wet and limber as an eel, turned in his arms, turned to him, turned against him, and swallowed him into sleep.

The battle washed across the desert as freely as water unbounded by shores, the war's tidal wrack of ruined bodies, tanks, and planes left like flotsam upon the dunes. The ancient, polluted city lay between the sea and that other, drier beach, and no-one knew yet where the high tide line would be. Already the streets were full of the walking wounded.

Graham had errands to run. His desert boots needed mending, he had a new dress tunic to collect from the tailor – trivial chores that, performed against the backdrop of conflict, reminded him in their surreality of lying with two other soldiers under an overhang that was too small to shelter one, seeing men torn apart by machine gun fire, and feeling the sand grit between his molars, the tickle of some insect across his hand, and his sergeant's boot heel drum against his kidney as the man shook, as they all shook, wanting to live, wanting not to die as the others died, wanting not to be eaten as the others were eaten by the vultures that wheeled down from an empty sky and that could not be trusted to report the enemy's absence, as they were brave enough to face the living when there was a meal at stake. In the tailor's shop he met a man he knew slightly, a major in another branch of Intelligence, and they went to a hotel bar for beer.

The place looked cool, with white tile, potted palms, lazy ceiling fans, but the look was a lie. Strips of flypaper that hung inconspicuously behind the bar twisted under the weight of captured flies. The major paid for two pints and led the way to an unoccupied table.

"Look at them all," he said between quick swallows.

Graham grunted acknowledgement, though he did not look around. He had already seen the scattered crowd of civilians, European refugees nervous as starlings under a hawk's wings.

"Terrified Jerry's going to come along and send them all back where they came from." The major sounded as if he rather liked the idea.

The beer felt good going down.

"As I see it," said the major, "this haphazard retreat of ours is actually going to work in our favour before the end. Think of it. The more scattered our forces are, the more thinly Jerry has to spread his own line. Right now they may look like a scythe sweeping up from the south and west," the major drew an arc in a puddle of spilled beer, "but they have to extend their line at every advance in order to keep any stragglers of ours from simply sitting tight until we're at their backs. Any day now they're going to find themselves overextended, and all we have to do is make a quick nip through a weak spot" – he bisected the arc – "and we'll have them in two pieces, both of them surrounded."

"And how do we find the weak spot?"

"Oh, well," the major said complacently, "that's a job for heroes like you, not desk wallahs like me."

Graham got up to buy the next round. When he came back to the table, the major had been joined by another man in uniform, a captain also wearing the *I* insignia. Graham put the glasses down and sat, and only then noticed the looks on their faces.

"I say, old man," the major said. "Rumour has it your section chief has just topped himself in his office."

"It's not a rumour," the captain said. "Colonel Tibbit-Noyse shot himself. I saw his desk. It was covered in his brains." He reached for Graham's beer and thirstily emptied the glass.

Major Healy, the colonel's aide, was impossible to find. Graham tracked him all over headquarters, but, although his progress allowed him to hear the evolving story of the colonel's death, he never managed to meet up with Healy. Eventually he came to his senses and let himself into Healy's cubbyhole of an office. The major kept a box of cigarettes on his desk. Graham seldom smoked, but, eaten by waiting, he lit one after another, the smoke dry and harsh as desert air flavoured with gunpowder. When Healy came in, not long before sundown, he shouted

"Bloody hell!" and slammed the door hard enough to rattle the window in its frame.

Graham put out his dog end in the overcrowded ashtray. Healy dropped into his desk chair, and it tipped him back with a groan.

"Go away, captain. I can't tell you anything, and if you stay I might shoot you and save Jerry the bother."

"Why did he do it?"

Healy jumped up and slammed his fist on his desk. "Out!" The chair rolled back to bump the wall.

"He sent the whole company to die on that slaughterground, and then he killed himself?" Graham shook his head.

The major wiped his face with his palms and went to stand at the window. "God knows what's in a man's mind at a time like that."

"Rumour has it he was the one who spilled our movements to the enemy." Graham was hoarse from cigarettes and thirst. "Rumour has him doing it for money, for sex, for loyalty to the other side. Because of blackmail, or stupidity, or threats."

"Rumour."

"I don't believe it."

Healy turned from the window. The last brass bars of light streaked the dusty glass. "Don't you?"

"Whatever he'd done, I don't believe he would have killed himself before he knew what had happened to the men."

"Don't you?"

"No, sir."

"If he was a spy, he wouldn't give a ha'penny damn about the men."

"Do you believe that, sir?"

Healy coughed and went to the box on his desk for a cigarette. When he saw how few were left he gave Graham a sour look. He chose one, lit it with a silver lighter from his pocket, blew out the smoke in a long thin stream.

"It doesn't matter what I believe," he said quietly. "Now give me some peace, will you? I have work to do."

The sun was almost gone. Graham got up and fumbled for the door.

★   ★   ★

Blackout enveloped the city. Even the stars were dim behind the scrim of cooking smoke that hazed the local sky. Though he might have wheedled a car and driver out of the motor pool, he decided to walk. Her compound was nearly a mile of crooked streets away, and it took all his concentration to recognize the turns in the darkness. Nearly all. He felt a kinship with the other men of his company, men who groped their way through the wind-built maze of dunes and bony sandstone ridges, led by a chancy map into what could be, at every furtive step, a trap. He had seen how blood pooled on earth too dry to drink, how it dulled under a skin of dust even before the flies came. Native eyes watched from dim doorways, and he touched the sidearm on his belt. With the war on the city's threshold, everyone was nervous.

Her doorway was as dim as all the rest. In the weak light that escaped her room her eyes were only a liquid gleam. She said his name uncertainly, and only when he answered did she step back to let him in.

"I didn't think you'd come."

"I'm still on leave." A fatuous thing to say, but it was all he could think of.

She led him into her room where, hidden by blinds, oil lamps added to the heat. The bare space was stifling, as if crowded by the invisible. On her bed, the blue shawl she used as a coverlet showed the wrinkles where she had lain.

"It's past curfew," she said. "And . . ." She stood with her elbows cupped in her palms, barefoot, her yellow cotton dress catching the light behind it. Graham went to her, put his arms about her, leaned his face against her hair. She smelled of tea leaves and cloves.

"Of course you've heard," he said.

"Heard?"

"About the colonel. Tibbit-Noyse's suicide."

She drew in a staggered breath and pulled her arms from between them. "Yes." She returned his embrace, tipped her head to put her cheek against his.

He pulled her tighter. She was slight and strong with bone. Some pent-up emotion began to shake its way out of his body.

As if to calm him, she kissed his neck, his mouth, her body alive against his. He could not discern whether she also shook or was only shaken by his tension. They stripped each other, clumsy, quick to reach the point of skin on skin. She began to kneel, but he caught her arms and lifted her to the bed.

He came closer than he ever had to ending it. Weighing her down, hard against the welling heat between her thighs, he wanted, he ached, he raged with some fury that was neither anger nor lust but some need, some absence without a name. Hard between her thighs. Hands tight against her face. Eyes on hers bright with oil flames. No, she said, and he was shaking again with the convulsive shudders of a fever, he'd seen malaria and thought this was some illness as well, some disease of heat and anguish and war, and she said "No!" and scratched his face.

He rolled onto his back and hardly had he moved but she was off the bed. Arms across his face, he heard her harsh breathing retreat across the room. The bathroom door slammed. Opened.
    "Do you know about Tibbit-Noyse?"
    Her voice shook. An answer to that uncertainty, at least.
    "Know what?" he asked.
    Her breathing was quieter, now.
    "Know what?"
    "That I have been ordered," she answered at last, "to resurrect him in the morning."
    He did not move.
    The bathroom door closed.
    She had broken his skin. The small wound stung with sweat, or maybe it was tears, there beside his eye.

When she stayed in the bathroom, and stayed, and stayed, he finally understood. He rose and dressed, and walked out into the curfew darkness where, apparently, he belonged.

Next morning, Graham ran up the stairs to Healy's office and collided with the major outside his door.

"Graham!" Major Healy exclaimed. "What the devil are you doing here? Don't tell me. I'm already late." He pushed past and started down the hall.

Graham stretched to catch up. "I know. They're bringing the colonel back."

Healy strode another step, two, then stopped. Graham stopped as well, so the two of them stood eye to eye in the corridor. Men in uniform brushed by on their own affairs. Healy said in a furious undertone, "How the hell do you know about that?"

"I want to be there."

"Impossible." The major started to turn.

Graham grabbed his arm. "Morale's already dangerously low. How do you think the troops would react if they knew their superiors were bringing back their own dead?"

Healy's eyes widened. "Are you blackmailing your superior officer? You could be shot!"

"Sir. David. Please." Graham took his hand off the other's arm.

Healy seemed to wilt. "It's nothing you ever want to see, John. Will you believe me? It's nothing you ever want to see."

"Neither is all your men being shot dead and eaten by vultures while you lie there and do *nothing*. I owe them this!"

Healy shut his eyes. "I don't know. You may be right." He coughed and started for the stairs. "You may be right."

Taking that for permission, Graham followed him down.

The company's staging area was a weird patch of quiet amidst the scramble of other units that had to equip and sustain their troops in the field. Trucks, jeeps, men raced overladen on crumbling streets, spewing exhaust and profanity as they went. By the nature of their missions, reconnaissance squads were on their own once deployed, and this was never truer than for Special Recon. No one wanted to involve themselves with the Dead Squad in the field. The nickname, Graham thought, was an irony no one was likely to pronounce aloud today.

He and Major Healy had driven to the staging area alone, late, as Healy had mentioned, but when they arrived they found only one staff car parked outside the necromancer's workshop. The general in charge of Intel was inside the vehicle with two men from his staff. When Healy parked his jeep next to the car, the three men got out, leaving the general's driver to slouch smoking behind the wheel. They formed a group on the square of rutted tarmac that was hemmed in by prefabricated wooden walls, empty windows, and blinding tin roofs. The compound stank of petrol fumes, hot tar, and an inadequate latrine.

The general, a short bulky man in a uniform limp with sweat, returned Graham's and Healy's salutes without enthusiasm. He didn't remark on Graham's presence. Graham supposed that Healy, as Special Recon's acting CO, was entitled to an aide.

The general checked his watch. "It's past time."

"Sorry, sir," Healy said. "We were detained at HQ."

The general grunted. He had cold pebble eyes in pouchy lids. "Any news of your men in the field?"

"No, sir. But I wouldn't expect to hear this early. None of the squads will have reached the line yet."

The general grunted again, and, though his face bore no expression, Graham realized he was reluctant to go in. His aides had the stiff faces and wide eyes of men about to go into battle. Healy looked tired and somewhat sick. Graham felt a twinge of adrenaline in his gut, his breath came a little short. The general gave a curt nod and headed for the necromancer's door.

Inside her workshop, the walls and the underside of the tin roof were clothed in woven reed mats. Even the windows were covered: the room was brilliantly and hotly lit by a klieg lamp in one corner. An electric fan whirred in another, stirring up a breeze that played among the mats, so that the long room was restless with motion, as if the pale brown mats were tent walls. This, the heat, the unmasked stink of decay, all recalled a dozen missions to Graham's mind. His gut clenched again and sweat sprang cool upon his skin. There was no sign of her, or of Tibbit-Noyse. An inner door stood slightly ajar.

The general cleared his throat once, and then again, as if he meant to call out, but he held his silence. Eventually the other door swung further open, and the girl put her head through.

Graham felt the shock when her eyes touched him. But she

was in some distant place, her eyelids heavy, her face open and serene. He saw that she knew him, but by her response his was only one face among five.

She said, "I'm ready to begin."

The general nodded. "Proceed."

"You know I have lodged a protest with the Sisterhood?"

The general's face clenched like a fist. "Proceed."

She stepped out of sight, leaving the door open, and in a moment she wheeled a hospital gurney into the room, handling the awkward thing with practiced ease. Tibbit-Noyse's corpse lay on its back, naked to the lamp's white glare. The heavy calibre bullet had made a ruin of the left side of his face and head. A ragged hole gaped from the outer corner of his eye to behind his temple. The cheekbone, cracked askew, whitely defined the lower margin of the wound. The whole of his face was distorted, the left eye open wide and strangely discoloured, while the right eye showed only a white crescent. Shrinking lips parted to show teeth and a grey hint of tongue beneath the crisp moustache. The body was the colour of paste and, barring an old appendectomy scar, intact.

The hole in Tibbit-Noyse's skull was open onto darkness. Graham remembered the Intel captain saying the man's brains had been scattered across his desk. But death was nothing new to him, and he realized he was examining the corpse so he could avoid seeing the girl. Spurred by the realization, then, he had to look at her.

She wore a prosaic bathrobe of worn blue velvet, tightly belted at her waist. Her dark hair was pinned at the base of her neck. Her feet, on the stained cement floor, were bare. She set the brakes on the gurney's wheels with her toes, and then stood at the corpse's head, studying it, arms folded with her elbows cupped in her palms, mouth a little pursed.

An expression he knew, a face he knew so well. Another wave of sweat washed over him. He wished he had not come.

The fan stirred the walls. The lamp glared. Trucks on the street behind the compound intermittently roared past.

The girl – the witch – nodded to herself and went back into the other room but reappeared almost at once, naked, bearing a

tray heavy with the tools of her craft. She set this down on the
floor at her feet, selected a small, hooked knife, and then glanced
at the men by the door.

"You might pray," she said softly. "It sometimes helps."

Helps the watchers, Graham understood her to mean. He
knew she needed no help from them.

Her nakedness spurred a rush of heat in his body, helpless
response to long conditioning, counter tide to the cold sweep of
horror. Blood started to sing in his ears.

She took up her knife and began.

There is no kindness between the living and the dead.

Graham had sat through the orientation lecture, he knew
the theory, at least the simplified version appropriate for
the uninitiated. To lay the foundation for the false link
between body and departed spirit the witch must claim the
flesh. She must possess the dead clay, she must absorb it
into her sphere of power, and so she must know it, know
it utterly.

The ritual was autopsy. Was intercourse. Was feast.

Not literally, not quite. But her excavation of the corpse was
intimate and brutal, a physical, sensual, savage act. As she
explored Tibbit-Noyse's face, his hands, his genitals, his skin,
Graham followed her on a tour of the lust they had known
together, he and she, the loving that they had enacted in the
privacy of her room and that was now laid bare. As the dead
man's secret tissues were stripped naked, so was Graham
exposed. He rode waves of disgust, of desire, of sheer scorching
humiliation, as if she fucked another man on the street – only
this was worse, unimaginably worse, steeped as it was in the
liquors of rot.

He also only stood, his shoulder by Healy's, his back to the
rough matted wall, and said nothing, did nothing, showed (he
thought) nothing . . . and watched.

When Tibbit-Noyse was open, when he was pierced and
wired and riddled with her tools and charms, when there was no
part of the man she had not seen and touched and claimed –
when the fan stirred not air but a swampy vapour of shit and bile

and decay – when she was slick with sweat and the clotting moistures of death – then she began the call.

She had a beautiful voice. Graham realized she had never sung for him, had not even hummed in the bath as she washed her hair. The men watching could see her throat swell as she drew in air, the muscles in her belly work as she sustained the long pure notes of the chant. The words were meaningless. The song was all.

When Tibbit-Noyse answered, it was with the voice of a child who weeps in the dark, alone.

The witch stepped back from the gurney, hands hanging at her sides, her face drawn with weariness but still serene.

"Ask," she said. "He will answer."

The general jerked his head, a marionette's parody of his usual brisk nod, and moved a step forward. He took a breath and then covered his mouth to catch a cough, the kind of cough that announces severe nausea. Carefully, he swallowed, and said, "Alfred Reginald Tibbit-Noyse. Do you hear me?"

A pause. "Y-ye-yes."

"Did you betray your country in a time of war?"

A pause. "Yes."

Graham could see the dead greyish lungs work inside the ribcage, the greyish tongue inside the mouth.

"How did you betray your country?"

A pause. "I sent my men." Pause. "To steal the dead." Pause. "Behind enemy lines."

The general sagged back on his heels. "That is a lie. Those men were sent out on my orders. How did you betray your country?"

A pause. "I sent my men." Pause. "To die." There was no emotion in the childish voice. It added calmly, "They were their mothers' sons."

"How did you know they were going to die?"

". . . How could they." Pause. "Not be doomed."

"Did you send them into a trap?"

". . . No."

"Did you betray their movements to the enemy?"

". . . No."

"Then why did you kill yourself?" Against the dead man's calm, the general's frustration was strident.

". . . I thought this war." Pause. "Would swallow us all." Pause. "I see now I was wrong."

Healy raised a hand to his eyes and whispered a curse. The general's shoulders bunched.

"Did you betray military secrets to the enemy?"

". . . No."

"To whom did you betray military secrets?"

". . . No one."

"Don't you lie to me!" the general bellowed at the riddled corpse.

"He cannot lie," the witch told him. Her voice was quietly reproachful. "He is dead."

". . . I do not lie."

The general, heeding neither the live woman nor the dead man, continued to rap out questions. Graham could bear no more. He brushed past Healy to slip through the door. In the clean hot light of noon he vomited spit and bile and sank down to sit with his back against the wall. After a minute, the general's driver climbed out of the staff car and offered him the last cigarette from a crumpled pack.

The battle became a part of history. The tide of the enemy's forces was turned before it swamped the city; a new frontline was drawn. The scattered squads of the Special Desert Reconnaissance Group returned in good time, missing no more men than most units who had fought in the desert sands and carrying their bounty of enemy dead. Graham was given a medal for bravery on a recommendation by the late Colonel Tibbit-Noyse, and a new command: twelve recruits from other units, men with stomachs already toughened by war. He led them out on a routine mission, by a stroke of luck found and recovered the withered husk of a major whose insignia promised useful intelligence, and on the morning of the scheduled resurrection, the second morning of his fourday leave, he went to the hotel bar where he had learned of Tibbit-Noyse's death and ordered a shot of whiskey and a beer.

He drank them, and several others like them, but the heat pressed the alcohol from his tissues before it could stupefy his mind. He gave up, paid his tab, and left. By this time the sunlight had thickened to the sticky amber of late afternoon. The ubiquitous flies made the only movement on the street. Graham settled his peaked cap on his head and blinked to accustom his eyes to the light, and when he looked again she was there.

She wore the yellow cotton dress. Her clean hair was soft about her face. Her eyes were wounded.

She said his name.

"Hello," he said after an awkward minute. "How are you?"

"My superiors have sent an official protest to the War Office."

"A protest?"

She looked down. "Because of the colonel's resurrection. It has made things . . . a little more difficult than usual."

"I'm sorry to hear that."

"You have not –" She broke off, then raised her eyes to his. "You have not come to see me."

"I'm sorry." The alcohol seemed to be having a delayed effect on him now. The street teetered sluggishly beneath his feet. His throat closed on a bubble of air.

"It was hard," she said. "It was the hardest I've ever had to do."

Her dark eyes grew darker, and then there were tears on her face. "Please, John, I don't want to do this any more. I don't think I can do this any more. Please, help me; help me break free."

She reached for him, and he knew what she meant. He remembered their nights together, his body remembered to the roots of his hair the night he almost took her completely. He also remembered the scratch her nails had left by his eye, and, more than anything, he remembered her gruesome infidelity with Tibbit-Noyse – with all the other dead men – and he flinched away.

She froze, still reaching.

"I'm sorry," he said.

She drew her arms across herself, clasped her elbows in her palms. "I understand."

He opened his mouth, then realized he had nothing more to say. He touched his cap and walked away. The street was uneasy beneath his feet, the sun a furnace burn against his face, and he was blind with the image he carried with him: the look of relief that had flickered in the virgin's eyes.

Blues in the Night

Sage Vivant

His penis beat against his palm as if it were his heart. Every pulse left him quaking and hornier but that didn't slow the rhythm of his hand up and down, up and down, tugging his shaft the way he imagined she might.

He'd beaten off to girls before but this was different. He'd randomly pick classmates to fantasize about when the urge to masturbate overtook him. Now, however, it was the fantasizing about Carla that inspired the spanking of the monkey.

Anybody who knew about this fixation (and nobody did) would have called it a crush and told him he'd outgrow it. Maybe they'd be right but before that elusive level of maturity descended upon him, he wanted to revel in his hard-ons and linger on his fantasies. He wanted to recall Carla's ethnic beauty gyrating above him on stage until his mind short-circuited from the repetition.

And what irony that his own parents were ultimately responsible for his rampant lust. On his eighteenth birthday last month, his father had given him tickets to *Blues in the Night* at the Rialto on opening night.

"I know how much you like opening nights," his father smiled, handing him the ticket.

"And Leslie Uggams," his mother added with a wink.

His playwright aspirations were no secret in the family, but the fact that he was drawn to comedy, not necessarily musicals, seemed to have escaped his parents. To them, one play was like any other – expensive.

He stroked himself now as he remembered that night in June, sitting in the front row, watching the dancers strut to "Stompin' at the Savoy," and being completely mesmerized by the dark-haired beauty with legs so perfect, he'd forgotten to breathe. He paid attention to the play only when she wasn't on stage. When she was present, his mind slipped into his crotch and concentration was a hopeless undertaking. His hand now gripped his tumescent appreciation and fueled his memory: the way her sculpted legs flexed and stretched as she moved, the sheen of her wild curls, the look on her face that suggested so much . . . experience.

She danced like some people spoke – effortlessly and concisely. Her movements were bold and confident and as the gap between her legs opened and closed with the music's rhythm, he pictured himself under her, watching the view from a much closer vantage point. Arms length, say.

He'd been with other women. Well, just one but he'd gotten into the pants of two others. So he knew how things could vary among women once you got past the clothing. Some were very hot and unbelievably wet. Others were willing enough but somehow lacking in heat and moisture. There was no doubt in his mind that not only did Carla have an abundance of both but she'd be happy to demonstrate how best to handle it.

He held on to the side of the sink as visions of her sensuous body undulated in his brain. With his free hand, he coaxed his desire from deep inside his balls until it slashed a gooey stripe against the tiled wall.

With his very limited income, he took in two more performances of *Blues in the Night* before the Fourth of July. He couldn't afford front row seats but his aunt let him borrow her opera glasses, so even from the second balcony, he could focus fairly effectively on the hot little vixen who shimmied her way into his heart.

After the third performance, he could think only about how he could get her to shimmy into his shorts.

He waited by the exit marked "stage door" one night after the show but soon discovered that it was more of an historical designation than a functioning door. So, the next night, he hung around the theater's front doors after the crowds poured out.

No luck then, either. He looked up her name in the phone book and found no Carla Capozzi but a few "C Capozzi"'s. When he dialed them, all three numbers were answered by men. He hung up at the sound of their voices.

His obsession had grown to the point where if he didn't have an erection, he was in the process of getting one. His pants were constantly tight and his mood irritable. His mother noticed only his demeanor and commented on it with aggravating regularity.

"Why don't you go to a play? You'll feel better," she'd say dismissively as she folded clothes or dried dishes. He wanted to yell that if she had a cock as raring to go as his, the last thing she'd recommend was more exposure to Carla.

One day she sent him to Bloomingdale's to find something for his father's upcoming birthday. Glad to have an excuse to get out of the house, he took the train into the city. As he walked west on East 60th Street, he saw the object of his affection walk by him on 3rd Avenue. She, too, was headed for Bloomingdale's.

Fighting his instinct to run away in abject terror, he followed her at what he believed was a safe distance. She browsed the cosmetic counters with a certain aimless quality he found endearing. He would have figured her for a more directed kind of shopper.

He knew he had to act quickly. He knew there would be no second chance.

"Aren't you Carla Capozzi?" He cocked his head in a gesture he'd seen among adults. It implied a nice mix of confusion and recollection, he'd always thought.

Her big brown eyes appraised him slowly, thoroughly. Even without her stage make-up, her dramatic features and coloring were striking. She read his face too well, for her mouth slipped into a wicked grin that made him feel naked.

"Yes," she drawled. "Did you maybe go to school with me?" Mischief sparked her gaze because both of them were well aware that a good ten years separated their ages.

He blushed and decided not to try to hide it. "No, no," he laughed. "I recognize you from *Blues in the Night*."

"Well, you're probably the only one," she commented. "The show's going to close next week. But thanks, anyway." She extended her hand. "And you are?"

"Donald Marron," he said distinctly in an attempt to keep from sputtering. His sweaty hand clasped her soft one, weakening his knees. Closing? How would he see her once that happened? The pressure to turn this meeting into something meaningful made his dick hard. Hard*er*.

"I'm so sorry to hear that," he continued. "Will you be in something new?"

"As a matter of fact, it looks like I will. It's called *Cats*. Andrew Lloyd Weber."

He'd read all about it. "I'd love to hear more about it. Would you like to have coffee?" His heartbeat threatened to drown out his words. He'd never asked a girl – a woman – out before and prayed he wasn't too eager.

The expression on her face wasn't promising and his heart began to climb up his throat. In the brief pause that hung between them, the pause that would determine so much of his future, some small morsel of curiosity, some tiny grain of intrigue must have lodged itself in her psyche and she smiled. "Sure. Why not?"

She told him about her career as a dancer. *Blues in the Night* had been her first Broadway gig. Prior to that, she'd done only community theater and off-Broadway productions. She also sang and hoped to find a role that showcased that talent. He told her about his dreams of being a screenwriter or playwright.

As she spoke, his eyes were as active as his ears. He took her in wholly, from her thick, Italian locks to her dark eyes flecked with amber, to her luscious lips. The Danskin top (or was it a bodysuit?) she wore plunged low enough to reveal the elegant contours of her modest cleavage.

"How'd you like to see what happens backstage at a Broadway show?" she asked.

"I'd love it! When?"

"No time like the present."

*　　*　　*

She whisked him off to the Winter Garden Theater, where the cast and crew of *Cats* scurried about with what seemed to be the most urgent of business. Half-built sets hung from the ceiling as whiskered men and women held impromptu conferences laced with song. Behind this cacophony were the remnants of an ice cream feast that had obviously been a crowd pleaser.

"Ice cream makes a great coffee chaser, don't you think?" Carla winked as she handed him a tub of what looked like strawberry ice cream. She picked up a can of whipped cream and a squeeze bottle of chocolate, then took his hand and led him toward the dressing rooms.

He expected the rooms to be buzzing with people but the one he entered with Carla was empty. She locked the door behind them and breezed into the room, placing the sweet condiments on the counter that served as a long vanity table before the mirror-lined wall.

"Do you have spoons?" He ventured, peering into the tub of soft, nearly liquid ice cream and wondering how they would eat it.

She shot him another one of those wonderfully crooked grins. "You're a creative person, Donald. Surely you can think of some way we could enjoy that ice cream."

If her remark didn't render him speechless, her peeling off her spandex top did the trick. She exposed her pretty breasts first, then slid the sleeves down her arms until they were off.

As his cock shot upward, a torrent of Catholic guilt showered down, engulfing him in a cloak of hot indecision. He knew what he wanted to do but the cloak, temporarily heavier than his lust, kept him immobile. She took the squeeze bottle and squirted chocolate lines across her pert breasts.

"Let me know when I look good enough to eat," she smirked.

Now! Now! his inner altar boy shouted. As she stood smiling at him with an enticing mixture of challenge and unabashed fun, he stepped toward her. Though he had no notion of what he would do next, she didn't seem put off by his confusion. Her steady gaze was fishing line to his flounder.

The closer he got to her, the more he realized his own power. His six foot one inch frame towering over her five foot six inch one notwithstanding, there was something in her eyes that communicated not just invitation but surrender. A silent, subtle shift occurred in his mind. Suddenly, gratefully, he knew how to proceed.

He grabbed the can of whipped cream and dotted her nipples with two air blasts of puffy white sweetness. She giggled and he laughed. Who knew going backstage would make him this happy?

He bent slightly toward her chest and traced the chocolate swirls with his tongue, savoring the slow infusion of cocoa and skin as it blended on his taste buds. He followed the swell of her breast until he reached the nipple and lapped like a kitten at the whipped cream until it was gone. He was beyond nervousness, beyond trembling. Everything in his brain and body was hard and compelling, propelling him into action without thought.

He unzipped his fly. She immediately dropped to her knees. It was she, not he, who whipped out his rock hardness and the sight as well as the heft of it shocked him. Had he ever been this excited before? No, never.

The familiar sputtering sound from the whipped cream can interrupted his penile fascination. The chilly cream nearly sizzled on his hot member but before he could register a real temperature change, her big brown eyes looked up at him boldly as his tip disappeared between her beautiful, full lips. She took the length of him down her throat – his head tickled the back of her throat. Her hands squeezed his ass cheeks while his own flailed for a place to land. Her head? The nearby table? The choice became moot as he erupted into her mouth in spurts of ecstasy that seemed to come from several cocks, for just when one stream stopped, another one began. Several rounds of gushing joy sent the room spinning. As if sensing his compromised balance, she held him firmly upright as she swallowed his satisfaction.

When he stopped calling out, he realized he'd been making too much noise. There he stood with his pants at his ankles, his still-hard cock bobbing near her face, and having possibly drawn unwanted attention to their little love nest. He felt himself blush.

"I'm sorry. I hope I wasn't too loud," he stammered, not nearly as contrite as he was euphoric.

She smiled, eyes still dancing but now glistening with something he couldn't identify. "Don't worry about it," she chuckled, getting to her feet. "There's so much going on out there, they can't even hear themselves think." She leaned her body, still sticky from the chocolate and cream, into his shirt. "Besides, I think you had fun." She kissed him with unexpected tenderness.

"God, yes! But I'm afraid I had more fun than you did."

"That may be true, but having you come like that was pretty damn fun for me, too. Anyway, who says we're finished?"

Someone tried to open the door. Encountering the lock, they knocked. Donald turned to Carla, panic-stricken.

"I'm sure it's just someone who needs to use the room. Zip up," she patted his cock affectionately. As he complied, she admitted a pretty young blonde woman into the room.

"Oh, sorry. I didn't know you were entertaining," the stranger said, surprised to find Donald there.

"It's okay, we were just leaving," Carla announced, dragging him by the hand and back among the cats.

"I need to get over to the Rialto now," she said, once they were back on the street.

His mind still reeled but he was sentient enough now to realize she was saying goodbye.

"Will I see you again?"

She laughed and pulled him toward her by his collar. "I should say so. You owe me an orgasm." She stuffed something in his pants pocket and sprinted away.

He walked the streets of Manhattan for a long time before heading home. He had no desire to be home, where even the air felt oppressive. Carla had left him with her business card: *Carla Capozzi, Dancer, Singer, Actress. 212–459–2221.* He ducked into the nearest phone booth and dialed the number, just to hear her voice on her answering machine. He left no message because he wasn't at all certain he could be coherent.

"What did you buy your father?" his mother said in greeting as he entered the front door.

"It's a surprise," he muttered, heading for his room, cursing the fact that he'd now have to make another shopping trip to buy a damn gift.

He dialed her phone number again, this time from his room. On the train, he'd decided what he was going to say.

"Hi, Carla. This is Donald. I just wanted to tell you what a wonderful time I had today. It was just fantastic." *Move along, Donald. Don't be so grateful. Act like a man.* "And I want to return the favor, so why don't you come over to my place after your show tomorrow?"

She'd know soon enough that it wasn't really *his* place, but he liked the way it sounded on the phone. He left her the address. He knew his parents had their bridge club meeting tomorrow night and, if memory served, it was scheduled to happen at the Edelstein's. The house would be his.

Predictably, she teased him about the house when she arrived, fingering doilies and pointing at china cabinets accusingly. "You've got such feminine taste, young man. Have you ever thought of going into interior design? Or theater?"

He laughed off her jokes. His goal was to get her into his bedroom. Once that mission was accomplished, he knew hormones would do the rest.

"So," she said, flopping her beautifully toned body onto the living room sofa and putting her feet up on the coffee table. "You wanted me on *your* turf this time. Thinking that will give you some kind of home court advantage?"

He loved her eyes. They always looked as if indescribable fun was about to burst from them.

"Maybe." Actually, he hadn't thought of that at all. This was just the only place he could think of where they could be alone. If he had enough money, he would've gotten a hotel room.

"Then I'll need to reassert my power somehow, won't I?" She wore no leggings or other dancer clothing today – just a white cotton blouse tied at her waist and a full, peasant-style skirt. She unbuttoned the blouse, revealing a stripe of flawless skin from neck to sternum. He could see the darker spots where her nipples lurked under the fabric.

He didn't answer her question. He knew she was going to make his response unnecessary, so he waited for her next move.

"When's the last time somebody took you over their knee to spank you?"

"It's been a while," he grinned.

"Then you're due. Take off your pants and come here." She patted her lap.

He wondered why he was bemused rather than mortified. He stripped as she asked and lay his mid-section over her thighs. The cool air taunted his upturned ass for a few seconds before her hand made contact with it. The playful slap stiffened his cock with unexpected efficiency and as it pressed against her thigh, she groaned.

"Mmmm, Donald. I see you take punishment very well . . ."

He slid off her lap and onto his knees, where he instantly slipped a hand under her skirt. Following the smooth contours of her calf, the back of her knee, and the underside of her thigh, he could feel the waves of heat from her pussy. She spread her legs to give him better access. He expected to find panties, but his hand brushed against soft pubic hair instead.

He disappeared under her skirt before she could object or even comment. With his face buried between her legs, he inhaled the tantalizing scent of her pussy before he put his lips to her swollen, slippery ones. Though he had little idea whether what he was doing was proper form (he hadn't read the oral sex chapter of *The Joy of Sex* as thoroughly as the penetration sections), he let her moans guide him. He found her clit easily and tongued it with exploratory tenderness. She seemed to like it.

She liked it so much, in fact, that her thighs soon clutched his head and her love button got noticeably harder. He dared not stop licking, even when she bucked her hips into his face and let out a series of gasps. His cock was now a bone, immovable and hard – he'd given a woman an orgasm!

When he came out from under her skirts, her head lay against the back of the sofa and her eyes were half-closed as she panted her recovery.

"Don't you have a bedroom?" she whispered, her face glowing with satisfaction.

He reminded himself not to let his jaw drop. He'd rehearsed all kinds of suave lines in the hopes of coercing her to his bedroom, and now to realize that he didn't need them made his head spin.

He escorted her upstairs and closed the door behind him. She slipped into his arms and he took the opportunity to slide her blouse off her shoulders until he heard it swoosh to the floor. They kissed in a long, slow burn of affection until she stepped away from him and slipped out of her skirt. She stood before him naked, skin beautifully taut, nipples erect, and her scent filling his room.

"Being naked by myself isn't much fun, you know," she commented, grinning at him with raised eyebrows.

He was naked faster than even he could have imagined and she wasted no time laying him down on his bed. His cock had assumed possession of his body – everything he was, everything he thought, resided in that seven-inch rod of volatile flesh. He feared that he'd explode the moment she touched him.

She kissed his aching member delicately and whisked away his pre-cum with her tongue. Her dark hair tumbled forward, brushing his abdomen.

"I'm going to fuck you, Donald," she purred as she straddled him. She slid her wet snatch along the length of him. "Would you like that?"

"Yes," he rasped, incredulous at the question. "Yes, fuck me. Please."

He wasn't likely to ever forget the sight of this delightful vixen, riding his cock with the kind of wild abandon he'd only dreamed of. Her small tits jiggled as she bounced on his ecstatic meat, which was accustomed to the tepid warmth of his hand as opposed to the fiery tropics of her pussy.

He bent his knees so he could thrust up into her. The moment he was as deep inside her steamy pussy as he could possibly get, the come in his balls shot feverishly up and out, filling her with what was surely pints. The walls of her cunt squeezed and massaged the last drops of joy from his cock. She leaned her body forward and rested her head on his chest. They both savored the glorious quiet of the moment.

His eyes shot open at the sound of his parents' voices downstairs. "Oh, shit!" He hissed. "My parents are home!"

She laughed and climbed off him. "Great! I can't wait to meet them!" She was already dressing.

He panicked. They'd never understand. They'd sense his happiness and know something had happened. They'd give him endless grief for seeing a woman Carla's age. But how could he ask her to leave? And how would he sneak her out?

She stood at the window and peered out. "Ever used that fire escape?" she asked him, nodding toward it.

"Well, no . . ."

"I'll let you know how sturdy it is. Call me tomorrow, okay?" She winked at him, opened the window, and climbed out. Seconds later, she was gone.

When his parents would later check in on him, they'd see their son napping. He fell asleep with a smile on his face, strains of the *Blues in the Night* overture swimming in his head.

The Wedding Dress

Don Rasner

All I could do was stare at the judge's cock. At my own wedding, standing next to my future husband.

That sounds horrible, I know. But don't blame me. Blame my mom; it was her wedding dress. Blame the judge, too. His erection was huge.

The trouble started because I promised my mom I'd wear her wedding dress when I finally got married. That wasn't the best idea. My mom and I don't have a lot in common, and that goes for our figures, too. My mom is petite. Me? I'm what you'd call curvy. And, as any guy will tell you, my breasts are my best feature.

I was in trouble as soon as Molly, my maid of honor, tried to wrap that dress around my monsters. My tits aren't just big; they're amazing. Giant. Juggernauts. Whatever word you want to use. When it's cold my nipples poke through the thickest sweaters. When I go swimming I can't put my head underwater. When I get my vision tested the doctor can't ever remember the color of my eyes. And in my mom's wedding dress – built for her flat, flat chest – my tits looked like over-pumped basketballs.

Molly and I have been friends for life. She looked great, her long blonde hair shimmering under the courthouse lights, the purple bridesmaid dress hugging her hips, the slit in its side showing off her strong legs. I'd never had any leanings toward the ladies, but Molly was hot that day.

And as she pulled my dress tighter and tighter, grunting with the effort of closing its back, I got a bit turned on. Well, that's not entirely true. I got totally turned on.

"Jesus, Suzanne, I can't get this thing shut," Molly said. "Pull harder."

Molly did. Stretched tight against my tits, the fabric rubbed against my already erect nipples. I must've gasped, because Molly suddenly stopped.

"You okay?"

"I'm nervous, that's all. Just get me into this thing."

Molly tugged even harder, nearly knocking me to the ground. Another gasp. And this time I couldn't help myself. I grabbed my tits, pressing hard against my nipples.

"Harder," I said through clenched teeth.

Molly hesitated. "What are you doing, Suze?"

"Pull harder," I repeated.

I knew it was wrong, this being my wedding day and all, but, like I said, blame it on that dress. I just couldn't help but reach my hand behind me and rub it – just a bit – along the swell of my bridesmaid's ass. I'd always been jealous of Molly's firm, muscular butt. Mine tended to be a bit on the "generous" side.

My touch shocked the shit out of Molly. She let go of my dress and tried to jump away, but by this time my little touch had become a choke-hold on those fine cheeks.

"Christ, Suzanne, what the fuck are you doing?" Molly asked.

I didn't answer. I just squeezed her ass harder, and then let my other hand run between her thighs. My mom's dress must've been doing something for her, too, because her underwear was already wet.

"Suzanne!" Molly hissed. "My God!"

"Shut up," I said. "It's this fucking dress." I pressed my hand hard against her crotch hard enough to make Molly groan. "Don't tell me you don't like it," I said.

Then I took the next step: I started stroking her cunt. She was getting wetter by the second. I could smell her. I swear, her turn-on scented the entire room. Outside, I could hear people milling about. My mom and dad were out there, and the judge who was performing the ceremony. The best man, too. And, of course, Greg, my husband-to-be.

I let go of Molly just long enough to spin her around so that our faces were inches apart. "You have to be quiet," I said. "I don't know how thick these walls are."

Molly's eyes were bugging. I shut her protests up by dropping the top of my dress. My tits rejoiced as they surged free of the frilly material. Molly stared, her mouth hanging open. She seemed in shock, so I sped things along by placing her hand on my tit. The feel of her palm against my nipple popped goosebumps along my arms.

"Shit, I must be hornier than hell," I said. "My knees are fucking knocking."

Molly didn't try to step away this time, I noticed, so I pulled her other hand to my other tit. And then, before she could say a word, I slipped my hand back between her legs. I wiggled my fingers past her underwear and into her wet slit, and then immediately slid to her clit. I didn't have time to fuck around; the wedding was in ten minutes. She gasped, but then squeezed both tits, tight. It hurt, and it felt good, real good. "Keep doing that," I said. "That dress makes my tits so fucking sensitive."

Molly wasn't resisting any more. She leaned against me, pushing me hard into the wall. I opened my mouth to tease her but she slapped her lips over me before I could get out a word. Our tongues touched. I squeezed my eyes shut and felt her body twitching as I flicked her clit with my fingers.

She pulled her mouth away. "Suzanne, this is so wrong. You're getting married – today."

I let my fingers trace slowly along the inside of her thigh. "I need it, baby. I can't be all horny during the ceremony. Just get me off, sweetie. Then I'll be fine."

I don't know how logical that argument was, but Molly was willing enough to buy it. Without another peep she knelt and yanked my dress down to my ankles. Then she did the same with my frilly lace underwear.

"Wow," I said, "you work fast."

She didn't waste time with foreplay, either. And what a touch. Her tongue immediately found my clit. She started at the base, then traveled slowly to its tip. There, she give a flick – just a tiny one – and moved back to the base. Then a kiss, gently puckering her lips over my clit. Like I said, Molly was a pro. Thank God I was leaning against the wall or I would've fallen on my ass.

I squeezed my rock-hard nipples. With my other hand I grabbed the back of Molly's head and shoved her mouth harder onto me. "Yes, sweetie," I whispered. "Suck it hard."

She did, swallowing my clit, letting it go, then licking up and down its length. She waited for my thighs to start quivering, then started licking faster, until my pelvis thrust forward and I came. It was the kind of orgasm that I'd normally celebrate with a scream, but this time I clenched my mouth and clamped my hands over my lips, too, just in case.

One thing, though. The orgasm made me fall onto my "generous" ass. Holding my scream in turned out to be kind of useless – the thump my keester made when it hit the ground was loud enough so that someone – maybe my dad – immediately banged on the door. "Everything okay in there?"

I couldn't answer. My breath was all ragged, like I'd been jogging. "It's okay," Molly hollered. Grinning, she added, "Just blowing off a little steam before the big moment."

"Shit," I whispered to her. "It was so hard not to scream. That was awesome, baby. Where's that been my whole life?" I struggled to my feet and started pulling my dress back up. "I still have to get this fucker on, though."

"Not so fast," Molly said.

I looked up. She was bent over a chair, ass in the air, her perfect cheeks facing me. She'd hiked her dress up and pulled her underwear down around her ankles.

"My turn," she said.

I looked at the clock. "Shit, Molly. The ceremony starts in five fucking minutes, and I still can't get this damn dress on."

"I don't give a shit," Molly said, rubbing that perfect ass. "Get your tongue over here or I tell everyone out there what just happened."

"You cunt," I hissed. But I was fucked and I knew it.

I had to make this fast. I pulled her legs apart and started licking. Pissed off? Sure, but Molly's cunt did taste damn good. And I did feel a twinge of heat when her clit stiffened under my tongue. And when she started whispering my name, I felt my own cunt getting soppy again. I must've gotten that girl all wound up, too, because her legs were shaking like two twigs in a tornado. In fact, she was too turned on: when I gave her a particularly good lick she let out a yelp.

Sure enough, someone pounded on the door again. "You girls all right in there?" This time it sounded like my mom.

I pulled my mouth away from Molly's cunt to answer, but she hissed, "Don't you stop for even a second."

"Girls? Girls?" My mom's voice for sure. But Molly's cunt wouldn't budge.

"We're fine!" Molly yelled, way too forcefully. "Give us a second!"

"C'mon, you bitch," Molly whispered, "finish me off."

I'd never heard Molly talk like that. She was captain of the fucking debate squad in high school, for Christ's sake. I'm sure she never used the word "cunt" arguing against nuclear weapons. When did she develop such a mouth?

That mystery would have to be tackled later. The clock was ticking. I needed to speed things up. That meant one thing: a little butt play. I slipped a finger into her asshole, surprised at how easily it slid in.

"God," she grunted as my finger slid into her. "Another one."

Who was I to argue? I slipped my index finger out, then put it and my middle finger in. This time Molly just leaned into the table. Good thing: the tabletop muffled her groans.

It was tough work. My neck hurt like hell, but I didn't want to move. I had a good rhythm going. I couldn't afford to lose my momentum.

Finally I hit the right spot – and Molly came. Boy, did she ever. The idiot screamed – on my wedding day! Not only that, she nearly sent the table flying across the room. What a huge fucking noise that made.

So it was no big surprise when someone came pounding again.

"Girls? What's going on?" This time it was – uh-ho – my future hubby.

"Nothing, dear! Molly just slipped, that's all. But she's fine."

She was. Actually, she seemed better than fine. She was lying on the floor, her dress still raised, eyes closed, and a huge smile across her face.

"Hey," I hissed, smacking her with my bouquet. "Get your ass up. We gotta get out of here."

Molly got up. We still had to struggle like hell to get my damn dress on, though. But finally, with me holding tight to the doorknob and Molly pulling with all her might, we got the dumb thing clasped. But my problems were far from solved. My tits were barely stuffed into the dress. My cleavage looked like it was going to rise up and strangle me. And my hair, which had been professionally done just an hour earlier, was poking all over the place. My face was flushed. I was as sweaty as if I'd just gotten home from the gym. A heel had snapped off one of my shoes.

Molly didn't look any better except her dress actually fit.

"I look like a fucking prostitute," I said, staring at the mirror.

"Just hold your bouquet in front of your tits. We gotta go."

So the two of us, sweaty, flushed, hair all over the place, opened the door. My husband-to-be looked like he was going to faint.

I smelled like sex. You know that scent. It lingers, that smell of a good fuck.

Molly reeked, too. Everyone must've sniffed it. How could they not?

My poor hubby-to-be kept giving me this look. It's hard to describe, but I'd say it was three parts sheer terror, one part ready-to-burst-into-tears and one part "Wow!" The best man couldn't take his eyes off my tits. Well, that's not true. Sometimes he'd take a break to glance at Molly's ass.

Mom and Dad? I couldn't even look at them.

And the judge? Well, I've already told you about his hard-on. It was one hell of a boner.

I mean, I could see the outline of his cock through his robes. That's pretty impressive. So don't think I'm a total slut when I tell you that I just couldn't stop myself from inching close enough during the ceremony to gently brush against that magnificent tool.

Greg has a nice dick. But nice is all it is. This judge's? Don't let any woman tell you size doesn't matter. Those robes were holding back a monster dick. Eight, nine inches? Maybe even the magical ten.

I tried to stop thinking about it or staring at it. Really, I did. But it was hopeless. It was like trying to ignore an elephant in your living room. So – and this is shameful stuff – I started to slowly rub that cock with my knee. I wanted to see if I could make it bigger. I could. And I did. I noticed then that I was licking my lips. And my cunt was getting wet all over again. I tried to ease some of the heat down there, but it was no good.

The judge was yakking away, all that wedding-ceremony babble that judges have to say to hitch two people. He must've said those same words thousands of times. But I could tell he was nervous. He kept stumbling over the phrases. I caught him saying the wrong word more than once.

I did a horrible thing, then. I made life even tougher for that poor judge. I jutted my chest forward, just enough to heave my tits directly in his line of vision. He could have counted the freckles if he'd been so inclined.

What was I doing? Good question. Watching the judge stutter, watching him try to tear his eyeballs away from my tits, watching the sweat bead on his forehead made me hotter than I'd been since . . . oh, five minutes earlier with Molly.

I'm not some heartless bitch. I did look over at my husband. Greg's a good man: hard-working, smart, kind. And, like I said, he doesn't have the worst dick in the world. But, and I can't emphasize this enough, that judge's dick was huge!

Next I did something really slutty. I dropped my bouquet so I'd have to pick it up. And I made sure to move slowly, giving the judge an even better look at my tits. He stopped talking and gasped.

There's something thrilling about being so bad. I was turned on something fierce. I wanted to grab the front of mom's wedding dress and tear it from my body. I wanted to jump the judge and feel his rock-hard dick pressing against my ass cheeks. I wanted to split those cheeks and force that cock inside me.

And as I grabbed my dropped flowers, a wicked thought hit me: "What if I accidentally bump the judge's dick on the way up?" So that's what I did. First, I grazed my head against his crotch, slow, along the length of his shaft. Then I tipped my head back so my eyes could feast on that amazing piece of meat. It was such a nice sight I took my sweet time moving the rest of my face up the judge's robes. Did anyone notice? I didn't give a damn. I could smell the judge's dick through his robes, for fuck's sake, could feel its heat against my skin. Nothing was going to keep my face from that monster.

I pictured his dick – long, thick, purple head, covered with crisscrossing blue veins. I imagined that salty pre-come that would dribble from its head. I imagined the erotic shock it would give my tongue.

And then I pictured that massive cock banging into my cunt. In my mind the judge was a wild lover, fierce. He'd slam into me over and over, not giving a damn whether he was being gentle or tender or kind, not giving a shit about my feelings. No, the judge of my fantasies was a sex machine, a robot with a horse cock. It would feel like my insides were going to split.

It was fucking awesome.

And hey, how bad was it, anyway? Bad enough to cancel a wedding? A wedding I'd spent the last six fucking months planning? To cancel a very expensive reception at the finest downtown hotel? I mean, what was it really? I just barely – the quickest, slightest flick of the tongue, really – gave his cock the tiniest lick. And, hell, I did it through all those robes. It's not like I opened his fly.

It's not my fault that the judge's stamina wasn't as big as his dick. And it's not my fault that the motherfucker yells like a girl when he comes, either. But that's what happened. I gave him the littlest lick. He shuddered all over, grunted a bit, and then – the moron – he screamed.

The best man dropped the rings. My Mom ran out of the room. My Dad swore, though he kind of tried to do it under his breath. Molly called me a slut, and didn't try to do it under her breath. And Greg? I thought he was going to die. He didn't, of course. He broke into tears, the pussy.

So, yeah, everyone knew what I was doing. And, yeah again, no one was all that pleased. (Well, maybe the judge.)

The upshot? I'm single again. Greg hasn't spoken to me. Neither has Molly, my Dad, or my Mom. The best man? He's called quite a few times, but I have Caller ID. It wasn't exactly the wedding of my dreams.

Worst of all, the judge won't return my calls. All that dick and no balls.

One good thing did come from it: I threw my mom's wedding dress in the trash. Next time I'll buy my own fucking dress.

Abstinence Makes the Heart Grow

J. D. Munro

"Pelvic rest," Dr Frank prescribes. Dr Frank is anything but frank. Despite a career based on the consequences of coitus, the obstetrician rarely mentions the carnal act that lands Lucy in stirrups. As if he can hide what his probing fingers are up to, he rearranges the drape between Lucy's spread knees every time she swats the paper sheet down. he unscrews his medieval instrument and snaps off his lubed latex glove. Rushing off to palpate his next patient, he leaves his assistant to translate the euphemistic instructions to Lucy.

"Pelvic rest," the nurse murmurs, handing Lucy a box of tissues. "No lifting, no intercourse, no exercise." She sandwiches the allusion to naked, intertwined limbs between two acts suitable for teatime small talk, sneaking in the indelicacy like unsuccessfully disguised vegetables in her children's dinner.

"No sex?" Lucy clamps the tissue between her legs. "You're *kidding*."

"Most women would be grateful," the nurse clucks. "Especially in your condition."

Dr Frank advises physical restraint because he can do little else other than monitor the baby's progress. Despite a barrage of tests, he can't diagnose the reason for Lucy's previous miscarriages. So he errs on the side of caution, recommending that she not rock the baby's boat. Although most expecting women can boff with abandon in between barfing and bathroom visits, refraining is advisable with Lucy's unfortunate history of early pregnancy losses. She agrees without legal counsel to everything he demands of her. As if she was in any position to argue, spread like a poked bug on the exam table.

Raised in the post-feminist era, Lucy had believed that her body was her own to operate as she saw fit. But Dr Frank orders the protection of Lucy's vaginal domain like her father issuing curfew twenty years ago, hitting her with the sledgehammer realization that emancipation was a deception. Once this miniature guppy takes up residence inside her, her pussy plays second fiddle. She no longer conducts desire's melody. Ian's staccato, long-tailed musicians can swarm her orchestra pit no more. One of the little buggers hit the right note and did the trick, and now her musical score shows only silence: a pelvic Rest mark stretching on for months.

Lucy resolves to make whatever sacrifices the butterfly heartbeat inside her requires. After all, her mommy friends complain that new parents surrender a great deal, including frequent and spontaneous sex, and none of them seem to mind. Now that Lucy's about to enter the holy ranks of motherhood, she determines to go cold turkey on profane language and lusty acts. But, once denied her, shtupping is all Lucy thinks about.

Lucy doesn't expect turning off the fucking faucet to be difficult, especially given her protective concern over the fluttering life inside her. Taken off guard by the unexpected medical instructions, she doesn't comprehend its ramifications until she goes home with her new living luggage and forces herself to ignore the waves of desire washing over her. If only she'd seen abstinence coming down the pike, she and Ian would have crash studied the *Kama Sutra* the night before instead of having a lukewarm quickie.

"Pelvic rest. Doctor's orders," Lucy informs Ian that night as he reaches for her boob. Her chest's transformation from pubescent to sex goddess proportions not only amazes and arouses them, but also awes them as the only wondrous visible sign of her three-month pregnancy. She backs away from his for the first time since they fought over Lucy's impetuous desire for a Chihuahua months ago.

"What's that mean?"

"No sex."

"Like, no coming, or, you know, like, no, um, the whole nine yards?" Like the doctor, Ian stumbles over precise terminology.

Lucy hadn't considered the various interpretations of the doctor's restriction. Ian thinks *"pelvic rest"* means no sexual intercourse, specifically, Ian keeping his perpetrating penis out of Lucy's vulnerable vagina. "Think of all the activity. It can't be good." He thrusts his hips to illustrate his point. He doesn't think "no sex" excludes sixty-nines. But Lucy believes that orgasm must be the dangerous part of the sex equation, because of the powerful contractions of the uterus.

"Well, okay, no sex, of any kind, period," Ian shrugs. "Whatever you think is best." Ian gives up pawing her body too easily for Lucy's liking. Shouldn't he look more wounded, like any romance hero would when his damsel rejects his passionate kiss because of nefarious secrets?

"What do you mean, it's *'okay'*?" Lucy cries. "It's not *okay*. You can give it up, just like *that*?"

"No, yes, I mean – Christ, look, what do you want me to say?" Ian rolls his eyes, a genetic behavioral predisposition Lucy hopes the baby will not inherit, although she prays the baby will be blessed with Ian's swift metabolism. "It *has* to be okay, right?" Ian folds her into a hug. "We'll get through this. We're having a *baby*." He squeezes her, hard. He squeezes the concern right out of her, deflating her irritation, and she knows everything will be all right despite the tiny pink judge between her thighs pounding her pearly-gavel and shouting, "Overruled!" Lucy's body is no longer a democracy of desire. The baby reigns as supreme dictator.

Lucy is too mortified to call the doctor's office for a more explicit definition of *"pelvic rest"*, as if she might give away the secret that she and Ian had copulated for more than the utilitarian purpose of replicating their gene pool. Lucy refrains from any suspect activity. She wants this baby above all else, and surely can handle carnal deprivation for a few months.

The pregnancy books taunt her, painting gleeful images of pregnant women who experience their first orgasms, most powerful orgasms, or first multiple orgasms once they're knocked up. With the "engorgement of genitals" (now there's a sexy term, Lucy thinks) caused by increased blood flow to the pelvic area, sexual response can be heightened. Lucy doesn't inform Ian that the tight fit may also increase the man's pleasure – better that he not know what he's missing. Lucy herself has never come twice. She rips the page out of the book and burns it.

She successfully ignores her bloated labia, but her swollen breasts torment her. She's gone from a buoyant B to a dense C cup. Rolling over in bed is sensual torture, as her mammary glands bump into her arms, the pillow, and Ian's side (how can he sleep so deeply with all this deprivation going on?). With one whispered touch they instantaneously communicate their demands via live wires to her clitoris. She cups her full and hefty breasts in wonder – they now overflow her small palms. Her hands pluck constantly at her underwires to give her enormous areolas room to breathe. Her knockers feel as noticeable as semi-truck headlights. And they're tender. One lick from her husband's expert tongue and she'd traverse interstellar erotic realms, transported by haywire hormonal wiring. It makes no sense to her. Once pregnancy is achieved, shouldn't nature tranquilize the clitoris? There's no evolutionary purpose in her yoni's incessant yammering. She surmises that maybe the body craves ample sex in early pregnancy in order to store pleasure before starvation, like Joseph and the grain, predicting sexual drought once the baby arrives.

Ian sometimes forgets the ban and cups her breasts. Their ardor increases at warp speed when they touch, their skin sizzles, but passion is now as forbidden as the early days of their romance when there was no safe place to do the nasty, not in the twin bed she'd grown up in or in his barracks' bunk. She pushes him away. Her breasts are a loaded camel marching across the desert tundra of her deprived body.

Nothing about Lucy's body signals her to knock off the screwing. Her amorousness increases rather than slackens. She hasn't had a single morning of nausea. To the contrary, she feels bountiful and ripe for the plucking. Her body wants the sexual congress to stay in session, before she grows as big as a house and Ian's cock can't reach her front door. She can hardly bear to give Ian a goodbye peck, she stands so close to the unforgivable gulf of temptation. She hovers on the precipice of sneaking in a quickie, but it's not like cheating on a diet, when one cookie can't hurt. If it weren't for the doctor's order, she wouldn't be able to keep her hands off herself.

Mundane events provoke her ardor. The almost undetectable vibration of water rushing through the garden hose sends her into a paroxysm of desire. Kneading bread dough reminds her of squeezing Ian's ass. "*Rear end*," Lucy mentally corrects herself. And forget the electric toothbrush – she switches to a manual Harry Potter brush so that she won't try anything under his watchful gaze. The blender, hair dryer, and battery-powered razor are all banned for the current they transmit to her clitoris.

To give an extra nourishing boost to the fœtus, she navigates progesterone suppositories up her twat twice a day, careful not to brush surrounding erogenous zones. Dr Frank's pharmaceutical prescription further aggravates her rabid lust, as if he and God are in on a cruel plot to test her forbearance, like giving Job a raging hard-on in addition to his other trials. At first Ian dispensed the pink pussy pills, on the excuse that his long fingers could push them closer to the baby, but Lucy put a stop to his lingering ministrations. Her vagina went into eager spasms at his probing hands, like a piranha sensing the proximity of fresh meat. She administers the bullet-shaped, waxy pills quickly while visualizing explicitly unerotic images such as St Bernards drooling or her cat's hairballs. But the instant she lies on the bed, her hands prying between her naked thighs, obscene images plague her: naked rock stars kidnapped and bound so that she can ride their pylon cocks; rolling with dark and tortured poets in the crashing surf; frontal and rear views of Antonio Banderas riding horseback nude while calling her name in his irresistible accent; and Ian on a long afternoon in bed with Belgian chocolate and an ice cold bottle of Veuve Clicquot champagne – Ian who knows exactly how to use his fingers or tongue or body to bring her to climax even on difficult days when she thinks she can't, when she's too overwhelmed with mundane distractions. He knows how to divert her attention to matters at hand, how to summon her mind to the core of herself that nestles between her legs – *ohh!* Lucy jumps out of bed, clinical hands smelling of her sex clamped in her armpit, and she furiously scours the toilet in order to redirect her unmatronly thoughts. She will *not* fuck this up. *Mess* it up, Lucy corrects herself.

Between her own fingers, the speculum, the doctor's gloved hands, test swabs, and the ultrasound wand, about the only thing that never sees the inside of Lucy's vagina is Ian's cock, the object that got them into this predicament in the first place. Lucy craves the intimacy of joined bodies, the return of the love act that unifies them each night after the long days in which their opposite personalities and habits drive them apart. He suggests that a blow job might not be against doctor's orders. The union would be a physical bonding of some sort, at least. But Lucy can't step down that dangerous road. She could not restrain herself from culminating the desire such an act would arouse. She would slip down the carnal crevasse as surely as a climber scaling Everest in bowling shoes. She calls Ian a typical male for his request. She can't stand herself.

"Sophia Loren went to bed," her mother tells her, "and she finally had a baby." If luscious, fertile-looking sex symbols like Loren and Marilyn Monroe had trouble maintaining a pregnancy, unremarkable Lucy doesn't think she stands a chance. Christ, their boobs were child-bearing billboards. Talk about Mother Nature practicing false advertising. Not being stacked, Lucy stacks the odds in her favor and goes to bed. Permanently. Although inactivity will hopefully improve the baby's chances, total bed rest also allows her to cave in to her growing depression. She worries that she's not fit for motherhood. What kind of sexual monster is she? What is wrong with her that makes her so goddamned painfully horny all the time? Maybe she is an undiagnosed nymphomaniac? Waves of peace and joy over impending motherhood battle breakers of resentful lust inside her, her Christmas-mind duking it out with her WWF groin. Maybe if she ceases to interact with the world, she can lure her mind out of the gutter. Even the bus driver in his brown polyester uniform looks hot to her. But going horizontal only gives her more time to fixate on not fucking.

She banishes Ian to the hard and lumpy couch because she can't stand the close proximity of his penis, which yearns towards her and stabs her under the sheets. She accuses his cock of communicating in sign language to her clitoris while they sleep. By all telltale signs his pecker is having as much of a problem forgetting its nerve endings as her pussy. His bulging basket knocks against her when they snuggle, like an insistent homing pigeon banging on her closed roost.

Lucy takes an extended absence from her job and rents a stack of subtitled foreign movies in order to dull her lascivious mind, but accidentally brings home a scorching Hispanic film. Raw sex scenes open and close abundant and explicit fucking throughout the story – she can't turn it off – and blister her thighs from the television screen across the room. Her clitoris doesn't need to read the captions to get the gist. Lucy sleeps with her hands pinned under her pillow so that they won't stray. Everything else that she watches or reads is littered with dead babies. Stillborn babies, miscarried babies, aborted babies. Have the sex and dead babies always been there, but she never noticed, just as she ignores billboards on road trips? Or is God testing her with malicious intent, manipulating her arousal and then hurling reminders at her of why she must not cave in to temptation? Lucy should be sainted – these mixed cosmic messages are worse than the arrows flung at Sebastian.

Amidst the rampant abstention and Lucy's heroic restraint, Lucy's healthy libido betrays her. A chronic insomniac most of her life, her sleep is deep now, and her dreams vibrant. After several weeks of abstinence, she has a blue dream too explicit even for the X-rated shelf of her mind. She awakens to a powerful orgasm.

The next day, Lucy doesn't know whether she wants to smash or fondle the calculatingly soothing, smooth, round artwork in Dr Frank's waiting room, the furniture all feminine curves before the rudeness of the exam room. "Everything's fine," Dr Frank reassures her after she haltingly and euphemistically explains her nocturnal explosion. The tiny heartbeat pulses on the ultrasound. "These preventative measures may be entirely unnecessary. Nothing you do will cause a problem unless you're lifting elephants. We just don't want you to do anything that will cause you to blame yourself if something happens. Better safe than sorry."

Lucy notices the doctor says "miscarriage" about as often as he mentions sex.

A week later, Lucy bleeds, a red river of loss.

Lucy will never crave sex again. Despite the doctor's assurance that nothing Lucy did could have caused the miscarriage, Lucy fears the baby stopped growing out of shock over Mom's bawdy telepathic signals. Deep down she knows that her turgid urges and sailor's vocabulary are not just cause for her sterility. Her baser instincts don't mean she lacks the maternal instinct. Despite her feelings of guilt, she believes she would have been a good mother. And Ian a good father. That they desire each other so profoundly after years together means the promise of a whole, lasting family for their child. A baby girl, Dr Frank tells her. Lucy names her Grace.

Weeks pass. She cannot remember the last time she felt remotely aroused. Sex will only remind her of what their union cannot bring, of what she wants but cannot have, of what she almost had but lost. She is undesirable. Damaged goods. How can Ian ever be aroused again by the crack in her body when he saw what fell out of it? No longer an erogenous zone, but a war zone. She's gained weight since the miscarriage, her metabolism as slow as a dirge. She feels flabby from her inactivity. Her dull and grey-flecked roots have grown out since her last hair color. Dye isn't recommended for pregnant women, and she can't summon the energy to call her stylist for an appointment now that she can douse her head in chemical baths to her heart's content. Low iron levels exhaust her. Pregnancy hormone mottles her face. Her breasts, back to their normal size, feel tiny and insignificant. When they are touched, she feels irritation, not arousal. If she could only have experienced one orgasm with Ian while they were beckoning, busty, lusty, fully charged creatures with a hotline wired straight to her groin. Her nipples with their own minds had prank-called the clitoris commissioner all those ceaseless weeks, but now the line is dead. The forfeit of that pleasurable experience is one loss amidst so much loss. She could have had a fuck-fest all that time and it wouldn't have made one fucking bit of difference.

How ironic that desire for sex consumed her during the weeks she could not indulge in pleasures of the flesh, yet eludes her now that she can make love whenever she wants. Now that her womb is open again for business, lust eludes her.

She has no excuse to refuse Ian. The doctor okays baths, swimming, intercourse, tampons, and exercise. (Linguistically true to form, the nurse wedges sex between mundane activities.) Lucy feels the presence of Ian's cock behind closed doors. He lurks around her with pained desire in his eyes, afraid to pressure her yet needing their union to heal himself – he has lost Grace, too. She misinterprets his respect for her needs as lack of desire for her, confirming her belief that she is no longer appealing – as a fat, ugly, small-breasted woman who apparently will never bear his children. Dr Frank recommends "mechanical birth control" for a few months – but *she* is mechanical, a robot with no human nerves, and condoms remain a non-issue. Ian remains on the couch. Lucy has no idea how to repair the growing gulf between them.

One night there is a tiny scratching at the bedroom door, with snuffling and high-pitched whining. Startled from the daze she sinks into nightly instead of sleep, she calls out.

"There's someone here to see you." The door muffles Ian's voice.

"I'm not dressed!" Lucy curls up in a corner of the bed, her body shrouded in long flannels.

"He doesn't care." Ian cracks open the door. "Arf arf." Ian is naked. With the hallway light spilling in through the doorway, Lucy makes out his cock – decorated like a Chihuahua. He stands uncertainly, hesitant of Lucy's reaction. She admires him for exposing himself so fully, wholly vulnerable though chances of rejection are high. She snaps on the bedside lamp. Ian has attached two huge ears tied on a soft cord around the shaft and drawn a happy face on the head with a marsh pen, with a red satin bow at the base for a collar and paws drawn on his balls. "I remembered you wanted a ChiWowWow."

Lucy laughs, as much at Ian's inability to pronounce foreign words as at his humor. His mispronunciation was the only thing that ended their argument when they last fought over Lucy's desire for the rat-sized dog, because neither of them could keep a straight face over his ridiculous slaughter of the dog's breed. The murmuring, surprised bubble of her laughter grows inside her until she cackles breathlessly, doubled up on the bed. She laughed like that the night they met, and her unrestrained glee sealed them for life more than the sex that swiftly followed. They could foresee a day far in the future when they would be too old to screw, but never too old to laugh.

Lucy catches her breath. "Man, I needed that. That was better than an orgasm." She hasn't so much as smiled in weeks. Though Ian had tried to make jokes about horny monks and nuns, she hadn't appreciated the humor.

As Ian's cock grows under the glow of Lucy's pleasure, the puppy's face distorts. Ian looks down. "Uh oh. He's drooling."

"Better than piddling. Does he know any commands?"

"Come."

Lucy makes kissy noises and pats the bed. "Come, Loco!"

Ian snuggles next to her on the bed, though her thick night-gown and the blankets separate them. "He likes to be petted."

"I wouldn't want to spoil him."

"There's no such thing as too much love for a puppy."

"His fur is so soft! Oh, dear. He's outgrowing his collar."

"I know a way to fix that." Ian's hand creeps under the blanket, up her gown, and down her panties. He rests the heel of his palm against her mons, his fingers cupped over her mound. At first Lucy winces. Her gash is now a raw wound, not a path to pleasure, but Ian does not nudge her open with his fingers. His hand simply rests low on her belly with only the pressure of its weight. She feels the cold arc of his wedding ring as his palm presses down against her, pushing her own small mound of flesh against her clitoris.

Lucy doesn't know where the orgasm comes from. It mounts inside her and explodes without warning, like a team of Clydesdales tearing around a bend in the road to knock her over. Their thundering, unforeseen passage leaves her sprawled and sloppy on the wayside of unleashed repression, her dress to her face and her hair in damp tangles. The breeze of their stampede dies down, and it is just Lucy and Ian together in the quiet bed.

Lucy blinks at him. "Okay, so maybe laughing isn't better than coming."

Ian smiles. "You can have both. Doctor's orders."

She catches her breath. "I think I needed that."

She cries when Ian crackles the condom packet, symbolizing the prevention of a pregnancy that she so badly wants but that can't be. "You'll suffocate Loco."

"He's a special mutant super-ninja ChiWowWow. He doesn't need air." They kick aside covers and clothing and Ian climbs on top of her. Ian has a hard time gaining entry, partly because he is being so careful, and partly because Lucy is closed like a fist. The condom chafes. "It won't work," Lucy weeps.

"Hold on." Ian squirts half a tube of K-Y between her legs. Her story starts and begins with lubricant. She should purchase stock in the goopy stuff. Lucy laughs.

Ian brushes her cheek. "I love your laugh. I've missed it."

Smeared with jelly, they slide in a slick puddle on the sheets. Ian is cautious and tender. His hesitant entrance hurts at first. "I thought he was a Chihuahua, not a St Bernard," Lucy gasps. Her vagina creaks, like a swollen door pushed open from its tight frame.

"You okay?" Ian asks. Lucy has forgotten how big and powerful he looks from this perspective, his protective body fully covering hers, when in daily life he is a small man.

"I'm like a virgin." Ian gets his tight fit, after all.

"Remember Sister Cyndy?"

Sister Cyndy, the self-proclaimed Born-Again Virgin who used to preach on the campus lawn where she and Ian first met during his ROTC days. Everything seemed possible, then, except Born-Again Virginity. But it turns out that Sister Cyndy was right. The return of the virginal state *is* possible, yet so much else that seemed possible is not. Lucy remembers the innocence of those days, sitting in the hot sun on the green lawn eating gloppy cafeteria food, when they hadn't yet thought about starting a family, when sex was simple, nothing but the joining of their two young, healthy, and perfect bodies. Sex is loaded now, fraught with repercussions and reminders.

Lucy welcomes the familiar fullness of Ian's body inside hers. There can be nothing sinful about her love of this act. She believes she is a decent person, despite indecent thoughts. She believes in her own goodness despite the lewd locomotive of her mind that pushed her into erotic torment for weeks on end, that broke up the smooth passage of their relationship like train cars derailing, that twisted her like the resulting wreckage into a ball-busting bitch. She believes in her marriage, in the man who won't let her go despite the baby that leaked away.

Another rolling thunderclap unleashes inside her. Her pelvic bone tilted up to Ian's belly as he barely moves, like slow dancing, the orgasm sneaks up on her and bursts.

"Making up for lost time?" Ian brushes the hair from her forehead.

"Shit, that *is* a Wow Wow," Lucy arches and sighs.

"Performs just for you." Sorrow hovers behind their smiles, but they let the hurt pass without sobering the light mood. Ian seems in no hurry for his own pleasure. His cock fills her but doesn't move inside her other than the pulse of his blood. "I love your hair like this. Don't dye it any more, okay?"

"But all the grey! I'm getting old."

"No, *we're* getting old. Together."

She had lost the baby, orgasms, laughter, and her own personality, but what she missed most was intimacy with Ian. They had always connected and healed through sex. Tonight won't make up for the loss of Grace, she knows, but in this at least she is blessed.